FAR FROM THE MADDING CROWD, THE MAYOR OF CASTERBRIDGE

THE GOLDEN HERITAGE SERIES

FAR FROM THE MADDING CROWD, THE MAYOR OF CASTERBRIDGE

THOMAS HARDY

Galley Press

Published in this edition by Galley Press, an imprint of
W. H. Smith Limited, Registered No. 237811 England.
Trading as W. H. Smith Distributors, St John's House
East Street, Leicester, LE1 6NE.

ISBN 0 86136 600 X

Production services by
Book Production Consultants, Cambridge

Printed and bound in Yugoslavia by Mladinska Knjiga

FAR FROM THE MADDING CROWD,

PREFACE

I N reprinting this story for a new edition I am reminded
that it was in the chapters of "Far from the Madding
Crowd," as they appeared month by month in a popular
magazine, that I first ventured to adopt the word "Wessex"
from the pages of early English history, and give it a
fictitious significance as the existing name of the district
once included in that extinct kingdom.   The series of
novels I projected being mainly of the kind called local,
they seemed to require a territorial definition of some sort
to lend unity to their scene.   Finding that the area of
a single county did not afford a canvas large enough for
this purpose, and that there were objections to an invented
name, I disinterred the old one.   The press and the
public were kind enough to welcome the fanciful plan,
and willingly joined me in the anachronism of imagining
a Wessex population living under Queen Victoria ;—a
modern Wessex of railways, the penny post, mowing and
reaping machines, union workhouses, lucifer matches,•
labourers who could read and write, and National school
children.   But I believe I am correct in stating that, until
the existence of this contemporaneous Wessex in place of
the usual counties was announced in the present story, in
1874, it had never been heard of in fiction and current

speech, if at all, and that the expression, "a Wessex peasant," or "a Wessex custom," would theretofore have been taken to refer to nothing later in date than the Norman Conquest.

I did not anticipate that this application of the word to modern story would extend outside the chapters of the chronicles themselves. But it was soon taken up elsewhere, the first to adopt it being the now defunct *Examiner*, which, in the impression bearing date July 15, 1876, entitled one of its articles "The Wessex Labourer," the article turning out to be no dissertation on farming during the Heptarchy, but on the modern peasant of the south-west counties.

Since then the appellation which I had thought to reserve to the horizons and landscapes of a partly real, partly dream-country, has become more and more popular as a practical provincial definition; and the dream-country has, by degrees, solidified into a utilitarian region which people can go to, take a house in, and write to the papers from. But I ask all good and gentle readers to forget this, and to refuse steadfastly to believe that there are any inhabitants of a Victorian Wessex outside these volumes in which their lives and conversations are detailed.

Moreover, the village called Weatherbury, wherein the scenes of the present story of the series are for the most part laid, would perhaps be hardly discernible by the explorer, without help, in any existing place nowadays; though at the time, comparatively recent, at which the tale was written, a sufficient reality to meet the descriptions, both of backgrounds and personages, might have been traced easily enough. The church remains, by great good fortune, unrestored and intact, and a few of the old houses; but the ancient malt-house, which was formerly so characteristic of the parish, has been pulled down these twenty years; also most of the thatched and dormered cottages that were once lifeholds. The heroine's fine old Jacobean house would be found in the story to have taken a witch's ride of a mile or more from its actual position; though with that difference its features are described as they still show themselves to the sun and moonlight. The game of prisoner's-base, which not so long ago seemed to enjoy a perennial vitality in front of the worn-out stocks, may, so far as I can say, be entirely unknown to the rising generation of school-boys there. The practice of divination by Bible and key, the regarding of valentines as things of serious import, the shearing-supper, the long smock-frocks, and the harvest-home, have, too, nearly disappeared in the wake of the old houses; and with them has gone, it is said, much of that love of fuddling to which the village at one time was notoriously prone. The change at the root of this has been the recent supplanting of the class of stationary cottagers, who carried on the local traditions and humours, by a population of more or less migratory labourers, which has led to a break of continuity in local history, more fatal than any other thing to the preservation of legend, folk-lore, close inter-social relations, and eccentric individualities. For these the indispensable conditions of existence are attachment to the soil of one particular spot by generation after generation.

T. H.

1895—1902.

CONTENTS

FAR FROM THE MADDING CROWD

CONTENTS

CHAPTER I

DESCRIPTION OF FARMER OAK—AN INCIDENT

WHEN Farmer Oak smiled, the corners of his mouth spread till they were within an unimportant distance of his ears, his eyes were reduced to mere chinks, and diverging wrinkles appeared round them, extending upon his countenance like the rays in a rudimentary sketch of the rising sun.

His Christian name was Gabriel, and on working days he was a young man of sound judgment, easy motions, proper dress, and general good character. On Sundays he was a man of misty views, rather given to postponing, and hampered by his best clothes and umbrella : upon the whole, one who felt himself to occupy morally that vast middle space of Laodicean neutrality which lay between the Communion people of the parish and the drunken section,—that is, he went to church, but yawned privately by the time the congregation reached the Nicene creed, and thought of what there would be for dinner when he meant to be listening to the sermon. Or, to state his character as it stood in the scale of public opinion, when his friends and critics were in tantrums, he was considered rather a bad man ; when they were pleased, he was rather a good man ; when they were neither, he was a man whose moral colour was a kind of pepper-and-salt mixture.

I

Since he lived six times as many working-days as Sundays, Oak's appearance in his old clothes was most peculiarly his own—the mental picture formed by his neighbours in imagining him being always dressed in that way. He wore a low-crowned felt hat, spread out at the base by tight jamming upon the head for security in high winds, and a coat like Dr. Johnson's; his lower extremities being encased in ordinary leather leggings and boots emphatically large, affording to each foot a roomy apartment so constructed that any wearer might stand in a river all day long and know nothing about it—their maker being a conscientious man who always endeavoured to compensate for any weakness in his cut by unstinted dimension and solidity.

Mr. Oak carried about him, by way of watch, what may be called a small silver clock; in other words, it was a watch as to shape and intention, and a small clock as to size. This instrument being several years older than Oak's grandfather, had the peculiarity of going either too fast or not at all. The smaller of its hands, too, occasionally slipped round on the pivot, and thus, though the minutes were told with the greatest precision, nobody could be quite certain of the hour they belonged to. The stopping peculiarity of his watch Oak remedied by thumps and shakes, and he escaped any evil consequences from the other two defects by constant comparisons with and observations of the sun and stars, and by pressing his face close to the glass of his neighbours' windows, till he could discern the hour marked by the green-faced timekeepers within. It may be mentioned that Oak's fob being painfully difficult of access, by reason of its somewhat high situation in the waistband of his trousers (which also lay at a remote height under his waistcoat), the watch was as a necessity pulled out by throwing the body extremely to one side, compressing the mouth and face to a mere mass of ruddy flesh on account of the exertion required, and drawing up the watch by its chain, like a bucket from a well.

But some thoughtful persons, who had seen him walking across one of his fields on a certain December morning—sunny and exceedingly mild—might have regarded Gabriel Oak in other aspects than these. In his face one might notice that many of the hues and curves of youth had tarried on to manhood: there even remained in his remoter crannies some relics of the boy. His height and breadth would have been sufficient to make his presence imposing, had they been exhibited with due consideration. But there is a way some men have, rural and urban alike, for which the mind is more responsible than flesh and sinew: it is a way of curtailing their dimensions by their manner of showing them. And from a quiet modesty that would have become a vestal, which seemed continually to impress upon him that he had no great claim on the world's room, Oak walked unassumingly, and with a faintly perceptible bend, quite distinct from a bowing of the shoulders. This may be said to be a defect in an individual if he depends for his valuation more upon his appearance than upon his capacity to wear well, which Oak did not.

He had just reached the time of life at which 'young' is ceasing to be the prefix of 'man' in speaking of one. He was at the brightest period of masculine growth, for his intellect and his emotions were clearly separated: he had passed the time during which the influence of youth indiscriminately mingles them in the character of impulse, and he had not yet arrived at the stage wherein they become united again, in the character of prejudice, by the influence of a wife and family. In short, he was twenty-eight, and a bachelor.

The field he was in this morning sloped steeply to a ridge called Norcombe Hill. Through a spur of this hill ran the highway from Norcombe to Casterbridge, sunk in a deep cutting. Casually glancing over the hedge, Oak saw coming down the incline before him an ornamental spring waggon, painted yellow and gaily marked, drawn by two horses, a waggoner walking alongside bearing a whip perpendicularly. The waggon was laden with household goods and window plants, and on the apex of the whole sat a woman, young and attractive. Gabriel had not beheld the sight for more than half a minute, when the vehicle was brought .to a standstill just beneath his eyes.

'The tailboard of the waggon is gone, Miss,' said the waggoner.

'Then I heard it fall,' said the girl, in a soft, though not particularly low voice. 'I heard a noise I could not account for when we were coming up the hill.'

'I'll run back.'

'Do,' she answered.

The sensible horses stood perfectly still, and the waggoner's steps sank fainter and fainter in the distance.

The girl on the summit of the load sat motionless, surrounded by tables and chairs with their legs upwards, backed by an oak settle, and ornamented in front by pots of geraniums, myrtles, and cactuses, together with a caged canary—all probably from the windows of the house just vacated. There was also a cat in a willow basket, from the partly-opened lid of which she gazed with half-closed eyes, and affectionately surveyed the small birds around.

The handsome girl waited for some time idly in her place, and the only sound heard in the stillness was the hopping of the canary up and down the perches of its prison. Then she looked attentively downwards. It was not at the bird, nor at the cat; it was at an oblong package tied in paper, and lying between them. She turned her head to learn if the waggoner were coming. He was not yet in sight; and her eyes crept back to the package, her thoughts seeming to run upon what was inside it. At length she drew the article into her

4

lap, and untied the paper covering; a small swing looking-glass was disclosed, in which she proceeded to survey herself attentively. She parted her lips and smiled.

It was a fine morning, and the sun lighted up to a scarlet glow the crimson jacket she wore, and painted a soft lustre upon her bright face and black hair. The myrtles, geraniums, and cactuses packed around her were fresh and green, and at such a leafless season they invested the whole concern of horses, waggon, furniture, and girl with a peculiar vernal charm. What possessed her to indulge in such a performance in the sight of the sparrows, blackbirds, and unperceived farmer who were alone its spectators,—whether the smile began as a factitious one, to test her capacity in that art,—nobody knows; it ended certainly in a real smile. She blushed at herself, and seeing her reflection blush, blushed the more.

The change from the customary spot and necessary occasion of such an act—from the dressing hour in a bedroom to a time of travelling out of doors—lent to the idle deed a novelty it certainly did not intrinsically possess. The picture was a delicate one. Woman's prescriptive infirmity had stalked into the sunlight, which had clothed it in the freshness of an originality. A cynical inference was irresistible by Gabriel Oak as he regarded the scene, generous though he fain would have been. There was no necessity whatever for her looking in the glass. She did not adjust her hat, or pat her hair, or press a dimple into shape, or do one thing to signify that any such intention had been her motive in taking up the glass. She simply observed herself as a fair product of Nature in the feminine kind, her thoughts seeming to glide into far-off though likely dramas in which men would play a part—vistas of probable triumphs—the smiles being of a phase suggesting that hearts were imagined as lost and won. Still, this was but conjecture, and the whole series of actions was so idly put forth as to make it rash to assert that intention had any part in them at all.

The waggoner's steps were heard returning. She put the glass in the paper, and the whole again into its place.

When the waggon had passed on, Gabriel withdrew from his point of espial, and descending into the road, followed the vehicle to the turnpike-gate at the bottom of the hill, where the object of his contemplation now halted for the payment of toll. About twenty steps still remained between him and the gate, when he heard a dispute. It was a difference concerning twopence between the persons with the waggon and the man at the toll-bar.

'Mis'ess's niece is upon the top of the things, and she says that's enough that I've offered ye, you great miser, and she won't pay any more.' These were the waggoner's words.

'Very well; then mis'ess's niece can't pass,' said the turnpike-keeper, closing the gate.

Oak looked from one to the other of the disputants, and fell into a reverie. There was something in the tone of twopence remarkably insignificant. Threepence had a definite value as money—it was an appreciable infringement on a day's wages, and, as such, a higgling matter; but twopence——'Here,' he said, stepping forward and handing twopence to the gatekeeper; 'let the young woman pass.' He looked up at her then; she heard his words, and looked down.

Gabriel's features adhered throughout their form so exactly to the middle line between the beauty of St. John and the ugliness of Judas Iscariot, as represented in a window of the church he attended, that not a single lineament could be selected and called worthy either of distinction or notoriety. The red-jacketed and dark-haired maiden seemed to think so too, for she carelessly

6

glanced over him, and told her man to drive on. She might have looked her thanks to Gabriel on a minute scale, but she did not speak them ; more probably she felt none, for in gaining her a passage he had lost her her point, and we know how women take a favour of that kind.

The gatekeeper surveyed the retreating vehicle. 'That's a handsome maid,' he said to Oak.

'But she has her faults,' said Gabriel.

'True, farmer.'

'And the greatest of them is—well, what it is always.'

'Beating people down? ay, 'tis so.'

'Oh no.'

'What, then?'

Gabriel, perhaps a little piqued by the comely traveller's indifference, glanced back to where he had witnessed her performance over the hedge, and said, 'Vanity.'

CHAPTER II

NIGHT—THE FLOCK—AN INTERIOR—ANOTHER INTERIOR

IT was nearly midnight on the eve of St. Thomas's, the shortest day in the year. A desolating wind wandered from the north over the hill whereon Oak had watched the yellow waggon and its occupant in the sunshine of a few days earlier.

Norcombe Hill—not far from lonely Toller-Down —was one of the spots which suggest to a passer-by that he is in the presence of a shape approaching the indestructible as nearly as any to be found on earth. It was a featureless convexity of chalk and soil—an ordinary specimen of those smoothly-outlined protuberances of the globe which may remain undisturbed on some great day of confusion, when far grander heights and dizzy granite precipices topple down.

The hill was covered on its northern side by an ancient and decaying plantation of beeches, whose upper verge formed a line over the crest, fringing its arched curve against the sky, like a mane. To-night these trees sheltered the southern slope from the keenest blasts, which smote the wood and floundered through it with a sound as of grumbling, or gushed over its crowning boughs in a weakened moan. The dry leaves in the ditch simmered and boiled in the same breezes, a tongue of air occasionally ferreting out a few, and sending them spinning across the grass. A group or two of the latest in date amongst this dead multitude had remained till this very mid-winter time on the twigs which bore them, and in falling rattled against the trunks with smart taps.

Between this half-wooded, half-naked hill, and the vague, still horizon that its summit indistinctly commanded, was a mysterious sheet of fathomless shade —the sounds from which suggested that what it concealed bore some humble resemblance to features here. The thin grasses, more or less coating the hill, were touched by the wind in breezes of differing powers, and almost of differing natures—one rubbing the blades heavily, another raking them piercingly, another brushing them like a soft broom. The instinctive act of humankind was to stand and listen, and learn how the trees on the right and the trees on the left wailed or chaunted to each other in the regular antiphonies of a cathedral choir; how hedges and other shapes to leeward then caught the note, lowering it to the tenderest sob; and how the hurrying gust then plunged into the south, to be heard no more.

The sky was clear—remarkably clear—and the twinkling of all the stars seemed to be but throbs of one body, timed by a common pulse. The North Star was directly in the wind's eye, and since evening the Bear had swung round it outwardly to the east, till he was now at a right angle with the meridian. A difference of colour in the stars—oftener read of than seen in England—was really perceptible here. The kingly brilliancy of Sirius pierced the eye with a steely glitter, the star called Capella was yellow, Aldebaran and Betelgueux shone with a fiery red.

To persons standing alone on a hill during a clear midnight such as this, the roll of the world eastward is almost a palpable movement. The sensation may be caused by the panoramic glide of the stars past earthly

objects, which is perceptible in a few minutes of stillness, or by the better outlook upon space that a hill
affords, or by the wind, or by the solitude ; but whatever
be its origin, the impression of riding along is vivid and
abiding. The poetry of motion is a phrase much in
use, and to enjoy the epic form of that gratification it
is necessary to stand on a hill at a small hour of the
night, and, having first expanded with a sense of difference from the mass of civilised mankind, who are
dreamwrapt and disregardful of all such proceedings at
this time, long and quietly watch your stately progress
through the stars. After such a nocturnal reconnoitre
it is hard to get back to earth, and to believe that the
consciousness of such majestic speeding is derived from
a tiny human frame.

Suddenly an unexpected series of sounds began to
be heard in this place up against the sky. They had a
clearness which was to be found nowhere in the wind,
and a sequence which was to be found nowhere in
nature. They were the notes of Farmer Oak's flute.

The tune was not floating unhindered into the open
air : it seemed muffled in some way, and was altogether
too curtailed in power to spread high or wide. It came
from the direction of a small dark object under the
plantation hedge—a shepherd's hut—now presenting
an outline to which an uninitiated person might have
been puzzled to attach either meaning or use.

The image as a whole was that of a small Noah's
Ark on a small Ararat, allowing the traditionary outlines
and general form of the Ark which are followed by toy-
makers—and by these means are established in men's
imaginations among their firmest, because earliest impressions—to pass as an approximate pattern. The
hut stood on small wheels, which raised its floor about a
foot from the ground. Such shepherds' huts are dragged
into the fields when the lambing season comes on, to
shelter the shepherd in his enforced nightly attendance.

It was only latterly that people had begun to call Gabriel 'Farmer' Oak. During the twelvemonth preceding this time he had been enabled by sustained efforts of industry and chronic good spirits to lease the small sheep-farm of which Norcombe Hill was a portion, and stock it with two hundred sheep. Previously he had been a bailiff for a short time, and earlier still a shepherd only, having from his childhood assisted his father in tending the flocks of large proprietors, till old Gabriel sank to rest.

This venture, unaided and alone, into the paths of farming as master and not as man, with an advance of sheep not yet paid for, was a critical juncture with Gabriel Oak, and he recognised his position clearly. The first movement in his new progress was the lambing of his ewes, and sheep having been his specialty from his youth, he wisely refrained from deputing the task of tending them at this season to a hireling or a novice.

The wind continued to beat about the corners of the hut, but the flute-playing ceased. A rectangular space of light appeared in the side of the hut, and in the opening the outline of Farmer Oak's figure. He carried a lantern in his hand, and closing the door behind him, came forward and busied himself about this nook of the field for nearly twenty minutes, the lantern light appearing and disappearing here and there, and brightening him or darkening him as he stood before or behind it.

Oak's motions, though they had a quiet energy, were slow, and their deliberateness accorded well with his occupation. Fitness being the basis of all beauty, nobody could have denied that his steady swings and turns in and about the flock had elements of grace. Yet, although if occasion demanded he could do or think a thing with as mercurial a dash as can the men of towns who are more to the manner born, his special power, morally, physically, and mentally, was static, owing little or nothing to momentum as a rule.

A close examination of the ground hereabout, even by the wan starlight only, revealed how a portion of what would have been casually called a wild slope had been appropriated by Farmer Oak for his great purpose this winter. Detached hurdles thatched with straw were stuck into the ground at various scattered points, amid and under which the whitish forms of his meek ewes moved and rustled. The ring of the sheep-bell, which had been silent during his absence, recommenced, in tones that had more mellowness than clearness, owing to an increasing growth of surrounding wool. This continued till Oak withdrew again from the flock. He returned to the hut, bringing in his arms a new-born lamb, consisting of four legs large enough for a full-grown sheep, united by an unimportant membrane about half the substance of the legs collectively, which constituted the animal's entire body just at present.

The little speck of life he placed on a wisp of hay before the small stove, where a can of milk was simmering. Oak extinguished the lantern by blowing into it and then pinching out the snuff, the cot being lighted by a candle suspended by a twisted wire. A rather hard couch, formed of a few corn sacks thrown carelessly down, covered half the floor of this little habitation, and here the young man stretched himself along, loosened his woollen cravat, and closed his eyes. In about the time a person unaccustomed to bodily labour would have decided upon which side to lie, Farmer Oak was asleep.

The inside of the hut, as it now presented itself, was cosy and alluring, and the scarlet handful of fire in addition to the candle, reflecting its own genial colour upon whatever it could reach, flung associations of enjoyment even over utensils and tools. In the corner stood the sheep-crook, and along a shelf at one side were ranged bottles and canisters of the simple preparations pertaining to ovine surgery and physic; spirits of wine, turpentine, tar, magnesia, ginger, and castor-oil being the chief. On a triangular shelf across the corner stood bread, bacon, cheese, and a cup for ale or cider, which was supplied from a flagon beneath. Beside the provisions lay the flute, whose notes had lately been called forth by the lonely watcher to beguile a tedious hour. The house was ventilated by two round holes, like the lights of a cabin, with wood slides.

The lamb, revived by the warmth, began to bleat, and the sound entered Gabriel's ears and brain with an instant meaning, as expected sounds will. Passing from the profoundest sleep to the most alert wakefulness with the same ease that had accompanied the reverse operation, he looked at his watch, found that the hour-hand had shifted again, put on his hat, took the lamb in his arms, and carried it into the darkness. After placing the little creature with its mother, he stood and carefully examined the sky, to ascertain the time of night from the altitudes of the stars.

The Dog-star and Aldebaran, pointing to the restless Pleiades, were half way up the Southern sky, and between them hung Orion, which gorgeous constellation never burnt more vividly than now, as it swung itself forth above the rim of the landscape. Castor and Pollux with their quiet shine were almost on the meridian: the barren and gloomy Square of Pegasus was creeping round to the north-west; far away through the plantation, Vega sparkled like a lamp suspended amid the leafless trees, and Cassiopeia's chair stood daintily poised on the uppermost boughs.

'One o'clock,' said Gabriel.

Being a man not without a frequent consciousness that there was some charm in this life he led, he stood still after looking at the sky as a useful instrument, and regarded it in an appreciative spirit, as a work of art superlatively beautiful. For a moment he seemed impressed with the speaking loneliness of the scene, or rather with the complete abstraction from all its compass

of the sights and sounds of man. Human shapes, inter-
ferences, troubles, and joys were all as if they were not,
and there seemed to be on the shaded hemisphere of
the globe no sentient being save himself; he could
fancy them all gone round to the sunny side.

Occupied thus, with eyes stretched afar, Oak gradually perceived that what he had previously taken to be
a star low down behind the outskirts of the plantation
was in reality no such thing. It was an artificial light,
almost close at hand.

To find themselves utterly alone at night where
company is desirable and expected makes some people
fearful; but a case more trying by far to the nerves
is to discover some mysterious companionship when
intuition, sensation, memory, analogy, testimony, probability, induction—every kind of evidence in the
logician's list—have united to persuade consciousness
that it is quite in isolation.

Farmer Oak went towards the plantation and pushed
through its lower boughs to the windy side. A dim
mass under the slope reminded him that a shed occupied a place here, the site being a cutting into the
slope of the hill, so that at its back part the roof was
almost level with the ground. In front it was formed
of boards nailed to posts and covered with tar as a
preservative. Through crevices in the roof and side
spread streaks and dots of light, a combination of
which made up the radiance that had attracted him.
Oak stepped up behind, where, leaning down upon the
roof and putting his eye close to a hole, he could see
into the interior clearly.

The place contained two women and two cows. By
the side of the latter a steaming bran-mash stood in a
bucket. One of the women was past middle age. Her
companion was apparently young and graceful; he could
form no decided opinion upon her looks, her position
being almost beneath his eye, so that he saw her in a

bird's-eye view, as Milton's Satan first saw Paradise. She wore no bonnet or hat, but had enveloped herself in a large cloak, which was carelessly flung over her head as a covering.

'There, now we'll go home,' said the elder of the two, resting her knuckles upon her hips, and looking at their goings-on as a whole. 'I do hope Daisy will fetch round again now. I have never been more frightened in my life, but I don't mind breaking my rest if she recovers.'

The young woman, whose eyelids were apparently inclined to fall together on the smallest provocation of silence, yawned without parting her lips to any inconvenient extent, whereupon Gabriel caught the infection and slightly yawned in sympathy.

'I wish we were rich enough to pay a man to do these things,' she said.

'As we are not, we must do them ourselves,' said the other; 'for you must help me if you stay.'

'Well, my hat is gone, however,' continued the younger. 'It went over the hedge, I think. The idea of such a slight wind catching it.'

The cow standing erect was of the Devon breed, and was encased in a tight warm hide of rich Indian red, as absolutely uniform from eyes to tail as if the animal had been dipped in a dye of that colour, her long back being mathematically level. The other was spotted, gray and white. Beside her Oak now noticed a little calf about a day old, looking idiotically at the two women, which showed that it had not long been accustomed to the phenomenon of eyesight, and often turning to the lantern, which it apparently mistook for the moon, inherited instinct having as yet had little time for correction by experience. Between the sheep and the cows, Lucina had been busy on Norcombe Hill lately.

'I think we had better send for some oatmeal,' said the elder woman; 'there's no more bran.'

'Yes, aunt; and I'll ride over for it as soon as it is light.'

'But there's no side-saddle.'

'I can ride on the other: trust me.'

Oak, upon hearing these remarks, became more curious to observe her features, but this prospect being denied him by the hooding effect of the cloak, and by his aërial position, he felt himself drawing upon his fancy for their details. In making even horizontal and clear inspections we colour and mould according to the wants within us whatever our eyes bring in. Had Gabriel been able from the first to get a distinct view of her countenance, his estimate of it as very handsome or slightly so would have been as his soul required a divinity at the moment or was ready supplied with one. Having for some time known the want of a satisfactory form to fill an increasing void within him, his position moreover affording the widest scope for his fancy, he painted her a beauty.

By one of those whimsical coincidences in which Nature, like a busy mother, seems to spare a moment from her unremitting labours to turn and make her children smile, the girl now dropped the cloak, and forth tumbled ropes of black hair over a red jacket. Oak knew her instantly as the heroine of the yellow waggon, myrtles, and looking-glass: prosily, as the woman who owed him twopence.

They placed the calf beside its mother again, took up the lantern, and went out, the light sinking down the hill till it was no more than a nebula. Gabriel Oak returned to his flock.

CHAPTER III

A GIRL ON HORSEBACK—CONVERSATION

THE sluggish day began to break. Even its position terrestrially is one of the elements of a new interest, and for no particular reason save that the incident of the night had occurred there, Oak went again into the plantation. Lingering and musing here, he heard the steps of a horse at the foot of the hill, and soon there appeared in view an auburn pony with a girl on its back, ascending by the path leading past the cattle-shed. She was the young woman of the night before. Gabriel instantly thought of the hat she had mentioned as having lost in the wind; possibly she had come to look for it. He hastily scanned the ditch, and after walking about ten yards along it, found the hat among the leaves. Gabriel took it in his hand and returned to his hut. Here he ensconced himself, and peeped through the loophole in the direction of the rider's approach.

She came up and looked around—then on the other side of the hedge. Gabriel was about to advance and restore the missing article, when an unexpected performance induced him to suspend the action for the present. The path, after passing the cowshed, bisected the plantation. It was not a bridle-path—merely a pedestrian's track, and the boughs spread horizontally at a height not greater than seven feet above the ground,

17

which made it impossible to ride erect beneath them. The girl, who wore no riding-habit, looked around for a moment, as if to assure herself that all humanity was out of view, then dexterously dropped backwards flat upon the pony's back, her head over its tail, her feet against its shoulder, and her eyes to the sky. The rapidity of her glide into this position was that of a kingfisher—its noiselessness that of a hawk. Gabriel's eyes had scarcely been able to follow her. The tall lank pony seemed used to such doings, and ambled along unconcerned. Thus she passed under the level boughs.

The performer seemed quite at home anywhere between a horse's head and its tail, and the necessity for this abnormal attitude having ceased with the passage of the plantation, she began to adopt another, even more obviously convenient than the first. She had no side-saddle, and it was very apparent that a firm seat upon the smooth leather beneath her was unattainable sideways. Springing to her accustomed perpendicular like a bowed sapling, and satisfying herself that nobody was in sight, she seated herself in the manner demanded by the saddle, though hardly expected of the woman, and trotted off in the direction of Tewnell Mill.

Oak was amused, perhaps a little astonished, and hanging up the hat in his hut, went again among his ewes. An hour passed, the girl returned, properly seated now, with a bag of bran in front of her. On nearing the cattle-shed she was met by a boy bringing a milking-pail, who held the reins of the pony whilst she slid off. The boy led away the horse, leaving the pail with the young woman.

Soon soft spirts alternating with loud spirts came in regular succession from within the shed. They were the sounds of a person milking a cow. Gabriel took the lost hat in his hand, and waited beside the path she would follow in leaving the hill.

CONVERSATION

She came, the pail in one hand, hanging against her knee. The left arm was extended as a balance, enough of it being shown bare to make Oak wish that the event had happened in the summer, when the whole would have been revealed. There was a bright air and manner about her now, by which she seemed to imply that the desirability of her existence could not be questioned; and this rather saucy assumption failed in being offensive, because a beholder felt it to be, upon the whole, true. Like exceptional emphasis in the tone of a genius, that which would have made mediocrity ridiculous was an addition to recognised power. It was with some surprise that she saw Gabriel's face rising like the moon behind the hedge.

The adjustment of the farmer's hazy conceptions of her charms to the portrait of herself she now presented him with was less a diminution than a difference. The starting-point selected by the judgment was her height. She seemed tall, but the pail was a small one, and the hedge diminutive; hence, making allowance for error by comparison with these, she could have been not above the height to be chosen by women as best. All features of consequence were severe and regular. It may have been observed by persons who go about the shires with eyes for beauty, that in Englishwomen a classically-formed face is seldom found to be united with a figure of the same pattern, the highly-finished features being generally too large for the remainder of the frame; that a graceful and proportionate figure of eight heads usually goes off into random facial curves. Without throwing a Nymphean tissue over a milkmaid, let it be said that here criticism checked itself as out of place, and looked at her proportions with a long consciousness of pleasure. From the contours of her figure in its upper part, she must have had a beautiful neck and shoulders; but since her infancy nobody had ever seen them. Had she been put into a low dress she would have run and thrust her head into a bush. Yet she was not a shy girl by any means; it was merely her instinct to draw the line dividing the seen from the unseen higher than they do it in towns.

That the girl's thoughts hovered about her face and form as soon as she caught Oak's eyes conning the same page was natural, and almost certain. The self-consciousness shown would have been vanity if a little more pronounced, dignity if a little less. Rays of male vision seem to have a tickling effect upon virgin faces in rural districts; she hastily brushed hers with her hand, as if Gabriel had been irritating its pink surface by actual touch, and the free air of her previous movements was reduced at the same time to a chastened phase of itself. Yet it was the man who blushed, the maid not at all.

'I found a hat,' said Oak.

'It is mine,' said she, and, from a sense of proportion, kept down to a small smile an inclination to laugh distinctly: 'it flew away last night.'

'One o'clock this morning?'

'Well—it was.' She was surprised. 'How did you know?' she said.

'I was here.'

'You are Farmer Oak, are you not?'

'That or thereabouts. I'm lately come to this place.'

'A large farm?' she inquired, casting her eyes round, and swinging back her hair, which was black in the shaded hollows of its mass; but it being now an hour past sunrise, the rays touched its prominent curves with a colour of their own.

'No; not large. About a hundred.' (In speaking of farms the word 'acres' is omitted by the natives, by analogy to such old expressions as 'a stag of ten.')

'I wanted my hat this morning,' she went on. 'I had to ride to Tewnell Mill.'

'Yes, you had.'

'How do you know?'

'I saw you.'

'Where?' she inquired, a misgiving bringing every muscle of her lineaments and frame to a standstill.

'Here—going through the plantation, and all down the hill,' said Farmer Oak, with an aspect excessively knowing with regard to some matter in his mind, as he gazed at a remote point in the direction named, and then turned back to meet his colloquist's eyes.

A perception caused him to withdraw his own eyes from hers as suddenly as if he had been caught in a theft. Recollection of the strange antics she had indulged in when passing through the trees, was succeeded in the girl by a nettled palpitation, and that by a hot face. It was a time to see a woman redden who was not given to reddening as a rule; not a point in the milkmaid but was of the deepest rose-colour. From the Maiden's Blush, through all varieties of the Provence down to the Crimson Tuscany, the countenance of Oak's acquaintance quickly graduated; whereupon he, in considerateness, turned away his head.

The sympathetic man still looked the other way, and wondered when she would recover coolness sufficient to justify him in facing her again. He heard what seemed to be the flitting of a dead leaf upon the breeze, and looked. She had gone away.

With an air between that of Tragedy and Comedy Gabriel returned to his work.

Five mornings and evenings passed. The young woman came regularly to milk the healthy cow or to attend to the sick one, but never allowed her vision to stray in the direction of Oak's person. His want of tact had deeply offended her—not by seeing what he could not help, but by letting her know that he had seen it. For, as without law there is no sin, without eyes there is no indecorum; and she appeared to feel that Gabriel's espial had made her an indecorous woman

21

without her own connivance. It was food for great regret with him; it was also a *contretemps* which touched into life a latent heat he had experienced in that direction.

The acquaintanceship might, however, have ended in a slow forgetting, but for an incident which occurred at the end of the same week. One afternoon it began to freeze, and the frost increased with evening, which drew on like a stealthy tightening of bonds. It was a time when in cottages the breath of the sleepers freezes to the sheets; when round the drawing-room fire of a thick-walled mansion the sitters' backs are cold, even whilst their faces are all aglow. Many a small bird went to bed supperless that night among the bare boughs.

As the milking-hour drew near, Oak kept his usual watch upon the cowshed. At last he felt cold, and shaking an extra quantity of bedding round the yeaning ewes he entered the hut and heaped more fuel upon the stove. The wind came in at the bottom of the door, and to prevent it Oak wheeled the cot round a little more to the south. Then the wind spouted in at a ventilating hole—of which there was one on each side of the hut.

Gabriel had always known that when the fire was lighted and the door closed one of these must be kept open—that chosen being always on the side away from the wind. Closing the slide to windward, he turned to open the other; on second thoughts the farmer considered that he would first sit down, leaving both closed for a minute or two, till the temperature of the hut was a little raised. He sat down.

His head began to ache in an unwonted manner, and, fancying himself weary by reason of the broken rests of the preceding nights, Oak decided to get up, open the slide, and then allow himself to fall asleep. He fell asleep without having performed the necessary preliminary.

How long he remained unconscious Gabriel never

knew. During the first stages of his return to perception peculiar deeds seemed to be in course of enactment. His dog was howling, his head was aching fearfully—somebody was pulling him about, hands were loosening his neckerchief.

On opening his eyes he found that evening had sunk to dusk in a strange manner of unexpectedness. The young girl with the remarkably pleasant lips and white teeth was beside him. More than this—astonishingly more—his head was upon her lap, his face and neck were disagreeably wet, and her fingers were unbuttoning his collar.

'Whatever is the matter?' said Oak, vacantly.

She seemed to experience mirth, but of too insignificant a kind to start the capacity of enjoyment.

'Nothing now,' she answered, 'since you are not dead. It was a wonder you were not suffocated in this hut of yours.'

'Ah, the hut!' murmured Gabriel. 'I gave ten pounds for that hut. But I'll sell it, and sit under thatched hurdles as they did in old times, and curl up to sleep in a lock of straw! It played me nearly the same trick the other day!' Gabriel, by way of emphasis, brought down his fist upon the floor.

'It was not exactly the fault of the hut,' she observed, speaking in a tone which showed her to be that novelty among women—one who finished a thought before beginning the sentence which was to convey it. 'You should, I think, have considered, and not have been so foolish as to leave the slides closed.'

'Yes, I suppose I should,' said Oak, absently. He was endeavouring to catch and appreciate the sensation of being thus with her, his head upon her dress, before the event passed on into the heap of bygone things. He wished she knew his impressions; but he would as soon have thought of carrying an odour in a net as of attempting to convey the intangibilities of his feeling in the coarse meshes of language. So he remained silent.

She made him sit up, and then Oak began wiping his face and shaking himself like a Samson. 'How can I thank ye?' he said at last, gratefully, some of the natural rusty red having returned to his face.

'Oh, never mind that,' said the girl, smiling, and allowing her smile to hold good for Gabriel's next remark, whatever that might prove to be.

'How did you find me?'

'I heard your dog howling and scratching at the door of the hut when I came to the milking (it was so lucky, Daisy's milking is almost over for the season, and I shall not come here after this week or the next). The dog saw me, and jumped over to me, and laid hold of my skirt. I came across and looked round the hut the very first thing to see if the slides were closed. My uncle has a hut like this one, and I have heard him tell his shepherd not to go to sleep without leaving a slide open. I opened the door, and there you were like dead. I threw the milk over you, as there was no water, forgetting it was warm, and no use.'

'I wonder if I should have died?' Gabriel said, in a low voice, which was rather meant to travel back to himself than on to her.

'Oh no,' the girl replied. She seemed to prefer a less tragic probability; to have saved a man from death involved talk that should harmonise with the dignity of such a deed—and she shunned it.

'I believe you saved my life, Miss——I don't know your name. I know your aunt's, but not yours.'

'I would just as soon not tell it—rather not. There is no reason either why I should, as you probably will never have much to do with me.'

'Still, I should like to know.'

'You can inquire at my aunt's—she will tell you.'

'My name is Gabriel Oak.'

'And mine isn't. You seem fond of yours in speaking it so decisively, Gabriel Oak.'

'You see, it is the only one I shall ever have, and I must make the most o' it.'

'I always think mine sounds odd and disagreeable.'

'I should think you might soon get a new one.'

'Mercy!—how many opinions you keep about you concerning other people, Gabriel Oak.'

'Well, Miss—excuse the words—I thought you would like them. But I can't match you, I know, in mapping out my mind upon my tongue, as I mid say. I never was very clever in my inside. But I thank you. Come, give me your hand!'

She hesitated, somewhat disconcerted at Oak's old-fashioned earnest conclusion to a dialogue lightly carried on. 'Very well,' she said, and gave him her hand, compressing her lips to a demure impassivity. He held it but an instant, and in his fear of being too demonstrative, swerved to the opposite extreme, touching her fingers with the lightness of a small-hearted person.

'I am sorry,' he said, the instant after, regretfully.

'What for?'

'Letting your hand go so quick.'

'You may have me again if you like; there it is.' She gave him her hand again.

Oak held it longer this time—indeed, curiously long. 'How soft it is—being winter time, too—not chapped or rough, or anything!' he said.

'There—that's long enough,' said she, though without pulling it away. 'But I suppose you are thinking you would like to kiss it? You may if you want to.'

'I wasn't thinking of any such thing,' said Gabriel, simply; 'but I will——'

'That you won't!' She snatched back her hand.

Gabriel felt himself guilty of another want of tact.

'Now find out my name,' she said, teasingly; and withdrew.

CHAPTER IV

GABRIEL'S RESOLVE—THE VISIT—THE MISTAKE

THE only superiority in women that is tolerable to the rival sex is, as a rule, that of the unconscious kind; but a superiority which recognizes itself may sometimes please by suggesting possibilities of capture to the subordinated man.

This well-favoured and comely girl soon made appreciable inroads upon the emotional constitution of young Farmer Oak.

Love, being an extremely exacting usurer (a sense of exorbitant profit, spiritually, by an exchange of hearts, being at the bottom of pure passions, as that of exorbitant profit, bodily or materially, is at the bottom of those of lower atmosphere), every morning Oak's feelings were as sensitive as the money-market in calculations upon his chances. His dog waited for his meals in a way so like that in which Oak waited for the girl's presence, that the farmer was quite struck with the resemblance, felt it lowering, and would not look at the dog. However, he continued to watch through the hedge at her regular coming, and thus his sentiments towards her were deepened without any corresponding effect being produced upon herself. Oak had nothing finished and ready to say as yet, and not being able to frame love phrases which end where they begin; passionate tales—

> —Full of sound and fury
> —Signifying nothing—

he said no word at all.

By making inquiries he found that the girl's name was Bathsheba Everdene, and that the cow would go dry in about seven days. He dreaded the eighth day.

At last the eighth day came. The cow had ceased to give milk for that year, and Bathsheba Everdene came up the hill no more. Gabriel had reached a pitch of existence he never could have anticipated a short time before. He liked saying 'Bathsheba' as a private enjoyment instead of whistling; turned over his taste to black hair, though he had sworn by brown ever since he was a boy, isolated himself till the space he filled in the public eye was contemptibly small. Love is a possible strength in an actual weakness. Marriage transforms a distraction into a support, the power of which should be, and happily often is, in direct proportion to the degree of imbecility it supplants. Oak began now to see light in this direction, and said to himself, 'I'll make her my wife, or upon my soul I shall be good for nothing!'

All this while he was perplexing himself about an errand on which he might consistently visit the cottage of Bathsheba's aunt.

He found his opportunity in the death of a ewe, mother of a living lamb. On a day which had a summer face and a winter constitution—a fine January morning, when there was just enough blue sky visible to make cheerfully-disposed people wish for more, and an occasional gleam of silvery sunshine, Oak put the lamb into a respectable Sunday basket, and stalked across the fields to the house of Mrs. Hurst, the aunt—George, the dog, walking behind, with a countenance of great concern at the serious turn pastoral affairs seemed to be taking.

Gabriel had watched the blue wood-smoke curling from the chimney with strange meditation. At evening he had fancifully traced it down the chimney to the spot of its origin—seen the hearth and Bathsheba beside it—beside it in her out-door dress; for the clothes she had worn on the hill were by association equally with her person included in the compass of his affection; they seemed at this early time of his love a necessary ingredient of the sweet mixture called Bathsheba Everdene.

He had made a toilet of a nicely-adjusted kind—of a nature between the carefully neat and the carelessly ornate—of a degree between fine-market-day and wet-Sunday selection. He thoroughly cleaned his silver watch-chain with whiting, put new lacing straps to his boots, looked to the brass eyelet-holes, went to the inmost heart of the plantation for a new walking-stick, and trimmed it vigorously on his way back; took a new handkerchief from the bottom of his clothes-box, put on the light waistcoat patterned all over with sprigs of an elegant flower uniting the beauties of both rose and lily without the defects of either, and used all the hair-oil he possessed upon his usually dry, sandy, and inextricably curly hair, till he had deepened it to a splendidly novel colour, between that of guano and Roman cement, making it stick to his head like mace round a nutmeg, or wet seaweed round a boulder after the ebb.

Nothing disturbed the stillness of the cottage save the chatter of a knot of sparrows on the eaves; one might fancy scandal and rumour to be no less the staple topic of these little coteries on roofs than of those under them. It seemed that the omen was an unpropitious one, for, as the rather untoward commencement of Oak's overtures, just as he arrived by the garden

28

gate, he saw a cat inside, going into various arched shapes and fiendish convulsions at the sight of his dog George. The dog took no notice, for he had arrived at an age at which all superfluous barking was cynically avoided as a waste of breath—in fact, he never barked even at the sheep except to order, when it was done with an absolutely neutral countenance, as a sort of Commination-service, which, though offensive, had to be gone through once now and then to frighten the flock for their own good.

A voice came from behind some laurel-bushes into' which the cat had run :

'Poor dear! Did a nasty brute of a dog want to kill it ;—did he, poor dear !'

'I beg yer pardon,' said Oak to the voice, 'but George was walking on behind me with a temper as mild as milk.'

Almost before he had ceased speaking, Oak was seized with a misgiving as to whose ear was the recipient of his answer. Nobody appeared, and he heard the person retreat among the bushes.

Gabriel meditated, and so deeply that he brought small furrows into his forehead by sheer force of reverie. Where the issue of an interview is as likely to be a vast change for the worse as for the better, any initial difference from expectation causes nipping sensations of failure. Oak went up to the door a little abashed : his mental rehearsal and the reality had had no common grounds of opening.

Bathsheba's aunt was indoors. 'Will you tell Miss Everdene that somebody would be glad to speak to her?' said Mr. Oak. (Calling one's self merely Somebody, without giving a name, is not to be taken as an example of the ill-breeding of the rural world : it springs from a refined sense of modesty, of which townspeople, with their cards and announcements, have no notion whatever.)

Bathsheba was out. The voice had evidently been hers.

'Will you come in, Mr. Oak?'

'Oh, thank ye,' said Gabriel, following her to the fireplace. 'I've brought a lamb for Miss Everdene. I thought she might like one to rear; girls do.'

'She might,' said Mrs. Hurst, musingly; 'though she's only a visitor here. If you will wait a minute, Bathsheba will be in.'

'Yes, I will wait,' said Gabriel, sitting down. 'The lamb isn't really the business I came about, Mrs. Hurst. In short, I was going to ask her if she'd like to be married.'

'And were you indeed?'

'Yes. Because if she would, I should be very glad to marry her. D'ye know if she's got any other young man hanging about her at all?'

'Let me think,' said Mrs. Hurst, poking the fire superfluously. . . . 'Yes—bless you, ever so many young men. You see, Farmer Oak, she's so good-looking, and an excellent scholar besides—she was going to be a governess once, you know, only she was too wild. Not that her young men ever come here—but, Lord, in the nature of women, she must have a dozen!'

'That's unfortunate,' said Farmer Oak, contemplating a crack in the stone floor with sorrow. 'I'm only an every-day sort of man, and my only chance was in being the first comer. . . . Well, there's no use in my waiting, for that was all I came about: so I'll take myself off home-along, Mrs. Hurst.'

When Gabriel had gone about two hundred yards along the down, he heard a 'hoi-hoi!' uttered behind him, in a piping note of more treble quality than that in which the exclamation usually embodies itself when shouted across a field. He looked round, and saw a girl racing after him, waving a white handkerchief.

Oak stood still—and the runner drew nearer. It was

Bathsheba Everdene. Gabriel's colour deepened : hers was already deep, not, as it appeared, from emotion, but from running.

'Farmer Oak—I——' she said, pausing for want of breath, pulling up in front of him with a slanted face, and putting her hand to her side.

'I have just called to see you,' said Gabriel, pending her further speech.

'Yes—I know that,' she said, panting like a robin, her face red and moist from her exertions, like a peony petal before the sun dries off the dew. 'I didn't know you had come to ask to have me, or I should have come in from the garden instantly. I ran after you to say— that my aunt made a mistake in sending you away from courting me——'

Gabriel expanded. 'I'm sorry to have made you run so fast, my dear,' he said, with a grateful sense of favours to come. 'Wait a bit till you've found your breath.'

'—It was quite a mistake—aunt's telling you I had a young man already,' Bathsheba went on. 'I haven't a sweetheart at all—and I never had one, and I thought that, as times go with women, it was *such* a pity to send you away thinking that I had several.'

'Really and truly I am glad to hear that!' said Farmer Oak, smiling one of his long special smiles, and blushing with gladness. He held out his hand to take hers, which, when she had eased her side by pressing it there, was prettily extended upon her bosom to still her loud-beating heart. Directly he seized it she put it behind her, so that it slipped through his fingers like an eel.

'I have a nice snug little farm,' said Gabriel, with half a degree less assurance than when he had seized her hand.

'Yes ; you have.'

'A man has advanced me money to begin with, but

31

still, it will soon be paid off, and though I am only an every-day sort of a man, I have got on a little since I was a boy.' Gabriel uttered 'a little' in a tone to show her that it was the complacent form of 'a great deal.' He continued: 'When we be married, I am quite sure I can work twice as hard as I do now.'

He went forward and stretched out his arm again. Bathsheba had overtaken him at a point beside which stood a low stunted holly bush, now laden with red berries. Seeing his advance take the form of an attitude threatening a possible enclosure, if not compression, of her person, she edged off round the bush.

'Why, Farmer Oak,' she said, over the top, looking at him with rounded eyes, 'I never said I was going to marry you.'

'Well—that *is* a tale!' said Oak, with dismay. 'To run after anybody like this, and then say you don't want me!'

'What I meant to tell you was only this,' she said eagerly, and yet half conscious of the absurdity of the position she had made for herself—'that nobody has got me yet as a sweetheart, instead of my having a dozen, as my aunt said; I *hate* to be thought men's property in that way, though possibly I shall be had some day. Why,.if I'd wanted you I shouldn't have run after you like this; 'twould have been the *forwardest* thing! But there was no harm in hurrying to correct a piece of false news that had been told you.'

'Oh no—no harm at all.' But there is such a thing as being too generous in expressing a judgment impuls-ively, and Oak added with a more appreciative sense of all the circumstances—'Well, I am not quite certain it was no harm.'

'Indeed, I hadn't time to think before starting whether I wanted to marry or not, for you'd have been gone over the hill.'

'Come,' said Gabriel, freshening again; 'think a

minute or two. I'll wait a while, Miss Everdene. Will you marry me? Do, Bathsheba. I love you far more than common!'

'I'll try to think,' she observed, rather more timorously; 'if I can think out of doors; but my mind spreads away so.'

'But you can give a guess.'

'Then give me time.' Bathsheba looked thoughtfully into the distance, away from the direction in which Gabriel stood.

'I can make you happy,' said he to the back of her head, across the bush. 'You shall have a piano in a year or two—farmers' wives are getting to have pianos now—and I'll practise up the flute right well to play with you in the evenings.'

'Yes; I should like that.'

'And have one of those little ten-pound gigs for market—and nice flowers, and birds—cocks and hens I mean, because they be useful,' continued Gabriel, feeling balanced between poetry and prose.

'I should like it very much.'

'And a frame for cucumbers—like a gentleman and lady.'

'Yes.'

'And when the wedding was over, we'd have it put in the newspaper list of marriages.'

'Dearly I should like that!'

'And the babies in the births—every man jack of 'em! And at home by the fire, whenever you look up, there I shall be—and whenever I look up, there will be you.'

'Wait, wait, and don't be improper!'

Her countenance fell, and she was silent awhile. He regarded the red berries between them over and over again, to such an extent, that holly seemed in his after life to be a cypher signifying a proposal of marriage. Bathsheba decisively turned to him.

'No; 'tis no use,' she said. 'I don't want to marry you.'

'Try.'

'I have tried hard all the time I've been thinking; for a marriage would be very nice in one sense. People would talk about me, and think I had won my battle, and I should feel triumphant, and all that. But a husband——'

'Well!'

'Why, he'd always be there, as you say; whenever I looked up, there he'd be.'

'Of course he would—I, that is.'

'Well, what I mean is that I shouldn't mind being a bride at a wedding, if I could be one without having a husband. But since a woman can't show off in that way by herself, I shan't marry—at least yet.'

'That's a terrible wooden story.'

At this criticism of her statement Bathsheba made an addition to her dignity by a slight sweep away from him.

'Upon my heart and soul, I don't know what a maid can say stupider than that,' said Oak. 'But dearest,' he continued in a palliative voice, 'don't be like it!' Oak sighed a deep honest sigh—none the less so in that, being like the sigh of a pine plantation, it was rather noticeable as a disturbance of the atmosphere. 'Why won't you have me?' he said appealingly, creeping round the holly to reach her side.

'I cannot,' she said, retreating.

'But why?' he persisted, standing still at last in despair of ever reaching her, and facing over the bush.

'Because I don't love you.'

'Yes, but——'

She contracted a yawn to an inoffensive smallness, so that it was hardly ill-mannered at all. 'I don't love you,' she said.

34

'But I love you—and, as for myself, I am content to be liked.'

'Oh, Mr. Oak—that's very fine! You'd get to despise me.'

'Never,' said Mr. Oak, so earnestly that he seemed to be coming, by the force of his words, straight through the bush and into her arms. 'I shall do one thing in this life—one thing certain—that is, love you, and long for you, and *keep wanting you* till I die.' His voice had a genuine pathos now, and his large brown hands perceptibly trembled.

'It seems dreadfully wrong not to have you when you feel so much!' she said with a little distress, and looking hopelessly around for some means of escape from her moral dilemma. 'How I wish I hadn't run after you!' However, she seemed to have a short cut for getting back to cheerfulness, and set her face to signify archness. 'It wouldn't do, Mr. Oak. I want somebody to tame me; I am too independent; and you would never be able to, I know.'

Oak cast his eyes down the field in a way implying that it was useless to attempt argument.

'Mr. Oak,' she said, with luminous distinctness and common sense, 'you are better off than I. I have hardly a penny in the world—I am staying with my aunt for my bare sustenance. I am better educated than you—and I don't love you a bit: that's my side of the case. Now yours: you are a farmer just beginning, and you ought in common prudence, if you marry at all (which you should certainly not think of doing at present) to marry a woman with money, who would stock a larger farm for you than you have now.'

Gabriel looked at her with a little surprise and much admiration.

'That's the very thing I had been thinking myself!' he naïvely said.

Farmer Oak had one-and-a-half Christian character-

35

istics too many to succeed with Bathsheba : his humility, and a superfluous moiety of honesty. Bathsheba was decidedly disconcerted.

'Well, then, why did you come and disturb me?' she said, almost angrily, if not quite, an enlarging red spot rising in each cheek.

'I can't do what I think would be—would be——'

'Right?'

'No: wise.'

'You have made an admission *now*, Mr. Oak,' she exclaimed, with even more hauteur, and rocking her head disdainfully. 'After that, do you think I could marry you? Not if I know it.'

He broke in passionately: 'But don't mistake me like that! Because I am open enough to own what every man in my shoes would have thought of, you make your colours come up your face, and get crabbed with me. That about your not being good enough for me is nonsense. You speak like a lady—all the parish notice it, and your uncle at Weatherbury is, I have heerd, a large farmer—much larger than ever I shall be. May I call in the evening, or will you walk along with me o' Sundays? I don't want you to make up your mind at once, if you'd rather not.'

'No—no—I cannot. Don't press me any more—don't. I don't love you—so 'twould be ridiculous,' she said, with a laugh.

No man likes to see his emotions the sport of a merry-go-round of skittishness. 'Very well,' said Oak, firmly, with the bearing of one who was going to give his days and nights to Ecclesiastes for ever. 'Then I'll ask you no more.'

CHAPTER V

DEPARTURE OF BATHSHEBA——A PASTORAL TRAGEDY

THE news which one day reached Gabriel, that Bath-sheba Everdene had left the neighbourhood, had an influence upon him which might have surprised any who never suspected that the more emphatic the renunciation the less absolute its character.

It may have been observed that there is no regular path for getting out of love as there is for getting in. Some people look upon marriage as a short cut that way, but it has been known to fail. Separation, which was the means that chance offered to Gabriel Oak by Bathsheba's disappearance, though effectual with people of certain humours, is apt to idealise the removed object with others—notably those whose affection, placid and regular as it may be, flows deep and long. Oak belonged to the even-tempered order of humanity, and felt the secret fusion of himself in Bathsheba to be burning with a finer flame now that she was gone—that was all.

His incipient friendship with her aunt had been nipped by the failure of his suit, and all that Oak learnt of Bathsheba's movements was done indirectly. It appeared that she had gone to a place called Weatherbury, more than twenty miles off, but in what capacity—whether as a visitor, or permanently, he could not discover.

Gabriel had two dogs. George, the elder, exhibited

37

an ebony-tipped nose, surrounded by a narrow margin of pink flesh, and a coat marked in random splotches approximating in colour to white and slaty grey; but the grey, after years of sun and rain, had been scorched and washed out of the more prominent locks, leaving them of a reddish-brown, as if the blue component of the grey had faded, like the indigo from the same kind of colour in Turner's pictures. In substance it had originally been hair, but long contact with sheep seemed to be turning it by degrees into wool of a poor quality and staple.

This dog had originally belonged to a shepherd of inferior morals and dreadful temper, and the result was that George knew the exact degrees of condemnation signified by cursing and swearing of all descriptions better than the wickedest old man in the neighbourhood. Long experience had so precisely taught the animal the difference between such exclamations as 'Come in!' and 'D—— ye, come in!' that he knew to a hair's breadth the rate of trotting back from the ewes' tails that each call involved, if a staggerer with the sheep-crook was to be escaped. Though old, he was clever and trustworthy still.

The young dog, George's son, might possibly have been the image of his mother, for there was not much resemblance between him and George. He was learning the sheep-keeping business, so as to follow on at the flock when the other should die, but had got no further than the rudiments as yet—still finding an insuperable difficulty in distinguishing between doing a thing well enough and doing it too well. So earnest and yet so wrong-headed was this young dog (he had no name in particular, and answered with perfect readiness to any pleasant interjection), that if sent behind the flock to help them on, he did it so thoroughly that he would have chased them across the whole county with the greatest pleasure if not called off, or reminded when to stop by the example of old George.

38

Thus much for the dogs. On the farther side of Norcombe Hill was a chalk-pit, from which chalk had been drawn for generations, and spread over adjacent farms. Two hedges converged upon it in the form of a V, but without quite meeting. The narrow opening left, which was immediately over the brow of the pit, was protected by a rough railing.

One night, when Farmer Oak had returned to his house, believing there would be no further necessity for his attendance on the down, he called as usual to the dogs, previously to shutting them up in the outhouse till next morning. Only one responded—old George; the other could not be found, either in the house, lane, or garden. Gabriel then remembered that he had left the two dogs on the hill eating a dead lamb (a kind of meat he usually kept from them, except when other food ran short), and concluding that the young one had not finished his meal, he went indoors to the luxury of a bed, which latterly he had only enjoyed on Sundays.

It was a still, moist night. Just before dawn he was assisted in waking by the abnormal reverberation of familiar music. To the shepherd, the note of the sheep-bell, like the ticking of the clock to other people, is a chronic sound that only makes itself noticed by ceasing or altering in some unusual manner from the well-known idle tinkle which signifies to the accustomed ear, however distant, that all is well in the fold. In the solemn calm of the awakening morn that note was heard by Gabriel, beating with unusual violence and rapidity. This exceptional ringing may be caused in two ways— by the rapid feeding of the sheep bearing the bell, as when the flock breaks into new pasture, which gives it an intermittent rapidity, or by the sheep starting off in a run, when the sound has a regular palpitation. The experienced ear of Oak knew the sound he now heard to be caused by the running of the flock with great velocity.

He jumped out of bed, dressed, tore down the lane through a foggy dawn, and ascended the hill. The forward ewes were kept apart from those among which the fall of lambs would be later, there being two hundred of the latter class in Gabriel's flock. These two hundred seemed to have absolutely vanished from the hill. There were the fifty with their lambs, enclosed at the other end as he had left them, but the rest, forming the bulk of the flock, were nowhere. Gabriel called at the top of his voice the shepherd's call.

'Ovey, ovey, ovey!'

Not a single bleat. He went to the hedge—a gap had been broken through it, and in the gap were the footprints of the sheep. Rather surprised to find them break fence at this season, yet putting it down instantly to their great fondness for ivy in winter-time, of which a great deal grew in the plantation, he followed through the hedge. They were not in the plantation. He called again : the valleys and farthest hills resounded as when the sailors invoked the lost Hylas on the Mysian shore ; but no sheep. He passed through the trees and along the ridge of the hill. On the extreme summit, where the ends of the two converging hedges of which we have spoken were stopped short by meeting the brow of the chalk-pit, he saw the younger dog standing against the sky — dark and motionless as Napoleon at St. Helena.

A horrible conviction darted through Oak. With a sensation of bodily faintness he advanced: at one point the rails were broken through, and there he saw the footprints of his ewes. The dog came up, licked his hand, and made signs implying that he expected some great reward for signal services rendered. Oak looked over the precipice. The ewes lay dead and dying at its foot—a heap of two hundred mangled carcases, representing in their condition just now at least two hundred more.

Oak was an intensely humane man: indeed, his humanity often tore in pieces any politic intentions of his which bordered on strategy, and carried him on as by gravitation. A shadow in his life had always been that his flock ended in mutton—that a day came and found every shepherd an arrant traitor to his defenceless sheep. His first feeling now was one of pity for the untimely fate of these gentle ewes and their unborn lambs.

It was a second to remember another phase of the matter. The sheep were not insured. All the savings of a frugal life had been dispersed at a blow; his hopes of being an independent farmer were laid low—possibly for ever. Gabriel's energies, patience, and industry had been so severely taxed during the years of his life between eighteen and eight-and-twenty, to reach his present stage of progress, that no more seemed to be left in him. He leant down upon a rail, and covered his face with his hands.

Stupors, however, do not last for ever, and Farmer Oak recovered from his. It was as remarkable as it was characteristic that the one sentence he uttered was in thankfulness :—

'Thank God I am not married: what would *she* have done in the poverty now coming upon me!'

Oak raised his head, and wondering what he could do, listlessly surveyed the scene. By the outer margin of the pit was an oval pond, and over it hung the attenuated skeleton of a chrome-yellow moon, which had only a few days to last—the morning star dogging her on the right hand. The pool glittered like a dead man's eye, and as the world awoke a breeze blew, shaking and elongating the reflection of the moon without breaking it, and turning the image of the star to a phosphoric streak upon the water. All this Oak saw and remembered.

As far as could be learnt it appeared that the poor

young dog, still under the impression that since he was kept for running after sheep, the more he ran after them the better, had at the end of his meal off the dead lamb, which may have given him additional energy and spirits, collected all the ewes into a corner, driven the timid creatures through the hedge, across the upper field, and by main force of worrying had given them momentum enough to break down a portion of the rotten railing, and so hurled them over the edge.

George's son had done his work so thoroughly that he was considered too good a workman to live, and was, in fact, taken and tragically shot at twelve o'clock that same day—another instance of the untoward fate which so often attends dogs and other philosophers who follow out a train of reasoning to its logical conclusion, and attempt perfectly consistent conduct in a world made up so largely of compromise.

Gabriel's farm had been stocked by a dealer—on the strength of Oak's promising look and character—who was receiving a percentage from the farmer till such time as the advance should be cleared off. Oak found that the value of stock, plant, and implements which were really his own would be about sufficient to pay his debts, leaving himself a free man with the clothes he stood up in, and nothing more.

CHAPTER VI

THE FAIR—THE JOURNEY—THE FIRE

TWO months passed away. We are brought on to a day in February, on which was held the yearly statute or hiring fair in the county-town of Casterbridge.

At one end of the street stood from two to three hundred blithe and hearty labourers waiting upon Chance —all men of the stamp to whom labour suggests nothing worse than a wrestle with gravitation, and pleasure nothing better than a renunciation of the same. Among these, carters and waggoners were distinguished by having a piece of whip-cord twisted round their hats; thatchers wore a fragment of woven straw; shepherds held their sheep-crooks in their hands; and thus the situation required was known to the hirers at a glance.

In the crowd was an athletic young fellow of somewhat superior appearance to the rest—in fact, his superiority was marked enough to lead several ruddy peasants standing by to speak to him inquiringly, as to a farmer, and to use 'Sir' as a finishing word. His answer always was,—

'I am looking for a place myself—a bailiff's. Do ye know of anybody who wants one?'

Gabriel was paler now. His eyes were more meditative, and his expression was more sad. He had passed through an ordeal of wretchedness which had given him more than it had taken away. He had sunk from his modest elevation as pastoral king into the very slime-pits of Siddim ; but there was left to him a dignified calm he had never before known, and that indifference to fate which, though it often makes a villain of a man, is the basis of his sublimity when it does not. And thus the abasement had been exaltation, and the loss gain.

In the morning a regiment of cavalry had left the town, and a sergeant and his party had been beating up for recruits through the four streets. As the end of the day drew on, and he found himself not hired, Gabriel almost wished that he had joined them, and gone off to serve his country. Weary of standing in the market-place, and not much minding the kind of work he turned his hand to, he decided to offer himself in some other capacity than that of bailiff.

All the farmers seemed to be wanting shepherds. Sheep-tending was Gabriel's specialty. Turning down an obscure street and entering an obscurer lane, he went up to a smith's shop.

'How long would it take you to make a shepherd's crook ? '

'Twenty minutes.'

'How much ? '

'Two shillings.'

He sat on a bench and the crook was made, a stem being given him into the bargain.

He then went to a ready-made clothes' shop, the owner of which had a large rural connection. As the crook had absorbed most of Gabriel's money, he attempted, and carried out, an exchange of his overcoat for a shepherd's regulation smock-frock.

This transaction having been completed, he again hurried off to the centre of the town, and stood on the kerb of the pavement, as a shepherd, crook in hand.

Now that Oak had turned himself into a shepherd, it seemed that bailiffs were most in demand. However, two or three farmers noticed him and drew near. Dialogues followed, more or less in the subjoined form :—

'Where do you come from?'

'Norcombe.'

'That's a long way.'

'Fifteen miles.'

'Who's farm were you upon last?'

'My own.'

This reply invariably operated like a rumour of cholera. The inquiring farmer would edge away and shake his head dubiously. Gabriel, like his dog, was too good to be trustworthy, and he never made advance beyond this point.

It is safer to accept any chance that offers itself, and extemporize a procedure to fit it, than to get a good plan matured, and wait for a chance of using it. Gabriel wished he had not nailed up his colours as a shepherd, but had laid himself out for anything in the whole cycle of labour that was required in the fair. It grew dusk. Some merry men were whistling and singing by the corn-exchange. Gabriel's hand, which had lain for some time idle in his smock-frock pocket, touched his flute, which he carried there. Here was an opportunity for putting his dearly bought wisdom into practice.

He drew out his flute and began to play 'Jockey to the Fair' in the style of a man who had never known a moment's sorrow. Oak could pipe with Arcadian sweetness, and the sound of the well-known notes cheered his own heart as well as those of the loungers. He played on with spirit, and in half an hour had earned in pence what was a small fortune to a destitute man.

By making inquiries he learnt that there was another fair at Shottsford the next day.

'How far is Shottsford?'

'Ten miles t'other side of Weatherbury.'

Weatherbury! It was where Bathsheba had gone two months before. This information was like coming from night into noon.

'How far is it to Weatherbury?'

'Five or six miles.'

Bathsheba had probably left Weatherbury long before this time, but the place had enough interest attaching to it to lead Oak to choose Shottsford fair as his next field of inquiry, because it lay in the Weatherbury quarter. Moreover, the Weatherbury folk were by no means uninteresting intrinsically. If report spoke truly they were as hardy, merry, thriving, wicked a set as any in the whole county. Oak resolved to sleep at Weatherbury that night on his way to Shottsford, and struck out at once into the high road which had been recommended as the direct route to the village in question.

The road stretched through water-meadows traversed by little brooks, whose quivering surfaces were braided along their centres, and folded into creases at the sides; or, where the flow was more rapid, the stream was pied with spots of white froth, which rode on in undisturbed serenity. On the higher levels the dead and dry carcases of leaves tapped the ground as they bowled along helter-skelter upon the shoulders of the wind, and little birds in the hedges were rustling their feathers and tucking themselves in comfortably for the night, retaining their places if Oak kept moving, but flying away if he stopped to look at them. He passed by Yalbury Wood where the game-birds were rising to their roosts, and heard the crack-voiced cock-pheasants' 'cu-uck, cuck,' and the wheezy whistle of the hens.

By the time he had walked three or four miles every shape in the landscape had assumed a uniform hue of blackness. He descended Yalbury Hill and could just

46

discern ahead of him a waggon, drawn up under a great over-hanging tree by the roadside.

On coming close, he found there were no horses attached to it, the spot being apparently quite deserted. The waggon, from its position, seemed to have been left there for the night, for beyond about half a truss of hay which was heaped in the bottom, it was quite empty. Gabriel sat down on the shafts of the vehicle and considered his position. He calculated that he had walked a very fair proportion of the journey; and having been on foot since daybreak, he felt tempted to lie down upon the hay in the waggon instead of pushing on to the village of Weatherbury, and having to pay for a lodging.

Eating his last slices of bread and ham, and drinking from the bottle of cider he had taken the precaution to bring with him, he got into the lonely waggon. Here he spread half of the hay as a bed, and, as well as he could in the darkness, pulled the other half over him by way of bed-clothes, covering himself entirely, and feeling, physically, as comfortable as ever he had been in his life. Inward melancholy it was impossible for a man like Oak, introspective far beyond his neighbours, to banish quite, whilst conning the present untoward page of his history. So, thinking of his misfortunes, amorous and pastoral, he fell asleep, shepherds enjoying, in common with sailors, the privilege of being able to summon the god instead of having to wait for him.

On somewhat suddenly awaking, after a sleep of whose length he had no idea, Oak found that the waggon was in motion. He was being carried along the road at a ·rate rather considerable for a vehicle without springs, and under circumstances of physical uneasiness, his head being dandled up and down on the bed of the waggon like a kettledrum-stick. He then distinguished voices in conversation, coming from the forepart of the waggon. His concern at this dilemma (which would have been alarm, had he been a thriving

47

man ; but misfortune is a fine opiate to personal terror)
led him to peer cautiously from the hay, and the first
sight he beheld was the stars above him. Charles's
Wain was getting towards a right angle with the Pole
star, and Gabriel concluded that it must be about nine
o'clock—in other words, that he had slept two hours.
This small astronomical calculation was made without
any positive effort, and whilst he was stealthily turning
to discover, if possible, into whose hands he had fallen.

Two figures were dimly visible in front, sitting with
their legs outside the waggon, one of whom was driving.
Gabriel soon found that this was the waggoner, and it
appeared they had come from Casterbridge fair, like
himself.

A conversation was in progress, which continued
thus :—

'Be as 'twill, she's a fine handsome body as far's
looks be concerned. But that's only the skin of the
woman, and these dandy cattle be as proud as a lucifer
in their insides.'

'Ay—so 'a do seem, Billy Smallbury—so 'a do seem.'
This utterance was very shaky by nature, and more so
by circumstance, the jolting of the waggon not being
without its effect upon the speaker's larynx. It came
from the man who held the reins.

'She's a very vain feymell—so 'tis said here and
there.'

'Ah, now. If so be 'tis like that, I can't look her in
the face. Lord, no: not I—heh-heh-heh ! Such a shy
man as I be !'

'Yes—she's very vain. 'Tis said that every night at
going to bed she looks in the glass to put on her nightcap properly.'

'And not a married woman. Oh, the world !'

'And 'a can play the peanner, so 'tis said. Can
play so clever that 'a can make a psalm tune sound as
well as the merriest loose song a man can wish for.'

'D'ye tell o't! A happy time for us, and I feel quite a new man! And how do she pay?'

'That I don't know, Master Poorgrass.'

On hearing these and other similar remarks, a wild thought flashed into Gabriel's mind that they might be speaking of Bathsheba. There were, however, no grounds for retaining such a supposition, for the waggon, though going in the direction of Weatherbury, might be going beyond it, and the woman alluded to seemed to be the mistress of some estate. They were now apparently close upon Weatherbury, and not to alarm the speakers unnecessarily, Gabriel slipped out of the waggon unseen.

He turned to an opening in the hedge, which he found to be a gate, and mounting thereon, he sat meditating whether to seek a cheap lodging in the village, or to ensure a cheaper one by lying under some hay or corn-stack. The crunching jangle of the waggon died upon his ear. He was about to walk on, when he noticed on his left hand an unusual light—appearing about half a mile distant. Oak watched it, and the glow increased. Something was on fire.

Gabriel again mounted the gate, and, leaping down on the other side upon what he found to be ploughed soil, made across the field in the exact direction of the fire. The blaze, enlarging in a double ratio by his approach and its own increase, showed him as he drew nearer the outlines of ricks beside it, lighted up to great distinctness. A rick-yard was the source of the fire. His weary face now began to be painted over with a rich orange glow, and the whole front of his smock-frock and gaiters was covered with a dancing shadow pattern of thorn-twigs—the light reaching him through a leafless intervening hedge—and the metallic curve of his sheep-crook shone silver-bright in the same abounding rays. He came up to the boundary fence, and stood to regain breath. It seemed as if the spot was unoccupied by a living soul.

49

The fire was issuing from a long straw-stack, which was so far gone as to preclude a possibility of saving it. A rick burns differently from a house. As the wind blows the fire inwards, the portion in flames completely disappears like melting sugar, and the outline is lost to the eye. However, a hay or a wheat-rick, well put together, will resist combustion for a length of time, if it begins on the outside.

This before Gabriel's eyes was a rick of straw, loosely put together, and the flames darted into it with lightning swiftness. It glowed on the windward side, rising and falling in intensity, like the coal of a cigar. Then a superincumbent bundle rolled down, with a whisking noise; flames elongated, and bent themselves about, with a quiet roar, but no crackle. Banks of smoke went off horizontally at the back like passing clouds, and behind these burned hidden pyres, illuminating the semi-transparent sheet of smoke to a lustrous yellow uniformity. Individual straws in the foreground were consumed in a creeping movement of ruddy heat, as if they were knots of red worms, and above shone imaginary fiery faces, tongues hanging from lips, glaring eyes, and other impish forms, from which at intervals sparks flew in clusters like birds from a nest.

Oak suddenly ceased from being a mere spectator by discovering the case to be more serious than he had at first imagined. A scroll of smoke blew aside and revealed to him a wheat-rick in startling juxtaposition with the decaying one, and behind this a series of others, composing the main corn produce of the farm; so that instead of the straw-stack standing, as he had imagined, comparatively isolated, there was a regular connection between it and the remaining stacks of the group.

Gabriel leapt over the hedge, and saw that he was not alone. The first man he came to was running about in a great hurry, as if his thoughts were several yards in advance of his body, which they could never drag on fast enough.

'Oh, man—fire, fire! A good master and a bad servant is fire, fire!—I mane a bad servant and a good master. Oh, Mark Clark—come! And you, Billy Smallbury—and you, Maryann Money—and you, Jan Coggan, and Matthew there!' Other figures now appeared behind this shouting man and among the smoke, and Gabriel found that, far from being alone, he was in a great company—whose shadows danced merrily up and down, timed by the jigging of the, flames, and not at all by their owners' movements. The assemblage—belonging to that class of society which casts its thoughts into the form of feeling, and its feelings into the form of commotion—set to work with a remarkable confusion of purpose.

'Stop the draught under the wheat-rick!' cried Gabriel to those nearest to him. The corn stood on stone staddles, and between these, tongues of yellow hue from the burning straw licked and darted playfully. If the fire once got *under* this stack, all would be lost.

'Get a tarpaulin—quick!' said Gabriel.

A rick-cloth was brought, and they hung it like a curtain across the channel. The flames immediately ceased to go under the bottom of the corn-stack, and stood up vertical.

'Stand here with a bucket of water and keep the cloth wet,' said Gabriel again.

The flames, now driven upwards, began to attack the angles of the huge roof covering the wheat-stack.

'A ladder,' cried Gabriel.

'The ladder was against the straw-rick and is burnt to a cinder,' said a spectre-like form in the smoke.

Oak seized the cut ends of the sheaves, as if he were going to engage in the operation of 'reed-drawing,' and digging in his feet, and occasionally sticking in the stem of his sheep-crook, he clambered up the beetling face. He at once sat astride the very apex, and began with his crook to beat off the fiery fragments which had lodged thereon, shouting to the others to get him a bough and a ladder, and some water.

Billy Smallbury—one of the men who had been on the waggon—by this time had found a ladder, which Mark Clark ascended, holding on beside Oak upon the thatch. The smoke at this corner was stifling, and Clark, a nimble fellow, having been handed a bucket of water, bathed Oak's face and sprinkled him generally, whilst Gabriel, now with a long beech-bough in one hand, in addition to his crook in the other, kept sweeping the stack and dislodging all fiery particles.

On the ground the groups of villagers were still occupied in doing all they could to keep down the conflagration, which was not much. They were all tinged orange, and backed up by shadows of varying pattern. Round the corner of the largest stack, out of the direct rays of the fire, stood a pony, bearing a young woman on its back. By her side was another woman, on foot. These two seemed to keep at a distance from the fire, that the horse might not become restive.

'He's a shepherd,' said the woman on foot. 'Yes—he is. See how his crook shines as he beats the rick with it. And his smock-frock is burnt in two holes, I declare! A fine young shepherd he is too, ma'am.'

'Whose shepherd is he?' said the equestrian in a clear voice.

'Don't know, ma'am.'

'Don't any of the others know?'

'Nobody at all—I've asked 'em. Quite a stranger, they say.'

The young woman on the pony rode out from the shade and looked anxiously around.

'Do you think the barn is safe?' she said.

'D'ye think the barn is safe, Jan Coggan?' said the second woman, passing on the question to the nearest man in that direction.

'Safe now—leastwise I think so. If this rick had gone the barn would have followed. 'Tis that bold shepherd up there that have done the most good—he sitting on the top o' rick, whizzing his great long arms about like a windmill.'

'He does work hard,' said the young woman on horseback, looking up at Gabriel through her thick woollen veil. 'I wish he was shepherd here. Don't any of you know his name.'

'Never heard the man's name in my life, or seed his form afore.'

The fire began to get worsted, and Gabriel's elevated position being no longer required of him, he made as if to descend.

'Maryann,' said the girl on horseback, 'go to him as he comes down, and say that the farmer wishes to thank him for the great service he has done.'

Maryann stalked off towards the rick and met Oak at the foot of the ladder. She delivered her message.

'Where is your master the farmer?' asked Gabriel, kindling with the idea of getting employment that seemed to strike him now.

''Tisn't a master; 'tis a mistress, shepherd.'

'A woman farmer?'

'Ay, 'a b'lieve, and a rich one too!' said a bystander. 'Lately 'a came here from a distance. Took on her uncle's farm, who died suddenly. Used to measure his money in half-pint cups. They say now that she've business in every bank in Casterbridge, and thinks no more of playing pitch-and-toss sovereign than you and I do pitch-halfpenny—not a bit in the world, shepherd.'

'That's she, back there upon the pony,' said Maryann ; 'wi' her face a-covered up in that black cloth with holes in it.'

Oak, his features smudged, grimy, and undiscoverable from the smoke and heat, his smock-frock burnt into holes and dripping with water, the ash stem of his sheep-crook charred six inches shorter, advanced with the humility stern adversity had thrust upon him up to the slight female form in the saddle. He lifted his hat with respect, and not without gallantry : stepping close to her hanging feet he said in a hesitating voice,—

'Do you happen to want a shepherd, ma'am ?'

She lifted the veil tied round her face, and looked all astonishment. Gabriel and his cold-hearted darling, Bathsheba Everdene, were face to face.

Bathsheba did not speak, and he mechanically repeated in an abashed and sad voice,—

'Do you want a shepherd, ma'am ?'

CHAPTER VII

RECOGNITION——A TIMID GIRL

BATHSHEBA withdrew into the shade. She scarcely knew whether most to be amused at the singularity of the meeting, or to be concerned at its awkwardness. There was room for a little pity, also for a very little exultation : the former at his position, the latter at her own. Embarrassed she was not, and she remembered Gabriel's declaration of love to her at Norcombe only to think she had nearly forgotten it.

'Yes,' she murmured, putting on an air of dignity, and turning again to him with a little warmth of cheek ; 'I do want a shepherd. But——'

'He's the very man, ma'am,' said one of the villagers, quietly.

Conviction breeds conviction. 'Ay, that 'a is,' said a second, decisively.

'The man, truly !' said a third, with heartiness.

'He's all there !' said number four, fervidly.

'Then will you tell him to speak to the bailiff,' said Bathsheba.

All was practical again now. A summer eve and loneliness would have been necessary to give the meeting its proper fulness of romance.

The bailiff was pointed out to Gabriel, who, checking the palpitation within his breast at discovering that this Ashtoreth of strange report was only a modification of

55

Venus the well-known and admired, retired with him to talk over the necessary preliminaries of hiring.

The fire before them wasted away. 'Men,' said Bathsheba, 'you shall take a little refreshment after this extra work. Will you come to the house?'

'We could knock in a bit and a drop a good deal freer, Miss, if so be ye'd send it to Warren's Malthouse,' replied the spokesman.

Bathsheba then rode off into the darkness, and the men straggled on to the village in twos and threes—Oak and the bailiff being left by the rick alone.

'And now,' said the bailiff, finally, 'all is settled, I think, about yer coming, and I am going home-along. Good-night to ye, shepherd.'

'Can you get me a lodging?' inquired Gabriel.

'That I can't, indeed,' he said, moving past Oak as a Christian edges past an offertory-plate when he does not mean to contribute. 'If you follow on the road till you come to Warren's Malthouse, where they are all gone to have their snap of victuals, I daresay some of 'em will tell you of a place. Good-night to ye, shepherd.'

The bailiff who showed this nervous dread of loving his neighbour as himself, went up the hill, and Oak walked on to the village, still astonished at the rencounter with Bathsheba, glad of his nearness to her, and perplexed at the rapidity with which the unpractised girl of Norcombe had developed into the supervising and cool woman here. But some women only require an emergency to make them fit for one.

Obliged, to some extent, to forego dreaming in order to find the way, he reached the churchyard, and passed round it under the wall where several ancient trees grew. There was a wide margin of grass along here, and Gabriel's footsteps were deadened by its softness, even at this indurating period of the year. When abreast of a trunk which appeared to be the oldest of the old, he became aware that a figure was standing behind it.

56

Gabriel did not pause in his walk, and in another moment he accidentally kicked a loose stone. The noise was enough to disturb the motionless stranger, who started and assumed a careless position.

It was a slim girl, rather thinly clad.

'Good-night to you,' said Gabriel, heartily.

'Good-night,' said the girl to Gabriel.

The voice was unexpectedly attractive; it was the low and dulcet note suggestive of romance ; common in descriptions, rare in experience.

'I'll thank you to tell me if I'm in the way for Warren's Malthouse ? ' Gabriel resumed, primarily to gain the information, indirectly to get more of the music.

'Quite right. It's at the bottom of the hill. And do you know——' The girl hesitated and then went on again. 'Do you know how late they keep open the Buck's Head Inn ? ' She seemed to be won by Gabriel's heartiness, as Gabriel had been won by her modulations.

'I don't know where the Buck's Head is, or anything about it. Do you think of going there to-night ? '

'Yes——' The woman again paused. There was no necessity for any continuance of speech, and the fact that she did add more seemed to proceed from an unconscious desire to show unconcern by making a remark, which is noticeable in the ingenuous when they are acting by stealth. 'You are not a Weatherbury man ? ' she said, timorously.

'I am not. I am the new shepherd—just arrived.'

'Only a shepherd—and you seem almost a farmer by your ways.'

'Only a shepherd,' Gabriel repeated, in a dull cadence of finality. His thoughts were directed to the past, his eyes to the feet of the girl ; and for the first time he saw lying there a bundle of some sort. She may have perceived the direction of his face, for she said coaxingly,—

'You won't say anything in the parish about having seen me here, will you—at least, not for a day or two?'

'I won't if you wish me not to,' said Oak.

'Thank you, indeed,' the other replied. 'I am rather poor, and I don't want people to know anything about me.' Then she was silent and shivered.

'You ought to have a cloak on such a cold night,' Gabriel observed. 'I would advise 'ee to get indoors.'

'Oh no! Would you mind going on and leaving me? I thank you much for what you have told me.'

'I will go on,' he said; adding hesitatingly,—'Since you are not very well off, perhaps you would accept this trifle from me. It is only a shilling, but it is all I have to spare.'

'Yes, I will take it,' said the stranger, gratefully.

She extended her hand; Gabriel his. In feeling for each other's palms in the gloom before the money could be passed, a minute incident occurred which told much. Gabriel's fingers alighted on the young woman's wrist. It was beating with a throb of tragic intensity. He had frequently felt the same quick, hard beat in the femoral artery of his lambs when overdriven. It suggested a consumption too great of a vitality which, to judge from her figure and stature, was already too little.

'What is the matter?'

'Nothing.'

'But there is?'

'No, no, no! Let your having seen me be a secret!'

'Very well; I will. Good-night, again.'

'Good-night.'

The young girl remained motionless by the tree, and Gabriel descended into the village of Weatherbury, or Lower Longpuddle as it was sometimes called. He fancied that he had felt himself in the penumbra of a very deep sadness when touching that slight and fragile creature. But wisdom lies in moderating mere impressions, and Gabriel endeavoured to think little of this.

CHAPTER VIII

THE MALTHOUSE—THE CHAT—NEWS

WARREN'S Malthouse was enclosed by an old wall inwrapped with ivy, and though not much of the exterior was visible at this hour, the character and purposes of the building were clearly enough shown by its outline upon the sky. From the walls an overhanging thatched roof sloped up to a point in the centre, upon which rose a small wooden lantern, fitted with louvre-boards on all the four sides, and from these openings a mist was dimly perceived to be escaping into the night air. There was no window in front ; but a square hole in the door was glazed with a single pane, through which red, comfortable rays now stretched out upon the ivied wall in front. Voices were to be heard inside.

Oak's hand skimmed the surface of the door with fingers extended to an Elymas-the-Sorcerer pattern, till he found a leathern strap, which he pulled. This lifted a wooden latch, and the door swung open.

The room inside was lighted only by the ruddy glow from the kiln mouth, which shone over the floor with the streaming horizontality of the setting sun, and threw upwards the shadows of all facial irregularities in those assembled around. The stone-flag floor was worn into a path from the doorway to the kiln, and into undulations everywhere. A curved settle of unplaned oak

59

stretched along one side, and in a remote corner was a small bed and bedstead, the owner and frequent occupier of which was the maltster.

This aged man was now sitting opposite the fire, his frosty white hair and beard overgrowing his gnarled figure like the grey moss and lichen upon a leafless apple-tree. He wore breeches and the laced-up shoes called ankle-jacks; he kept his eyes fixed upon the fire.

Gabriel's nose was greeted by an atmosphere laden with the sweet smell of new malt. The conversation (which seemed to have been concerning the origin of the fire) immediately ceased, and every one ocularly criticised him to the degree expressed by contracting the flesh of their foreheads and looking at him with narrowed eyelids, as if he had been a light too strong for their sight. Several exclaimed meditatively, after this operation had been completed :—

'Oh, 'tis the new shepherd, 'a b'lieve.'

'We thought we heard a hand pawing about the door for the bobbin, but weren't sure 'twere not a dead leaf blowed across,' said another. 'Come in, shepherd; sure ye be welcome, though we don't know yer name.'

'Gabriel Oak, that's my name, neighbours.'

The ancient maltster sitting in the midst turned at this—his turning being as the turning of a rusty crane.

'That's never Gable Oak's grandson over at Norcombe—never!' he said, as a formula expressive of surprise, which nobody was supposed for a moment to take literally.

'My father and my grandfather were old men of the name of Gabriel,' said the shepherd, placidly.

'Thought I knowed the man's face as I seed him on the rick!—thought I did! And where be ye trading o't to now, shepherd?'

'I'm thinking of biding here,' said Mr. Oak.

'Knowed yer grandfather for years and years!'

continued the maltster, the words coming forth of their
own accord as if the momentum previously imparted
had been sufficient.

'Ah—and did you!'

'Knowed yer grandmother.'

'And her too!'

'Likewise knowed yer father when he was a child.
Why, my boy Jacob there and your father were sworn
brothers—that they were sure—weren't ye, Jacob?'

'Ay, sure,' said his son, a young man about sixty-
five, with a semi-bald head and one tooth in the left
centre of his upper jaw, which made much of itself by
standing prominent, like a milestone in a bank. 'But
'twas Joe had most to do with him. However, my son
William must have knowed the very man afore us—
didn't ye, Billy, afore ye left Norcombe?'

'No, 'twas Andrew,' said Jacob's son Billy, a child
of forty, or thereabouts, who manifested the peculiarity
of possessing a cheerful soul in a gloomy body, and
whose whiskers were assuming a chinchilla shade here
and there.

'I can mind Andrew,' said Oak, 'as being a man in
the place when I was quite a child.'

'Ay—the other day I and my youngest daughter,
Liddy, were over at my grandson's christening,' continued
Billy. 'We were talking about this very family, and
'twas only last Purification Day in this very world, when
the use-money is gied away to the second-best poor
folk, you know, shepherd, and I can mind the day
because they all had to traypse up to the vestry—yes,
this very man's family.'

'Come, shepherd, and drink. 'Tis gape and
swaller with us—a drap of sommit, but not of much
account,' said the maltster, removing from the fire his
eyes, which were vermilion-red and bleared by gazing
into it for so many years. 'Take up the God-forgive-
me, Jacob. See if 'tis warm, Jacob.'

Jacob stooped to the God-forgive-me, which was a two-handled tall mug standing in the ashes, cracked and charred with heat : it was rather furred with extraneous matter about the outside, especially in the crevices of the handles, the innermost curves of which may not have seen daylight for several years by reason of this encrustation thereon—formed of ashes accidentally wetted with cider and baked hard ; but to the mind of any sensible drinker the cup was no worse for that, being incontestably clean on the inside and about the rim. It may be observed that such a class of mug is called a God-forgive-me in Weatherbury and its vicinity for uncertain reasons ; probably because its size makes any given toper feel ashamed of himself when he sees its bottom in drinking it empty.

Jacob, on receiving the order to see if the liquor was warm enough, placidly dipped his forefinger into it by way of thermometer, and having pronounced it nearly of the proper degree, raised the cup and very civilly attempted to dust some of the ashes from the bottom with the skirt of his smock-frock, because Shepherd Oak was a stranger.

'A clane cup for the shepherd,' said the maltster commandingly.

'No—not at all,' said Gabriel, in a reproving tone of considerateness. 'I never fuss about dirt in its pure state, and when I know what sort it is.' Taking the mug he drank an inch or more from the depth of its contents, and duly passed it to the next man. 'I wouldn't think of giving such trouble to neighbours in washing up when there's so much work to be done in the world already,' continued Oak in a moister tone, after recovering from the stoppage of breath which is occasioned by pulls at large mugs.

'A right sensible man,' said Jacob.

'True, true ; it can't be gainsaid !' observed a brisk young man—Mark Clark by name, a genial and pleasant gentleman, whom to meet anywhere in your travels was to know, to know was to drink with, and to drink with was, unfortunately, to pay for.

'And here's a mouthful of bread and bacon that mis'ess have sent, shepherd. The cider will go down better with a bit of victuals. Don't ye chaw quite close, shepherd, for I let the bacon fall in the road outside as I was bringing it along, and may be 'tis rather gritty. There, 'tis clane dirt; and we all know what that is, as you say, and you bain't a particular man we see, shepherd.'

'True, true—not at all,' said the friendly Oak.

'Don't let your teeth quite meet, and you won't feel the sandiness at all. Ah! 'tis wonderful what can be done by contrivance!'

'My own mind exactly, neighbour.'

'Ah, he's his grandfer's own grandson!—his grandfer were just such a nice unparticular man!' said the maltster.

'Drink, Henry Fray—drink,' magnanimously said Jan Coggan, a person who held Saint-Simonian notions of share and share alike where liquor was concerned, as the vessel showed signs of approaching him in its gradual revolution among them.

Having at this moment reached the end of a wistful gaze into mid-air, Henry did not refuse. He was a man of more than middle age, with eyebrows high up in his forehead, who laid it down that the law of the world was bad, with a long-suffering look through his listeners at the world alluded to, as it presented itself to his imagination. He always signed his name 'Henery'— strenuously insisting upon that spelling, and if any passing schoolmaster ventured to remark that the second 'e' was superfluous and old-fashioned, he received the reply that 'H-e-n-e-r-y' was the name he was christened and the name he would stick to—in the tone of one to whom orthographical differences were matters which had a great deal to do with personal character.

Mr. Jan Coggan, who had passed the cup to Henery, was a crimson man with a spacious countenance, and private glimmer in his eye, whose name had appeared on the marriage register of Weatherbury and neighbouring parishes as best man and chief witness in countless unions of the previous twenty years; he also very frequently filled the post of head godfather in baptisms of the subtly-jovial kind.

'Come, Mark Clark—come. Ther's plenty more in the barrel,' said Jan.

'Ay—that I will; 'tis my only doctor,' replied Mr. Clark, who, twenty years younger than Jan Coggan, revolved in the same orbit. He secreted mirth on all occasions for special discharge at popular parties.

'Why, Joseph Poorgrass, ye han't had a drop!' said Mr. Coggan to a self-conscious man in the background, thrusting the cup towards him.

'Such a modest man as he is!' said Jacob Smallbury. 'Why, ye've hardly had strength of eye enough to look in our young mis'ess's face, so I hear, Joseph?'

All looked at Joseph Poorgrass with pitying reproach.

'No—I've hardly looked at her at all,' simpered Joseph, reducing his body smaller whilst talking, apparently from a meek sense of undue prominence. 'And when I seed her, 'twas nothing but blushes with me!'

'Poor feller,' said Mr. Clark.

''Tis a curious nature for a man,' said Jan Coggan.

'Yes,' continued Joseph Poorgrass—his shyness, which was so painful as a defect, filling him with a mild complacency now that it was regarded as an interesting study. ''Twere blush, blush, blush with me every minute of the time, when she was speaking to me.'

'I believe ye, Joseph Poorgrass, for we all know ye to be a very bashful man.'

''Tis a' awkward gift for a man, poor soul,' said the

64

maltster. 'And how long have ye suffered from it, Joseph?'

'Oh, ever since I was a boy. Yes—mother was concerned to her heart about it—yes. But 'twas all nought.'

'Did ye ever go into the world to try and stop it, Joseph Poorgrass?'

'Oh ay, tried all sorts o' company. They took me to Greenhill Fair, and into a great large jerry-go-nimble show, where there were women-folk riding round—standing upon horses, with hardly anything on but their smocks; but it didn't cure me a morsel. And then I was put errand-man at the Woman's Skittle Alley at the back of the Tailor's Arms in Casterbridge. 'Twas a horrible evil situation, and a very curious place for a good man. I had to stand and look ba'dy people in the face from morning till night; but 'twas no use—I was just as bad as ever after all. Blushes hev been in the family for generations. There, 'tis a happy providence that I be no worse, and I feel the blessing.'

'True,' said Jacob Smallbury, deepening his thoughts to a profounder view of the subject. ''Tis a thought to look at, that ye might have been worse; but even as you be, 'tis a very bad affliction for ye, Joseph. For ye see, shepherd, though 'tis very well for a woman, dang it all, 'tis awkward for a man like him, poor feller?' He appealed to the shepherd by a feeling glance.

''Tis—'tis,' said Gabriel, recovering from a meditation. 'Yes, very awkward for the man.'

'Ay, and he's very timid, too,' observed Jan Coggan. 'Once he had been working late at Yalbury Bottom, and had had a drap of drink, and lost his way as he was coming home-along through Yalbury Wood, didn't ye, Master Poorgrass?'

'No, no, no; not that story!' expostulated the modest man, forcing a laugh to bury his concern.

'—— And so 'a lost himself quite,' continued Mr.

65

Coggan, with an impassive face, implying that a true narrative, like time and tide, must run its course and would respect no man. 'And as he was coming along in the middle of the night, much afeared, and not able to find his way out of the trees nohow, 'a cried out, "Man-a-lost! man-a-lost!" A owl in a tree happened to be crying "Whoo-whoo-whoo!" as owls do, you know, shepherd' (Gabriel nodded), 'and Joseph, all in a tremble, said, "Joseph Poorgrass, of Weatherbury, sir!"'

'No, no, now—that's too much!' said the timid man, becoming a man of brazen courage all of a sudden. 'I didn't say *sir*. I'll take my oath I didn't say "Joseph Poorgrass o' Weatherbury, sir." No, no; what's right is right, and I never said sir to the bird, knowing very well that no man of a gentleman's rank would be hollering there at that time o' night. "Joseph Poorgrass of Weatherbury,"—that's every word I said, and I shouldn't ha' said that if 't hadn't been for Keeper Day's metheglin. . . . There, 'twas a merciful thing it ended where it did.'

The question of which was right being tacitly waived by the company, Jan went on meditatively:—

'And he's the fearfullest man, bain't ye, Joseph? Ay, another time ye were lost by Lambing-Down Gate, weren't ye, Joseph?'

'I was,' replied Poorgrass, as if there were some conditions too serious even for modesty to remember itself under, this being one.

'Yes; that were the middle of the night, too. The gate would not open, try how he would, and knowing there was the Devil's hand in it, he kneeled down.'

'Ay,' said Joseph, acquiring confidence from the warmth of the fire, the cider, and a perception of the narrative capabilities of the experience alluded to. 'My heart died within me, that time; but I kneeled down and said the Lord's Prayer, and then the Belief

66

right through, and then the Ten Commandments, in earnest prayer. But no, the gate wouldn't open ; and then I went on with Dearly Beloved Brethren, and, thinks I, this makes four, and 'tis all I know out of book, and if this don't do it nothing will, and I'm a lost man. Well, when I got to Saying After Me, I rose from my knees and found the gate would open —yes, neighbours, the gate opened the same as ever.'

A meditation on the obvious inference was indulged in by all, and during its continuance each directed his vision into the ashpit, which glowed like a desert in the tropics under a vertical sun, shaping their eyes long and liny, partly because of the light, partly from the depth of the subject discussed.

Gabriel broke the silence. 'What sort of a place is this to live at, and what sort of a mis'ess is she to work under?' Gabriel's bosom thrilled gently as he thus slipped under the notice of the assembly the innermost subject of his heart.

'We d' know little of her—nothing. She only showed herself a few days ago. Her uncle was took bad, and the doctor was called with his world-wide skill; but he couldn't save the man. As I take it, she's going to keep on the farm.'

'That's about the shape o't, 'a b'lieve,' said Jan Coggan. 'Ay, 'tis a very good family. I'd as soon be under 'em as under one here and there. Her uncle was a very fair sort of man. Did ye know en, shepherd—a bachelor-man?'

'Not at all.'

'I used to go to his house a-courting my first wife, Charlotte, who was his dairymaid. Well, a very good-hearted man were Farmer Everdene, and I being a respectable young fellow was allowed to call and see her and drink as much ale as I liked, but not to carry away any—outside my skin I mane, of course.'

'Ay, ay, Jan Coggan ; we know yer maning.'

'And so you see 'twas beautiful ale, and I wished to value his kindness as much as I could, and not to be so ill-mannered as to drink only a thimbleful, which would have been insulting the man's generosity——'

'True, Master Coggan, 'twould so,' corroborated Mark Clark.

'——And so I used to eat a lot of salt fish afore going, and then by the time I got there I were as dry as a lime-basket—so thorough dry that that ale would slip down — ah, 'twould slip down sweet! Happy times! heavenly times! Such lovely drunks as I used to have at that house! You can mind, Jacob? You used to go wi' me sometimes.'

'I can—I can,' said Jacob. 'That one, too, that we had at Buck's Head on a White Monday was a pretty tipple.'

''Twas. But for a drunk of really a noble class that brought you no nearer to the dark man than you were afore you begun, there was none like those in Farmer Everdene's kitchen. Not a single damn allowed; no, not a bare poor one, even at the most cheerful moment when all were blindest, though the good old word of sin thrown in here and there at such times is a great relief to a merry soul.'

'True,' said the maltster. 'Nater requires her swearing at the regular times, or she's not herself; and unholy exclamations is a necessity of life.'

'But Charlotte,' continued Coggan—'not a word of the sort would Charlotte allow, nor the smallest item of taking in vain. . . . Ay, poor Charlotte, I wonder if she had the good fortune to get into Heaven when 'a died! But 'a was never much in luck's way, and perhaps 'a went downwards after all, poor soul.'

'And did any of you know Miss Everdene's father and mother?' inquired the shepherd, who found some difficulty in keeping the conversation in the desired channel.

'I knew them a little,' said Jacob Smallbury; 'but they were townsfolk, and didn't live here. They've been dead for years. Father, what sort of people were mis'ess' father and mother?'

'Well,' said the maltster, 'he wasn't much to look at; but she was a lovely woman. He was fond enough of her as his sweetheart.'

'Used to kiss her in scores and long-hundreds, so 'twas said here and there,' observed Coggan.

'He was very proud of her, too, when they were married, as I've been told,' said the maltster.

'Ay,' said Coggan. 'He admired her so much that he used to light the candle three times a night to look at her.'

'Boundless love; I shouldn't have supposed it in the world's universe!' murmured Joseph Poorgrass, who habitually spoke on a large scale in his moral reflections.

'Well, to be sure,' said Gabriel.

'Oh, 'tis true enough. I knowed the man and woman both well. Levi Everdene—that was the man's name, sure enough. "Man," saith I in my hurry, but he were of a higher circle of life than that—'a was a gentleman-tailor really, worth scores of pounds. And he became a very celebrated bankrupt two or three times.'

'Oh, I thought he was quite a common man!' said Joseph.

'Oh, no, no! That man failed for heaps of money; hundreds in gold and silver.'

The maltster being rather short of breath, Mr. Coggan, after absently scrutinising a coal which had fallen among the ashes, took up the narrative, with a private twirl of his eye:—

'Well, now, you'd hardly believe it, but that man— our Miss Everdene's father—was one of the ficklest husbands alive, after a while. Understand, 'a didn't want to be fickle, but he couldn't help it. The pore

69

feller were faithful and true enough to her in his wish, but his heart would rove, do what he would. Ay, 'a spoke to me in real tribulation about it once. "Coggan," he said, "I could never wish for a handsomer woman than I've got, but feeling she's ticketed as my lawful wife, I can't help my wicked heart wandering, do what I will." But at last I believe he cured it by making her take off her wedding-ring and calling her by her maiden name as they sat together after the shop was shut, and so 'a would get to fancy she was only his sweetheart, and not married to him at all. And as soon as he could thoroughly fancy he was doing wrong and committing the seventh, 'a got to like her as well as ever, and they lived on a perfect picture of mutel love.'

'Well, 'twas a most ungodly remedy,' murmured Joseph Poorgrass; 'but we ought to feel deep cheerfulness, as I may say, that a happy Providence kept it from being any worse. You see, he might have gone the bad road and given his eyes to unlawfulness entirely —yes, gross unlawfulness, so to say it.'

'You see,' said Billy Smallbury, 'the man's will was to do right, sure enough, but his heart didn't chime in.'

'He got so much better, that he was quite religious in his later years, wasn't he, Jan?' said Joseph Poorgrass. 'He got himself confirmed over again in a more serious way, and took to saying "Amen" almost as loud as a clerk, and he liked to copy comforting verses from the tombstones. He used, too, to hold the money-plate at Let Your Light so Shine, and stand godfather to poor little come-by-chance children; and he kept a missionary box upon his table to nab folks unawares when they called; yes, and he would box the charity-boys' ears, if they laughed in church, till they could hardly stand upright, and do other deeds of piety natural to the saintly inclined.'

'Ay, at that time he thought of nothing but such things,' added Billy Smallbury. 'One day Parson Thirdly

met him and said, " Good-morning, Mister Everdene ; 'tis
a fine day ! " " Amen," said Everdene, quite absent-
like, thinking only of religion when he seed a parson.
Yes, he was a very Christian man.'

'Their daughter was not at all a pretty chiel at that
time,' said Henery Fray. 'Never should have thought
she'd have growed up such a handsome body as she is.'

' 'Tis to be hoped her temper is as good as her face.'

'Well, yes ; but the baily will have most to do with
the business and ourselves. Ah !' Henery shook his
head, gazed into the ashpit, and smiled volumes of
ironical knowledge.

'A queer Christian, like the Devil's head in a cowl,
as the saying is,' volunteered Mark Clark.

'He is,' said Henery, with a manner implying that
irony must necessarily cease at a certain point. 'Between
we two, man and man, I believe that man would as soon
tell a lie Sundays as working-days—that I do so.'

'Good faith, you do talk ! ' said Gabriel.

'True enough,' said the man of bitter moods, looking
round upon the company with the antithetic laughter
that comes from a keener appreciation of the miseries
of life than ordinary men are capable of. 'Ah, there's
people of one sort, and people of another, but that man
—bless your souls ! '

Gabriel thought fit to change the subject. 'You
must be a very aged man, malter, to have sons growed
up so old and ancient,' he remarked.

'Father's so old that 'a can't mind his age, can ye,
father ? ' interposed Jacob. 'And he's growed terrible
crooked, too, lately,' Jacob continued, surveying his
father's figure, which was rather more bowed than his own.
'Really, one may say that father there is three-double.'

'Crooked folk will last a long while,' said the maltster,
grimly, and not in the best humour.

'Shepherd would like to hear the pedigree of yer
life, father—wouldn't ye, shepherd ? '

'Ay, that I should,' said Gabriel, with the heartiness of a man who had longed to hear it for several months. 'What may your age be, malter?'

The maltster cleared his throat in an exaggerated form for emphasis, and elongating his gaze to the remotest point of the ashpit, said, in the slow speech justifiable when the importance of a subject is so generally felt that any mannèrism must be tolerated in getting at it, 'Well, I don't mind the year I were born in, but perhaps I can reckon up the places I've lived at, and so get it that way. I bode at Upper Long-puddle across there' (nodding to the north) 'till I were eleven. I bode seven at Kingsbere' (nodding to the east) 'where I took to malting. I went therefrom to Norcombe, and malted there two-and-twenty years, and two-and-twenty years I was there turnip-hoeing and harvesting. Ah, I knowed that old place, Norcombe, years afore you were thought of, Master Oak' (Oak smiled a corroboration of the fact). 'Then I malted at Dur-nover four year, and four year turnip-hoeing; and I was fourteen times eleven months at Millpond St. Jude's' (nodding north-west-by-north). 'Old Twills wouldn't hire me for more than eleven months at a time, to keep me from being chargeable to the parish if so be I was disabled. Then I was three year at Mellstock, and I've been here one-and-thirty year come Candlemas. How much is that?'

'Hundred and seventeen,' chuckled another old gentleman, given to mental arithmetic and little con-versation, who had hitherto sat unobserved in a corner.

'Well, then, that's my age,' said the maltster, em-phatically.

'Oh, no, father!' said Jacob. 'Your turnip-hoeing were in the summer and your malting in the winter of the same years, and ye don't ought to count both halves, father.'

'Chok' it all! I lived through the summers, didn't

72

I? That's my question. I suppose ye'll say next I be no age at all to speak of?'

'Sure we shan't,' said Gabriel, soothingly.

'Ye be a very old aged person, malter,' attested Jan Coggan, also soothingly. 'We all know that, and ye must have a wonderful talented constitution to be able to live so long, mustn't he, neighbours?'

'True, true; ye must, malter, wonderful;' said the meeting unanimously.

The maltster, being now pacified, was even generous enough to voluntarily disparage in a slight degree the virtue of having lived a great many years, by mentioning that the cup they were drinking out of was three years older than he.

While the cup was being examined, the end of Gabriel Oak's flute became visible over his smock-frock pocket, and Henery Fray exclaimed, 'Surely, shepherd, I seed you blowing into a great flute by now at Casterbridge?'

'You did,' said Gabriel, blushing faintly. 'I've been in great trouble, neighbours, and was driven to it. I used not to be so poor as I be now.'

'Never mind, heart!' said Mark Clark. 'You should take it careless-like, shepherd, and your time will come. But we could thank ye for a tune, if ye bain't too tired?'

'Neither drum nor trumpet have I heard this Christmas,' said Jan Coggan. 'Come, raise a tune, Master Oak!'

'Ay, that I will,' said Gabriel readily, pulling out his flute and putting it together. 'A poor tool, neighbours; but such as I can do ye shall have and welcome.'

Oak then struck up 'Jockey to the Fair,' and played that sparkling melody three times through, accenting the notes in the third round in a most artistic and lively manner by bending his body in small jerks and tapping with his foot to beat time.

'He can blow the flute very well—that 'a can,' said a young married man, who having no individuality worth mentioning was known as 'Susan Tall's husband.' He continued admiringly, 'I'd as lief as not be able to blow into a flute as well as that.'

'He's a clever man, and 'tis a true comfort for us to have such a shepherd,' murmured Joseph Poorgrass, in a soft cadence. 'We ought to feel real thanksgiving that he's not a player of ba'dy songs instead of these merry tunes; for 'twould have been just as easy for God to have made the shepherd a loose low man—a man of iniquity, so to speak it—as what he is. Yes, for our wives' and daughters' sakes we should feel real thanksgiving.'

'True, true,—real thanksgiving!' dashed in Mark Clark conclusively, not feeling it to be of any consequence to his opinion that he had only heard about a word and three-quarters of what Joseph had said.

'Yes,' added Joseph, beginning to feel like a man in the Bible; 'for evil do thrive so in these times that ye may be as much deceived in the clanest shaved and whitest shirted man as in the raggedest tramp upon the turnpike, if I may term it so.'

'Ay, I can mind yer face now, shepherd,' said Henery Fray, criticising Gabriel with misty eyes as he entered upon his second tune. 'Yes—now I see ye blowing into the flute I know ye to be the same man I see play at Casterbridge, for yer mouth were scrimped up and yer eyes a-staring out like a strangled man's— just as they be now.'

''Tis a pity that playing the flute should make a man look such a scarecrow,' observed Mr. Mark Clark, with additional criticism of Gabriel's countenance, the latter person jerking out, with the ghastly grimace required by the instrument, the chorus of 'Dame Durden:'—

'Twas Moll' and Bet', and Doll' and Kate',
And Dor'-othy Drag'-gle Tail'.

'I hope you don't mind that young man Mark Clark's bad manners in naming your features?' whispered Joseph to Gabriel privately.

'Not at all,' said Mr. Oak.

'For by nature ye be a very handsome man, shepherd,' continued Joseph Poorgrass, with winning suavity.

'Ay, that ye be, shepherd,' said the company.

'Thank you very much,' said Oak, in the modest tone good manners demanded, thinking, however, that he would never let Bathsheba see him playing the flute ; in this resolve showing a discretion equal to that related of its sagacious inventress, the divine Minerva herself.

'Ah, when I and my wife were married at Norcombe Church,' said the old maltster, not pleased at finding himself left out of the subject, 'we were called the handsomest couple in the neighbourhood—everybody said so.'

'Danged if ye bain't altered now, malter,' said a voice with the vigour natural to the enunciation of a remarkably evident truism. It came from the old man in the background, whose offensiveness and spiteful ways were barely atoned for by the occasional chuckle he contributed to general laughs.

'Oh, no, no,' said Gabriel.

'Don't ye play no more, shepherd,' said Susan Tall's husband, the young married man who had spoken once before. 'I must be moving, and when there's tunes going on I seem as if hung in wires. If I thought after I'd left that music was still playing, and I not there, I should be quite melancholy-like.'

'What's yer hurry then, Laban?' inquired Coggan. 'You used to bide as late as the latest.'

'Well, ye see, neighbours, I was lately married to a woman, and she's my vocation now, and so ye see——' The young man halted lamely.

'New lords new laws, as the saying is, I suppose,'

75

remarked Coggan, with a very compressed countenance.

'Ay, 'a b'lieve—ha, ha!' said Susan Tall's husband, in a tone intended to imply his habitual reception of jokes without minding them at all. The young man then wished them good-night and withdrew.

Henery Fray was the first to follow. Then Gabriel arose and went off with Jan Coggan, who had offered him a lodging. A few minutes later, when the remaining ones were on their legs and about to depart, Fray came back again in a hurry. Flourishing his finger ominously he threw a gaze teeming with tidings just where his eye alighted by accident, which happened to be in Joseph Poorgrass's face.

'Oh—what's the matter, what's the matter, Henery?' said Joseph, starting back.

'What's a-brewing, Henery?' asked Jacob and Mark Clark.

'Baily Pennyways—Baily Pennyways—I said so; yes, I said so!'

'What, found out stealing anything?'

'Stealing it is. The news is, that after Miss Everdene got home she went out again to see all was safe, as she usually do, and coming in found Baily Pennyways creeping down the granary steps with half a bushel of barley. She fleed at him like a cat—never such a tomboy as she is—of course I speak with closed doors?'

'You do—you do, Henery.'

'She fleed at him, and, to cut a long story short, he owned to having carried off five sack altogether, upon her promising not to persecute him. Well, he's turned out neck and crop, and my question is, who's going to be baily now?'

The question was such a profound one that Henery was obliged to drink there and then from the large cup till the bottom was distinctly visible inside. Before

76

he had replaced it on the table, in came the young man, Susan Tall's husband, in a still greater hurry.

'Have ye heard the news that's all over parish?'

'About Baily Pennyways?'

'Ah—but besides that?'

'No—not a morsel of it!' they all replied, looking into the very midst of Laban Tall as if to meet his words half-way down his throat.

'What a night of horrors!' murmured Joseph Poorgrass, waving his hands spasmodically. 'I've had the news-bell ringing in my left ear quite bad enough for a murder, and I've seed a magpie all alone!'

'Fanny Robin—Miss Everdene's youngest servant—can't be found. They've been wanting to lock up the door these two hours, but she isn't come in. And they don't know what to do about going to bed for fear of locking her out. They wouldn't be so concerned if she hadn't been noticed in such low spirits these last few days, and Maryann d' think the beginning of a crowner's inquest has happened to the poor girl.'

'Oh—'tis burned—'tis burned!' said Joseph Poorgrass with dry lips.

'No—'tis drowned!' said Tall.

'Or 'tis her father's razor!' suggested Billy Smallbury, with a vivid sense of detail.

'Well—Miss Everdene wants to speak to one or two of us before we go to bed. What with this trouble about the baily, and now about the girl, mis'ess is almost wild.'

They all hastened up the rise to the farmhouse, excepting the old maltster, whom neither news, fire, rain, nor thunder could draw from his hole. There, as the others' footsteps died away, he sat down again, and continued gazing as usual into the furnace with his red, bleared eyes.

From the bedroom window above their heads Bathsheba's head and shoulders, robed in mystic white, were dimly seen extended into the air.

'Are any of my men among you?' she said anxiously.

'Yes, ma'am, several,' said Susan Tall's husband.

'To-morrow morning I wish two or three of you to make inquiries in the villages round if they have seen such a person as Fanny Robin. Do it quietly; there is no reason for alarm as yet. She must have left whilst we were all at the fire.'

'I beg yer pardon, but had she any young man courting her in the parish, ma'am?' asked Jacob Smallbury.

'I don't know,' said Bathsheba.

'I've never heard of any such thing, ma'am,' said two or three.

'It is hardly likely, either,' continued Bathsheba. 'For any lover of hers might have come to the house if he had been a respectable lad. The most mysterious matter connected with her absence—indeed, the only thing which gives me serious alarm—is that she was seen to go out of the house by Maryann with only her indoor working gown on—not even a bonnet.'

'And you mean, ma'am, excusing my words, that a young woman would hardly go to see her young man without dressing up,' said Jacob, turning his mental vision upon past experiences. 'That's true—she would not, ma'am.'

'She had, I think, a bundle, though I couldn't see very well,' said a female voice from another window, which seemed that of Maryann. 'But she had no young man about here. Hers lives in Casterbridge, and I believe he's a soldier.'

'Do you know his name?' Bathsheba said.

'No, mistress; she was very close about it.'

'Perhaps I might be able to find out if I went to Casterbridge barracks,' said William Smallbury.

'Very well; if she doesn't return to-morrow, mind you go there and try to discover which man it is, and see him. I feel more responsible than I should if she had had any friends or relations alive. I do hope she

has come to no harm through a man of that kind. . . .
And then there's this disgraceful affair of the bailiff—
but I can't speak of him now.'

Bathsheba had so many reasons for uneasiness that
it seemed she did not think it worth while to dwell
upon any particular one. 'Do as I told you, then,'
she said in conclusion, closing the casement.˗

'Ay, ay, mistress; we will,' they replied, and moved
away.

That night at Coggan's, Gabriel Oak, beneath the
screen of closed eyelids, was busy with fancies, and full
of movement, like a river flowing rapidly under its ice.
Night had always been the time at which he saw Bathsheba most vividly, and through the slow hours of
shadow he tenderly regarded her image now. It is
rarely that the pleasures of the imagination will compensate for the pain of sleeplessness, but they possibly did
with Oak to-night, for the delight of merely seeing her
effaced for the time his perception of the great difference between seeing and possessing.

He also thought of plans for fetching his few utensils
and books from Norcombe. *The Young Man's Best
Companion*, *The Farrier's Sure Guide*, *The Veterinary
Surgeon*, *Paradise Lost*, *The Pilgrim's Progress*, *Robinson
Crusoe*, Ash's *Dictionary*, and Walkingame's *Arithmetic*,
constituted his library ; and though a limited series, it was
one from which he had acquired more sound information by diligent perusal than many a man of opportunities
has done from a furlong of laden shelves.

CHAPTER IX

THE HOMESTEAD—A VISITOR—HALF-CONFIDENCES

By daylight, the bower of Oak's new-found mistress, Bathsheba Everdene, presented itself as a hoary building, of the Jacobean stage of Classic Renaissance as regards its architecture, and of a proportion which told at a glance that, as is so frequently the case, it had once been the manorial hall upon a small estate around it, now altogether effaced as a distinct property, and merged in the vast tract of a non-resident landlord, which comprised several such modest demesnes.

Fluted pilasters, worked from the solid stone, decorated its front, and above the roof pairs of chimneys were here and there linked by an arch, some gables and other unmanageable features · still retaining traces of their Gothic extraction. Soft brown mosses, like faded velveteen, formed cushions upon the stone tiling, and tufts of the houseleek or sengreen sprouted from the eaves of the low surrounding buildings. A gravel walk leading from the door to the road in front was encrusted at the sides with more moss—here it was a silver-green variety, the nut-brown of the gravel being visible to the width of only a foot or two in the centre. This circumstance, and the generally sleepy air of the whole prospect here, together with the animated and contrasting state of the reverse façade, suggested to the imagination that on the adaptation of the building for farming purposes the vital principle of the house had turned round inside its body to face the other way. Reversals of this kind, strange deformities, tremendous paralyses, are often seen to be inflicted by trade upon edifices—either individual or in the aggregate as streets and towns—which were originally planned for pleasure alone.

Lively voices were heard this morning in the upper rooms, the main staircase to which was of hard oak, the balusters, heavy as bed-posts, being turned and moulded in the quaint fashion of their century, the handrail as stout as a parapet-top, and the stairs themselves continually twisting round like a person trying to look over his shoulder. Going up, the floors above were found to have a very irregular surface, rising to ridges, sinking into valleys; and being just then uncarpeted, the face of the boards was seen to be eaten into innumerable vermiculations. Every window replied by a clang to the opening and shutting of every door, a tremble followed every bustling movement, and a creak accompanied a walker about the house, like a spirit, wherever he went.

In the room from which the conversation proceeded, Bathsheba and her servant-companion, Liddy Smallbury, were to be discovered sitting upon the floor, and sorting a complication of papers, books, bottles, and rubbish spread out thereon—remnants from the household stores of the late occupier. Liddy, the maltster's great-granddaughter, was about Bathsheba's equal in age, and her face was a prominent advertisement of the light-hearted English country girl. The beauty her features might have lacked in form was amply made up for by perfection of hue, which at this winter-time was the softened ruddiness on a surface of high rotundity that we meet with in a Terburg or a Gerard Douw; and, like the presentations of those great colourists, it was a face which kept well back from the boundary between comeliness and the ideal. Though elastic in nature she was less daring than Bathsheba, and occasionally showed some earnestness, which consisted half of genuine feeling, and half of mannerliness superadded by way of duty.

Through a partly-opened door the noise of a scrubbing-brush led up to the charwoman, Maryann Money, a person who for a face had a circular disc, furrowed less by age than by long gazes of perplexity at distant objects. To think of her was to get good-humoured; to speak of her was to raise the image of a dried Normandy pippin.

'Stop your scrubbing a moment,' said Bathsheba through the door to her. 'I hear something.'

Maryann suspended the brush.

The tramp of a horse was apparent, approaching the front of the building. The paces slackened, turned in at the wicket, and, what was most unusual, came up the mossy path close to the door. The door was tapped with the end of a crop or stick.

'What impertinence!' said Liddy, in a low voice. 'To ride up the footpath like that! Why didn't he stop at the gate? Lord! 'tis a gentleman! I see the top of his hat.'

'Be quiet!' said Bathsheba.

The further expression of Liddy's concern was continued by aspect instead of narrative.

'Why doesn't Mrs. Coggan go to the door?' Bathsheba continued.

Rat-tat-tat-tat, resounded more decisively from Bathsheba's oak.

'Maryann, you go!' said she, fluttering under the onset of a crowd of romantic possibilities.

'Oh, ma'am—see, here's a mess!'

The argument was unanswerable after a glance at Maryann.

'Liddy—you must,' said Bathsheba.

Liddy held up her hands and arms, coated with dust from the rubbish they were sorting, and looked imploringly at her mistress.

'There—Mrs. Coggan is going!' said Bathsheba, exhaling her relief in the form of a long breath which had lain in her bosom a minute or more.

The door opened, and a deep voice said—

'Is Miss Everdene at home?'

'I'll see, sir,' said Mrs. Coggan, and in a minute appeared in the room.

'Dear, what a thirtover place this world is!' continued Mrs. Coggan (a wholesome-looking lady who had a voice for each class of remark according to the emotion involved; who could toss a pancake or twirl a mop with the accuracy of pure mathematics, and who at this moment showed hands shaggy with fragments of dough and arms encrusted with flour). 'I am never up to my elbows, Miss, in making a pudding but one of two things do happen—either my nose must needs begin tickling, and I can't live without scratching it, or somebody knocks at the door. Here's Mr. Boldwood wanting to see you, Miss Everdene.'

A woman's dress being a part of her countenance, and any disorder in the one being of the same nature with a malformation or wound in the other, Bathsheba said at once—

'I can't see him in this state. Whatever shall I do?'

Not-at-homes were hardly naturalized in Weatherbury farmhouses, so Liddy suggested—'Say you're a fright with dust, and can't come down.'

'Yes—that sounds very well,' said Mrs. Coggan, critically.

'Say I can't see him—that will do.'

Mrs. Coggan went downstairs, and returned the answer as requested, adding, however, on her own responsibility, 'Miss is dusting bottles, sir, and is quite a object—that's why 'tis.'

'Oh, very well,' said the deep voice, indifferently. 'All I wanted to ask was, if anything had been heard of Fanny Robin?'

'Nothing, sir—but we may know to-night. William Smallbury is gone to Casterbridge, where her young man lives, as is supposed, and the other men be inquiring about everywhere.'

The horse's tramp then recommenced and retreated, and the door closed.

'Who is Mr. Boldwood?' said Bathsheba.

'A gentleman-farmer at Little Weatherbury.'

'Married?'

'No, miss.'

'How old is he?'

'Forty, I should say—very handsome—rather stern-looking—and rich.'

'What a bother this dusting is! I am always in some unfortunate plight or other,' Bathsheba said, complainingly. 'Why should he inquire about Fanny?'

'Oh, because, as she had no friends in her childhood, he took her and put her to school, and got her her place here under your uncle. He's a very kind man that way, but Lord—there!'

'What?'

'Never was such a hopeless man for a woman! He's been courted by sixes and sevens—all the girls, gentle and simple, for miles round, have tried him. Jane Perkins worked at him for two months like a slave, and the two Miss Taylors spent a year upon him, and he cost Farmer Ives's daughter nights of tears and twenty pounds' worth of new clothes; but Lord—the money might as well have been thrown out of the window.'

A little boy came up at this moment and looked in upon them. This child was one of the Coggans, who, with the Smallburys, were as common among the families of this district as the Avons and Derwents among our rivers. He always had a loosened tooth or a cut finger to show to particular friends, which he did with an air of being thereby elevated above the common herd of afflictionless humanity—to which exhibition people were expected to say 'Poor child!' with a dash of congratulation as well as pity.

'I've got a pen-nee!' said Master Coggan in a scanning measure.

'Well—who gave it you, Teddy?' said Liddy.

'Mis-terr Bold-wood! He gave it to me for opening the gate.'

'What did he say?'

'He said, "Where are you going, my little man?" and I said, "To Miss Everdene's, please;" and he said, "She is a staid woman, isn't she, my little man?" and I said, "Yes."'

'You naughty child! What did you say that for?'

''Cause he gave me the penny!'

'What a pucker everything is in!' said Bathsheba, discontentedly, when the child had gone. 'Get away, Maryann, or go on with your scrubbing, or do something! You ought to be married by this time, and not here troubling me!'

'Ay, mistress—so I did. But what between the poor men I won't have, and the rich men who won't have me, I stand forlorn. Ah, poor soul of me!'

'Did anybody ever want to marry you, miss?' Liddy ventured to ask when they were again alone. 'Lots of 'em, I daresay?'

Bathsheba paused, as if about to refuse a reply, but the temptation to say yes, since it really was in her power, was irresistible by aspiring virginity, in spite of her spleen at having been published as old.

'A man wanted to once,' she said, in a highly experienced tone, and the image of Gabriel Oak, as the farmer, rose before her.

'How nice it must seem!' said Liddy, with the fixed

features of mental realization. 'And you wouldn't have him?'

'He wasn't quite good enough for me.'

'How sweet to be able to disdain, when most of us are glad to say, "Thank you!" I seem I hear it. "No, sir—I'm your better," or "Kiss my foot, sir; my face is for mouths of consequence." And did you love him, miss?'

'Oh no. But I rather liked him.'

'Do you now?'

'Of course not—what footsteps are those I hear?'

Liddy looked from a back window into the courtyard behind, which was now getting low-toned and dim with the earliest films of night. A crooked file of men was approaching the back door. The whole string of trailing individuals advanced in the completest balance of intention, like the remarkable creatures known as Chain Salpæ, which, distinctly organized in other respects, have one will common to a whole family. Some were, as usual, in snow-white smock-frocks of Russia duck, and some in whitey-brown ones of drabbet—marked on the wrists, breasts, backs, and sleeves with honeycomb-work. Two or three women in pattens brought up the rear.

'The Philistines be upon us,' said Liddy, making her nose white against the glass.

'Oh, very well. Maryann, go down and keep them in the kitchen till I am dressed, and then show them in to me in the hall.'

CHAPTER X

MISTRESS AND MEN

HALF-AN-HOUR later Bathsheba, in finished dress, and followed by Liddy, entered the upper end of the old hall to find that her men had all deposited themselves on a long form and a settle at the lower extremity. She sat down at a table and opened the time-book, pen in her hand, with a canvas money-bag beside her. From this she poured a small heap of coin. Liddy chose a position at her elbow and began to sew, sometimes pausing and looking round, or with the air of a privileged person, taking up one of the half-sovereigns lying before her, and merely surveying it as a work of art, while strictly preventing her countenance from expressing any wish to possess it as money.

'Now, before I begin, men,' said Bathsheba, 'I have two matters to speak of. The first is that the bailiff is dismissed for thieving, and that I have formed a resolution to have no bailiff at all, but to manage everything with my own head and hands.'

The men breathed an audible breath of amazement.

'The next matter is, have you heard anything of Fanny?'

'Nothing, ma'am.'

'Have you done anything?'

'I met Farmer Boldwood,' said Jacob Smallbury, 'and

87

I went with him and two of his men, and dragged New-mill Pond, but we found nothing.'

'And the new shepherd have been to Buck's Head, by Yalbury, thinking she had gone there, but nobody had seed her,' said Laban Tall.

'Hasn't William Smallbury been to Casterbridge?'

'Yes, ma'am, but he's not yet come home. He promised to be back by six.'

'It wants a quarter to six at present,' said Bathsheba, looking at her watch. 'I daresay he'll be in directly. Well, now then'—she looked into the book—'Joseph Poorgrass, are you there?'

'Yes, sir—ma'am I mane,' said the person addressed. 'I be the personal name of Poorgrass.'

'And what are you?'

'Nothing in my own eye. In the eye of other people —well, I don't say it; though public thought will out.'

'What do you do on the farm?'

'I do do carting things all the year, and in seed time I shoots the rooks and sparrows, and helps at pig-killing, sir.'

'How much to you?'

'Please nine and ninepence and a good halfpenny where 'twas a bad one, sir—ma'am I mane.'

'Quite correct. Now here are ten shillings in addition as a small present, as I am a new comer.'

Bathsheba blushed slightly at the sense of being generous in public, and Henery Fray, who had drawn up towards her chair, lifted his eyebrows and fingers to express amazement on a small scale.

'How much do I owe you—that man in the corner— what's your name?' continued Bathsheba.

'Matthew Moon, ma'am,' said a singular framework of clothes with nothing of any consequence inside them, which advanced with the toes in no definite direction forwards, but turned in or out as they chanced to swing.

'Matthew Mark, did you say?—speak out—I shall not hurt you,' inquired the young farmer, kindly.

'Matthew Moon, mem,' said Henery Fray, correctingly, from behind her chair, to which point he had edged himself.

'Matthew Moon,' murmured Bathsheba, turning her bright eyes to the book. 'Ten and twopence halfpenny is the sum put down to you, I see?'

'Yes, mis'ess,' said Matthew, as the rustle of wind among dead leaves.

'Here it is, and ten shillings. Now the next—Andrew Randle, you are a new man, I hear. How came you to leave your last farm?'

'P-p-p-p-p-pl-pl-pl-pl-l-l-l-l-ease, ma'am, p-p-p-p-pl-pl-pl-pl-please, ma'am-please'm-please'm——'

''A's a stammering man, mem,' said Henery Fray in an undertone, 'and they turned him away because the only time he ever did speak plain he said his soul was his own, and other iniquities, to the squire. 'A can cuss, mem, as well as you or I, but 'a can't speak a common speech to save his life.'

'Andrew Randle, here's yours—finish thanking me in a day or two. Temperance Miller—oh, here's another, Soberness—both women, I suppose?'

'Yes'm. Here we be, 'a b'lieve,' was echoed in shrill unison.

'What have you been doing?'

'Tending thrashing-machine, and wimbling haybonds, and saying "Hoosh!" to the cocks and hens when they go upon your seeds, and planting Early Flourballs and Thompson's Wonderfuls with a dibble.'

'Yes—I see. Are they satisfactory women?' she inquired softly of Henery Fray.

'Oh, mem—don't ask me! Yielding women—as scarlet a pair as ever was!' groaned Henery under his breath.

'Sit down.'

'Who, mem.'

'Sit down.'

Joseph Poorgrass, in the background, twitched, and his lips became dry with fear of some terrible consequences, as he saw Bathsheba summarily speaking, and Henery slinking off to a corner.

'Now the next. Laban Tall, you'll stay on working for me?'

'For you or anybody that pays me well, ma'am,' replied the young married man.

'True—the man must live!' said a woman in the back quarter, who had just entered with clicking pattens.

'What woman is that?' Bathsheba asked.

'I be his lawful wife!' continued the voice with greater prominence of manner and tone. This lady called herself five-and-twenty, looked thirty, passed as thirty-five, and was forty. She was a woman who never, like some newly married, showed conjugal tenderness in public, perhaps because she had none to show.

'Oh, you are,' said Bathsheba. 'Well, Laban, will you stay on?'

'Yes, he'll stay, ma'am!' said again the shrill tongue of Laban's lawful wife.

'Well, he can speak for himself, I suppose.'

'Oh, Lord, no, ma'am! A simple tool. Well enough, but a poor gawkhammer mortal,' the wife replied.

'Heh-heh-heh!' laughed the married man with a hideous effort of appreciation, for he was as irrepressibly good-humoured under ghastly snubs as a parliamentary candidate on the hustings.

The names remaining were called in the same manner.

'Now I think I have done with you,' said Bathsheba, closing the book and shaking back a stray twine of hair. 'Has William Smallbury returned?'

'No, ma'am.'

'The new shepherd will want a man under him,' suggested Henery Fray, trying to make himself official again by a sideway approach towards her chair.

'Oh—he will. Who can he have?'

'Young Cain Ball is a very good lad,' Henery said, 'and Shepherd Oak don't mind his youth?' he added, turning with an apologetic smile to the shepherd, who had just appeared on the scene, and was now leaning against the doorpost with his arms folded.

'No, I don't mind that,' said Gabriel.

'How did Cain come by such a name?' asked Bathsheba.

'Oh you see, mem, his pore mother, not being a Scripture-read woman, made a mistake at his christening, thinking 'twas Abel killed Cain, and called en Cain, meaning Abel all the time. The parson put it right, but 'twas too late, for the name could never be got rid of in the parish. 'Tis very unfortunate for the boy.'

'It is rather unfortunate.'

'Yes. However, we soften it down as much as we can, and call him Cainey. Ah, pore widow-woman! she cried her heart out about it almost. She was brought up by a very heathen father and mother, who never sent her to church or school, and it shows how the sins of the parents are visited upon the children, mem.'

Mr. Fray here drew up his features to the mild degree of melancholy required when the persons involved in the given misfortune do not belong to your own family.

'Very well then, Cainey Ball to be under-shepherd. And you quite understand your duties?—you I mean, Gabriel Oak?'

'Quite well, I thank you, Miss Everdene,' said Shepherd Oak from the doorpost. 'If I don't, I'll inquire.' Gabriel was rather staggered by the remarkable coolness of her manner. Certainly nobody without previous information would have dreamt that Oak and the handsome woman before whom he stood had ever been other than strangers. But perhaps her air was the inevitable result of the social rise which had advanced her from a cottage to a large house and fields. The case is not unexampled in high places. When, in the writings of the later poets, Jove and his family are found to have moved from their cramped quarters on the peak of Olympus into the wide sky above it, their words show a proportionate increase of arrogance and reserve.

Footsteps were heard in the passage, combining in their character the qualities both of weight and measure, rather at the expense of velocity.

(All). 'Here's Billy Smallbury come from Caster-bridge.'

'And what's the news?' said Bathsheba, as William, after marching to the middle of the hall, took a hand-kerchief from his hat and wiped his forehead from its centre to its remoter boundaries.

'I should have been sooner, miss,' he said, 'if it hadn't been for the weather.' He then stamped with each foot severely, and on looking down his boots were perceived to be clogged with snow.

'Come at last, is it?' said Henery.

'Well, what about Fanny?' said Bathsheba.

'Well, ma'am, in round numbers, she's run away with the soldiers,' said William.

'No; not a steady girl like Fanny!'

'I'll tell ye all particulars. When I got to Caster-bridge Barracks, they said, "The Eleventh Dragoon-Guards be gone away, and new troops have come." The Eleventh left last week for Melchester and onwards. The Route came from Government like a thief in the night, as is his nature to, and afore the Eleventh knew it almost, they were on the march. They passed near here.'

Gabriel had listened with interest. 'I saw them go,' he said.

'Yes,' continued William, 'they pranced down the street playing "The Girl I Left Behind Me," so 'tis said, in glorious notes of triumph. Every looker-on's inside shook with the blows of the great drum to his deepest vitals, and there was not a dry eye throughout the town among the public-house people and the nameless women!'

'But they're not gone to any war?'

'No, ma'am; but they be gone to take the places of them who may, which is very close connected. And so I said to myself, Fanny's young man was one of the regiment, and she's gone after him. There, ma'am, that's it in black and white.'

'Did you find out his name?'

'No; nobody knew it. I believe he was higher in rank than a private.'

Gabriel remained musing and said nothing, for he was in doubt.

'Well, we are not likely to know more to-night, at any rate,' said Bathsheba. 'But one of you had better run across to Farmer Boldwood's and tell him that much.'

She then rose; but before retiring, addressed a few words to them with a pretty dignity, to which her mourning dress added a soberness that was hardly to be found in the words themselves.

'Now mind, you have a mistress instead of a master. I don't yet know my powers or my talents in farming; but I shall do my best, and if you serve me well, so shall I serve you. Don't any unfair ones among you (if there are any such, but I hope not) suppose that because I'm a woman I don't understand the difference between bad goings-on and good.'

(All). 'No'm!'

(Liddy). 'Excellent well said.'

'I shall be up before you are awake; I shall be afield before you are up; and I shall have breakfasted before you are afield. In short, I shall astonish you all.'

(All). 'Yes'm!'

'And so good-night.'

93

(All). 'Good-night, ma'am.'

Then this small thesmothete stepped from the table, and surged out of the hall, her black silk dress licking up a few straws and dragging them along with a scratching noise upon the floor. Liddy, elevating her feelings to the occasion from a sense of grandeur, floated off behind Bathsheba with a milder dignity not entirely free from travesty, and the door was closed.

CHAPTER XI

OUTSIDE THE BARRACKS—SNOW—A MEETING

FOR dreariness nothing could surpass a prospect in the outskirts of a certain town and military station, many miles north of Weatherbury, at a later hour on this same snowy evening—if that may be called a prospect of which the chief constituent was darkness.

It was a night when sorrow may come to the brightest without causing any great sense of incongruity: when, with impressible persons, love becomes solicitousness, hope sinks to misgiving, and faith to hope: when the exercise of memory does not stir feelings of regret at opportunities for ambition that have been passed by, and anticipation does not prompt to enterprise.

The scene was a public path, bordered on the left hand by a river, behind which rose a high wall. On the right was a tract of land, partly meadow and partly moor, reaching, at its remote verge, to a wide undulating upland.

The changes of the seasons are less obtrusive on spots of this kind than amid woodland scenery. Still, to a close observer, they are just as perceptible; the difference is that their media of manifestation are less trite and familiar than such well-known ones as the bursting of the buds or the fall of the leaf. Many are not so stealthy and gradual as we may be apt to imagine in considering the general torpidity of a moor or waste. Winter, in coming to the country hereabout, advanced in well-marked stages, wherein might have been successively observed the retreat of the snakes, the transformation of the ferns, the filling of the pools, a rising of fogs, the embrowning by frost, the collapse of the fungi, and an obliteration by snow.

This climax of the series had been reached to-night on the aforesaid moor, and for the first time in the season its irregularities were forms without features ; suggestive of anything, proclaiming nothing, and without more character than that of being the limit of something else—the lowest layer of a firmament of snow. From this chaotic skyful of crowding flakes the mead and moor momentarily received additional clothing, only to appear momentarily more naked thereby. The vast dome of cloud above was strangely low, and formed as it were the roof of a large dark cavern, gradually sinking in upon its floor ; for the instinctive thought was that the snow lining the heavens and that encrusting the earth would soon unite into one mass without any intervening stratum of air at all.

We turn our attention to the left-hand characteristics ; which were flatness in respect of the river, verticality in respect of the wall behind it, and darkness as to both. These features made up the mass. If anything could be darker than the sky, it was the wall, and if any-thing could be gloomier than the wall it was the river beneath. The indistinct summit of the façade was notched and pronged by chimneys here and there, and upon its face were faintly signified the oblong shapes of windows, though only in the upper part. Below, down to the water's edge, the flat was unbroken by hole or projection.

An indescribable succession of dull blows, perplexing in their regularity, sent their sound with difficulty through the fluffy atmosphere. It was a neighbouring clock striking ten. The bell was in the open air, and being overlaid with several inches of muffling snow, had lost its voice for the time.

About this hour the snow abated: ten flakes fell where twenty had fallen, then one had the room of ten. Not long after a form moved by the brink of the river.

By its outline upon the colourless background, a close observer might have seen that it was small. This was all that was positively discoverable, though it seemed human.

The shape went slowly along, but without much exertion, for the snow, though sudden, was not as yet more than two inches deep. At this time some words were spoken aloud:—

'One. Two. Three. Four. Five.'

Between each utterance the little shape advanced about half a dozen yards. It was evident now that the windows high in the wall were being counted. The word 'Five' represented the fifth window from the end of the wall.

Here the spot stopped, and dwindled smaller. The figure was stooping. Then a morsel of snow flew across the river towards the fifth window. It smacked against the wall at a point several yards from its mark. The throw was the idea of a man conjoined with the execution of a woman. No man who had ever seen bird, rabbit, or squirrel in his childhood, could possibly have thrown with such utter imbecility as was shown here.

Another attempt, and another; till by degrees the wall must have become pimpled with the adhering lumps of snow. At last one fragment struck the fifth window.

The river would have been seen by day to be of that deep smooth sort which races middle and sides with the same gliding precision, any irregularities of speed being immediately corrected by a small whirlpool. Nothing was heard in reply to the signal but the gurgle and cluck of one of these invisible wheels—together with a few small sounds which a sad man would have called moans, and a happy man laughter—caused by the flapping of the waters against trifling objects in other parts of the stream.

The window was struck again in the same manner.

Then a noise was heard, apparently produced by the opening of the window. This was followed by a voice from the same quarter.

'Who's there?'

The tones were masculine, and not those of surprise. The high wall being that of a barrack, and marriage being looked upon with disfavour in the army, assignations and communications had probably been made across the river before to-night.

'Is it Sergeant Troy?' said the blurred spot in the snow, tremulously.

This person was so much like a mere shade upon the earth, and the other speaker so much a part of the building, that one would have said the wall was holding a conversation with the snow.

'Yes,' came suspiciously from the shadow. 'What girl are you?'

'Oh, Frank—don't you know me?' said the spot. 'Your wife, Fanny Robin.'

'Fanny!' said the wall, in utter astonishment.

'Yes,' said the girl, with a half-suppressed gasp of emotion.

There was something in the woman's tone which is not that of the wife, and there was a manner in the man which is rarely a husband's. The dialogue went on.

'How did you come here?'

'I asked which was your window. Forgive me!'

'I did not expect you to-night. Indeed, I did not think you would come at all. It was a wonder you found me here. I am orderly to-morrow.'

'You said I was to come.'

'Well—I said that you might.'

'Yes, I mean that I might. You are glad to see me, Frank?'

'Oh yes—of course.'

'Can you—come to me!'

'My dear Fan, no! The bugle has sounded, the barrack gates are closed, and I have no leave. We are all of us as good as in the county gaol till to-morrow morning.'

'Then I shan't see you till then!' The words were in a faltering tone of disappointment.

'How did you get here from Weatherbury?'

'I walked—some part of the way—the rest by the carriers.'

'I am surprised.'

'Yes—so am I. And Frank, when will it be?'

'What?'

'That you promised.'

'I don't quite recollect.'

'Oh you do! Don't speak like that. It weighs me to the earth. It makes me say what ought to be said first by you.'

'Never mind—say it.'

'Oh, must I?—it is, when shall we be married, Frank?'

'Oh, I see. Well — you have to get proper clothes.'

'I have money. Will it be by banns or license?'

'Banns, I should think.'

'And we live in two parishes.'

'Do we? What then?'

'My lodgings are in St. Mary's, and this is not. So they will have to be published in both.'

'Is that the law?'

'Yes. Oh, Frank—you think me forward, I am afraid! Don't, dear Frank—will you—for I love you so.

99

And you said lots of times you would marry me, and—and—I—I—I—— '

'Don't cry, now! It is foolish. If I said so, of course I will.'

'And shall I put up the banns in my parish, and will you in yours?'

'Yes.'

'To-morrow?'

'Not to-morrow. We'll settle in a few days.'

'You have the permission of the officers?'

'No—not yet.'

'Oh—how is it? You said you almost had before you left Casterbridge.'

'The fact is, I forgot to ask. Your coming like this is so sudden and unexpected.'

'Yes—yes—it is. It was wrong of me to worry you. I'll go away now. Will you come and see me to-morrow, at Mrs. Twills's, in North Street? I don't like to come to the Barracks. There are bad women about, and they think me one.'

'Quite so. I'll come to you, my dear. Good-night.'

'Good-night, Frank—good-night!'

And the noise was again heard of a window closing. The little spot moved away. When she passed the corner a subdued exclamation was heard inside the wall.

'Ho—ho—Sergeant—ho—ho!' An expostulation followed, but it was indistinct; and it became lost amid a low peal of laughter, which was hardly distinguishable from the gurgle of the tiny whirlpools outside.

CHAPTER XII

FARMERS—A RULE—AN EXCEPTION

THE first public evidence of Bathsheba's decision to be a farmer in her own person and by proxy no more was her appearance the following market-day in the cornmarket at Casterbridge.

The low though extensive hall, supported by beams and pillars, and latterly dignified by the name of Corn Exchange, was thronged with hot men who talked among each other in twos and threes, the speaker of the minute looking sideways into his auditor's face and concentrating his argument by a contraction of one eyelid during delivery. The greater number carried in their hands ground-ash saplings, using them partly as walking-sticks and partly for poking up pigs, sheep, neighbours with their backs turned, and restful things in general, which seemed to require such treatment in the course of their peregrinations. During conversations each subjected his sapling to great varieties of usage—bending it round his back, forming an arch of it between his two hands, overweighting it on the ground till it reached nearly a semicircle ; or perhaps it was hastily tucked under the arm whilst the sample-bag was pulled forth and a handful of corn poured into the palm, which, after criticism, was flung upon the floor, an issue of events perfectly well known to half-a-dozen acute town-bred fowls which had as usual crept into the building unobserved, and waited the fulfilment of their anticipations with a high-stretched neck and oblique eye.

Among these heavy yeomen a feminine figure glided, the single one of her sex that the room contained. She was prettily and even daintily dressed. She moved between them as a chaise between carts, was heard after them as a romance after sermons, was felt among them like a breeze among furnaces. It had required a little determination—far more than she had at first imagined —to take up a position here, for at her first entry the lumbering dialogues had ceased, nearly every face had been turned towards her, and those that were already turned rigidly fixed there.

Two or three only of the farmers were personally known to Bathsheba, and to these she had made her way. But if she was to be the practical woman she had intended to show herself, business must be carried on, introductions or none, and she ultimately acquired confidence enough to speak and reply boldly to men merely known to her by hearsay. Bathsheba too had her sample-bags, and by degrees adopted the professional pour into the hand—holding up the grains in her narrow palm for inspection, in perfect Casterbridge manner.

Something in the exact arch of her upper unbroken row of teeth, and in the keenly pointed corners of her red mouth when, with parted lips, she somewhat defiantly turned up her face to argue a point with a tall man, suggested that there was depth enough in that lithe slip of humanity for alarming exploits, and daring enough to carry them out. But her eyes had a softness —invariably a softness—which, had they not been dark, would have seemed mistiness; as they were, it lowered an expression that might have been piercing to simple clearness.

Strange to say of a woman in full bloom and vigour, she always allowed her interlocutors to finish their statements before rejoining with hers. In arguing on prices, she held to her own firmly, as was natural in a dealer, and reduced theirs persistently, as was inevitable in a woman. But there was an elasticity in her firmness which removed it from obstinacy, as there was a *naïveté* in her cheapening which saved it from meanness.

Those of the farmers with whom she had no dealings (by far the greater part) were continually asking each other, 'Who is she?' The reply would be—

'Farmer Everdene's niece; took on Weatherbury Upper Farm; turned away the baily, and swears she'll do everything herself.'

The other man would then shake his head.

'Yes, 'tis a pity she's so headstrong,' the first would say. 'But we ought to be proud of her here—she lightens up the old place. 'Tis such a shapely maid, however, that she'll soon get picked up.'

It would be ungallant to suggest that the novelty of her engagement in such an occupation had almost as much to do with the magnetism as had the beauty of her face and movements. However, the interest was general, and this Saturday's *début* in the forum, whatever it may have been to Bathsheba as the buying and selling farmer, was unquestionably a triumph to her as the maiden. Indeed, the sensation was so pronounced that her instinct on two or three occasions was to merely walk as a queen among these gods of the fallow, like a little sister of a little Jove, and to neglect closing prices altogether.

The numerous evidences of her power to attract were only thrown into greater relief by a marked exception. Women seem to have eyes in their ribbons for such matters as these. Bathsheba, without looking within a right angle of him, was conscious of a black sheep among the flock.

It perplexed her first. If there had been a respectable minority on either side, the case would have been most natural. If nobody had regarded her, she would have taken the matter indifferently—such cases had occurred. If everybody, this man included, she would have taken it as a matter of course—people had done so before. But the smallness of the exception made the mystery.

She soon knew thus much of the recusant's appearance. He was a gentlemanly man, with full and distinctly outlined Roman features, the prominences of which glowed in the sun with a bronze-like richness of tone. He was erect in attitude, and quiet in demeanour. One characteristic pre-eminently marked him—dignity.

Apparently he had some time ago reached that entrance to middle age at which a man's aspect naturally ceases to alter for the term of a dozen years or so ; and, artificially, a woman's does likewise. Thirty-five and fifty were his limits of variation—he might have been either, or anywhere between the two.

It may be said that married men of forty are usually ready and generous enough to fling passing glances at any specimen of moderate beauty they may discern by the way. Probably, as with persons playing whist for love, the consciousness of a certain immunity under any circumstances from that worst possible ultimate, the having to pay, makes them unduly speculative. Bathsheba was convinced that this unmoved person was not a married man.

When marketing was over, she rushed off to Liddy, who was waiting for her beside the yellow gig in which they had driven to town. The horse was put in, and on they trotted—Bathsheba's sugar, tea, and drapery parcels being packed behind, and expressing in some indescribable manner, by their colour, shape, and general lineaments, that they were that young lady-farmer's property, and the grocer's and draper's no more.

'I've been through it, Liddy, and it is over. I shan't mind it again, for they will all have grown accustomed to seeing me there; but this morning it was as bad as being married—eyes everywhere!'

'I knowed it would be,' Liddy said. 'Men be such a terrible class of society to look at a body.'

'But there was one man who had more sense than to waste his time upon me.' The information was put in this form that Liddy might not for a moment suppose her mistress was at all piqued. 'A very good-looking man,' she continued, 'upright; about forty, I should think. Do you know at all who he could be?'

Liddy couldn't think.

'Can't you guess at all?' said Bathsheba with some disappointment.

'I haven't a notion; besides, 'tis no difference, since he took less notice of you than any of the rest. Now, if he'd taken more, it would have mattered a great deal.'

Bathsheba was suffering from the reverse feeling just then, and they bowled along in silence. A low carriage, bowling along still more rapidly behind a horse of unimpeachable breed, overtook and passed them.

'Why, there he is!' she said.

Liddy looked. 'That! That's Farmer Boldwood—of course 'tis—the man you couldn't see the other day when he called.'

'Oh, Farmer Boldwood,' murmured Bathsheba, and looked at him as he outstripped them. The farmer had never turned his head once, but with eyes fixed on the most advanced point along the road, passed as unconsciously and abstractedly as if Bathsheba and her charms were thin air.

'He's an interesting man—don't you think so?' she remarked.

'Oh yes, very. Everybody owns it,' replied Liddy.

'I wonder why he is so wrapt up and indifferent, and seemingly so far away from all he sees around him.'

'It is said—but not known for certain—that he met with some bitter disappointment when he was a young man and merry. A woman jilted him, they say.'

'People always say that—and we know very well women scarcely ever jilt men; 'tis the men who jilt us. I expect it is simply his nature to be so reserved.'

'Simply his nature—I expect so, miss—nothing else in the world.'

'Still, 'tis more romantic to think he has been served cruelly, poor thing! Perhaps, after all, he has.'

'Depend upon it he has. Oh yes, miss, he has! I feel he must have.'

'However, we are very apt to think extremes of people. I shouldn't wonder after all if it wasn't a little of both—just between the two—rather cruelly used and rather reserved.'

'Oh dear no, miss—I can't think it between the two!'

'That's most likely.'

'Well, yes, so it is. I am convinced it is most likely. You may take my word, miss, that that's what's the matter with him.'

CHAPTER XIII

SORTES SANCTORUM—THE VALENTINE

IT was Sunday afternoon in the farmhouse, on the thirteenth of February. Dinner being over, Bathsheba, for want of a better companion, had asked Liddy to come and sit with her. The mouldy pile was dreary in winter-time before the candles were lighted and the shutters closed; the atmosphere of the place seemed as old as the walls; every nook behind the furniture had a temperature of its own, for the fire was not kindled in this part of the house early in the day; and Bathsheba's new piano, which was an old one in other annals, looked particularly sloping and out of level on the warped floor before night threw a shade over its less prominent angles and hid the unpleasantness. Liddy, like a little brook, though shallow, was always rippling; her presence had not so much weight as to task thought, and yet enough to exercise it.

On the table lay an old quarto Bible, bound in leather. Liddy looking at it said,—

'Did you ever find out, miss, who you are going to marry by means of the Bible and key?'

'Don't be so foolish, Liddy. As if such things could be.'

'Well, there's a good deal in it, all the same.'

'Nonsense, child.'

'And it makes your heart beat fearful. Some believe in it; some don't; I do.'

'Very well, let's try it,' said Bathsheba, bounding from her seat with that total disregard of consistency which can be indulged in towards a dependent, and entering into the spirit of divination at once. 'Go and get the front door key.'

Liddy fetched it. 'I wish it wasn't Sunday,' she said, on returning. 'Perhaps 'tis wrong.'

'What's right week days is right Sundays,' replied her mistress in a tone which was a proof in itself.

The book was opened—the leaves, drab with age, being quite worn away at much-read verses by the fore-fingers of unpractised readers in former days, where they were moved along under the line as an aid to the vision. The special verse in the Book of Ruth was sought out by Bathsheba, and the sublime words met her eye. They slightly thrilled and abashed her. It was Wisdom in the abstract facing Folly in the concrete. Folly in the concrete blushed, persisted in her intention, and placed the key on the book. A rusty patch immediately upon the verse, caused by previous pressure of an iron substance thereon, told that this was not the first time the old volume had been used for the purpose.

'Now keep steady, and be silent,' said Bathsheba.

The verse was repeated; the book turned round; Bathsheba blushed guiltily.

'Who did you try?' said Liddy curiously.

'I shall not tell you.'

'Did you notice Mr. Boldwood's doings in church this morning, miss?' Liddy continued, adumbrating by the remark the track her thoughts had taken.

'No, indeed,' said Bathsheba, with serene indifference.

'His pew is exactly opposite yours, miss.'

'I know it.'

'And you did not see his goings on!'

'Certainly I did not, I tell you.'

Liddy assumed a smaller physiognomy, and shut her lips decisively.

This move was unexpected, and proportionately disconcerting. 'What did he do?' Bathsheba said perforce.

'Didn't turn his head to look at you once all the service.'

'Why should he?' again demanded her mistress, wearing a nettled look. 'I didn't ask him to.'

'Oh no. But everybody else was noticing you; and it was odd he didn't. There, 'tis like him. Rich and gentlemanly, what does he care?'

Bathsheba dropped into a silence intended to express that she had opinions on the matter too abstruse for Liddy's comprehension, rather than that she had nothing to say.

'Dear me—I had nearly forgotten the valentine I bought yesterday,' she exclaimed at length.

'Valentine! who for, miss?' said Liddy, 'Farmer Boldwood?'

It was the single name among all possible wrong ones that just at this moment seemed to Bathsheba more pertinent than the right.

'Well, no. It is only for little Teddy Coggan. I have promised him something, and this will be a pretty surprise for him. Liddy, you may as well bring me my desk and I'll direct it at once.'

Bathsheba took from her desk a gorgeously illuminated and embossed design in post-octavo, which had been bought on the previous market-day at the chief stationer's in Casterbridge. In the centre was a small oval enclosure; this was left blank, that the sender might insert tender words more appropriate to the special occasion than any generalities by a printer could possibly be.

'Here's a place for writing,' said Bathsheba. 'What shall I put?'

'Something of this sort, I should think,' returned Liddy promptly :—

> 'The rose is red,
> The violet blue,
> Carnation's sweet,
> And so are you.'

'Yes, that shall be it. It just suits itself to a chubby-faced child like him,' said Bathsheba. She inserted the words in a small though legible handwriting; enclosed the sheet in an envelope, and dipped her pen for the direction.

'What fun it would be to send it to the stupid old Boldwood, and how he would wonder!' said the irrepressible Liddy, lifting her eyebrows, and indulging in an awful mirth on the verge of fear as she thought of the moral and social magnitude of the man contemplated.

Bathsheba paused to regard the idea at full length. Boldwood's had begun to be a troublesome image—a species of Daniel in her kingdom who persisted in kneeling eastward when reason and common sense said that he might just as well follow suit with the rest, and afford her the official glance of admiration which cost nothing at all. She was far from being seriously concerned about his nonconformity. Still, it was faintly depressing that the most dignified and valuable man in the parish should withhold his eyes, and that a girl like Liddy should talk about it. So Liddy's idea was at first rather harassing than piquant.

'No, I won't do that. He wouldn't see any humour in it.'

'He'd worry to death,' said the persistent Liddy.

'Really, I don't care particularly to send it to Teddy,' remarked her mistress. 'He's rather a naughty child sometimes.'

'Yes—that he is.'

'Let's toss, as men do,' said Bathsheba, idly. 'Now then, head, Boldwood; tail, Teddy. No, we won't toss money on a Sunday, that would be tempting the devil indeed.'

'Toss this hymn-book; there can't be no sinfulness in that, miss.'

'Very well. Open, Boldwood—shut, Teddy. No; it's more likely to fall open. Open, Teddy—shut, Boldwood.'

The book went fluttering in the air and came down shut.

Bathsheba, a small yawn upon her mouth, took the pen, and with off-hand serenity directed the missive to Boldwood.

'Now light a candle, Liddy. Which seal shall we use? Here's a unicorn's head—there's nothing in that. What's this?—two doves—no. It ought to be something extraordinary, ought it not, Lidd? Here's one with a motto—I remember it is some funny one, but I can't read it. We'll try this, and if it doesn't do we'll have another.'

A large red seal was duly affixed. Bathsheba looked closely at the hot wax to discover the words.

'Capital!' she exclaimed, throwing down the letter frolicsomely. ''Twould upset the solemnity of a parson and clerk too.'

Liddy looked at the words of the seal, and read—

'MARRY ME.'

The same evening the letter was sent, and was duly sorted in Casterbridge post-office that night, to be returned to Weatherbury again in the morning.

So very idly and unreflectingly was this deed done. Of love as a spectacle Bathsheba had a fair knowledge; but of love subjectively she knew nothing.

CHAPTER XIV

EFFECT OF THE LETTER—SUNRISE

At dusk, on the evening of St. Valentine's Day, Bold-wood sat down to supper as usual, by a beaming fire of aged logs. Upon the mantel-shelf before him was a time-piece, surmounted by a spread eagle, and upon the eagle's wings was the letter Bathsheba had sent. Here the bachelor's gaze was continually fastening itself, till the large red seal became as a blot of blood on the retina of his eye ; and as he ate and drank he still read in fancy the words thereon, although they were too remote for his sight—

'Marry Me.'

The pert injunction was like those crystal substances which, colourless themselves, assume the tone of objects about them. Here, in the quiet of Boldwood's parlour, where everything that was not grave was extraneous, and where the atmosphere was that of a Puritan Sunday lasting all the week, the letter and its dictum changed their tenor from the thoughtlessness of their origin to a deep solemnity, imbibed from their accessories now.

Since the receipt of the missive in the morning, Boldwood had felt the symmetry of his existence to be slowly getting distorted in the direction of an ideal passion. The disturbance was as the first floating weed to Columbus—the contemptibly little suggesting possibilities of the infinitely great.

The letter must have had an origin and a motive. That the latter was of the smallest magnitude compatible with its existence at all, Boldwood, of course, did not know. And such an explanation did not strike him as a possibility even. It is foreign to a mystified condition of mind to realize of the mystifier that the processes of approving a course suggested by circumstance, and of striking out a course from inner impulse, would look the same in the result. The vast difference between starting a train of events, and directing into a particular groove a series already started, is rarely apparent to the person confounded by the issue.

When Boldwood went to bed he placed the valentine in the corner of the looking-glass. He was conscious of its presence, even when his back was turned upon it. It was the first time in Boldwood's life that such an event had occurred. The same fascination that caused him to think it an act which had a deliberate motive prevented him from regarding it as an impertinence. He looked again at the direction. The mysterious influences of night invested the writing with the presence of the unknown writer. Somebody's —some *woman's*—hand had travelled softly over the paper bearing his name; her unrevealed eyes had watched every curve as she formed it; her brain had seen him in imagination the while. Why should she have imagined him? Her mouth—were the lips red or pale, plump or creased?—had curved itself to a certain expression as the pen went on—the corners had moved with all their natural tremulousness: what had been the expression?

The vision of the woman writing, as a supplement to the words written, had no individuality. She was a

113

misty shape, and well she might be, considering that her original was at that moment sound asleep and oblivious of all love and letter-writing under the sky. Whenever Boldwood dozed she took a form, and comparatively ceased to be a vision : when he awoke there was the letter justifying the dream.

The moon shone to-night, and its light was not of a customary kind. His window admitted only a reflection of its rays, and the pale sheen had that reversed direction which snow gives, coming upward and lighting up his ceiling in an unnatural way, casting shadows in strange places, and putting lights where shadows had used to be.

The substance of the epistle had occupied him but little in comparison with the fact of its arrival. He suddenly wondered if anything more might be found in the envelope than what he had withdrawn. He jumped out of bed in the weird light, took the letter, pulled out the flimsy sheet, shook the envelope—searched it. Nothing more was there. Boldwood looked, as he had a hundred times the preceding day, at the insistent red seal : ' Marry me,' he said aloud.

The solemn and reserved yeoman again closed the letter, and stuck it in the frame of the glass. In doing so he caught sight of his reflected features, wan in expression, and insubstantial in form. He saw how closely compressed was his mouth, and that his eyes were wide-spread and vacant. Feeling uneasy and dissatisfied with himself for this nervous excitability, he returned to bed.

Then the dawn drew on. The full power of the clear heaven was not equal to that of a cloudy sky at noon, when Boldwood arose and dressed himself. He descended the stairs and went out towards the gate of a field to the east, leaning over which he paused and looked around.

It was one of the usual slow sunrises of this time of

the year, and the sky, pure violet in the zenith, was
leaden to the northward, and murky to the east, where,
over the snowy down or ewe-lease on Weatherbury
Upper Farm, and apparently resting upon the ridge, the
only half of the sun yet visible burnt rayless, like a red
and flameless fire shining over a white hearthstone.
The whole effect resembled a sunset as childhood
resembles age.

In other directions, the fields and sky were so much
of one colour by the snow, that it was difficult in a
hasty glance to tell whereabouts the horizon occurred,;
and in general there was here, too, that before-mentioned
preternatural inversion of light and shade which attends
the prospect when the garish brightness commonly in
the sky is found on the earth, and the shades of earth
are in the sky. Over the west hung the wasting moon,
now dull and greenish-yellow, like tarnished brass.

Boldwood was listlessly noting how the frost had
hardened and glazed the surface of the snow, till it
shone in the red eastern light with the polish of marble ;
how, in some portions of the slope, withered grass-bents,
encased in icicles, bristled through the smooth wan
coverlet in the twisted and curved shapes of old
Venetian glass ; and how the footprints of a few birds,
which had hopped over the snow whilst it lay in the
state of a soft fleece, were now frozen to a short perma-
nency. A half-muffled noise of light wheels interrupted
him. Boldwood turned back into the road. It was
the mail-cart—a crazy, two-wheeled vehicle, hardly
heavy enough to resist a puff of wind. The driver held
out a letter. Boldwood seized it and opened it, expecting another anonymous one—so greatly are people's
ideas of probability a mere sense that precedent will
repeat itself.

'I don't think it is for you, sir,' said the man, when
he saw Boldwood's action. 'Though there is no name,
I think it is for your shepherd.'

Boldwood looked then at the address—

To the New Shepherd,
Weatherbury Farm,
Near Casterbridge.

'Oh—what a mistake!—it is not mine. Nor is it for my shepherd. It is for Miss Everdene's. You had better take it on to him—Gabriel Oak—and say I opened it in mistake.'

At this moment, on the ridge, up against the blazing sky, a figure was visible, like the black snuff in the midst of a candle-flame. Then it moved and began to bustle about vigorously from place to place, carrying square skeleton masses, which were riddled by the same rays. A small figure on all fours followed behind. The tall form was that of Gabriel Oak; the small one that of George; the articles in course of transit were hurdles.

'Wait,' said Boldwood. 'That's the man on the hill. I'll take the letter to him myself.'

To Boldwood it was now no longer merely a letter to another man. It was an opportunity. Exhibiting a face pregnant with intention, he entered the snowy field.

Gabriel, at that minute, descended the hill towards the right. The glow stretched down in this direction now, and touched the distant roof of Warren's Malthouse —whither the shepherd was apparently bent. Boldwood followed at a distance.

CHAPTER XV

A MORNING MEETING—THE LETTER AGAIN

THE scarlet and orange light outside the malthouse did not penetrate to its interior, which was, as usual, lighted by a rival glow of similar hue, radiating from the hearth.

The maltster, after having lain down in his clothes for a few hours, was now sitting beside a three-legged table, breakfasting off bread and bacon. This was eaten on the plateless system, which is performed by placing a slice of bread upon the table, the meat flat upon the bread, a mustard plaster upon the meat, and a pinch of salt upon the whole, then cutting them vertically downwards with a large pocket-knife till wood is reached, when the severed lump is impaled on the knife, elevated, and sent the proper way of food.

The maltster's lack of teeth appeared not to sensibly diminish his powers as a mill. He had been without them for so many years that toothlessness was felt less to be a defect than hard gums an acquisition. Indeed, he seemed to approach the grave as a hyperbolic curve approaches a line—less directly as he got nearer, till it was doubtful if he would ever reach it at all.

In the ashpit was a heap of potatoes roasting, and a boiling pipkin of charred bread, called 'coffee,' for the benefit of whomsoever should call, for Warren's was a sort of clubhouse, used as an alternative to the inn.

'I say, says I, we get a fine day, and then down comes a snapper at night,' was a remark now suddenly heard spreading into the malthouse from the door, which had been opened the previous moment. The form of Henery Fray advanced to the fire, stamping the snow from his boots when about half-way there. The speech and entry had not seemed to be at all an abrupt begin· ning to the maltster, introductory matter being often omitted in this neighbourhood, both from word and deed, and the maltster having the same latitude allowed him, did not hurry to reply. He picked up a fragment of cheese, by pecking upon it with his knife, as a butcher picks up skewers.

Henery appeared in a drab kerseymere great-coat, buttoned over his smock-frock, the white skirts of the latter being visible to the distance of about a foot below the coat-tails, which, when you got used to the style of dress, looked natural enough, and even ornamental—it certainly was comfortable.

Matthew Moon, Joseph Poorgrass, and other carters and waggoners followed at his heels, with great lanterns dangling from their hands, which showed that they had just come from the cart-horse stables, where they had been busily engaged since four o'clock that morning.

'And how is she getting on without a baily?' the maltster inquired.

Henery shook his head, and smiled one of the bitter smiles, dragging all the flesh of his forehead into a corrugated heap in the centre.

'She'll rue it—surely, surely!' he said. 'Benjy Pennyways were not a true man or an honest baily— as big a betrayer as Joey Iscariot himself. But to think she can carr' on alone!' He allowed his head to swing laterally three or four times in silence. 'Never in all my creeping up—never!'

This was recognized by all as the conclusion of some gloomy speech which had been expressed in thought alone during the shake of the head; Henery meanwhile retained several marks of despair upon his face, to imply that they would be required for use again directly he should go on speaking.

'All will be ruined, and ourselves too, or there's no meat in gentlemen's houses!' said Mark Clark, in the manner of a man ready to burst all links of habit.

'A headstrong maid, that's what she is—and won't listen to no advice at all. Pride and vanity have ruined many a cobbler's dog. Dear, dear, when I think o' it, I sorrows like a man in travel!'

'True, Henery, you do, I've heard ye,' said Joseph Poorgrass, in a voice of thorough attestation, and with a wire-drawn smile of misery.

'"Twould do a martel man no harm to have what's under her bonnet,' said Billy Smallbury, who had just entered, bearing his one tooth before him. 'She can spaik real language, and must have some sense somewhere. Do ye foller me?'

'I do, I do; but no baily—I deserved that place,' wailed Henery, signifying wasted genius by gazing blankly at visions of a high destiny apparently visible to him on Billy Smallbury's smock-frock. 'There, 'twas to be, I suppose. Your lot is your lot, and Scripture is nothing; for if you do good you don't get rewarded according to your works, but be cheated in some mean way out of your recompense.'

'No, no; I don't agree with'ee there,' said Mark Clark, decisively. 'God's a perfect gentleman in that respect.'

'Good works good pay, so to speak it,' attested Joseph Poorgrass.

A short pause ensued, and as a sort of *entr'acte* Henery turned and blew out the lanterns, which the increase of daylight rendered no longer necessary even in the malthouse, with its one pane of glass.

'I wonder what a farmer-woman can want with a

harpsichord, dulcimer, pianner, or whatever 'tis they d'call it?' said the maltster. 'Liddy saith she've a new one.'

'Got a pianner?'

'Ay. Seems her old uncle's things were not good enough for her. She've bought all but everything new. There's heavy chairs for the stout, weak and wiry ones for the slender; great watches, getting on to the size of clocks, to stand upon the chimbley-piece.'

'Pictures, for the most part wonderful frames.'

'And long horse-hair settles for the drunk, with horse-hair pillows at each end,' said Mr. Clark. 'Likewise looking-glasses for the pretty, and lying books for the wicked.'

A firm loud tread was now heard stamping outside; the door was opened about six inches, and somebody on the other side exclaimed—

'Neighbours, have ye got room for a few new-born lambs?'

'Ay, sure, shepherd,' said the conclave.

The door was flung back till it kicked the wall and trembled from top ·to bottom with the blow. Mr. Oak appeared in the entry with a steaming face, hay-bands wound about his ankles to keep out the snow, a leather strap round his waist outside the smock-frock, and looking altogether an epitome of the world's health and vigour. Four lambs hung in various embarrassing attitudes over his shoulders, and the dog George, whom Gabriel had contrived to fetch from Norcombe, stalked solemnly behind.

'Well, Shepherd Oak, and how's lambing this year, if I mid say it?' inquired Joseph Poorgrass.

'Terrible trying,' said Oak. 'I've been wet through twice a-day, either in snow or rain, this last fortnight. Cainy and I haven't tined our eyes to-night.'

'A good few twins, too, I hear?'

'Too many by half. Yes; 'tis a very queer lambing this year. We shan't have done by Lady Day.'

'And last year 'twer all over by Sexajessamine Sunday,' Joseph remarked.

'Bring on the rest, Cain,' said Gabriel, 'and then run back to the ewes. I'll follow you soon.'

Cainy Ball—a cherry-faced young lad, with a small circular orifice by way of mouth, advanced and deposited two others, and retired as he was bidden. Oak lowered the lambs from their unnatural elevation, wrapped them in hay, and placed them round the fire.

'We've no lambing-hut here, as I used to have at Norcombe,' said Gabriel, 'and 'tis such a plague to bring the weakly ones to a house. If 'twasn't for your place here, malter, I don't know what I should do, this keen weather. And how is it with you to-day, malter?'

'Oh, neither sick nor sorry, shepherd; but no younger.'

'Ay—I understand.'

'Sit down, Shepherd Oak,' continued the ancient man of malt. 'And how was the old place at Norcombe, when ye went for your dog? I should like to see the old familiar spot; but faith, I shouldn't know a soul there now.'

'I suppose you wouldn't. 'Tis altered very much.'

'Is it true that Dicky Hill's wooden cider-house is pulled down?'

'Oh yes—years ago, and Dicky's cottage just above it.'

'Well, to be sure!'

'Yes; and Tompkins's old apple-tree is rooted that used to bear two hogsheads of cider, and no help from other trees.'

'Rooted?—you don't say it! Ah! stirring times we live in—stirring times.'

'And you can mind the old well that used to be in the middle of the place? That's turned into a solid iron pump with a large stone trough, and all complete.'

'Dear, dear—how the face of nations alter, and what great revolutions we live to see nowadays! Yes—and 'tis the same here. They've been talking but now of the mis'ess's strange doings.'

'What have you been saying about her?' inquired Oak, sharply turning to the rest, and getting very warm.

'These middle-aged men have been pulling her over the coals for pride and vanity,' said Mark Clark; 'but I say, let her have rope enough. Bless her pretty face —shouldn't I like to do so—upon her cherry lips!' The gallant Mark Clark here made a peculiar and well-known sound with his own.

'Mark,' said Gabriel, sternly, 'now you mind this: none of that dalliance-talk — that dandle-smack-and-coddle style of yours—about Miss Everdene. I don't allow it. Do you hear?'

'With all my heart, as I've got no chance,' replied Mr. Clark, cordially.

'I suppose you've been speaking against her?' said Oak, turning to Joseph Poorgrass with a very grim look.

'No, no—not a word I—'tis a real joyful thing that she's no worse, that's what I say,' said Joseph, trembling and blushing with terror. 'Matthew just said——'

'Matthew Moon, what have you been saying?' asked Oak.

'I? Why ye know I wouldn't harm a worm—no, not one underground worm?' said Matthew Moon, looking very uneasy.

'Well, somebody has—and look here, neighbours.' Gabriel, though one of the quietest and most gentle men on earth, rose to the occasion, with martial promptness and vigour. 'That's my fist.' Here he placed his fist, rather smaller in size than a common loaf, in the mathematical centre of the maltster's little table, and with it gave a bump or two thereon, as if to ensure that their eyes all thoroughly took in the idea of fistiness before he went further. 'Now—the first man in the parish that I hear prophesying bad of our mistress, why' (here the fist was raised and let fall, as Thor might have done with his hammer in assaying it)—'he'll smell and taste that—or I'm a Dutchman.'

All earnestly expressed by their features that their minds did not wander to Holland for a moment on account of this statement, but were deploring the difference which gave rise to the figure; and Mark Clark cried 'Hear, hear; just what I should ha' said.' The dog George looked up at the same time after the shepherd's menace, and though he understood English but imperfectly, began to growl.

'Now, don't ye take on so, shepherd, and sit down!' said Henery, with a deprecating peacefulness equal to anything of the kind in Christianity.

'We hear that ye be a extraordinary good and clever man, shepherd,' said Joseph Poorgrass with considerable anxiety from behind the maltster's bedstead, whither he had retired for safety. ''Tis a great thing to be clever, I'm sure,' he added, making movements associated with states of mind rather than body; 'we wish we were, don't we, neighbours?'

'Ay, that we do, sure,' said Matthew Moon, with a small anxious laugh towards Oak, to show how very friendly disposed he was likewise.

'Who's been telling you I'm clever?' said Oak.

''Tis blowed about from pillar to post quite common,' said Matthew. 'We hear that ye can tell the time as well by the stars as we can by the sun and moon, shepherd.'

'Yes, I can do a little that way,' said Gabriel, as a man of medium sentiments on the subject.

'And that ye can make sun-dials, and prent folks' names upon their waggons almost like copper-plate, with beautiful flourishes, and great long tails. A excellent fine thing for ye to be such a clever man, shepherd. Joseph Poorgrass used to prent to Farmer James .Everdene's waggons before you came, and 'a could never mind which way to turn the J's and E's

—could ye, Joseph?' Joseph shook his head to express how absolute was the fact that he couldn't. 'And so you used to do 'em the wrong way, like this, didn't ye, Joseph?' Matthew marked on the dusty floor with his whip-handle

ᒐ A M Ǝ S

'And how Farmer James would cuss, and call thee a fool, wouldn't he, Joseph, when 'a seed his name looking so inside-out-like?' continued Matthew Moon, with feeling.

'Ay—'a would,' said Joseph, meekly. 'But, you see, I wasn't so much to blame, for them J's and E's be such trying sons o' witches for the memory to mind whether they face backward or forward; and I always had such a forgetful memory, too.'

''Tis a very bad affliction for ye, being such a man of calamities in other ways.'

'Well, 'tis; but a happy Providence ordered that it should be no worse, and I feel my thanks. As to shepherd, there, I'm sure mis'ess ought to have made ye her baily—such a fitting man for't as you be.'

'I don't mind owning that I expected it,' said Oak, frankly. 'Indeed, I hoped for the place. At the same time, Miss Everdene has a right to be her own baily if she choose—and to keep me down to be a common shepherd only.' Oak drew a slow breath, looked sadly into the bright ashpit, and seemed lost in thoughts not of the most hopeful hue.

The genial warmth of the fire now began to stimulate the nearly lifeless lambs to bleat and move their limbs briskly upon the hay, and to recognize for the first time the fact that they were born. Their noise increased to a chorus of baas, upon which Oak pulled the milk-can from before the fire, and taking a small tea-pot from the pocket of his smock-frock, filled it with milk, and taught those of the helpless creatures which were not to be restored to their dams how to drink from the spout—a trick they acquired with astonishing aptitude.

'And she don't even let ye have the skins of the dead lambs, I hear?' resumed Joseph Poorgrass, his eyes lingering on the operations of Oak with the necessary melancholy.

'I don't have them,' said Gabriel.

'Ye be very badly used, shepherd,' hazarded Joseph again, in the hope of getting Oak as an ally in lamentation after all. 'I think she's took against ye—that I do.'

'Oh no—not at all,' replied Gabriel, hastily, and a sigh escaped him, which the deprivation of lamb skins could hardly have caused.

Before any further remark had been added a shade darkened the door, and Boldwood entered the malthouse, bestowing upon each a nod of a quality between friendliness and condescension.

'Ah! Oak, I thought you were here,' he said. 'I met the mail-cart ten minutes ago, and a letter was put into my hand, which I opened without reading the address. I believe it is yours. You must excuse the accident, please.'

'Oh yes—not a bit of difference, Mr. Boldwood—not a bit,' said Gabriel, readily. He had not a correspondent on earth, nor was there a possible letter coming to him whose contents the whole parish would not have been welcome to peruse.

Oak stepped aside, and read the following in an unknown hand:—

'DEAR FRIEND,—I do not know your name, but I think these few lines will reach you, which I write to thank you for your kindness to me the night I left Weatherbury in a reckless way. I also return the money I owe you, which you will excuse my not keeping as a gift. All has ended well, and I am happy to say I am going to be married to the young man who has courted me for some time—Sergeant

125

Troy, of the 11th Dragoon Guards, now quartered in this town. He would, I know, object to my having received anything except as a loan, being a man of great respectability and high honour—indeed, a nobleman by blood.

'I should be much obliged to you if you would keep the contents of this letter a secret for the present, dear friend. We mean to surprise Weatherbury by coming there soon as husband and wife, though I blush to state it to one nearly a stranger. The sergeant grew up in Weatherbury. Thanking you again for your kindness,

        'I am, your sincere well-wisher,

                'FANNY ROBIN.'

'Have you read it, Mr. Boldwood?' said Gabriel; 'if not, you had better do so. I know you are interested in Fanny Robin.'

Boldwood read the letter and looked grieved.

'Fanny—poor Fanny! the end she is so confident of has not yet come, she should remember—and may never come. I see she gives no address.'

'What sort of a man is this Sergeant Troy?' said Gabriel.

'H'm—I'm afraid not one to build much hope upon in such a case as this,' the farmer murmured, 'though he's a clever fellow, and up to everything. A slight romance attaches to him, too. His mother was a French governess, and it seems that a secret attachment existed between her and the late Lord Severn. She was married to a poor medical man, and soon after an infant was born; and while money was forthcoming all went on well. Unfortunately for her boy, his best friends died; and he got then a situation as second clerk at a lawyer's in Casterbridge. He stayed there for some time, and might have worked himself into a dignified position of some sort had he not indulged in the wild freak of enlisting. I have much doubt if ever little Fanny will surprise us in the way she mentions—very much doubt. A silly girl—silly girl!'

The door was hurriedly burst open again, and in came running Cainy Ball out of breath, his mouth red and open, like the bell of a penny trumpet, from which he coughed with noisy vigour and great distension of face.

'Now, Cain Ball,' said Oak, sternly, 'why will you run so fast and lose your breath so? I'm always telling you of it.'

'Oh—I—A puff of mee breath—went—the wrong way, please, Mister Oak, and made me cough—hok—hok!'

'Well—what have you come for?'

'I've run to tell ye,' said the junior shepherd, supporting his exhausted youthful frame against the doorpost, 'that you must come directly. Two more ewes have twinned—that's what's the matter, Shepherd Oak.'

'Oh, that's it,' said Oak, jumping up, and dismissing for the present his thoughts on poor Fanny. 'You are a good boy to run and tell me, Cain, and you shall smell a large plum pudding some day as a treat. But, before we go, Cainy, bring the tarpot, and we'll mark this lot and have done with 'em.'

Oak took from his illimitable pockets a marking iron, dipped it into the pot, and imprinted on the buttocks of the infant sheep the initials of her he delighted to muse on—'B. E.,' which signified to all the region round that henceforth the lambs belonged to Farmer Bathsheba Everdene, and to no one else.

'Now, Cainy, shoulder your two, and off. Good morning, Mr. Boldwood.' The shepherd lifted the sixteen large legs and four small bodies he had himself brought, and vanished with them in the direction of the lambing field hard by—their frames being now in a sleek and hopeful state, pleasantly contrasting with their death's-door plight of half an hour before.

Boldwood followed him a little way up the field, hesitated, and turned back. He followed him again with a last resolve, annihilating return. On approaching

127

the nook in which the fold was constructed, the farmer drew out his pocket-book, unfastened it, and allowed it to lie open on his hand. A letter was revealed—Bathsheba's.

'I was going to ask you, Oak,' he said, with unreal carelessness, 'if you know whose writing this is?'

Oak glanced into the book, and replied instantly, with a flushed face, 'Miss Everdene's.'

Oak had coloured simply at the consciousness of sounding her name. He now felt a strangely distressing qualm from a new thought. The letter could of course be no other than anonymous, or the inquiry would not have been necessary.

Boldwood mistook his confusion: sensitive persons are always ready with their 'Is it I?' in preference to objective reasoning.

'The question was perfectly fair,' he returned—and there was something incongruous in the serious earnestness with which he applied himself to an argument on a valentine. 'You know it is always expected that privy inquiries will be made: that's where the—fun lies.' If the word 'fun' had been 'torture,' it could not have been uttered with a more constrained and restless countenance than was Boldwood's then.

Soon parting from Gabriel, the lonely and reserved man returned to his house to breakfast—feeling twinges of shame and regret at having so far exposed his mood by those fevered questions to a stranger. He again placed the letter on the mantelpiece, and sat down to think of the circumstances attending it by the light of Gabriel's information.

CHAPTER XVI

ALL SAINTS' AND ALL SOULS'

ON a week-day morning a small congregation, consisting mainly of women and girls, rose from its knees
in the mouldy nave of a church called All Saints', in
the distant barrack-town before mentioned, at the end
of a service without a sermon. They were about to
disperse, when a smart footstep, entering the porch and
coming up the central passage, arrested their attention.
The step echoed with a ring unusual in a church; it
was the clink of spurs. Everybody looked. A young
cavalry soldier in a red uniform, with the three chevrons
of a sergeant upon his sleeve, strode up the aisle, with
an embarrassment which was only the more marked
by the intense vigour of his step, and by the determination upon his face to show none. A slight flush
had mounted his cheek by the time he had run the
gauntlet between these women; but, passing on through
the chancel arch, he never paused till he came close
to the altar railing. Here for a moment he stood
alone.

The officiating curate, who had not yet doffed his
surplice, perceived the new-comer, and followed him
to the communion-space. He whispered to the soldier,
and then beckoned to the clerk, who in his turn
whispered to an elderly woman, apparently his wife, and
they also went up the chancel steps.

"'Tis a wedding!' murmured some of the women, brightening. 'Let's wait!'

The majority again sat down.

There was a creaking of machinery behind, and some of the young ones turned their heads. From the interior face of the west wall of the tower projected a little canopy with a quarter-jack and small bell beneath it, the automaton being driven by the same clock machinery that struck the large bell in the tower. Between the tower and the church was a close screen, the door of which was kept shut during services, hiding this grotesque clockwork from sight. At present, however, the door was open, and the egress of the jack, the blows on the bell, and the mannikin's retreat into the nook again, were visible to many, and audible throughout the church.

The jack had struck half-past eleven.

'Where's the woman?' whispered some of the spectators.

The young sergeant stood still with the abnormal rigidity of the old pillars around. He faced the southeast, and was as silent as he was still.

The silence grew to be a noticeable thing as the minutes went on, and nobody else appeared, and not a soul moved. The rattle of the quarter-jack again from its niche, its blows for three-quarters, its fussy retreat, were almost painfully abrupt, and caused many of the congregation to start palpably.

'I wonder where the woman is!' a voice whispered again.

There began now that slight shifting of feet, that artificial coughing among several, which betrays a nervous suspense. At length there was a titter. But the soldier never moved. There he stood, his face to the south-east, upright as a column, his cap in his hand.

The clock ticked on. The women threw off their nervousness, and titters and giggling became more

130

frequent. Then came a dead silence. Every one was waiting for the end. Some persons may have noticed how extraordinarily the striking of quarters seems to quicken the flight of time. It was hardly credible that the jack had not got wrong with the minutes when the rattle began again, the puppet emerged, and the four quarters were struck fitfully as before. One could almost be positive that there was a malicious leer upon the hideous creature's face, and a mischievous delight in its twitchings. Then followed the dull and remote resonance of the twelve heavy strokes in the tower above. The women were impressed, and there was no giggle this time.

The clergyman glided into the vestry, and the clerk vanished. The sergeant had not yet turned; every woman in the church was waiting to see his face, and he appeared to know it. At last he did turn, and stalked resolutely down the nave, braving them all, with a compressed lip. Two bowed and toothless old almsmen then looked at each other and chuckled, innocently enough; but the sound had a strange weird effect in that place.

Opposite to the church was a paved square, around which several overhanging wood buildings of old time cast a picturesque shade. The young man on leaving the door went to cross the square, when, in the middle, he met a little woman. The expression of her face, which had been one of intense anxiety, sank at the sight of his nearly to terror.

'Well?' he said, in a suppressed passion, fixedly looking at her.

'Oh, Frank—I made a mistake!—I thought that church with the spire was All Saints', and I was at the door at half-past eleven to a minute as you said. I waited till a quarter to twelve, and found then that I was in All Souls'. But I wasn't much frightened, for I thought it could be to-morrow as well.'

'You fool, for so fooling me! But say no more.'

'Shall it be to-morrow, Frank?' she asked blankly.

'To-morrow!' and he gave vent to a hoarse laugh. 'I don't go through that experience again for some time, I warrant you!'

'But after all,' she expostulated in a trembling voice, 'the mistake was not such a terrible thing! Now, dear Frank, when shall it be?'

'Ah, when? God knows!' he said, with a light irony, and turning from her walked rapidly away.

CHAPTER XVII

IN THE MARKET-PLACE

ON Saturday Boldwood was in Casterbridge market-house as usual, when the disturber of his dreams entered, and became visible to him. Adam had awakened from his deep sleep, and behold! there was Eve. The farmer took courage, and for the first time really looked at her.

Material causes and emotional effects are not to be arranged in regular equation. The result from capital employed in the production of any movement of a mental nature is sometimes as tremendous as the cause itself is absurdly minute. When women are in a freakish mood, their usual intuition, either from carelessness or inherent defect, seemingly fails to teach them this, and hence it was that Bathsheba was fated to be astonished to-day.

Boldwood looked at her—not slily, critically, or understandingly, but blankly at gaze, in the way a reaper looks up at a passing train—as something foreign to his element, and but dimly understood. To Boldwood women had been remote phenomena rather than necessary complements — comets of such uncertain aspect, movement, and permanence, that whether their orbits were as geometrical, unchangeable, and as subject to laws as his own, or as absolutely erratic as they superficially appeared, he had not deemed it his duty to consider.

He saw her black hair, her correct facial curves and profile, and the roundness of her chin and throat. He saw then the side of her eyelids, eyes, and lashes, and the shape of her ear. Next he noticed her figure, her skirt, and the very soles of her shoes.

Boldwood thought her beautiful, but wondered whether he was right in his thought, for it seemed impossible that this romance in the flesh, if so sweet as he imagined, could have been going on long without creating a commotion of delight among men, and provoking more inquiry than Bathsheba had done, even though that was not a little. To the best of his judgment neither nature nor art could improve this perfect one of an imperfect many. His heart began to move within him. Boldwood, it must be remembered, though forty years of age, had never before inspected a woman with the very centre and force of his glance; they had struck upon all his senses at wide angles.

Was she really beautiful? He could not assure himself that his opinion was true even now. He furtively said to a neighbour, 'Is Miss Everdene considered handsome?'

'Oh, yes; she was a good deal noticed the first time she came, if you remember. A very handsome girl indeed.'

A man is never more credulous than in receiving favourable opinions on the beauty of a woman he is half, or quite, in love with; a mere child's word on the point has the weight of an R.A.'s. Boldwood was satisfied now.

And this charming woman had in effect said to him, 'Marry me.' Why should she have done that strange thing? Boldwood's blindness to the difference between approving of what circumstances suggest, and originating what they do not suggest, was well matched by Bathsheba's insensibility to the possibly great issues of little beginnings.

She was at this moment coolly dealing with a dashing young farmer, adding up accounts with him as indifferently as if his face had been the pages of a ledger. It was evident that such a nature as his had no attraction for a woman of Bathsheba's taste. But Boldwood grew hot down to his hands with an incipient jealousy; he trod for the first time the threshold of 'the injured lover's hell.' His first impulse was to go and thrust himself between them. This could be done, but only in one way—by asking to see a sample of her corn. Boldwood renounced the idea. He could not make the request; it was debasing loveliness to ask it to buy and sell, and jarred with his conceptions of her.

All this time Bathsheba was conscious of having broken into that dignified stronghold at last. His eyes, she knew, were following her everywhere. This was a triumph; and had it come naturally, such a triumph would have been the sweeter to her for this piquing delay. But it had been brought about by misdirected ingenuity, and she valued it only as she valued an artificial flower or a wax fruit.

Being a woman with some good sense in reasoning on subjects wherein her heart was not involved, Bathsheba genuinely repented that a freak which had owed its existence as much to Liddy as to herself, should ever have been undertaken, to disturb the placidity of a man she respected too highly to deliberately tease.

She that day nearly formed the intention of begging his pardon on the very next occasion of their meeting. The worst features of this arrangement were that, if he thought she ridiculed him, an apology would increase the offence by being disbelieved; and if he thought she wanted him to woo her, it would read like additional evidence of her forwardness.

CHAPTER XVIII

BOLDWOOD IN MEDITATION—REGRET

BOLDWOOD was tenant of what was called Little Weatherbury Farm, and his person was the nearest approach to aristocracy that this remoter quarter of the parish could boast of. Genteel strangers, whose god was their town, who might happen to be compelled to linger about this nook for a day, heard the sound of light wheels, and prayed to see good society, to the degree of a solitary lord, or squire at the very least, but it was only Mr. Boldwood going out for the day. They heard the sound of wheels yet once more, and were re-animated to expectancy: it was only Mr. Boldwood coming home again.

His house stood recessed from the road, and the stables, which are to a farm what a fireplace is to a room, were behind, their lower portions being lost amid bushes of laurel. Inside the blue door, open half-way down, were to be seen at this time the backs and tails of half-a-dozen warm and contented horses standing in their stalls; and as thus viewed, they presented alternations of roan and bay, in shapes like a Moorish arch, the tail being a streak down the midst of each. Over these, and lost to the eye gazing in from the outer light, the mouths of the same animals could be heard busily sustaining the above-named

warmth and plumpness by quantities of oats and hay.
The restless and shadowy figure of a colt wandered
about a loose-box at the end, whilst the steady grind
of all the eaters was occasionally diversified by the
rattle of a rope or the stamp of a foot.

Pacing up and down at the heels of the animals was
Farmer Boldwood himself. This place was his almonry
and cloister in one : here, after looking to the feeding
of his four-footed dependants, the celibate would walk
and meditate of an evening till the moon's rays streamed
in through the cobwebbed windows, or total darkness
enveloped the scene.

His square-framed perpendicularity showed more fully
now than in the crowd and bustle of the market-house.
In this meditative walk his foot met the floor with heel
and toe simultaneously, and his fine reddish-fleshed face
was bent downwards just enough to render obscure the
still mouth and the well-rounded though rather prominent
and broad chin. A few clear and thread-like horizontal
lines were the only interruption to the otherwise smooth
surface of his large forehead.

The phases of Boldwood's life were ordinary enough,
but his was not an ordinary nature. That stillness,
which struck casual observers more than anything else
in his character and habit, and seemed so precisely
like the rest of inanition, may have been the perfect
balance of enormous antagonistic forces—positives and
negatives in fine adjustment. His equilibrium disturbed,
he was in extremity at once. If an emotion possessed
him at all, it ruled him ; a feeling not mastering him
was entirely latent. Stagnant or rapid, it was never
slow. He was always hit mortally, or he was missed.

He had no light and careless touches in his constitution, either for good or for evil. Stern in the outlines of
action, mild in the details, he was serious throughout all.
He saw no absurd sides to the follies of life, and thus,
though not quite companionable in the eyes of merry

men and scoffers, and those to whom all things show
life as a jest, he was not intolerable to the earnest and
those acquainted with grief. Being a man who read
all the dramas of life seriously, if he failed to please
when they were comedies, there was no frivolous treatment to reproach him for when they chanced to end
tragically.

Bathsheba was far from dreaming that the dark and
silent shape upon which she had so carelessly thrown a
seed was a hotbed of tropic intensity. Had she known
Boldwood's moods, her blame would have been fearful,
and the stain upon her heart ineradicable. Moreover,
had she known her present power for good or evil over
this man, she would have trembled at her responsibility.
Luckily for her present, unluckily for her future tranquillity, her understanding had not yet told her what
Boldwood was. Nobody knew entirely ; for though it
was possible to form guesses concerning his wild capabilities from old floodmarks faintly visible, he had never
been seen at the high tides which caused them.

Farmer Boldwood came to the stable-door and looked
forth across the level fields. Beyond the first enclosure
was a hedge, and on the other side of this a meadow
belonging to Bathsheba's farm.

It was now early spring—the time of going to grass
with the sheep, when they have the first feed of the
meadows, before these are laid up for mowing. The
wind, which had been blowing east for several weeks,
had veered to the southward, and the middle of spring
had come abruptly—almost without a beginning. It
was that period in the vernal quarter when we may
suppose the Dryads to be waking for the season. The
vegetable world begins to move and swell and the saps
to rise, till in the completest silence of lone gardens
and trackless plantations, where everything seems helpless and still after the bond and slavery of frost, there
are bustlings, strainings, united thrusts, and pulls-all-

138

together, in comparison with which the powerful tugs of cranes and pulleys in a noisy city are but pigmy efforts.

Boldwood, looking into the distant meadows, saw there three figures. They were those of Miss Everdene, Shepherd Oak, and Cainy Ball.

When Bathsheba's figure shone upon the farmer's eyes it lighted him up as the moon lights up a great tower. A man's body is as the shell, or the tablet, of his soul, as he is reserved or ingenuous, overflowing or self-contained. There was a change in Boldwood's exterior from its former impassibleness; and his face showed that he was now living outside his defences for the first time, and with a fearful sense of exposure. It is the usual experience of strong natures when they love.

At last he arrived at a conclusion. It was to go across and inquire boldly of her.

The insulation of his heart by reserve during these many years, without a channel of any kind for disposable emotion, had worked its effect. It has been observed more than once that the causes of love are chiefly subjective, and Boldwood was a living testimony to the truth of the proposition. No mother existed to absorb his devotion, no sister for his tenderness, no idle ties for sense. He became surcharged with the compound, which was genuine lover's love.

He approached the gate of the meadow. Beyond it the ground was melodious with ripples, and the sky with larks; the low bleating of the flock mingling with both. Mistress and man were engaged in the operation of making a lamb 'take,' which is performed whenever an ewe has lost her own offspring, one of the twins of another ewe being given her as a substitute. Gabriel had skinned the dead lamb, and was tying the skin over the body of the live lamb, in the customary manner, whilst Bathsheba was holding open a little pen of four hurdles, into which the mother and foisted lamb were driven, where they would remain till the old sheep conceived an affection for the young one.

Bathsheba looked up at the completion of the manœuvre, and saw the farmer by the gate, where he was overhung by a willow tree in full bloom. Gabriel, to whom her face was as the uncertain glory of an April day, was ever regardful of its faintest changes, and instantly discerned thereon the mark of some influence from without, in the form of a keenly self-conscious reddening. He also turned and beheld Boldwood.

At once connecting these signs with the letter Boldwood had shown him, Gabriel suspected her of some coquettish procedure begun by that means, and carried on since, he knew not how.

Farmer Boldwood had read the pantomime denoting that they were aware of his presence, and the perception was as too much light turned upon his new sensibility. He was still in the road, and by moving on he hoped that neither would recognize that he had originally intended to enter the field. He passed by with an utter and overwhelming sensation of ignorance, shyness, and doubt. Perhaps in her manner there were signs that she wished to see him—perhaps not—he could not read a woman. The cabala of this erotic philosophy seemed to consist of the subtlest meanings expressed in misleading ways. Every turn, look, word, and accent contained a mystery quite distinct from its obvious import, and not one had ever been pondered by him until now.

As for Bathsheba, she was not deceived into the belief that Farmer Boldwood had walked by on business or in idleness. She collected the probabilities of the case, and concluded that she was herself responsible for Boldwood's appearance there. It troubled her much to see what a great flame a little wildfire was likely to kindle. Bathsheba was no schemer for marriage, nor was she deliberately a trifler with the affections of men, and a censor's experience on seeing an actual flirt after observing her would have been a feeling of surprise that Bathsheba could be so different from such a one, and yet so like what a flirt is supposed to be.

She resolved never again, by look or by sign, to interrupt the steady flow of this man's life. But a resolution to avoid an evil is seldom framed till the evil is so far advanced as to make avoidance impossible.

CHAPTER XIX

THE SHEEP-WASHING—THE OFFER

BOLDWOOD did eventually call upon her. She was not at home. 'Of course not,' he murmured. In contemplating Bathsheba as a woman, he had forgotten the accidents of her position as an agriculturist—that being as much of a farmer, and as extensive a farmer, as himself, her probable whereabouts was out-of-doors at this time of the year. This, and the other oversights Boldwood was guilty of, were natural to the mood, and still more natural to the circumstances. The great aids to idealization in love were present here: occasional observation of her from a distance, and the absence of social intercourse with her—visual familiarity, oral strangeness. The smaller human elements were kept out of sight; the pettinesses that enter so largely into all earthly living and doing were disguised by the accident of lover and loved-one not being on visiting terms; and there was hardly awakened a thought in Boldwood that sorry household realities appertained to her, or that she, like all others, had moments of commonplace, when to be least plainly seen was to be most prettily remembered. Thus a mild sort of apotheosis took place in his fancy, whilst she still lived and breathed within his own horizon, a troubled creature like himself.

It was the end of May when the farmer determined to be no longer repulsed by trivialities or distracted by suspense. He had by this time grown used to being in love; the passion now startled him less even when it tortured him more, and he felt himself adequate to the situation. On inquiring for her at her house they had told him she was at the sheep-washing, and he went off to seek her there.

The sheep-washing pool was a perfectly circular basin of brickwork in the meadows, full of the clearest water. To birds on the wing its glassy surface, reflecting the light sky, must have been visible for miles around as a glistening Cyclops' eye in a green face. The grass about the margin at this season was a sight to remember long—in a minor sort of way. Its activity in sucking the moisture from the rich damp sod was almost a process observable by the eye. The outskirts of this level water-meadow were diversified by rounded and hollow pastures, where just now every flower that was not a buttercup was a daisy. The river slid along noiselessly as a shade, the swelling reeds and sedge forming a flexible palisade along its moist brink. To the north of the mead were trees, the leaves of which were new, soft, and moist, not yet having stiffened and darkened under summer sun and drought, their colour being yellow beside a green—green beside a yellow. From the recesses of this knot of foliage the loud notes of three cuckoos were resounding through the still air.

Boldwood went meditating down the slopes with his eyes on his boots, which the yellow pollen from the buttercups had bronzed in artistic gradations. A tributary of the main stream flowed through the basin of the pool by an inlet and outlet at opposite points of its diameter. Shepherd Oak, Jan Coggan, Moon, Poorgrass, Cain Ball, and several others were assembled here, all dripping wet to the very roots of their hair,

and Bathsheba was standing by in a new riding-habit—
the most elegant she had ever worn—the reins of her
horse being looped over her arm. Flagons of cider
were rolling about upon the green. The meek sheep
were pushed into the pool by Coggan and Matthew
Moon, who stood by the lower hatch, immersed to their
waists; then Gabriel, who stood on the brink, thrust
them under as they swam along, with an instrument
like a crutch, formed for the purpose, and also for
assisting the exhausted animals when the wool became
saturated and they began to sink. They were let out
against the stream, and through the upper opening, all
impurities flowing away below. Cainy Ball and Joseph,
who performed this latter operation, were if possible
wetter than the rest; they resembled dolphins under a
fountain, every protuberance and angle of their clothes
dribbling forth a small rill.

Boldwood came close and bade her good-morning, with
such constraint that she could not but think he had
stepped across to the washing for its own sake, hoping
not to find her there; more, she fancied his brow severe
and his eye slighting. Bathsheba immediately contrived
to withdraw, and glided along by the river till she was
a stone's throw off. She heard footsteps brushing the
grass, and had a consciousness that love was encircling
her like a perfume. Instead of turning or waiting,
Bathsheba went further among the high sedges, but
Boldwood seemed determined, and pressed on till they
were completely past the bend of the river. Here,
without being seen, they could hear the splashing and
shouts of the washers above.

'Miss Everdene!' said the farmer.

She trembled, turned, and said 'Good morning.'
His tone was so utterly removed from all she had
expected as a beginning. It was lowness and quiet
accentuated: an emphasis of deep meanings, their form,
at the same time, being scarcely expressed. Silence

has sometimes a remarkable power of showing itself as the disembodied soul of feeling wandering without its carcase, and it is then more impressive than speech. In the same way, to say a little is often to tell more than to say a great deal. Boldwood told everything in that word.

As the consciousness expands on learning that what was fancied to be the rumble of wheels is the reverberation of thunder, so did Bathsheba's at her intuitive conviction.

'I feel—almost too much—to think,' he said, with a solemn simplicity. 'I have come to speak to you without preface. My life is not my own since I have beheld you clearly, Miss Everdene—I come to make you an offer of marriage.'

Bathsheba tried to preserve an absolutely neutral countenance, and all the motion she made was that of closing lips which had previously been a little parted.

'I am now forty-one years old,' he went on. 'I may have been called a confirmed bachelor, and I was a confirmed bachelor. I had never any views of myself as a husband in my earlier days, nor have I made any calculation on the subject since I have been older. But we all change, and my change, in this matter, came with seeing you. I have felt lately, more and more, that my present way of living is bad in every respect. Beyond all things, I want you as my wife.'

'I feel, Mr. Boldwood, that though I respect you much, I do not feel—what would justify me to—in accepting your offer,' she stammered.

This giving back of dignity for dignity seemed to open the sluices of feeling that Boldwood had as yet kept closed.

'My life is a burden without you,' he exclaimed, in a low voice. 'I want you—I want you to let me say I love you again and again!'

Bathsheba answered nothing, and the horse upon

145

her arm seemed so impressed that instead of cropping the herbage he looked up.

'I think and hope you care enough for me to listen to what I have to tell!'

Bathsheba's momentary impulse at hearing this was to ask why he thought that, till she remembered that, far from being a conceited assumption on Boldwood's part, it was but the natural conclusion of serious reflection based on deceptive premises of her own offering.

'I wish I could say courteous flatteries to you,' the farmer continued in an easier tone, 'and put my rugged feeling into a graceful shape: but I have neither power nor patience to learn such things. I want you for my wife—so wildly that no other feeling can abide in me; but I should not have spoken out had I not been led to hope.'

'The valentine again! Oh that valentine!' she said to herself, but not a word to him.

'If you can love me say so, Miss Everdene. If not —don't say no!'

'Mr. Boldwood, it is painful to have to say I am surprised, so that I don't know how to answer you with propriety and respect—but am only just able to speak out my feeling—I mean my meaning; that I am afraid I can't marry you, much as I respect you. You are too dignified for me to suit you, sir.'

'But, Miss Everdene!'

'I—I didn't—I know I ought never to have dreamt of sending that valentine—forgive me, sir—it was a wanton thing which no woman with any self-respect should have done. If you will only pardon my thoughtlessness, I promise never to——'

'No, no, no. Don't say thoughtlessness! Make me think it was something more—that it was a sort of prophetic instinct—the beginning of a feeling that you would like me. You torture me to say it was done in thoughtlessness—I never thought of it in that light, and

I can't endure it. Ah! I wish I knew how to win you! but that I can't do—I can only ask if I have already got you. If I have not, and it is not true that you have come unwittingly to me as I have to you, I can say no more.'

'I have not fallen in love with you, Mr. Boldwood— certainly I must say that.' She allowed a very small smile to creep for the first time over her serious face in saying this, and the white row of upper teeth, and keenly-cut lips already noticed, suggested an idea of heartless-ness, which was immediately contradicted by the pleasant eyes.

'But you will just think—in kindness and conde-scension think—if you cannot bear with me as a husband! I fear I am too old for you, but believe me I will take more care of you than would many a man of your own age. I will protect and cherish you with all my strength —I will indeed! You shall have no cares—be worried by no household affairs, and live quite at ease, Miss Everdene. The dairy superintendence shall be done by a man—I can afford it well—you shall never have so much as to look out of doors at haymaking time, or to think of weather in the harvest. I rather cling to the chaise, because it is the same my poor father and mother drove, but if you don't like it I will sell it, and you shall have a pony-carriage of your own. I cannot say how far above every other idea and object on earth you seem to me—nobody knows—God only knows—how much you are to me!'

Bathsheba's heart was young, and it swelled with sympathy for the deep-natured man who spoke so simply.

'Don't say it: don't! I cannot bear you to feel so much, and me to feel nothing. And I am afraid they will notice us, Mr. Boldwood. Will you let the matter rest now? I cannot think collectedly. I did not know you were going to say this to me. Oh, I am wicked to

147

have made you suffer so!' She was frightened as well as agitated at his vehemence.

'Say then, that you don't absolutely refuse. Do not quite refuse?'

'I can do nothing. I cannot answer.'

'I may speak to you again on the subject?'

'Yes.'

'I may think of you?'

'Yes, I suppose you may think of me.'

'And hope to obtain you?'

'No—do not hope! Let us go on.'

'I will call upon you again to-morrow.'

'No—please not. Give me time.'

'Yes—I will give you any time,' he said earnestly and gratefully. 'I am happier now.'

'No—I beg you! Don't be happier if happiness only comes from my agreeing. Be neutral, Mr. Boldwood! I must think.'

'I will wait,' he said.

And then she turned away. Boldwood dropped his gaze to the ground, and stood long like a man who did not know where he was. Realities then returned upon him like the pain of a wound received in an excitement which eclipses it, and he, too, then went on.

CHAPTER XX

PERPLEXITY—GRINDING THE SHEARS—A QUARREL

'HE is so disinterested and kind to offer me all that I can desire,' Bathsheba said, musingly.

Yet Farmer Boldwood, whether by nature kind or the reverse to kind, did not exercise kindness here. The rarest offerings of the purest loves are but a self-indulgence, and no generosity at all.

Bathsheba, not being the least in love with him, was eventually able to look calmly at his offer. It was one which many women of her own station in the neighbourhood, and not a few of higher rank, would have been wild to accept and proud to publish. In every point of view, ranging from politic to passionate, it was desirable that she, a lonely girl, should marry, and marry this earnest, well-to-do, and respected man. He was close to her doors: his standing was sufficient: his qualities were even supererogatory. Had she felt, which she did not, any wish whatever for the married state in the abstract, she could not reasonably have rejected him, being a woman who frequently appealed to her understanding for deliverance from her whims. Boldwood as a means to marriage was unexceptionable: she esteemed and liked him, yet she did not want him. It appears that ordinary men take wives because possession is not possible without marriage, and that ordinary women

149

accept husbands because marriage is not possible without possession ; with totally differing aims the method is the same on both sides. But the understood incentive on the woman's part was wanting here. Besides, Bathsheba's position as absolute mistress of a farm and house was a novel one, and the novelty had not yet begun to wear off.

But a disquiet filled her which was somewhat to her credit, for it would have affected few. Beyond the mentioned reasons with which she combated her objections, she had a strong feeling that, having been the one who began the game, she ought in honesty to accept the consequences. Still the reluctance remained. She said in the same breath that it would be ungenerous not to marry Boldwood, and that she couldn't do it to save her life.

Bathsheba's was an impulsive nature under a deliberative aspect. An Elizabeth in brain and a Mary Stuart in spirit, she often performed actions of the greatest temerity with a manner of extreme discretion. Many of her thoughts were perfect syllogisms ; unluckily they always remained thoughts. Only a few were irrational assumptions ; but, unfortunately, they were the ones which most frequently grew into deeds.

The next day to that of the declaration she found Gabriel Oak at the bottom of her garden, grinding his shears for the sheep-shearing. All the surrounding cottages were more or less scenes of the same operation; the scurr of whetting spread into the sky from all parts of the village as from an armoury previous to a campaign. Peace and war kiss each other at their hours of preparation—sickles, scythes, shears, and pruning-hooks, ranking with swords, bayonets, and lances, in their common necessity for point and edge.

Cainy Ball turned the handle of Gabriel's grindstone, his head performing a melancholy see-saw up and down with each turn of the wheel. Oak stood somewhat as Eros is represented when in the act of sharpening his arrows : his figure slightly bent, the weight of his body thrown over on the shears, and his head balanced sideways, with a critical compression of the lips and contraction of the eyelids to crown the attitude.

His mistress came up and looked upon them in silence for a minute or two ; then she said—

'Cain, go to the lower mead and catch the bay mare. I'll turn the winch of the grindstone. I want to speak to you, Gabriel.'

Cain departed, and Bathsheba took the handle. Gabriel had glanced up in intense surprise, quelled its expression, and looked down again. Bathsheba turned the winch, and Gabriel applied the shears.

The peculiar motion involved in turning a wheel has a wonderful tendency to benumb the mind. It is a sort of attenuated variety of Ixion's punishment, and contributes a dismal chapter to the history of gaols. The brain gets muddled, the head grows heavy, and the body's centre of gravity seems to settle by degrees in a leaden lump somewhere between the eyebrows and the crown. Bathsheba felt the unpleasant symptoms after two or three dozen turns.

'Will you turn, Gabriel, and let me hold the shears ? ' she said. 'My head is in a whirl, and I can't talk.'

Gabriel turned. Bathsheba then began, with some awkwardness, allowing her thoughts to stray occasionally from her story to attend to the shears, which required a little nicety in sharpening.

'I wanted to ask you if the men made any observations on my going behind the sedge with Mr. Boldwood yesterday ? '

'Yes, they did,' said Gabriel. 'You don't hold the shears right, miss—I knew you wouldn't know the way—hold like this.'

He relinquished the winch, and inclosing her two hands completely in his own (taking each as we sometimes clasp a child's hand in teaching him to write), grasped the shears with her. 'Incline the edge so,' he said.

Hands and shears were inclined to suit the words, and held thus for a peculiarly long time by the instructor as he spoke.

'That will do,' exclaimed Bathsheba. 'Loose my hands. I won't have them held! Turn the winch.'

Gabriel freed her hands quietly, retired to his handle, and the grinding went on.

'Did the men think it odd?' she said again.

'Odd was not the idea, miss.'

'What did they say?'

'That Farmer Boldwood's name and your own were likely to be flung over pulpit together before the year was out.'

'I thought so by the look of them! Why, there's nothing in it. A more foolish remark was never made, and I want you to contradict it: that's what I came for.'

Gabriel looked incredulous and sad, but between his moments of incredulity, relieved.

'They must have heard our conversation,' she continued.

'Well, then, Bathsheba!' said Oak, stopping the handle, and gazing into her face with astonishment.

'Miss Everdene, you mean,' she said, with dignity.

'I mean this, that if Mr. Boldwood really spoke of marriage, I am not going to tell a story and say he didn't to please you. I have already tried to please you too much for my own good!'

Bathsheba regarded him with round-eyed perplexity. She did not know whether to pity him for disappointed love of her, or to be angry with him for having got over it—his tone being ambiguous.

'I said I wanted you just to mention that it was not true I was going to be married to him,' she murmured, with a slight decline in her assurance.

'I can say that to them if you wish, Miss Everdene. And I could likewise give an opinion to you on what you have done.'

'I daresay. But I don't want your opinion.'

'I suppose not,' said Gabriel bitterly, and going on with his turning, his words rising and falling in a regular swell and cadence as he stooped or rose with the winch, which directed them, according to his position, perpendicularly into the earth, or horizontally along the garden, his eyes being fixed on a leaf upon the ground.

With Bathsheba a hastened act was a rash act; but, as does not always happen, time gained was prudence insured. It must be added, however, that time was very seldom gained. At this period the single opinion in the parish on herself and her doings that she valued as sounder than her own was Gabriel Oak's. And the outspoken honesty of his character was such that on any subject, even that of her love for, or marriage with, another man, the same disinterestedness of opinion might be calculated on, and be had for the asking. Thoroughly convinced of the impossibility of his own suit, a high resolve constrained him not to injure that of another. This is a lover's most stoical virtue, as the lack of it is a lover's most venial sin. Knowing he would reply truly, she asked the question, painful as she must have known the subject would be. Such is the selfishness of some charming women. Perhaps it was some excuse for her thus torturing honesty to her own advantage, that she had absolutely no other sound judgment within easy reach.

'Well, what is your opinion of my conduct,' she said, quietly.

'That it is unworthy of any thoughtful, and meek, and comely woman.'

In an instant Bathsheba's face coloured with the angry crimson of a Danby sunset. But she forbore to utter this feeling, and the reticence of her tongue only made the loquacity of her face the more noticeable.

The next thing Gabriel did was to make a mistake.

'Perhaps you don't like the rudeness of my reprimanding you, for I know it is rudeness; but I thought it would do good.'

She instantly replied sarcastically—

'On the contrary, my opinion of you is so low, that I see in your abuse the praise of discerning people!'

'I am glad you don't mind it, for I said it honestly and with every serious meaning.'

'I see. But, unfortunately, when you try not to speak in jest you are amusing—just as when you wish to avoid seriousness you sometimes say a sensible word.'

It was a hard hit, but Bathsheba had unmistakably lost her temper, and on that account Gabriel had never in his life kept his own better. He said nothing. She then broke out—

'I may ask, I suppose, where in particular my unworthiness lies? In my not marrying you, perhaps!'

'Not by any means,' said Gabriel quietly. 'I have long given up thinking of that matter.'

'Or wishing it, I suppose,' she said; and it was apparent that she expected an unhesitating denial of this supposition.

Whatever Gabriel felt, he coolly echoed her words—

'Or wishing it either.'

A woman may be treated with a bitterness which is sweet to her, and with a rudeness which is not offensive. Bathsheba would have submitted to an indignant chastisement for her levity had Gabriel protested that he was loving her at the same time; the impetuosity of passion unrequited is bearable, even if it stings and anathematizes—there is a triumph in the humiliation, and a tenderness in the strife. This was what she had been expecting, and what she had not got. To be lectured because the lecturer saw her in the cold morning light of open-shuttered disillusion was exasperating. He had not finished, either. He continued in a more agitated voice :—

'My opinion is (since you ask it) that you are greatly to blame for playing pranks upon a man like Mr. Boldwood, merely as a pastime. Leading on a man you don't care for is not a praiseworthy action. And even, Miss Everdene, if you seriously inclined towards him, you might have let him discover it in some way of true loving-kindness, and not by sending him a valentine's letter.'

Bathsheba laid down the shears.

'I cannot allow any man to—to criticize my private conduct!' she exclaimed. 'Nor will I for a minute. So you'll please leave the farm at the end of the week!'

It may have been a peculiarity—at any rate it was a fact—that when Bathsheba was swayed by an emotion of an earthly sort her lower lip trembled : when by a refined emotion, her upper or heavenward one. Her nether lip quivered now.

'Very well, so I will,' said Gabriel calmly. He had been held to her by a beautiful thread which it pained him to spoil by breaking, rather than by a chain he could not break. 'I should be even better pleased to go at once,' he added.

'Go at once then, in Heaven's name!' said she, her eyes flashing at his, though never meeting them. 'Don't let me see your face any more.'

'Very well, Miss Everdene—so it shall be.'

And he took his shears and went away from her in placid dignity, as Moses left the presence of Pharaoh.

CHAPTER XXI

TROUBLES IN THE FOLD—A MESSAGE

GABRIEL OAK had ceased to feed the Weatherbury flock for about four-and-twenty hours, when on Sunday afternoon the elderly gentlemen Joseph Poorgrass, Matthew Moon, Fray, and half-a-dozen others, came running up to the house of the mistress of the Upper Farm.

'Whatever *is* the matter, men?' she said, meeting them at the door just as she was coming out on her way to church, and ceasing in a moment from the close compression of her two red lips, with which she had accompanied the exertion of pulling on a tight glove.

'Sixty!' said Joseph Poorgrass.

'Seventy!' said Moon.

'Fifty-nine!' said Susan Tall's husband.

'—Sheep have broke fence,' said Fray.

'—And got into a field of young clover,' said Tall.

'—Young clover!' said Moon.

'—Clover!' said Joseph Poorgrass.

'And they be getting blasted,' said Henery Fray.

'That they be,' said Joseph.

'And will all die as dead as nits, if ·they bain't got out and cured!' said Tall.

Joseph's countance was drawn into lines and puckers by his concern. Fray's forehead was wrinkled both perpendicularly and crosswise, after the pattern of a portcullis, expressive of a double despair. Laban Tall's lips were thin, and his face was rigid. Matthew's jaws sank, and his eyes turned whichever way the strongest muscle happened to pull them.

'Yes,' said Joseph, 'and I was sitting at home, looking for Ephesians, and says I to myself, "'Tis nothing but Corinthians and Thessalonians in this danged Testament," when who should come in but Henery there: "Joseph," he said, "the sheep have blasted theirselves——"'

With Bathsheba it was a moment when thought was speech and speech exclamation. Moreover, she had hardly recovered her equanimity since the disturbance which she had suffered from Oak's remarks.

'That's enough—that's enough!—oh, you fools!' she cried, throwing the parasol and Prayer-book into the passage, and running out of doors in the direction signified. 'To come to me, and not go and get them out directly! Oh, the stupid numskulls!'

Her eyes were at their darkest and brightest now. Bathsheba's beauty belonging rather to the demonian than to the angelic school, she never looked so well as when she was angry—and particularly when the effect was heightened by a rather dashing velvet dress, carefully put on before a glass.

All the ancient men ran in a jumbled throng after her to the clover-field, Joseph sinking down in the midst when about half-way, like an individual withering in a world which was more and more insupportable. Having once received the stimulus that her presence always gave them they went round among the sheep with a will. The majority of the afflicted animals were lying down, and could not be stirred. These were bodily lifted out, and the others driven into the adjoining field. Here, after the lapse of a few minutes, several more fell down, and lay helpless and livid as the rest.

Bathsheba, with a sad, bursting heart, looked at these primest specimens of her prime flock as they rolled there—

Swoln with wind and the rank mist they drew.

Many of them foamed at the mouth, their breathing being quick and short, whilst the bodies of all were fearfully distended.

'Oh, what can I do, what can I do!' said Bathsheba, helplessly. 'Sheep are such unfortunate animals!—there's always something happening to them! I never knew a flock pass a year without getting into some scrape or other.'

'There's only one way of saving them,' said Tall.

'What way? Tell me quick!'

'They must be pierced in the side with a thing made on purpose.'

'Can you do it? Can I?'

'No, ma'am. We can't, nor you neither. It must be done in a particular spot. If ye go to the right or left but an inch you stab the ewe and kill her. Not even a shepherd can do it, as a rule.'

'Then they must die,' she said, in a resigned tone.

'Only one man in the neighbourhood knows the way,' said Joseph, now just come up. 'He could cure 'em all if he were here.'

'Who is he? Let's get him!'

'Shepherd Oak,' said Matthew. 'Ah, he's a clever man in talents!'

'Ah, that he is so!' said Joseph Poorgrass.

'True—he's the man,' said Laban Tall.

'How dare you name that man in my presence!' she said excitedly. 'I told you never to allude to him, nor shall you if you stay with me. Ah!' she added, brightening, 'Farmer Boldwood knows!'

'Oh no, ma'am,' said Matthew. 'Two of his store ewes got into some vetches t'other day, and were just like these. He sent a man on horseback here post-haste for Gable, and Gable went and saved 'em. Farmer Boldwood hev got the thing they do it with. 'Tis a holler pipe, with a sharp pricker inside. Isn't it, Joseph?'

'Ay—a holler pipe,' echoed Joseph. 'That's what 'tis.'

'Ay, sure—that's the machine,' chimed in Henery Fray, reflectively, with an Oriental indifference to the flight of time.

'Well,' burst out Bathsheba, 'don't stand there with your "ayes" and your "sures," talking at me! Get somebody to cure the sheep instantly!'

All then stalked off in consternation, to get somebody as directed, without any idea of who it was to be. In a minute they had vanished through the gate, and she stood alone with the dying flock.

'Never will I send for him—never!' she said, firmly.

One of the ewes here contracted its muscles horribly, extended itself, and jumped high into the air. The leap was an astonishing one. The ewe fell heavily, and lay still.

Bathsheba went up to it. The sheep was dead.

'Oh, what shall I do—what shall I do!' she again exclaimed, wringing her hands. 'I won't send for him. No, I won't!'

The most vigorous expression of a resolution does not always coincide with the greatest vigour of the resolution itself. It is often flung out as a sort of prop to support a decaying conviction which, whilst strong, required no enunciation to prove it so. The 'No, I won't' of Bathsheba meant virtually, 'I think I must.'

She followed her assistants through the gate, and lifted her hand to one of them. Laban answered to her signal.

'Where is Oak staying?'

'Across the valley at Nest Cottage.'

'Jump on the bay mare, and ride across, and say he must return instantly—that I say so.'

Tall scrambled off to the field, and in two minutes was on Poll, the bay, bare-backed, and with only a halter by way of rein. He diminished down the hill.

Bathsheba watched. So did all the rest. Tall cantered along the bridle-path through Sixteen Acres, Sheeplands, Middle Field, The Flats, Cappel's Piece, shrank almost to a point, crossed the bridge, and ascended from the valley through Springmead and Whitepits on the other side. The cottage to which Gabriel had retired before taking his final departure from the locality was visible as a white spot on the opposite hill, backed by blue firs. Bathsheba walked up and down. The men entered the field and endeavoured to ease the anguish of the dumb creatures by rubbing them. Nothing availed.

Bathsheba continued walking. The horse was seen descending the hill, and the wearisome series had to be repeated in reverse order: Whitepits, Springmead, Cappel's Piece, The Flats, Middle Field, Sheeplands, Sixteen Acres. She hoped Tall had had presence of mind enough to give the mare up to Gabriel, and return himself on foot. The rider neared them. It was Tall.

'Oh, what folly!' said Bathsheba.

Gabriel was not visible anywhere.

'Perhaps he is already gone!' she said.

Tall came into the inclosure, and leapt off, his face tragic as Morton's after the battle of Shrewsbury.

'Well?' said Bathsheba, unwilling to believe that her verbal *lettre-de-cachet* could possibly have miscarried.

'He says *beggars mustn't be choosers*,' replied Laban.

'What!' said the young farmer, opening her eyes and drawing in her breath for an outburst. Joseph Poorgrass retired a few steps behind a hurdle.

'He says he shall not come onless you request en

to come civilly and in a proper manner, as becomes any
'ooman begging a favour.'

'Oh, oh, that's his answer! Where does he get his
airs? Who am I, then, to be treated like that? Shall
I beg to a man who has begged to me?'

Another of the flock sprang into the air, and fell
dead.

The men looked grave, as if they suppressed opinion.

Bathsheba turned aside, her eyes full of tears. The
strait she was in through pride and shrewishness could
not be disguised longer: she burst out crying bitterly;
they all saw it; and she attempted no further concealment.

'I wouldn't cry about it, miss,' said William Smallbury, compassionately. 'Why not ask him softer like?
I'm sure he'd come then. Gable is a true man in that
way.'

Bathsheba checked her grief and wiped her eyes.
'Oh, it is a wicked cruelty to me—it is—it is!' she
murmured. 'And he drives me to do what I wouldn't;
yes, he does!—Tall, come indoors.'

After this collapse, not very dignified for the head
of an establishment, she went into the house, Tall at
· her heels. Here she sat down and hastily scribbled a
note between the small convulsive sobs of convalescence
which follow a fit of crying as a ground-swell follows a
storm. The note was none the less polite for being
written in a hurry. She held it ˙at a distance, was
about to fold it, then added these words at the
bottom :—

' Do not desert me, Gabriel !'

She looked a little redder in refolding it, and closed
her lips, as if thereby to suspend till too late the action
of conscience in examining whether such strategy were
justifiable. The note was despatched as the message
had been, and Bathsheba waited indoors for the result.

It was an anxious quarter of an hour that intervened

between the messenger's departure and the sound of the horse's tramp again outside. She could not watch this time, but, leaning over the old bureau at which she had written the letter, closed her eyes, as if to keep out both hope and fear.

The case, however, was a promising one. Gabriel was not angry: he was simply neutral, although her first command had been so haughty. Such imperiousness would have damned a little less beauty; and on the other hand, such beauty would have redeemed a little less imperiousness.

She went out when the horse was heard, and looked up. A mounted figure passed between her and the sky, and went on towards the field of sheep, the rider turning his face in receding. Gabriel looked at her. It was a moment when a woman's eyes and tongue tell distinctly opposite tales. Bathsheba looked full of gratitude, and she said :—

'Oh, Gabriel, how could you serve me so unkindly!'

Such a tenderly-shaped reproach for his previous delay was the one speech in the language that he could pardon for not being commendation of his readiness now.

Gabriel murmured a confused reply, and hastened on. She knew from the look which sentence in her note had brought him. Bathsheba followed to the field.

Gabriel was already among the turgid, prostrate forms. He had flung off his coat, rolled up his shirt-sleeves, and taken from his pocket the instrument of salvation. It was a small tube or trochar, with a lance passing down the inside; and Gabriel began to use it with a dexterity that would have graced a hospital-surgeon. Passing his hand over the sheep's left flank, and selecting the proper point, he punctured the skin and rumen with the lance as it stood in the tube; then he suddenly withdrew the lance, retaining the tube in its place. A current of air rushed up the tube, forcible enough to have extinguished a candle held at the orifice.

It has been said that mere ease after torment is delight for a time; and the countenances of these poor creatures expressed it now. Forty-nine operations were successfully performed. Owing to the great hurry necessitated by the far-gone state of some of the flock, Gabriel missed his aim in one case, and in one only— striking wide of the mark, and inflicting a mortal blow at once upon the suffering ewe. Four had died; three recovered without an operation. The total number of sheep which had thus strayed and injured themselves so dangerously was fifty-seven.

When the love-led man had ceased from his labours, Bathsheba came and looked him in the face.

'Gabriel, will you stay on with me?' she said, smiling winningly, and not troubling to bring her lips quite together again at the end, because there was going to be another smile soon.

'I will,' said Gabriel.

And she smiled on him again.

CHAPTER XXII

THE GREAT BARN AND THE SHEEP-SHEARERS

M EN thin away to insignificance and oblivion quite as often by not making the most of good spirits when they have them as by lacking good spirits when they are indispensable. Gabriel lately, for the first time since his prostration by misfortune, had been independent in thought and vigorous in action to a marked extent— conditions which, powerless without an opportunity as an opportunity without them is barren, would have given him a sure lift upwards when the favourable con- junction should have occurred. But this incurable loitering beside Bathsheba Everdene stole his time ruinously. The spring tides were going by without floating him off, and the neap might soon come which could not.

It was the first day of June, and the sheep-shearing season culminated, the landscape, even to the leanest pasture, being all health and colour. Every green was young, every pore was open, and every stalk was swollen with racing currents of juice. God was palpably present in the country, and the devil had gone with the world to town. Flossy catkins of the later kinds, fern-sprouts like bishops' crooks, the square-headed moschatel, the odd cuckoo-pint,—like an apoplectic saint in a niche of malachite,—clear white ladies'-smocks, the toothwort, approximating to human flesh, the enchanter's night-shade, and the black-petaled doleful-bells, were among the quainter objects of the vegetable world in and about Weatherbury at this teeming time; and of the animal, the metamorphosed figures of Mr. Jan Coggan, the master-shearer; the second and third shearers, who travelled in the exercise of their calling, and do not require definition by name; Henery Fray the fourth shearer, Susan Tall's husband the fifth, Joseph Poorgrass the sixth, young Cain Ball as assistant-shearer, and Gabriel Oak as general supervisor. None of these were clothed to any extent worth mentioning, each appearing to have hit in the matter of raiment the decent mean between a high and low caste Hindoo. An angularity of lineament, and a fixity of facial machinery in general, proclaimed that serious work was the order of the day.

They sheared in the great barn, called for the nonce the Shearing-barn, which on ground-plan resembled a church with transepts. It not only emulated the form of the neighbouring church of the parish, but vied with it in antiquity. Whether the barn had ever formed one of a group of conventual buildings nobody seemed to be aware; no trace of such surroundings remained. The vast porches at the sides, lofty enough to admit a waggon laden to its highest with corn in the sheaf, were spanned by heavy-pointed arches of stone, broadly and boldly cut, whose very simplicity was the origin of a grandeur not apparent in erections where more ornament has been attempted. The dusky, filmed, chestnut roof, braced and tied in by huge collars, curves, and diagonals, was far nobler in design, because more wealthy in material, than nine-tenths of those in our modern churches. Along each side wall was a range of striding buttresses, throwing deep shadows on the spaces between them, which were perforated by lancet openings, combining in their proportions the precise requirements both of beauty and ventilation.

One could say about this barn, what could hardly be said of either the church or the castle, akin to it in age and style, that the purpose which had dictated its original erection was the same with that to which it was still applied. Unlike and superior to either of those two typical remnants of mediævalism, the old barn embodied practices which had suffered no mutilation at the hands of time. Here at least the spirit of the ancient builders was at one with the spirit of the modern beholder. Standing before this abraded pile, the eye regarded its present usage, the mind dwelt upon its past history, with a satisfied sense of functional continuity throughout—a feeling almost of gratitude, and quite of pride, at the permanence of the idea which had heaped it up. The fact that four centuries had neither proved it to be founded on a mistake, inspired any hatred of its purpose, nor given rise to any reaction that had battered it down, invested this simple grey effort of old minds with a repose, if not a grandeur, which a too curious reflection was apt to disturb in its ecclesiastical and military compeers. For once mediævalism and modernism had a common standpoint. The lanceolate windows, the time-eaten archstones and chamfers, the orientation of the axis, the misty chestnut work of the rafters, referred to no exploded fortifying art or worn-out religious creed. The defence and salvation of the body by daily bread is still a study, a religion, and a desire.

To-day the large side doors were thrown open towards the sun to admit a bountiful light to the immediate spot of the shearers' operations, which was the wood threshing-floor in the centre, formed of thick oak, black with age and polished by the beating of flails for many generations, till it had grown as slippery and as rich in hue as the state-room floors of an Elizabethan mansion. Here the shearers knelt, the sun slanting in upon their bleached shirts, tanned arms, and the polished shears they flourished, causing them to bristle with a thousand rays strong enough to blind a weak-eyed man. Beneath them a captive sheep lay panting, quickening its pants as misgiving merged in terror, till it quivered like the hot landscape outside.

This picture of to-day in its frame of four hundred years ago did not produce that marked contrast between ancient and modern which is implied by the contrast of date. In comparison with cities, Weatherbury was immutable. The citizen's *Then* is the rustic's *Now*. In London, twenty or thirty years ago are old times; in Paris ten years, or five; in Weatherbury three or four score years were included in the mere present, and nothing less than a century set a mark on its face or tone. Five decades hardly modified the cut of a gaiter, the embroidery of a smock-frock, by the breadth of a hair. Ten generations failed to alter the turn of a single phrase. In these Wessex nooks the busy outsider's ancient times are only old; his old times are still new; his present is futurity.

So the barn was natural to the shearers, and the shearers were in harmony with the barn.

The spacious ends of the building, answering ecclesiastically to nave and chancel extremities, were fenced off with hurdles, the sheep being all collected in a crowd within these two enclosures; and in one angle a catching-pen was formed, in which three or four sheep were continuously kept ready for the shearers to seize without loss of time. In the background, mellowed by tawny shade, were the three women, Maryann Money, and Temperance and Soberness Miller, gathering up the fleeces and twisting ropes of wool with a wimble for tying them round. They were indifferently well assisted by the old maltster, who, when the malting season from October to April had passed, made himself useful upon any of the bordering farmsteads.

Behind all was Bathsheba, carefully watching the

men to see that there was no cutting or wounding through carelessness, and that the animals were shorn close. Gabriel, who flitted and hovered under her bright eyes like a moth, did not shear continuously, half his time being spent in attending to the others and selecting the sheep for them. At the present moment he was engaged in handing round a mug of mild liquor, supplied from a barrel in the corner, and cut pieces of bread and cheese.

Bathsheba, after throwing a glance here, a caution there, and lecturing one of the younger operators who had allowed his last finished sheep to go off among the flock without re-stamping it with her initials, came again to Gabriel, as he put down the luncheon to drag a frightened ewe to his shear-station, flinging it over upon its back with a dexterous twist of the arm. He lopped off the tresses about its head, and opened up the neck and collar, his mistress quietly looking on.

'She blushes at the insult,' murmured Bathsheba, watching the pink flush which arose and overspread the neck and shoulders of the ewe where they were left bare by the clicking shears—a flush which was enviable, for its delicacy, by many queens of coteries, and would have been creditable, for its promptness, to any woman in the world.

Poor Gabriel's soul was fed with a luxury of content by having her over him, her eyes critically regarding his skilful shears, which apparently were going to gather up a piece of the flesh at every close, and yet never did so. Like Guildenstern, Oak was happy in that he was not over happy. He had no wish to converse with her: that his bright lady and himself formed one group, exclusively their own, and containing no others in the world, was enough.

So the chatter was all on her side. There is a loquacity that tells nothing, which was Bathsheba's;

and there is a silence which says much : that was
Gabriel's. Full of this dim and temperate bliss, he
went on to fling the ewe over upon her other side,
covering her head with his knee, gradually running
the shears line after line round her dewlap, thence
about her flank and back, and finishing over the tail.

'Well done, and done quickly !' said Bathsheba,
looking at her watch as the last snip resounded.

' How long, miss ?' said Gabriel, wiping his brow.

' Three-and-twenty minutes and a half since you took
the first lock from its forehead. It is the first time that
I have ever seen one done in less than half an hour.'

The clean, sleek creature arose from its fleece—how
perfectly like Aphrodite rising from the foam should
have been seen to be realized—looking startled and
shy at the loss of its garment, which lay on the floor
in one soft cloud, united throughout, the portion visible
being the inner surface only, which, never before exposed,
was white as snow, and without flaw or blemish of the
minutest kind.

' Cain Ball !'

' Yes, Mister Oak ; here I be !'

Cainy now runs forward with the tar-pot. ' B. E.' is
newly stamped upon the shorn skin, and away the simple
dam leaps, panting, over the board into the shirtless
flock outside. Then up comes Maryann ; throws the
loose locks into the middle of the fleece, rolls it up,
and carries it into the background as three-and-a-half
pounds of unadulterated warmth for the winter enjoyment of persons unknown and far away, who will,
however, never experience the superlative comfort
derivable from the wool as it here exists, new and pure
—before the unctuousness of its nature whilst in a
living state has dried, stiffened, and been washed out
—rendering it just now as superior to anything *woollen*
as cream is superior to milk-and-water.

But heartless circumstance could not leave entire

Gabriel's happiness of this morning. The rams, old ewes, and two-shear ewes had duly undergone their stripping, and the men were proceeding with the shearlings and hogs, when Oak's belief that she was going to stand pleasantly by and time him through another performance was painfully interrupted by Farmer Boldwood's appearance in the extremest corner of the barn. Nobody seemed to have perceived his entry, but there he certainly was. Boldwood always carried with him a social atmosphere of his own, which everybody felt who came near him; and the talk, which Bathsheba's presence had somewhat suppressed, was now totally suspended.

He crossed over towards Bathsheba, who turned to greet him with a carriage of perfect ease. He spoke to her in low tones, and she instinctively modulated her own to the same pitch, and her voice ultimately even caught the inflection of his. She was far from having a wish to appear mysteriously connected with him; but woman at the impressionable age gravitates to the larger body not only in her choice of words, which is apparent every day, but even in her shades of tone and humour, when the influence is great.

What they conversed about was not audible to Gabriel, who was too independent to get near, though too concerned to disregard. The issue of their dialogue was the taking of her hand by the courteous farmer to help her over the spreading-board into the bright June sunlight outside. Standing beside the sheep already shorn, they went on talking again. Concerning the flock? Apparently not. Gabriel theorized, not without truth, that in quiet discussion of any matter within reach of the speakers' eyes, these are usually fixed upon it. Bathsheba demurely regarded a contemptible straw lying upon the ground, in a way which suggested less ovine criticism than womanly embarrassment. She became more or less red in the cheek, the blood wavering in uncertain flux and reflux over the sensitive space between ebb and flood. Gabriel sheared on, constrained and sad.

She left Boldwood's side, and he walked up and down alone for nearly a quarter of an hour. Then she reappeared in her new riding-habit of myrtle-green, which fitted her to the waist as a rind fits its fruit; and young Bob Coggan led on her mare, Boldwood fetching his own horse from the tree under which it had been tied.

Oak's eyes could not forsake them; and in endeavouring to continue his shearing at the same time that he watched Boldwood's manner, he snipped the sheep in the groin. The animal plunged; Bathsheba instantly gazed towards it, and saw the blood.

'Oh Gabriel!' she exclaimed, with severe remonstrance, 'you who are so strict with the other men—see what you are doing yourself!'

To an outsider there was not much to complain of in this remark; but to Oak, who knew Bathsheba to be well aware that she herself was the cause of the poor ewe's wound, because she had wounded the ewe's shearer in a still more vital part, it had a sting which the abiding sense of his inferiority to both herself and Boldwood was not calculated to heal. But a manly resolve to recognize boldly that he had no longer a lover's interest in her, helped him occasionally to conceal a feeling.

'Bottle!' he shouted, in an unmoved voice of routine. Cainy Ball ran up, the wound was anointed, and the shearing continued.

Boldwood gently tossed Bathsheba into the saddle, and before they turned away she again spoke out to Oak with the same dominative and tantalizing graciousness.

'I am going now to see Mr. Boldwood's Leicesters. Take my place in the barn, Gabriel, and keep the men carefully to their work.'

The horses' heads were put about, and they trotted away.

Boldwood's deep attachment was a matter of great interest among all around him; but, after having been pointed out for so many years as the perfect exemplar, of thriving bachelorship, his lapse was an anticlimax somewhat resembling that of St. John Long's death by consumption in the midst of his proofs that it was not a fatal disease.

'That means matrimony,' said Temperance Miller, following them out of sight with her eyes.

'I reckon that's the size o,'t,' said Coggan, working along without looking up.

'Well, better wed over the mixen than over the moor,' said Laban Tall, turning his sheep.

Henery Fray spoke, exhibiting miserable eyes at the same time: 'I don't see why a maid should take a husband when she's bold enough to fight her own battles, and don't want a home; for 'tis keeping another woman out. But let it be, for 'tis a pity he and she should trouble two houses.'

As usual with decided characters, Bathsheba invariably provoked the criticism of individuals like Henery Fray. Her emblazoned fault was to be too pronounced in her objections, and not sufficiently overt in her likings. We learn that it is not the rays which bodies absorb, but those which they reject, that give them the colours they are known by; and in the same way people are specialized by their dislikes and antagonisms, whilst their goodwill is looked upon as no attribute at all.

Henery continued in a more complaisant mood: 'I once hinted my mind to her on a few things, as nearly as a battered frame dared to do so to such a froward piece. You all know, neighbours, what a man I be, and how I come down with my powerful words when my pride is boiling wi' scarn?'

'We do, we do, Henery.'

'So I said, " Mistress Everdene, there's places empty, and there's gifted men willing; but the spite "—no, not

172

the spite—I didn't say spite—"but the villainy of the contrarikind," I said (meaning womankind), "keeps 'em out." That wasn't too strong for her, say?'

'Passably well put.'

'Yes; and I would have said it, had death and salvation overtook me for it. Such is my spirit when I have a mind.'

'A true man, and proud as a lucifer.'

'You see the artfulness? Why, 'twas about being baily really; but I didn't put it so plain that she could understand my meaning, so I could lay it on all the stronger. That was my depth! . . . However, let her marry an she will. Perhaps 'tis high time. I believe Farmer Boldwood kissed her behind the spear-bed at the sheep-washing t'other day—that I do.'

'What a lie!' said Gabriel.

'Ah, neighbour Oak—how'st know?' said Henery, mildly.

'Because she told me all that passed,' said Oak, with a pharisaical sense that he was not as other shearers in this matter.

'Ye have a right to believe it,' said Henery, with dudgeon; 'a very true right. But I mid see a little distance into things! To be long-headed enough for a baily's place is a poor mere trifle—yet a trifle more than nothing. However, I look round upon life quite cool. Do you heed me, neighbours? My words, though made as simple as I can, mid be rather deep for some heads.'

'Oh, yes, Henery, we quite heed ye.'

'A strange old piece, goodmen—whirléd about from here to yonder, as if I were nothing! A little warped, too. But I have my depths; ha, and even my great depths! I might gird at a certain shepherd, brain to brain. But no—Oh no!'

'A strange old piece, ye say!' interposed the maltster, in a querulous voice. 'At the same time ye be no old man worth naming—no old man at all. Yer teeth baint half gone yet; and what's a old man's standing if so be his teeth baint gone? Weren't I stale in wedlock afore ye were out of arms? 'Tis a poor thing to be sixty, when there's people far past four-score—a boast weak as water.'

It was the unvarying custom in Weatherbury to sink minor differences when the maltster had to be pacified.

'Weak as water! yes,' said Jan Coggan. 'Malter, we feel ye to be a wonderful veteran man, and nobody can gainsay it.'

'Nobody,' said Joseph Poorgrass. 'Ye be a very rare old spectacle, malter, and we all respect ye for that gift.'

'Ay, and as a young man, when my senses were in prosperity, I was likewise liked by a good-few who knowed me,' said the maltster.

''Ithout doubt you was—'ithout doubt.'

The bent and hoary man was satisfied, and so apparently was Henery Fray. That matters should continue pleasant Maryann spoke, who, what with her brown complexion, and the working wrapper of rusty linsey, had at present the mellow hue of an old sketch in oils—notably some of Nicholas Poussin's :—

'Do anybody know of a crooked man, or a lame, or any second-hand fellow at all that would do for poor me?' said Maryann. 'A perfect one I don't expect to get at my time of life. If I could hear of such a thing 'twould do me more good than toast and ale.'

Coggan furnished a suitable reply. Oak went on with his shearing, and said not another word. Pestilent moods had come, and teased away his quiet. Bathsheba had shown indications of anointing him above his fellows by installing him as the bailiff that the farm imperatively required. He did not covet the post relatively to the farm : in relation to herself, as beloved by him and unmarried to another, he had coveted it.

His readings of her seemed now to be vapoury and indistinct. His lecture to her was, he thought, one of the absurdest mistakes. Far from coquetting with Boldwood, she had trifled with himself in thus feigning that she had trifled with another. He was inwardly convinced that, in accordance with the anticipations of his easy-going and worse-educated comrades, that day would see Boldwood the accepted husband of Miss Everdene. Gabriel at this time of his life had outgrown the instinctive dislike which every Christian boy has for reading the Bible, perusing it now quite frequently, and he inwardly said, '"I find more bitter than death the woman whose heart is snares and nets!"' This was mere exclamation—the froth of the storm. He adored Bathsheba just the same.

'We workfolk shall have some lordly junketing to-night,' said Cainy Ball, casting forth his thoughts in a new direction. 'This morning I see 'em making the great puddens in the milking-pails—lumps of fat as big as yer thumb, Mister Oak! I've never seed such splendid large knobs of fat before in the days of my life—they never used to be bigger than a horse-bean. And there was a great black crock upon the brandise with his legs a-sticking out, but I don't know what was in within.'

'And there's two bushels of biffins for apple-pies,' said Maryann.

'Well, I hope to do my duty by it all,' said Joseph Poorgrass, in a pleasant, masticating manner of anticipation. 'Yes; victuals and drink is a cheerful thing, and gives nerves to the nerveless, if the form of words may be used. 'Tis the gospel of the body, without which we perish, so to speak it.'

CHAPTER XXIII

EVENTIDE—A SECOND DECLARATION

For the shearing-supper a long table was placed on the grass-plot beside the house, the end of the table being thrust over the sill of the wide parlour window and a foot or two into the room.   Miss Everdene sat inside the window, facing down the table.   She was thus at the head without mingling with the men.

This evening Bathsheba was unusually excited, her red cheeks and lips contrasting lustrously with the mazy skeins of her shadowy hair.   She seemed to expect assistance, and the seat at the bottom of the table was at her request left vacant until after they had begun the meal.   She then asked Gabriel to take the place and the duties appertaining to that end, which he did with great readiness.

At this moment Mr. Boldwood came in at the gate, and crossed the green to Bathsheba at the window. He apologized for his lateness : his arrival was evidently by arrangement.

'Gabriel,' said she, 'will you move again, please, and let Mr. Boldwood come there ? '

Oak moved in silence back to his original seat.

The gentleman-farmer was dressed in cheerful style, in a new coat and white waistcoat, quite contrasting with his usual sober suits of grey.   Inwardly, too, he

176

was blithe, and consequently chatty to an exceptional degree. So also was Bathsheba now that he had come, though the uninvited presence of Pennyways, the bailiff who had been dismissed for theft, disturbed her equanimity for a while.

Supper being ended, Coggan began on his own private account, without reference to listeners :—

> I've lost my love, and I care not,
> I've lost my love, and I care not ;
> I shall soon have another
> That's better than t'other ;
> I've lost my love, and I care not.

This lyric, when concluded, was received with a silently appreciative gaze at the table, implying that the performance, like a work by those established authors who are independent of notices in the papers, was a well-known delight which required no applause.

'Now, Master Poorgrass, your song !' said Coggan.

'I be all but in liquor, and the gift is wanting in me,' said Joseph, diminishing himself.

'Nonsense ; wou'st never be so ungrateful, Joseph— never !' said Coggan, expressing hurt feelings by an inflection of voice. 'And mistress is looking hard at ye, as much as to say, "Sing at once, Joseph Poorgrass."'

'Faith, so she is ; well, I must suffer it ! . . . Just eye my features, and see if the tell-tale blood overheats me much, neighbours ? '

'No, yer blushes be quite reasonable,' said Coggan.

'I always tries to keep my colours from rising when a beauty's eyes get fixed on me,' said Joseph, diffidently ; 'but if so be 'tis willed they do, they must.'

'Now, Joseph, your song, please,' said Bathsheba, from the window.

'Well, really, ma'am,' he replied, in a yielding tone,

'I don't know what to say. It would be a poor plain ballet of my own composure.'

'Hear, hear!' said the supper-party.

Poorgrass, thus assured, trilled forth a flickering yet commendable piece of sentiment, the tune of which consisted of the key-note and another, the latter being the sound chiefly dwelt upon. This was so successful that he rashly plunged into a, second in the same breath, after a few false starts :—

> I sow'-ed th'-e . . . . . .
> I sow'-ed . . . . .
> I sow'-ed the'-e seeds' of' love',
>   I-it was' all' i'-in the'-e spring',
>   I-in A'-pril', Ma'-ay, a'-nd sun'-ny' June',
>   When sma'-all bi'-irds they' do' sing.

'Well put out of hand,' said Coggan, at the end of the verse. ' "They do sing" was a very taking paragraph.'

'Ay; and there was a pretty place at "seeds of love," and 'twas well heaved out. Though "love" is a nasty high corner when a man's voice is getting crazed. Next verse, Master Poorgrass.'

But during this rendering young Bob Coggan exhibited one of those anomalies which will afflict little people when other persons are particularly serious: in trying to check his laughter, he pushed down his throat as much of the tablecloth as he could get hold of, when, after continuing hermetically sealed for a short time, his mirth burst out through his nose. Joseph perceived it, and with hectic cheeks of indignation instantly ceased singing. Coggan boxed Bob's ears immediately.

'Go on, Joseph—go on, and never mind the young scamp,' said Coggan. ''Tis a very catching ballet. Now then again—the next bar; I'll help ye to flourish up the shrill notes where yer wind is rather wheezy :—

> Oh the wi'-il-lo'-ow tree' will' twist',
> And the wil'-low' tre'-ee wi'-ill twine'.

But the singer could not be set going again. Bob Coggan was sent home for his ill manners, and tranquillity was restored by Jacob Smallbury, who volunteered a ballad as inclusive and interminable as that with which the worthy toper old Silenus amused on a similar occasion the swains Chromis and Mnasylus, and other jolly dogs of his day.

It was still the beaming time of evening, though night was stealthily making itself visible low down upon the ground, the western lines of light raking the earth without alighting upon it to any extent, or illuminating the dead levels at all. The sun had crept round the tree as a last effort before death, and then began to sink, the shearers' lower parts becoming steeped in embrowning twilight, whilst their heads and shoulders were still enjoying day, touched with a yellow of self-sustained brilliancy that seemed inherent rather than acquired.

The sun went down in an ochreous mist; but they sat, and talked on, and grew as merry as the gods in Homer's heaven. Bathsheba still remained enthroned inside the window, and occupied herself in knitting, from which she sometimes looked up to view the fading scene outside. The slow twilight expanded and enveloped them completely before the signs of moving were shown.

Gabriel suddenly missed Farmer Boldwood from his place at the bottom of the table. How long he had been gone Oak did not know; but he had apparently withdrawn into the encircling dusk. Whilst he was thinking of this, Liddy brought candles into the back part of the room overlooking the shearers, and their lively new flames shone down the table and over the men, and dispersed among the green shadows behind. Bathsheba's form, still in its original position, was now again distinct between their eyes and the light, which revealed that Boldwood had gone inside the room, and was sitting near her.

Next came the question of the evening. Would Miss Everdene sing to them the song she always sang so charmingly—'The Banks of Allan Water'—before they went home?

After a moment's consideration Bathsheba assented, beckoning to Gabriel, who hastened up into the coveted atmosphere at once.

'Have you brought your flute?' she whispered.

'Yes, miss.'

'Play to my singing, then.'

She stood up in the window-opening, facing the men, the candles behind her, Gabriel on her right hand, immediately outside the sash-frame. Boldwood had drawn up on her left, within the room. Her singing was soft and rather tremulous at first, but it soon swelled to a steady clearness. Subsequent events caused one of the verses to be remembered for many months, and even years, by more than one of those who were gathered there :—

> For his bride a soldier sought her,
> And a winning tongue had he :
> On the banks of Allan Water
> None was gay as she !

In addition to the dulcet piping of Gabriel's flute, Boldwood supplied a bass in his customary profound voice, uttering his notes so softly, however, as to abstain entirely from making anything like an ordinary duet of the song ; they rather formed a rich unexplored shadow, which threw her tones into relief. The shearers reclined against each other as at suppers in the early ages of the world, and so silent and absorbed were they that her breathing could almost be heard between the bars ; and at the end of the ballad, when the last tone loitered on to an inexpressible close, there arose that buzz of pleasure which is the attar of applause.

It is scarcely necessary to state that Gabriel could

not avoid noting the farmer's bearing to-night towards their entertainer. Yet there was nothing exceptional in his actions beyond what appertained to his time of performing them. It was when the rest were all looking away that Boldwood observed her ; when they regarded her he turned aside ; when they thanked or praised he was silent ; when they were inattentive he murmured his thanks. The meaning lay in the difference between actions, none of which had any meaning of themselves ; and the necessity of being jealous, which lovers are troubled with, did not lead Oak to underestimate these signs.

Bathsheba then wished them good-night, withdrew from the window, and retired to the back part of the room, Boldwood thereupon closing the sash and the shutters, and remaining inside with her. Oak wandered away under the quiet and scented trees. Recovering from the softer impressions produced by Bathsheba's voice, the shearers rose to leave, Coggan turning to Pennyways as he pushed back the bench to pass out :—

'I like to give praise where praise is due, and the man deserves it—that 'a do so,' he remarked, looking at the worthy thief, as if he were the masterpiece of some world-renowned artist.

'I'm sure I should never have believed it if we hadn't proved it, so to allude,' whispered Joseph Poorgrass, 'that every cup, every one of the best knives and forks, and every empty bottle be in their place as perfect now as at the beginning, and not one stole at all.'

'I'm sure I don't deserve half the praise you give me,' said the virtuous thief, grimly.

'Well, I'll say this for Pennyways,' added Coggan, 'that whenever he do really make up his mind to do a noble thing in the shape of a good action, as I could see by his face he did to-night afore sitting down, he's generally able to carry it out. Yes, I'm proud to say, neighbours, that he's stole nothing at all.'

'Well, 'tis an honest deed, and we thank ye for it, Pennyways,' said Joseph ; to which opinion the remainder of the company subscribed unanimously.

At this time of departure, when nothing more was visible of the inside of the parlour than a thin and still chink of light between the shutters, a passionate scene was in course of enactment there.

Miss Everdene and Boldwood were alone. Her cheeks had lost a great deal of their healthful fire from the very seriousness of her position ; but her eye was bright with the excitement of a triumph—though it was a triumph which had rather been contemplated than desired.

She was standing behind a low arm-chair, from which she had just risen, and he was kneeling in it—inclining himself over its back towards her, and holding her hand in both his own. His body moved restlessly, and it was with what the poet Keats calls a too happy happiness. This unwonted abstraction by love of all dignity from a man of whom it had ever seemed the chief component, was, in its distressing incongruity, a pain to her which quenched much of the pleasure she derived from the proof that she was idolized.

'I will try to love you,' she was saying, in a trembling voice quite unlike her usual self-confidence. 'And if I can believe in any way that I shall make you a good wife I shall indeed be willing to marry you. But, Mr. Boldwood, hesitation on so high a matter is honourable in any woman, and I don't want to give a solemn promise to-night. I would rather ask you to wait a few weeks till I can see my situation better.'

'But you have every reason to believe that *then*——'

'I have every reason to hope that at the end of the five or six weeks, between this time and harvest, that you say you are going to be away from home, I shall be able to promise to be your wife,' she said, firmly. 'But remember this distinctly, I don't promise yet.'

'It is enough; I don't ask more. I can wait on those dear words. And now, Miss Everdene, good-night!'

'Good-night,' she said, graciously—almost tenderly; and Boldwood withdrew with a serene smile.

Bathsheba knew more of him now; he had entirely bared his heart before her, even until he had almost worn in her eyes the sorry look of a grand bird without the feathers that make it grand. She had been awe-struck at her past temerity, and was struggling to make amends without thinking whether the sin quite deserved the penalty she was schooling herself to pay. To have brought all this about her ears was terrible; but after a while the situation was not without a fearful joy. The facility with which even the most timid women some-times acquire a relish for the dreadful when that is amalgamated with a little triumph, is marvellous.

CHAPTER XXIV

THE SAME NIGHT—THE FIR PLANTATION

AMONG the multifarious duties which Bathsheba had voluntarily imposed upon herself by dispensing with the services of a bailiff, was the particular one of looking round the homestead before going to bed, to see that all was right and safe for the night. Gabriel had almost constantly preceded her in this tour every evening, watching her affairs as carefully as any specially appointed officer of surveillance could have done ; but this tender devotion was to a great extent unknown to his mistress, and as much as was known was somewhat thanklessly received. Women are never tired of bewailing man's fickleness in love, but they only seem to snub his constancy.

As watching is best done invisibly, she usually carried a dark lantern in her hand, and every now and then turned on the light to examine nooks and corners with the coolness of a metropolitan policeman. This coolness may have owed its existence not so much to her fearlessness of expected danger as to her freedom from the suspicion of any ; her worst anticipated discovery being that a horse might not be well bedded, the fowls not all in, or a door not closed.

This night the buildings were inspected as usual, and she went round to the farm paddock. Here the

only sounds disturbing the stillness were steady munch-
ings of many mouths, and stentorian breathings from all
but invisible noses, ending in snores and puffs like the
blowing of bellows slowly. Then the munching would
recommence, when the lively imagination might assist
the eye to discern a group of pink-white nostrils, large
as caverns, and very clammy and humid on their surfaces, not exactly pleasant to the touch until one got
used to them; the mouths beneath having a great
partiality for closing upon any fragment of Bathsheba's
apparel which came within reach of their tongues.
Above each of these a still keener vision suggested a
brown forehead and two staring though not unfriendly
eyes, and above all a pair of whitish crescent-shaped
horns like two particularly new moons, an occasional
stolid 'moo!' proclaiming beyond the shade of a doubt
that these phenomena were the features and persons of
Daisy, Whitefoot, Bonny-lass, Jolly-O, Spot, Twinkle-eye,
etc., etc.—the respectable dairy of Devon cows belonging
to Bathsheba aforesaid.

Her way back to the house was by a path through a
young plantation of tapering firs, which had been planted
some years earlier to shelter the premises from the north
wind. By reason of the density of the interwoven foliage
overhead, it was gloomy there at cloudless noontide,
twilight in the evening, dark as midnight at dusk, and
black as the ninth plague of Egypt at midnight. To
describe the spot is to call it a vast, low, naturally formed
hall, the plumy ceiling of which was supported by slender
pillars of living wood, the floor being covered with a soft
dun carpet of dead spikelets and mildewed cones, with
a tuft of grass-blades here and there.

This bit of the path was always the crux of the
night's ramble, though, before starting, her apprehen-
sions of danger were not vivid enough to lead her to
take a companion. Slipping along here covertly as
Time, Bathsheba fancied she could hear footsteps enter-

ing the track at the opposite end. It was certainly a rustle of footsteps. Her own instantly fell as gently as snowflakes. She reassured herself by a remembrance that the path was public, and that the traveller was probably some villager returning home; regretting, at the same time, that the meeting should be about to occur in the darkest point of her route, even though only just outside her own door.

The noise approached, came close, and a figure was apparently on the point of gliding past her when something tugged at her skirt and pinned it forcibly to the ground. The instantaneous check nearly threw Bathsheba off her balance. In recovering she struck against warm clothes and buttons.

'A rum start, upon my soul!' said a masculine voice, a foot or so above her head. 'Have I hurt you, mate?'

'No,' said Bathsheba, attempting to shrink away.

'We have got hitched together somehow, I think.'

'Yes.'

'Are you a woman?'

'Yes.'

'A lady, I should have said.'

'It doesn't matter.'

'I am a man.'

'Oh!'

Bathsheba softly tugged again, but to no purpose.

'Is that a dark lantern you have? I fancy so,' said the man.

'Yes.'

'If you'll allow me I'll open it, and set you free.'

A hand seized the lantern, the door was opened, the rays burst out from their prison, and Bathsheba beheld her position with astonishment.

The man to whom she was hooked was brilliant in brass and scarlet. He was a soldier. His sudden appearance was to darkness what the sound of a trumpet is to silence. Gloom, the *genius loci* at all times hitherto, was now totally overthrown, less by the lantern-light than by what the lantern lighted. The contrast of this revelation with her anticipations of some sinister figure in sombre garb was so great that it had upon her the effect of a fairy transformation.

It was immediately apparent that the military man's spur had become entangled in the gimp which decorated the skirt of her dress. He caught a view of her face.

'I'll unfasten you in one moment, miss,' he said, with new-born gallantry.

'Oh no—I can do it, thank you,' she hastily replied, and stooped for the performance.

The unfastening was not such a trifling affair. The rowel of the spur had so wound itself among the gimp cords in those few moments, that separation was likely to be a matter of time.

He too stooped, and the lantern standing on the ground betwixt them threw the gleam from its open side among the fir-tree needles and the blades of long damp grass with the effect of a large glowworm. It radiated upwards into their faces, and sent over half the plantation gigantic shadows of both man and woman, each dusky shape becoming distorted and mangled upon the tree-trunks till it wasted to nothing.

He looked hard into her eyes when she raised them for a moment; Bathsheba looked down again, for his gaze was too strong to be received pointblank with her own. But she had obliquely noticed that he was young and slim, and that he wore three chevrons upon his sleeve.

Bathsheba pulled again.

'You are a prisoner, miss; it is no use blinking the matter,' said the soldier, drily. 'I must cut your dress if you are in such a hurry.'

'Yes—please do!' she exclaimed, helplessly.

'It wouldn't be necessary if you could wait a moment;' and he unwound a cord from the little wheel. She withdrew her own hand, but, whether by accident or design, he touched it. Bathsheba was vexed; she hardly knew why.

His unravelling went on, but it nevertheless seemed coming to no end. She looked at him again.

'Thank you for the sight of such a beautiful face!' said the young sergeant, without ceremony.

She coloured with embarrassment. ''Twas unwillingly shown,' she replied, stiffly, and with as much dignity—which was very little—as she could infuse into a position of utter captivity.

'I like you the better for that incivility, miss,' he said.

'I should have liked—I wish—you had never shown yourself to me by intruding here!' She pulled again, and the gathers of her dress began to give way like liliputian musketry.

'I deserve the chastisement your words give me. But why should such a fair and dutiful girl have such an aversion to her father's sex?'

'Go on your way, please.'

'What, Beauty, and drag you after me? Do but look; I never saw such a tangle!'

'Oh, 'tis shameful of you; you have been making it worse on purpose to keep me here—you have!'

'Indeed, I don't think so,' said the sergeant, with a merry twinkle.

'I tell you you have!' she exclaimed, in high temper. 'I insist upon undoing it. Now, allow me!'

'Certainly, miss; I am not of steel.' He added a sigh which had as much archness in it as a sigh could possess without losing its nature altogether. 'I am thankful for beauty, even when 'tis thrown to me like a bone to a dog. These moments will be over too soon!'

She closed her lips in a determined silence.

Bathsheba was revolving in her mind whether by a

bold and desperate rush she could free herself at the risk of leaving her skirt bodily behind her. The thought was too dreadful. The dress—which she had put on to appear stately at the supper—was the head and front of her wardrobe; not another in her stock became her so well. What woman in Bathsheba's position, not naturally timid, and within call of her retainers, would have bought escape from a dashing soldier at so dear a price?

'All in good time; it will soon be done, I perceive,' said her cool friend.

'This trifling provokes, and—and——'

'Not too cruel!'

'— Insults me!'

'It is done in order that I may have the pleasure of apologizing to so charming a woman, which I straightway do most humbly, madam,' he said, bowing low.

Bathsheba really knew not what to say.

'I've seen a good many women in my time,' continued the young man in a murmur, and more thoughtfully than hitherto, critically regarding her bent head at the same time; 'but I've never seen a woman so beautiful as you. Take it or leave it—be offended or like it—I don't care.'

'Who are you, then, who can so well afford to despise opinion?'

'No stranger. Sergeant Troy. I am staying in this place.—There! it is undone at last, you see. Your light fingers were more eager than mine. I wish it had been the knot of knots, which there's no untying!'

This was worse and worse. She started up, and so did he. How to decently get away from him—that was her difficulty now. She sidled off inch by inch, the lantern in her hand, till she could see the redness of his coat no longer.

'Ah, Beauty; good-bye!' he said.

189

She made no reply, and, reaching a distance of twenty or thirty yards, turned about, and ran indoors.

Liddy had just retired to rest. In ascending to her own chamber, Bathsheba opened the girl's door an inch or two, and, panting, said—

' Liddy, is any soldier staying in the village—sergeant somebody—rather gentlemanly for a sergeant, and good looking—a red coat with blue facings ? '

' No, miss . . . No, I say; but really it might be Sergeant Troy home on furlough, though I have not seen him. He was here once in that way when the regiment was at Casterbridge.'

' Yes; that's the name. Had he a moustache—no whiskers or beard ? '

' He had.'

' What kind of a person is he ? '

' Oh ! miss—I blush to name it—a gay man ! But I know him to be very quick and trim, who might have made his thousands, like a squire. Such a clever young dand as he is ! He's a doctor's son by name, which is a great deal; and he's an earl's son by nature !'

' Which is a great deal more. Fancy ! Is it true ? '

' Yes. And he was brought up so well, and sent to Casterbridge Grammar School for years and years. Learnt all languages while he was there ; and it was said he got on so far that he could take down Chinese in shorthand ; but that I don't answer for, as it was only reported. However, he wasted his gifted lot, and listed a soldier ; but even then he rose to be a sergeant without trying at all. Ah ! such a blessing it is to be high-born ; nobility of blood will shine out even in the ranks and files. And is he really come home, miss ? '

' I believe so. Good-night, Liddy.'

After all, how could a cheerful wearer of skirts be permanently offended with the man ? There are occasions when girls like Bathsheba will put up with a great deal of unconventional behaviour. When they want to be praised, which is often ; when they want to be mastered, which is sometimes; and when they want no nonsense, which is seldom. Just now the first feeling was in the ascendant with Bathsheba, with a dash of the second. Moreover, by chance or by devilry, the ministrant was antecedently made interesting by being a handsome stranger who had evidently seen better days.

So she could not clearly decide whether it was her opinion that he had insulted her or not.

'Was ever anything so odd !' she at last exclaimed to herself, in her own room. 'And was ever anything so meanly done as what I did—to skulk away like that from a man who was only civil and kind !' Clearly she did not think his barefaced praise of her person an insult now.

It was a fatal omission of Boldwood's that he had never once told her she was beautiful.

CHAPTER XXV

THE NEW ACQUAINTANCE DESCRIBED

IDIOSYNCRASY and vicissitude had combined to stamp Sergeant Troy as an exceptional being.

He was a man to whom memories were an incumbrance, and anticipations a superfluity. Simply feeling, considering, and caring for what was before his eyes, he was vulnerable only in the present. His outlook upon time was as a transient flash of the eye now and then : that projection of consciousness into days gone by and to come, which makes the past a synonym for the pathetic and the future a word for circumspection, was foreign to Troy. With him the past was yesterday; the future, to-morrow; never, the day after.

On this account he might, in certain lights, have been regarded as one of the most fortunate of his order. For it may be argued with great plausibility that reminiscence is less an endowment than a disease, and that expectation in its only comfortable form—that of absolute faith—is practically an impossibility; whilst in the form of hope and the secondary compounds, patience, impatience, resolve, curiosity, it is a constant fluctuation between pleasure and pain.

Sergeant Troy, being entirely innocent of the practice of expectation, was never disappointed. To set against this negative gain there may have been some positive losses from a certain narrowing of the higher tastes and sensations which it entailed. But limitation of the capacity is never recognized as a loss by the loser therefrom: in this attribute moral or æsthetic poverty contrasts plausibly with material, since those who suffer do not mind it, whilst those who mind it soon cease to suffer. It is not a denial of anything to have been always without it, and what Troy had never enjoyed he did not miss; but, being fully conscious that what sober people missed he enjoyed, his capacity, though really less, seemed greater than theirs.

He was moderately truthful towards men, but to women lied like a Cretan—a system of ethics above all others calculated to win popularity at the first flush of admission into lively society; and the possibility of the favour gained being transitory had reference only to the future.

He never passed the line which divides the spruce vices from the ugly; and hence, though his morals had hardly been applauded, disapproval of them had frequently been tempered with a smile. This treatment had led to his becoming a sort of regrater of other men's gallantries, to his own aggrandizement as a Corinthian, rather than to the moral profit of his hearers.

His reason and his propensities had seldom any reciprocating influence, having separated by mutual consent long ago: thence it sometimes happened that, while his intentions were as honourable as could be wished, any particular deed formed a dark background which threw them into fine relief. The sergeant's vicious phases being the offspring of impulse, and his virtuous phases of cool meditation, the latter had a modest tendency to be oftener heard of than seen.

Troy was full of activity, but his activities were less of a locomotive than a vegetative nature; and, never being based upon any original choice of foundation or direction, they were exercised on whatever object chance might place in their way. Hence, whilst he sometimes reached the brilliant in speech because that was spontaneous, he fell below the commonplace in action, from inability to guide incipient effort. He had a quick comprehension and considerable force of character; but, being without the power to combine them, the comprehension became engaged with trivialities whilst waiting for the will to direct it, and the force wasted itself in useless grooves through unheeding the comprehension.

He was a fairly well-educated man for one of middle class—exceptionally well educated for a common soldier. He spoke fluently and unceasingly. He could in this way be one thing and seem another: for instance, he could speak of love and think of dinner; call on the husband to look at the wife; be eager to pay and intend to owe.

The wondrous power of flattery in *passados* at woman is a perception so universal as to be remarked upon by many people almost as automatically as they repeat a proverb, or say that they are Christians and the like, without thinking much of the enormous corollaries which spring from the proposition. Still less is it acted upon for the good of the complemental being alluded to. With the majority such an opinion is shelved with all those trite aphorisms which require some catastrophe to bring their tremendous meanings thoroughly home. When expressed with some amount of reflectiveness it seems co-ordinate with a belief that this flattery must be reasonable to be effective. It is to the credit of men that few attempt to settle the question by experiment, and it is for their happiness, perhaps, that accident has never settled it for them. Nevertheless, that a male dissembler who by deluging her with untenable fictions charms the female wisely, may acquire powers reaching to the extremity of perdition, is a truth taught to many by unsought and wringing occurrences. And some profess to have attained to the same knowledge by experiment as aforesaid, and jauntily continue their indulgence in such experiments with terrible effect. Sergeant Troy was one.

He had been known to observe casually that in dealing with womankind the only alternative to flattery was cursing and swearing. There was no third method. 'Treat them fairly, and you are a lost man,' he would say.

This person's public appearance in Weatherbury promptly followed his arrival there. A week or two after the shearing, Bathsheba, feeling a nameless relief of spirits on account of Boldwood's absence, approached her hayfields and looked over the hedge towards the haymakers. They consisted in about equal proportions of gnarled and flexuous forms, the former being the men, the latter the women, who wore tilt bonnets covered with nankeen, which hung in a curtain upon their shoulders. Coggan and Mark Clark were mowing in a less forward meadow, Clark humming a tune to the strokes of his scythe, to which Jan made no attempt to keep time with his. In the first mead they were already loading hay, the women raking it into cocks and windrows, and the men tossing it upon the waggon.

From behind the waggon a bright scarlet spot emerged, and went on loading unconcernedly with the rest. It was the gallant sergeant, who had come haymaking for pleasure ; and nobody could deny that he was doing the mistress of the farm real knight-service by this voluntary contribution of his labour at a busy time.

As soon as she had entered the field Troy saw her,

and sticking his pitchfork into the ground and picking up his walking-cane, he came forward. Bathsheba blushed with half-angry embarrassment, and adjusted her eyes as well as her feet to the direct line of her path.

CHAPTER XXVI

SCENE ON THE VERGE OF THE HAY-MEAD

'AH, Miss Everdene!' said the sergeant, touching his diminutive cap. 'Little did I think it was you I was speaking to the other night. And yet, if I had reflected, the "Queen of the Corn-market" (truth is truth at any hour of the day or night, and I heard you so named in Casterbridge yesterday), the "Queen of the Corn-market," I say, could be no other woman. I step across now to beg your forgiveness a thousand times for having been led by my feelings to express myself too strongly for a stranger. To be sure I am no stranger to the place— I am Sergeant Troy, as I told you, and I have assisted your uncle in these fields no end of times when I was a lad. I have been doing the same for you to-day.'

'I suppose I must thank you for that, Sergeant Troy,' said the Queen of the Corn-market, in an indifferently grateful tone.

The sergeant looked hurt and sad. 'Indeed you must not, Miss Everdene,' he said. 'Why could you think such a thing necessary?'

'I am glad it is not.'

'Why? if I may ask without offence.'

'Because I don't much want to thank you for anything.'

'I am afraid I have made a hole with my tongue

that my heart will never mend. Oh these intolerable times: that ill-luck should follow a man for honestly telling a woman she is beautiful! 'Twas the most I said—you must own that; and the least I could say—that I own myself.'

'There is some talk I could do without more easily than money.'

'Indeed. That remark is a sort of digression.'

'No. It means that I would rather have your room than your company.'

'And I would rather have curses from you than kisses from any other woman; so I'll stay here.'

Bathsheba was absolutely speechless. And yet she could not help feeling that the assistance he was rendering forbade a harsh repulse.

'Well,' continued Troy, 'I suppose there is a praise which is rudeness, and that may be mine. At the same time there is a treatment which is injustice, and that may be yours. Because a plain blunt man, who has never been taught concealment, speaks out his mind without exactly intending it, he's to be snapped off like the son of a sinner.'

'Indeed there's no such case between us,' she said, turning away. 'I don't allow strangers to be bold and impudent—even in praise of me.'

'Ah—it is not the fact but the method which offends you,' he said, carelessly. 'But I have the sad satisfaction of knowing that my words, whether pleasing or offensive, are unmistakably true. Would you have had me look at you, and tell my acquaintance that you are quite a common-place woman, to save you the embarrassment of being stared at if they come near you? Not I. I couldn't tell any such ridiculous lie about a beauty to encourage a single woman in England in too excessive a modesty.'

'It is all pretence—what you are saying!' exclaimed Bathsheba, laughing in spite of herself at the sergeant's

198

sly method. 'You have a rare invention, Sergeant Troy. Why couldn't you have passed by me that night, and said nothing?—that was all I meant to reproach you for.'

'Because I wasn't going to. Half the pleasure of a feeling lies in being able to express it on the spur of the moment, and I let out mine. It would have been just the same if you had been the reverse person—ugly and old—I should have exclaimed about it in the same way.'

'How long is it since you have been so afflicted with strong feeling, then?'

'Oh, ever since I was big enough to know loveliness from deformity.'

''Tis to be hoped your sense of the difference you speak of doesn't stop at faces, but extends to morals as well.'

'I won't speak of morals or religion—my own or anybody else's. Though perhaps I should have been a very good Christian if you pretty women hadn't made me an idolater.'

Bathsheba moved on to hide the irrepressible dimplings of merriment. Troy followed, whirling his cane.

'But—Miss Everdene—you do forgive me?'

'Hardly.'

'Why?'

'You say such things.'

'I said you were beautiful, and I'll say so still, for, by— so you are! The most beautiful ever I saw, or may I fall dead this instant! Why, upon my——'

'Don't—don't! I won't listen to you—you are so profane!' she said, in a restless state between distress at hearing him and a *penchant* to hear more.

'I again say you are a most fascinating woman. There's nothing remarkable in my saying so, is there? I'm sure the fact is evident enough. Miss Everdene, my opinion may be too forcibly let out to please you, and, for the matter of that, too insignificant to convince you, but surely it is honest, and why can't it be excused?'

'Because it—it isn't a correct one,' she femininely murmured.

'Oh, fie—fie! Am I any worse for breaking the third of that Terrible Ten than you for breaking the ninth?'

'Well, it doesn't seem *quite* true to me that I am fascinating,' she replied evasively.

'Not so to you: then I say with all respect that, if so, it is owing to your modesty, Miss Everdene. But surely you must have been told by everybody of what everybody notices? and you should take their words for it.'

'They don't say so exactly.'

'Oh yes, they must!'

'Well, I mean to my face, as you do,' she went on, allowing herself to be further lured into a conversation that intention had rigorously forbidden.

'But you know they think so?'

'No—that is—I certainly have heard Liddy say they do, but——' She paused.

Capitulation—that was the purport of the simple reply, guarded as it was—capitulation, unknown to herself. Never did a fragile tailless sentence convey a more perfect meaning. The careless sergeant smiled within himself, and probably too the devil smiled from a loop-hole in Tophet, for the moment was the turning-point of a career. Her tone and mien signified beyond mistake that the seed which was to lift the foundation had taken root in the chink: the remainder was a mere question of time and natural changes.

'There the truth comes out!' said the soldier, in reply. 'Never tell me that a young lady can live in a buzz of admiration without knowing something about it. Ah, well, Miss Everdene, you are—pardon my blunt way—you are rather an injury to our race than otherwise.'

'How—indeed?' she said, opening her eyes.

'Oh, it is true enough. I may as well be hung for a sheep as a lamb (an old country saying, not of much account, but it will do for a rough soldier), and so I will speak my mind, regardless of your pleasure, and without hoping or intending to get your pardon. Why, Miss Everdene, it is in this manner that your good looks may do more harm than good in the world.' The sergeant looked down the mead in critical abstraction. 'Probably some one man on an average falls in love with each ordinary woman. She can marry him : he is content, and leads a useful life. Such women as you a hundred men always covet—your eyes will bewitch scores on scores into an unavailing fancy for you —you can only marry one of that many. Out of these say twenty will endeavour to drown the bitterness of despised love in drink ; twenty more will mope away their lives without a wish or attempt to make a mark in the world, because they have no ambition apart from their attachment to you ; twenty more—the susceptible person myself possibly among them—will be always draggling after you, getting where they may just see you, doing desperate things. Men are such constant fools ! The rest may try to get over their passion with more or less success. But all these men will be saddened. And not only those ninety-nine men, but the ninety-nine women they might have married are saddened with them. There's my tale. That's why I say that a woman so charming as yourself, Miss Everdene, is hardly a blessing to her race.'

The handsome sergeant's features were during this speech as rigid and stern as John Knox's in addressing his gay young queen.

Seeing she made no reply, he said, 'Do you read French?'

'No; I began, but when I got to the verbs, father died,' she said simply.

'I do—when I have an opportunity, which latterly has not been often (my mother was a Parisienne)—and there's a proverb they have, *Qui aime bien châtie bien* —"He chastens who loves well." Do you understand me?'

'Ah!' she replied, and there was even a little tremulousness in the usually cool girl's voice; 'if you can only fight half as winningly as you can talk, you are able to make a pleasure of a bayonet wound!' And then poor Bathsheba instantly perceived her slip in making this admission: in hastily trying to retrieve it, she went from bad to worse. 'Don't, however, suppose that *I* derive any pleasure from what you tell me.'

'I know you do not—I know it perfectly,' said Troy, with much hearty conviction on the exterior of his face: and altering the expression to moodiness; 'when a dozen men are ready to speak tenderly to you, and give the admiration you deserve without adding the warning you need, it stands to reason that my poor rough-and-ready mixture of praise and blame cannot convey much pleasure. Fool as I may be, I am not so conceited as to suppose that!'

'I think you—are conceited, nevertheless,' said Bathsheba, hesitatingly, and looking askance at a reed she was fitfully pulling with one hand, having lately grown feverish under the soldier's system of procedure —not because the nature of his cajolery was entirely unperceived, but because its vigour was overwhelming.

'I would not own it to anybody else—nor do I exactly to you. Still, there might have been some self-conceit in my foolish supposition the other night. I knew that what I said in admiration might be an opinion too often forced upon you to give any pleasure, but I certainly did think that the kindness of your nature might prevent you judging an uncontrolled tongue harshly—which you have done—and thinking badly of me and wounding me this morning, when I am working hard to save your hay.'

'Well, you need not think more of that: perhaps you did not mean to be rude to me by speaking out your mind: indeed, I believe you did not,' said the shrewd woman, in painfully innocent earnest. 'And I thank you for giving help here. But—but mind you don't speak to me again in that way, or in any other, unless I speak to you.'

'Oh, Miss Bathsheba! That is too hard!'

'No, it isn't. Why is it?'

'You will never speak to me; for I shall not be here long. I am soon going back again to the miserable monotony of drill—and perhaps our regiment will be ordered out soon. And yet you take away the one little ewe-lamb of pleasure that I have in this dull life of mine. Well, perhaps generosity is not a woman's most marked characteristic.'

'When are you going from here?' she asked, with some interest.

'In a month.'

'But how can it give you pleasure to speak to me?'

'Can you ask, Miss Everdene—knowing as you do —what my offence is based on?'

'If you do care so much for a silly trifle of that kind, then, I don't mind doing it,' she uncertainly and doubtingly answered. 'But you can't really care for a word from me? you only say so—I think you only say so.'

'That's unjust—but I won't repeat the remark. I am too gratified to get such a mark of your friendship at any price to cavil at the tone. I *do*, Miss Everdene, care for it. You may think a man foolish to want a mere word—just a good morning. Perhaps he is—I don't know. But you have never been a man looking upon a woman, and that woman yourself.'

'Well.'

'Then you know nothing of what such an experience is like—and Heaven forbid that you ever should!'

'Nonsense, flatterer! What is it like? I am interested in knowing.'

'Put shortly, it is not being able to think, hear, or look in any direction except one without wretchedness, nor there without torture.'

'Ah, sergeant, it won't do—you are pretending!' she said, shaking her head dubiously. 'Your words are too dashing to be true.'

'I am not, upon the honour of a soldier.'

'But *why* is it so?—Of course I ask for mere past-time.'

'Because you are so distracting—and I am so distracted.'

'You look like it.'

'I am indeed.'

'Why, you only saw me the other night!'

'That makes no difference. The lightning works in-stantaneously. I loved you then, at once—as I do now.'

Bathsheba surveyed him curiously, from the feet upward, as high as she liked to venture her glance, which was not quite so high as his eyes.

'You cannot and you don't,' she said demurely. 'There is no such sudden feeling in people. I won't listen to you any longer. Dear me, I wish I knew what o'clock it is—I am going—I have wasted too much time here already!'

The sergeant looked at his watch and told her. 'What, haven't you a watch, miss?' he inquired.

'I have not just at present—I am about to get a new one.'

'No. You shall be given one. Yes—you shall. A gift, Miss Everdene—a gift.'

And before she knew what the young man was intending, a heavy gold watch was in her hand.

'It is an unusually good one for a man like me to possess,' he quietly said. 'That watch has a history. Press the spring and open the back.'

She did so.

'What do you see?'

'A crest and a motto.'

'A coronet with five points, and beneath, *Cedit amor rebus*—" Love yields to circumstance." It's the motto of the Earls of Severn. That watch belonged to the last lord, and was given to my mother's husband, a medical man, for his use till I came of age, when it was to be given to me. It was all the fortune that ever I inherited. That watch has regulated imperial interests in its time—the stately ceremonial, the courtly assignation, pompous travels, and lordly sleeps. Now it is yours.'

'But, Sergeant Troy, I cannot take this—I cannot!' she exclaimed, with round-eyed wonder. 'A gold watch! What are you doing? Don't be such a dissembler!'

The sergeant retreated to avoid receiving back his gift, which she held out persistently towards him. Bathsheba followed as he retired.

'Keep it—do, Miss Everdene—keep it!' said the erratic child of impulse. 'The fact of your possessing it makes it worth ten times as much to me. A more plebeian one will answer my purpose just as well, and the pleasure of knowing whose heart my old one beats against—well, I won't speak of that. It is in far worthier hands than ever it has been in before.'

'But indeed I can't have it!' she said, in a perfect simmer of distress. 'Oh, how can you do such a thing; that is, if you really mean it! Give me your dead father's watch, and such a valuable one! You should not be so reckless, indeed, Sergeant Troy!'

'I loved my father: good; but better, I love you more. That's how I can do it,' said the sergeant, with an intonation of such exquisite fidelity to nature that it was evidently not all acted now. Her beauty, which, whilst it had been quiescent, he had praised in jest, had in its animated phases moved him to earnest; and though his seriousness was less than she imagined, it was probably more than he imagined himself.

Bathsheba was brimming with agitated bewilderment, and she said, in half-suspicious accents of feeling, 'Can it be! Oh, how can it be, that you care for me, and so suddenly! You have seen so little of me: I may not be really so—so nice-looking as I seem to you. Please, do take it; oh, do! I cannot and will not have it. Believe me, your generosity is too great. I have never done you a single kindness, and why should you be so kind to me?'

A factitious reply had been again upon his lips, but it was again suspended, and he looked at her with an arrested eye. The truth was, that as she now stood— excited, wild, and honest as the day—her alluring beauty bore out so fully the epithets he had bestowed upon it that he was quite startled at his temerity in advancing them as false. He said mechanically, 'Ah, why?' and continued to look at her.

'And my workfolk see me following you about the field, and are wondering. Oh, this is dreadful!' she went on, unconscious of the transmutation she was effecting.

'I did not quite mean you to accept it at first, for it was my one poor patent of nobility,' he broke out, bluntly; 'but, upon my soul, I wish you would now. Without any shamming, come! Don't deny me the happiness of wearing it for my sake? But you are too lovely even to care to be kind as others are.'

'No, no; don't say so! I have reasons for reserve which I cannot explain.'

'Let it be, then, let it be,' he said, receiving back the watch at last; 'I must be leaving you now. And will you speak to me for these few weeks of my stay?'

206

'Indeed I will. Yet, I don't know if I will! Oh, why did you come and disturb me so!'

'Perhaps in setting a gin, I have caught myself. Such things have happened. Well, will you let me work in your fields?' he coaxed.

'Yes, I suppose so; if it is any pleasure to you.'

'Miss Everdene, I thank you.'

'No, no.'

'Good-bye!'

The sergeant brought his hand to the cap on the slope of his head, saluted, and returned to the distant group of haymakers.

Bathsheba could not face the haymakers now. Her heart erratically flitting hither and thither from perplexed excitement, hot, and almost tearful, she retreated homeward, murmuring, 'Oh, what have I done! What does it mean! I wish I knew how much of it was true!'

CHAPTER XXVII

HIVING THE BEES

THE Weatherbury bees were late in their swarming this year. It was in the latter part of June, and the day after the interview with Troy in the hayfield, that Bathsheba was standing in her garden, watching a swarm in the air and guessing their probable settling place. Not only were they late this year, but unruly. Sometimes throughout a whole season all the swarms would alight on the lowest attainable bough—such as part of a currant-bush or espalier apple-tree; next year they would, with just the same unanimity, make straight off to the uppermost member of some tall, gaunt costard, or quarrenden, and there defy all invaders who did not come armed with ladders and staves to take them.

This was the case at present. Bathsheba's eyes, shaded by one hand, were following the ascending multitude against the unexplorable stretch of blue till they ultimately halted by one of the unwieldy trees spoken of. A process somewhat analogous to that of alleged formations of the universe, time and times ago, was observable. The bustling swarm had swept the sky in a scattered and uniform haze, which now thickened to a nebulous centre : this glided on to a bough and grew still denser, till it formed a solid black spot upon the light.

The men and women being all busily engaged in saving the hay—even Liddy had left the house for the purpose of lending a hand—Bathsheba resolved to hive the bees herself, if possible. She had dressed the hive with herbs and honey, fetched a ladder, brush, and crook, made herself impregnable with armour of leather gloves, straw hat, and large gauze veil—once green but now faded to snuff colour—and ascended a dozen rungs of the ladder. At once she heard, not ten yards off, a voice that was beginning to have a strange power in agitating her.

'Miss Everdene, let me assist you; you should not attempt such a thing alone.'

Troy was just opening the garden gate.

Bathsheba flung down the brush, crook, and empty hive, pulled the skirt of her dress tightly round her ankles in a tremendous flurry, and as well as she could slid down the ladder. By the time she reached the bottom Troy was there also, and he stooped to pick up the hive.

'How fortunate I am to have dropped in at this moment!' exclaimed the sergeant.

She found her voice in a minute. 'What! and will you shake them in for me?' she asked, in what, for a defiant girl, was a faltering way; though, for a timid girl, it would have seemed a brave way enough.

'Will I!' said Troy. 'Why, of course I will. How blooming you are to-day!' Troy flung down his cane and put his foot on the ladder to ascend.

'But you must have on the veil and gloves, or you'll be stung fearfully!'

'Ah, yes. I must put on the veil and gloves. Will you kindly show me how to fix them properly?'

'And you must have the broad-brimmed hat, too; for your cap has no brim to keep the veil off, and they'd reach your face.'

'The broad-brimmed hat, too, by all means.'

So a whimsical fate ordered that her hat should be taken off—veil and all attached—and placed upon his head, Troy tossing his own into a gooseberry bush. Then the veil had to be tied at its lower edge round his collar and the gloves put on him.

He looked such an extraordinary object in this guise that, flurried as she was, she could not avoid laughing outright. It was the removal of yet another stake from the palisade of cold manners which had kept him off.

Bathsheba looked on from the ground whilst he was busy sweeping and shaking the bees from the tree, holding up the hive with the other hand for them to fall into. She made use of an unobserved minute whilst his attention was absorbed in the operation to arrange her plumes a little. He came down holding the hive at arm's length, behind which trailed a cloud of bees.

'Upon my life,' said Troy, through the veil, 'holding up this hive makes one's arm ache worse than a week of sword-exercise.' When the manœuvre was complete he approached her. 'Would you be good enough to untie me and let me out? I am nearly stifled inside this silk cage.'

To hide her embarrassment during the unwonted process of untying the string about his neck, she said :—

'I have never seen that you spoke of.'

'What?'

'The sword-exercise.'

'Ah! would you like to?' said Troy.

Bathsheba hesitated. She had heard wondrous reports from time to time by dwellers in Weatherbury, who had by chance sojourned awhile in Casterbridge, near the barracks, of this strange and glorious perform-ance, the sword-exercise Men and boys who had peeped through chinks or over walls into the barrack-yard returned with accounts of its being the most flashing affair conceivable ; accoutrements and weapons glistening like stars—here, there, around—yet all by rule and compass. So she said mildly what she felt strongly.

'Yes; I should like to see it very much.'

'And so you shall; you shall see me go through it.'

'No! How?'

'Let me consider.'

'Not with a walking-stick—I don't care to see that. It must be a real sword.'

'Yes, I know; and I have no sword here; but I think I could get 'one by the evening. Now, will you do this?'

Troy bent over her and murmured some suggestion in a low voice.

'Oh no, indeed!' said Bathsheba, blushing. 'Thank you very much, but I couldn't on any account.'

'Surely you might? Nobody would know.'

She shook her head, but with a weakened negation. 'If I were to,' she said, 'I must bring Liddy too. Might I not?'

Troy looked far away. 'I don't see why you want to bring her,' he said coldly.

An unconscious look of assent in Bathsheba's eyes betrayed that something more than his coldness had made her also feel that Liddy would be superfluous in the suggested scene. She had felt it, even whilst making the proposal.

'Well, I won't bring Liddy—and I'll come. But only for a very short time,' she added; 'a very short time.'

'It will not take five minutes,' said Troy.

CHAPTER XXVIII

THE HOLLOW AMID THE FERNS

THE hill opposite Bathsheba's dwelling extended, a mile off, into an uncultivated tract of land, dotted at this season with tall thickets of brake fern, plump and diaphanous from recent rapid growth, and radiant in hues of clear and untainted green.

At eight o'clock this midsummer evening, whilst the bristling ball of gold in the west still swept the tips of the ferns with its long, luxuriant rays, a soft brushing-by of garments might have been heard among them, and Bathsheba appeared in their midst, their soft, feathery arms caressing her up to her shoulders. She paused, turned, went back over the hill and half-way to her own door, whence she cast a farewell glance upon the spot she had just left, having resolved not to remain near the place after all.

She saw a dim spot of artificial red moving round the shoulder of the rise. It disappeared on the other side.

She waited one minute—two minutes—thought of Troy's disappointment at her non-fulfilment of a promised engagement, till she again ran along the field, clambered over the bank, and followed the original direction. She was now literally trembling and panting at this her temerity in such an errant undertaking; her breath

212

came and went quickly, and her eyes shone with an infrequent light. Yet go she must. She reached the verge of a pit in the middle of the ferns. Troy stood in the bottom, looking up towards her.

'I heard you rustling through the fern before I saw you,' he said, coming up and giving her his hand to help her down the slope.

The pit was a saucer-shaped concave, naturally formed, with a top diameter of about thirty feet, and shallow enough to allow the sunshine to reach their heads. Standing in the centre, the sky overhead was met by a circular horizon of fern: this grew nearly to the bottom of the slope and then abruptly ceased. The middle within the belt of verdure was floored with a thick flossy carpet of moss and grass intermingled, so yielding that the foot was half-buried within it.

'Now,' said Troy, producing the sword, which, as he raised it into the sunlight, gleamed a sort of greeting, like a living thing, 'first, we have four right and four left cuts; four right and four left thrusts. Infantry cuts and guards are more interesting than ours, to my mind; but they are not so swashing. They have seven cuts and three thrusts. So much as a preliminary. Well, next, our cut one is as if you were sowing your corn—so.' Bathsheba saw a sort of rainbow, upside down in the air, and Troy's arm was still again. 'Cut two, as if you were hedging—so. Three, as if you were reaping—so. Four, as if you were threshing—in that way. Then the same on the left. The thrusts are these: one, two, three, four, right; one, two, three, four, left.' He repeated them. 'Have 'em again?' he said. 'One, two——'

She hurriedly interrupted: 'I'd rather not; though I don't mind your twos and fours; but your ones and threes are terrible!'

'Very well. I'll let you off the ones and threes. Next, cuts, points and guards altogether.' Troy duly

213

exhibited them. 'Then there's pursuing practice, in this way.' He gave the movements as before. 'There, those are the stereotyped forms. The infantry have two most diabolical upward cuts, which we are too humane to use. Like this—three, four.'

'How murderous and bloodthirsty!'

'They are rather deathy. Now I'll be more interesting, and let you see some loose play—giving all the cuts and points, infantry and cavalry, quicker than lightning, and as promiscuously—with just enough rule to regulate instinct and yet not to fetter it. You are my antagonist, with this difference from real warfare, that I shall miss you every time by one hair's breadth, or perhaps two. Mind you don't flinch, whatever you do.'

'I'll be sure not to!' she said invincibly.

He pointed to about a yard in front of him.

Bathsheba's adventurous spirit was beginning to find some grains of relish in these highly novel proceedings. She took up her position as directed, facing Troy.

'Now just to learn whether you have pluck enough to let me do what I wish, I'll give you a preliminary test.'

He flourished the sword by way of introduction number two, and the next thing of which she was conscious was that the point and blade of the sword were darting with a gleam towards her left side, just above her hip; then of their reappearance on her right side, emerging as it were from between her ribs, having apparently passed through her body. The third item of consciousness was that of seeing the same sword, perfectly clean and free from blood held vertically in Troy's hand (in the position technically called 'recover swords'). All was as quick as electricity.

'Oh!' she cried out in affright, pressing her hand to her side. 'Have you run me through?—no, you have not! Whatever have you done!'

'I have not touched you,' said Troy, quietly. 'It was mere sleight of hand. The sword passed behind you. Now you are not afraid, are you? Because if you are I can't perform. I give my word that I will not only not hurt you, but not once touch you.'

'I don't think I am afraid. You are quite sure you will not hurt me?'

'Quite sure.'

'Is the sword very sharp?'

'Oh no—only stand as still as a statue. Now!'

In an instant the atmosphere was transformed to Bathsheba's eyes. Beams of light caught from the low sun's rays, above, around, in front of her, well-nigh shut out earth and heaven—all emitted in the marvellous evolutions of Troy's reflecting blade, which seemed everywhere at once, and yet nowhere specially. These circling gleams were accompanied by a keen rush that was almost a whistling—also springing from all sides of her at once. In short, she was enclosed in a firmament of light, and of sharp hisses, resembling a sky-full of meteors close at hand.

Never since the broadsword became the national weapon had there been more dexterity shown in its management than by the hands of Sergeant Troy, and never had he been in such splendid temper for the performance as now in the evening sunshine among the ferns with Bathsheba. It may safely be asserted with respect to the closeness of his cuts, that had it been possible for the edge of the sword to leave in the air a permanent substance wherever it flew past, the space left untouched would have been almost a mould of Bathsheba's figure.

Behind the luminous streams of this *aurora militaris*, she could see the hue of Troy's sword arm, spread in a scarlet haze over the space covered by its motions, like a twanged harpstring, and behind all Troy himself, mostly facing her; sometimes, to show the rear cuts,

215

half turned away, his eye nevertheless always keenly measuring her breadth and outline, and his lips tightly closed in sustained effort. Next, his movements lapsed slower, and she could see them individually. The hissing of the sword had ceased, and he stopped entirely.

'That outer loose lock of hair wants tidying,' he said, before she had moved or spoken. 'Wait: I'll do it for you.'

An arc of silver shone on her right side: the sword had descended. The lock dropped to the ground.

'Bravely borne!' said Troy. 'You didn't flinch a shade's thickness. Wonderful in a woman!'

'It was because I didn't expect it. Oh, you have spoilt my hair!'

'Only once more.'

'No—no! I am afraid of you—indeed I am!' she cried.

'I won't touch you at all—not even your hair. I am only going to kill that caterpillar settling on you. Now: still!'

It appeared that a caterpillar had come from the fern and chosen the front of her bodice as his resting place. She saw the point glisten towards her bosom, and seemingly enter it. Bathsheba closed her eyes in the full persuasion that she was killed at last. However, feeling just as usual, she opened them again.

'There it is, look,' said the sergeant, holding his sword before her eyes.

The caterpillar was spitted upon its point.

'Why, it is magic!' said Bathsheba, amazed.

'Oh no—dexterity. I merely gave point to your bosom where the caterpillar was, and instead of running you through checked the extension a thousandth of an inch short of your surface.'

'But how could you chop off a curl of my hair with a sword that has no edge?'

'No edge! This sword will shave like a razor. Look here.'

He touched the palm of his hand with the blade, and then, lifting it, showed her a thin shaving of scarf-skin dangling therefrom.

'But you said before beginning that it was blunt and couldn't cut me!'

'That was to get you to stand still, and so ensure your safety. The risk of injuring you through your moving was too great not to force me to tell you an untruth to obviate it.'

She shuddered. 'I have been within an inch of my life, and didn't know it!'

'More precisely speaking, you have been within half an inch of being pared alive two hundred and ninety-five times.'

'Cruel, cruel, 'tis of you!'

'You have been perfectly safe, nevertheless. My sword never errs.' And Troy returned the weapon to the scabbard.

Bathsheba, overcome by a hundred tumultuous feelings resulting from the scene, abstractedly sat down on a tuft of heather.

'I must leave you now,' said Troy, softly. 'And I'll venture to take and keep this in remembrance of you.'

She saw him stoop to the grass, pick up the winding lock which he had severed from her manifold tresses, twist it round his fingers, unfasten a button in the breast of his coat, and carefully put it inside. She felt powerless to withstand or deny him. He was altogether too much for her, and Bathsheba seemed as one who, facing a reviving wind, finds it blow so strongly that it stops the breath.

He drew near and said, 'I must be leaving you.' He drew nearer still. A minute later and she saw his scarlet form disappear amid the ferny thicket, almost in a flash, like a brand swiftly waved.

That minute's interval had brought the blood beating into her face, set her stinging as if aflame to the very hollows of her feet, and enlarged emotion to a compass which quite swamped thought. It had brought upon her a stroke resulting, as did that of Moses in Horeb, in a liquid stream—here a stream of tears. She felt like one who has sinned a great sin.

The circumstance had been the gentle dip of Troy's mouth downwards upon her own. He had kissed her.

CHAPTER XXIX

ARTICULARS OF A TWILIGHT WALK

WE now see the element of folly distinctly mingling with the many varying particulars which made up the character of Bathsheba Everdene. It was almost foreign to her intrinsic nature. Introduced as lymph on the dart of Eros, it eventually permeated and coloured her whole constitution. Bathsheba, though she had too much understanding to be entirely governed by her womanliness, had too much womanliness to use her understanding to the best advantage. Perhaps in no minor point does woman astonish her helpmate more than in the strange power she possesses of believing cajoleries that she knows to be false—except, indeed, in that of being utterly sceptical on strictures that she knows to be true.

Bathsheba loved Troy in the way that only self-reliant women love when they abandon their self-reliance. When a strong woman recklessly throws away her strength she is worse than a weak woman who has never had any strength to throw away. One source of her inadequacy is the novelty of the occasion. She has never had practice in making the best of such a condition. Weakness is doubly weak by being new.

Bathsheba was not conscious of guile in this matter. Though in one sense a woman of the world, it was, after all, that world of daylight coteries and green carpets wherein cattle form the passing crowd and winds the busy hum ; where a quiet family of rabbits or hares lives on the other side of your party-wall, where your neighbour is everybody in the tything, and where calculation is confined to market-days. Of the fabricated tastes of good fashionable society she knew but little, and of the formulated self-indulgence of bad, nothing at all. Had her utmost thoughts in this direction been distinctly worded (and by herself they never were), they would only have amounted to such a matter as that she felt her impulses to be pleasanter guides than her discretion. Her love was entire as a child's, and though warm as summer it was fresh as spring. Her culpability lay in her making no attempt to control feeling by subtle and careful inquiry into consequences. She could show others the steep and thorny way, but 'reck'd not her own rede.'

And Troy's deformities lay deep down from a woman's vision, whilst his embellishments were upon the very surface ; thus contrasting with homely Oak, whose defects were patent to the blindest, and whose virtues were as metals in a mine.

The difference between love and respect was markedly shown in her conduct. Bathsheba had spoken of her interest in Boldwood with the greatest freedom to Liddy, but she had only communed with her own heart concerning Troy.

All this infatuation Gabriel saw, and was troubled thereby from the time of his daily journey a-field to the time of his return, and on to the small hours of many a night. That he was not beloved had hitherto been his great sorrow ; that Bathsheba was getting into the toils was now a sorrow greater than the first, and one which nearly obscured it. It was a result which paralleled the oft-quoted observation of Hippocrates concerning physical pains.

That is a noble though perhaps an unpromising love

which not even the fear of breeding aversion in the bosom of the one beloved can deter from combating his or her errors. Oak determined to speak to his mistress. He would base his appeal on what he considered her unfair treatment of Farmer Boldwood, now absent from home.

An opportunity occurred one evening when she had gone for a short walk by a path through the neighbouring cornfields. It was dusk when Oak, who had not been far a-field that day, took the same path and met her returning, quite pensively, as he thought.

The wheat was now tall, and the path was narrow; thus the way was quite a sunken groove between the embowing thicket on either side. Two persons could not walk abreast without damaging the crop, and Oak stood aside to let her pass.

'Oh, is it Gabriel?' she said. 'You are taking a walk too. Good-night.'

'I thought I would come to meet you, as it is rather late,' said Oak, turning and following at her heels when she had brushed somewhat quickly by him.

'Thank you, indeed, but I am not very fearful.'

'Oh no ; but there are bad characters about.'

'I never meet them.'

Now Oak, with marvellous ingenuity, had been going to introduce the gallant sergeant through the channel of 'bad characters.' But all at once the scheme broke down, it suddenly occurring to him that this was rather a clumsy way, and too barefaced to begin with. He tried another preamble.

'And as the man who would naturally come to meet you is away from home, too—I mean Farmer Boldwood —why, thinks I, I'll go,' he said.

'Ah, yes.' She walked on without turning her head, and for many steps nothing further was heard from her quarter than the rustle of her dress against the heavy corn-ears. Then she resumed rather tartly—

'I don't quite understand what you meant by saying that Mr. Boldwood would naturally come to meet me.'

'I meant on account of the wedding which they say is likely to take place between you and him, miss. Forgive my speaking plainly.'

'They say what is not true,' she returned quickly. 'No marriage is likely to take place between us.'

Gabriel now put forth his unobscured opinion, for the moment had come. 'Well, Miss Everdene,' he said, 'putting aside what people say, I never in my life saw any courting if his is not a courting of you.'

Bathsheba would probably have terminated the conversation there and then by flatly forbidding the subject, had not her conscious weakness of position allured her to palter and argue in endeavours to better it.

'Since this subject has been mentioned,' she said very emphatically, 'I am glad of the opportunity of clearing up a mistake which is very common and very provoking. I didn't definitely promise Mr. Boldwood anything. I have never cared for him. I respect him, and he has urged me to marry him. But I have given him no distinct answer. As soon as he returns I shall do so ; and the answer will be that I cannot think of marrying him.'

'People are full of mistakes, seemingly.'

'They are.'

'The other day they said you were trifling with him, and you almost proved that you were not ; lately they have said that you be not, and you straightway begin to show——'

'That I am, I suppose you mean.'

'Well, I hope they speak the truth.'

'They do, but wrongly applied. I don't trifle with him ; but then, I have nothing to do with him.'

Oak was unfortunately led on to speak of Boldwood's rival in a wrong tone to her after all. 'I wish you had never met that young Sergeant Troy, miss,' he sighed.

Bathsheba's steps became faintly spasmodic. 'Why?' she asked.

'He is not good enough for 'ee.'

'Did any one tell you to speak to me like this?'

'Nobody at all.'

'Then it appears to me that Sergeant Troy does not concern us here,' she said, intractably. 'Yet I must say that Sergeant Troy is an educated man, and quite worthy of any woman. He is well born.'

'His being higher in learning and birth than the ruck o' soldiers is anything but a proof of his worth. It shows his course to be down'ard.'

'I cannot see what this has to do with our conversation. Mr. Troy's course is not by any means downward; and his superiority *is* a proof of his worth!'

'I believe him to have no conscience at all. And I cannot help begging you, miss, to have nothing to do with him. Listen to me this once—only this once! I don't say he's such a bad man as I have fancied—I pray to God he is not. But since we don't exactly know what he is, why not behave as if he *might* be bad, simply for your own safety? Don't trust him, mistress; I ask you not to trust him so.'

'Why, pray?'

'I like soldiers, but this one I do not like,' he said, sturdily. 'The nature of his calling may have tempted him astray, and what is mirth to the neighbours is ruin to the woman. When he tries to talk to 'ee again, why not turn away with a short "Good day;" and when you see him coming one way, turn the other. When he says anything laughable, fail to see the point and don't smile, and speak of him before those who will report your talk as "that fantastical man," or "that Sergeant What's-his-name." "That man of a family that has come to the dogs." Don't be unmannerly towards en, but harmless-uncivil, and so get rid of the man.'

No Christmas robin detained by a window-pane ever pulsed as did Bathsheba now.

'I say—I say again—that it doesn't become you to talk about him. Why he should be mentioned passes me quite!' she exclaimed desperately. 'I know this, th-th-that he is a thoroughly conscientious man—blunt sometimes even to rudeness—but always speaking his mind about you plain to your face!'

'Oh.'

'He is as good as anybody in this parish! He is very particular, too, about going to church—yes, he is!'

'I am afeard nobody ever saw him there. I never did, certainly.'

'The reason of that is,' she said eagerly, 'that he goes in privately by the old tower door, just when the service commences, and sits at the back of the gallery. He told me so.'

This supreme instance of Troy's goodness fell upon Gabriel's ears like the thirteenth stroke of a crazy clock. It was not only received with utter incredulity as regarded itself, but threw a doubt on all the assurances that had preceded it.

Oak was grieved to find how entirely she trusted him. He brimmed with deep feeling as he replied in a steady voice, the steadiness of which was spoilt by the palpableness of his great effort to keep it so :—

'You know, mistress, that I love you, and shall love you always. I only mention this to bring to your mind that at any rate I would wish to do you no harm: beyond that I put it aside. I have lost in the race for money and good things, and I am not such a fool as to pretend to 'ee now I am poor, and you have got altogether above me. But Bathsheba, dear mistress, this I beg you to consider—that, both to keep yourself well honoured among the workfolk, and in common generosity to an honourable man who loves you as well as I, you should be more discreet in your bearing towards this soldier.'

'Don't, don't, don't!' she exclaimed, in a choking voice.

'Are ye not more to me than my own affairs, and even life!' he went on. 'Come, listen to me! I am six years older than you, and Mr. Boldwood is ten years older than I, and consider—I do beg of 'ee to consider before it is too late—how safe you would be in his hands!'

Oak's allusion to his own love for her lessened, to some extent, her anger at his interference; but she could not really forgive him for letting his wish to marry her be eclipsed by his wish to do her good, any more than for his slighting treatment of Troy.

'I wish you to go elsewhere,' she said, a paleness of face invisible to the eye being suggested by the trembling words. 'Do not remain on this farm any longer. I don't want you—I beg you to go!'

'That's nonsense,' said Oak, calmly. 'This is the second time you have pretended to dismiss me; and what's the use o' it?'

'Pretended! You shall go, sir—your lecturing I will not hear! I am mistress here.'

'Go, indeed—what folly will you say next? Treating me like Dick, Tom and Harry when you know that a short time ago my position was as good as yours! Upon my life, Bathsheba, it is too barefaced. You know, too, that I can't go without putting things in such a strait as you wouldn't get out of I can't tell when. Unless, indeed, you'll promise to have an understanding man as bailiff, or manager, or something. I'll go at once if you'll promise that.'

'I shall have no bailiff; I shall continue to be my own manager,' she said decisively.

'Very well, then; you should be thankful to me for biding. How would the farm go on with nobody to mind it but a woman? But mind this, I don't wish 'ee to feel you owe me anything. Not I. What I do, I do. Sometimes I say I should be as glad as a bird to leave the place—for don't suppose I'm content to be a nobody. I was made for better things. However, I don't like to see your concerns going to ruin, as they must if you keep in this mind. . . . I hate taking my own measure so plain, but upon my life, your provoking ways make a man say what he wouldn't dream of at other times! I own to being rather interfering. But you know well enough how it is, and who she is that I like too well, and feel too much like a fool about to be civil to her!'

It is more than probable that she privately and unconsciously respected him a little for this grim fidelity, which had been shown in his tone even more than in his words. At any rate she murmured something to the effect that he might stay if he wished. She said more distinctly, 'Will you leave me alone now? I don't order it as a mistress—I ask it as a woman, and I expect you not to be so uncourteous as to refuse.'

'Certainly I will, Miss Everdene,' said Gabriel, gently. He wondered that the request should have come at this moment, for the strife was over, and they were on a most desolate hill, far from every human habitation, and the hour was getting late. He stood still and allowed her to get far ahead of him till he could only see her form upon the sky.

A distressing explanation of this anxiety to be rid of him at that point now ensued. A figure apparently rose from the earth beside her. The shape beyond all doubt was Troy's. Oak would not be even a possible listener, and at once turned back till a good two hundred yards were between the lovers and himself.

Gabriel went home by way of the churchyard. In passing the tower he thought of what she had said about the sergeant's virtuous habit of entering the church unperceived at the beginning of service. Believing that the little gallery door alluded to was quite disused, he ascended the external flight of steps at the top of which it stood, and examined it. The pale lustre yet hanging in the north-western heaven was sufficient to show that a sprig of ivy had grown from the wall across the door to a length of more than a foot, delicately tying the panel to the stone jamb. It was a decisive proof that the door had not been opened at least since Troy came back to Weatherbury.

CHAPTER XXX

HOT CHEEKS AND TEARFUL EYES

HALF an hour later Bathsheba entered her own house. There burnt upon her face when she met the light of the candles the flush and excitement which were little less than chronic with her now. The farewell words of Troy, who had accompanied her to the very door, still lingered in her ears. He had bidden her adieu for two days, which were, so he stated, to be spent at Bath in visiting some friends. He had also kissed her a second time.

It is only fair to Bathsheba to explain here a little fact which did not come to light till a long time afterwards: that Troy's presentation of himself so aptly at the roadside this evening was not by any distinctly preconcerted arrangement. He had hinted—she had forbidden; and it was only on the chance of his still coming that she had dismissed Oak, fearing a meeting between them just then.

She now sank down into a chair, wild and perturbed by all these new and fevering sequences. Then she jumped up with a manner of decision, and fetched her desk from a side table.

In three minutes, without pause or modification, she had written a letter to Boldwood, at his address beyond Casterbridge, saying mildly but firmly that she had well considered the whole subject he had brought before her and kindly given her time to decide upon; that her final decision was that she could not marry him. She had expressed to Oak an intention to wait till Boldwood came home before communicating to him her conclusive reply. But Bathsheba found that she could not wait.

It was impossible to send this letter till the next day; yet to quell her uneasiness by getting it out of her hands, and so, as it were, setting the act in motion at once, she arose to take it to any one of the women who might be in the kitchen.

She paused in the passage. A dialogue was going on in the kitchen, and Bathsheba and Troy were the subject of it.

'If he marry her, she'll gie up farming.'

' 'Twill be a gallant life, but may bring some trouble between the mirth—so say I.'

'Well, I wish I had half such a husband.'

Bathsheba had too much sense to mind seriously what her servitors said about her; but too much womanly redundance of speech to leave alone what was said till it died the natural death of unminded things. She burst in upon them.

'Who are you speaking of?' she asked.

There was a pause before anybody replied. At last Liddy said frankly, 'What was passing was a bit of a word about yourself, miss.'

'I thought so! Maryann and Liddy and Temperance—now I forbid you to suppose such things. You know I don't care the least for Mr. Troy—not I. Everybody knows how much I hate him.—Yes,' repeated the froward young person, '*hate* him!'

'We know you do, miss,' said Liddy; 'and so do we all.'

'I hate him too,' said Maryann.

'Maryann—Oh you perjured woman! How can you speak that wicked story!' said Bathsheba, excitedly.

'You admired him from your heart only this morning in the very world, you did. Yes, Maryann, you know it!'

'Yes, miss, but so did you. He is a wild scamp now, and you are right to hate him.'

'He's *not* a wild scamp! How dare you to my face! I have no right to hate him, nor you, nor anybody. But I am a silly woman! What is it to me what he is? You know it is nothing. I don't care for him; I don't mean to defend his good name, not I. Mind this, if any of you say a word against him you'll be dismissed instantly!'

She flung down the letter and surged back into the parlour, with a big heart and tearful eyes, Liddy following her.

'Oh miss!' said mild Liddy, looking pitifully into Bathsheba's face. 'I am sorry we mistook you so! I did think you cared for him; but I see you don't now.'

'Shut the door, Liddy.'

Liddy closed the door, and went on: 'People always say such foolery, miss. I'll make answer hencefor'ard, "Of course a lady like Miss Everdene can't love him;" I'll say it out in plain black and white.'

Bathsheba burst out: 'O Liddy, are you such a simpleton? Can't you read riddles? Can't you see? Are you a woman yourself?'

Liddy's clear eyes rounded with wonderment.

'Yes; you must be a blind thing, Liddy!' she said, in reckless abandonment and grief. 'Oh, I love him to very distraction and misery and agony! Don't be frightened at me, though perhaps I am enough to frighten any innocent woman. Come closer—closer.' She put her arms round Liddy's neck. 'I must let it out to somebody; it is wearing me away! Don't you yet know enough of me to see through that miserable denial of mine? O God, what a lie it was! Heaven and my Love forgive me. And don't you know that a woman who loves at all thinks nothing of perjury when it is

balanced against her love? There, go out of the room;
I want to be quite alone.'

Liddy went towards the door.

'Liddy, come here. Solemnly swear to me that he's
not a bad man; that it is all lies they say about him!'

'But, miss, how can I say he is not if——'

'You graceless girl! How can you have the cruel
heart to repeat what they say? Unfeeling thing that
you are. . . . But *I'll* see if you or anybody else in the
village, or town either, dare do such a thing!' She
started off, pacing from fireplace to door, and back
again.

'No, miss. I don't—I know it is not true!' said
Liddy, frightened at Bathsheba's unwonted vehemence.

'I suppose you only agree with me like that to please
me. But, Liddy, he *cannot be* bad, as is said. Do you
hear?'

'Yes, miss, yes.'

'And you don't believe he is?'

'I don't know what to say, miss,' said Liddy, beginning to cry. 'If I say No, you don't believe me;
and if I say Yes, you rage at me!'

'Say you don't believe it—say you don't!'

'I don't believe him to be so bad as they make out.'

'He is not bad at all. . . . My poor life and heart,
how weak I am!' she moaned, in a relaxed, desultory
way, heedless of Liddy's presence. 'Oh, how I wish I
had never seen him! Loving is misery for women
always. I shall never forgive God for making me a
woman, and dearly am I beginning to pay for the honour
of owning a pretty face.' She freshened and turned to
Liddy suddenly. 'Mind this, Lydia Smallbury, if you
repeat anywhere a single word of what I have said to
you inside this closed door, I'll never trust you, or love
you, or have you with me a moment longer—not a
moment!'

'I don't want to repeat anything,' said Liddy, with

womanly dignity of a diminutive order; 'but I don't wish to stay with you. And, if you please, I'll go at the end of the harvest, or this week, or to-day. . . . I don't see that I deserve to be put upon and stormed at for nothing!' concluded the small woman, bigly.

'No, no, Liddy; you must stay!' said Bathsheba, dropping from haughtiness to entreaty with capricious inconsequence. 'You must not notice my being in a taking just now. You are not as a servant—you are a companion to me. Dear, dear—I don't know what I am doing since this miserable ache o' my heart has weighted and worn upon me so! What shall I come to! I suppose I shall get further and further into troubles. I wonder sometimes if I am doomed to die in the Union. I am friendless enough, God knows!'

'I won't notice anything, nor will I leave you!' sobbed Liddy, impulsively putting up her lips to Bathsheba's, and kissing her.

Then Bathsheba kissed Liddy, and all was smooth again.

'I don't often cry, do I, Lidd? but you have made tears come into my eyes,' she said, a smile shining through the moisture. 'Try to think him a good man, won't you, dear Liddy?'

'I will, miss, indeed.'

'He is a sort of steady man in a wild way, you know. That's better than to be as some are, wild in a steady way. I am afraid that's how I am. And promise me to keep my secret—do, Liddy! And do not let them know that I have been crying about him, because it will be dreadful for me, and no good to him, poor thing!'

'Death's head himself shan't wring it from me, mistress, if I've a mind to keep anything; and I'll always be your friend,' replied Liddy, emphatically, at the same time bringing a few more tears into her own eyes, not from any particular necessity, but from an artistic sense of making herself in keeping with the remainder of the picture, which seems to influence women at such times. 'I think God likes us to be good friends, don't you?'

'Indeed I do.'

'And, dear miss, you won't harry me and storm at me, will you? because you seem to swell so tall as a lion then, and it frightens me! Do you know, I fancy you would be a match for any man when you are in one o' your takings.'

'Never! do you?' said Bathsheba, slightly laughing, though somewhat seriously alarmed by this Amazonian picture of herself. 'I hope I am not a bold sort of maid—mannish?' she continued with some anxiety.

'Oh no, not mannish; but so almighty womanish that 'tis getting on that way sometimes. Ah! miss,' she said, after having drawn her breath very sadly in and sent it very sadly out, 'I wish I had half your failing that way. 'Tis a great protection to a poor maid in these days!'

CHAPTER XXXI

BLAME—FURY

THE next evening Bathsheba, with the idea of getting out of the way of Mr. Boldwood in the event of his returning to answer her note in person, proceeded to fulfil an engagement made with Liddy some few hours earlier. Bathsheba's companion, as a gage of their reconciliation, had been granted a week's holiday to visit her sister, who was married to a thriving hurdler and cattle-crib-maker living in a delightful labyrinth of hazel copse not far beyond Yalbury. The arrangement was that Miss Everdene should honour them by coming there for a day or two to inspect some ingenious contrivances which this man of the woods had introduced into his wares.

Leaving her instructions with Gabriel and Maryann, that they were to see everything carefully locked up for the night, she went out of the house just at the close of a timely thunder-shower, which had refined the air, and daintily bathed the coat of the land, though all beneath was dry as ever. Freshness was exhaled in an essence from the varied contours of bank and hollow, as if the earth breathed maiden breath; and the pleased birds were hymning to the scene. Before her, among the clouds, there was a contrast in the shape of lairs of fierce light which showed themselves in the neighbourhood of a hidden sun, lingering on to the farthest north-west corner of the heavens that this midsummer season allowed.

She had walked nearly two miles of her journey, watching how the day was retreating, and thinking how the time of deeds was quietly melting into the time of thought, to give place in its turn to the time of prayer and sleep, when she beheld advancing over the hill the very man she sought so anxiously to elude. Boldwood was stepping on, not with that quiet tread of reserved strength which was his customary gait, in which he always seemed to be balancing two thoughts. His manner was stunned and sluggish now.

Boldwood had for the first time been awakened to woman's privileges in tergiversation even when it involves another person's possible blight. That Bathsheba was a firm and positive girl, far less inconsequent than her fellows, had been the very lung of his hope; for he had held that these qualities would lead her to adhere to a straight course for consistency's sake, and accept him, though her fancy might not flood him with the iridescent hues of uncritical love. But the argument now came back as sorry gleams from a broken mirror. The discovery was no less a scourge than a surprise.

He came on looking upon the ground, and did not see Bathsheba till they were less than a stone's throw apart. He looked up at the sound of her pit-pat, and his changed appearance sufficiently denoted to her the depth and strength of the feelings paralyzed by her letter.

'Oh; is it you, Mr. Boldwood?' she faltered, a guilty warmth pulsing in her face.

Those who have the power of reproaching in silence may find it a means more effective than words. There are accents in the eye which are not on the tongue, and more tales come from pale lips than can enter an ear. It is both the grandeur and the pain of the remoter

235

moods that they avoid the pathway of sound. Boldwood's look was unanswerable.

Seeing she turned a little aside, he said, 'What, are
you afraid of me?'

'Why should you say that?' said Bathsheba.

'I fancied you looked so,' said he. 'And it is most
strange, because of its contrast with my feeling for you.'

She regained self-possession, fixed her eyes calmly,
and waited.

'You know what that feeling is,' continued Boldwood,
deliberately. 'A thing strong as death. No dismissal
by a hasty letter affects that.'

'I wish you did not feel so strongly about me,' she
murmured. 'It is generous of you, and more than I
deserve, but I must not hear it now.'

'Hear it? What do you think I have to say, then?
I am not to marry you, and that's enough. Your letter
was excellently plain. I want you to hear nothing—
not I.'

Bathsheba was unable to direct her will into any
definite groove for freeing herself from this fearfully
awkward position. She confusedly said, 'Good evening,'
and was moving on. Boldwood walked up to her heavily
and dully.

'Bathsheba—darling—is it final indeed?'

'Indeed it is.'

'Oh Bathsheba—have pity upon me!' Boldwood
burst out. 'God's sake, yes—I am come to that low,
lowest stage—to ask a woman for pity! Still, she is
you—she is you.'

Bathsheba commanded herself well. But she could
hardly get a clear voice for what came instinctively to
her lips: 'There is little honour to the woman in that
speech.' It was only whispered, for something unutter-
ably mournful no less than distressing in this spectacle
of a man showing himself to be so entirely the vane of a
passion enervated the feminine instinct for punctilios.

'I am beyond myself about this, and am mad,' he said. 'I am no stoic at all to be supplicating here; but I do supplicate to you. I wish you knew what is in me of devotion to you; but it is impossible, that. In bare human mercy to a lonely man, don't throw me off now!'

'I don't throw you off—indeed, how can I? I never had you.' In her noon-clear sense that she had never loved him she forgot for a moment her thoughtless angle on that day in February.

'But there was a time when you turned to me, before I thought of you! I don't reproach you, for even now I feel that the ignorant and cold darkness that I should have lived in if you had not attracted me by that letter—valentine you call it—would have been worse than my knowledge of you, though it has brought this misery. But, I say, there was a time when I knew nothing of you, and cared nothing for you, and yet you drew me on. And if you say you gave me no encouragement, I cannot but contradict you.'

'What you call encouragement was the childish game of an idle minute. I have bitterly repented of it —ay, bitterly, and in tears. Can you still go on reminding me?'

'I don't accuse you of it—I deplore it. I took for earnest what you insist was jest, and now this that I pray to be jest you say is awful, wretched earnest. Our moods meet at wrong places. I wish your feeling was more like mine, or my feeling more like yours! Oh, could I but have foreseen the torture that trifling trick was going to lead me into, how I should have cursed you; but only having been able to see it since, I cannot do that, for I love you too well! But it is weak, idle drivelling to go on like this. . . . Bathsheba, you are the first woman of any shade or nature that I have ever looked at to love, and it is the having been so near claiming you for my own that makes this denial so hard to bear. How nearly you promised me! But I don't speak now to move your heart, and make you grieve because of my pain ; it is no use, that. I must bear it; my pain would get no less by paining you.'

'But I do pity you—deeply—oh, so deeply!' she earnestly said.

'Do no such thing—do no such thing. Your dear love, Bathsheba, is such a vast thing beside your pity, that the loss of your pity as well as your love is no great addition to my sorrow, nor does the gain of your pity make it sensibly less. Oh. sweet—how dearly you spoke to me behind the spear-bed at the washing-pool, and in the barn at the shearing, and that dearest last time in the evening at your home! Where are your pleasant words all gone—your earnest hope to be able to love me? Where is your firm conviction that you would get to care for me very much? Really forgotten? —really?'

She checked emotion, looked him quietly and clearly in the face, and said in her low, firm voice, 'Mr. Boldwood, I promised you nothing. Would you have had me a woman of clay when you paid me that furthest, highest compliment a man can pay a woman—telling her he loves her? I was bound to show some feeling, if I would not be a graceless shrew. Yet each of those pleasures was just for the day—the day just for the pleasure. How was I to know that what is a pastime to all other men was death to you? Have reason, do, and think more kindly of me!'

'Well, never mind arguing—never mind. One thing is sure : you were all but mine, and now you are not nearly mine. Everything is changed, and that by you alone, remember. You were nothing to me once, and I was contented ; you are now nothing to me again, and how different the second nothing is from the first! Would to God you had never taken me up, since it was only to throw me down!'

Bathsheba, in spite of her mettle, began to feel unmistakable signs that she was inherently the weaker vessel. She strove miserably against this femininity which would insist upon supplying unbidden emotions in stronger and stronger current. She had tried to elude agitation by fixing her mind on the trees, sky, any trivial object before her eyes, whilst his reproaches fell, but ingenuity could not save her now.

'I did not take you up—surely I did not!' she answered as heroically as she could. 'But don't be in this mood with me. I can endure being told I am in the wrong, if you will only tell it me gently! Oh sir, will you not kindly forgive me, and look at it cheerfully?'

'Cheerfully! Can a man fooled to utter heart-burning find a reason for being merry? If I have lost, how can I be as if I had won? Heavens, you must be heartless quite! Had I known what a fearfully bitter sweet this was to be, how I would have avoided you, and never seen you, and been deaf to you. I tell you all this, but what do you care! You don't care.'

She returned silent and weak denials to his charges, and swayed her head desperately, as if to thrust away the words as they came showering about her ears from the lips of the trembling man in the climax of life, with his bronzed Roman face and fine frame.

'Dearest, dearest, I am wavering even now between the two opposites of recklessly renouncing you, and labouring humbly for you again. Forget that you have said No, and let it be as it was! Say, Bathsheba, that you only wrote that refusal to me in fun—come, say it to me!'

'It would be untrue, and painful to both of us. You overrate my capacity for love. I don't possess half the warmth of nature you believe me to have. An unprotected childhood in a cold world has beaten gentleness out of me.'

He immediately said with more resentment: 'That may be true, somewhat; but ah, Miss Everdene, it won't do as a reason! You are not the cold woman you would have me believe. No, no! It isn't because you have no feeling in you that you don't love me. You naturally would have me think so—you would hide from me that you have a burning heart like mine. You have love enough, but it is turned into a new channel. I know where.'

The swift music of her heart became hubbub now, and she throbbed to extremity. He was coming to Troy. He did then know what had occurred! And the name fell from his lips the next moment.

'Why did Troy not leave my treasure alone?' he asked, fiercely. 'When I had no thought of injuring him, why did he force himself upon your notice! Before he worried you your inclination was to have me; when next I should have come to you your answer would have been Yes. Can you deny it—I ask, can you deny it?'

She delayed the reply, but was too honest to withhold it. 'I cannot,' she whispered.

'I know you cannot. But he stole in in my absence and robbed me. Why didn't he win you away before, when nobody would have been grieved?—when nobody would have been set tale-bearing. Now the people sneer at me—the very hills and sky seem to laugh at me till I blush shamefully for my folly. I have lost my respect, my good name, my standing—lost it, never to get it again. Go and marry your man—go on!'

'Oh, sir—Mr. Boldwood!'

'You may as well. I have no further claim upon you. As for me, I had better go somewhere alone, and hide—and pray. I loved a woman once. I am now ashamed. When I am dead they'll say, Miserable love-sick man that he was. Heaven—heaven—if I had got jilted secretly, and the dishonour not known, and my position kept! But no matter, it is gone, and the woman not gained. Shame upon him—shame!'

His unreasonable anger terrified her, and she glided from him, without obviously moving, as she said, 'I am only a girl—do not speak to me so!'

'All the time you knew—how very well you knew—that your new freak was my misery. Dazzled by brass and scarlet—Oh, Bathsheba—this is woman's folly indeed!'

She fired up at once. 'You are taking too much upon yourself!' she said, vehemently. 'Everybody is upon me — everybody. It is unmanly to attack a woman so! I have nobody in the world to fight my battles for me; but no mercy is shown. Yet if a thousand of you sneer and say things against me, I *will not* be put down!'

'You'll chatter with him doubtless about me. Say to him, "Boldwood would have died for me." Yes, and you have given way to him, knowing him to be not the man for you. He has kissed you—claimed you as his. Do you hear—he has kissed you. Deny it!'

The most tragic woman is cowed by a tragic man, and although Boldwood was, in vehemence and glow, nearly her own self rendered into another sex, Bathsheba's cheek quivered. She gasped, 'Leave me, sir—leave me! I am nothing to you. Let me go on!'

'Deny that he has kissed you.'

'I shall not.'

'Ha—then he has!' came hoarsely from the farmer.

'He has,' she said, slowly, and, in spite of her fear, defiantly. 'I am not ashamed to speak the truth.'

'Then curse him; and curse him!' said Boldwood, breaking into a whispered fury. 'Whilst I would have given worlds to touch your hand, you have let a rake come in without right or ceremony and—kiss you! Heaven's mercy—kiss you! . . . Ah, a time of his life shall come when he will have to repent, and think wretchedly of the pain he has caused another man ; and then may he ache, and wish, and curse, and yearn—as I do now !'

'Don't, don't, oh, don't pray down evil upon him !' she implored in a miserable cry. 'Anything but that—anything. Oh, be kind to him, sir, for I love him true !'

Boldwood's ideas had reached that point of fusion at which outline and consistency entirely disappear. The impending night appeared to concentrate in his eye. He did not hear her at all now.

'I'll punish him—by my soul, that will I ! I'll meet him, soldier or no, and I'll horsewhip the untimely stripling for this reckless theft of my one delight. If he were a hundred men I'd horsewhip him——' He dropped his voice suddenly and unnaturally. 'Bathsheba, sweet, lost coquette, pardon me ! I've been blaming you, threatening you, behaving like a churl to you, when he's the greatest sinner. He stole your dear heart away with his unfathomable lies ! . . . . It is a fortunate thing for him that he's gone back to his regiment—that he's away up the country, and not here ! I hope he may not return here just yet. I pray God he may not come into my sight, for I may be tempted beyond myself. Oh, Bathsheba, keep him away—yes, keep him away from me !'

For a moment Boldwood stood so inertly after this that his soul seemed to have been entirely exhaled with the breath of his passionate words. He turned his face away, and withdrew, and his form was soon covered over by the twilight as his footsteps mixed in with the low hiss of the leafy trees.

Bathsheba, who had been standing motionless as a model all this latter time, flung her hands to her face, and wildly attempted to ponder on the exhibition which had just passed away. Such astounding wells of fevered feeling in a still man like Mr. Boldwood were incomprehensible, dreadful. Instead of being a man trained to repression he was—what she had seen him.

The force of the farmer's threats lay in their relation to a circumstance known at present only to herself: her lover was coming back to Weatherbury in the course of the very next day or two. Troy had not returned to his distant barracks as Boldwood and others supposed, but had merely gone to visit some acquaintance in Bath, and had yet a week or more remaining to his furlough.

She felt wretchedly certain that if he revisited her just at this nick of time, and came into contact with Boldwood, a fierce quarrel would be the consequence. She panted with solicitude when she thought of possible injury to Troy. The least spark would kindle the farmer's swift feelings of rage and jealousy; he would lose his self-mastery as he had this evening; Troy's blitheness might become aggressive; it might take the direction of derision, and Boldwood's anger might then take the direction of revenge.

With almost a morbid dread of being thought a gushing girl, this guideless woman too well concealed from the world under a manner of carelessness the warm depths of her strong emotions. But now there was no reserve. In her distraction, instead of advancing further, she walked up and down, beating the air with her fingers, pressing her brow, and sobbing brokenly to herself. Then she sat down on a heap of stones by the wayside to think. There she remained long. Above the dark margin of the earth appeared foreshores and promontories of coppery cloud, bounding a green and pellucid expanse in the western sky. Amaranthine glosses came over them then, and the unresting world wheeled her round to a contrasting prospect eastward, in the shape of indecisive and palpitating stars. She gazed upon their silent throes amid the shades of space, but realized none at all. Her troubled spirit was far away with Troy.

CHAPTER XXXII

NIGHT—HORSES TRAMPING

THE village of Weatherbury was quiet as the graveyard in its midst, and the living were lying well-nigh as still as the dead. The church clock struck eleven. The air was so empty of other sounds that the whirr of the clock-work immediately before the strokes was distinct, and so was also the click of the same at their close. The notes flew forth with the usual blind obtuseness of inanimate things—flapping and rebounding among walls, undulating against the scattered clouds, spreading through their interstices into unexplored miles of space.

Bathsheba's crannied and mouldly halls were to-night occupied only by Maryann, Liddy being, as was stated, with her sister, whom Bathsheba had set out to visit. A few minutes after eleven had struck, Maryann turned in her bed with a sense of being disturbed. She was totally unconscious of the nature of the interruption to her sleep. It led to a dream, and the dream to an awakening, with an uneasy sensation that something had happened. She left her bed and looked out of the window. The paddock abutted on this end of the building, and in the paddock she could just discern by the uncertain gray a moving figure approaching the horse that was feeding there. The figure seized the horse by the forelock, and led it to the corner of the

244

field. Here she could see some object which circumstances proved to be a vehicle, for after a few minutes spent apparently in harnessing, she heard the trot of the horse down the road, mingled with the sound of light wheels.

Two varieties only of humanity could have entered the paddock with the ghost-like glide of that mysterious figure. They were a woman and a gipsy man. A woman was out of the question in such an occupation at this hour, and the comer could be no less than a thief, who might probably have known the weakness of the household on this particular night, and have chosen it on that account for his daring attempt. Moreover, to raise suspicion to conviction itself, there were gipsies in Weatherbury Bottom.

Maryann, who had been afraid to shout in the robber's presence, having seen him depart had no fear. She hastily slipped on her clothes, stumped down the disjointed staircase with its hundred creaks, ran to Coggan's, the nearest house, and raised an alarm. Coggan called Gabriel, who now again lodged in his house as at first, and together they went to the paddock. Beyond all doubt the horse was gone.

'Hark!' said Gabriel.

They listened. Distinct upon the stagnant air came the sounds of a trotting horse passing up Longpuddle Lane—just beyond the gipsies' encampment in Weatherbury Bottom.

'That's our Dainty—I'll swear to her step,' said Jan.

'Mighty me! Won't mis'ess storm and call us stupids when she comes back!' moaned Maryann. 'How I wish it had happened when she was at home, and none of us had been answerable!'

'We must ride after,' said Gabriel, decisively. 'I'll be responsible to Miss Everdene for what we do. Yes, we'll follow.'

'Faith, I don't see how,' said Coggan. 'All our

horses are too heavy for that trick except little Poppet, and what's she between two of us?—If we only had that pair over the hedge we might do something.'

'Which pair?'

'Mr. Boldwood's Tidy and Moll.'

'Then wait here till I come hither again,' said Gabriel. He ran down the hill towards Farmer Boldwood's.

'Farmer Boldwood is not at home,' said Maryann.

'All the better,' said Coggan. 'I know what he's gone for.'

Less than five minutes brought up Oak again, running at the same pace, with two halters dangling from his hand.

'Where did you find 'em?' said Coggan, turning round and leaping upon the hedge without waiting for an answer.

'Under the eaves. I knew where they were kept,' said Gabriel, following him. 'Coggan, you can ride bare-backed? there's no time to look for saddles.'

'Like a hero!' said Jan.

'Maryann, you go to bed,' Gabriel shouted to her from the top of the hedge.

Springing down into Boldwood's pastures, each pocketed his halter to hide it from the horses, who, seeing the men empty-handed, docilely allowed themselves to be seized by the mane, when the halters were dexterously slipped on. Having neither bit nor bridle, Oak and Coggan extemporized the former by passing the rope in each case through the animal's mouth and looping it on the other side. Oak vaulted astride, and Coggan clambered up by aid of the bank, when they ascended to the gate and galloped off in the direction taken by Bathsheba's horse and the robber. Whose vehicle the horse had been harnessed to was a matter of some uncertainty.

Weatherbury Bottom was reached in three or four minutes. They scanned the shady green patch by the roadside. The gipsies were gone.

'The villains!' said Gabriel. 'Which way have they gone, I wonder?'

'Straight on, as sure as God made little apples,' said Jan.

'Very well; we are better mounted, and must overtake 'em,' said Oak. 'Now, on at full speed!'

No sound of the rider in their van could now be discovered. The road-metal grew softer and more clayey as Weatherbury was left behind, and the late rain had wetted its surface to a somewhat plastic, but not muddy state. They came to cross-roads. Coggan suddenly pulled up Moll and slipped off.

'What's the matter?' said Gabriel.

'We must try to track 'em, since we can't hear 'em,' said Jan, fumbling in his pockets. He struck a light, and held the match to the ground. The rain had been heavier here, and all foot and horse tracks made previous to the storm had been abraded and blurred by the drops, and they were now so many little scoops of water, which reflected the flame of the match like eyes. One set of tracks was fresh and had no water in them; one pair of ruts was also empty, and not small canals, like the others. The footprints forming this recent impression were full of information as to pace; they were in equidistant pairs, three or four feet apart, the right and left foot of each pair being exactly opposite one another.

'Straight on!' Jan exclaimed. 'Tracks like that mean a stiff gallop. No wonder we don't hear him. And the horse is harnessed—look at the ruts. Ay, that's our mare, sure enough!'

'How do you know?'

'Old Jimmy Harris only shoed her last week, and I'd swear to his make among ten thousand.'

'The rest of the gipsies must ha' gone on earlier, or some other way,' said Oak. 'You saw there were no other tracks?'

'True.' They rode along silently for a long weary

time. Coggan carried an old pinchbeck repeater which he had inherited from some genius in his family; and it now struck one. He lighted another match, and examined the ground again.

''Tis a canter now,' he said, throwing away the light. 'A twisty, rickety pace for a gig. The fact is, they overdrove her at starting; we shall catch 'em yet.'

Again they hastened on, and entered Blackmore Vale. Coggan's watch struck one. When they looked again the hoof-marks were so spaced as to form a sort of zigzag if united, like the lamps along a street.

'That's a trot, I know,' said Gabriel.

'Only a trot now,' said Coggan, cheerfully. 'We shall overtake him in time.'

They pushed rapidly on for yet two or three miles. 'Ah! a moment,' said Jan. 'Let's see how she was driven up this hill. 'Twill help us.' A light was promptly struck upon his gaiters as before, and the examination made.

'Hurrah!' said Coggan. 'She walked up here—and well she might. We shall get them in two miles, for a crown.'

They rode three, and listened. No sound was to be heard save a mill-pond trickling hoarsely through a hatch, and suggesting gloomy possibilities of drowning by jumping in. Gabriel dismounted when they came to a turning. The tracks were absolutely the only guide as to the direction that they now had, and great caution was necessary to avoid confusing them with some others which had made their appearance lately.

'What does this mean?—though I guess,' said Gabriel, looking up at Coggan as he moved the match over the ground about the turning. Coggan, who, no less than the panting horses, had latterly shown signs of weariness, again scrutinized the mystic characters. This time only three were of the regular horseshoe shape. Every fourth was a dot.

He screwed up his face, and emitted a long
'whew-w-w!'

'Lame,' said Oak.

'Yes. Dainty is lamed; the near-foot-afore,' said
Coggan, slowly, staring still at the footprints.

'We'll push on,' said Gabriel, remounting his humid
steed.

Although the road along its greater part had been as
good as any turnpike-road in the country, it was nomin-
ally only a byway. The last turning had brought them
into the high road leading to Bath. Coggan recollected
himself.

'We shall have him now!' he exclaimed.

'Where?'

'Sherton Turnpike. The keeper of that gate is the
sleepiest man between here and London—Dan Randall,
that's his name—knowed en for years, when he was at
Casterbridge gate. Between the lameness and the gate
'tis a done job.'

They now advanced with extreme caution. Nothing
was said until, against a shady background of foliage,
five white bars were visible, crossing their route a little
way ahead.

'Hush—we are almost close!' said Gabriel.

'Amble on upon the grass,' said Coggan.

The white bars were blotted out in the midst by a
dark shape in front of them. The silence of this lonely
time was pierced by an exclamation from that quarter.

'Hoy-a-hoy! Gate!'

It appeared that there had been a previous call which
they had not noticed, for on their close approach the
door of the turnpike-house opened, and the keeper
came out half-dressed, with a candle in his hand. The
rays illumined the whole group.

'Keep the gate close!' shouted Gabriel. 'He has
stolen the horse!'

'Who?' said the turnpike-man.

Gabriel looked at the driver of the gig, and saw a woman—Bathsheba, his. mistress.

On hearing his voice she had turned her face away from the light. Coggan had, however, caught sight of her in the meanwhile.

'Why, 'tis mistress—I'll take my oath!' he said, amazed.

Bathsheba it certainly was, and she had by this time done the trick she could do so well in crises not of love, namely, mask a surprise by coolness of manner.

'Well, Gabriel,' she inquired quietly, 'where are you going?'

'We thought——' began Gabriel.

'I am driving to Bath,' she said, taking for her own use the assurance that Gabriel lacked. 'An important matter made it necessary for me to give up my visit to Liddy, and go off at once. What, then, were you following me?'

'We thought the horse was stole.'

'Well—what a thing! How very foolish of you not to know that I had taken the trap and horse. I could neither wake Maryann nor get into the house, though I hammered for ten minutes against her window-sill. Fortunately, I could get the key of the coach-house, so I troubled no one further. Didn't you think it might be me?'

'Why should we, miss?'

'Perhaps not. Why, those are never Farmer Bold-wood's horses! Goodness mercy! what have you been doing—bringing trouble upon me in this way? What! mustn't a lady move an inch from her door without being dogged like a thief?'

'But how was we to know, if you left no account of your doings?' expostulated Coggan, 'and ladies don't drive at these hours as a jineral rule of society.'

'I did leave an account—and you would have seen it in the morning. I wrote in chalk on the coach-house doors that I had come back for the horse and gig, and driven off; that I could arouse nobody, and should return soon.'

'But you'll consider, ma'am, that we couldn't see that till it got daylight.'

'True,' she said, and though vexed at first she had too much sense to blame them long or seriously for a devotion to her that was as valuable as it was rare. She added with a very pretty grace, 'Well, I really thank you heartily for taking all this trouble; but I wish you had borrowed anybody's horses but Mr. Boldwood's.'

'Dainty is lame, miss,' said Coggan. 'Can ye go on?'

'It was only a stone in her shoe. I got down and pulled it out a hundred yards back. I can manage very well, thank you. I shall be in Bath by daylight. Will you now return, please?'

She turned her head—the gateman's candle shimmering upon her quick, clear eyes as she did so—passed through the gate, and was soon wrapped in the embowering shades of mysterious summer boughs. Coggan and Gabriel put about their horses, and, fanned by the velvety air of this July night, retraced the road by which they had come.

'A strange vagary, this of hers, isn't it, Oak?' said Coggan, curiously.

'Yes,' said Gabriel, shortly.

'She won't be in Bath by no daylight!'

'Coggan, suppose we keep this night's work as quiet as we can?'

'I am of one and the same mind.'

'Very well. We shall be home by three o'clock or so, and can creep into the parish like lambs.'

Bathsheba's perturbed meditations by the roadside had ultimately evolved a conclusion that there were only two remedies for the present desperate state of affairs.

The first was merely to keep Troy away from Weatherbury till Boldwood's indignation had cooled; the second to listen to Oak's entreaties, and Boldwood's denunciations, and give up Troy altogether.

Alas! Could she give up this new love—induce him to renounce her by saying she did not like him—could no more speak to him, and beg him, for her good, to end his furlough in Bath, and see her and Weatherbury no more?

It was a picture full of misery, but for a while she contemplated it firmly, allowing herself, nevertheless, as girls will, to dwell upon the happy life she would have enjoyed had Troy been Boldwood, and the path of love the path of duty—inflicting upon herself gratuitous tortures by imagining him the lover of another woman after forgetting her; for she had penetrated Troy's nature so far as to estimate his tendencies pretty accurately, but unfortunately loved him no less in thinking that he might soon cease to love her—indeed, considerably more.

She jumped to her feet. She would see him at once. Yes, she would implore him by word of mouth to assist her in this dilemma. A letter to keep him away could not reach him in time, even if he should be disposed to listen to it.

Was Bathsheba altogether blind to the obvious fact that the support of a lover's arms is not of a kind best calculated to assist a resolve to renounce him? Or was she sophistically sensible, with a thrill of pleasure, that by adopting this course for getting rid of him she was ensuring a meeting with him, at any rate, once more?

It was now dark, and the hour must have been nearly ten. The only way to accomplish her purpose was to give up her idea of visiting Liddy at Yalbury, return to Weatherbury Farm, put the horse into the gig, and drive at once to Bath. The scheme seemed at first impossible: the journey was a fearfully heavy one, even for a strong horse, at her own estimate; and she much underrated the distance. It was most venturesome for a woman, at night, and alone.

But could she go on to Liddy's and leave things to take their course? No, no; anything but that. Bathsheba was full of a stimulating turbulence, beside which caution vainly prayed for a hearing. She turned back towards the village.

Her walk was slow, for she wished not to enter Weatherbury till the cottagers were in bed, and, particularly, till Boldwood was secure. Her plan was now to drive to Bath during the night, see Sergeant Troy in the morning before he set out to come to her, bid him farewell, and dismiss him: then to rest the horse thoroughly (herself to weep the while, she thought), starting early the next morning on her return journey. By this arrangement she could trot Dainty gently all the day, reach Liddy at Yalbury in the evening, and come home to Weatherbury with her whenever they chose—so nobody would know she had been to Bath at all.

This idea she proceeded to carry out, with what success we have already seen.

CHAPTER XXXIII

IN THE SUN—A HARBINGER

A WEEK passed, and there were no tidings of Bath- sheba; nor was there any explanation of her Gilpin's rig.

Then a note came for Maryann, stating that the business which had called her mistress to Bath still detained her there; but that she hoped to return in the course of another week.

Another week passed. The oat-harvest began, and all the men were a-field under a monochromatic Lammas sky, amid the trembling air and short shadows of noon. Indoors nothing was to be heard save the droning of blue-bottle flies; out-of-doors the whetting of scythes and the hiss of tressy oat-ears rubbing together as their perpendicular stalks of amber-yellow fell heavily to each swath. Every drop of moisture not in the men's bottles and flagons in the form of cider was raining as perspiration from their foreheads and cheeks. Drought was everywhere else.

They were about to withdraw for a while into the charitable shade of a tree in the fence, when Coggan saw a figure in a blue coat and brass buttons running to them across the field.

'I wonder who that is?' he said.

'I hope nothing is wrong about mistress,' said

254

Maryann, who with some other women was tying the bundles (oats being always sheafed on this farm), 'but an unlucky token came to me indoors this morning. I went to unlock the door and dropped the key, and it fell upon the stone floor and broke into two pieces. Breaking a key is a dreadful bodement. I wish mis'ess was home.'

''Tis Cain Ball,' said Gabriel, pausing from whetting his reaphook.

Oak was not bound by his agreement to assist in the corn-field; but the harvest month is an anxious time for a farmer, and the corn was Bathsheba's, so he lent a hand.

'He's dressed up in his best clothes,' said Matthew Moon. 'He hev been away from home for a few days, since he's had that felon upon his finger; for 'a said, since I can't work I'll have a hollerday.'

'A good time for one—a' excellent time,' said Joseph Poorgrass, straightening his back; for he, like some of the others, had a way of resting a while from his labour on such hot days for reasons preternaturally small; of which Cain Ball's advent on a week-day in his Sunday-clothes was one of the first magnitude. ''Twas a bad leg allowed me to read the *Pilgrim's Progress*, and Mark Clark learnt All-Fours in a whitlow.'

'Ay, and my father put his arm out of joint to have time to go courting,' said Jan Coggan, in an eclipsing tone, wiping his face with his shirt-sleeve and thrusting back his hat upon the nape of his neck.

By this time Cainy was nearing the group of harvesters, and was perceived to be carrying a large slice of bread and ham in one hand, from which he took mouthfuls as he ran, the other being wrapped in a bandage. When he came close, his mouth assumed the bell shape, and he began to cough violently.

'Now, Cainy!' said Gabriel, sternly 'How many more times must I tell you to keep from running so fast when you be eating? You'll choke yourself some day, that's what you'll do, Cain Ball.'

'Hok-hok-hok!' replied Cain. 'A crumb of my victuals went the wrong way—hok-hok! That's what 'tis, Mister Oak! And I've been visiting to Bath because I had a felon on my thumb; yes, and I've seen—ahok-hok!'

Directly Cain mentioned Bath, they all threw down their hooks and forks and drew round him. Unfortunately the erratic crumb did not improve his narrative powers, and a supplementary hindrance was that of a sneeze, jerking from his pocket his rather large watch, which dangled in front of the young man pendulum-wise.

'Yes,' he continued, directing his thoughts to Bath and letting his eyes follow, 'I've seed the world at last —yes—and I've seed our mis'ess—ahok-hok-hok!'

'Bother the boy!' said Gabriel. 'Something is always going the wrong way down your throat, so that you can't tell what's necessary to be told.'

'Ahok! there! Please, Mister Oak, a gnat have just fleed into my stomach and brought the cough on again!'

'Yes, that's just it. Your mouth is always open, you young rascal!'

''Tis terrible bad to have a gnat fly down yer throat, pore boy!' said Matthew Moon.

'Well, at Bath you saw——' prompted Gabriel.

'I saw our mistress,' continued the junior shepherd, 'and a sojer, walking along. And bymeby they got closer and closer, and then they went arm-in-crook, like courting complete—hok-hok! like courting complete— hok!—courting complete——' Losing the thread of his narrative at this point simultaneously with his loss of breath, their informant looked up and down the field apparently for some clue to it. 'Well, I see our mis'ess and a soldier—a-ha-a-wk!'

'Damn the boy!' said Gabriel.

''Tis only my manner, Mister Oak, if ye'll excuse it,' said Cain Ball, looking reproachfully at Oak, with eyes drenched in their own dew.

'Here's some cider for him—that'll cure his throat,' said Jan Coggan, lifting a flagon of cider, pulling out the cork, and applying the hole to Cainy's mouth; Joseph Poorgrass in the meantime beginning to think apprehensively of the serious consequences that would follow Cainy Ball's strangulation in his cough, and the history of his Bath adventures dying with him.

'For my poor self, I always say "please God" afore I do anything,' said Joseph, in an unboastful voice; 'and so should you, Cain Ball. 'Tis a great safeguard, and might perhaps save you from being choked to death some day.'

Mr. Coggan poured the liquor with unstinted liberality at the suffering Cain's circular mouth; half of it running down the side of the flagon, and half of what reached his mouth running down outside his throat, and half of what ran in going the wrong way, and being coughed and sneezed around the persons of the gathered reapers in the form of a cider fog, which for a moment hung in the sunny air like a small exhalation.

'There's a great clumsy sneeze! Why can't ye have better manners, you young dog!' said Coggan, withdrawing the flagon.

'The cider went up my nose!' cried Cainy, as soon as he could speak; 'and now 'tis gone down my neck, and into my poor dumb felon, and over my shiny buttons and all my best cloze!'

'The poor lad's cough is terrible onfortunate,' said Matthew Moon. 'And a great history on hand, too. Bump his back, shepherd.'

''Tis my nater,' mourned Cain. 'Mother says I always was so excitable when my feelings were worked up to a point!'

'True, true,' said Joseph Poorgrass. 'The Balls were always a very excitable family. I knowed the boy's grandfather—a truly nervous and modest man, even to genteel refinery. 'Twas blush, blush with him, almost as much as 'tis with me—not but that 'tis a fault in me!'

'Not at all, Master Poorgrass,' said Coggan. ''Tis a very noble quality in ye.'

'Heh-heh! well, I wish to noise nothing abroad— nothing at all,' murmured Poorgrass, diffidently. 'But we be born to things—that's true. Yet I would rather my trifle were hid; though, perhaps, a high nater is a little high, and at my birth all things were possible to my Maker, and he may have begrudged no gifts. . . . But under your bushel, Joseph! under your bushel with 'ee! A strange desire, neighbours, this desire to hide, and no praise due. Yet there is a Sermon on the Mount with a calendar of the blessed at the head, and certain meek men may be named therein.'

'Cainy's grandfather was a very clever man,' said Matthew Moon. 'Invented a' apple-tree out of his own head, which is called by his name to this day—the Early Ball. You know 'em, Jan? A Quarrenden grafted on a Tom Putt, and a Rathe-ripe upon top o' that again. 'Tis trew 'a used to bide about in a public-house in a way he had no business to by rights, but there—'a were a clever man in the sense of the term.'

'Now then,' said Gabriel, impatiently, 'what did you see, Cain?'

'I seed our mis'ess go into a sort of a park place, where there's seats, and shrubs and flowers, arm-in-crook with a sojer,' continued Cainy, firmly, and with a dim sense that his words were very effective as regarded Gabriel's emotions. 'And I think the sojer was Sergeant Troy. And they sat there together for more than half-an-hour, talking moving things, and she once was crying a'most to death. And when they came out

her eyes were shining and she was as white as a lily;
and they looked into one another's faces, as far-gone
friendly as a man and woman can be.'

Gabriel's features seemed to get thinner. 'Well,
what did you see besides?'

'Oh, all sorts.'

'White as a lily? You are sure 'twas she?'

'Yes.'

'Well, what besides?'

'Great glass windows to the shops, and great clouds
in the sky, full of rain, and old wooden trees in the
country round.'

'You stun-poll! What will ye say next?' said
Coggan.

'Let en alone,' interposed Joseph Poorgrass. 'The
boy's maning is that the sky and the earth in the
kingdom of Bath is not altogether different from ours
here. 'Tis for our good to gain knowledge of strange
cities, and as such the boy's words should be suffered,
so to speak it.'

'And the people of Bath,' continued Cain, 'never
need to light their fires except as a luxury, for the
water springs up out of the earth ready boiled for
use.'

''Tis true as the light,' testified Matthew Moon. 'I've
heard other navigators say the same thing.'

'They drink nothing else there,' said Cain, 'and seem
to enjoy it, to see how they swaller it down.'

'Well, it seems a barbarian practice enough to us,
but I daresay the natives think nothing o' it,' said
Matthew.

'And don't victuals spring up as well as drink?'
asked Coggan, twirling his eye.

'No—I own to a blot there in Bath—a true blot.
God didn't provide 'em with victuals as well as drink,
and 'twas a drawback I couldn't get over at all.'

'Well, 'tis a curious place, to say the least,' observed

Moon; 'and it must be a curious people that live therein.'

'Miss Everdene and the soldier were walking about together, you say?' said Gabriel, returning to the group.

'Ay, and she wore a beautiful gold-colour silk gown, trimmed with black lace, that would have stood alone 'ithout legs inside if required. 'Twas a very winsome sight; and her hair was brushed splendid. And when the sun shone upon the bright gown and his red coat—my! how handsome they looked. You could see 'em all the length of the street.'

'And what then?' murmured Gabriel.

'And then I went into Griffin's to hae my boots hobbed, and then I went to Riggs's batty-cake shop, and asked 'em for a penneth of the cheapest and nicest stales, that were all but blue-mouldy, but not quite. And whilst I was chawing 'em down I walked on and seed a clock with a face as big as a baking trendle——'

'But that's nothing to do with mistress!'

'I'm coming to that, if you'll leave me alone, Mister Oak!' remonstrated Cainy. 'If you excites me, perhaps you'll bring on my cough, and then I shan't be able to tell ye nothing.'

'Yes—let him tell it his own way,' said Coggan.

Gabriel settled into a despairing attitude of patience, and Cainy went on :—

'And there were great large houses, and more people all the week long than at Weatherbury club-walking on White Tuesdays. And I went to grand churches and chapels. And how the parson would pray! Yes; he would kneel down and put up his hands together, and make the holy gold rings on his fingers gleam and twinkle in yer eyes, that he'd earned by praying so excellent well!—Ah yes, I wish I lived there.'

'Our poor Parson Thirdly can't get no money to

buy such rings,' said Matthew Moon, thoughtfully.
'And as good a man as ever walked. I don't believe
poor Thirdly have a single one, even of humblest tin or
copper. Such a great ornament as they'd be to him on
a dull a'ternoon, when he's up in the pulpit lighted by
the wax candles! But 'tis impossible, poor man. Ah,
to think how unequal things be.'

'Perhaps he's made of different stuff than to wear
'em,' said Gabriel, grimly. 'Well, that's enough of this.
Go on, Cainy—quick.'

'Oh—and the new style of pa'sons wear moustaches
and long beards,' continued the illustrious traveller,
'and look like Moses and Aaron complete, and make
we fokes in the congregation feel all over like the
children of Israel.'

'A very right feeling—very,' said Joseph Poorgrass.

'And there's two religions going on in the nation
now—High Church and High Chapel. And, thinks I,
I'll play fair; so I went to High Church in the morning,
and High Chapel in the afternoon.'

'A right and proper boy,' said Joseph Poorgrass.

'Well, at High Church they pray singing, and worship
all the colours of the rainbow; and at High Chapel they
pray preaching, and worship drab and whitewash only.
And then—I didn't see no more of Miss Everdene at
all.'

'Why didn't you say so afore, then?' exclaimed Oak,
with much disappointment.

'Ah,' said Matthew Moon, 'she'll wish her cake
dough if so be she's over intimate with that man.'

'She's not over intimate with him,' said Gabriel,
indignantly.

'She would know better,' said Coggan. 'Our
mis'ess has too much sense under they knots of black
hair to do such a mad thing.'

'You see, he's not a coarse, ignorant man, for he
was well brought up,' said Matthew, dubiously. ''Twas

only wildness that made him a soldier, and maids rather like your man of sin.'

'Now, Cain Ball,' said Gabriel restlessly, 'can you swear in the most awful form that the woman you saw was Miss Everdene?'

'Cain Ball, you be no longer a babe and suckling,' said Joseph in the sepulchral tone the circumstances demanded, 'and you know what taking an oath is. 'Tis a horrible testament mind ye, which you say and seal with your blood-stone, and the prophet Matthew tells us that on whomsoever it shall fall it will grind him to powder. Now, before all the work-folk here assembled, can you swear to your words as the shepherd asks ye?'

'Please no, Mister Oak!' said Cainy, looking from one to the other with great uneasiness at the spiritual magnitude of the position. 'I don't mind saying 'tis true, but I don't like to say 'tis damn true, if that's what you mane.'

'Cain, Cain, how can you!' asked Joseph sternly. 'You be asked to swear in a holy manner, and you swear like wicked Shimei, the son of Gera, who cursed as he came. Young man, fie!'

'No, I don't! 'Tis you want to squander a pore boy's soul, Joseph Poorgrass—that's what 'tis!' said Cain, beginning to cry. 'All I mane is that in common truth 'twas Miss Everdene and Sergeant Troy, but in the horrible so-help-me truth that ye want to make of it perhaps 'twas somebody else!'

'There's no getting at the rights of it,' said Gabriel, turning to his work.

'Cain Ball, you'll come to a bit of bread!' groaned Joseph Poorgrass.

Then the reapers' hooks were flourished again, and the old sounds went on. Gabriel, without making any pretence of being lively, did nothing to show that he was particularly dull. However, Coggan knew pretty nearly how the land lay, and when they were in a nook together he said—

'Don't take on about her, Gabriel. What difference does it make whose sweetheart she is, since she can't be yours?'

'That's the very thing I say to myself,' said Gabriel.

CHAPTER XXXIV

HOME AGAIN—A TRICKSTER

THAT same evening at dusk Gabriel was leaning over Coggan's garden-gate, taking an up-and-down survey before retiring to rest.

A vehicle of some kind was softly creeping along the grassy margin of the lane. From it spread the tones of two women talking. The tones were natural and not at all suppressed. Oak instantly knew the voices to be those of Bathsheba and Liddy.

The carriage came opposite and passed by. It was Miss Everdene's gig, and Liddy and her mistress were the only occupants of the seat. Liddy was asking questions about the city of Bath, and her companion was answering them listlessly and unconcernedly. Both Bathsheba and the horse seemed weary.

The exquisite relief of finding that she was here again, safe and sound, overpowered all reflection, and Oak could only luxuriate in the sense of it. All grave reports were forgotten.

He lingered and lingered on, till there was no difference between the eastern and western expanses of sky, and the timid hares began to limp courageously round the dim hillocks. Gabriel might have been there an additional half-hour when a dark form walked slowly by. 'Good-night, Gabriel,' the passer said.

It was Boldwood. 'Good-night, sir,' said Gabriel.

Boldwood likewise vanished up the road, and Oak shortly afterwards turned indoors to bed.

Farmer Boldwood went on towards Miss Everdene's house. He reached the front, and approaching the entrance, saw a light in the parlour. The blind was not drawn down, and inside the room was Bathsheba, looking over some papers or letters. Her back was towards Boldwood. He went to the door, knocked, and waited with tense muscles and an aching brow.

Boldwood had not been outside his garden since his meeting with Bathsheba in the road to Yalbury. Silent and alone, he had remained in moody meditation on woman's ways, deeming as essentials of the whole sex the accidents of the single one of their number he had ever closely beheld. By degrees a more charitable temper had pervaded him, and this was the reason of his sally to-night. He had come to apologize and beg forgiveness of Bathsheba with something like a sense of shame at his violence, having but just now learnt that she had returned—only from a visit to Liddy, as he supposed, the Bath escapade being quite unknown to him.

He inquired for Miss Everdene. Liddy's manner was odd, but he did not notice it. She went in, leaving him standing there, and in her absence the blind of the room containing Bathsheba was pulled down. Boldwood augured ill from that sign. Liddy came out.

'My mistress cannot see you, sir,' she said.

The farmer instantly went out by the gate. He was unforgiven—that was the issue of it all. He had seen her who was to him simultaneously a delight and a torture, sitting in the room he had shared with her as a peculiarly privileged guest only a little earlier in the summer, and she had denied him an entrance there now.

Boldwood did not hurry homeward. It was ten

o'clock at least, when, walking deliberately through the lower part of Weatherbury, he heard the carrier's spring van entering the village. The van ran to and from a town in a northern direction, and it was owned and driven by a Weatherbury man, at the door of whose house it now pulled up. The lamp fixed to the head of the hood illuminated a scarlet and gilded form, who was the first to alight.

'Ah !' said Boldwood to himself, 'come to see her again.'

Troy entered the carrier's house, which had been the place of his lodging on his last visit to his native place. Boldwood was moved by a sudden determination. He hastened home. In ten minutes he was back again, and made as if he were going to call upon Troy at the carrier's. But as he approached, some one opened the door and came out. He heard this person say 'Good-night' to the inmates, and the voice was Troy's. This was strange, coming so immediately after his arrival. Boldwood, however, hastened up to him. Troy had what appeared to be a carpet-bag in his hand—the same that he had brought with him. It seemed as if he were going to leave again this very night.

Troy turned up the hill and quickened his pace. Boldwood stepped forward.

'Sergeant Troy?'

'Yes—I'm Sergeant Troy.'

'Just arrived from up the country, I think?'

'Just arrived from Bath.'

'I am William Boldwood.'

'Indeed.'

The tone in which this word was uttered was all that had been wanted to bring Boldwood to the point.

'I wish to speak a word with you,' he said.

'What about?'

'About her who lives just ahead there—and about a woman you have wronged.'

'I wonder at your impertinence,' said Troy, moving on.

'Now look here,' said Boldwood, standing in front of him, 'wonder or not, you are going to hold a conversation with me.'

Troy heard the dull determination in Boldwood's voice, looked at his stalwart frame, then at the thick cudgel he carried in his hand. He remembered it was past ten o'clock. It seemed worth while to be civil to Boldwood.

'Very well, I'll listen with pleasure,' said Troy, placing his bag on the ground, 'only speak low, for somebody or other may overhear us in the farmhouse there.'

'Well then—I know a good deal concerning your—Fanny Robin's attachment to you. I may say, too, that I believe I am the only person in the village, excepting Gabriel Oak, who does know it. You ought to marry her.'

'I suppose I ought. Indeed, I wish to, but I cannot.'

'Why?'

Troy was about to utter something hastily; he then checked himself and said, 'I am too poor.' His voice was changed. Previously it had had a devil-may-care tone. It was the voice of a trickster now.

Boldwood's present mood was not critical enough to notice tones. He continued, 'I may as well speak plainly; and understand, I don't wish to enter into the questions of right or wrong, woman's honour and shame, or to express any opinion on your conduct. I intend a business transaction with you.'

'I see,' said Troy. 'Suppose we sit down here.'

An old tree trunk lay under the hedge immediately opposite, and they sat down.

'I was engaged to be married to Miss Everdene,' said Boldwood, 'but you came and——'

'Not engaged,' said Troy.

'As good as engaged.'

'If I had not turned up she might have become engaged to you.'

'Hang might!'

'Would, then.'

'If you had not come I should certainly—yes, *certainly*—have been accepted by this time. If you had not seen her you might have been married to Fanny. Well, there's too much difference between Miss Everdene's station and your own for this flirtation with her ever to benefit you by ending in marriage. So all I ask is, don't molest her any more. Marry Fanny. I'll make it worth your while.'

'How will you?'

'I'll pay you well now, I'll settle a sum of money upon her, and I'll see that you don't suffer from poverty in the future. I'll put it clearly. Bathsheba is only playing with you : you are too poor for her as I said ; so give up wasting your time about a great match you'll never make for a moderate and rightful match you may make to-morrow ; take up your carpet-bag, turn about, leave Weatherbury now, this night, and you shall take fifty pounds with you. Fanny shall have fifty to enable her to prepare for the wedding, when you have told me where she is living, and she shall have five hundred paid down on her wedding-day.'

In making this statement Boldwood's voice revealed only too clearly a consciousness of the weakness of his position, his aims, and his method. His manner had lapsed quite from that of the firm and dignified Boldwood of former times ; and such a scheme as he had now engaged in he would have condemned as childishly imbecile only a few months ago. We discern a grand force in the lover which he lacks whilst a free man ; but there is a breadth of vision in the free man which in the lover we vainly seek. Where there is much bias there must be some narrowness, and love, though added emotion, is subtracted capacity. Boldwood exemplified this to an abnormal degree : he knew nothing of Fanny Robin's circumstances or whereabouts, he knew nothing of Troy's possibilities, yet that was what he said.

'I like Fanny best,' said Troy; 'and if, as you say, Miss Everdene is out of my reach, why I have all to gain by accepting your money, and marrying Fan. But she's only a servant.'

'Never mind—do you agree to my arrangement?'

'I do.'

'Ah!' said Boldwood, in a more elastic voice. 'Oh Troy, if you like her best, why then did you step in here and injure my happiness?'

'I love Fanny best now,' said Troy. 'But Bathsh——Miss Everdene inflamed me, and displaced Fanny for a time. It is over now.'

'Why should it be over so soon? And why then did you come here again?'

'There are weighty reasons. Fifty pounds at once, you said!'

'I did,' said Boldwood, 'and here they are—fifty sovereigns.' He handed Troy a small packet.

'You have everything ready—it seems that you calculated on my accepting them,' said the sergeant, taking the packet.

'I thought you might accept them,' said Boldwood.

'You've only my word that the programme shall be adhered to, whilst I at any rate have fifty pounds.'

'I had thought of that, and I have considered that if I can't appeal to your honour I can trust to your— well, shrewdness we'll call it—not to lose five hundred pounds in prospèct, and also make a bitter enemy of a man who is willing to be an extremely useful friend.'

'Stop, listen!' said Troy in a whisper.

A light pit-pat was audible upon the road just above them.

'By George—'tis she,' he continued. 'I must go on and meet her.'

'She—who?'

'Bathsheba.'

'Bathsheba—out alone at this time o' night!' said Boldwood in amazement, and starting up. 'Why must you meet her?'

'She was expecting me to-night—and I must now speak to her, and wish her good-bye, according to your wish.'

'I don't see the necessity of speaking.'

'It can do no harm—and she'll be wandering about looking for me if I don't. You shall hear all I say to her. It will help you in your love-making when I am gone.'

'Your tone is mocking.'

'Oh no. And remember this, if she does not know what has become of me, she will think more about me than if I tell her flatly I have come to give her up.'

'Will you confine your words to that one point?—Shall I hear every word you say?'

'Every word. Now sit still there, and hold my carpet bag for me, and mark what you hear.'

The light footstep came closer, halting occasionally, as if the walker listened for a sound. Troy whistled a double note in a soft, fluty tone.

'Come to that, is it!' murmured Boldwood, uneasily.

'You promised silence,' said Troy.

'I promise again.'

Troy stepped forward.

'Frank, dearest, is that you?' The tones were Bathsheba's.

'O God!' said Boldwood.

'Yes,' said Troy to her.

'How late you are,' she continued, tenderly. 'Did you come by the carrier? I listened and heard his wheels entering the village, but it was some time ago, and I had almost given you up, Frank.'

'I was sure to come,' said Frank. 'You knew I should, did you not?'

'Well, I thought you would,' she said, playfully; 'and, Frank, it is so lucky! There's not a soul in my house but me to-night. I've packed them all off, so nobody on earth will know of your visit to your lady's bower. Liddy wanted to go to her grandfather's to tell him about her holiday, and I said she might stay with them till to-morrow—when you'll be gone again.'

'Capital,' said Troy. 'But, dear me, I had better go back for my bag, because my slippers and brush and comb are in it; you run home whilst I fetch it, and I'll promise to be in your parlour in ten minutes.'

'Yes.' She turned and tripped up the hill again.

During the progress of this dialogue there was a nervous twitching of Boldwood's tightly closed lips, and his face became bathed in a clammy dew. He now started forward towards Troy. Troy turned to him and took up the bag.

'Shall I tell her I have come to give her up and cannot marry her?' said the soldier, mockingly.

'No, no; wait a minute. I want to say more to you—more to you!' said Boldwood, in a hoarse whisper.

'Now,' said Troy, 'you see my dilemma. Perhaps I am a bad man—the victim of my impulses—led away to do what I ought to leave undone. I can't, however, marry them both. And I have two reasons for choosing Fanny. First, I like her best upon the whole, and second, you make it worth my while.'

At the same instant Boldwood sprang upon him, and held him by the neck. Troy felt Boldwood's grasp slowly tightening. The move was absolutely unexpected.

'A moment,' he gasped. 'You are injuring her you love!'

'Well, what do you mean?' said the farmer.

'Give me breath,' said Troy.

Boldwood loosened his hand, saying, 'By Heaven, I've a mind to kill you!'

'And ruin her.'

'Save her.'

'Oh, how can she be saved now, unless I marry her?'

Boldwood groaned. He reluctantly released the soldier, and flung him back against the hedge. 'Devil, you torture me!' said he.

Troy rebounded like a ball, and was about to make a dash at the farmer; but he checked himself, saying lightly—

'It is not worth while to measure my strength with you. Indeed it is a barbarous way of settling a quarrel. I shall shortly leave the army because of the same conviction. Now after that revelation of how the land lies with Bathsheba, 'twould be a mistake to kill me, would it not?'

''Twould be a mistake to kill you,' repeated Boldwood, mechanically, with a bowed head.

'Better kill yourself.'

'Far better.'

'I'm glad you see it.'

'Troy, make her your wife, and don't act upon what I arranged just now. The alternative is dreadful, but take Bathsheba; I give her up! She must love you indeed to sell soul and body to you so utterly as she has done. Wretched woman—deluded woman—you are, Bathsheba!'

'But about Fanny?'

'Bathsheba is a woman well to do,' continued Boldwood, in nervous anxiety, 'and, Troy, she will make a good wife; and, indeed, she is worth your hastening on your marriage with her!'

'But she has a will—not to say a temper, and I shall be a mere slave to her. I could do anything with poor Fanny Robin.'

'Troy,' said Boldwood, imploringly, 'I'll do anything for you, only don't desert her; pray don't desert her, Troy.'

'Which, poor Fanny?'

'No; Bathsheba Everdene. Love her best! Love her tenderly! How shall I get you to see how advantageous it will be to you to secure her at once?'

'I don't wish to secure her in any new way.'

Boldwood's arm moved spasmodically towards Troy's person again. He repressed the instinct, and his form drooped as with pain.

Troy went on—

'I shall soon purchase my discharge, and then——'

'But I wish you to hasten on this marriage! It will be better for you both. You love each other, and you must let me help you to do it.'

'How?'

'Why, by settling the five hundred on Bathsheba instead of Fanny, to enable you to marry at once. No; she wouldn't have it of me. I'll pay it down to you on the wedding-day.'

Troy paused in secret amazement at Boldwood's wild infatuation. He carelessly said, 'And am I to have anything now?'

'Yes, if you wish to. But I have not much additional money with me. I did not expect this; but all I have is yours.'

Boldwood, more like a somnambulist than a wakeful man, pulled out the large canvas bag he carried by way of a purse, and searched it.

'I have twenty-one pounds more with me,' he said. 'Two notes and a sovereign. But before I leave you I must have a paper signed——'

'Pay me the money, and we'll go straight to her parlour, and make any arrangement you please to secure my compliance with your wishes. But she must know nothing of this cash business.'

'Nothing, nothing,' said Boldwood, hastily. 'Here is the sum, and if you'll come to my house we'll write out the agreement for the remainder, and the terms also.'

'First we'll call upon her.'

'But why? Come with me to-night, and go with me to-morrow to the surrogate's.'.

'But she must be consulted; at any rate informed.'

'Very well; go on.'

They went up the hill to Bathsheba's house. When they stood at the entrance, Troy said, 'Wait here a moment.' Opening the door, he glided inside, leaving the door ajar.

Boldwood waited. In two minutes a light appeared in the passage. Boldwood then saw that the chain had been fastened across the door. Troy appeared inside, carrying a bedroom candlestick.

'What, did you think I should break in?' said Boldwood, contemptuously.

'Oh no; it is merely my humour to secure things. Will you read this a moment? I'll hold the light.'

Troy handed a folded newspaper through the slit between door and doorpost, and put the candle close. 'That's the paragraph,' he said, placing his finger on a line.

Boldwood looked and read—

'MARRIAGES.

'On the 17th inst., at St. Ambrose's Church, Bath, by the Rev. G. Mincing, B.A., Francis Troy, only son of the late Edward Troy, Esq., M.D., of Weatherbury, and sergeant 11th Dragoon Guards, to Bathsheba, only surviving daughter of the late Mr. John Everdene, of Casterbridge.'

'This may be called Fort meeting Feeble, hey, Boldwood?' said Troy. A low gurgle of derisive laughter followed the words.

The paper fell from Boldwood's hands. Troy continued—

'Fifty pounds to marry Fanny. Good. Twenty-one pounds not to marry Fanny, but Bathsheba. Good. Finale: already Bathsheba's husband. Now, Boldwood, yours is the ridiculous fate which always attends interference between a man and his wife. And another word. Bad as I am, I am not such a villain as to make the marriage or misery of any woman a matter of huckster and sale. Fanny has long ago left me. I don't know where she is. I have searched everywhere. Another word yet. You say you love Bathsheba; yet on the merest apparent evidence you instantly believe in her dishonour. A fig for such love! Now that I've taught you a lesson, take your money back again.'

'I will not; I will not!' said Boldwood, in a hiss.

'Anyhow I won't have it,' said Troy, contemptuously. He wrapped the packet of gold in the notes, and threw the whole into the road.

Boldwood shook his clenched fist at him. 'You juggler of Satan! You black hound! But I'll punish you yet; mark me, I'll punish you yet!'

Another peal of laughter. Troy then closed the door, and locked himself in.

Throughout the whole of that night Boldwood's dark form might have been seen walking about the hills and downs of Weatherbury like an unhappy Shade in the Mournful Fields by Acheron.

CHAPTER XXXV

AT AN UPPER WINDOW

IT was very early the next morning—a time of sun and dew. The confused beginnings of many birds' songs spread into the healthy air, and the wan blue of the heaven was here and there coated with thin webs of incorporeal cloud which were of no effect in obscuring day. All the lights in the scene were yellow as to colour, and all the shadows were attenuated as to form. The creeping plants about the old manor-house were bowed with rows of heavy water drops, which had upon objects behind them the effect of minute lenses of high magnifying power.

Just before the clock struck five Gabriel Oak and Coggan passed the village cross, and went on together to the fields. They were yet barely in view of their mistress's house, when Oak fancied he saw the opening of a casement in one of the upper windows. The two men were at this moment partially screened by an elder bush, now beginning to be enriched with black bunches of fruit, and they paused before emerging from its shade.

A handsome man leaned idly from the lattice. He looked east and then west, in the manner of one who makes a first morning survey. The man was Sergeant Troy. His red jacket was loosely thrown on, but not buttoned, and he had altogether the relaxed bearing of a soldier taking his ease.

Coggan spoke first, looking quietly at the window. 'She has married him!' he said.

Gabriel had previously beheld the sight, and he now stood with his back turned, making no reply.

'I fancied we should know something to-day,' continued Coggan. 'I heard wheels pass my door just after dark—you were out somewhere.' He glanced round upon Gabriel. 'Good heavens above us, Oak, how white your face is; you look like a corpse!'

'Do I?' said Oak, with a faint smile.

'Lean on the gate: I'll wait a bit.'

'All right, all right.'

They stood by the gate awhile, Gabriel listlessly staring at the ground. His mind sped into the future, and saw there enacted in years of leisure the scenes of repentance that would ensue from this work of haste. That they were married he had instantly decided. Why had it been so mysteriously managed? It had become known that she had had a fearful journey to Bath, owing to her miscalculating the distance: that the horse had broken down, and that she had been more than two days getting there. It was not Bathsheba's way to do things furtively. With all her faults, she was candour itself. Could she have been entrapped? The union was not only an unutterable grief to him: it amazed him, notwithstanding that he had passed the preceding week in a suspicion that such might be the issue of Troy's meeting her away from home. Her quiet return with Liddy had to some extent dispersed the dread. Just as that imperceptible motion which appears like stillness is infinitely divided in its properties from stillness itself, so had his hope undistinguishable from despair differed from despair indeed.

In a few minutes they moved on again towards the house. The sergeant still looked from the window.

'Morning, comrades!' he shouted, in a cheery voice, when they came up.

Coggan replied to the greeting. 'Baint ye going to answer the man?' he then said to Gabriel. 'I'd say good morning—you needn't spend a hapeth of meaning upon it, and yet keep the man civil.'

Gabriel soon decided too that, since the deed was done, to put the best face upon the matter would be the greatest kindness to her he loved.

'Good morning, Sergeant Troy,' he returned, in a ghastly voice.

'A rambling, gloomy house this,' said Troy, smiling.

'Why—they *may* not be married!' suggested Coggan. 'Perhaps she's not there.'

Gabriel shook his head. The soldier turned a little towards the east, and the sun kindled his scarlet coat to an orange glow.

'But it is a nice old house,' responded Gabriel.

'Yes—I suppose so; but I feel like new wine in an old bottle here. My notion is that sash-windows should be put throughout, and these old wainscoted walls brightened up a bit; or the oak cleared quite away, and the walls papered.'

'It would be a pity, I think.'

'Well, no. A philosopher once said in my hearing that the old builders, who worked when art was a living thing, had no respect for the work of builders who went before them, but pulled down and altered as they thought fit; and why shouldn't we? "Creation and preservation don't do well together," says he, "and a million of antiquarians can't invent a style." My mind exactly. I am for making this place more modern, that we may be cheerful whilst we can.'

The military man turned and surveyed the interior of the room, to assist his ideas of improvement in this direction. Gabriel and Coggan began to move on.

'Oh, Coggan,' said Troy, as if inspired by a recollection, ' do you know if insanity has ever appeared in Mr. Boldwood's family ? '

Jan reflected for a moment.

'I once heard that an uncle of his was queer in his head, but I don't know the rights o't,' he said.

'It is of no importance,' said Troy, lightly. 'Well, I shall be down in the fields with you some time this week ; but I have a few matters to attend to first. So good-day to you. We shall, of course, keep on just as friendly terms as usual. I'm not a proud man : nobody is ever able to say that of Sergeant Troy. However, what is must be, and here's half-a-crown to drink my health, men.'

Troy threw the coin dexterously across the front plot and over the fence towards Gabriel, who shunned it in its fall, his face turning to an angry red. Coggan twirled his eye, edged forward, and caught the money in its ricochet upon the road.

'Very well—you keep it, Coggan,' said Gabriel with disdain, and almost fiercely. 'As for me, I'll do without gifts from him ! '

'Don't show it too much,' said Coggan, musingly. 'For if he's married to her, mark my words, he'll buy his discharge and be our master here. Therefore 'tis well to say "Friend" outwardly, though you say "Troublehouse" within.'

'Well—perhaps it is best to be silent ; but I can't go further than that. I can't flatter, and if my place here is only to be kept by smoothing him down, my place must be lost.'

A horseman, whom they had for some time seen in the distance, now appeared close beside them.

'There's Mr. Boldwood,' said Oak. 'I wonder what Troy meant by his question.'

Coggan and Oak nodded respectfully to the farmer, just checked their paces to discover if they were wanted, and finding they were not, stood back to let him pass on.

The only signs of the terrible sorrow Boldwood had been combating through the night, and was combating now, were the want of colour in his well-defined face, the enlarged appearance of the veins in his forehead and temples, and the sharper lines about his mouth. The horse bore him away, and the very step of the animal seemed significant of dogged despair. Gabriel, for a minute, rose above his own grief in noticing Boldwood's. He saw the square figure sitting erect upon the horse, the head turned to neither side, the elbows steady by the hips, the brim of the hat level and undisturbed in its onward glide, until the keen edges of Boldwood's shape sank by degrees over the hill. To one who knew the man and his story there was something more striking in this immobility than in a collapse. The clash of discord between mood and matter here was forced painfully home to the heart; and, as in laughter there are more dreadful phases than in tears, so was there in the steadiness of this agonized man an expression deeper than a cry.

CHAPTER XXXVI

WEALTH IN JEOPARDY—THE REVEL

ONE night, at the end of August, when Bathsheba's experiences as a married woman were still new, and when the weather was yet dry and sultry, a man stood motionless in the stackyard of Weatherbury Upper Farm, looking at the moon and sky.

The night had a sinister aspect. A heated breeze from the south slowly fanned the summits of lofty objects, and in the sky dashes of buoyant cloud were sailing in a course at right angles to that of another stratum, neither of them in the direction of the breeze below. The moon, as seen through these films, had a lurid metallic look. The fields were sallow with the impure light, and all were tinged in monochrome, as if beheld through stained glass. The same evening the sheep had trailed homeward head to tail, the behaviour of the rooks had been confused, and the horses had moved with timidity and caution.

Thunder was imminent, and, taking some secondary appearances into consideration, it was likely to be followed by one of the lengthened rains which mark the close of dry weather for the season. Before twelve hours had passed a harvest atmosphere would be a bygone thing.

Oak gazed with misgiving at eight naked and unprotected ricks, massive and heavy with the rich produce of one-half the farm for that year. He went on to the barn.

This was the night which had been selected by Sergeant Troy—ruling now in the room of his wife—for giving the harvest supper and dance. As Oak approached the building the sound of violins and a tambourine, and the regular jigging of many feet, grew more distinct. He came close to the large doors, one of which stood slightly ajar, and looked in.

The central space, together with the recess at one end, was emptied of all incumbrances, and this area, covering about two-thirds of the whole, was appropriated for the gathering, the remaining end, which was piled to the ceiling with oats, being screened off with sail-cloth. Tufts and garlands of green foliage decorated the walls, beams, and extemporized chandeliers, and immediately opposite to Oak a rostrum had been erected, bearing a table and chairs. Here sat three fiddlers, and beside them stood a frantic man with his hair on end, perspiration streaming down his cheeks, and a tambourine quivering in his hand.

The dance ended, and on the black oak floor in the midst a new row of couples formed for another.

'Now, ma'am, and no offence I hope, I ask what dance you would like next?' said the first violin.

'Really, it makes no difference,' said the clear voice of Bathsheba, who stood at the inner end of the building, observing the scene from behind a table covered with cups and viands. Troy was lolling beside her.

'Then,' said the fiddler, 'I'll venture to name that the right and proper thing is "The Soldier's Joy"—there being a gallant soldier married into the farm—hey, my sonnies, and gentlemen all?'

'It shall be "The Soldier's Joy,"' exclaimed a chorus.

'Thanks for the compliment,' said the sergeant

gaily, taking Bathsheba by the hand and leading her to the top of the dance. 'For though I have pur- chased my discharge from Her Most Gracious Majesty's regiment of cavalry the 11th Dragoon Guards, to attend to the new duties awaiting me here, I shall continue a soldier in spirit and feeling as long as I live.'

So the dance began. As to the merits of 'The Soldier's Joy,' there cannot be, and never were, two opinions. It has been observed in the musical circles of Weatherbury and its vicinity that this melody, at the end of three-quarters of an hour of thunderous footing, still possesses more stimulative properties for the heel and toe than the majority of other dances at their first opening. 'The Soldier's Joy' has, too, an additional charm, in being so admirably adapted to the tambourine aforesaid—no mean instrument in the hands of a performer who understands the proper convulsions, spasms, St. Vitus's dances, and fearful frenzies necessary when exhibiting its tones in their highest perfection.

The immortal tune ended, a fine DD rolling forth from the bass-viol with the sonorousness of a cannonade, and Gabriel delayed his entry no longer. He avoided Bathsheba, and got as near as possible to the platform, where Sergeant Troy was now seated, drinking brandy- and-water, though the others drank without exception cider and ale. Gabriel could not easily thrust himself within speaking distance of the sergeant, and he sent a message, asking him to come down for a moment. The sergeant said he could not attend.

'Will you tell him, then,' said Gabriel, 'that I only stepped ath'art to say that a heavy rain is sure to fall soon, and that something should be done to protect the ricks?'

'Mr. Troy says it will not rain,' returned the messenger, 'and he cannot stop to talk to you about such fidgets.'

In juxtaposition with Troy, Oak had a melancholy tendency to look like a candle beside gas, and ill at ease, he went out again, thinking he would go home; for, under the circumstances, he had no heart for the scene in the barn. At the door he paused for a moment: Troy was speaking.

'Friends, it is not only the harvest home that we are celebrating to-night; but this is also a Wedding Feast. A short time ago I had the happiness to lead to the altar this lady, your mistress, and not until now have we been able to give any public flourish to the event in Weatherbury. That it may be thoroughly well done, and that every man may go happy to bed, I have ordered to be brought here some bottles of brandy and kettles of hot water. A treble-strong goblet will be handed round to each guest.'

Bathsheba put her hand upon his arm, and, with upturned pale face, said imploringly, 'No—don't give it to them—pray don't, Frank! It will only do them harm: they have had enough of everything.'

'True—we don't wish for no more, thank ye,' said one or two.

'Pooh!' said the sergeant contemptuously, and raised his voice as if lighted up by a new idea. 'Friends,' he said, 'we'll send the women-folk home! 'Tis time they were in bed. Then we cockbirds will have a jolly carouse to ourselves! If any of the men show the white feather, let them look elsewhere for a winter's work.'

Bathsheba indignantly left the barn, followed by all the women and children. The musicians, not looking upon themselves as 'company,' slipped quietly away to their spring waggon and put in the horse. Thus Troy and the men on the farm were left sole occupants of the place. Oak, not to appear unnecessarily disagreeable, stayed a little while; then he, too, arose and quietly took his departure, followed by a friendly oath from the sergeant for not staying to a second round of grog.

Gabriel proceeded towards his home. In approaching the door, his toe kicked something which felt and sounded soft, leathery, and distended, like a boxing-glove. It was a large toad humbly travelling across the path. Oak took it up, thinking it might be better to kill the creature to save it from pain ; but finding it uninjured, he placed it again among the grass. He knew what this direct message from the Great Mother meant. And soon came another.

When he struck a light indoors there appeared upon the table a thin glistening streak, as if a brush of varnish had been lightly dragged across it. Oak's eyes followed the serpentine sheen to the other side, where it led up to a huge brown garden-slug, which had come indoors to-night for reasons of its own. It was Nature's second way of hinting to him that he was to prepare for foul weather.

Oak sat down meditating for nearly an hour. During this time two black spiders, of the kind common in thatched houses, promenaded the ceiling, ultimately dropping to the floor. This reminded him that if there was one class of manifestation on this matter that he thoroughly understood, it was the instincts of sheep. He left the room, ran across two or three fields towards the flock, got upon a hedge, and looked over among them.

They were crowded close together on the other side around some furze bushes, and the first peculiarity observable was that, on the sudden appearance of Oak's head over the fence, they did not stir or run away. They had now a terror of something greater than their terror of man. But this was not the most noteworthy feature : they were all grouped in such a way that their tails, without a single exception, were towards that half of the horizon from which the storm threatened. There was an inner circle closely huddled, and outside these they radiated wider apart, the pattern formed by the flock as a whole not being unlike a vandyked lace collar, to which the clump of furze-bushes stood in the position of a wearer's neck.

This was enough to re-establish him in his original opinion. He knew now that he was right, and that Troy was wrong. Every voice in nature was unanimous in bespeaking change. But two distinct translations attached to these dumb expressions. Apparently there was to be a thunder-storm, and afterwards a cold continuous rain. The creeping things seemed to know all about the later rain, but little of the interpolated thunder-storm; whilst the sheep knew all about the thunder-storm and nothing of the later rain.

This complication of weathers being uncommon, was all the more to be feared. Oak returned to the stack-yard. All was silent here, and the conical tips of the ricks jutted darkly into the sky. There were five wheat-ricks in this yard, and three stacks of barley. The wheat when threshed would average about thirty quarters to each stack; the barley, at least forty. Their value to Bathsheba, and indeed to anybody, Oak mentally estimated by the following simple calculation :—

$$5 \times 30 = 150 \text{ quarters} = 500l.$$
$$3 \times 40 = 120 \text{ quarters} = 250l.$$

Total . . 750l.

Seven hundred and fifty pounds in the divinest form that money can wear—that of necessary food for man and beast: should the risk be run of deteriorating this bulk of corn to less than half its value, because of the instability of a woman? 'Never, if I can prevent it!' said Gabriel.

Such was the argument that Oak set outwardly before

him. But man, even to himself, is a palimpsest, having an ostensible writing, and another beneath the lines. It is possible that there was this golden legend under the utilitarian one: 'I will help to my last effort the woman I have loved so dearly.'

He went back to the barn to endeavour to obtain assistance for covering the ricks that very night. All was silent within, and he would have passed on in the belief that the party had broken up, had not a dim light, yellow as saffron by contrast with the greenish whiteness outside, streamed through a knot-hole in the folding doors.

Gabriel looked in. An unusual picture met his eye.

The candles suspended among the evergreens had burnt down to their sockets, and in some cases the leaves tied about them were scorched. Many of the lights had quite gone out, others smoked and stank, grease dropping from them upon the floor. Here, under the table, and leaning against forms and chairs in every conceivable attitude except the perpendicular, were the wretched persons of all the work-folk, the hair of their heads at such low levels being suggestive of mops and brooms. In the midst of these shone red and distinct the figure of Sergeant Troy, leaning back in a chair. Coggan was on his back, with his mouth open, buzzing forth snores, as were several others; the united breathings of the horizonal assemblage forming a subdued roar like London from a distance. Joseph Poorgrass was curled round in the fashion of a hedge-hog, apparently in attempts to present the least possible portion of his surface to the air; and behind him was dimly visible an unimportant remnant of William Small-bury. The glasses and cups still stood upon the table, a water-jug being overturned, from which a small rill, after tracing its course with marvellous precision down the centre of the long table, fell into the neck of the unconscious Mark Clark, in a steady, monotonous drip, like the dripping of a stalactite in a cave.

Gabriel glanced hopelessly at the group, which, with one or two exceptions, composed all the able-bodied men upon the farm. He saw at once that if the ricks were to be saved that night, or even the next morning, he must save them with his own hands.

A faint 'ting-ting' resounded from under Coggan's waistcoat. It was Coggan's watch striking the hour of two.

Oak went to the recumbent form of Matthew Moon, who usually undertook the rough thatching of the homestead, and shook him. The shaking was without effect.

Gabriel shouted in his ear, 'Where's your thatching-beetle and rick-stick and spars?'

'Under the staddles,' said Moon, mechanically, with the unconscious promptness of a medium.

Gabriel let go his head, and it dropped upon the floor like a bowl. He then went to Susan Tall's husband.

'Where's the key of the granary?'

No answer. The question was repeated, with the same result. To be shouted to at night was evidently less of a novelty to Susan Tall's husband than to Matthew Moon. Oak flung down Tall's head into the corner again and turned away.

To be just, the men were not greatly to blame for this painful and demoralizing termination to the evening's entertainment. Sergeant Troy had so strenuously insisted, glass in hand, that drinking should be the bond of their union, that those who wished to refuse hardly liked to be so unmannerly under the circumstances. Having from their youth up been entirely unaccustomed to any liquor stronger than cider or mild ale, it was no wonder that they had succumbed, one and all, with extraordinary uniformity, after the lapse of about an hour.

Gabriel was greatly depressed. This debauch boded ill for that wilful and fascinating mistress whom the faithful man even now felt within him as the embodiment of all that was sweet and bright and hopeless.

He put out the expiring lights, that the barn might not be endangered, closed the door upon the men in their deep and oblivious sleep, and went again into the lone night. A hot breeze, as if breathed from the parted lips of some dragon about to swallow the globe, fanned him from the south, while directly opposite in the north rose a grim misshapen body of cloud, in the very teeth of the wind. So unnaturally did it rise that one could fancy it to be lifted by machinery from below. Meanwhile the faint cloudlets had flown back into the south-east corner of the sky, as if in terror of the large cloud, like a young brood gazed in upon by some monster.

Going on to the village, Oak flung a small stone against the window of Laban Tall's bedroom, expecting Susan to open it; but nobody stirred. He went round to the back door, which had been left unfastened for Laban's entry, and passed in to the foot of the staircase.

'Mrs. Tall, I've come for the key of the granary, to get at the rick-cloths,' said Oak, in a stentorian voice.

'Is that you?' said Mrs. Susan Tall, half awake.

'Yes,' said Gabriel.

'Come along to bed, do, you draw-latching rogue— keeping a body awake like this!'

'It isn't Laban——'tis Gabriel Oak. I want the key of the granary.'

'Gabriel! What in the name of fortune did you pretend to be Laban for?'

'I didn't. I thought you meant——'

'Yes you did! What do you want here?'

'The key of the granary.'

'Take it then. 'Tis on the nail. People coming disturbing women at this time of night ought——'

Gabriel took the key, without waiting to hear the conclusion of the tirade. Ten minutes later his lonely figure might have been seen dragging four large waterproof coverings across the yard, and soon two of these heaps of treasure in grain were covered snug—two cloths to each. Two hundred pounds were secured. Three wheat-stacks remained open, and there were no more cloths. Oak looked under the staddles and found a fork. He mounted the third pile of wealth and began operating, adopting the plan of sloping the upper sheaves one over the other; and, in addition, filling the interstices with the material of some untied sheaves.

So far all was well. By this hurried contrivance Bathsheba's property in wheat was safe for at any rate a week or two, provided always that there was not much wind.

Next came the barley. This it was only possible to protect by systematic thatching. Time went on, and the moon vanished not to reappear. It was the farewell of the ambassador previous to war. The night had a haggard look, like a sick thing; and there came finally an utter expiration of air from the whole heaven in the form of a slow breeze, which might have been likened to a death. And now nothing was heard in the yard but the dull thuds of the beetle which drove in the spars, and the rustle of thatch in the intervals.

CHAPTER XXXVII

THE STORM—THE TWO TOGETHER

A LIGHT flapped over the scene, as if reflected from phosphorescent wings crossing the sky, and a rumble filled the air. It was the first move of the approaching storm.

The second peal was noisy, with comparatively little visible lightning. Gabriel saw a candle shining in Bathsheba's bedroom, and soon a shadow swept to and fro upon the blind.

Then there came a third flash. Manœuvres of a most extraordinary kind were going on in the vast firmamental hollows overhead. The lightning now was the colour of silver, and gleamed in the heavens like a mailed army. Rumbles became rattles. Gabriel from his elevated position could see over the landscape at least half-a-dozen miles in front. Every hedge, bush, and tree was distinct as in a line engraving. In a paddock in the same direction was a herd of heifers, and the forms of these were visible at this moment in the act of galloping about in the wildest and maddest confusion, flinging their heels and tails high into the air, their heads to earth. A poplar in the immediate foreground was like an ink stroke on burnished tin. Then the picture vanished, leaving the darkness so intense that Gabriel worked entirely by feeling with his hands.

He had stuck his ricking-rod, groom, or poniard, as it was indifferently called—a long iron lance, sharp at the extremity and polished by handling—into the stack to support the sheaves. A blue light appeared in the zenith, and in some indescribable manner flickered down near the top of the rod. It was the fourth of the larger flashes. A moment later and there was a smack—smart, clear, and short. Gabriel felt his position to be anything but a safe one, and he resolved to descend.

Not a drop of rain had fallen as yet. He wiped his weary brow, and looked again at the black forms of the unprotected stacks. Was his life so valuable to him after all? What were his prospects that he should be so chary of running risk, when important and urgent labour could not be carried on without such risk? He resolved to stick to the stack. However, he took a precaution. Under the staddles was a long tethering chain, used to prevent the escape of errant horses. This he carried up the ladder, and sticking his rod through the clog at one end, allowed the other end of the chain to trail upon the ground. The spike attached to it he drove in. Under the shadow of this extemporized lightning-conductor he felt himself comparatively safe.

Before Oak had laid his hands upon his tools again out leapt the fifth flash, with the spring of a serpent and the shout of a fiend. It was green as an emerald, and the reverberation was stunning. What was this the light revealed to him? In the open ground before him, as he looked over the ridge of the rick, was a dark and apparently female form. Could it be that of the only venturesome woman in the parish—Bathsheba? The form moved on a step: then he could see no more.

'Is that you, ma'am?' said Gabriel to the darkness.

'Who is there?' said the voice of Bathsheba.

'Gabriel. I am on the rick, thatching.'

'Oh, Gabriel!—and are you? I have come about them. The weather awoke me, and I thought of the corn. I am so distressed about it—can we save it any-how? I cannot find my husband. Is he with you?'

'He is not here.'

'Do you know where he is?'

'Asleep in the barn.'

'He promised that the stacks should be seen to, and now they are all neglected! Can I do anything to help? Liddy is afraid to come out. Fancy finding you here at such an hour! Surely I can do something?'

'You can bring up some reed-sheaves to me, one by one, ma'am; if you are not afraid to come up the ladder in the dark,' said Gabriel. 'Every moment is precious now, and that would save a good deal of time. It is not very dark when the lightning has been gone a bit.'

'I'll do anything!' she said, resolutely. She instantly took a sheaf upon her shoulder, clambered up close to his heels, placed it behind the rod, and descended for another. At her third ascent the rick suddenly brightened with the brazen glare of shining majolica—every knot in every straw was visible. On the slope in front of him appeared two human shapes, black as jet. The rick lost its sheen—the shapes vanished. Gabriel turned his head. It had been the sixth flash which had come from the east behind him, and the two dark forms on the slope had been the shadows of himself and Bathsheba.

Then came the peal. It hardly was credible that such a heavenly light could be the parent of such a diabolical sound.

'How terrible!' she exclaimed, and clutched him by the sleeve. Gabriel turned, and steadied her on her aërial perch by holding her arm. At the same moment, while he was still reversed in his attitude, there was more light, and he saw, as it were, a copy of the tall poplar tree on the hill drawn in black on the wall of the barn. It was the shadow of that tree, thrown across by a secondary flash in the west.

The next flare came. Bathsheba was on the ground now, shouldering another sheaf, and she bore its dazzle without flinching—thunder and all—and again ascended with the load. There was then a silence everywhere for four or five minutes, and the crunch of the spars, as Gabriel hastily drove them in, could again be distinctly heard. He thought the crisis of the storm had passed. But there came a burst of light.

'Hold on!' said Gabriel, taking the sheaf from her shoulder, and grasping her arm again.

Heaven opened then, indeed. The flash was almost too novel for its inexpressibly dangerous nature to be at once realized, and they could only comprehend the magnificence of its beauty. It sprang from east, west, north, south. It was a perfect dance of death. The forms of skeletons appeared in the air, shaped with blue fire for bones—dancing, leaping, striding, racing around, and mingling altogether in unparalleled confusion. With these were intertwined undulating snakes of green. Behind these was a broad mass of lesser light. Simultaneously came from every part of the tumbling sky what may be called a shout; since, though no shout ever came near it, it was more of the nature of a shout than of anything else earthly. In the meantime one of the grisly forms had alighted upon the point of Gabriel's rod, to run invisibly down it, down the chain, and into the earth. Gabriel was almost blinded, and he could feel Bathsheba's warm arm tremble in his hand—a sensation novel and thrilling enough; but love, life, everything human, seemed small and trifling in such close juxtaposition with an infuriated universe.

Oak had hardly time to gather up these impressions into a thought, and to see how strangely the red feather of her hat shone in this light, when the tall tree on the hill before mentioned seemed on fire to a white heat, and a new one among these terrible voices mingled with the last crash of those preceding. It was a stupefying blast, harsh and pitiless, and it fell upon their ears in a dead, flat blow, without that reverberation which lends the tones of a drum to more distant thunder. By the lustre reflected from every part of the earth and from the wide domical scoop above it, he saw that the tree was sliced down the whole length of its tall, straight stem, a huge riband of bark being apparently flung off. The other portion remained erect, and revealed the bared surface as a strip of white down the front. The lightning had struck the tree. A sulphurous smell filled the air; then all was silent, and black as a cave in Hinnom.

'We had a narrow escape!' said Gabriel, hurriedly. 'You had better go down.'

Bathsheba said nothing; but he could distinctly hear her rhythmical pants, and the recurrent rustle of the sheaf beside her in response to her frightened pulsations. She descended the ladder, and, on second thoughts, he followed her. The darkness was now impenetrable by the sharpest vision. They both stood still at the bottom, side by side. Bathsheba appeared to think only of the weather—Oak thought only of her just then. At last he said—

'The storm seems to have passed now, at any rate.'

'I think so too,' said Bathsheba. 'Though there are multitudes of gleams, look!'

The sky was now filled with an incessant light, frequent repetition melting into complete continuity, as an unbroken sound results from the successive strokes on a gong.

'Nothing serious,' said he. 'I cannot understand no rain falling. But Heaven be praised, it is all the better for us. I am now going up again.'

'Gabriel, you are kinder than I deserve! I will stay

and help you yet. Oh, why are not some of the others here!'

'They would have been here if they could,' said Oak, in a hesitating way.

'Oh, I know it all—all,' she said, adding slowly: 'They are all asleep in the barn, in a drunken sleep, and my husband among them. That's it, is it not? Don't think I am a timid woman and can't endure things.'

'I am not certain,' said Gabriel. 'I will go and see.'

He crossed to the barn, leaving her there alone. He looked through the chinks of the door. All was in total darkness, as he had left it, and there still arose, as at the former time, the steady buzz of many snores.

He felt a zephyr curling about his cheek, and turned. It was Bathsheba's breath—she had followed him, and was looking into the same chink.

He endeavoured to put off the immediate and painful subject of their thoughts by remarking gently, 'If you'll come back again, miss—ma'am, and hand up a few more; it would save much time.'

Then Oak went back again, ascended to the top, stepped off the ladder for greater expedition, and went on thatching. She followed, but without a sheaf.

'Gabriel,' she said, in a strange and impressive voice.

Oak looked up at her. She had not spoken since he left the barn. The soft and continual shimmer of the dying lightning showed a marble face high against the black sky of the opposite quarter. Bathsheba was sitting almost on the apex of the stack, her feet gathered up beneath her, and resting on the top round of the ladder.

'Yes, mistress,' he said.

'I suppose you thought that when I galloped away to Bath that night it was on purpose to be married?'

'I did at last—not at first,' he answered, somewhat surprised at the abruptness with which this new subject was broached.

'And others thought so, too?'

'Yes.'

'And you blamed me for it?'

'Well—a little.'

'I thought so. Now, I care a little for your good opinion, and I want to explain something—I have longed to do it ever since I returned, and you looked so gravely at me. For if I were to die—and I may die soon—it would be dreadful that you should always think mistakenly of me. Now, listen.'

Gabriel ceased his rustling.

'I went to Bath that night in the full intention of breaking off my engagement to Mr. Troy. It was owing to circumstances which occurred after I got there that—that we were married. Now, do you see the matter in a new light?'

'I do—somewhat.'

'I must, I suppose, say more, now that I have begun. And perhaps it's no harm, for you are certainly under no delusion that I ever loved you, or that I can have any object in speaking, more than that object I have mentioned. Well, I was alone in a strange city, and the horse was lame. And at last I didn't know what to do. I saw, when it was too late, that scandal might seize hold of me for meeting him alone in that way. But I was coming away, when he suddenly said he had that day seen a woman more beautiful than I, and that his constancy could not be counted on unless I at once became his. . . . And I was grieved and troubled——' She cleared her voice, and waited a moment, as if to gather breath. 'And then, between jealousy and distraction, I married him!' she whispered with desperate impetuosity.

Gabriel made no reply.

'He was not to blame, for it was perfectly true about —about his seeing somebody else,' she quickly added. 'And now I don't wish for a single remark from you upon the subject—indeed, I forbid it. I only wanted you to know that misunderstood bit of my history before a time comes when you could never know it.—You want some more sheaves?'

She went down the ladder, and the work proceeded. Gabriel soon perceived a languor in the movements of his mistress up and down, and he said to her, gently as a mother—

'I think you had better go indoors now, you are tired. I can finish the rest alone. If the wind does not change the rain is likely to keep off.'

'If I am useless I will go,' said Bathsheba, in a flagging cadence. 'But oh, if your life should be lost!'

'You are not useless; but I would rather not tire you longer. You have done well.'

'And you better!' she said, gratefully. 'Thank you for your devotion, a thousand times, Gabriel! Good-night—I know you are doing your very best for me.'

She diminished in the gloom, and vanished, and he heard the latch of the gate fall as she passed through. He worked in a reverie now, musing upon her story, and upon the contradictoriness of that feminine heart which had caused her to speak more warmly to him to-night than she ever had done whilst unmarried and free to speak as warmly as she chose.

He was disturbed in his meditation by a grating noise from the coach-house. It was the vane on the roof turning round, and this change in the wind was the signal for a disastrous rain.

CHAPTER XXXVIII

RAIN—ONE SOLITARY MEETS ANOTHER

IT was now five o'clock, and the dawn was promising to break in hues of drab and ash. The air changed its temperature and stirred itself more vigorously. Cool breezes coursed in transparent eddies round Oak's face. The wind shifted yet a point or two and blew stronger. In ten minutes every wind of heaven seemed to be roaming at large. Some of the thatching on the wheat-stacks was now whirled fantastically aloft, and had to be replaced and weighted with some rails that lay near at hand. This done, Oak slaved away again at the barley. A huge drop of rain smote his face, the wind snarled round every corner, the trees rocked to the bases of their trunks, and the twigs clashed in strife. Driving in spars at any point and on any system, inch by inch he covered more and more safely from ruin this distracting impersonation of seven hundred pounds. The rain came on in earnest, and Oak soon felt the water to be tracking cold and clammy routes down his back. Ultimately he was reduced well-nigh to a homogeneous sop, and the dyes of his clothes trickled down and stood in a pool at the foot of the ladder. The rain stretched obliquely through the dull atmosphere in liquid spines, unbroken in continuity between their beginnings in the clouds and their points in him.

Oak suddenly remembered that eight months before this time he had been fighting against fire in the same spot as desperately as he was fighting against water now—and for a futile love of the same woman. As for her—— But Oak was generous and true, and dismissed his reflections.

It was about seven o'clock in the dark leaden morning when Gabriel came down from the last stack, and thankfully exclaimed, 'It is done!' He was drenched, weary, and sad, and yet not so sad as drenched and weary, for he was cheered by a sense of success in a good cause.

Faint sounds came from the barn, and he looked that way. Figures stepped singly and in pairs through the doors—all walking awkwardly, and abashed, save the foremost, who wore a red jacket, and advanced with his hands in his pockets, whistling. The others shambled after with a conscience-stricken air : the whole procession was not unlike Flaxman's group of the suitors tottering on towards the infernal regions under the conduct of Mercury. The gnarled shapes passed into the village, Troy, their leader, entering the farmhouse. Not a single one of them had turned his face to the ricks, or apparently bestowed one thought upon their condition.

Soon Oak too went homeward, by a different route from theirs. In front of him against the wet glazed surface of the lane he saw a person walking yet more slowly than himself under an umbrella. The man turned and plainly started ; he was Boldwood.

'How are you this morning, sir ? ' said Oak.

'Yes, it is a wet day.—Oh, I am well, very well, I thank you ; quite well.'

'I am glad to hear it, sir.'

Boldwood seemed to awake to the present by degrees. 'You look tired and ill, Oak,' he said then, desultorily regarding his companion.

'I am tired. You look strangely altered, sir.'

'I? Not a bit of it: I am well enough. What put that into your head?'

'I thought you didn't look quite so topping as you used to, that was all.'

'Indeed, then you are mistaken,' said Boldwood, shortly. 'Nothing hurts me. My constitution is an iron one.'

'I've been working hard to get our ricks covered, and was barely in time. Never had such a struggle in my life. . . . Yours of course are safe, sir.'

'Oh, yes.' Boldwood added, after an interval of silence: 'What did you ask, Oak?'

'Your ricks are all covered before this time?'

'No.'

'At any rate, the large ones upon the stone staddles?'

'They are not.'

'Them under the hedge?'

'No. I forgot to tell the thatcher to set about it.'

'Nor the little one by the stile?'

'Nor the little one by the stile. I overlooked the ricks this year.'

'Then not a tenth of your corn will come to measure, sir.'

'Possibly not.'

'Overlooked them,' repeated Gabriel slowly to himself. It is difficult to describe the intensely dramatic effect that announcement had upon Oak at such a moment. All the night he had been feeling that the neglect he was labouring to repair was abnormal and isolated—the only instance of the kind within the circuit of the county. Yet at this very time, within the same parish, a greater waste had been going on, uncomplained of and disregarded. A few months earlier Boldwood's forgetting his husbandry would have been as preposterous an idea as a sailor forgetting he was in a ship. Oak was just thinking that whatever he himself might have suffered from Bathsheba's marriage, here was a man who had suffered more, when Boldwood spoke in a changed voice—that of one who yearned to make a confidence and relieve his heart by an outpouring.

'Oak, you know as well as I that things have gone wrong with me lately. I may as well own it. I was going to get a little settled in life; but in some way my plan has come to nothing.'

'I thought my mistress would have married you,' said Gabriel, not knowing enough of the full depths of Boldwood's love to keep silence on the farmer's account, and determined not to evade discipline by doing so on his own. 'However, it is so sometimes, and nothing happens that we expect,' he added, with the repose of a man whom misfortune had inured rather than subdued.

'I daresay I am a joke about the parish,' said Boldwood, as if the subject came irresistibly to his tongue, and with a miserable lightness meant to express his indifference.

'Oh no—I don't think that.'

'—But the real truth of the matter is that there was not, as some fancy, any jilting on—her part. No engagement ever existed between me and Miss Everdene. People say so, but it is untrue: she never promised me!' Boldwood stood still now and turned his wild face to Oak. 'Oh, Gabriel,' he continued, 'I am weak and foolish, and I don't know what, and I can't fend off my miserable grief! . . . I had some faint belief in the mercy of God till I lost that woman. Yes, He prepared a gourd to shade me, and like the prophet I thanked Him and was glad. But the next day He prepared a worm to smite the gourd and wither it; and I feel it is better to die than to live!'

A silence followed. Boldwood aroused himself from the momentary mood of confidence into which he had drifted, and walked on again, resuming his usual reserve.

'No, Gabriel,' he resumed, with a carelessness which was like the smile on the countenance of a skull: 'it was made more of by other people than ever it was by us. I do feel a little regret occasionally, but no woman ever had power over me for any length of time. Well, good morning; I can trust you not to mention to others what has passed between us two here.'

CHAPTER XXXIX

COMING HOME—A CRY

ON the turnpike road, between Casterbridge and Weatherbury, and about three miles from the former place, is Yalbury Hill, one of those steep long ascents which pervade the highways of this undulating part of South Wessex. In returning from market it is usual for the farmers and other gig-gentry to alight at the bottom and walk up.

One Saturday evening in the month of October Bathsheba's vehicle was duly creeping up this incline. She was sitting listlessly in the second seat of the gig, whilst walking beside her in a farmer's marketing suit of unusually fashionable cut was an erect, well-made young man. Though on foot, he held the reins and whip, and occasionally aimed light cuts at the horse's ear with the end of the lash, as a recreation. This man was her husband, formerly Sergeant Troy, who, having bought his discharge with Bathsheba's money, was gradually transforming himself into a farmer of a spirited and very modern school. People of unalterable ideas still insisted upon calling him 'Sergeant' when they met him, which was in some degree owing to his having still retained the well-shaped moustache of his military days, and the soldierly bearing inseparable from his form.

'Yes, if it hadn't been for that wretched rain I should have cleared two hundred as easy as looking, my love,' he was saying. 'Don't you see, it altered all the chances? To speak like a book I once read, wet weather is the narrative, and fine days are the episodes, of our country's history; now, isn't that true?'

'But the time of year is come for changeable weather.'

'Well, yes. The fact is, these autumn races are the ruin of everybody. Never did I see such a day as 'twas! 'Tis a wild open place, just out of Budmouth, and a drab sea rolled in towards us like liquid misery. Wind and rain—good Lord! Dark? Why, 'twas as black as my hat before the last race was run. 'Twas five o'clock, and you couldn't see the horses till they were almost in, leave alone colours. The ground was as heavy as lead, and all judgment from a fellow's experience went for nothing. Horses, riders, people, were all blown about like ships at sea. Three booths were blown over, and the wretched folk inside crawled out upon their hands and knees; and in the next field were as many as a dozen hats at one time. Aye, Pimpernel regularly stuck fast, when about sixty yards off, and when I saw Policy stepping on, it did knock my heart against the lining of my ribs, I assure you, my love!'

'And you mean, Frank,' said Bathsheba, sadly— her voice was painfully lowered from the fulness and vivacity of the previous summer—'that you have lost more than a hundred pounds in a month by this dreadful horse-racing? Oh, Frank, it is cruel; it is foolish of you to take away my money so. We shall have to leave the farm; that will be the end of it!'

'Humbug about cruel. Now, there 'tis again— turn on the waterworks; that's just like you.'

'But you'll promise me not to go to Budmouth second meeting, won't you?' she implored. Bathsheba was at the full depth for tears, but she maintained a dry eye.

'I don't see why I should; in fact, if it turns out to be a fine day, I was thinking of taking you.'

'Never, never! I'll go a hundred miles the other way first. I hate the sound of the very word!'

'But the question of going to see the race or staying at home has very little to do with the matter. Bets are all booked safely enough before the race begins, you may depend. Whether it is a bad race for me or a good one, will have very little to do with our going there next Monday.'

'But you don't mean to say that you have risked anything on this one too!' she exclaimed, with an agonized look.

'There now, don't you be a little fool. Wait till you are told. Why, Bathsheba, you have lost all the pluck and sauciness you formerly had, and upon my life if I had known what a chicken-hearted creature you were under all your boldness, I'd never have—I know what.'

A flash of indignation might have been seen in Bathsheba's dark eyes as she looked resolutely ahead after this reply. They moved on without further speech, some early-withered leaves from the trees which hooded the road at this spot occasionally spinning downward across their path to the earth.

A woman appeared on the brow of the hill. The ridge was in a cutting, so that she was very near the husband and wife before she became visible. Troy had turned towards the gig to remount, and whilst putting his foot on the step the woman passed behind him.

Though the overshadowing trees and the approach of eventide enveloped them in gloom, Bathsheba could see plainly enough to discern the extreme poverty of the woman's garb, and the sadness of her face.

'Please, sir, do you know at what time Casterbridge Union-house closes at night?'

The woman said these words to Troy over his shoulder.

Troy started visibly at the sound of the voice; yet he seemed to recover presence of mind sufficient to prevent himself from giving way to his impulse to suddenly turn and face her. He said, slowly—

'I don't know.'

The woman, on hearing him speak, quickly looked up, examined the side of his face, and recognized the soldier under the yeoman's garb. Her face was drawn into an expression which had gladness and agony both among its elements. She uttered an hysterical cry, and fell down.

'Oh, poor thing!' exclaimed Bathsheba, instantly preparing to alight.

'Stay where you are, and attend to the horse!' said Troy, peremptorily, throwing her the reins and the whip. 'Walk the horse to the top: I'll see to the woman.'

'But I——'

'Do you hear? Clk—Poppet!'

The horse, gig, and Bathsheba moved on.

'How on earth did you come here? I thought you were miles away, or dead! Why didn't you write to me?' said Troy to the woman, in a strangely gentle, yet hurried voice, as he lifted her up.

'I feared to.'

'Have you any money?'

'None.'

'Good Heaven—I wish I had more to give you! Here's — wretched — the merest trifle. It is every farthing I have left. I have none but what my wife gives me, you know, and I can't ask her now.'

The woman made no answer.

'I have only another moment,' continued Troy; 'and now listen. Where are you going to-night? Casterbridge Union?'

'Yes; I thought to go there.'

'You shan't go there; yet, wait. Yes, perhaps for to-night; I can do nothing better—worse luck! Sleep there to-night, and stay there to-morrow. Monday is the first free day I have; and on Monday morning, at ten exactly, meet me on Casterbridge Bridge. I'll bring all the money I can muster. You shan't want— I'll see that, Fanny; then I'll get you a lodging somewhere. Good-bye till then. I am a brute—but good-bye!'

After advancing the distance which completed the ascent of the hill, Bathsheba turned her head. The woman was upon her feet, and Bathsheba saw her withdrawing from Troy, and going feebly down the hill by the third milestone from Casterbridge. Troy then came on towards his wife, stepped into the gig, took the reins from her hand, and without making any observation whipped the horse into a trot. He was rather pale.

'Do you know who that woman was?' said Bathsheba, looking searchingly into his face.

'I do,' he said, looking boldly back into hers.

'I thought you did,' said she, with angry hauteur, and still regarding him. 'Who is she?'

He suddenly seemed to think that frankness would benefit neither of the women.

'Nothing to either of us,' he said. 'I know her by sight.'

'What is her name?'

'How should I know her name?'

'I think you do.'

'Think if you will, and be——' The sentence was completed by a smart cut of the whip round Poppet's flank, which caused the animal to start forward at a wild pace. No more was said.

CHAPTER XL

ON CASTERBRIDGE HIGHWAY

FOR a considerable time the woman walked on. Her steps became feebler, and she strained her eyes to look afar upon the naked road, now indistinct amid the penumbræ of night. At length her onward walk dwindled to the merest totter, and she opened a gate within which was a haystack. Underneath this she sat down and presently slept.

When the woman awoke it was to find herself in the depths of a moonless and starless night. A heavy unbroken crust of cloud stretched across the sky, shutting out every speck of heaven; and a distant halo which hung over the town of Casterbridge was visible against the black concave, the luminosity appearing the brighter by its great contrast with the circumscribing darkness. Towards this weak, soft glow the woman turned her eyes.

'If I could only get there!' she said. 'Meet him the day after to-morrow: God help me! Perhaps I shall be in my grave before then.'

A manor-house clock from the far depths of shadow struck the hour, one, in a small, attenuated tone. After midnight the voice of a clock seems to lose in breadth as much as in length, and to diminish its sonorousness to a thin falsetto.

Afterwards a light—two lights—arose from the remote shade, and grew larger. A carriage rolled along the road, and passed the gate. It probably contained some late diners-out. The beams from one lamp shone for a moment upon the crouching woman, and threw her face into vivid relief. The face was young in the groundwork, old in the finish; the general contours were flexuous and childlike, but the finer lineaments had begun to be sharp and thin.

The pedestrian stood up, apparently with a revived determination, and looked around. The road appeared to be familiar to her, and she carefully scanned the fence as she slowly walked along. Presently there became visible a dim white shape; it was another milestone. She drew her fingers across its face to feel the marks.

'Two more !' she said.

She leant against the stone as a means of rest for a short interval, then bestirred herself, and again pursued her way. For a lengthy distance she bore up bravely, afterwards flagging as before. This was beside a lone copsewood, wherein heaps of white chips strewn upon the leafy ground showed that woodmen had been faggoting and making hurdles during the day. Now there was not a rustle, not a breeze, not the faintest clash of twigs to keep her company. The woman looked over the gate, opened it, and went in. Close to the entrance stood a row of faggots, bound and unbound, together with stakes of all sizes.

For a few seconds the wayfarer stood with that tense stillness which signifies itself to be not the end, but merely the suspension, of a previous motion. Her attitude was that of a person who listens, either to the external world of sound, or to the imagined discourse of thought. A close criticism might have detected signs proving that she was intent on the latter alternative. Moreover, as was shown by what followed, she was oddly exercising the faculty of invention upon the speciality of the clever Jacquet Droz, the designer of automatic substitutes for human limbs.

By the aid of the Casterbridge aurora, and by feeling with her hands, the woman selected two sticks from the heaps. These sticks were nearly straight to the height of three or four feet, where each branched into a fork like the letter Y. She sat down, snapped off the small upper twigs, and carried the remainder with her into the road. She placed one of these forks under each arm as a crutch, tested them, timidly threw her whole weight upon them—so little that it was—and swung herself forward. The girl had made for herself a material aid.

The crutches answered well. The pat of her feet, and the tap of her sticks upon the highway, were all the sounds that came from the traveller now. She had passed the last milestone by a good long distance, and began to look wistfully towards the bank as if calculating upon another milestone soon. The crutches, though so very useful, had their limits of power. Mechanism only transfers labour, being powerless to supersede it, and the original amount of exertion was not cleared away; it was thrown into the body and arms. She was exhausted, and each swing forward became fainter. At last she swayed sideways, and fell.

Here she lay, a shapeless heap, for ten minutes and more. The morning wind began to boom dully over the flats, and to move afresh dead leaves which had lain still since yesterday. The woman desperately turned round upon her knees, and next rose to her feet. Steadying herself by the help of one crutch, she essayed a step, then another, then a third, using the crutches now as walking-sticks only. Thus she progressed till descending Mellstock Hill another milestone appeared, and soon the beginning of an iron-railed fence came into view. She staggered across to the first post, clung to it, and looked around.

The Casterbridge lights were now individually visible. It was getting towards morning, and vehicles might be hoped for, if not expected soon. She listened. There was not a sound of life save that acme and sublimation of all dismal sounds, the bark of a fox, its three hollow notes being rendered at intervals of a minute with the precision of a funeral bell.

'Less than a mile!' the woman murmured. 'No; more,' she added, after a pause. 'The mile is to the town hall, and my resting-place is on the other side Casterbridge. A little over a mile, and there I am!' After an interval she again spoke. 'Five or six steps to a yard—six perhaps. I have to go seventeen hundred yards. A hundred times six, six hundred. Seventeen times that. Oh, pity me, Lord!'

Holding to the rails, she advanced, thrusting one hand forward upon the rail, then the other, then leaning over it whilst she dragged her feet on beneath.

This woman was not given to soliloquy; but extremity of feeling lessens the individuality of the weak, as it increases that of the strong. She said again in the same tone, 'I'll believe that the end lies five posts forward, and no further, and so get strength to pass them.'

This was a practical application of the principle that a half-feigned and fictitious faith is better than no faith at all.

She passed five posts and held on to the fifth.

'I'll pass five more by believing my longed-for spot is at the next fifth. I can do it.'

She passed five more.

'It lies only five further.'

She passed five more.

'But it is five further.'

She passed them.

'That stone bridge is the end of my journey,' she said, when the bridge over the Froom was in view.

She crawled to the bridge. During the effort each

breath of the woman went into the air as if never to return again.

'Now for the truth of the matter,' she said, sitting down. 'The truth is, that I have less than half a mile.' Self-beguilement with what she had known all the time to be false had given her strength to come over half a mile that she would have been powerless to face in the lump. The artifice showed that the woman, by some mysterious intuition, had grasped the paradoxical truth that blindness may operate more vigorously than prescience, and the short-sighted effect more than the far-seeing; that limitation, and not comprehensiveness, is needed for striking a blow.

The half-mile stood now before the sick and weary woman like a stolid Juggernaut. It was an impassive King of her world. The road here ran across Durnover Moor, open to the road on either side. She surveyed the wide space, the lights, herself, sighed, and lay down against a guard-stone of the bridge.

Never was ingenuity exercised so sorely as the traveller here exercised hers. Every conceivable aid, method, stratagem, mechanism, by which these last desperate eight hundred yards could be overpassed by a human being unperceived, was revolved in her busy brain, and dismissed as impracticable. She thought of sticks, wheels, crawling—she even thought of rolling. But the exertion demanded by either of these latter two was greater than to walk erect. The faculty of contrivance was worn out. Hopelessness had come at last.

'No further!' she whispered, and closed her eyes.

From the stripe of shadow on the opposite side of the way a portion of shade seemed to detach itself and move into isolation upon the pale white of the road. It glided noiselessly towards the recumbent woman.

She became conscious of something touching her hand; it was softness and it was warmth. She opened her eyes, and the substance touched her face. A dog was licking her cheek.

He was a huge, heavy, and quiet creature, standing darkly against the low horizon, and at least two feet higher than the present position of her eyes. Whether Newfoundland, mastiff, bloodhound, or what not, it was impossible to say. He seemed to be of too strange and mysterious a nature to belong to any variety among those of popular nomenclature. Being thus assignable to no breed, he was the ideal embodiment of canine greatness —a generalization from what was common to all. Night, in its sad, solemn, and benevolent aspect, apart from its stealthy and cruel side, was personified in this form. Darkness endows the small and ordinary ones among mankind with poetical power, and even the suffering woman threw her idea into figure.

In her reclining position she looked up to him just as in earlier times she had, when standing, looked up to a man. The animal, who was as homeless as she, respectfully withdrew a step or two when the woman moved, and, seeing that she did not repulse him, he licked her hand again.

A thought moved within her like lightning. ' Perhaps I can make use of him—I might do it then ! '

She pointed in the direction of Casterbridge, and the dog seemed to misunderstand : he trotted on. Then, finding she could not follow, he came back and whined.

The ultimate and saddest singularity of woman's effort and invention was reached when, with a quickened breathing, she rose to a stooping posture, and, resting her two little arms upon the shoulders of the dog, leant firmly thereon, and murmured stimulating words. Whilst she sorrowed in her heart she cheered with her voice, and what was stranger than that the strong should need encouragement from the weak was that cheerfulness should be so well stimulated by such utter dejection. Her friend moved forward slowly, and she with small mincing steps moved forward beside him, half her weight being thrown upon the animal. Sometimes she sank as she had sunk from walking erect, from the crutches, from the rails. The dog, who now thoroughly understood her desire and her incapacity, was frantic in his distress on these occasions; he would tug at her dress and run forward. She always called him back, and it was now to be observed that the woman listened for human sounds only to avoid them. It was evident that she had an object in keeping her presence on the road and her forlorn state unknown.

Their progress was necessarily very slow. They reached the bottom of the town, and the Casterbridge lamps lay before them like fallen Pleiads as they turned to the left into the dense shade of a deserted avenue of chestnuts, and so skirted the borough. Thus the town was passed, and the goal was reached.

On this much-desired spot outside the town rose a picturesque building. Originally it had been a mere case to hold people. The shell had been so thin, so devoid of excrescence, and so closely drawn over the accommodation granted, that the grim character of what was beneath showed through it, as the shape of a body is visible under a winding-sheet.

Then Nature, as if offended, lent a hand. Masses of ivy grew up, completely covering the walls, till the place looked like an abbey; and it was discovered that the view from the front, over the Casterbridge chimneys, was one of the most magnificent in the county. A neighbouring earl once said that he would give up a year's rental to have at his own door the view enjoyed by the inmates from theirs—and very probably the inmates would have given up the view for his year's rental.

This stone edifice consisted of a central mass and two wings, whereon stood as sentinels a few slim chimneys, now gurgling sorrowfully to the slow wind.

In the wall was a gate, and by the gate a bell-pull formed of a hanging wire. The woman raised herself as high as possible upon her knees, and could just reach the handle. She moved it and fell forwards in a bowed attitude, her face upon her bosom.

It was getting on towards six o'clock, and sounds of movement were to be heard inside the building which was the haven of rest to this wearied soul. A little door by the large one was opened, and a man appeared inside. He discerned the panting heap of clothes, went back for a light, and came again. He entered a second time, and returned with two women.

These lifted the prostrate figure and assisted her in through the doorway. The man then closed the door.

'How did she get here?' said one of the women.

'The Lord knows,' said the other.

'There is a dog outside,' murmured the overcome traveller. 'Where is he gone? He helped me.'

'I stoned him away,' said the man.

The little procession then moved forward—the man in front bearing the light, the two bony women next, supporting between them the small and supple one. Thus they entered the house and disappeared.

CHAPTER XLI

SUSPICION—FANNY IS SENT FOR

BATHSHEBA said very little to her husband all that evening of their return from market, and he was not disposed to say much to her. He exhibited the unpleasant combination of a restless condition with a silent tongue. The next day, which was Sunday, passed nearly in the same manner as regarded their taciturnity, Bathsheba going to church both morning and afternoon. This was the day before the Budmouth races. In the evening Troy said, suddenly—

'Bathsheba, could you let me have twenty pounds?'

Her countenance instantly sank. 'Twenty pounds?' she said.

'The fact is, I want it badly.' The anxiety upon Troy's face was unusual and very marked. It was a culmination of the mood he had been in all the day.

'Ah! for those races to-morrow.'

Troy for the moment made no reply. Her mistake had its advantages to a man who shrank from having his mind inspected as he did now. 'Well, suppose I do want it for races?' he said, at last.

'Oh, Frank!' Bathsheba replied, and there was such a volume of entreaty in the words. 'Only such a few weeks ago you said that I was far sweeter than all your other pleasures put together, and that you would give

317

them all up for me; and now, won't you give up this
one, which is more a worry than a pleasure? Do,
Frank. Come, let me fascinate you by all I can do
—by pretty words and pretty looks, and everything I
can think of—to stay at home. Say yes to your wife—
say yes!'

The tenderest and softest phases of Bathsheba's
nature were prominent now—advanced impulsively for
his acceptance, without any of the disguises and defences
which the wariness of her character when she was cool
too frequently threw over them. Few men could have
resisted the arch yet dignified entreaty of the beautiful
face, thrown a little back and sideways in the well-
known attitude that expresses more than the words it
accompanies, and which seems to have been designed
for these special occasions. Had the woman not been
his wife, Troy would have succumbed instantly; as it
was, he thought he would not deceive her longer.

'The money is not wanted for racing debts at all,'
he said.

'What is it for?' she asked. 'You worry me a great
deal by these mysterious responsibilities, Frank.'

Troy hesitated. He did not now love her enough
to allow himself to be carried too far by her ways. Yet
it was necessary to be civil. 'You wrong me by such
a suspicious manner,' he said. 'Such strait-waistcoating
as you treat me to is not becoming in you at so early a
date.'

'I think that I have a right to grumble a little if I
pay,' she said, with features between a smile and a
pout.

'Exactly; and, the former being done, suppose we
proceed to the latter. Bathsheba, fun is all very well,
but don't go too far, or you may have cause to regret
something.'

She reddened. 'I do that already,' she said, quickly.

'What do you regret?'

318

'That my romance has come to an end.'

'All romances end at marriage.'

'I wish you wouldn't talk like that. You grieve me to my soul by being smart at my expense.'

'You are dull enough at mine. I believe you hate me.'

'Not you—only your vices. I do hate them.'

''Twould be much more becoming if you set yourself to cure them. Come, let's strike a balance with the twenty pounds, and be friends.'

She gave a sigh of resignation. 'I have about that sum here for household expenses. If you must have it, take it.'

'Very good. Thank you. I expect I shall have gone away before you are in to breakfast to-morrow.'

'And must you go? Ah! there was a time, Frank, when it would have taken a good many promises to other people to drag you away from me. You used to call me darling, then. But it doesn't matter to you how my days are passed now.'

'I must go, in spite of sentiment.' Troy, as he spoke, looked at his watch, and, apparently actuated by *non lucendo* principles, opened the case at the back, revealing, snugly stowed within it, a small coil of hair.

Bathsheba's eyes had been accidentally lifted at that moment, and she saw the action and saw the hair. She flushed in pain and surprise, and some words escaped her before she had thought whether or not it was wise to utter them. 'A woman's curl of hair!' she said. 'Oh, Frank, whose is that?'

Troy had instantly closed his watch. He carelessly replied, as one who cloaked some feelings that the sight had stirred. 'Why, yours, of course. Whose should it be? I had quite forgotten that I had it.'

'What a dreadful fib, Frank!'

'I tell you I had forgotten it!' he said, loudly.

'I don't mean that—it was yellow hair.'

'Nonsense.'

'That's insulting me. I know it was yellow. Now whose was it? I want to know.'

'Very well—I'll tell you, so make no more ado. It is the hair of a young woman I was going to marry before I knew you.'

'You ought to tell me her name, then'

'I cannot do that.'

'Is she married yet?'

'No.'

'Is she alive?'

'Yes.'

'Is she pretty?'

'Yes.'

'It is wonderful how she can be, poor thing, under such an awful affliction!'

'Affliction—what affliction?' he inquired, quickly.

'Having hair of that dreadful colour.'

'Oh—ho—I like that!' said Troy, recovering himself. 'Why, her hair has been admired by everybody who has seen her since she has worn it loose, which has not been long. It is beautiful hair. People used to turn their heads to look at it, poor girl!'

'Pooh! that's nothing — that's nothing!' she exclaimed, in incipient accents of pique. 'If I cared for your love as much as I used to I could say people had turned to look at mine.'

'Bathsheba, don't be so fitful and jealous. You knew what married life would be like, and shouldn't have entered it if you feared these contingencies.'

Troy had by this time driven her to bitterness: her heart was big in her throat, and the ducts to her eyes were painfully full. Ashamed as she was to show emotion, at last she burst out :—

'This is all I get for loving you so well! Ah! when I married you your life was dearer to me than my own. I would have died for you—how truly I can say that I

would have died for you! And now you sneer at my
foolishness in marrying you. Oh! is it kind to me to
throw my mistake in my face? Whatever opinion you
may have of my wisdom, you should not tell me of it so
mercilessly, now that I am in your power.'

'I can't help how things fall out,' said Troy; 'upon
my heart, women will be the death of me!'

'Well, you shouldn't keep people's hair. You'll
burn it, won't you, Frank?'

Frank went on as if he had not heard her. 'There
are considerations even before my consideration for you;
reparations to be made—ties you know nothing of. If
you repent of marrying, so do I.'

Trembling now, she put her hand upon his arm,
saying, in mingled tones of wretchedness and coaxing,
'I only repent it if you don't love me better than any
woman in the world! I don't otherwise, Frank. You
don't repent because you already love somebody better
than you love me, do you?'

'I don't know. Why do you say that?'

'You won't burn that curl. You like the woman
who owns that pretty hair—yes; it is pretty—more
beautiful than my miserable black mane! Well, it is
no use; I can't help being ugly. You must like her
best, if you will!'

'Until to-day, when I took it from a drawer, I have
never looked upon that bit of hair for several months—
that I am ready to swear.'

'But just now you said "ties;" and then—that
woman we met?'

''Twas the meeting with her that reminded me of
the hair.'

'Is it hers, then?'

'Yes. There, now that you have wormed it out of
me, I hope you are content.'

'And what are the ties?'

'Oh! that meant nothing—a mere jest.'

'A mere jest!' she said, in mournful astonishment. 'Can you jest when I am so wretchedly in earnest? Tell me the truth, Frank. I am not a fool, you know, although I am a woman, and have my woman's moments. Come! treat me fairly,' she said, looking honestly and fearlessly into his face. 'I don't want much; bare justice—that's all! Ah! once I felt I could be content with nothing less than the highest homage from the husband I should choose. Now, anything short of cruelty will content me. Yes! the independent and spirited Bathsheba is come to this!'

'For Heaven's sake don't be so desperate!' Troy said, snappishly, rising as he did so, and leaving the room.

Directly he had gone, Bathsheba burst into great sobs—dry-eyed sobs, which cut as they came, without any softening by tears. But she determined to repress all evidences of feeling. She was conquered; but she would never own it as long as she lived. Her pride was indeed brought low by despairing discoveries of her spoliation by marriage with a less pure nature than her own. She chafed to and fro in rebelliousness, like a caged leopard; her whole soul was in arms, and the blood fired her face. Until she had met Troy, Bathsheba had been proud of her position as a woman; it had been a glory to her to know that her lips had been touched by no man's on earth—that her waist had never been encircled by a lover's arm. She hated herself now. In those earlier days she had always nourished a secret contempt for girls who were the slaves of the first good-looking young fellow who should choose to salute them. She had never taken kindly to the idea of marriage in the abstract as did the majority of women she saw about her. In the turmoil of her anxiety for her lover she had agreed to marry him; but the perception that had accompanied her happiest hours on this account was rather that of self-sacrifice than of promotion and honour. Although she scarcely knew the divinity's name, Diana was the goddess whom Bathsheba instinctively adored. That she had never, by look, word, or sign, encouraged a man to approach her—that she had felt herself sufficient to herself, and had in the independence of her girlish heart fancied there was a certain degradation in renouncing the simplicity of a maiden existence to become the humbler half of an indifferent matrimonial whole—were facts now bitterly remembered. Oh, if she had never stooped to folly of this kind, respectable as it was, and could only stand again, as she had stood on the hill at Norcombe, and dare Troy or any other man to pollute a hair of her head by his interference!

The next morning she rose earlier than usual, and had the horse saddled for her ride round the farm in the customary way. When she came in at half-past eight—their usual hour for breakfasting—she was informed that her husband had risen, taken his breakfast, and driven off to Casterbridge with the gig and Poppet.

After breakfast she was cool and collected—quite herself in fact—and she rambled to the gate, intending to walk to another quarter of the farm, which she still personally superintended as well as her duties in the house would permit, continually, however, finding herself preceded in forethought by Gabriel Oak, for whom she began to entertain the genuine friendship of a sister. Of course, she sometimes thought of him in the light of an old lover, and had momentary imaginings of what life with him as a husband would have been like; also of life with Boldwood under the same conditions. But Bathsheba, though she could feel, was not much given to futile dreaming, and her musings under this head were short and entirely confined to the times when Troy's neglect was more than ordinarily evident.

She saw coming up the road a man like Mr. Boldwood. It was Mr. Boldwood. Bathsheba blushed painfully, and watched. The farmer stopped when still a long way off, and held up his hand to Gabriel Oak, who was in a footpath across the field. The two men then approached each other and seemed to engage in earnest conversation.

Thus they continued for a long time. Joseph Poorgrass now passed near them, wheeling a barrow of apples up the hill to Bathsheba's residence. Boldwood and Gabriel called to him, spoke to him for a few minutes, and then all three parted, Joseph immediately coming up the hill with his barrow.

Bathsheba, who had seen this pantomime with some surprise, experienced great relief when Boldwood turned back again. 'Well, what's the message, Joseph?' she said.

He set down his barrow, and, putting upon himself the refined aspect that a conversation with a lady required, spoke to Bathsheba over the gate.

'You'll never see Fanny Robin no more—use nor principal—ma'am.'

'Why?'

'Because she's dead in the Union.'

'Fanny dead—never!'

'Yes, ma'am.'

'What did she die from?'

'I don't know for certain; but I should be inclined to think it was from general neshness of constitution. She was such a limber maid that 'a could stand no hardship, even when I knowed her, and 'a went like a candle-snoff, so 'tis said. She was took bad in the morning, and, being quite feeble and worn out, she died in the evening. She belongs by law to our parish; and Mr. Boldwood is going to send a waggon at three this afternoon to fetch her home here and bury her.'

'Indeed I shall not let Mr. Boldwood do any such thing—I shall do it! Fanny was my uncle's servant, and, although I only knew her for a couple of days,

she belongs to me. How very, very sad this is!—
the idea of Fanny being in a workhouse.' Bathsheba
had begun to know what suffering was, and she spoke
with real feeling. . . . 'Send across to Mr. Boldwood's,
and say that Mrs. Troy will take upon herself the duty
of fetching an old servant of the family. . . . We
ought not to put her in a waggon ; we'll get a hearse.'

'There will hardly be time, ma'am, will there?'

'Perhaps not,' she said, musingly. 'When did you
say we must be at the door—three o'clock?'

'Three o'clock this afternoon, ma'am, so to speak it.'

'Very well—you go with it. A pretty waggon is
better than an ugly hearse, after all. Joseph, have the
new spring waggon with the blue body and red wheels,
and wash it very clean. And, Joseph——'

'Yes, ma'am.'

'Carry with you some evergreens and flowers to put
upon her coffin — indeed, gather a great many, and
completely bury her in them. Get some boughs of
laurustinus, and variegated box, and yew, and boy's-love;
ay, and some bunches of chrysanthemum. And let old
Pleasant draw her, because she knew him so well.'

'I will, ma'am. I ought to have said that the
Union, in the form of four labouring men, will meet me
when I gets to our churchyard gate, and take her and
bury her according to the rites of the Board of Guardians,
as by law ordained.'

'Dear me—Casterbridge Union—and is Fanny come
to this?' said Bathsheba, musing. 'I wish I had known
of it sooner. I thought she was far away. How long
has she lived there?'

'On'y been there a day or two.'

'Oh!—then she has not been staying there as a
regular inmate?'

'No. She first went to live in a garrison-town t'other
side o' Wessex, and since then she's been picking up a
living at seampstering in Melchester for several months,

at the house of a very respectable widow-woman who takes in work of that sort. She only got handy the Union-house on Sunday morning 'a b'lieve, and 'tis supposed here and there that she had traipsed every step of the way from Melchester. Why she left her place, I can't say, for I don't know; and as to a lie, why, I wouldn't tell it. That's the short of the story, ma'am.'

'Ah-h!'

No gem ever flashed from a rosy ray to a white one more rapidly than changed the young wife's countenance whilst this word came from her in a long-drawn breath. 'Did she walk along our turnpike-road?' she said, in a suddenly restless and eager voice.

'I believe she did. . . . Ma'am, shall I call Liddy? You bain't well, ma'am, surely? You look like a lily— so pale and fainty!'

'No; don't call her; it is nothing. When did she pass Weatherbury?'

'Last Saturday night.'

'That will do, Joseph; now you may go.'

'Certainly, ma'am.'

'Joseph, come hither a moment. What was the colour of Fanny Robin's hair?'

'Really, mistress, now that 'tis put to me so judge-and-jury like, I can't call to mind, if ye'll believe me!'

'Never mind; go on and do what I told you. Stop —well no, go on.'

She turned herself away from him, that he might no longer notice the mood which had set its sign so visibly upon her, and went indoors with a distressing sense of faintness and a beating brow. About an hour after, she heard the noise of the waggon and went out, still with a painful consciousness of her bewildered and troubled look. Joseph, dressed in his best suit of clothes, was putting in the horse to start. The shrubs and flowers were all piled in the waggon, as she had directed. Bathsheba hardly saw them now.

'Whose sweetheart did you say, Joseph?'

'I don't know, ma'am.'

'Are you quite sure?'

'Yes, ma'am, quite sure.'

'Sure of what?'

'I'm sure that all I know is that she arrived in the morning and died in the evening without further parley. What Oak and Mr. Boldwood told me was only these few words. "Little Fanny Robin is dead, Joseph," Gabriel said, looking in my face in his steady old way. I was very sorry, and I said, "Ah!—and how did she come to die?" "Well, she's dead in Casterbridge Union," he said; "and perhaps 'tisn't much matter about how she came to die. She reached the Union early Sunday morning, and died in the afternoon—that's clear enough." Then I asked what she'd been doing lately, and Mr. Boldwood turned round to me then, and left off spitting a thistle with the end of his stick. He told me about her having lived by seampstering in Melchester, as I mentioned to you, and that she walked therefrom at the end of last week, passing near here Saturday night in the dusk. They then said I had better just name a hent of her death to you, and away they went. Her death might have been brought on by biding in the night wind, you know, ma'am; for people used to say she'd go off in a decline: she used to cough a good deal in winter time. However, 'tisn't much odds to us about that now, for 'tis all over.'

'Have you heard a different story at all?' She looked at him so intently that Joseph's eyes quailed.

'Not a word, mistress, I assure 'ee!' he said. 'Hardly anybody in the parish knows the news yet.'

'I wonder why Gabriel didn't bring the message to me himself. He mostly makes a point of seeing me upon the most trifling errand.' These words were merely murmured, and she was looking upon the ground.

'Perhaps he was busy, ma'am,' Joseph suggested.

327

'And sometimes he seems to suffer from things upon his mind, connected with the time when he was better off than 'a is now. 'A's rather a curious item, but a very understanding shepherd, and learned in books.'

'Did anything seem upon his mind whilst he was speaking to you about this?'

'I cannot but say that there did, ma'am. He was terrible down, and so was Farmer Boldwood.'

'Thank you, Joseph. That will do. Go on now, or you'll be late.'

Bathsheba, still unhappy, went indoors again. In the course of the afternoon she said to Liddy, who had been informed of the occurrence, 'What was the colour of poor Fanny Robin's hair? Do you know? I cannot recollect—I only saw her for a day or two.'

'It was light, ma'am; but she wore it rather short, and packed away under her cap, so that you would hardly notice it. But I have seen her let it down when she was going to bed, and it looked beautiful then. Real golden hair.'

'Her young man was a soldier, was he not?'

'Yes. In the same regiment as Mr. Troy. He says he knew him very well.'

'What, Mr. Troy says so? How came he to say that?'

'One day I just named it to him, and asked him if he knew Fanny's young man. He said, "Oh yes, he knew the young man as well as he knew himself, and that there wasn't a man in the regiment he liked better."'

'Ah! Said that, did he?'

'Yes; and he said there was a strong likeness between himself and the other young man, so that sometimes people mistook them——'

'Liddy, for Heaven's sake stop your talking!' said Bathsheba, with the nervous petulance that comes from worrying perceptions.

CHAPTER XLII

JOSEPH AND HIS BURDEN—BUCK'S HEAD

A WALL bounded the site of Casterbridge Union-house, except along a portion of the end. Here a high gable stood prominent, and it was covered like the front with a mat of ivy. In this gable was no window, chimney, ornament, or protuberance of any kind. The single feature appertaining to it, beyond the expanse of dark green leaves, was a small door.

The situation of the door was peculiar. The sill was three or four feet above the ground, and for a moment one was at a loss for an explanation of this exceptional altitude, till ruts immediately beneath suggested that the door was used solely for the passage of articles and persons to and from the level of a vehicle standing on the outside. Upon the whole, the door seemed to advertise itself as a species of Traitor's Gate translated to another sphere. That entry and exit hereby was only at rare intervals became apparent on noting that tufts of grass were allowed to flourish undisturbed in the chinks of the sill.

As the clock over the South-street Alms-house pointed to five minutes to three, a blue spring waggon, picked out with red, and containing boughs and flowers, passed the end of the street, and up towards this side of the building. Whilst the chimes were yet stammering out a shattered form of 'Malbrook,' Joseph Poorgrass rang the bell, and received directions to back his waggon against the high door under the gable. The door then opened, and a plain elm coffin was slowly thrust forth, and laid by two men in fustian along the middle of the vehicle.

One of the men then stepped up beside it, took from his pocket a lump of chalk, and wrote upon the cover the name and a few other words in a large scrawling hand. (We believe that they do these things more tenderly now, and provide a plate.) He covered the whole with a black cloth, threadbare, but decent, the tail-board of the waggon was returned to its place, one of the men handed a certificate of registry to Poorgrass, and both entered the door, closing it behind them. Their connection with her, short as it had been, was over for ever.

Joseph then placed the flowers as enjoined, and the evergreens around the flowers, till it was difficult to divine what the waggon contained; he smacked his whip, and the rather pleasing funeral car crept down the hill, and along the road to Weatherbury.

The afternoon drew on apace, and, looking to the right towards the sea as he walked beside the horse, Poorgrass saw strange clouds and scrolls of mist rolling over the long ridges· which girt the landscape in that quarter. They came in yet greater volumes, and indolently crept across the intervening valleys, and around the withered papery flags of the sloughs and river brinks. Then their dank spongy forms closed in upon the sky. It was a sudden overgrowth of atmospheric fungi which had their roots in the neighbouring sea, and by the time that horse, man, and corpse entered Yalbury Great Wood, these silent workings of an invisible hand had reached them, and they were completely enveloped. It was the first arrival of the autumn fogs, and the first fog of the series.

The air was as an eye suddenly struck blind. The waggon and its load rolled no longer on the horizontal division between clearness and opacity. They were imbedded in an elastic body of a monotonous pallor throughout. There was no perceptible motion in the air, not a visible drop of water fell upon a leaf of the beeches, birches, and firs composing the wood on either side. The trees stood in an attitude of intentness, as if they waited longingly for a wind to come and rock them. A startling quiet overhung all surrounding things —so completely, that the crunching of the waggon-wheels was as a great noise, and small rustles, which had never obtained a hearing except by night, were distinctly individualized.

Joseph Poorgrass looked round upon his sad burden as it loomed faintly through the flowering laurustinus, then at the unfathomable gloom amid the high trees on each hand, indistinct, shadowless, and spectre-like in their monochrome of grey. He felt anything but cheerful, and wished he had the company even of a child or dog. Stopping the horse, he listened. Not a footstep or wheel was audible anywhere around, and the dead silence was broken only by a heavy particle falling from a tree through the evergreens and alighting with a smart rap upon the coffin of poor Fanny. The fog had by this time saturated the trees, and this was the first dropping of water from the overbrimming leaves. The hollow echo of its fall reminded the waggoner painfully of the grim Leveller. Then hard by came down another drop, then two or three. Presently there was a continual tapping of these heavy drops upon the dead leaves, the road, and the travellers. The nearer boughs were beaded with the mist to the greyness of aged men, and the rusty-red leaves of the beeches were hung with similar drops, like diamonds on auburn hair.

At the roadside hamlet called Roy-town, just beyond this wood, was the old inn Buck's Head. It was about a mile and a half from Weatherbury, and in the meridian times of stage-coach travelling had been the place where many coaches changed and kept their relays of horses. All the old stabling was now pulled down, and little remained besides the habitable inn itself, which, standing a little way back from the road, signified its existence to people far up and down the highway by a sign hanging from the horizontal bough of an elm on the opposite side of the way.

Travellers — for the variety *tourist* had hardly developed into a distinct species at this date—sometimes said in passing, when they cast their eyes up to the sign-bearing tree, that artists were fond of representing the signboard hanging thus, but that they themselves had never before noticed so perfect an instance in actual working order. It was near this tree that the waggon was standing into which Gabriel Oak crept on his first journey to Weatherbury; but, owing to the darkness, the sign and the inn had been unobserved.

The manners of the inn were of the old-established type. Indeed, in the minds of its frequenters they existed as unalterable formulæ: *e.g.*—

Rap with the bottom of your pint for more liquor.
For tobacco, shout.
In calling for the girl in waiting, say, ' Maid ! '
Ditto for the landlady, ' Old Soul ! ' etc., etc.

It was a relief to Joseph's heart when the friendly signboard came in view, and, stopping his horse immediately beneath it, he proceeded to fulfil an intention made a long time before. His spirits were oozing out of him quite. He turned the horse's head to the green bank, and entered the hostel for a mug of ale.

Going down into the kitchen of the inn, the floor of which was a step below the passage, which in its turn was a step below the road outside, what should Joseph see to gladden his eyes but two copper-coloured discs, in the form of the countenances of Mr. Jan Coggan and Mr. Mark Clark. These owners of the two most appreciative throats in the neighbourhood, within the pale of respectability, were now sitting face to face over a three-legged circular table, having an iron rim to keep cups and pots from being accidentally elbowed off; they might have been said to resemble the setting sun and the full moon shining *vis-à-vis* across the globe.

'Why, 'tis neighbour Poorgrass!' said Mark Clark. 'I'm sure your face don't praise your mistress's table, Joseph.'

'I've had a very pale companion for the last five miles,' said Joseph, indulging in a shudder toned down by resignation. 'And to speak the truth, 'twas beginning to tell upon me. I assure ye, I ha'n't seed the colour of victuals or drink since breakfast time this morning, and that was no more than a dew-bit afield.'

'Then drink, Joseph, and don't restrain yourself!' said Coggan, handing him a hooped mug three-quarters full.

Joseph drank for a moderately long time, then for a longer time, saying, as he lowered the jug, ''Tis pretty drinking—very pretty drinking, and is more than cheerful on my melancholy errand, so to speak it.'

'True, drink is a pleasant comfort,' said Jan, as one who repeated a truism so familiar to his brain that he hardly noticed its passage over his tongue; and, lifting the cup, Coggan tilted his head gradually backwards, with closed eyes, that his expectant soul might not be diverted for one instant from its bliss by irrelevant surroundings.

'Well, I must be on again,' said Poorgrass. 'Not but that I should like another nip with ye; but the country might lose confidence in me if I was seed here.'

'Where be ye trading o't to to-day, then, Joseph?'

'Back to Weatherbury. I've got poor little Fanny Robin in my waggon outside, and I must be at the churchyard gates at a quarter to five with her.'

'Ay—I've heard of it. And so she's nailed up in parish boards after all, and nobody to pay the bell shilling and the grave half-crown.'

'The parish pays the grave half-crown, but not the bell shilling, because the bell's a luxery: but 'a can hardly do without the grave, poor body. However, I expect our mistress will pay all.'

'A pretty maid as ever I see! But what's yer hurry, Joseph? The pore woman's dead, and you can't bring her to life, and you may as well sit down comfortable, and finish another with us.'

'I don't mind taking just the least thimbleful ye can dream of more with ye, sonnies. But only a few minutes, because 'tis as 'tis.'

'Of course, you'll have another drop. A man's twice the man afterwards. You feel so warm and glorious, and you whop and slap at your work without any trouble, and everything goes on like sticks a-breaking. Too much liquor is bad, and leads us to that horned man in the smoky house; but after all, many people haven't the gift of enjoying a soak, and since we be highly favoured with a power that way, we should make the most o't.'

'True,' said Mark Clark. ''Tis a talent the Lord has mercifully bestowed upon us, and we ought not to neglect it. But, what with the parsons and clerks and school-people and serious tea-parties, the merry old ways of good life have gone to the dogs—upon my carcase, they have!'

'Well, really, I must be onward again now,' said Joseph.

'Now, now, Joseph; nonsense! The poor woman is dead, isn't she, and what's your hurry?'

'Well, I hope Providence won't be in a way with me for my doings,' said Joseph, again sitting down. 'I've been troubled with weak moments lately, 'tis true. I've been drinky once this month already, and I did not go to church a-Sunday, and I dropped a curse or two yesterday; so I don't want to go too far for my safety. Your next world is your next world, and not to be squandered offhand.'

'I believe ye to be a chapel-member, Joseph. That I do.'

'Oh, no, no! I don't go so far as that.'

'For my part,' said Coggan, 'I'm staunch Church of England.'

'Ay, and faith, so be I,' said Mark Clark.

'I won't say much for myself; I don't wish to,' Coggan continued, with that tendency to talk on principles which is characteristic of the barley-corn. 'But I've never changed a single doctrine: I've stuck like a plaster to the old faith I was born in. Yes; there's this to be said for the Church, a man can belong to the Church and bide in his cheerful old inn, and never trouble or worry his mind about doctrines at all. But to be a meetinger, you must go to chapel in all winds and weathers, and make yerself as frantic as a skit. Not but that chapel-members be clever chaps enough in their way. They can lift up beautiful prayers out of their own heads, all about their families and shipwracks in the newspaper.'

'They can—they can,' said Mark Clark, with corroborative feeling; 'but we Churchmen, you see, must have it all printed aforehand, or, dang it all, we should no more know what to say to a great gaffer like the Lord than babes unborn.'

'Chapel-folk be more hand-in-glove with them above than we,' said Joseph, thoughtfully.

'Yes,' said Coggan. 'We know very well that if anybody do go to heaven, they will. They've worked hard for it, and they deserve to have it, such as 'tis. I baint such a fool as to pretend that we who stick to the Church have the same chance as they, because we know we have not. But I hate a feller who'll change his old ancient doctrines for the sake of getting to heaven. I'd as soon turn king's-evidence for the few pounds you get. Why, neighbours, when every one of my taties were frosted, our Pa'son Thirdly were the man who gave me a sack for seed, though he hardly had one for his own use, and no money to buy 'em. If it hadn't been for him, I shouldn't hae had a tatie to put in my garden. D'ye think I'd turn after that? No, I'll stick to my side; and if we be in the wrong, so be it: I'll fall with the fallen!'

'Well said—very well said,' observed Joseph.— 'However, folks, I must be moving now: upon my life I must. Pa'son Thirdly will be waiting at the church gates, and there's the woman a-biding outside in the waggon.'

'Joseph Poorgrass, don't be so miserable! Pa'son Thirdly won't mind. He's a generous man; he's found me in tracts for years, and I've consumed a good many in the course of a long and shady life; but he's never been the man to cry out at the expense. Sit down.'

The longer Joseph Poorgrass remained, the less his spirit was troubled by the duties which devolved upon him this afternoon. The minutes glided by uncounted, until the evening shades began perceptibly to deepen, and the eyes of the three were but sparkling points on the surface of darkness. Coggan's watch struck six from his pocket in the usual still small tones.

At that moment hasty steps were heard in the entry, and the door opened to admit the figure of Gabriel Oak, followed by the maid of the inn bearing a candle. He stared sternly at the one lengthy and two round faces

336

of the sitters, which confronted him with the expressions of a fiddle and a couple of warming-pans. Joseph Poorgrass blinked, and shrank several inches into the background.

'Upon my soul, I'm ashamed of you; 'tis disgraceful, Joseph, disgraceful!' said Gabriel, indignantly. 'Coggan, you call yourself a man, and don't know better than this.'

Coggan looked up indefinitely at Oak, one or other of his eyes occasionally opening and closing of its own accord, as if it were not a member, but a dozy individual with a distinct personality.

'Don't take on so, shepherd!' said Mark Clark, looking reproachfully at the candle, which appeared to possess special features of interest for his eyes.

'Nobody can hurt a dead woman,' at length said Coggan, with the precision of a machine. 'All that could be done for her is done—she's beyond us: and why should a man put himself in a tearing hurry for lifeless clay that can neither feel nor see, and don't know what you do with her at all? If she'd been alive, I would have been the first to help her. If she now wanted victuals and drink, I'd pay for it, money down. But she's dead, and no speed of ours will bring her to life. The woman's past us—time spent upon her is throwed away: why should we hurry to do what's not required? Drink, shepherd, and be friends, for to-morrow we may be like her.'

'We may,' added Mark Clark, emphatically, at once drinking himself, to run no further risk of losing his chance by the event alluded to, Jan meanwhile merging his additional thoughts of to-morrow in a song:—

To-mor-row, to-mor-row!
And while peace and plen-ty I find at my board,
With a heart free from sick-ness and sor-row,
With my friends will I share what to-day may af-ford,
And let them spread the ta-ble to-mor-row.
To-mor-row, to-mor——

337

'Do hold thy horning, Jan!' said Oak; and turning upon Poorgrass, 'as for you, Joseph, who do your wicked deeds in such confoundedly holy ways, you are as drunk as you can stand.'

'No, Shepherd Oak, no! Listen to reason, shepherd. All that's the matter with me is the affliction called a multiplying eye, and that's how it is I look double to you—I mean, you look double to me.'

'A multiplying eye is a very bad thing,' said Mark Clark.

'It always comes on when I have been in a public-house a little time,' said Joseph Poorgrass, meekly. 'Yes; I see two of every sort, as if I were some holy man living in the times of King Noah and entering into the ark. . . . Y-y-y-yes,' he added, becoming much affected by the picture of himself as a person thrown away, and shedding tears; 'I feel too good for England: I ought to have lived in Genesis by rights, like the other men of sacrifice, and then I shouldn't have b-b-been called a d-d-drunkard in such a way!'

'I wish you'd show yourself a man of spirit, and not sit whining there!'

'Show myself a man of spirit? . . . Ah, well! let me take the name of drunkard humbly—let me be a man of contrite knees—let it be! I know that I always do say "Please God" afore I do anything, from my getting up to my going down of the same, and I be willing to take as much disgrace as there is in that holy act. Hah, yes! . . . But not a man of spirit? Have I ever allowed the toe of pride to be lifted against my hinder parts without groaning manfully that I question the right to do so? I inquire that query boldly?'

'We can't say that you have, Hero Poorgrass,' admitted Jan.

'Never have I allowed such treatment to pass un-questioned! Yet the shepherd says in the face of that

rich testimony that I be not a man of spirit! Well,
let it pass by, and death is a real release!'

Gabriel, seeing that neither of the three was in a fit
state to take charge of the waggon for the remainder of
the journey, made no reply, but, closing the door again
upon them, went across to where the vehicle stood, now
getting indistinct in the fog and gloom of this mildewy
time. He pulled the horse's head from the large patch
of turf it had eaten bare, readjusted the boughs over
the coffin, and drove along through the unwholesome
night.

It had gradually become rumoured in the village
that the body to be brought and buried that day was
all that was left of the unfortunate Fanny Robin who
had followed the Eleventh from Casterbridge through
Melchester and onwards. But, thanks to Boldwood's
reticence and Oak's generosity, the lover she had followed
had never been individualized as Troy. Gabriel hoped
that the whole truth of the matter might not be published
till at any rate the girl had been in her grave for a few
days, when the interposing barriers of earth and time,
and a sense that the events had been somewhat shut
into oblivion, would deaden the sting that revelation and
invidious remark would have for Bathsheba just now.

By the time that Gabriel reached the old manor-
house, her residence, which lay in his way to the church,
it was quite dark. A man came from the gate and said
through the fog, which hung between them like blown
flour—

'Is that Poorgrass with the corpse?'

Gabriel recognized the voice as that of the parson.

'The corpse is here, sir,' said Gabriel.

'I have just been to inquire of Mrs. Troy if she could
tell me the reason of the delay. I am afraid it is too
late now for the funeral to be performed with proper
decency. Have you the registrar's certificate?'

'No,' said Gabriel. 'I expect Poorgrass has that;

339

and he's at the Buck's Head. I forgot to ask him for it.'

'Then that settles the matter. We'll put off the funeral till to-morrow morning. The body may be brought on to the church, or it may be left here at the farm and fetched by the bearers in the morning. They waited more than an hour, and have now gone home.'

Gabriel had his reasons for thinking the latter a most objectionable plan, notwithstanding that Fanny had been an inmate of the farm-house for several years in the lifetime of Bathsheba's uncle. Visions of several unhappy contingencies which might arise from this delay flitted before him. But his will was not law, and he went indoors to inquire of his mistress what were her wishes on the subject. He found her in an unusual mood: her eyes as she looked up to him were suspicious and perplexed as with some antecedent thought. Troy had not yet returned. At first Bathsheba assented with a mien of indifference to his proposition that they should go on to the church at once with their burden; but immediately afterwards, following Gabriel to the gate, she swerved to the extreme of solicitousness on Fanny's account, and desired that the girl might be brought into the house. Oak argued upon the convenience of leaving her in the waggon, just as she lay now, with her flowers and green leaves about her, merely wheeling the vehicle into the coach-house till the morning, but to no purpose. 'It is unkind and unchristian,' she said, 'to leave the poor thing in a coach-house all night.'

'Very well, then,' said the parson. 'And I will arrange that the funeral shall take place early to-morrow. Perhaps Mrs. Troy is right in feeling that we cannot treat a dead fellow-creature too thoughtfully. We must remember that though she may have erred grievously in leaving her home, she is still our sister; and it is to be believed that God's uncovenanted mercies are extended towards her, and that she is a member of the flock of Christ.'

The parson's words spread into the heavy air with a sad yet unperturbed cadence, and Gabriel shed an honest tear. Bathsheba seemed unmoved. Mr. Thirdly then left them, and Gabriel lighted a lantern. Fetching three other men to assist him, they bore the unconscious truant indoors, placing the coffin on two benches in the middle of a little sitting-room next the hall, as Bathsheba directed.

Every one except Gabriel Oak then left the room. He still indecisively lingered beside the body. He was deeply troubled at the wretchedly ironical aspect that circumstances were putting on with regard to Troy's wife, and at his own powerlessness to counteract them. In spite of his careful manœuvring all this day, the very worst event that could in any way have happened in connection with the burial had happened now. Oak imagined a terrible discovery resulting from this afternoon's work that might cast over Bathsheba's life a shade which the interposition of many lapsing years might but indifferently lighten, and which nothing at all might altogether remove.

Suddenly, as in a last attempt to save Bathsheba from, at any rate, immediate anguish, he looked again, as he had looked before, at the chalk writing upon the coffin-lid. The scrawl was this simple one, '*Fanny Robin and child.*' Gabriel took his handkerchief and carefully rubbed out the two latter words, leaving visible the inscription '*Fanny Robin*' only. He then left the room, and went out quietly by the front door.

CHAPTER XLIII

FANNY'S REVENGE

'Do you want me any longer, ma'am?' inquired Liddy, at a later hour the same evening, standing by the door with a chamber candlestick in her hand, and addressing Bathsheba, who sat cheerless and alone in the large parlour beside the first fire of the season.

'No more to-night, Liddy.'

'I'll sit up for master if you like, ma'am. I am not at all afraid of Fanny, if I may sit in my own room and have a candle. She was such a childlike, nesh young thing that her spirit couldn't appear to anybody if it tried, I'm quite sure.'

'Oh no, no! You go to bed. I'll sit up for him myself till twelve o'clock, and if he has not arrived by that time, I shall give him up and go to bed too.'

'It is half-past ten now.'

'Oh! is it?'

'Why don't you sit upstairs, ma'am?'

'Why don't I?' said Bathsheba, desultorily. 'It isn't worth while—there's a fire here, Liddy.' She suddenly exclaimed in an impulsive and excited whisper, 'Have you heard anything strange said of Fanny?' The words had no sooner escaped her than an expression of unutterable regret crossed her face, and she burst into tears.

'No—not a word!' said Liddy, looking at the weeping woman with astonishment. 'What is it makes you cry so, ma'am; has anything hurt you?' She came to Bathsheba's side with a face full of sympathy.

'No, Liddy—I don't want you any more. I can hardly say why I have taken so to crying lately: I never used to cry. Good-night.'

Liddy then left the parlour and closed the door.

Bathsheba was lonely and miserable now; not lonelier actually than she had been before her marriage; but her loneliness then was to that of the present time as the solitude of a mountain is to the solitude of a cave. And within the last day or two had come these disquieting thoughts about her husband's past. Her wayward sentiment that evening concerning Fanny's temporary resting-place had been the result of a strange complication of impulses in Bathsheba's bosom. Perhaps it would be more accurately described as a determined rebellion against her prejudices, a revulsion from a lower instinct of uncharitableness, which would have withheld all sympathy from the dead woman, because in life she had preceded Bathsheba in the attentions of a man whom Bathsheba had by no means ceased from loving, though her love was sick to death just now with the gravity of a further misgiving.

In five or ten minutes there was another tap at the door. Liddy reappeared, and coming in a little way stood hesitating, until at length she said, 'Maryann has just heard something very strange, but I know it isn't true. And we shall be sure to know the rights of it in a day or two.'

'What is it?'

'Oh, nothing connected with you or us, ma'am. It is about Fanny. That same thing you have heard.'

'I have heard nothing.'

'I mean that a wicked story is got to Weatherbury within this last hour—that——' Liddy came close to her mistress and whispered the remainder of the sentence slowly into her ear, inclining her head as she spoke in the direction of the room where Fanny lay.

Bathsheba trembled from head to foot.

'I don't believe it!' she said, excitedly. 'And there's only one name written on the coffin-cover.'

'Nor I, ma'am. And a good many others don't; for we should surely have been told more about it if it had been true—don't you think so, ma'am?'

'We might or we might not.'

Bathsheba turned and looked into the fire, that Liddy might not see her face. Finding that her mistress was going to say no more, Liddy glided out, closed the door softly, and went to bed.

Bathsheba's face, as she continued looking into the fire that evening, might have excited solicitousness on her account even among those who loved her least. The sadness of Fanny Robin's fate did not make Bathsheba's glorious, although she was the Esther to this poor Vashti, and their fates might be supposed to stand in some respects as contrasts to each other. When Liddy came into the room a second time the beautiful eyes which met hers had worn a listless, weary look. When she went out after telling the story they had expressed wretchedness in full activity. This also sank to apathy after a time. But her thoughts, sluggish and confused at first, acquired more life as the minutes passed, and the dull misgiving in her brow and eyes suddenly gave way to the stillness of concentration.

Bathsheba had grounds for conjecturing a connection between her own history and the dimly suspected tragedy of Fanny's end which Oak and Boldwood never for a moment credited her with possessing. The meeting with the lonely woman on the previous Saturday night had been unwitnessed and unspoken of. Oak may have had the best of intentions in withholding for as many days as possible the details of what had happened to Fanny; but had he known that Bathsheba's perceptions had already been exercised in the matter, he would have done nothing to lengthen the minutes of suspense she was now undergoing, when the certainty which must terminate it would be the worst fact suspected after all.

She suddenly felt a longing desire to speak to some one stronger than herself, and so get strength to sustain her surmised position with dignity and her carking doubts with stoicism. Where could she find such a friend? nowhere in the house. She was by far the coolest of the women under her roof. Patience and suspension of judgment for a few hours were what she wanted to learn, and there was nobody to teach her. Might she but go to Gabriel Oak!—but that could not be. What a way Oak had, she thought, of enduring things. Boldwood, who seemed so much deeper and higher and stronger in feeling than Gabriel, had not yet learnt, any more than she herself, the simple lesson which Oak showed a mastery of by every turn and look he gave—that among the multitude of interests by which he was surrounded, those which affected his personal well-being were not the most absorbing and important in his eyes. Oak meditatively looked upon the horizon of circumstances without any special regard to his own standpoint in the midst. That was how she would wish to be. But then Oak was not racked by incertitude upon the inmost matter of his bosom, as she was at this moment. Oak knew all about Fanny that she wished to know—she felt convinced of that. If she were to go to him now at once and say no more than these few words, 'What is the truth of the story?' he would feel bound in honour to tell her. It would be an inexpressible relief. No further speech would need to be uttered. He knew her so well that no eccentricity of behaviour in her would alarm him.

She flung a cloak round her, went to the door and

opened it. Every blade, every twig was still. The air
was yet thick with moisture, though somewhat less dense
than during the afternoon, and a steady smack of drops
upon the fallen leaves under the boughs was almost
musical in its soothing regularity. It seemed better to
be out of the house than within it, and Bathsheba closed
the door, and walked slowly down the lane till she came
opposite to Gabriel's cottage, where he now lived alone,
having left Coggan's house through being pinched for
room. There was a light in one window only, and that
was downstairs. The shutters were not closed, nor was
any blind or curtain drawn over the window, neither
robbery nor observation being a contingency which could
do much injury to the occupant of the domicile. Yes,
it was Gabriel himself who was sitting up : he was reading.
From her standing-place in the road she could see him
plainly, sitting quite still, his light curly head upon his
hand, and only occasionally looking up to snuff the
candle which stood beside him. At length he looked
at the clock, seemed surprised at the lateness of the
hour, closed his book, and arose. He was going to bed,
she knew, and if she tapped it must be done at once.

Alas for her resolve ! She felt she could not do it.
Not for worlds now could she give a hint about her
misery to him, much less ask him plainly for information
on the cause of Fanny's death. She must suspect, and
guess, and chafe, and bear it all alone.

Like a homeless wanderer she lingered by the bank,
as if lulled and fascinated by the atmosphere of content
which seemed to spread from that little dwelling, and
was so sadly lacking in her own. Gabriel appeared in
an upper room, placed his light in the window-bench,
and then—knelt down to pray. The contrast of the
picture with her rebellious and agitated existence at this
same time was too much for her to bear to look upon
longer. It was not for her to make a truce with
trouble by any such means. She must tread her giddy

distracting measure to its last note, as she had begun it.
With a swollen heart she went again up the lane, and
entered her own door.

More fevered now by a reaction from the first feelings
which Oak's example had raised in her, she paused in
the hall, looking at the door of the room wherein Fanny
lay. She locked her fingers, threw back her head, and
strained her hot hands rigidly across her forehead, saying,
with a hysterical sob, 'Would to God you would speak
and tell me your secret, Fanny! . . . Oh, I hope, hope
it is not true that there are two of you! . . . If I could
only look in upon you for one little minute, I should
know all!'

A few moments passed, and she added, slowly, '*And
I will.*'

Bathsheba in after times could never gauge the mood
which carried her through the actions following this
murmured resolution on this memorable evening of her
life. She went to the lumber-closet for a screw-driver.
At the end of a short though undefined time she found
herself in the small room, quivering with emotion, a mist
before her eyes, and an excruciating pulsation in her
brain, standing beside the uncovered coffin of the girl
whose conjectured end had so entirely engrossed her, and
saying to herself in a husky voice as she gazed within—

'It was best to know the worst, and I know it now!'

She was conscious of having brought about this
situation by a series of actions done as by one in an
extravagant dream ; of following that idea as to method,
which had burst upon her in the hall with glaring
obviousness, by gliding to the top of the stairs, assuring
herself by listening to the heavy breathing of her maids
that they were asleep, gliding down again, turning the
handle of the door within which the young girl lay, and
deliberately setting herself to do what, if she had anticipated any such undertaking at night and alone, would
have horrified her, but which, when done, was not so

347

dreadful as was the conclusive proof of her husband's conduct which came with knowing beyond doubt the last chapter of Fanny's story.

Bathsheba's head sank upon her bosom, and the breath which had been bated in suspense, curiosity, and interest, was exhaled now in the form of a whispered wail: 'Oh-h-h!' she said, and the silent room added length to her moan.

Her tears fell fast beside the unconscious pair in the coffin: tears of a complicated origin, of a nature indescribable, almost indefinable except as other than those of simple sorrow. Assuredly their wonted fires must have lived in Fanny's ashes when events were so shaped as to chariot her hither in this natural, unobtrusive, yet effectual manner. The one feat alone—that of dying—by which a mean condition could be resolved into a grand one, Fanny had achieved. And to that had destiny subjoined this rencounter to-night, which had, in Bathsheba's wild imagining, turned her companion's failure to success, her humiliation to triumph, her lucklessness to ascendency; it had thrown over herself a garish light of mockery, and set upon all things about her an ironical smile.

Fanny's face was framed in by that yellow hair of hers; and there was no longer much room for doubt as to the origin of the curl owned by Troy. In Bathsheba's heated fancy the innocent white countenance expressed a dim triumphant consciousness of the pain she was retaliating for her pain with all the merciless rigour of the Mosaic law: 'Burning for burning; wound for wound; strife for strife.'

Bathsheba indulged in contemplations of escape from her position by immediate death, which, thought she, though it was an inconvenient and awful way, had limits to its inconvenience and awfulness that could not be overpassed; whilst the shames of life were measureless. Yet even this scheme of extinction by death was but tamely copying her rival's method without the reasons which had glorified it in her rival's case. She glided rapidly up and down the room, as was mostly her habit when excited, her hands hanging clasped in front of her, as she thought and in part expressed in broken words: 'Oh, I hate her, yet I don't mean that I hate her, for it is grievous and wicked; and yet I hate her a little! Yes, my flesh insists upon hating her, whether my spirit is willing or no! . . . If she had only lived, I could have been angry and cruel towards her with some justification; but to be vindictive towards a poor dead woman recoils upon myself. O God, have mercy! I am miserable at all this!'

Bathsheba became at this moment so terrified at her own state of mind that she looked around for some sort of refuge from herself. The vision of Oak kneeling down that night recurred to her, and with the imitative instinct which animates women she seized upon the idea, resolved to kneel, and, if possible, pray. Gabriel had prayed; so would she.

She knelt beside the coffin, covered her face with her hands, and for a time the room was silent as a tomb. Whether from a purely mechanical, or from any other cause, when Bathsheba arose it was with a quieted spirit, and a regret for the antagonistic instincts which had seized upon her just before.

In her desire to make atonement she took flowers from a vase by the window, and began laying them around the dead girl's head. Bathsheba knew no other way of showing kindness to persons departed than by giving them flowers. She knew not how long she remained engaged thus. She forgot time, life, where she was, what she was doing. A slamming together of the coach-house doors in the yard brought her to herself again. An instant after, the front door opened and closed, steps crossed the hall, and her husband appeared at the entrance to the room, looking in upon her.

He beheld it all by degrees, stared in stupefaction at the scene, as if he thought it an illusion raised by some fiendish incantation. Bathsheba, pallid as a corpse on end, gazed back at him in the same wild way.

So little are instinctive guesses the fruit of a legitimate induction, that at this moment, as he stood with the door in his hand, Troy never once thought of Fanny in connection with what he saw. His first confused idea was that somebody in the house had died.

'Well—what?' said Troy, blankly.

'I must go! I must go!' said Bathsheba, to herself more than to him. She came with a dilated eye towards the door, to push past him.

'What's the matter, in God's name? who's dead?' said Troy.

'I cannot say; let me go out. I want air!' she continued.

'But no; stay, I insist!' He seized her hand, and then volition seemed to leave her, and she went off into a state of passivity. He, still holding her, came up the room, and thus, hand in hand, Troy and Bathsheba approached the coffin's side.

The candle was standing on a bureau close by them, and the light slanted down, distinctly enkindling the cold features of both mother and babe. Troy looked in, dropped his wife's hand, knowledge of it all came over him in a lurid sheen, and he stood still.

So still he remained that he could be imagined to have left in him no motive power whatever. The clashes of feeling in all directions confounded one another, produced a neutrality, and there was motion in none.

'Do you know her?' said Bathsheba, in a small enclosed echo, as from the interior of a cell.

'I do,' said Troy.

'Is it she?'

'It is.'

350

He had originally stood perfectly erect. And now, in the well-nigh congealed immobility of his frame could be discerned an incipient movement, as in the darkest night may be discerned light after a while. He was gradually sinking forwards. The lines of his features softened, and dismay modulated to illimitable sadness. Bathsheba was regarding him from the other side, still with parted lips and distracted eyes. Capacity for intense feeling is proportionate to the general intensity of the nature, and perhaps in all Fanny's sufferings, much greater relatively to her strength, there never was a time when she suffered in an absolute sense what Bathsheba suffered now.

This is what Troy did. He sank upon his knees with an indefinable union of remorse and reverence upon his face, and, bending over Fanny Robin, gently kissed her, as one would kiss an infant asleep to avoid awakening it.

At the sight and sound of that, to her, unendurable act, Bathsheba sprang towards him. All the strong feelings which had been scattered over her existence since she knew what feeling was, seemed gathered together into one pulsation now. The revulsion from her indignant mood a little earlier, when she had meditated upon compromised honour, forestalment, eclipse in maternity by another, was violent and entire. All that was forgotten in the simple and still strong attachment of wife to husband. She had sighed for her self-completeness then, and now she cried aloud against the severance of the union she had deplored. She flung her arms round Troy's neck, exclaiming wildly from the deepest deep of her heart—

'Don't—don't kiss them! Oh, Frank, I can't bear it—I can't! I love you better than she did: kiss me too, Frank—kiss me! *You will, Frank, kiss me too!*'

There was something so abnormal and startling in the childlike pain and simplicity of this appeal from a woman of Bathsheba's calibre and independence, that Troy, loosening her tightly clasped arms from his neck, looked at her in bewilderment. It was such an unexpected revelation of all women being alike at heart, even those so different in their accessories as Fanny and this one beside him, that Troy could hardly seem to believe her to be his proud wife Bathsheba. Fanny's own spirit seemed to be animating her frame. But this was the mood of a few instants only. When the momentary surprise had passed, his expression changed to a silencing imperious gaze.

'I will not kiss you!' he said, pushing her away.

Had the wife now but gone no further. Yet, perhaps, under the harrowing circumstances, to speak out was the one wrong act which can be better understood, if not forgiven in her, than the right and politic one. All the feeling she had been betrayed into showing she drew back to herself again by a strenuous effort of self-command.

'What have you to say as your reason?' she asked, her bitter voice being strangely low—quite that of another woman now.

'I have to say that I have been a bad, black-hearted man,' he answered.

'And that this woman is your victim; and I not less than she.'

'Ah! don't taunt me, madam. This woman is more to me, dead as she is, than ever you were, or are, or can be. If Satan had not tempted me with that face of yours, and those cursed coquetries, I should have married her. I never had another thought till you came in my way. Would to God that I had; but it is all too late! I deserve to live in torment for this!' He turned to Fanny then. 'But never mind, darling,' he said; 'in the sight of Heaven you are my very, very wife!'

At these words there arose from Bathsheba's lips a

long, low cry of measureless despair and indignation, such a wail of anguish as had never before been heard within those old-inhabited walls. It was the Τετέλεσται of her union with Troy.

'If she's — that,—what—am I?' she added, as a continuation of the same cry, and sobbing pitifully: and the rarity with her of such abandonment only made the condition more dire.

'You are nothing to me — nothing,' said Troy, heartlessly. 'A ceremony before a priest doesn't make a marriage. I am not morally yours.'

A vehement impulse to flee from him, to run from this place, hide, and escape his words at any price, not stopping short of death itself, mastered Bathsheba now. She waited not an instant, but turned to the door and ran out.

CHAPTER XLIV

UNDER A TREE—REACTION

BATHSHEBA went along the dark road, neither knowing nor caring about the direction or issue of her flight.
The first time that she definitely noticed her position
was when she reached a gate leading into a thicket overhung by some large oak and beech trees. On looking
into the place, it occurred to her that she had seen it
by daylight on some previous occasion, and that what
appeared like an impassable thicket was in reality a
brake of fern now withering fast. She could think of
nothing better to do with her palpitating self than to go
in here and hide; and entering, she lighted on a spot
sheltered from the damp fog by a reclining trunk, where
she sank down upon a tangled couch of fronds and
stems. She mechanically pulled some armfuls round
her to keep off the breezes, and closed her eyes.

Whether she slept or not that night Bathsheba was
not clearly aware. But it was with a freshened existence and a cooler brain that, a long time afterwards, she
became conscious of some interesting proceedings which
were going on in the trees above her head and around.

A coarse-throated chatter was the first sound.

It was a sparrow just waking.

Next: 'Chee-weeze-weeze-weeze!' from another
retreat.

It was a finch.

Third : 'Tink-tink-tink-tink-a-chink !' from the hedge.

It was a robin.

'Chuck-chuck-chuck !' overhead.

A squirrel.

Then, from the road, 'With my ra-ta-ta, and my rum-tum-tum !'

It was a ploughboy. Presently he came opposite, and she believed from his voice that he was one of the boys on her own farm. He was followed by a shambling tramp of heavy feet, and looking through the ferns Bathsheba could just discern in the wan light of daybreak a team of her own horses. They stopped to drink at a pond on the other side of the way. She watched them flouncing into the pool, drinking, tossing up their heads, drinking again, the water dribbling from their lips in silver threads. There was another flounce, and they came out of the pond, and turned back again towards the farm.

She looked further around. Day was just dawning, and beside its cool air and colours her heated actions and resolves of the night stood out in lurid contrast. She perceived that in her lap, and clinging to her hair, were red and yellow leaves which had come down from the tree and settled silently upon her during her partial sleep. Bathsheba shook her dress to get rid of them, when multitudes of the same family lying round about her rose and fluttered away in the breeze thus created, 'like ghosts from an enchanter fleeing.'

There was an opening towards the east, and the glow from the as yet unrisen sun attracted her eyes thither. From her feet, and between the beautiful yellowing ferns with their feathery arms, the ground sloped downwards to a hollow, in which was a species of swamp, dotted with fungi. A morning mist hung over it now—a fulsome yet magnificent silvery veil, full of light from the sun, yet semi-opaque—the hedge behind it being in some measure hidden by its hazy luminousness. Up the sides of this depression grew sheaves of the common rush, and here and there a peculiar species of flag, the blades of which glistened in the emerging sun, like scythes. But the general aspect of the swamp was malignant. From its moist and poisonous coat seemed to be exhaled the essences of evil things in the earth, and in the waters under the earth. The fungi grew in all manner of positions from rotting leaves and tree stumps, some exhibiting to her listless gaze their clammy tops, others their oozing gills. Some were marked with great splotches, red as arterial blood, others were saffron yellow, and others tall and attenuated, with stems like macaroni. Some were leathery and of richest browns. The hollow seemed a nursery of pestilences small and great, in the immediate neighbourhood of comfort and health, and Bathsheba arose with a tremor at the thought of having passed the night on the brink of so dismal a place.

There were now other footsteps to be heard along the road. Bathsheba's nerves were still unstrung: she crouched down out of sight again, and the pedestrian came into view. He was a schoolboy, with a bag slung over his shoulder containing his dinner, and a book in his hand. He paused by the gate, and, without looking up, continued murmuring words in tones quite loud enough to reach her ears.

'"O Lord, O Lord, O Lord, O Lord, O Lord":— that I know out o' book. "Give us, give us, give us, give us, give us":—that I know. "Grace that, grace that, grace that, grace that":—that I know.' Other words followed to the same effect. The boy was of the dunce class apparently; the book was a psalter, and this was his way of learning the collect. In the worst attacks of trouble there appears to be always a superficial film of consciousness which is left disengaged

and open to the notice of trifles, and Bathsheba was
faintly amused at the boy's method, till he too passed on.

By this time stupor had given place to anxiety, and
anxiety began to make room for hunger and thirst.
A form now appeared upon the rise on the other side
of the swamp, half-hidden by the mist, and came
towards Bathsheba. The woman—for it was a woman
—approached with her face askance, as if looking
earnestly on all sides of her. When she got a little
further round to the left, and drew nearer, Bathsheba
could see the newcomer's profile against the sunny
sky, and knew the wavy sweep from forehead to chin,
with neither angle nor decisive line anywhere about
it, to be the familiar contour of Liddy Smallbury.

Bathsheba's heart bounded with gratitude in the
thought that she was not altogether deserted, and she
jumped up. 'Oh, Liddy!' she said, or attempted to say;
but the words had only been framed by her lips; there
came no sound. She had lost her voice by exposure
to the clogged atmosphere all these hours of night.

'Oh, ma'am! I am so glad I have found you,' said
the girl, as soon as she saw Bathsheba.

'You can't come across,' Bathsheba said in a whisper,
which she vainly endeavoured to make loud enough to
reach Liddy's ears. Liddy, not knowing this, stepped
down upon the swamp, saying, as she did so, 'It will
bear me up, I think.'

Bathsheba never forgot that transient little picture
of Liddy crossing the swamp to her there in the
morning light. Iridescent bubbles of dank subter-
ranean breath rose from the sweating sod beside the
waiting maid's feet as she trod, hissing as they burst
and expanded away to join the vapoury firmament above.
Liddy did not sink, as Bathsheba had anticipated.

She landed safely on the other side, and looked up
at the beautiful though pale and weary face of her
young mistress.

'Poor thing!' said Liddy, with tears in her eyes. 'Do hearten yourself up a little, ma'am. However did——'

'I can't speak above a whisper—my voice is gone for the present,' said Bathsheba, hurriedly. 'I suppose the damp air from that hollow has taken it away. Liddy, don't question me, mind. Who sent you—anybody?'

'Nobody. I thought, when I found you were not at home, that something cruel had happened. I fancy I heard his voice late last night; and so, knowing something was wrong——'

'Is he at home?'

'No; he left just before I came out.'

'Is Fanny taken away?'

'Not yet. She will soon be—at nine o'clock.'

'We won't go home at present, then. Suppose we walk about in this wood?'

Liddy, without exactly understanding everything, or anything, in this episode, assented, and they walked together further among the trees.

'But you had better come in, ma'am, and have something to eat. You will die of a chill!'

'I shall not come indoors yet—perhaps never.'

'Shall I get you something to eat, and something else to put over your head besides that little shawl?'

'If you will, Liddy.'

Liddy vanished, and at the end of twenty minutes returned with a cloak, hat, some slices of bread and butter, a tea-cup, and some hot tea in a little china jug.

'Is Fanny gone?' said Bathsheba.

'No,' said her companion, pouring out the tea.

Bathsheba wrapped herself up and ate and drank sparingly. Her voice was then a little clearer, and a trifling colour returned to her face. 'Now we'll walk about again,' she said.

They wandered about the wood for nearly two

hours, Bathsheba replying in monosyllables to Liddy's prattle, for her mind ran on one subject, and one only. She interrupted with—

'I wonder if Fanny is gone by this time?'

'I will go and see.'

She came back with the information that the men were just taking away the corpse; that Bathsheba had been inquired for; that she had replied to the effect that her mistress was unwell and could not be seen.

'Then they think I am in my bedroom?'

'Yes.' Liddy then ventured to add: 'You said when I first found you that you might never go home again—you didn't mean it, ma'am?'

'No; I've altered my mind. It is only women with no pride in them who run away from their husbands. There is one position worse than that of being found dead in your husband's house from his ill-usage, and that is, to be found alive through having gone away to the house of somebody else. I've thought of it all this morning, and I've chosen my course. A runaway wife is an encumbrance to everybody, a burden to herself and a byword—all of which make up a heap of misery greater than any that comes by staying at home— though this may include the trifling items of insult, beating, and starvation. Liddy, if ever you marry— God forbid that you ever should!—you'll find yourself in a fearful situation; but mind this, don't you flinch. Stand your ground, and be cut to pieces. That's what I'm going to do.'

'Oh, mistress, don't talk so!' said Liddy, taking her hand; 'but I knew you had too much sense to bide away. May I ask what dreadful thing it is that has happened between you and him?'

'You may ask; but I may not tell.'

In about ten minutes they returned to the house by a circuitous route, entering at the rear. Bathsheba glided up the back stairs to a disused attic, and her companion followed.

'Liddy,' she said, with a lighter heart, for youth and hope had begun to reassert themselves; 'you are to be my confidante for the present—somebody must be—and I choose you. Well, I shall take up my abode here for a while. Will you get a fire lighted, put down a piece of carpet, and help me to make the place comfortable? Afterwards, I want you and Maryann to bring up that little stump bedstead in the small room, and the bed belonging to it, and a table, and some other things. . . . What shall I do to pass the heavy time away?'

'Hemming handkerchiefs is a very good thing,' said Liddy.

'Oh no, no! I hate needlework—I always did.'

'Knitting?'

'And that, too.'

'You might finish your sampler. Only the carnations and peacocks want filling in; and then it could be framed and glazed, and hung beside your aunt's, ma'am.'

'Samplers are out of date—horribly countrified. No, Liddy, I'll read. Bring up some books—not new ones. I haven't heart to read anything new.'

'Some of your uncle's old ones, ma'am?'

'Yes. Some of those we stowed away in boxes.' A faint gleam of humour passed over her face as she said: 'Bring Beaumont and Fletcher's *Maid's Tragedy;* and the *Mourning Bride;* and—let me see—*Night Thoughts*, and the *Vanity of Human Wishes.*'

'And that story of the black man, who murdered his wife Desdemona? It is a nice dismal one that would suit you excellent just now.'

'Now, Lidd, you've been looking into my books, without telling me; and I said you were not to! How do you know it would suit me? It wouldn't suit me at all.'

'But if the others do———'

'No, they don't; and I won't read dismal books. Why should I read dismal books, indeed? Bring me *Love in a Village*, and the *Maid of the Mill*, and *Doctor Syntax*, and some volumes of the *Spectator*.'

All that day Bathsheba and Liddy lived in the attic in a state of barricade; a precaution which proved to be needless as against Troy, for he did not appear in the neighbourhood or trouble them at all. Bathsheba sat at the window till sunset, sometimes attempting to read, at other times watching every movement outside without much purpose, and listening without much interest to every sound.

The sun went down almost blood-red that night, and a livid cloud received its rays in the east. Up against this dark background the west front of the church tower—the only part of the edifice visible from the farm-house windows—rose distinct and lustrous, the vane upon the summit bristling with rays. Hereabouts, at six o'clock, the young men of the village gathered, as was their custom, for a game of Prisoners' base. The spot had been consecrated to this ancient diversion from time immemorial, the old stocks conveniently forming a base facing the boundary of the churchyard, in front of which the ground was trodden hard and bare as a pavement by the players. She could see the brown and black heads of the young lads darting about right and left, their white shirt-sleeves gleaming in the sun; whilst occasionally a shout and a peal of hearty laughter varied the stillness of the evening air. They continued playing for a quarter of an hour or so, when the game concluded abruptly, and the players leapt over the wall and vanished round to the other side behind a yew-tree, which was also half behind a beech, now spreading in one mass of golden foliage, on which the branches traced black lines.

'Why did the base-players finish their game so

suddenly?' Bathsheba inquired, the next time that Liddy entered the room.

'I think 'twas because two men came just then from Casterbridge and began putting up a grand carved tombstone,' said Liddy. 'The lads went to see whose it was.'

'Do you know?' Bathsheba asked.

'I don't,' said Liddy.

CHAPTER XLV

TROY'S ROMANTICISM

WHEN Troy's wife had left the house at the previous midnight his first act was to cover the dead from sight. This done he ascended the stairs, and throwing himself down upon the bed dressed as he was, he waited miserably for the morning.

Fate had dealt grimly with him through the last four-and-twenty hours. His day had been spent in a way which varied very materially from his intentions regarding it. There is always an inertia to be overcome in striking out a new line of conduct—not more in ourselves, it seems, than in circumscribing events, which appear as if leagued together to allow no novelties in the way of amelioration.

Twenty pounds having been secured from Bathsheba, he had managed to add to the sum every farthing he could muster on his own account, which had been seven pounds ten. With this money, twenty-seven pounds ten in all, he had hastily driven from the gate that morning to keep his appointment with Fanny Robin.

On reaching Casterbridge he left the horse and trap at an inn, and at five minutes before ten went to the bridge at the lower end of the town, and sat himself upon the parapet. The clocks struck the hour, and no Fanny appeared. In fact, at that moment she was being robed in her grave-clothes by two attendants at the Union poorhouse—the first and last tiring-women the gentle creature had ever been honoured with. The quarter went, the half hour. A rush of recollection came upon Troy as he waited : this was the second time she had broken a serious engagement with him. In anger he vowed it should be the last, and at eleven o'clock, when he had lingered and watched the stones of the bridge till he knew every lichen upon their faces, and heard the chink of the ripples underneath till they oppressed him, he jumped from his seat, went to the inn for his gig, and in a bitter mood of indifference concerning the past, and recklessness about the future, drove on to Budmouth races.

He reached the race-course at two o'clock, and remained either there or in the town till nine. But Fanny's image, as it had appeared to him in the sombre shadows of that Saturday evening, returned to his mind, backed up by Bathsheba's reproaches. He vowed he would not bet, and he kept his vow, for on leaving the town at nine o'clock in the evening he had diminished his cash only to the extent of a few shillings.

He trotted slowly homeward, and it was now that he was struck for the first time with a thought that Fanny had been really prevented by illness from keeping her promise. This time she could have made no mistake. He regretted that he had not remained in Casterbridge and made inquiries. Reaching home he quietly unharnessed the horse and came indoors, as we have seen, to the fearful shock that awaited him.

As soon as it grew light enough to distinguish objects, Troy arose from the coverlet of the bed, and in a mood of absolute indifference to Bathsheba's whereabouts, and almost oblivious of her existence, he stalked downstairs and left the house by the back door. His walk was towards the churchyard, entering which he searched around till he found a newly dug unoccupied grave— the grave dug the day before for Fanny. The position of this having been marked, he hastened on to Caster-bridge, only pausing and musing for a while at the hill whereon he had last seen Fanny alive.

Reaching the town, Troy descended into a side street and entered a pair of gates surmounted by a board bearing the words, 'Lester, stone and marble mason.' Within were lying about stones of all sizes and designs, inscribed as being sacred to the memory of unnamed persons who had not yet died.

Troy was so unlike himself now in look, word, and deed, that the want of likeness was perceptible even to his own consciousness. His method of engaging himself in this business of purchasing a tomb was that of an absolutely unpractised man. He could not bring himself to consider, calculate, or economize. He waywardly wished for something, and he set about obtaining it like a child in a nursery. 'I want a good tomb,' he said to the man who stood in a little office within the yard. 'I want as good a one as you can give me for twenty-seven pounds.'

It was all the money he possessed.

'That sum to include everything?'

'Everything. Cutting the name, carriage to Weather-bury, and erection. And I want it now, at once.'

'We could not get anything special worked this week.'

'I must have it now.'

'If you would like one of these in stock it could be got ready immediately.'

'Very well,' said Troy, impatiently. 'Let's see what you have.'

'The best I have in stock is this one,' said the stone-cutter, going into a shed. 'Here's a marble headstone beautifully crocketed, with medallions beneath of typical subjects; here's the footstone after the same pattern, and here's the coping to enclose the grave. The polishing alone of the set cost me eleven pounds—the slabs are the best of their kind, and I can warrant them to resist rain and frost for a hundred years without flying.'

'And how much?'

'Well, I could add the name, and put it up at Weatherbury for the sum you mention.'

'Get it done to-day, and I'll pay the money now.'

The man agreed, and wondered at such a mood in a visitor who wore not a shred of mourning. Troy then wrote the words which were to form the inscription, settled the account and went away. In the afternoon he came back again, and found that the lettering was almost done. He waited in the yard till the tomb was packed, and saw it placed in the cart and starting on its way to Weatherbury, giving directions to the two men who were to accompany it to inquire of the sexton for the grave of the person named in the inscription.

It was quite dark when Troy came out of Caster-bridge. He carried rather a heavy basket upon his arm, with which he strode moodily along the road, resting occasionally at bridges and gates, whereon he deposited his burden for a time. Midway on his journey he met, returning in the darkness, the men and the waggon which had conveyed the tomb. He merely inquired if the work was done, and, on being assured that it was, passed on again.

Troy entered Weatherbury churchyard about ten o'clock, and went immediately to the corner where he had marked the vacant grave early in the morning. It was on the obscure side of the tower, screened to a great extent from the view of passers along the road—a spot which until lately had been abandoned to heaps of stones and bushes of alder, but now it was cleared and made orderly for interments, by reason of the rapid filling of the ground elsewhere.

Here now stood the tomb as the men had stated, snow-white and shapely in the gloom, with a head and foot-stone, and enclosing border of marble-work uniting them. In the midst was mould, suitable for plants.

Troy deposited his basket beside the tomb, and vanished for a few minutes. When he returned he carried a spade and a lantern, the light of which he directed for a few moments upon the tomb, whilst he read the inscription. He hung his lantern on the lowest bough of the yew-tree, and took from his basket flower-roots of several varieties. There were bundles of snow-drop, hyacinth and crocus bulbs, violets and double daisies, which were to bloom in early spring, and of carnations, pinks, picotees, lilies of the valley, forget-me-not, summer's-farewell, meadow-saffron and others, for the later seasons of the year.

Troy laid these out upon the grass, and with an impassive face set to work to plant them. The snowdrops were arranged in a line on the outside of the coping, the remainder within the enclosure of the grave. The crocuses and hyacinths were to grow in rows; some of the summer flowers he placed over her head and feet, the lilies and forget-me-nots over her heart. The remainder were dispersed in the spaces between these.

Troy, in his prostration at this time, had no perception that in the futility of these romantic doings, dictated by a remorseful reaction from previous indifference, there was any element of absurdity. Deriving his idiosyncrasies from both sides of the Channel, he showed at such junctures as the present the inelasticity of the Englishman, together with that blindness to the line where sentiment verges on mawkishness, characteristic of the French.

It was a cloudy, muggy, and very dark night, and the rays from Troy's lantern spread into the two old yews with a strange illuminating power, flickering, as it seemed, up to the black ceiling of cloud above. He felt a large drop of rain upon the back of his hand, and presently one came and entered one of the holes of the lantern, whereupon the candle sputtered and went out. Troy was weary, and it being now not far from midnight, and the rain threatening to increase, he resolved to leave the finishing touches of his labour until the day should break. He groped along the wall and over the graves in the dark till he found himself round at the north side. Here he entered the porch, and, reclining upon the bench within, fell asleep.

CHAPTER XLVI

THE GURGOYLE: ITS DOINGS

THE tower of Weatherbury Church was a square erection of fourteenth-century date, having two stone gurgoyles on each of the four faces of its parapet. Of these eight carved protuberances only two at this time continued to serve the purpose of their erection—that of spouting the water from the lead roof within. One mouth in each front had been closed by bygone church-wardens as superfluous, and two others were broken away and choked—a matter not of much consequence to the well-being of the tower, for the two mouths which still remained open and active were gaping enough to do all the work.

It has been sometimes argued that there is no truer criterion of the vitality of any given art-period than the power of the master-spirits of that time in grotesque; and certainly in the instance of Gothic art there is no disputing the proposition. Weatherbury tower was a somewhat early instance of the use of an ornamental parapet in parish as distinct from cathedral churches, and the gurgoyles, which are the necessary correlatives of a parapet, were exceptionally prominent—of the boldest cut that the hand could shape, and of the most original design that a human brain could conceive. There was, so to speak, that symmetry in their distortion which is less the characteristic of British than of Continental grotesques of the period. All the eight were different from each other. A beholder was convinced that nothing on earth could be more hideous than those he saw on the north side until he went round to the south. Of the two on this latter face, only that at the south-eastern corner concerns the story. It was too human to be called like a dragon, too impish to be like a man, too animal to be like a fiend, and not enough like a bird to be called a griffin. This horrible stone entity was fashioned as if covered with a wrinkled hide; it had short, erect ears, eyes starting from their sockets, and its fingers and hands were seizing the corners of its mouth, which they thus seemed to pull open to give free passage to the water it vomited. The lower row of teeth was quite washed away, though the upper still remained. Here and thus, jutting a couple of feet from the wall against which its feet rested as a support, the creature had for four hundred years laughed at the surrounding landscape, voicelessly in dry weather, and in wet with a gurgling and snorting sound.

Troy slept on in the porch, and the rain increased outside. Presently the gurgoyle spat. In due time a small stream began to trickle through the seventy feet of aërial space between its mouth and the ground, which the water-drops smote like duckshot in their accelerated velocity. The stream thickened in substance, and increased in power, gradually spouting farther and yet farther from the side of the tower. When the rain fell in a steady and ceaseless torrent the stream dashed downward in volumes.

We follow its course to the ground at this point of time. The base of the liquid parabola has come forward from the wall, has advanced over the plinth mouldings, over a heap of stones, over the marble border, into the midst of Fanny Robin's grave.

The force of the stream had, until very lately, been received upon some loose stones spread thereabout, which had acted as a shield to the soil under the onset. These during the summer had been cleared from the ground, and there was now nothing to resist the downfall but the bare earth. For several years the stream had not spouted so far from the tower as it was doing on this night, and such a contingency had been overlooked. Sometimes this obscure corner received no inhabitant for the space of two or three years, and then it was usually but a pauper, a poacher, or other sinner of undignified sins.

The persistent torrent from the gurgoyle's jaws directed all its vengeance into the grave. The rich tawny mould was stirred into motion, and boiled like chocolate. The water accumulated and washed deeper down, and the roar of the pool thus formed spread into the night as the head and chief among other noises of the kind created by the deluging rain. The flowers so carefully planted by Fanny's repentant lover began to move and writhe in their bed. The winter-violets turned slowly upside down, and became a mere mat of mud. Soon the snowdrop and other bulbs danced in the boiling mass like ingredients in a cauldron. Plants of the tufted species were loosened, rose to the surface, and floated off.

Troy did not awake from his comfortless sleep till it was broad day. Not having been in bed for two nights his shoulders felt stiff, his feet tender, and his head heavy. He remembered his position, arose, shivered, took the spade, and again went out.

The rain had quite ceased, and the sun was shining through the green, brown, and yellow leaves, now sparkling and varnished by the raindrops to the brightness of similar effects in the landscapes of Ruysdael and Hobbema, and full of all those infinite beauties that arise from the union of water and colour with high

371

lights. The air was rendered so transparent by the heavy fall of rain that the autumn hues of the middle distance were as rich as those near at hand, and the remote fields intercepted by the angle of the tower appeared in the same plane as the tower itself.

He entered the gravel path which would take him behind the tower. The path, instead of being stony as it had been the night before, was browned over with a thin coating of mud. At one place in the path he saw a tuft of stringy roots washed white and clean as a bundle of tendons. He picked it up—surely it could not be one of the primroses he had planted? He saw a bulb, another, and another as he advanced. Beyond doubt they were the crocuses. With a face of perplexed dismay Troy turned the corner and then beheld the wreck the stream had made.

The pool upon the grave had soaked away into the ground, and in its place was a hollow. The disturbed earth was washed over the grass and pathway in the guise of the brown mud he had already seen, and it spotted the marble tombstone with the same stains. Nearly all the flowers were washed clean out of the ground, and they lay, roots upwards, on the spots whither they had been splashed by the stream.

Troy's brow became heavily contracted. He set his teeth closely, and his compressed lips moved as those of one in great pain. This singular accident, by a strange confluence of emotions in him, was felt as the sharpest sting of all. Troy's face was very expressive, and any observer who had seen him now would hardly have believed him to be a man who had laughed, and sung, and poured love-trifles into a woman's ear. To curse his miserable lot was at first his impulse, but even that lowest stage of rebellion needed an activity whose absence was necessarily antecedent to the existence of the morbid misery which wrung him. The sight, coming as it did, superimposed upon the other dark scenery of the previous days, formed a sort of climax to the whole panorama, and it was more than he could endure. Sanguine by nature, Troy had a power of eluding grief by simply adjourning it. He could put off the consideration of any particular spectre till the matter had become old and softened by time. The planting of flowers on Fanny's grave had been perhaps but a species of elusion of the primary grief, and now it was as if his intention had been known and circumvented.

Almost for the first time in his life, Troy, as he stood by this dismantled grave, wished himself another man. It is seldom that a person with much animal spirit does not feel that the fact of his life being his own is the one qualification which singles it out as a more hopeful life than that of others who may actually resemble him in every particular. Troy had felt, in his transient way, hundreds of times, that he could not envy other people their condition, because the possession of that condition would have necessitated a different personality, when he desired no other than his own. He had not minded the peculiarities of his birth, the vicissitudes of his life, the meteor-like uncertainty of all that related to him, because these appertained to the hero of his story, without whom there would have been no story at all for him ; and it seemed to be only in the nature of things that matters would right themselves at some proper date and wind up well. This very morning the illusion completed its disappearance, and, as it were, all of a sudden, Troy hated himself. The suddenness was probably more apparent than real. A coral reef which just comes short of the ocean surface is no more to the horizon than if it had never been begun, and the mere finishing stroke is what often appears to create an event which has long been potentially an accomplished thing.

He stood and meditated—a miserable man. Whither should he go ? ' He that is accursed, let him be accursed still,' was the pitiless anathema written in this spoliated effort of his new-born solicitousness. A man who has spent his primal strength in journeying in one direction has not much spirit left for reversing his course. Troy had, since yesterday, faintly reversed his; but the merest opposition had disheartened him. To turn about would have been hard enough under the greatest providential encouragement; but to find that Providence, far from helping him into a new course, or showing any wish that he might adopt one, actually jeered his first trembling and critical attempt in that kind, was more than nature could bear.

He slowly withdrew from the grave. He did not attempt to fill up the hole, replace the flowers, or do anything at all. He simply threw up his cards and forswore his game for that time and always. Going out of the churchyard silently and unobserved—none of the villagers having yet risen—he passed down some fields at the back, and emerged just as secretly upon the high road. Shortly afterwards he had gone from the village.

Meanwhile, Bathsheba remained a voluntary prisoner in the attic. The door was kept locked, except during the entries and exits of Liddy, for whom a bed had been arranged in a small adjoining room. The light of Troy's lantern in the churchyard was noticed about ten o'clock by the maid-servant, who casually glanced from the window in that direction whilst taking her supper, and she called Bathsheba's attention to it. They looked curiously at the phenomenon for a time, until Liddy was sent to bed.

Bathsheba did not sleep very heavily that night. When her attendant was unconscious and softly breathing in the next room, the mistress of the house was still looking out of the window at the faint gleam spreading from among the trees—not in a steady shine, but blinking like a revolving coast-light, though this appearance failed to suggest to her that a person was passing and repassing in front of it. Bathsheba sat here till it began to rain, and the light vanished, when she withdrew to lie restlessly in her bed and re-enact in a worn mind the lurid scene of yesternight.

Almost before the first faint sign of dawn appeared she arose again, and opened the window to obtain a full breathing of the new morning air, the panes being now wet with trembling tears left by the night rain, each one rounded with a pale lustre caught from primrose-hued slashes through a cloud low down in the awakening sky. From the trees came the sound of steady dripping upon the drifted leaves under them, and from the direction of the church she could hear another noise —peculiar, and not intermittent like the rest, the purl of water falling into a pool.

Liddy knocked at eight o'clock, and Bathsheba unlocked the door.

'What a heavy rain we've had in the night, ma'am!' said Liddy, when her inquiries about breakfast had been made.

'Yes; very heavy.'

'Did you hear the strange noise from the church-yard?'

'I heard one strange noise. I've been thinking it must have been the water from the tower spouts.'

'Well, that's what the shepherd was saying, ma'am. He's now gone on to see.'

'Oh! Gabriel has been here this morning!'

'Only just looked in in passing—quite in his old way, which I thought he had left off lately. But the tower spouts used to spatter on the stones, and we are puzzled, for this was like the boiling of a pot.'

Not being able to read, think, or work, Bathsheba asked Liddy to stay and breakfast with her. The tongue of the more childish woman still ran upon recent events. 'Are you going across to the church, ma'am?' she asked.

'Not that I know of,' said Bathsheba.

'I thought you might like to go and see where they have put Fanny. The trees hide the place from your window.'

Bathsheba had all sorts of dreads about meeting her husband. 'Has Mr. Troy been in to-night?' she said.

'No, ma'am; I think he's gone to Budmouth.'

Budmouth! The sound of the word carried with it a much diminished perspective of him and his deeds; there were fifteen miles interval betwixt them now. She hated questioning Liddy about her husband's movements, and indeed had hitherto sedulously avoided doing so; but now all the house knew that there had been some dreadful disagreement between them, and it was futile to attempt disguise. Bathsheba had reached a stage at which people cease to have any appreciative regard for public opinion.

'What makes you think he has gone there?' she said.

'Laban Tall saw him on the Budmouth road this morning before breakfast.'

Bathsheba was momentarily relieved of that wayward heaviness of the past twenty-four hours which had quenched the vitality of youth in her without substituting the philosophy of maturer years, and she resolved to go out and walk a little way. So when breakfast was over, she put on her bonnet, and took a direction towards the church. It was nine o'clock, and the men having returned to work again from their first meal, she was not likely to meet many of them in the road. Knowing that Fanny had been laid in the reprobates' quarter of the graveyard, called in the parish 'behind church,' which was invisible from the road, it was impossible to resist the impulse to enter and look upon a spot which, from nameless feelings, she at the same time dreaded to see. She had been unable to overcome an impression that some connection existed between her rival and the light through the trees.

Bathsheba skirted the buttress, and beheld the hole and the tomb, its delicately veined surface splashed and stained just as Troy had seen it and left it two hours earlier. On the other side of the scene stood Gabriel. His eyes, too, were fixed on the tomb, and her arrival having been noiseless, she had not as yet attracted his attention. Bathsheba did not at once perceive that the grand tomb and the disturbed grave were Fanny's, and she looked on both sides and around for some humbler mound, earthed up and clodded in the usual way. Then her eye followed Oak's, and she read the words with which the inscription opened :—

> 'Erected by Francis Troy in Beloved Memory of Fanny Robin.'

Oak saw her, and his first act was to gaze inquiringly and learn how she received this knowledge of the authorship of the work, which to himself had caused considerable astonishment. But such discoveries did not much affect her now. Emotional convulsions seemed to have become the commonplaces of her history, and she bade him good morning, and asked him to fill in the hole with the spade which was standing by. Whilst Oak was doing as she desired, Bathsheba collected the flowers, and began planting them with that sympathetic manipulation of roots and leaves which is so conspicuous in a woman's gardening, and which flowers seem to understand and thrive upon. She requested Oak to get the churchwardens to turn the leadwork at the mouth of the gurgoyle that hung gaping down upon them, that by this means the stream might be directed sideways, and a repetition of the accident prevented. Finally, with the superfluous magnanimity of a woman whose narrower instincts have brought down bitterness upon her instead of love, she wiped the mud spots from the tomb as if she rather liked its words than otherwise, and went home again.

CHAPTER XLVII

ADVENTURES BY THE SHORE

Troy wandered along towards the south. A composite feeling, made up of disgust with the, to him, humdrum tediousness of a farmer's life, gloomy images of her who lay in the churchyard, remorse, and a general averseness to his wife's society, impelled him to seek a home in any place on earth save Weatherbury. The sad accessories of Fanny's end confronted him as vivid pictures which threatened to be indelible, and made life in Bathsheba's house intolerable. At three in the afternoon he found himself at the foot of a slope more than a mile in length, which ran to the ridge of a range of hills lying parallel with the shore, and forming a monotonous barrier between the basin of cultivated country inland and the wilder scenery of the coast. Up the hill stretched a road perfectly straight and perfectly white, the two sides approaching each other in a gradual taper till they met the sky at the top about two miles off. Throughout the length of this narrow and irksome inclined plane not a sign of life was visible on this garish afternoon. Troy toiled up the road with a languor and depression greater than any he had experienced for many a day and year before. The air was warm and muggy, and the top seemed to recede as he approached.

At last he reached the summit, and a wide and

novel prospect burst upon him with an effect almost like
that of the Pacific upon Balboa's gaze. The broad
steely sea, marked only by faint lines, which had a
semblance of being etched thereon to a degree not deep
enough to disturb its general evenness, stretched the
whole width of his front and round to the right, where,
near the town and port of Budmouth, the sun bristled
down upon it, and banished all colour, to substitute in
its place a clear oily polish. Nothing moved in sky,
land, or sea, except a frill of milkwhite foam along the
nearer angles of the shore, shreds of which licked the
contiguous stones like tongues.

He descended and came to a small basin of sea
enclosed by the cliffs. Troy's nature freshened within
him ; he thought he would rest and bathe here before
going farther. He undressed and plunged in. Inside
the cove the water was uninteresting to a swimmer,
being smooth as a pond, and to get a little of the ocean
swell, Troy presently swam between the two projecting
spurs of rock which formed the pillars of Hercules to
this miniature Mediterranean. Unfortunately for Troy
a current unknown to him existed outside, which, unimportant to craft of any burden, was awkward for a
swimmer who might be taken in it unawares. Troy
found himself carried to the left and then round in a
swoop out to sea.

He now recollected the place and its sinister
character. Many bathers had there prayed for a dry
death from time to time, and, like Gonzalo also, had
been unanswered ; and Troy began to deem it possible
that he might be added to their number. Not a boat
of any kind was at present within sight, but far in the
distance Budmouth lay upon the sea, as it were quietly
regarding his efforts, and beside the town the harbour
showed its position by a dim meshwork of ropes and
spars. After well-nigh exhausting himself in attempts
to get back to the mouth of the cove, in his weakness

swimming several inches deeper than was his wont, keeping up his breathing entirely by his nostrils, turning upon his back a dozen times over, swimming *en papillon*, and so on, Troy resolved as a last resource to tread water at a slight incline, and so endeavour to reach the shore at any point, merely giving himself a gentle impetus inwards whilst carried on in the general direction of the tide. This, necessarily a slow process, he found to be not altogether so difficult, and though there was no choice of a landing-place—the objects on shore passing by him in a sad and slow procession—he perceptibly approached the extremity of a spit of land yet further to the right, now well defined against the sunny portion of the horizon. While the swimmer's eyes were fixed upon the spit as his only means of salvation on this side of the Unknown, a moving object broke the outline of the extremity, and immediately a ship's boat appeared, manned with several sailor lads, her bows towards the sea.

All Troy's vigour spasmodically revived to prolong the struggle yet a little further. Swimming with his right arm, he held up his left to hail them, splashing upon the waves, and shouting with all his might. From the position of the setting sun his white form was distinctly visible upon the now deep-hued bosom of the sea to the east of the boat, and the men saw him at once. Backing their oars and putting the boat about, they pulled towards him with a will, and in five or six minutes from the time of his first halloo, two of the sailors hauled him in over the stern.

They formed part of a brig's crew, and had come ashore for sand. Lending him what little clothing they could spare among them as a slight protection against the rapidly cooling air, they agreed to land him in the morning ; and without further delay, for it was growing late, they made again towards the roadstead where their vessel lay.

And now night drooped slowly upon the wide watery levels in front; and at no great distance from them, where the shore-line curved round, and formed a long riband of shade upon the horizon, a series of points of yellow light began to start into existence, denoting the spot to be the site of Budmouth, where the lamps were being lighted along the parade. The cluck of their oars was the only sound of any distinctness upon the sea, and as they laboured amid the thickening shades the lamp-lights grew larger, each appearing to send a flaming sword deep down into the waves before it, until there arose, among other dim shapes of the kind, the form of the vessel for which they were bound.

CHAPTER XLVIII

DOUBTS ARISE—DOUBTS VANISH

BATHSHEBA underwent the enlargement of her husband's absence from hours to days with a slight feeling of surprise, and a slight feeling of relief; yet neither sensation rose at any time far above the level commonly designated as indifference. She belonged to him : the certainties of that position were so well defined, and the reasonable probabilities of its issue so bounded, that she could not speculate on contingencies. Taking no further interest in herself as a splendid woman, she acquired the indifferent feelings of an outsider in contemplating her probable fate as a singular wretch ; for Bathsheba drew herself and her future in colours that no reality could exceed for darkness. Her original vigorous pride of youth had sickened, and with it had declined all her anxieties about coming years, since anxiety recognizes a better and a worse alternative, and Bathsheba had made up her mind that alternatives on any noteworthy scale had ceased for her. Soon, or later— and that not very late—her husband would be home again. And then the days of their tenancy of the Upper Farm would be numbered. There had originally been shown by the agent to the estate some distrust of Bathsheba's tenure as James Everdene's successor, on the score of her sex, and her youth, and her beauty ;

but the peculiar nature of her uncle's will, his own frequent testimony before his death to her cleverness in such a pursuit, and her vigorous marshalling of the numerous flocks and herds which came suddenly into her hands before negotiations were concluded, had won confidence in her powers, and no further objections had been raised. She had latterly been in great doubt as to what the legal effects of her marriage would be upon her position; but no notice had been taken as yet of her change of name, and only one point was clear—that in the event of her own or her husband's inability to meet the agent at the forthcoming January rent-day, very little consideration would be shown, and, for that matter, very little would be deserved. Once out of the farm, the approach of poverty would be sure.

Hence Bathsheba lived in a perception that her purposes were broken off. She was not a woman who could hope on without good materials for the process, differing thus from the less far-sighted and energetic, though more petted ones of the sex, with whom hope goes on as a sort of clockwork which the merest food and shelter are sufficient to wind up; and perceiving clearly that her mistake had been a fatal one, she accepted her position, and waited coldly for the end.

The first Saturday after Troy's departure she went to Casterbridge alone, a journey she had not before taken since her marriage. On this Saturday Bathsheba was passing slowly on foot through the crowd of rural business-men gathered as usual in front of the market-house, who were as usual gazed upon by the burghers with feelings that those healthy lives were dearly paid for by exclusion from possible aldermanship, when a man, who had apparently been following her, said some words to another on her left hand. Bathsheba's ears were keen as those of any wild animal, and she distinctly heard what the speaker said, though her back was towards him.

'I am looking for Mrs. Troy. Is that she there?'

'Yes; that's the young lady, I believe,' said the person addressed.

'I have some awkward news to break to her. Her husband is drowned.'

As if endowed with the spirit of prophecy, Bathsheba gasped out, 'Oh, it is not true; it cannot be true!' Then she said and heard no more. The ice of self-command which had latterly gathered over her was broken, and the currents burst forth again, and overwhelmed her. A darkness came into her eyes, and she fell.

But not to the ground. A gloomy man, who had been observing her from under the portico of the old corn-exchange when she passed through the group without, stepped quickly to her side at the moment of her exclamation, and caught her in his arms as she sank down.

'What is it?' said Boldwood, looking up at the bringer of the big news, as he supported her.

'Her husband was drowned this week while bathing in Lulstead Cove. A coastguardsman found his clothes, and brought them into Budmouth yesterday.'

Thereupon a strange fire lighted up Boldwood's eye, and his face flushed with the suppressed excitement of an unutterable thought. Everybody's glance was now centred upon him and the unconscious Bathsheba. He lifted her bodily off the ground, and smoothed down the folds of her dress as a child might have taken a storm-beaten bird and arranged its ruffled plumes, and bore her along the pavement to the King's Arms Inn. Here he passed with her under the archway into a private room; and by the time he had deposited—so lothly—the precious burden upon a sofa, Bathsheba had opened her eyes. Remembering all that had occurred, she murmured, 'I want to go home!'

Boldwood left the room. He stood for a moment in

the passage to recover his senses. The experience had been too much for his consciousness to keep up with, and now that he had grasped it it had gone again. For those few heavenly, golden moments she had been in his arms. What did it matter about her not knowing it? She had been close to his breast; he had been close to hers.

He started onward again, and sending a woman to her, went out to ascertain all the facts of the case. These appeared to be limited to what he had already heard. He then ordered her horse to be put into the gig, and when all was ready returned to inform her. He found that, though still pale and unwell, she had in the meantime sent for the Budmouth man who brought the tidings, and learnt from him all there was to know.

Being hardly in a condition to drive home as she had driven to town, Boldwood, with every delicacy of manner and feeling, offered to get her a driver, or to give her a seat in his phaeton, which was more comfortable than her own conveyance. These proposals Bathsheba gently declined, and the farmer at once departed.

About half-an-hour later she invigorated herself by an effort, and took her seat and the reins as usual—in external appearance much as if nothing had happened. She went out of the town by a tortuous back street, and drove slowly along, unconscious of the road and the scene. The first shades of evening were showing themselves when Bathsheba reached home, where, silently alighting and leaving the horse in the hands of the boy, she proceeded at once upstairs. Liddy met her on the landing. The news had preceded Bathsheba to Weatherbury by half-an-hour, and Liddy looked inquiringly into her mistress's face. Bathsheba had nothing to say.

She entered her bedroom and sat by the window, and thought and thought till night enveloped her, and the extreme lines only of her shape were visible. Somebody came to the door, knocked, and opened it.

'Well, what is it, Liddy?' she said.

'I was thinking there must be something got for you to wear,' said Liddy, with hesitation.

'What do you mean?'

'Mourning.'

'No, no, no,' said Bathsheba, hurriedly.

'But I suppose there must be something done for poor——'

'Not at present, I think.   It is not necessary.'

'Why not, ma'am?'

'Because he's still alive.'

'How do you know that?' said Liddy, amazed.

'I don't know it.   But wouldn't it have been different, or shouldn't I have heard more, or wouldn't they have found him, Liddy?—or—I don't know how it is, but death would have been different from how this is.   I am full of a feeling that he is still alive!'

Bathsheba remained firm in this opinion till Monday, when two circumstances conjoined to shake it.   The first was a short paragraph in the local newspaper, which, beyond making by a methodizing pen formidable presumptive evidence of Troy's death by drowning, contained the important testimony of a young Mr. Barker, M.D., of Budmouth, who spoke to being an eyewitness of the accident, in a letter to the editor.   In this he stated that he was passing over the cliff on the remoter side of the cove just as the sun was setting.   At that time he saw a bather carried along in the current outside the mouth of the cove, and guessed in an instant that there was but a poor chance for him unless he should be possessed of unusual muscular powers.   He drifted behind a projection of the coast, and Mr. Barker followed along the shore in the same direction.   But by the time that he could reach an elevation sufficiently great to command a view of the sea beyond, dusk had set in, and nothing further was to be seen.

The other circumstance was the arrival of his clothes, when it became necessary for her to examine and identify them—though this had virtually been done long before by those who inspected the letters in his pockets. It was so evident to her in the midst of her agitation that Troy had undressed in the full conviction of dressing again almost immediately, that the notion that anything but death could have prevented him was hard to entertain.

Then Bathsheba said to herself that others were assured in their opinion, and why should not she be? A strange reflection occurred to her, causing her face to flush. Suppose that Troy had followed Fanny into another world. Had he done this intentionally, yet contrived to make his death appear like an accident? Nevertheless, this thought of how the apparent might differ from the real—made vivid by her bygone jealousy of Fanny, and the remorse he had shown that night—did not blind her to the perception of a likelier difference, less tragic, but to herself far more terrible.

When alone late that evening beside a small fire, and much calmed down, Bathsheba took Troy's watch into her hand, which had been restored to her with the rest of the articles belonging to him. She opened the case as he had opened it before her a week ago. There was the little coil of pale hair which had been as the fuze to this great explosion.

'He was hers and she was his; they should be gone together,' she said. 'I am nothing to either of them, and why should I keep her hair?' She took it in her hand, and held it over the fire. 'No—I'll not burn it—I'll keep it in memory of her, poor thing!' she added, snatching back her hand.

CHAPTER XLIX

OAK'S ADVANCEMENT—A GREAT HOPE

THE later autumn and the winter drew on apace, and the leaves lay thick upon the turf of the glades and the mosses of the woods. Bathsheba, having previously been living in a state of suspended feeling which was not suspense, now lived in a mood of quietude which was not precisely peacefulness. While she had known him to be alive she could have thought of his death with equanimity; but now that it might be she had lost him, she regretted that he was not hers still. She kept the farm going, raked in her profits without caring keenly about them, and expended money on ventures because she had done so in bygone days, which, though not long gone by, seemed infinitely removed from her present. She looked back upon that past over a great gulf, as if she were now a dead person, having the faculty of meditation still left in her, by means of which, like the mouldering gentlefolk of the poet's story, she could sit and ponder what a gift life used to be.

However, one excellent result of her general apathy was the long-delayed installation of Oak as bailiff; but he having virtually exercised that function for a long time already, the change, beyond the substantial in-

388

crease of wages it brought, was little more than a nominal one addressed to the outside world.

Boldwood lived secluded and inactive. Much of his wheat and all his barley of that season had been spoilt by the rain. It sprouted, grew into intricate mats, and was ultimately thrown to the pigs in armfuls. The strange neglect which had produced this ruin and waste became the subject of whispered talk among all the people round; and it was elicited from one of Boldwood's men that forgetfulness had nothing to do with it, for he had been reminded of the danger to his corn as many times and as persistently as inferiors dared to do. The sight of the pigs turning in disgust from the rotten ears seemed to arouse Boldwood, and he one evening sent for Oak. Whether it was suggested by Bathsheba's recent act of promotion or not, the farmer proposed at the interview that Gabriel should undertake the superintendence of the Lower Farm as well as of Bathsheba's, because of the necessity Boldwood felt for such aid, and the impossibility of discovering a more trustworthy man. Gabriel's malignant star was assuredly setting fast.

Bathsheba, when she learnt of this proposal—for Oak was obliged to consult her—at first languidly objected. She considered that the two farms together were too extensive for the observation of one man. Boldwood, who was apparently determined by personal rather than commercial reasons, suggested that Oak should be furnished with a horse for his sole use, when the plan would present no difficulty, the two farms lying side by side. Boldwood did not directly communicate with her during these negotiations, only speaking to Oak, who was the go-between throughout. All was harmoniously arranged at last, and we now see Oak mounted on a strong cob, and daily trotting the length and breadth of about two thousand acres in a cheerful spirit of surveillance, as if the crops all belonged to him—the actual mistress of the one-half, and the master of the other, sitting in their respective homes in gloomy and sad seclusion.

Out of this there arose, during the spring succeeding, a talk in the parish that Gabriel Oak was feathering his nest fast.

'Whatever d'ye think,' said Susan Tall, 'Gable Oak is coming it quite the dand. He now wears shining boots with hardly a hob in 'em, two or three times a-week, and a tall hat a-Sundays, and 'a hardly knows the name of smockfrock. When I see people strut enough to be cut up into bantam cocks, I stand dormant with wonder, and says no more!'

It was eventually known that Gabriel, though paid a fixed wage by Bathsheba independent of the fluctuations of agricultural profits, had made an engagement with Boldwood by which Oak was to receive a share of the receipts—a small share certainly, yet it was money of a higher quality than mere wages, and capable of expansion in a way that wages were not. Some were beginning to consider Oak a 'near' man, for though his condition had thus far improved, he lived in no better style than before, occupying the same cottage, paring his own potatoes, mending his stockings, and sometimes even making his bed with his own hands. But as Oak was not only provokingly indifferent to public opinion, but a man who clung persistently to old habits and usages, simply because they were old, there was room for doubt as to his motives.

A great hope had latterly germinated in Boldwood, whose unreasoning devotion to Bathsheba could only be characterized as a fond madness which neither time nor circumstance, evil nor good report, could weaken or destroy. This fevered hope had grown up again like a grain of mustard-seed during the quiet which followed the hasty conjecture that Troy was drowned. He nourished it fearfully, and almost shunned the contemplation of it in earnest, lest facts should reveal the wildness of the dream. Bathsheba having at last been persuaded to wear mourning, her appearance as she entered the church in that guise was in itself a weekly addition to his faith that a time was coming—very far off perhaps, yet surely nearing—when his waiting on events should have its reward. How long he might have to wait he had not yet closely considered. What he would try to recognize was that the severe schooling she had been subjected to had made Bathsheba much more considerate than she had formerly been of the feelings of others, and he trusted that, should she be willing at any time in the future to marry any man at all, that man would be himself. There was a substratum of good feeling in her: her self-reproach for the injury she had thoughtlessly done him might be depended upon now to a much greater extent than before her infatuation and disappointment. It would be possible to approach her by the channel of her good nature, and to suggest a friendly business-like compact between them for fulfilment at some future day, keeping the passionate side of his desire entirely out of her sight. Such was Boldwood's hope.

To the eyes of the middle-aged, Bathsheba was perhaps additionally charming just now. Her exuberance of spirit was pruned down; the original phantom of delight had shown herself to be not too bright for human nature's daily food, and she had been able to enter this second poetical phase without losing much of the first in the process.

Bathsheba's return from a two months' visit to her old aunt at Norcombe afforded the impassioned and yearning farmer a pretext for inquiring directly after her—now possibly in the ninth month of her widowhood—and endeavouring to get a notion of her state of mind regarding him. This occurred in the middle of the haymaking, and Boldwood contrived to be near Liddy, who was assisting in the fields.

'I am glad to see you out of doors, Lydia,' he said, pleasantly.

She simpered, and wondered in her heart why he should speak so frankly to her.

'I hope Mrs. Troy is quite well after her long absence,' he continued, in a manner expressing that the coldest-hearted neighbour could scarcely say less about her.

'She is quite well, sir.'

'And cheerful, I suppose.'

'Yes, cheerful.'

'Fearful, did you say?'

'Oh no. I merely said she was cheerful.'

'Tells you all her affairs?'

'No, sir.'

'Some of them?'

'Yes, sir.'

'Mrs. Troy puts much confidence in you, Lydia; and very wisely, perhaps.'

'She do, sir. I've been with her all through her troubles, and was with her at the time of Mr. Troy's going and all. And if she were to marry again I expect I should bide with her.'

'She promises that you shall—quite natural,' said the strategic lover, throbbing throughout him at the presumption which Liddy's words appeared to warrant —that his darling had thought of re-marriage.

'No—she doesn't promise it exactly. I merely judge on my own account.'

'Yes, yes, I understand. When she alludes to the possibility of marrying again, you conclude——'

'She never do allude to it, sir,' said Liddy, thinking how very stupid Mr. Boldwood was getting.

'Of course not,' he returned hastily, his hope falling

again. 'You needn't take quite such long reaches with your rake, Lydia—short and quick ones are best. Well, perhaps, as she is absolute mistress again now, it is wise of her to resolve never to give up her freedom.'

'My mistress did certainly once say, though not seriously, that she supposed she might marry again at the end of seven years from last year, if she wished.'

'Ah, six years from the present time. Said that she might. She might marry at once in every reasonable person's opinion, whatever the lawyers may say to the contrary.'

'Have you been to ask them?' said Liddy, innocently.

'Not I,' said Boldwood, growing red. 'Liddy, you needn't stay here a minute later than you wish, so Mr. Oak says. I am now going on a little farther. Good-afternoon.'

He went away vexed with himself, and ashamed of having for this one time in his life done anything which could be called underhand. Poor Boldwood had no more skill in finesse than a battering-ram, and he was uneasy with a sense of having made himself to appear stupid and, what was worse, mean. But he had, after all, lighted upon one fact by way of repayment. It was a singularly fresh and fascinating fact, and though not without its sadness it was pertinent and real. In little more than six years from this time Bathsheba might certainly marry him. There was something definite in that hope, for admitting that there might have been no deep thought in her words to Liddy about marriage, they showed at least her creed on the matter.

This pleasant notion was now continually in his mind. Six years were a long time, but how much shorter than never, the idea he had for so long been obliged to endure! Jacob had served twice seven years for Rachel: what were six for such a woman as this? He tried to like the notion of waiting for her better than that of winning her at once. Boldwood felt his love to be so deep and strong and eternal, that it was possible she had never yet known its full volume, and this patience in delay would afford him an opportunity of giving sweet proof on the point. He would annihilate the six years of his life as if they were minutes—so little did he value his time on earth beside her love. He would let her see, all those six years of intangible ethereal courtship, how little care he had for anything but as it bore upon the consummation.

Meanwhile the early and the late summer brought round the week in which Greenhill Fair was held. This fair was frequently attended by the folk of Weatherbury.

CHAPTER L

THE SHEEP FAIR—TROY TOUCHES HIS WIFE'S HAND

GREENHILL was the Nijni Novgorod of South Wessex; and the busiest, merriest, noisiest day of the whole statute number was the day of the sheep fair. This yearly gathering was upon the summit of a hill which retained in good preservation the remains of an ancient earthwork, consisting of a huge rampart and entrenchment of an oval form encircling the top of the hill, though somewhat broken down here and there. To each of the two chief openings on opposite sides a winding road ascended, and the level green space of twenty or thirty acres enclosed by the bank was the site of the fair. A few permanent erections dotted the spot, but the majority of visitors patronized canvas alone for resting and feeding under during the time of their sojourn here.

Shepherds who attended with their flocks from long distances started from home two or three days, or even a week, before the fair, driving their charges a few miles each day—not more than ten or twelve—and resting them at night in hired fields by the wayside at previously chosen points, where they fed, having fasted since morning. The shepherd of each flock marched behind, a bundle containing his kit for the week strapped upon his shoulders, and in his hand his crook, which he used

395

as the staff of his pilgrimage. Several of the sheep would get worn and lame, and occasionally a lambing occurred on the road. To meet these contingencies, there was frequently provided, to accompany the flocks from the remoter points, a pony and waggon into which the weakly ones were taken for the remainder of the journey.

The Weatherbury Farms, however, were no such long distance from the hill, and those arrangements were not necessary in their case. But the large united flocks of Bathsheba and Farmer Boldwood formed a valuable and imposing multitude which demanded much attention, and on this account Gabriel, in addition to Boldwood's shepherd and Cain Ball, accompanied them along the way, through the decayed old town of Kingsbere, and upward to the plateau,—old George the dog of course behind them.

When the autumn sun slanted over Greenhill this morning and lighted the dewy flat upon its crest, nebulous clouds of dust were to be seen floating between the pairs of hedges which streaked the wide prospect around in all directions. These gradually converged upon the base of the hill, and the flocks became individually visible, climbing the serpentine ways which led to the top. Thus, in a slow procession, they entered the opening to which the roads tended, multitude after multitude, horned and hornless—blue flocks and red flocks, buff flocks and brown flocks, even green and salmon-tinted flocks, according to the fancy of the colourist and custom of the farm. Men were shouting, dogs were barking, with greatest animation, but the thronging travellers in so long a journey had grown nearly indifferent to such terrors; though they still bleated piteously at the unwontedness of their experiences, a tall shepherd rising here and there in the midst of them, like a gigantic idol amid a crowd of prostrate devotees.

The great mass of sheep in the fair consisted of South Downs and the old Wessex horned breeds; to the latter class Bathsheba's and Farmer Boldwood's mainly belonged. These filed in about nine o'clock, their vermiculated horns lopping gracefully on each side of their cheeks in geometrically perfect spirals, a small pink and white ear nestling under each horn. Before and behind came other varieties, perfect leopards as to the full rich substance of their coats, and only lacking the spots. There were also a few of the Oxfordshire breed, whose wool was beginning to curl like a child's flaxen hair, though surpassed in this respect by the effeminate Leicesters, which were in turn less curly than the Cotswolds. But the most picturesque by far was a small flock of Exmoors, which chanced to be there this year. Their pied faces and legs, dark and heavy horns, tresses of wool hanging round their swarthy foreheads, quite relieved the monotony of the flocks in that quarter.

All these bleating, panting, and weary thousands had entered and were penned before the morning had far advanced, the dog belonging to each flock being tied to the corner of the pen containing it. Alleys for pedestrians intersected the pens, which soon became crowded with buyers and sellers from far and near.

In another part of the hill an altogether different scene began to force itself upon the eye towards midday. A circular tent, of exceptional newness and size, was in course of erection here. As the day drew on, the flocks began to change hands, lightening the shepherd's responsibilities; and they turned their attention to this tent and inquired of a man at work there, whose soul seemed concentrated on tying a bothering knot in no time, what was going on.

'The Royal Hippodrome Performance of Turpin's Ride to York and the Death of Black Bess,' replied the man promptly, without turning his eyes or leaving off tying.

As soon as the tent was completed the band struck up highly stimulating harmonies, and the announcement was publicly made, Black Bess standing in a conspicuous position on the outside, as a living proof, if proof were wanted, of the truth of the oracular utterances from the stage over which the people were to enter. These were so convinced by such genuine appeals to heart and understanding both that they soon began to crowd in abundantly, among the foremost being visible Jan Coggan and Joseph Poorgrass, who were holiday keeping here to-day.

'That's the great ruffen pushing me!' screamed a woman in front of Jan over her shoulder at him when the rush was at its fiercest.

'How can I help pushing ye when the folk behind push me?' said Coggan, in a deprecating tone, turning his head towards the aforesaid folk as far as he could without turning his body, which was jammed as in a vice.

There was a silence; then the drums and trumpets again sent forth their echoing notes. The crowd was again ecstasied, and gave another lurch in which Coggan and Poorgrass were again thrust by those behind upon the women in front.

'Oh that helpless feymels should be at the mercy of such ruffens!' exclaimed one of these ladies again, as she swayed like a reed shaken by the wind.

'Now,' said Coggan, appealing in an earnest voice to the public at large as it stood clustered about his shoulder-blades, 'did ye ever hear such a onreasonable woman as that? Upon my carcase, neighbours, if I could only get out of this cheesewring, the damn women might eat the show for me!'

'Don't ye lose yer temper, Jan!' implored Joseph Poorgrass, in a whisper. 'They might get their men to murder us, for I think by the shine of their eyes that they be a sinful form of womankind.'

Jan held his tongue, as if he had no objection to be

pacified to please a friend, and they gradually reached the foot of the ladder, Poorgrass being flattened like a jumping-jack, and the sixpence, for admission, which he had got ready half-an-hour earlier, having become so reeking hot in the tight squeeze of his excited hand that the woman in spangles, brazen rings set with glass diamonds, and with chalked face and shoulders, who took the money of him, hastily dropped it again from a fear that some trick had been played to burn her fingers. So they all entered, and the cloth of the tent, to the eyes of an observer on the outside, became bulged into innumerable pimples such as we observe on a sack of potatoes, caused by the various human heads, backs, and elbows at high pressure within.

At the rear of the large tent there were two small dressing-tents. One of these, allotted to the male performers, was partitioned into halves by a cloth ; and in one of the divisions there was sitting on the grass, pulling on a pair of jack-boots, a young man whom we instantly recognize as Sergeant Troy.

Troy's appearance in this position may be briefly accounted for. The brig aboard which he was taken in Budmouth Roads was about to start on a voyage, though somewhat short of hands. Troy read the articles and joined, but before they sailed a boat was despatched across the bay to Lulstead Cove ; as he had half expected, his clothes were gone. He ultimately worked his passage to the United States, where he made a precarious living in various towns as Professor of Gymnastics, Sword Exercise, Fencing, and Pugilism. A few months were sufficient to give him a distaste for this kind of life. There was a certain animal form of refinement in his nature ; and however pleasant a strange condition might be whilst privations were easily warded off, it was disadvantageously coarse when money was short. There was ever present, too, the idea that he could claim a home and its comforts did he but choose to return to

England and Weatherbury Farm. Whether Bathsheba
thought him dead was a frequent subject of curious
conjecture. To England he did return at last; but the
fact of drawing nearer to Weatherbury abstracted its
fascinations, and his intention to enter his old groove at
that place became modified. It was with gloom he considered on landing at Liverpool that if he were to go home
his reception would be of a kind very unpleasant to contemplate; for what Troy had in the way of emotion was
an occasional fitful sentiment which sometimes caused
him as much inconvenience as emotion of a strong and
healthy kind. Bathsheba was not a woman to be made
a fool of, or a woman to suffer in silence; and how
could he endure existence with a spirited wife to whom
at first entering he would be beholden for food and
lodging? Moreover, it was not at all unlikely that his
wife would fail at her farming, if she had not already
done so; and he would then become liable for her
maintenance: and what a life such a future of poverty
with her would be, the spectre of Fanny constantly between them, harrowing his temper and embittering her
words! Thus, for reasons touching on distaste, regret,
and shame commingled, he put off his return from day
to day, and would have decided to put it off altogether
if he could have found anywhere else the ready-made
establishment which existed for him there.

At this time—the July preceding the September in
which we find him at Greenhill Fair—he fell in with a
travelling circus which was performing in the outskirts of
a northern town. Troy introduced himself to the
manager by taming a restive horse of the troupe, hitting
a suspended apple with a pistol-bullet fired from the
animal's back when in full gallop, and other feats. For
his merits in these—all more or less based upon his experiences as a dragoon-guardsman—Troy was taken into
the company, and the play of Turpin was prepared with
a view to his personation of the chief character. Troy

was not greatly elated by the appreciative spirit in which he was undoubtedly treated, but he thought the engagement might afford him a few weeks for consideration. It was thus carelessly, and without having formed any definite plan for the future, that Troy found himself at Greenhill Fair with the rest of the company on this day.

And now the mild autumn sun got lower, and in front of the pavilion the following incident had taken place. Bathsheba—who was driven to the fair that day by her odd man Poorgrass—had, like every one else, read or heard the announcement that Mr. Francis, the Great Cosmopolitan Equestrian and Roughrider, would enact the part of Turpin, and she was not yet too old and careworn to be without a little curiosity to see him. This particular show was by far the largest and grandest in the fair, a horde of little shows grouping themselves under its shade like chickens around a hen. The crowd had passed in, and Boldwood, who had been watching all the day for an opportunity of speaking to her, seeing her comparatively isolated, came up to her side.

'I hope the sheep have done well to-day, Mrs. Troy?' he said, nervously.

'Oh yes, thank you,' said Bathsheba, colour springing up in the centre of her cheeks. 'I was fortunate enough to sell them all just as we got upon the hill, so we hadn't to pen at all.'

'And now you are entirely at leisure?'

'Yes, except that I have to see one more dealer in two hours' time : otherwise I should be going home. I was looking at this large tent and the announcement. Have you ever seen the play of "Turpin's Ride to York?" Turpin was a real man, was he not?'

'Oh yes, perfectly true—all of it. Indeed, I think I've heard Jan Coggan say that a relation of his knew Tom King, Turpin's friend, quite well.'

'Coggan is rather given to strange stories connected

with his relations, we must remember. I hope they can all be believed.'

'Yes, yes; we know Coggan. But Turpin is true enough. You have never seen it played, I suppose?'

'Never. I was not allowed to go into these places when I was young. Hark! What's that prancing? How they shout!'

'Black Bess just started off, I suppose. Am I right in supposing you would like to see the performance, Mrs. Troy? Please excuse my mistake, if it is one; but if you would like to, I'll get a seat for you with pleasure.' Perceiving that she hesitated, he added, 'I myself shall not stay to see it: I've seen it before.'

Now Bathsheba did care a little to see the show, and had only withheld her feet from the ladder because she feared to go in alone. She had been hoping that Oak might appear, whose assistance in such cases was always accepted as an inalienable right, but Oak was nowhere to be seen; and hence it was that she said, 'Then if you will just look in first, to see if there's room, I think I will go in for a minute or two.'

And so a short time after this Bathsheba appeared in the tent with Boldwood at her elbow, who, taking her to a 'reserved' seat, again withdrew.

This feature consisted of one raised bench in a very conspicuous part of the circle, covered with red cloth, and floored with a piece of carpet, and Bathsheba immediately found, to her confusion, that she was the single reserved individual in the tent, the rest of the crowded spectators, one and all, standing on their legs on the borders of the arena, where they got twice as good a view of the performance for half the money. Hence as many eyes were turned upon her, enthroned alone in this place of honour, against a scarlet background, as upon the ponies and clown who were engaged in preliminary exploits in the centre, Turpin not having yet appeared. Once there, Bathsheba was forced to make the best of it and remain: she sat down, spreading her skirts with some dignity over the unoccupied space on each side of her, and giving a new and feminine aspect to the pavilion. In a few minutes she noticed the fat red nape of Coggan's neck among those standing just below her, and Joseph Poorgrass's saintly profile a little further on.

The interior was shadowy with a peculiar shade. The strange luminous semi-opacities of fine autumn afternoons and eves intensified into Rembrandt effects the few yellow sunbeams which came through holes and divisions in the canvas, and spirted like jets of gold-dust across the dusky blue atmosphere of haze pervading the tent, until they alighted on inner surfaces of cloth opposite, and shone like little lamps suspended there.

Troy, on peeping from his dressing-tent through a slit for a reconnoitre before entering, saw his unconscious wife on high before him as described, sitting as queen of the tournament. He started back in utter confusion, for although his disguise effectually concealed his personality, he instantly felt that she would be sure to recognize his voice. He had several times during the day thought of the possibility of some Weatherbury person or other appearing and recognizing him; but he had taken the risk carelessly. If they see me, let them, he had said. But here was Bathsheba in her own person; and the reality of the scene was so much intenser than any of his prefigurings that he felt he had not half enough considered the point.

She looked so charming and fair that his cool mood about Weatherbury people was changed. He had not expected her to exercise this power over him in the twinkling of an eye. Should he go on, and care nothing? He could not bring himself to do that. Beyond a politic wish to remain unknown, there suddenly arose in him now a sense of shame at the possibility that his attractive young wife, who already despised him, should despise him more by discovering him in so mean a condition after so long a time. He actually blushed at the thought, and was vexed beyond measure that his sentiments of dislike towards Weatherbury should have led him to dally about the country in this way.

But Troy was never more clever than when absolutely at his wit's end. He hastily thrust aside the curtain dividing his own little dressing space from that of the manager and proprietor, who now appeared as the individual called Tom King as far down as his waist, and as the aforesaid respectable manager thence to his toes.

'Here's the devil to pay!' said Troy.

'How's that?'

'Why, there's a blackguard creditor in the tent I don't want to see, who'll discover me and nab me as sure as Satan if I open my mouth. What's to be done?'

'You must appear now, I think.'

'I can't.'

'But the play must proceed.'

'Do you give out that Turpin has got a bad cold, and can't speak his part, but that he'll perform it just the same without speaking.'

The proprietor shook his head.

'Anyhow, play or no play, I won't open my mouth,' said Troy, firmly.

'Very well, then let me see. I tell you how we'll manage,' said the other, who perhaps felt it would be extremely awkward to offend his leading man just at this time. 'I won't tell 'em anything about your keeping silence; go on with the piece and say nothing, doing what you can by a judicious wink now and then, and a few indomitable nods in the heroic places, you know. They'll never find out that the speeches are omitted.'

This seemed feasible enough, for Turpin's speeches were not many or long, the fascination of the piece lying entirely in the action; and accordingly the play began, and at the appointed time Black Bess leapt into the grassy circle amid the plaudits of the spectators. At the turnpike scene, where Bess and Turpin are hotly pursued at midnight by the officers, and the half-awake gatekeeper in his tasselled nightcap denies that any horseman has passed, Coggan uttered a broad-chested 'Well done!' which could be heard all over the fair above the bleating, and Poorgrass smiled delightedly with a nice sense of dramatic contrast between our hero, who coolly leaps the gate, and halting justice in the form of his enemies, who must needs pull up cumbersomely and wait to be let through. At the death of Tom King, he could not refrain from seizing Coggan by the hand, and whispering, with tears in his eyes, 'Of course he's not really shot, Jan — only seemingly!' And when the last sad scene came on, and the body of the gallant and faithful Bess had to be carried out on a shutter by twelve volunteers from among the spectators, nothing could restrain Poorgrass from lending a hand, exclaiming, as he asked Jan to join him, ''Twill be something to tell of at Warren's in future years, Jan, and hand down to our children.' For many a year in Weatherbury, Joseph told, with the air of a man who had had experiences in his time, that he touched with his own hand the hoof of Bess as she lay upon the board upon his shoulder. If, as some thinkers hold, immortality consists in being enshrined in others' memories, then did Black Bess become immortal that day if she never had done so before.

Meanwhile Troy had added a few touches to his ordinary make-up for the character, the more effectually to disguise himself, and though he had felt faint qualms on first entering, the metamorphosis effected by judiciously 'lining' his face with a wire rendered him safe from the eyes of Bathsheba and her men. Nevertheless, he was relieved when it was got through.

There was a second performance in the evening, and
the tent was lighted up. Troy had taken his part very
quietly this time, venturing to introduce a few speeches
on occasion; and was just concluding it when, whilst
standing at the edge of the circle contiguous to the first
row of spectators, he observed within a yard of him the
eye of a man darted keenly into his side features. Troy
hastily shifted his position, after having recognized in
the scrutineer the knavish bailiff Pennyways, his wife's
sworn enemy, who still hung about the outskirts of
Weatherbury.

At first Troy resolved to take no notice and abide
by circumstances. That he had been recognized by
this man was highly probable; yet there was room for
a doubt. Then the great objection he had felt to
allowing news of his proximity to precede him to
Weatherbury in the event of his return, based on a
feeling that knowledge of his present occupation would
discredit him still further in his wife's eyes, returned
in full force. Moreover, should he resolve not to
return at all, a tale of his being alive and being in
the neighbourhood would be awkward; and he was
anxious to acquire a knowledge of his wife's temporal
affairs before deciding which to do.

In this dilemma Troy at once went out to reconnoitre. It occurred to him that to find Pennyways, and
make a friend of him if possible, would be a very wise
act. He had put on a thick beard borrowed from the
establishment, and in this he wandered about the fair-
field. It was now almost dark, and respectable people
were getting their carts and gigs ready to go home.

The largest refreshment booth in the fair was provided
by an innkeeper from a neighbouring town. This was
considered an unexceptionable place for obtaining the
necessary food and rest: Host Trencher (as he was
jauntily called by the local newspaper) being a substantial man of high repute for catering through all the

country round. The tent was divided into first and second-class compartments, and at the end of the first-class division was a yet further enclosure for the most exclusive, fenced off from the body of the tent by a luncheon-bar, behind which the host himself stood, bustling about in white apron and shirt-sleeves, and looking as if he had never lived anywhere but under canvas all his life. In these penetralia were chairs and a table, which, on candles being lighted, made quite a cozy and luxurious show, with an urn, silver tea and coffee pots, china teacups, and plum cakes.

Troy stood at the entrance to the booth, where a gipsy-woman was frying pancakes over a little fire of sticks and selling them at a penny a-piece, and looked over the heads of the people within. He could see nothing of Pennyways, but he soon discerned Bathsheba through an opening into the reserved space at the further end. Troy thereupon retreated, went round the tent into the darkness, and listened. He could hear Bathsheba's voice immediately inside the canvas; she was conversing with a man. A warmth overspread his face: surely she was not so unprincipled as to flirt in a fair! He wondered if, then, she reckoned upon his death as an absolute certainty. To get at the root of the matter, Troy took a penknife from his pocket and softly made two little cuts crosswise in the cloth, which, by folding back the corners left a hole the size of a wafer. Close to this he placed his face, withdrawing it again in a movement of surprise; for his eye had been within twelve inches of the top of Bathsheba's head. It was too near to be convenient. He made another hole a little to one side and lower down, in a shaded place beside her chair, from which it was easy and safe to survey her by looking horizontally.

Troy took in the scene completely now. She was leaning back, sipping a cup of tea that she held in her hand, and the owner of the male voice was Boldwood, who had apparently just brought the cup to her. Bathsheba, being in a negligent mood, leant so idly against the canvas that it was pressed to the shape of her shoulder, and she was, in fact, as good as in Troy's arms; and he was obliged to keep his breast carefully backward that she might not feel its warmth through the cloth as he gazed in.

Troy found unexpected chords of feeling to be stirred again within him as they had been stirred earlier in the day. She was handsome as ever, and she was his. It was some minutes before he could counteract his sudden wish to go in, and claim her. Then he thought how the proud girl who had always looked down upon him even whilst it was to love him, would hate him on discovering him to be a strolling player. Were he to make himself known, that chapter of his life must at all risks be kept for ever from her and from the Weatherbury people, or his name would be a byword throughout the parish. He would be nicknamed 'Turpin' as long as he lived. Assuredly before he could claim her these few past months of his existence must be entirely blotted out.

'Shall I get you another cup before you start, ma'am?' said Farmer Boldwood.

'Thank you,' said Bathsheba. 'But I must be going at once. It was great neglect in that man to keep me waiting here till so late. I should have gone two hours ago, if it had not been for him. I had no idea of coming in here; but there's nothing so refreshing as a cup of tea, though I should never have got one if you hadn't helped me.'

Troy scrutinized her cheek as lit by the candles, and watched each varying shade thereon, and the white shell-like sinuosities of her little ear. She took out her purse and was insisting to Boldwood on paying for her tea for herself, when at this moment Pennyways entered the tent. Troy trembled: here was his scheme for respectability endangered at once. He was about to leave his hole of espial, attempt to follow Pennyways, and find out if the ex-bailiff had recognized him, when he was arrested by the conversation, and found he was too late.

'Excuse me, ma'am,' said Pennyways; 'I've some private information for your ear alone.'

'I cannot hear it now,' she said, coldly. That Bathsheba could not endure this man was evident; in fact, he was continually coming to her with some tale or other, by which he might creep into favour at the expense of persons maligned.

'I'll write it down,' said Pennyways, confidently. He stooped over the table, pulled a leaf from a warped pocket-book, and wrote upon the paper, in a round hand—

'*Your husband is here. I've seen him. Who's the fool now ?*'

This he folded small, and handed towards her. Bathsheba would not read it; she would not even put out her hand to take it. Pennyways, then, with a laugh of derision, tossed it into her lap, and, turning away, left her.

From the words and action of Pennyways, Troy, though he had not been able to see what the ex-bailiff wrote, had not a moment's doubt that the note referred to him. Nothing that he could think of could be done to check the exposure. 'Curse my luck !' he whispered, and added imprecations which rustled in the gloom like a pestilent wind. Meanwhile Boldwood said, taking up the note from her lap—

'Don't you wish to read it, Mrs. Troy? If not, I'll destroy it.'

'Oh, well,' said Bathsheba, carelessly, 'perhaps it is unjust not to read it; but I can guess what it is about. He wants me to recommend him, or it is to tell me of some little scandal or another connected with my work-people. He's always doing that.'

Bathsheba held the note in her right hand. Bold-wood handed towards her a plate of cut bread-and-butter; when, in order to take a slice, she put the note into her left hand, where she was still holding the purse, and then allowed her hand to drop beside her close to the canvas. The moment had come for saving his game, and Troy impulsively felt that he would play the card. For yet another time he looked at the fair hand, and saw the pink finger-tips, and the blue veins of the wrist, encircled by a bracelet of coral chippings which she wore: how familiar it all was to him! Then, with the lightning action in which he was such an adept, he noiselessly slipped his hand under the bottom of the tent-cloth, which was far from being pinned tightly down, lifted it a little way, keeping his eye to the hole, snatched the note from her fingers, dropped the canvas, and ran away in the gloom towards the bank and ditch, smiling at the scream of astonishment which burst from her. Troy then slid down on the outside of the rampart, hastened round in the bottom of the entrenchment to a distance of a hundred yards, ascended again, and crossed boldly in a slow walk towards the front entrance of the tent. His object was now to get to Pennyways, and prevent a repetition of the announcement until such time as he should choose.

Troy reached the tent door, and standing among the groups there gathered, looked anxiously for Pennyways, evidently not wishing to make himself prominent by inquiring for him. One or two men were speaking of a daring attempt that had just been made to rob a young lady by lifting the canvas of the tent beside her. It was supposed that the rogue had imagined a slip of paper which she held in her hand to be a bank note, for he had seized it, and made off with it, leaving her purse behind. His chagrin and disappointment at dis-covering its worthlessness would be a good joke, it was said. However, the occurrence seemed to have become known to few, for it had not interrupted a fiddler, who had lately begun playing by the door of the tent, nor the four bowed old men with grim countenances and walking‑sticks in hand, who were dancing 'Major Malley's Reel' to the tune. Behind these stood Pernyways. Troy glided up to him, beckoned, and whispered a few words; and with a mutual glance of concurrence the two men went into the night together.

CHAPTER LI

BATHSHEBA TALKS WITH HER OUTRIDER

THE arrangement for getting back again to Weatherbury had been that Oak should take the place of Poorgrass in Bathsheba's conveyance and drive her home, it being discovered late in the afternoon that Joseph was suffering from his old complaint, a multiplying eye, and was, therefore, hardly trustworthy as coachman and protector to a woman. But Oak had found himself so occupied, and was full of so many cares relative to those portions of Boldwood's flocks that were not disposed of, that Bathsheba, without telling Oak or anybody, resolved to drive home herself, as she had many times done from Casterbridge Market, and trust to her good angel for performing the journey unmolested. But having fallen in with Farmer Boldwood accidentally (on her part at least) at the refreshment-tent, she found it impossible to refuse his offer to ride on horseback beside her as escort. It had grown twilight before she was aware, but Boldwood assured her that there was no cause for uneasiness, as the moon would be up in half-an-hour.

Immediately after the incident in the tent, she had risen to go—now absolutely alarmed and really grateful for her old lover's protection—though regretting Gabriel's absence, whose company she would have much preferred, as being more proper as well as more pleasant, since he was her own managing-man and servant. This, however, could not be helped; she would not, on any consideration, treat Boldwood harshly, having once already ill-used him, and the moon having risen, and the gig being ready, she drove across the hill-top in the wending ways which led downwards—to oblivious obscurity, as it seemed, for the moon and the hill it flooded with light were in appearance on a level, the rest of the world lying as a vast shady concave between them. Boldwood mounted his horse, and followed in close attendance behind. Thus they descended into the lowlands, and the sounds of those left on the hill came like voices from the sky, and the lights were as those of a camp in heaven. They soon passed the merry stragglers in the immediate vicinity of the hill, traversed Kingsbere, and got upon the high road.

The keen instincts of Bathsheba had perceived that the farmer's staunch devotion to herself was still undiminished, and she sympathized deeply. The sight had quite depressed her this evening; had reminded her of her folly; she wished anew, as she had wished many months ago, for some means of making reparation for her fault. Hence her pity for the man who so persistently loved on to his own injury and permanent gloom had betrayed Bathsheba into an injudicious considerateness of manner, which appeared almost like tenderness, and gave new vigour to the exquisite dream of a Jacob's seven years' service in poor Boldwood's mind.

He soon found an excuse for advancing from his position in the rear, and rode close by her side. They had gone two or three miles in the moonlight, speaking desultorily across the wheel of her gig concerning the fair, farming, Oak's usefulness to them both, and other indifferent subjects, when Boldwood said suddenly and simply—

'Mrs. Troy, you will marry again some day?'

This point-blank query unmistakably confused her, and it was not till a minute or more had elapsed that she said, 'I have not seriously thought of any such subject.'

'I quite understand that. Yet your late husband has been dead nearly one year, and——'

'You forget that his death was never absolutely proved, and so I suppose I am not legally a widow,' she said, catching at the straw of escape that the fact afforded.

'Not absolutely proved, perhaps, but it was proved circumstantially. A man saw him drowning, too. No reasonable person has any doubt of his death; nor have you, ma'am, I should imagine.'

'I have less now, or I should have acted differently,' she said, gently. 'I certainly, at first, had a strange unaccountable feeling that he could not have perished, but I have been able to explain that in several ways since. But though I am half persuaded that I shall see him no more, I am far from thinking of marriage with another. I should be very contemptible to indulge in such a thought.'

They were silent now awhile, and having struck into an unfrequented track across a common, the creaks of Boldwood's saddle and her gig springs were all the sounds to be heard. Boldwood ended the pause.

'Do you remember when I carried you fainting in my arms into the King's Arms, in Casterbridge? Every dog has his day: that was mine.'

'I know—I know it all,' she said, hurriedly.

'I, for one, shall never cease regretting that events so fell out as to deny you to me.'

'I, too, am very sorry,' she said, and then checked herself. 'I mean, you know, I am sorry you thought I——'

'I have always this dreary pleasure in thinking over

those past times with you—that I was something to you before *he* was anything, and that you belonged *almost* to me. But, of course, that's nothing. You never liked me.'

'I did; and respected you, too.'

'Do you now?'

'Yes.'

'Which?'

'How do you mean which?'

'Do you like me, or do you respect me?'

'I don't know—at least, I cannot tell you. It is difficult for a woman to define her feelings in language which is chiefly made by men to express theirs. My treatment of you was thoughtless, inexcusable, wicked! I shall eternally regret it. If there had been anything I could have done to make amends I would most gladly have done it—there was nothing on earth I so longed to do as to repair the error. But that was not possible.'

'Don't blame yourself—you were not so far in the wrong as you suppose. Bathsheba, suppose you had real complete proof that you are what, in fact, you are —a widow—would you repair the old wrong to me by marrying me?'

'I cannot say. I shouldn't yet, at any rate.'

'But you might at some future time of your life?'

'Oh yes, I might at some time.'

'Well, then, do you know that without further proof of any kind you may marry again in about six years from the present—subject to nobody's objection or blame?'

'Oh yes,' she said, quickly. 'I know all that. But don't talk of it—seven or six years—where may we all be by that time?'

'They will soon glide by, and it will seem an astonishingly short time to look back upon when they are past—much less than to look forward to now.'

'Yes, yes; I have found that in my own experience.'

'Now, listen once more,' Boldwood pleaded. 'If I wait that time, will you marry me? You own that you owe me amends—let that be your way of making them.'

'But, Mr. Boldwood—six years——'

'Do you want to be the wife of any other man?'

'No indeed! I mean, that I don't like to talk about this matter now. Perhaps it is not proper, and I ought not to allow it. Let us drop it for the present, please do!'

'Of course, I'll drop the subject if you wish. But propriety has nothing to do with reasons. I am a middle-aged man, willing to protect you for the remainder of our lives. On your side, at least, there is no passion or blamable haste—on mine, perhaps, there is. But I can't help seeing that if you choose from a feeling of pity, and, as you say, a wish to make amends, to make a bargain with me for a far-ahead time—an agreement which will set all things right and make me happy, late though it may be—there is no fault to be found with you as a woman. Hadn't I the first place beside you? Haven't you been almost mine once already? Surely you can say to me as much as this, you will have me back again should circumstances permit? Now, pray speak! O Bathsheba, promise—it is only a little promise—that if you marry again, you will marry me!'

His tone was so excited that she almost feared him at this moment, even whilst she sympathized. It was a simple physical fear—the weak of the strong; there was no emotional aversion or inner repugnance. She said, with some distress in her voice, for she remembered vividly his outburst on the Yalbury Road, and shrank from a repetition of his anger:—

'I will never marry another man whilst you wish me to be your wife, whatever comes—but to say more—you have taken me so by surprise——'

416

'But let it stand in these simple words—that in six years' time you will be my wife? Unexpected accidents we'll not mention, because those, of course, must be given way to. Now, this time I know you will keep your word.'

'That's why I hesitate to give it.'

'But do give it! Remember the past, and be kind.'

She breathed; and then said mournfully: 'Oh what shall I do? I don't love you, and I much fear that I never shall love you as much as a woman ought to love a husband. If you, sir, know that, and I can yet give you happiness by a mere promise to marry at the end of six years, if my husband should not come back, it is a great honour to me. And if you value such an act of friendship from a woman who doesn't esteem herself as she did, and has little love left, why I—I will—— '

'Promise!'

'—Consider, if I cannot promise soon.'

'But soon is perhaps never?'

'Oh no, it is not! I mean soon. Christmas, we'll say.'

'Christmas!' He said nothing further till he added: 'Well, I'll say no more to you about it till that time.'

Bathsheba was in a very peculiar state of mind, which showed how entirely the soul is the slave of the body, the ethereal spirit dependent for its quality upon the tangible flesh and blood. It is hardly too much to say that she felt coerced by a force stronger than her own will, not only into the act of promising upon this singularly remote and vague matter, but into the emotion of fancying that she ought to promise. When the weeks intervening between the night of this conversation and Christmas day began perceptibly to diminish, her anxiety and perplexity increased.

One day she was led by an accident into an oddly confidential dialogue with Gabriel about her difficulty. It afforded her a little relief—of a dull and cheerless kind. They were auditing accounts, and something occurred in the course of their labours which led Oak to say, speaking of Boldwood, 'He'll never forget you, ma'am, never.'

Then out came her trouble before she was aware; and she told him how she had again got into the toils; what Boldwood had asked her, and how he was expecting her assent. 'The most mournful reason of all for my agreeing to it,' she said sadly, 'and the true reason why I think to do so for good or for evil, is this —it is a thing I have not breathed to a living soul as yet—I believe that if I don't give my word, he'll go out of his mind.'

'Really, do ye?' said Gabriel, gravely.

'I believe this,' she continued, with reckless frankness; 'and Heaven knows I say it in a spirit the very reverse of vain, for I am grieved and troubled to my soul about it—I believe I hold that man's future in my hand. His career depends entirely upon my treatment of him. O Gabriel, I tremble at my responsibility, for it is terrible!'

'Well, I think this much, ma'am, as I told you years ago,' said Oak, 'that his life is a total blank whenever he isn't hoping for 'ee; but I can't suppose—I hope that nothing so dreadful hangs on to it as you fancy. His natural manner has always been dark and strange, you know. But since the case is so sad and odd-like, why don't ye give the conditional promise? I think I would.'

'But is it right? Some rash acts of my past life have taught me that a watched woman must have very much circumspection to retain only a very little credit, and I do want and long to be discreet in this! And six years—why we may all be in our graves by that time, or Mr. Troy may even be back again! Such thoughts give a sort of absurdity to the scheme. Now, isn't it preposterous, Gabriel? However he came to dream of it, I cannot think. But is it wrong? You know—you are older than I.'

'Eight years older, ma'am.'

'Yes, eight years—and is it wrong?'

'Perhaps it would be an uncommon agreement for a man and woman to make: I don't see anything really wrong about it,' said Oak, slowly. 'In fact the very thing that makes it doubtful if you ought to marry en under any condition, that is, your not caring about him —for I mid suppose——'

'Yes, you may suppose that love is wanting,' she said shortly. 'Love is an utterly bygone, sorry, worn-out, miserable thing with me—for him or any one else.'

'Well, your want of love seems to me the one thing that takes away harm from such an agreement with him. If wild heat had to do wi' it, making ye long to over-come the awkwardness about your husband's death, it mid be wrong; but a cold-hearted agreement to oblige a man seems different, somehow. The real sin, ma'am, in my mind, lies in thinking of ever wedding wi' a man you don't love honest and true.'

'That I'm willing to pay the penalty of,' said Bath-sheba, firmly. 'You know, Gabriel, this is what I can-not get off my conscience—that I once seriously injured him in sheer idleness. If I had never played a trick upon him, he would never have wanted to marry me. Oh! if I could only pay some heavy damages in money to him for the harm I did, and so get the sin off my soul that way! . . . Well, there's the debt, which can only be discharged in one way, and I believe I am bound to do it if it honestly lies in my power, without any consideration of my own future at all. When a rake gambles away his expectations, the fact that it is an inconvenient debt doesn't make him the less liable.

I've been a rake, and the single point I ask you is, considering that my own scruples, and the fact that in the eye of the law my husband is only missing, will keep any man from marrying me until seven years have passed—am I free to entertain such an idea, even though 'tis a sort of penance—for it will be that? I *hate* the act of marriage under such circumstances, and the class of women I should seem to belong to by doing it!'

'It seems to me that all depends upon whe'r you think, as everybody else do, that your husband is dead.'

'I am getting to, because I cannot help feeling what would have brought him back long before this time if he had lived.'

'Well, then, in a religious sense you must be as free to think o' marrying again as any real widow of one year's standing. But why don't ye ask Mr. Thirdly's advice on how to treat Mr. Boldwood?'

'No. When I want a broad-minded opinion for general enlightenment, distinct from special advice, I never go to a man who deals in the subject professionally. So I like the parson's opinion on law, the lawyer's on doctoring, the doctor's on business, and my business-man's—that is, yours—on morals.'

'And on love——'

'My own.'

'I'm afraid there's a hitch in that arg'ment,' said Oak, with a grave smile.

She did not reply at once, and then saying, 'Good evening, Mr. Oak,' went away.

She had spoken frankly, and neither asked nor expected any reply from Gabriel more satisfactory than that she had obtained. Yet in the centremost parts of her complicated heart there existed at this minute a little pang of disappointment, for a reason she would not allow herself to recognize. Oak had not once wished her free that he might marry her himself—had not once said 'I could wait for you as well as he.' That was the insect sting. Not that she would have listened to any such hypothesis. Oh no—for wasn't she saying all the time that such thoughts of the future were improper, and wasn't Gabriel far too poor a man to speak sentiment to her? Yet he might have just hinted about that old love of his, and asked, in a playful off-hand way, if he might speak of it. It would have seemed pretty and sweet, if no more; and then she would have shown how kind and inoffensive a woman's 'No' can sometimes be. But to give such cool advice —the very advice she had asked for—it ruffled our heroine all the afternoon.

CHAPTER LII

CONVERGING COURSES

I

CHRISTMAS-EVE came, and a party that Boldwood was to give in the evening was the great subject of talk in Weatherbury. It was not that the rarity of Christmas parties in the parish made this one a wonder, but that Boldwood should be the giver. The announcement had had an abnormal and incongruous sound, as if one should hear of croquet-playing in a cathedral aisle, or that some much-respected judge was going upon the stage. That the party was intended to be a truly jovial one there was no room for doubt. A large bough of mistletoe had been brought from the woods that day, and suspended in the hall of the bachelor's home. Holly and ivy had followed in armfuls. From six that morning till past noon the huge wood fire in the kitchen roared and sparkled at its highest, the kettle, the saucepan, and the three-legged pot appearing in the midst of the flames like Shadrach, Meshach, and Abednego; moreover, roasting and basting operations were continually carried on in front of the genial blaze.

As it grew later the fire was made up in the large long hall into which the staircase descended, and all encumbrances were cleared out for dancing. The log

422

which was to form the back-brand of the evening fire
was the uncleft trunk of a tree, so unwieldy that it could
be neither brought nor rolled to its place; and accordingly four men were to be observed dragging and heaving
it in by chains and levers as the hour of assembly drew
near.

In spite of all this, the spirit of revelry was wanting
in the atmosphere of the house. Such a thing had
never been attempted before by its owner, and it was
now done as by a wrench. Intended gaieties would
insist upon appearing like solemn grandeurs, the organ-
ization of the whole effort was carried out coldly by
hirelings, and a shadow seemed to move about the
rooms, saying that the proceedings were unnatural to
the place and the lone man who lived therein, and hence
not good.

II

Bathsheba was at this time in her room, dressing for
the event. She had called for candles, and Liddy
entered and placed one on each side of her mistress's
glass.

'Don't go away, Liddy,' said Bathsheba, almost
timidly. 'I am foolishly agitated—I cannot tell why.
I wish I had not been obliged to go to this dance; but
there's no escaping now. I have not spoken to Mr.
Boldwood since the autumn, when I promised to see
him at Christmas on business, but I had no idea there
was to be anything of this kind.'

'But I would go now,' said Liddy, who was going
with her; for Boldwood had been indiscriminate in his
invitations.

'Yes, I shall make my appearance, of course,' said
Bathsheba. 'But I am *the cause* of the party, and that
upsets me!—Don't tell, Liddy.'

'Oh no, ma'am. You the cause of it, ma'am?'

'Yes. I am the reason of the party—I. If it had

not been for me, there would never have been one. I can't explain any more—there's no more to be explained. I wish I had never seen Weatherbury.'

'That's wicked of you—to wish to be worse off than you are.'

'No, Liddy. I have never been free from trouble since I have lived here, and this party is likely to bring me more. Now, fetch my black silk dress, and see how it sits upon me.'

'But you will leave off that, surely, ma'am? You have been a widow-lady fourteen months, and ought to brighten up a little on such a night as this.'

'Is it necessary? No; I will appear as usual, for if I were to wear any light dress people would say things about me, and I should seem to be rejoicing when I am solemn all the time. The party doesn't suit me a bit; but never mind, stay and help to finish me off.'

III

Boldwood was dressing also at this hour. A tailor from Casterbridge was with him, assisting him in the operation of trying on a new coat that had just been brought home.

Never had Boldwood been so fastidious, unreasonable about the fit, and generally difficult to please. The tailor walked round and round him, tugged at the waist, pulled the sleeve, pressed out the collar, and for the first time in his experience Boldwood was not bored. Times had been when the farmer had exclaimed against all such niceties as childish, but now no philosophic or hasty rebuke whatever was provoked by this man for attaching as much importance to a crease in the coat as to an earthquake in South America. Boldwood at last expressed himself nearly satisfied, and paid the bill, the tailor passing out of the door just as Oak came in to report progress for the day.

'Oh, Oak,' said Boldwood. 'I shall of course see you here to-night. Make yourself merry. I am determined that neither expense nor trouble shall be spared.'

'I'll try to be here, sir, though perhaps it may not be very early,' said Gabriel, quietly. 'I am glad indeed to see such a change in 'ee from what it used to be.'

'Yes—I must own it—I am bright to-night: cheerful and more than cheerful—so much so that I am almost sad again with the sense that all of it is passing away. And sometimes, when I am excessively hopeful and blithe, a trouble is looming in the distance: so that I often get to look upon gloom in me with content, and to fear a happy mood. Still this may be absurd—I feel that it is absurd. Perhaps my day is dawning at last.'

'I hope it 'ill be a long and a fair one.'

'Thank you—thank you. Yet perhaps my cheerfulness rests on a slender hope. And yet I trust my hope. It is faith, not hope. I think this time I reckon with my host.—Oak, my hands are a little shaky, or something: I can't tie this neckerchief properly. Perhaps you will tie it for me. The fact is, I have not been well lately, you know.'

'I am sorry to hear that, sir.'

'Oh, it's nothing. I want it done as well as you can, please. Is there any late knot in fashion, Oak?'

'I don't know, sir,' said Oak. His tone had sunk to sadness.

Boldwood approached Gabriel, and as Oak tied the neckerchief the farmer went on feverishly—

'Does a woman keep her promise, Gabriel?'

'If it is not inconvenient to her she may.'

'—Or rather an implied promise.'

'I won't answer for her implying,' said Oak, with faint bitterness. 'That's a word as full o' holes as a sieve with them.'

'Oak, don't talk like that. You have got quite cynical lately—how is it? We seem to have shifted our positions: I have become the young and hopeful man, and you the old and unbelieving one. However, does a woman keep a promise, not to marry, but to enter on an engagement to marry at some time? Now you know women better than I—tell me.'

'I am afeard you honour my understanding too much. However, she may keep such a promise, if it is made with an honest maning to repair a wrong.'

'It has not gone far yet, but I think it will soon—yes, I know it will,' he said, in an impulsive whisper. 'I have pressed her upon the subject, and she inclines to be kind to me, and to think of me as a husband at a long future time, and that's enough for me. How can I expect more? She has a notion that a widow should not marry within seven years of her husband's death—that her own self shouldn't, I mean—because his body was not found. It may be merely this legal reason which influences her, or it may be a religious one, but she is reluctant to talk on the point. Yet she has promised—implied—that she will ratify an engagement to-night.'

'Seven years,' murmured Oak.

'No, no—it's no such thing!' he said, with impatience. 'Five years, nine months, and a few days. Fifteen months nearly have passed since his death, and is there anything so wonderful in an engagement of little more than five years?'

'It seems long in a forward view. Don't build too much upon such promises, sir. Remember, you have once be'n deceived. Her maning may be good; but there—she's young yet.'

'Deceived? Never!' said Boldwood, vehemently. 'She never promised me at that first time, and hence she did not break her promise! If she promises me, she'll marry me. Bathsheba is a woman to her word.'

IV

Troy was sitting in a corner of The White Hart tavern at Casterbridge, smoking and drinking a steaming mixture from a glass. A knock was given at the door, and Pennyways entered.

'Well, have you seen him?' Troy inquired, pointing to a chair.

'Boldwood?'

'No—Lawyer Long.'

'He wadn' at home. I went there first, too.'

'That's a nuisance.'

''Tis rather, I suppose.'

'Yet I don't see that, because a man appears to be drowned and was not, he should be liable for anything. I shan't ask any lawyer—not I.'

'But that's not it, exactly. If a man changes his name and so forth, and takes steps to deceive the world and his own wife, he's a cheat, and that in the eye of the law is ayless a rogue, and that is ayless a lammocken vagabond; and that's a punishable situation.'

'Ha-ha! Well done, Pennyways.' Troy had laughed, but it was with some anxiety that he said, 'Now, what I want to know is this, do you think there's really anything going on between her and Boldwood? Upon my soul, I should never have believed it! How she must detest me! Have you found out whether she has encouraged him?'

'I haen't been able to learn. There's a deal of feeling on his side seemingly, but I don't answer for her. I didn't know a word about any such thing till yesterday, and all I heard then was that she was gwine to the party at his house to-night. This is the first time she has ever gone there, they say. And they say that she've not so much as spoke to him since they were at Greenhill Fair: but what can folk believe o't? How-

427

ever, she's not fond of him—quite offish and quite careless, I know.'

'I'm not so sure of that. . . . She's a handsome
woman, Pennyways, is she not? Own that you never
saw a finer or more splendid creature in your life.
Upon my honour, when I set eyes upon her that day
I wondered what I could have been made of to be able
to leave her by herself so long. And then I was
hampered with that bothering show, which I'm free of
at last, thank the stars.' He smoked on awhile, and
then added, 'How did she look when you passed by
yesterday?'

'Oh, she took no great heed of me, ye may well
fancy; but she looked well enough, far's I know. Just
flashed her haughty eyes upon my poor scram body, and
then let them go past me to what was yond, much as if
I'd been no more than a leafless tree. She had just got
off her mare to look at the last wring-down of cider for
the year; she had been riding, and so her colours were
up and her breath rather quick, so that her bosom
plimmed and fell—plimmed and fell—every time plain
to my eye. Ay, and there were the fellers round her
wringing down the cheese and bustling about and
saying, "Ware o' the pommy, ma'am: 'twill spoil yer
gown." "Never mind me," says she. Then Gabe
brought her some of the new cider, and she must
needs go drinking it through a strawmote, and not in
a nateral way at all. "Liddy," says she, "bring indoors
a few gallons, and I'll make some cider-wine." Sergeant,
I was no more to her than a morsel of scroff in the fuel-
house!'

'I must go and find her out at once—Oh yes, I see
that—I must go. Oak is head man still, isn't he?'

'Yes, 'a b'lieve. And at Little Weatherbury Farm
too. He manages everything.'

''Twill puzzle him to manage her, or any other man
of his compass!'

'I don't know about that. She can't do without him, and knowing it well he's pretty independent. And she've a few soft corners to her mind, though I've never been able to get into one, the devil's in't!'

'Ah, baily, she's a notch above you, and you must own it: a higher class of animal—a finer tissue. However, stick to me, and neither this haughty goddess, dashing piece of womanhood, Juno-wife of mine (Juno was a goddess, you know), nor anybody else shall hurt you. But all this wants looking into, I perceive. What with one thing and another, I see that my work is well cut out for me.'

V

'How do I look to-night, Liddy?' said Bathsheba, giving a final adjustment to her dress before leaving the glass.

'I never saw you look so well before. Yes—I'll tell you when you looked like it—that night, a year and a half ago, when you came in so wild-like, and scolded us for making remarks about you and Mr. Troy.'

'Everybody will think that I am setting myself to captivate Mr. Boldwood, I suppose,' she murmured. 'At least they'll say so. Can't my hair be brushed down a little flatter? I dread going—yet I dread the risk of wounding him by staying away.'

'Anyhow, ma'am, you can't well be dressed plainer than you are, unless you go in sackcloth at once. 'Tis your excitement is what makes you look so noticeable to-night.'

'I don't know what's the matter, I feel wretched at one time, and buoyant at another. I wish I could have continued quite.alone as I have been for the last year or so, with no hopes and no fears, and no pleasure and no grief.'

'Now just suppose Mr. Boldwood should ask you

429

—only just suppose it—to run away with him, what
would you do, ma'am?'

'Liddy—none of that,' said Bathsheba, gravely.
'Mind, I won't hear joking on any such matter. Do
you hear?'

'I beg pardon, ma'am. But knowing what rum
things we women be, I just said—however, I won't
speak of it again.'

'No marrying for me yet for many a year; if ever,
'twill be for reasons very, very different from those you
think, or others will believe! Now get my cloak, for it
is time to go.'

VI

'Oak,' said Boldwood, 'before you go I want to
mention what has been passing in my mind lately—
that little arrangement we made about your share in the
farm I mean. That share is small, too small, considering how little I attend to business now, and how much
time and thought you give to it. Well, since the world
is brightening for me, I want to show my sense of it
by increasing your proportion in the partnership. I'll
make a memorandum of the arrangement which struck
me as likely to be convenient, for I haven't time to talk
about it now; and then we'll discuss it at our leisure.
My intention is ultimately to retire from the management altogether, and until you can take all the expendi-
ture upon your shoulders, I'll be a sleeping partner in
the stock. Then, if I marry her—and I hope—I feel I
shall, why——'

'Pray don't speak of it, sir,' said Oak, hastily. 'We
don't know what may happen. So many upsets may
befall 'ee. There's many a slip, as they say—and I
would advise you—I know you'll pardon me this once—
not to be *too sure*.'

'I know, I know. But the feeling I have about increasing your share is on account of what I know of you.

Oak, I have learnt a little about your secret: your interest in her is more than that of bailiff for an employer. But you have behaved like a man, and I, as a sort of successful rival—successful partly through your goodness of heart—should like definitely to show my sense of your friendship under what must have been a great pain to you.'

'Oh, that's not necessary, thank 'ee,' said Oak, hurriedly. 'I must get used to such as that; other men have, and so shall I.'

Oak then left him. He was uneasy on Boldwood's account, for he saw anew that this constant passion of the farmer made him not the man he once had been.

As Boldwood continued awhile in his room alone— ready and dressed to receive his company—the mood of anxiety about his appearance seemed to pass away, and to be succeeded by a deep solemnity. He looked out of the window, and regarded the dim outline of the trees upon the sky, and the twilight deepening to darkness.

Then he went to a locked closet, and took from a locked drawer therein a small circular case the size of a pill-box, and was about to put it into his pocket. But he lingered to open the cover and take a momentary glance inside. It contained a woman's finger-ring, set all the way round with small diamonds, and from its appearance had evidently been recently purchased. Boldwood's eyes dwelt upon its many sparkles a long time, though that its material aspect concerned him little was plain from his manner and mien, which were those of a mind following out the presumed thread of that jewel's future history.

The noise of wheels at the front of the house became audible. Boldwood closed the box, stowed it away carefully in his pocket, and went out upon the landing. The old man who was his indoor factotum came at the same moment to the foot of the stairs.

'They be coming, sir—lots of 'em—a-foot and a-driving!'

'I was coming down this moment. Those wheels I heard—is it Mrs. Troy?'

'No, sir—'tis not she yet.'

A reserved and sombre expression had returned to Boldwood's face again, but it poorly cloaked his feelings when he pronounced Bathsheba's name; and his feverish anxiety continued to show its existence by a galloping motion of his fingers upon the side of his thigh as he went down the stairs.

VII

'How does this cover me?' said Troy to Pennyways. 'Nobody would recognize me now, I'm sure.'

He was buttoning on a heavy grey overcoat of Noachian cut, with cape and high collar, the latter being erect and rigid, like a girdling wall, and nearly reaching to the verge of a travelling cap which was pulled down over his ears.

Pennyways snuffed the candle, and then looked up and deliberately inspected Troy.

'You've made up your mind to go then?' he said.

'Made up my mind? Yes; of course I have.'

'Why not write to her? 'Tis a very queer corner that you have got into, sergeant. You see all these things will come to light if you go back, and they won't sound well at all. Faith, if I was you I'd even bide as you be —a single man of the name of Francis. A good wife is good, but the best wife is not so good as no wife at all. Now that's my outspoke mind, and I've been called a long-headed feller here and there.'

'All nonsense!' said Troy, angrily. 'There she is with plenty of money, and a house and farm, and horses, and comfort, and here am I living from hand to mouth—a needy adventurer. Besides, it is no use talking now; it is too late, and I am glad of it; I've been seen and recognized here this very afternoon. I should have gone back to her the day after the fair, if it hadn't been for you talking about the law, and rubbish about getting a separation; and I don't put it off any longer. What the deuce put it into my head to run away at all, I can't think! Humbugging sentiment—that's what it was. But what man on earth was to know that his wife would be in such a hurry to get rid of his name!'

'I should have known it. She's bad enough for anything.'

'Pennyways, mind who you are talking to.'

'Well, sergeant, all I say is this, that if I were you I'd go abroad again where I came from—'tisn't too late to do it now. I wouldn't stir up the business and get a bad name for the sake of living with her—for all that about your play-acting is sure to come out, you know, although you think otherwise. My eyes and limbs, there'll be a racket if you go back just now—in the middle of Bold-wood's Christmasing!'

'H'm, yes. I expect I shall not be a very welcome guest if he has her there,' said the sergeant, with a slight laugh. 'A sort of Alonzo the Brave; and when I go in the guests will sit in silence and fear, and all laughter and pleasure will be hushed, and the lights in the chamber burn blue, and the worms—Ugh, horrible!— Ring for some more brandy, Pennyways, I felt an awful shudder just then! Well, what is there besides? A stick—I must have a walking-stick.'

Pennyways now felt himself to be in something of a difficulty, for should Bathsheba and Troy become reconciled it would be necessary to regain her good opinion if he would secure the patronage of her husband. 'I sometimes think she likes you yet, and is a good woman at bottom,' he said, as a saving sentence. 'But there's no telling to a certainty from a body's outside. Well, you'll do as you like about going, of course, sergeant, and as for me, I'll do as you tell me.'

'Now, let me see what the time is,' said Troy, after emptying his glass in one draught as he stood. 'Half-past six o'clock. I shall not hurry along the road, and shall be there then before nine.'

CHAPTER LIII

CONCURRITUR—HORÆ MOMENTO

OUTSIDE the front of Boldwood's house a group of men stood in the dark, with their faces towards the door, which occasionally opened and closed for the passage of some guest or servant, when a golden rod of light would stripe the ground for the moment and vanish again, leaving nothing outside but the glowworm shine of the pale lamp amid the evergreens over the door.

'He was seen in Casterbridge this afternoon—so the boy said,' one of them remarked in a whisper. 'And I for one believe it. His body was never found, you know.'

''Tis a strange story,' said the next. 'You may depend upon't that she knows nothing about it.'

'Not a word.'

'Perhaps he don't mean that she shall,' said another man.

'If he's alive and here in the neighbourhood, he means mischief,' said the first. 'Poor young thing: I do pity her, if 'tis true. He'll drag her to the dogs.'

'Oh, no; he'll settle down quiet enough,' said one disposed to take a more hopeful view of the case.

'What a fool she must have been ever to have had anything to do with the man! She is so self-willed and independent too, that one is more minded to say it serves her right than pity her.'

'No, no! I don't hold with ye there. She was no otherwise than a girl mind, and how could she tell what the man was made of? If 'tis really true, 'tis too hard a punishment, and more than she ought to hae.—Hullo, who's that?' This was to some footsteps that were heard approaching.

'William Smallbury,' said a dim figure in the shades, coming up and joining them. 'Dark as a hedge, to-night, isn't it? I all but missed the plank over the river ath'art there in the bottom—never did such a thing before in my life. Be ye any of Boldwood's workfolk?' He peered into their faces.

'Yes—all o' us. We met here a few minutes ago.'

'Oh, I hear now—that's Sam Samway: thought I knowed the voice, too. Going in?'

'Presently. But I say, William,' Samway whispered, 'have ye heard this strange tale?'

'What—that about Sergeant Troy being seen, d'ye mean, souls?' said Smallbury, also lowering his voice.

'Ay: in Casterbridge.'

'Yes, I have. Laban Tall named a hint of it to me but now—but I don't think it. Hark, here Laban comes himself, 'a b'lieve.' A footstep drew near.

'Laban?'

'Yes, 'tis I,' said Tall.

'Have ye heard any more about that?'

'No,' said Tall, joining the group. 'And I'm in-clined to think we'd better keep quiet. If so be 'tis not true, 'twill flurry her, and do her much harm to repeat it; and if so be 'tis true, 'twill do no good to forestall her time o' trouble. God send that it mid be a lie, for though Henery Fray and some of 'em do speak against her, she's never been anything but fair to me. She's hot and hasty, but she's a brave girl who'll never tell a lie however much the truth may harm her, and I've no cause to wish her evil.'

'She never do tell women's little lies, that's true; and

'tis a thing that can be said of very few. Ay, all the harm she thinks she says to yer face: there's nothing underhand wi' her.'

They stood silent then, every man busied with his own thoughts, during which interval sounds of merriment could be heard within. Then the front door again opened, the rays streamed out, the well-known form of Boldwood was seen in the rectangular area of light, the door closed, and Boldwood walked slowly down the path.

''Tis master,' one of the men whispered, as he neared them. 'We'd better stand quiet—he'll go in again directly. He would think it unseemly o' us to be loitering here.'

Boldwood came on, and passed by the men without seeing them, they being under the bushes on the grass. He paused, leant over the gate, and breathed a long breath. They heard low words come from him.

'I hope to God she'll come, or this night will be nothing but misery to me! Oh, my darling, my darling, why do you keep me in suspense like this?'

He said this to himself, and they all distinctly heard it. Boldwood remained silent after that, and the noise from indoors was again just audible, until, a few minutes later, light wheels could be distinguished coming down the hill. They drew nearer, and ceased at the gate. Boldwood hastened back to the door, and opened it; and the light shone upon Bathsheba coming up the path.

Boldwood compressed his emotion to mere welcome: the men marked her light laugh and apology as she met him: he took her into the house; and the door closed again.

'Gracious heaven, I didn't know it was like that with him!' said one of the men. 'I thought that fancy of his was over long ago.'

'You don't know much of master, if you thought that,' said Samway.

437

'I wouldn't he should know we heard what 'a said for the world,' remarked a third.

'I wish we had told of the report at once,' the first uneasily continued. 'More harm may come of this than we know of. Poor Mr. Boldwood, it will be hard upon en. I wish Troy was in —— Well, God forgive me for such a wish! A scoundrel to play a poor wife such tricks. Nothing has prospered in Weatherbury since he came here. And now I've no heart to go in. Let's look into Warren's, shall us, neighbours?'

Samway, Tall, and Smallbury agreed to go to Warren's, and went out at the gate, the remaining ones entering the house. The three soon drew near the malt-house, approaching it from the adjoining orchard, and not by way of the street. The pane of glass was illuminated as usual. Smallbury was a little in advance of the rest, when, pausing, he turned suddenly to his companions and said, 'Hist! See there.'

The light from the pane was now perceived to be shining not upon the ivied wall as usual, but upon some object close to the glass. It was a human face.

'Let's come closer,' whispered Samway; and they approached on tiptoe. There was no disbelieving the report any longer. Troy's face was almost close to the pane, and he was looking in. Not only was he looking in, but he appeared to have been arrested by a conversation which was in progress in the malt-house, the voices of the interlocutors being those of Oak and the maltster.

'The spree is all in her honour, isn't it—hey?' said the old man. 'Although he made believe 'tis only keeping up o' Christmas?'

'I cannot say,' replied Oak.

'Oh 'tis true enough, faith. I cannot understand Farmer Boldwood being such a fool at his time of life as to ho and hanker after thik woman in the way 'a do, and she not care a bit about en.'

The men, after recognizing Troy's features, withdrew across the orchard as quietly as they had come. The air was big with Bathsheba's fortunes to-night : every word everywhere concerned her. When they were quite out of earshot all by one instinct paused.

'It gave me quite a turn—his face,' said Tall, breathing.

'And so it did me,' said Samway. 'What's to be done?'

'I don't see that 'tis any business of ours,' Smallbury murmured dubiously.

'Oh yes. 'Tis a thing which is everybody's business,' said Samway. 'We know very well that master's on a wrong tack, and that she's quite in the dark, and we should let 'em know at once. Laban, you know her best—you'd better go and ask to speak to her.'

'I bain't fit for any such thing,' said Laban, nervously. 'I should think William ought to do it if anybody. He's oldest.'

'I shall have nothing to do with it,' said Smallbury. ''Tis a ticklish business altogether. Why, he'll go on to her himself in a few minutes, ye'll see.'

'We don't know that he will. Come, Laban.'

'Very well, if I must I must, I suppose,' Tall reluctantly answered. 'What must I say?'

'Just ask to see master.'

'Oh no; I shan't speak to Mr. Boldwood. If I tell anybody, 'twill be mistress.'

'Very well,' said Samway.

Laban then went to the door. When he opened it the hum of bustle rolled out as a wave upon a still strand—the assemblage being immediately inside the hall—and was deadened to a murmur as he closed it again. Each man waited intently, and looked around at the dark tree tops gently rocking against the sky and occasionally shivering in a slight wind, as if he took interest in the scene, which neither did. One of them began walking up and down, and then came to where he started from and stopped again, with a sense that walking was a thing not worth doing now.

'I should think Laban must have seen mistress by this time,' said Smallbury, breaking the silence. 'Perhaps she won't come and speak to him.'

The door opened. Tall appeared, and joined them. 'Well?' said both.

'I didn't like to ask for her after all,' Laban faltered out. 'They were all in such a stir, trying to put a little spirit into the party. Somehow the fun seems to hang fire, though everything's there that a heart can desire, and I couldn't for my soul interfere and throw damp upon it—if 'twas to save my life, I couldn't!'

'I suppose we had better all go in together,' said Samway, gloomily. 'Perhaps I may have a chance of saying a word to master.'

So the men entered the hall, which was the room selected and arranged for the gathering because of its size. The younger men and maids were at last just beginning a dance. Bathsheba had been perplexed how to act, for she was not much more than a slim young maid herself, and the weight of stateliness sat heavy upon her. Sometimes she thought she ought not to have come under any circumstances; then she considered what cold unkindness that would have been, and finally resolved upon the middle course of staying for about an hour only, and gliding off unobserved, having from the first made up her mind that she could on no account dance, sing, or take any active part in the proceedings.

Her allotted hour having been passed in chatting and looking on, Bathsheba told Liddy not to hurry herself, and went to the small parlour to prepare for departure, which, like the hall, was decorated with holly and ivy, and well lighted up.

Nobody was in the room, but she had hardly

been there a moment when the master of the house entered.

'Mrs. Troy—you are not going?' he said. 'We've hardly begun!'

'If you'll excuse me, I should like to go now.' Her manner was restive, for she remembered her promise, and imagined what he was about to say. 'But as it is not late,' she added, 'I can walk home, and leave my man and Liddy to come when they choose.'

'I've been trying to get an opportunity of speaking to you,' said Boldwood. 'You know perhaps what I long to say?'

Bathsheba silently looked on the floor.

'You do give it?' he said, eagerly.

'What?' she whispered.

'Now, that's evasion! Why, the promise. I don't want to intrude upon you at all, or to let it become known to anybody. But do give your word! A mere business compact, you know, between two people who are beyond the influence of passion.' Boldwood knew how false this picture was as regarded himself; but he had proved that it was the only tone in which she would allow him to approach her. 'A promise to marry me at the end of five years and three-quarters. You owe it to me!'

'I feel that I do,' said Bathsheba; 'that is, if you demand it. But I am a changed woman—an unhappy woman—and not—not——'

'You are still a very beautiful woman,' said Boldwood. Honesty and pure conviction suggested the remark, unaccompanied by any perception that it might have been adopted by blunt flattery to soothe and win her.

However, it had not much effect now, for she said, in a passionless murmur which was in itself a proof of her words: 'I have no feeling in the matter at all. And I don't at all know what is right to do in my difficult position, and I have nobody to advise me. But

I give my promise, if I must. I give it as the rendering of a debt, conditionally, of course, on my being a widow.'

'You'll marry me between five and six years hence?'

'Don't press me too hard. I'll marry nobody else.'

'But surely you will name the time, or there's nothing in the promise at all?'

'Oh, I don't know, pray let me go!' she said, her bosom beginning to rise. 'I am afraid what to do! I want to be just to you, and to be that seems to be wronging myself, and perhaps it is breaking the commandments. There is considerable doubt of his death, and then it is dreadful; let me ask a solicitor, Mr. Boldwood, if I ought or no!'

'Say the words, dear one, and the subject shall be dismissed; a blissful loving intimacy of six years, and then marriage—O Bathsheba, say them!' he begged in a husky voice, unable to sustain the forms of mere friendship any longer. 'Promise yourself to me; I deserve it, indeed I do, for I have loved you more than anybody in the world! And if I said hasty words and showed uncalled-for heat of manner towards you, believe me, dear, I did not mean to distress you; I was in agony, Bathsheba, and I did not know what I said. You wouldn't let a dog suffer what I have suffered, could you but know it! Sometimes I shrink from your knowing what I have felt for you, and sometimes I am distressed that all of it you never will know. Be gracious, and give up a little to me, when I would give up my life for you!'

The trimmings of her dress, as they quivered against the light, showed how agitated she was, and at last she burst out crying. 'And you'll not—press me—about anything more—if I say in five or six years?' she sobbed, when she had power to frame the words.

'Yes, then I'll leave it to time.'

'Very well. If he does not return, I'll marry you

442

in six years from this day, if we both live,' she said solemnly.

'And you'll take this as a token from me.'

Boldwood had come close to her side, and now he clasped one of her hands in both his own, and lifted it to his breast.

'What is it? Oh I cannot wear a ring!' she exclaimed, on seeing what he held; 'besides, I wouldn't have a soul know that it's an engagement! Perhaps it is improper? Besides, we are not engaged in the usual sense, are we? Don't insist, Mr. Boldwood—don't!' In her trouble at not being able to get her hand away from him at once, she stamped passionately on the floor with one foot, and tears crowded to her eyes again.

'It means simply a pledge—no sentiment—the seal of a practical compact,' he said more quietly, but still retaining her hand in his firm grasp. 'Come, now!' And Boldwood slipped the ring on her finger.

'I cannot wear it,' she said, weeping as if her heart would break. 'You frighten me, almost. So wild a scheme! Please let me go home!'

'Only to-night: wear it just to-night, to please me!'

Bathsheba sat down in a chair, and buried her face in her handkerchief, though Boldwood kept her hand yet. At length she said, in a sort of hopeless whisper—

'Very well, then, I will to-night, if you wish it so earnestly. Now loosen my hand; I will, indeed I will wear it to-night.'

'And it shall be the beginning of a pleasant secret courtship of six years, with a wedding at the end?'

'It must be, I suppose, since you will have it so!' she said, fairly beaten into non-resistance.

Boldwood pressed her hand, and allowed it to drop in her lap. 'I am happy now,' he said. 'God bless you!'

He left the room, and when he thought she might be sufficiently composed sent one of the maids to her.

Bathsheba cloaked the effects of the late scene as she best could, followed the girl, and in a few moments came downstairs with her hat and cloak on, ready to go. To get to the door it was necessary to pass through the hall, and before doing so she paused on the bottom of the staircase which descended into one corner, to take a last look at the gathering.

There was no music or dancing in progress just now. At the lower end, which had been arranged for the work-folk specially, a group conversed in whispers, and with clouded looks. Boldwood was standing by the fireplace, and he, too, though so absorbed in visions arising from her promise that he scarcely saw anything, seemed at that moment to have observed their peculiar manner, and their looks askance.

'What is it you are in doubt about, men?' he said.

One of them turned and replied uneasily: 'It was something Laban heard of, that's all, sir.'

'News? Anybody married or engaged, born or dead?' inquired the farmer, gaily. 'Tell it to us, Tall. One would think from your looks and mysterious ways that it was something very dreadful indeed.'

'Oh no, sir, nobody is dead,' said Tall.

'I wish somebody was,' said Samway, in a whisper.

'What do you say, Samway?' asked Boldwood, somewhat sharply. 'If you have anything to say, speak out; if not, get up another dance.'

'Mrs. Troy has come downstairs,' said Samway to Tall. 'If you want to tell her, you had better do it now.'

'Do you know what they mean?' the farmer asked Bathsheba, across the room.

'I don't in the least,' said Bathsheba.

There was a smart rapping at the door. One of the men opened it instantly, and went outside.

'Mrs. Troy is wanted,' he said, on returning.

'Quite ready,' said Bathsheba. 'Though I didn't tell them to send.'

'It is a stranger, ma'am,' said the man by the door.

'A stranger?' she said.

'Ask him to come in,' said Boldwood.

The message was given, and Troy, wrapped up to his eyes as we have seen him, stood in the doorway.

There was an unearthly silence, all looking towards the newcomer. Those who had just learnt that he was in the neighbourhood recognized him instantly; those who did not were perplexed. Nobody noted Bathsheba. She was leaning on the stairs. Her brow had heavily contracted; her whole face was pallid, her lips apart, her eyes rigidly staring at their visitor.

Boldwood was among those who did not notice that he was Troy. 'Come in, come in!' he repeated, cheerfully, 'and drain a Christmas beaker with us, stranger!'

Troy next advanced into the middle of the room, took off his cap, turned down his coat-collar, and looked Boldwood in the face. Even then Boldwood did not recognize that the impersonator of Heaven's persistent irony towards him, who had once before broken in upon his bliss, scourged him, and snatched his delight away, had come to do these things a second time. Troy began to laugh a mechanical laugh: Boldwood recognized him now.

Troy turned to Bathsheba. The poor girl's wretchedness at this time was beyond all fancy or narration. She had sunk down on the lowest stair; and there she sat, her mouth blue and dry, and her dark eyes fixed vacantly upon him, as if she wondered whether it were not all a terrible illusion.

Then Troy spoke. 'Bathsheba, I come here for you!'

She made no reply.

'Come home with me: come!'

Bathsheba moved her feet a little, but did not rise. Troy went across to her.

'Come, madam, do you hear what I say?' he said, peremptorily.

A strange voice came from the fireplace—a voice sounding far off and confined, as if from a dungeon. Hardly a soul in the assembly recognized the thin tones to be those of Boldwood. Sudden despair had transformed him.

'Bathsheba, go with your husband!'

Nevertheless, she did not move. The truth was that Bathsheba was beyond the pale of activity—and yet not in a swoon. She was in a state of mental *gutta serena*; her mind was for the minute totally deprived of light at the same time that no obscuration was apparent from without.

Troy stretched out his hand to pull her towards him, when she quickly shrank back. This visible dread of him seemed to irritate Troy, and he seized her arm and pulled it sharply. Whether his grasp pinched her, or whether his mere touch was the cause, was never known, but at the moment of his seizure she writhed, and gave a quick, low scream.

The scream had been heard but a few seconds when it was followed by a sudden deafening report that echoed through the room and stupefied them all. The oak partition shook with the concussion, and the place was filled with grey smoke.

In bewilderment they turned their eyes to Boldwood. At his back, as he stood before the fireplace, was a gun-rack, as is usual in farmhouses, constructed to hold two guns. When Bathsheba had cried out in her husband's grasp, Boldwood's face of gnashing despair had changed. The veins had swollen, and a frenzied look had gleamed in his eye. He had turned quickly, taken one of the guns, cocked it, and at once discharged it at Troy.

Troy fell. The distance apart of the two men was so small that the charge of shot did not spread in the least, but passed like a bullet into his body. He uttered a long guttural sigh—there was a contraction—an extension—then his muscles relaxed, and he lay still.

Boldwood was seen through the smoke to be now again engaged with the gun. It was double-barrelled, and he had, meanwhile, in some way fastened his handkerchief to the trigger, and with his foot on the other end was in the act of turning the second barrel upon himself. Samway his man was the first to see this, and in the midst of the general horror darted up to him. Boldwood had already twitched the handkerchief, and the gun exploded a second time, sending its contents, by a timely blow from Samway, into the beam which crossed the ceiling.

'Well, it makes no difference!' Boldwood gasped. 'There is another way for me to die.'

Then he broke from Samway, crossed the room to Bathsheba, and kissed her hand. He put on his hat, opened the door, and went into the darkness, nobody thinking of preventing him.

CHAPTER LIV

AFTER THE SHOCK

BOLDWOOD passed into the high road, and turned in the direction of Casterbridge. Here he walked at an even, steady pace over Yalbury Hill, along the dead level beyond, mounted Mellstock Hill, and between eleven and twelve o'clock crossed the Moor into the town. The streets were nearly deserted now, and the waving lamp-flames only lighted up rows of grey shop-shutters, and strips of white paving upon which his step echoed as he passed along. He turned to the right, and halted before an archway of heavy stonework, which was closed by an iron studded pair of doors. This was the entrance to the gaol, and over it a lamp was fixed, the light enabling the wretched traveller to find a bell-pull.

The small wicket at last opened, and a porter appeared. Boldwood stepped forward, and said something in a low tone, when, after a delay, another man came. Boldwood entered, and the door was closed behind him, and he walked the world no more.

Long before this time Weatherbury had been thoroughly aroused, and the wild deed which had terminated Boldwood's merrymaking became known to all. Of those out of the house Oak was one of the first to hear of the catastrophe, and when he entered the room, which was about five minutes after Boldwood's exit, the scene was terrible.   All the female guests were huddled aghast against the walls like sheep in a storm, and the men were bewildered as to what to do.   As for Bathsheba, she had changed.   She was sitting on the floor beside the body of Troy, his head pillowed in her lap, where she had herself lifted it.   With one hand she held her handkerchief to his breast and covered the wound, though scarcely a single drop of blood had flowed, and with the other she tightly clasped one of his.   The household convulsion had made her herself again.   The temporary coma had ceased, and activity had come with the necessity for it.   Deeds of endurance, which seem ordinary in philosophy, are rare in conduct, and Bathsheba was astonishing all around her now, for her philosophy was her conduct, and she seldom thought practicable what she did not practise. She was of the stuff of which great men's mothers are made.   She was indispensable to high generation, hated at tea parties, feared in shops, and loved at crises. Troy recumbent in his wife's lap formed now the sole spectacle in the middle of the spacious room.

'Gabriel,' she said, automatically, when he entered, turning up a face of which only the well-known lines remained to tell him it was hers, all else in the picture having faded quite.   'Ride to Casterbridge instantly for a surgeon.   It is, I believe, useless, but go.   Mr. Boldwood has shot my husband.'

Her statement of the fact in such quiet and simple words came with more force than a tragic declamation, and had somewhat the effect of setting the distorted images in each mind present into proper focus.   Oak, almost before he had comprehended anything beyond the briefest abstract of the event, hurried out of the room, saddled a horse and rode away.   Not till he had ridden more than a mile did it occur to him that he would have done better by sending some other man on this errand, remaining himself in the house.   What had become of Boldwood? He should have been looked after. Was he mad—had there been a quarrel? Then how had Troy got there? Where had he come from? How did this remarkable reappearance effect itself when he was supposed to be at the bottom of the sea? Oak had in some slight measure been prepared for the presence of Troy by hearing a rumour of his return just before entering Boldwood's house; but before he had weighed that information, this fatal event had been superimposed. However, it was too late now to think of sending another messenger, and he rode on, in the excitement of these self-inquiries not discerning, when about three miles from Casterbridge, a square-figured pedestrian passing along under the dark hedge in the same direction as his own.

The miles necessary to be traversed, and other hindrances incidental to the lateness of the hour and the darkness of the night, delayed the arrival of Mr. Aldritch, the surgeon; and more than three hours passed between the time at which the shot was fired and that of his entering the house. Oak was additionally detained in Casterbridge through having to give notice to the authorities of what had happened; and he then found that Boldwood had also entered the town, and delivered himself up.

In the meantime the surgeon, having hastened into the hall at Boldwood's, found it in darkness and quite deserted. He went on to the back of the house, where he discovered in the kitchen an old man, of whom he made inquiries.

'She's had him took away to her own house, sir,' said his informant.

'Who has?' said the doctor.

'Mrs. Troy. 'A was quite dead, sir.'

This was astonishing information. 'She had no right to do that,' said the doctor. 'There will have to be an inquest, and she should have waited to know what to do.'

'Yes, sir; it was hinted to her that she had better wait till the law was known. But she said law was nothing to her, and she wouldn't let her dear husband's corpse bide neglected for folks to stare at for all the crowners in England.'

Mr. Aldritch drove at once back again up the hill to Bathsheba's. The first person he met was poor Liddy, who seemed literally to have dwindled smaller in these few latter hours. 'What has been done?' he said.

'I don't know, sir,' said Liddy, with suspended breath. 'My mistress has done it all.'

'Where is she?'

'Upstairs with him, sir. When he was brought home and taken upstairs, she said she wanted no further help from the men. And then she called me, and made me fill the bath, and after that told me I had better go and lie down because I looked so ill. Then she locked herself into the room alone with him, and would not let a nurse come in, or anybody at all. But I thought I'd wait in the next room in case she should want me. I heard her moving about inside for more than an hour, but she only came out once, and that was for more candles, because hers had burnt down into the socket. She said we were to let her know when you or Mr. Thirdly came, sir.'

Oak entered with the parson at this moment, and they all went upstairs together, preceded by Liddy Smallbury. Everything was silent as the grave when they paused on the landing. Liddy knocked, and Bathsheba's dress was heard rustling across the room: the key turned in the lock, and she opened the door. Her looks were calm and nearly rigid, like a slightly animated bust of Melpomene.

'Oh, Mr. Aldritch, you have come at last,' she

murmured from her lips merely, and threw back the door. 'Ah, and Mr. Thirdly. Well, all is done, and anybody in the world may see him now.' She then passed by him, crossed the landing, and entered another room.

Looking into the chamber of death she had vacated they saw by the light of the candles which were on the drawers a tall straight shape lying at the further end of the bedroom, wrapped in white. Everything around was quite orderly. The doctor went in, and after a few minutes returned to the landing again, where Oak and the parson still waited.

'It is all done, indeed, as she says,' remarked Mr. Aldritch, in a subdued voice. 'The body has been undressed and properly laid out in grave clothes. Gracious Heaven—this mere girl! She must have the nerve of a stoic!'

'The heart of a wife merely,' floated in a whisper about the ears of the three, and turning they saw Bathsheba in the midst of them. Then, as if at that instant to prove that her fortitude had been more of will than of spontaneity, she silently sank down between them and was a shapeless heap of drapery on the floor. The simple consciousness that superhuman strain was no longer required had at once put a period to her power to continue it.

They took her away into a further room, and the medical attendance which had been useless in Troy's case was invaluable in Bathsheba's, who fell into a series of fainting-fits that had a serious aspect for a time. The sufferer was got to bed, and Oak, finding from the bulletins that nothing really dreadful was to be apprehended on her score, left the house. Liddy kept watch in Bathsheba's chamber, where she heard her mistress, moaning in whispers through the dull slow hours of that wretched night: 'Oh, it is my fault —how can I live! Oh Heaven, how can I live!'

CHAPTER LV

THE MARCH FOLLOWING—'BATHSHEBA BOLDWOOD'

WE pass rapidly on into the month of March, to a breezy day without sunshine, frost, or dew. On Yalbury Hill, about midway between Weatherbury and Casterbridge, where the turnpike road passes over the crest, a numerous concourse of people had gathered, the eyes of the greater number being frequently stretched afar in a northerly direction. The groups consisted of a throng of idlers, a party of javelin-men, and two trumpeters, and in the midst were carriages, one of which contained the high sheriff. With the idlers, many of whom had mounted to the top of a cutting formed for the road, were several Weatherbury men and boys—among others Poorgrass, Coggan, and Cain Ball.

At the end of half-an-hour a faint dust was seen in the expected quarter, and shortly after a travelling-carriage, bringing one of the two judges on the Western Circuit, came up the hill and halted on the top. The judge changed carriages whilst a flourish was blown by the big-cheeked trumpeters, and a procession being formed of the vehicles and javelin-men, they all proceeded towards the town, excepting the Weatherbury men, who as soon as they had seen the judge move off returned home again to their work.

'Joseph, I zeed you squeezing close to the carriage,' said Coggan, as they walked. 'Did ye notice my lord judge's face?'

'I did,' said Poorgrass. 'I looked hard at en, as if I would read his very soul; and there was mercy in his eyes—or to speak with the exact truth required of us at this solemn time, in the eye that was towards me.'

'Well, I hope for the best,' said Coggan, though bad that must be. However, I shan't go to the trial, and I'd advise the rest of ye that bain't wanted to bide away. 'Twill disturb his mind more than anything to see us there staring at him as if he were a show.'

'The very thing I said this morning,' observed Joseph. '"Justice is come to weigh him in the balance," I said in my reflectious way, "and if he's found wanting, so be it unto him," and a bystander said "Hear, hear! A man who can talk like that ought to be heard." But I don't like dwelling upon it, for my few words are my few words, and not much; though the speech of some men is rumoured abroad, as though by nature formed for such.'

'So 'tis, Joseph. And now, neighbours, as I said, every man bide at home.'

The resolution was adhered to; and all waited anxiously for the news next day. Their suspense was diverted, however, by a discovery which was made in the afternoon, throwing more light on Boldwood's conduct and condition than any details which had preceded it.

That he had been from the time of Greenhill Fair until the fatal Christmas Eve in excited and unusual moods was known to those who had been intimate with him; but nobody imagined that there had shown in him unequivocal symptoms of the mental derangement which Bathsheba and Troy, alone of all others and at different times, had momentarily suspected.

In a locked closet was now discovered an extraordinary collection of articles. There were several sets of ladies' dresses in the piece, of sundry expensive materials; silks and satins, poplins and velvets, all of colours which from Bathsheba's style of dress might have been judged to be her favourites. There were two muffs, sable and ermine. Above all there was a case of jewellery, containing four heavy gold bracelets and several lockets and rings, all of fine quality and manufacture. These things had been bought in Bath and other towns from time to time, and brought home by stealth. They were all carefully packed in paper, and each package was labelled ' Bathsheba Boldwood,' a date being subjoined six years in advance in every instance.

These somewhat pathetic evidences of a mind crazed with care and love were the subject of discourse in Warren's malt-house when Oak entered from Caster-bridge with tidings of the sentence. He came in the afternoon, and his face, as the kiln glow shone upon it, told the tale sufficiently well. Boldwood, as every one supposed he would do, had pleaded guilty, and had been sentenced to death.

The conviction that Boldwood had not been morally responsible for his later acts now became general. Facts elicited previous to the trial had pointed strongly in the same direction, but they had not been of sufficient weight to lead to an order for an examination into the state of Boldwood's mind. It was astonishing, now that a presumption of insanity was raised, how many collateral circumstances were remembered to which a condition of mental disease seemed to afford the only explanation —among others, the unprecedented neglect of his corn. stacks in the previous summer.

A petition was addressed to the Home Secretary, advancing the circumstances which appeared to justify a request for a reconsideration of the sentence. It was

not 'numerously signed' by the inhabitants of Casterbridge, as is usual in such cases, for Boldwood had
never made many friends over the counter. The shops
thought it very natural that a man who, by importing
direct from the producer, had daringly set aside the
first great principle of provincial existence, namely,
that God made country villages to supply customers
to country towns, should have confused ideas about
the Decalogue. The prompters were a few merciful
men who had perhaps too feelingly considered the
facts latterly unearthed, and the result was that evidence
was taken which it was hoped might remove the crime,
in a moral point of view, out of the category of wilful
murder, and lead it to be regarded as a sheer outcome
of madness.

The upshot of the petition was waited for in Weatherbury with solicitous interest. The execution had been
fixed for eight o'clock on a Saturday morning about a
fortnight after the sentence was passed, and up to
Friday afternoon no answer had been received. At
that time Gabriel came from Casterbridge Gaol, whither
he had been to wish Boldwood good-bye, and turned
down a by-street to avoid the town. When past the last
house he heard a hammering, and lifting his bowed
head he looked back for a moment. Over the chimneys
he could see the upper part of the gaol entrance, rich
and glowing in the afternoon sun, and some moving
figures were there. They were carpenters lifting a post
into a vertical position within the parapet. He withdrew his eyes quickly, and hastened on.

It was dark when he reached home, and half the
village was out to meet him.

'No tidings,' Gabriel said, wearily. 'And I'm afraid
there's no hope. I've been with him more than two
hours.'

'Do ye think he *really* was out of his mind when he
did it?' said Smallbury.

' I can't honestly say that I do,' Oak replied. ' However, that we can talk of another time. Has there been any change in mistress this afternoon ? '

' None at all.'

' Is she downstairs ? '

' No. And getting on so nicely as she was too. She's but very little better now again than she was a-Christmas. She keeps on asking if you be come, and if there's news, till one's wearied out wi' answering her. Shall I go and say you've come ? '

' No,' said Oak. ' There's a chance yet; but I couldn't stay in town any longer—after seeing him too. So Laban—Laban is here, isn't he ? '

' Yes,' said Tall.

' What I've arranged is, that you shall ride to town the last thing to-night; leave here about nine, and wait a while there, getting home about twelve. If nothing has been received by eleven to-night, they say there's no chance at all.'

' I do so hope his life will be spared,' said Liddy. ' If it is not, she'll go out of her mind too. Poor thing; her sufferings have been dreadful; she deserves anybody's pity.'

' Is she altered much ? ' said Coggan.

' If you haven't seen poor mistress since Christmas, you wouldn't know her,' said Liddy. ' Her eyes are so miserable that she's not the same woman. Only two years ago she was a romping girl, and now she's this ! '

Laban departed as directed, and at eleven o'clock that night several of the villagers strolled along the road to Casterbridge and awaited his arrival—among them Oak, and nearly all the rest of Bathsheba's men. Gabriel's anxiety was great that Boldwood might be saved, even though in his conscience he felt that he ought to die; for there had been qualities in the farmer which Oak loved. At last, when they all were weary the tramp of a horse was heard in the distance—

First dead, as if on turf it trode,
Then, clattering, on the village road
In other pace than forth he yode.

'We shall soon know now, one way or other,' said Coggan, and they all stepped down from the bank on which they had been standing into the road, and the rider pranced into the midst of them.

'Is that you, Laban?' said Gabriel.

'Yes—'tis come. He's not to die. 'Tis confinement during her Majesty's pleasure.'

'Hurrah!' said Coggan, with a swelling heart. 'God's above the devil yet!'

CHAPTER LVI

BEAUTY IN LONELINESS—AFTER ALL

BATHSHEBA revived with the spring. The utter prostration that had followed the low fever from which she had suffered diminished perceptibly when all uncertainty upon every subject had come to an end.

But she remained alone now for the greater part of her time, and stayed in the house, or at furthest went into the garden. She shunned every one, even Liddy, and could be brought to make no confidences, and to ask for no sympathy.

As the summer drew on she passed more of her time in the open air, and began to examine into farming matters from sheer necessity, though she never rode out or personally superintended as at former times. One Friday evening in August she walked a little way along the road and entered the village for the first time since the sombre event of the preceding Christmas. None of the old colour had as yet come to her cheek, and its absolute paleness was heightened by the jet black of her gown, till it appeared preternatural. When she reached a little shop at the other end of the place, which stood nearly opposite to the churchyard, Bathsheba heard singing inside the church, and she knew that the singers were practising. She crossed the road, opened the gate, and entered the graveyard, the high sills of the church windows effectually screening her from the eyes of those gathered within. Her stealthy walk was to the nook wherein Troy had worked at planting flowers upon Fanny Robin's grave, and she came to the marble tombstone.

A motion of satisfaction enlivened her face as she read the complete inscription. First came the words of Troy himself:—

ERECTED BY FRANCIS TROY
IN BELOVED MEMORY OF
FANNY ROBIN,
WHO DIED OCTOBER 9, 18—,
AGED 20 YEARS.

Underneath this was now inscribed in new letters:—

IN THE SAME GRAVE LIE
THE REMAINS OF THE AFORESAID
FRANCIS TROY,
WHO DIED DECEMBER 24TH, 18—,
AGED 26 YEARS.

Whilst she stood and read and meditated the tones of the organ began again in the church, and she went with the same light step round to the porch and listened. The door was closed, and the choir was learning a new hymn. Bathsheba was stirred by emotions which latterly she had assumed to be altogether dead within her. The little attenuated voices of the children brought to her ear in distinct utterance the words they sang without thought or comprehension—

Lead, kindly Light, amid the encircling gloom,
Lead Thou me on.

Bathsheba's feeling was always to some extent dependent upon her whim, as is the case with many other women. Something big came into her throat and an uprising to her eyes—and she thought that she would

allow the imminent tears to flow if they wished. They
did flow and plenteously, and one fell upon the stone
bench beside her. Once that she had begun to cry for
she hardly knew what, she could not leave off for crowding thoughts she knew too well. She would have given
anything in the world to be, as those children were, unconcerned at the meaning of their words, because too
innocent to feel the necessity for any such expression.
All the impassioned scenes of her brief experience
seemed to revive with added emotion at that moment,
and those scenes which had been without emotion
during enactment had emotion then. Yet grief came
to her rather as a luxury than as the scourge of former
times.

Owing to Bathsheba's face being buried in her hands
she did not notice a form which came quietly into the
porch, and on seeing her, first moved as if to retreat,
then paused and regarded her. Bathsheba did not raise
her head for some time, and when she looked round
her face was wet, and her eyes drowned and dim. 'Mr.
Oak,' exclaimed she, disconcerted, 'how long have you
been here?'

'A few minutes, ma'am,' said Oak, respectfully.

'Are you going in?' said Bathsheba; and there came
from within the church as from a prompter—

> I loved the garish day, and, spite of fears,
> Pride ruled my will: remember not past years.

'I was,' said Gabriel. 'I am one of the bass singers,
you know. I have sung bass for several months.'

'Indeed: I wasn't aware of that. I'll leave you, then.'

> Which I have loved long since, and lost awhile,

sang the children.

'Don't let me drive you away, mistress. I think I
won't go in to-night.'

'Oh no—you don't drive me away.'

461

Then they stood in a state of some embarrassment, Bathsheba trying to wipe her dreadfully drenched and inflamed face without his noticing her. At length Oak said, 'I've not seen you—I mean spoken to you—since ever so long, have I?' But he feared to bring distressing memories back, and interrupted himself with: 'Were you going into church?'

'No,' she said. 'I came to see the tombstone privately—to see if they had cut the inscription as I wished. Mr. Oak, you needn't mind speaking to me, if you wish to, on the matter which is in both our minds at this moment.'

'And have they done it as you wished?' said Oak.

'Yes. Come and see it, if you have not already.'

So together they went and read the tomb. 'Eight months ago!' Gabriel murmured when he saw the date. 'It seems like yesterday to me.'

'And to me as if it were years ago—long years, and I had been dead between. And now I am going home, Mr. Oak.'

Oak walked after her. 'I wanted to name a small matter to you as soon as I could,' he said, with hesitation. 'Merely about business, and I think I may just mention it now, if you'll allow me.'

'Oh yes, certainly.'

'It is that I may soon have to give up the management of your farm, Mrs. Troy. The fact is, I am thinking of leaving England—not yet, you know—next spring.'

'Leaving England!' she said, in surprise and genuine disappointment. 'Why, Gabriel, what are you going to do that for?'

'Well, I've thought it best,' Oak stammered out. 'California is the spot I've had in my mind to try.'

'But it is understood everywhere that you are going to take poor Mr. Boldwood's farm on your own account.'

'I've had the refusal o' it 'tis true; but nothing is

462

settled yet, and I have reasons for gieing up. I shall
finish out my year there as manager for the trustees,
but no more.'

'And what shall I do without you? Oh Gabriel, I
don't think you ought to go away. You've been with
me so long—through bright times and dark times—such
old friends as we are—that it seems unkind almost. I
had fancied that if you leased the other farm as master,
you might still give a helping look across at mine. And
now going away!'

'I would have willingly.'

'Yet now that I am more helpless than ever you go
away!'

'Yes, that's the ill fortune o' it,' said Gabriel, in a
distressed tone. 'And it is because of that very help-
lessness that I feel bound to go. Good afternoon,
ma'am,' he concluded, in evident anxiety to get
away, and at once went out of the churchyard by a
path she could follow on no pretence whatever.

Bathsheba went home, her mind occupied with a
new trouble, which being rather harassing than deadly
was calculated to do good by diverting her from the
chronic gloom of her life. She was set thinking a great
deal about Oak and of his wish to shun her; and there
occurred to Bathsheba several incidents of her latter intercourse with him, which, trivial when singly viewed,
amounted together to a perceptible disinclination for
her society. It broke upon her at length as a great
pain that her last old disciple was about to forsake her
and flee. He who had believed in her and argued on
her side when all the rest of the world was against her,
had at last like the others become weary and neglectful
of the old cause, and was leaving her to fight her battles
alone.

Three weeks went on, and more evidence of his
want of interest in her was forthcoming. She noticed
that instead of entering the small parlour or office

where the farm accounts were kept, and waiting, or leaving a memorandum as he had hitherto done during her seclusion, Oak never came at all when she was likely to be there, only entering at unseasonable hours when her presence in that part of the house was least to be expected. Whenever he wanted directions he sent a message, or note with neither heading nor signature, to which she was obliged to reply in the same off-hand style. Poor Bathsheba began to suffer now from the most torturing sting of all—a sensation that she was despised.

The autumn wore away gloomily enough amid these melancholy conjectures, and Christmas-day came, completing a year of her legal widowhood, and two years and a quarter of her life alone. On examining her heart it appeared beyond measure strange that the subject of which the season might have been supposed suggestive—the event in the hall at Boldwood's—was not agitating her at all; but instead, an agonizing conviction that everybody abjured her—for what she could not tell—and that Oak was the ringleader of the recusants. Coming out of church that day she looked round in hope that Oak, whose bass voice she had heard rolling out from the gallery overhead in a most unconcerned manner, might chance to linger in her path in the old way. There he was, as usual, coming down the path behind her. But on seeing Bathsheba turn, he looked aside, and as soon as he got beyond the gate, and there was the barest excuse for a divergence, he made one, and vanished.

The next morning brought the culminating stroke; she had been expecting it long. It was a formal notice by letter from him that he should not renew his engagement with her for the following Lady-day.

Bathsheba actually sat and cried over this letter most bitterly. She was aggrieved and wounded that the possession of hopeless love from Gabriel, which she had grown to regard as her inalienable right for life, should have been withdrawn just at his own pleasure in this way. She was bewildered too by the prospect of having to rely on her own resources again : it seemed to herself that she never could again acquire energy sufficient to go to market, barter, and sell. Since Troy's death Oak had attended all sales and fairs for her, transacting her business at the same time with his own. What should she do now? Her life was becoming a desolation.

So desolate was Bathsheba this evening, that in an absolute hunger for pity and sympathy, and miserable in that she appeared to have outlived the only true friendship she had ever owned, she put on her bonnet and cloak and went down to Oak's house just after sunset, guided on her way by the pale primrose rays of a crescent moon a few days old.

A lively firelight shone from the window, but nobody was visible in the room. She tapped nervously, and then thought it doubtful if it were right for a single woman to call upon a bachelor who lived alone, although he was her manager, and she might be supposed to call on business without any real impropriety. Gabriel opened the door, and the moon shone upon his forehead.

'Mr. Oak,' said Bathsheba, faintly.

'Yes; I am Mr. Oak,' said Gabriel. 'Who have I the honour—Oh! how stupid of me, not to know you, mistress!'

'I shall not be your mistress much longer, shall I, Gabriel?' she said, in pathetic tones.

'Well, no. I suppose—But come in, ma'am. Oh— and I'll get a light,' Oak replied, with some awkwardness.

'No ; not on my account.'

'It is so seldom that I get a lady visitor that I'm afraid I haven't proper accommodation. Will you sit down, please? Here's a chair, and there's one, too. I am sorry that my chairs all have wood seats, and are

465

rather hard, but I—was thinking of getting some new ones.' Oak placed two or three for her.

'They are quite easy enough for me.'

So down she sat, and down sat he, the fire dancing in their faces, and upon the old furniture,

> all a-sheenen
> Wi' long years o' handlen,[1]

that formed Oak's array of household possessions, which sent back a dancing reflection in reply. It was very odd to these two persons, who knew each other passing well, that the mere circumstance of their meeting in a new place and in a new way should make them so awkward and constrained. In the fields, or at her house, there had never been any embarrassment; but now that Oak had become the entertainer their lives seemed to be moved back again to the days when they were strangers.

'You'll think it strange that I have come, but——'

'Oh, no; not at all.'

'But I thought—Gabriel, I have been uneasy in the belief that I have offended you, and that you are going away on that account. It grieved me very much, and I couldn't help coming.'

'Offended me! As if you could do that, Bathsheba!'

'Haven't I?' she asked, gladly. 'But, what are you going away for else?'

'I am not going to emigrate, you know; I wasn't aware that you would wish me not to when I told 'ee, or I shouldn't ha' thought of doing it,' he said, simply. 'I have arranged for Little Weatherbury Farm, and shall have it in my own hands at Lady-day. You know I've had a share in it for some time. Still, that wouldn't prevent my attending to your business as before, hadn't it been that things have been said about us.'

'What?' said Bathsheba, in surprise. 'Things said about you and me! What are they?'

[1] W. Barnes.

'I cannot tell you.'

'It would be wiser if you were to, I think. You have played the part of mentor to me many times, and I don't see why you should fear to do it now.'

'It is nothing that you have done, this time. The top and tail o't is this—that I am sniffing about here, and waiting for poor Boldwood's farm, with a thought of getting you some day.'

'Getting me! What does that mean?'

'Marrying o' 'ee, in plain British. You asked me to tell, so you mustn't blame me.'

Bathsheba did not look quite so alarmed as if a cannon had been discharged by her ear, which was what Oak had expected. 'Marrying me! I didn't know it was that you meant,' she said, quietly. 'Such a thing as that is too absurd—too soon—to think of, by far!'

'Yes; of course, it is too absurd. I don't desire any such thing; I should think that was plain enough by this time. Surely, surely you be the last person in the world I think of marrying. It is too absurd, as you say.'

' " Too—s-s-soon " were the words I used.'

'I must beg your pardon for correcting you, but you said, "too absurd," and so do I.'

'I beg your pardon too!' she returned, with tears in her eyes. ' "Too soon " was what I said. But it doesn't matter a bit—not at all—but I only meant, "too soon." Indeed, I didn't, Mr. Oak, and you must believe me!'

Gabriel looked her long in the face, but the firelight being faint there was not much to be seen. 'Bathsheba,' he said, tenderly and in surprise, and coming closer: 'if I only knew one thing—whether you would allow me to love you and win you, and marry you after all—if I only knew that!'

'But you never will know,' she murmured.

'Why?'

'Because you never ask.'

'Oh—Oh!' said Gabriel, with a low laugh of joyousness. 'My own dear——'

'You ought not to have sent me that harsh letter this morning,' she interrupted. 'It shows you didn't care a bit about me, and were ready to desert me like all the rest of them! It was very cruel of you, considering I was the first sweetheart that you ever had, and you were the first I ever had; and I shall not forget it!'

'Now, Bathsheba, was ever anybody so provoking?' he said, laughing. 'You know it was purely that I, as an unmarried man, carrying on a business for you as a very taking young woman, had a proper hard part to play—more particular that people knew I had a sort of feeling for 'ee; and I fancied, from the way we were mentioned together, that it might injure your good name. Nobody knows the heat and fret I have been caused by it.'

'And was that all?'

'All.'

'Oh, how glad I am I came!' she exclaimed, thankfully, as she rose from her seat. 'I have thought so much more of you since I fancied you did not want even to see me again. But I must be going now, or I shall be missed. Why, Gabriel,' she said, with a slight laugh, as they went to the door, 'it seems exactly as if I had come courting you—how dreadful!'

'And quite right, too,' said Oak. 'I've danced at your skittish heels, my beautiful Bathsheba, for many a long mile, and many a long day; and it is hard to begrudge me this one visit.'

He accompanied her up the hill, explaining to her the details of his forthcoming tenure of the other farm. They spoke very little of their mutual feelings; pretty phrases and warm expressions being probably unnecessary between such tried friends. Theirs was that substantial affection which arises (if any arises at all) when the two who are thrown together begin first by

468

knowing the rougher sides of each other's character, and not the best till further on, the romance growing up in the interstices of a mass of hard prosaic reality. This good-fellowship—*camaraderie*—usually occurring through similarity of pursuits, is unfortunately seldom superadded to love between the sexes, because men and women associate, not in their labours, but in their pleasures merely. Where, however, happy circumstance permits its development, the compounded feeling proves itself to be the only love which is strong as death—that love which many waters cannot quench, nor the floods drown, beside which the passion usually called by the name is evanescent as steam.

CHAPTER LVII

A FOGGY NIGHT AND MORNING—CONCLUSION

'THE most private, secret, plainest wedding that it is possible to have.'

Those had been Bathsheba's words to Oak one evening, some time after the event of the preceding chapter, and he meditated a full hour by the clock upon how to carry out her wishes to the letter.

'A license—Oh yes, it must be a license,' he said to himself at last. 'Very well, then ; first, a license.'

On a dark night, a few days later, Oak came with mysterious steps from the surrogate's door, in Caster-bridge. On the way home he heard a heavy tread in front of him, and, overtaking the man, found him to be Coggan. They walked together into the village until they came to a little lane behind the church, leading down to the cottage of Laban Tall, who had lately been installed as clerk of the parish, and was yet in mortal terror at church on Sundays when he heard his lone voice among certain hard words of the Psalms, whither no man ventured to follow him.

'Well, good-night, Coggan,' said Oak, 'I'm going down this way.'

'Oh !' said Coggan, surprised ; 'what's going on to-night, then, make so bold, Mr. Oak ?'

It seemed rather ungenerous not to tell Coggan,

under the circumstances, for Coggan had been true as steel all through the time of Gabriel's unhappiness about Bathsheba, and Gabriel said, 'You can keep a secret, Coggan?'

'You've proved me, and you know.'

'Yes, I have, and I do know. Well, then, mistress and I mean to get married to-morrow morning.'

'Heaven's high tower! And yet I've thought of such a thing from time to time; true, I have. But keeping it so close! Well, there, 'tis no consarn of mine, and I wish 'ee joy o' her.'

'Thank you, Coggan. But I assure 'ee that this great hush is not what I wished for at all, or what either of us would have wished if it hadn't been for certain things that would make a gay wedding seem hardly the thing. Bathsheba has a great wish that all the parish shall not be in church, looking at her—she's shy-like and nervous about it, in fact—so I be doing this to humour her.'

'Ay, I see: quite right, too, I suppose I must say. And you be now going down to the clerk.'

'Yes; you may as well come with me.'

'I am afeard your labour in keeping it close will be throwed away,' said Coggan, as they walked along. 'Labe Tall's old woman will horn it all over parish in half-an-hour.'

'So she will, upon my life; I never thought of that,' said Oak, pausing. 'Yet I must tell him to-night, I suppose, for he's working so far off, and leaves early.'

'I'll tell 'ee how we could tackle her,' said Coggan. 'I'll knock and ask to speak to Laban outside the door, you standing in the background. Then he'll come out, and you can tell yer tale. She'll never guess what I want en for; and I'll make up a few words about the farm-work, as a blind.'

This scheme was considered feasible; and Coggan

advanced boldly, and rapped at Mrs. Tall's door. Mrs. Tall herself opened it.

'I wanted to have a word with Laban.'

'He's not at home, and won't be this side of eleven o'clock. He've been forced to go over to Yalbury since shutting out work. I shall do quite as well.'

'I hardly think you will. Stop a moment;' and Coggan stepped round the corner of the porch to consult Oak.

'Who's t'other man, then?' said Mrs. Tall.

'Only a friend,' said Coggan.

'Say he's wanted to meet mistress near church-hatch to-morrow morning at ten,' said Oak, in a · whisper. 'That he must come without fail, and wear his best clothes.'

'The clothes will floor us as safe as houses!' said Coggan.

'It can't be helped,' said Oak. 'Tell her.'

So Coggan delivered the message. 'Mind, het or wet, blow or snow, he must .come,' added Jan. ''Tis very particular, indeed. The fact is, 'tis to witness her sign some law-work about taking shares wi' another farmer for a long span o' years. There, that's what 'tis, and now I've told 'ee, Mother Tall, in a way I shouldn't ha' done if I hadn't loved 'ee so hopeless well.'

Coggan retired before she could ask any further; and next they called at the vicar's in a manner which excited no curiosity at all. Then Gabriel went home, and prepared for the morrow.

'Liddy,' said Bathsheba, on going to bed that night, 'I want you to call me at seven o'clock to-morrow, in case I shouldn't wake.'

'But you always do wake afore then, ma'am.'

'Yes, but I have something important to do, which I'll tell you of when the time comes, and it's best to make sure.'

Bathsheba, however, awoke voluntarily at four, nor could she by any contrivance get to sleep again. About six, being quite positive that her watch had stopped during the night, she could wait no longer. She went and tapped at Liddy's door, and after some labour awoke her.

'But I thought it was I who had to call you?' said the bewildered Liddy. 'And it isn't six yet.'

'Indeed it is; how can you tell such a story, Liddy? I know it must be ever so much past seven. Come to my room as soon as you can; I want you to give my hair a good brushing.'

When Liddy came to Bathsheba's room her mistress was already waiting. Liddy could not understand this extraordinary promptness. 'Whatever *is* going on, ma'am?' she said.

'Well, I'll tell you,' said Bathsheba, with a mischievous smile in her bright eyes. 'Farmer Oak is coming here to dine with me to-day!'

'Farmer Oak—and nobody else?—you two alone?'

'Yes.'

'But is it safe, ma'am?' said her companion, dubiously. 'A woman's good name is such a perishable article that——'

Bathsheba laughed with a flushed cheek, and whispered in Liddy's ear, although there was nobody present. Then Liddy stared and exclaimed, 'Souls alive, what news! It makes my heart go quite bumpity-bump!'

'It makes mine rather furious, too,' said Bathsheba. 'However, there's no getting out of it now!'

It was a damp disagreeable morning. Nevertheless, at twenty minutes to ten o'clock, Oak came out of his house, and

Went up the hill side
With that sort of stride
A man puts out when walking in search of a bride,

473

and knocked at Bathsheba's door. Ten minutes later a large and a smaller umbrella might have been seen moving from the same door, and through the mist along the road to the church. The distance was not more than a quarter of a mile, and these two sensible persons deemed it unnecessary to drive. An observer must have been very close indeed to discover that the forms under the umbrellas were those of Oak and Bathsheba, arm-in-arm for the first time in their lives, Oak in a greatcoat extending to his knees, and Bathsheba in a cloak that reached her clogs. Yet, though so plainly dressed, there was a certain rejuvenated appearance about her :—

As though a rose should shut and be a bud again.

Repose had again incarnadined her cheeks ; and having, at Gabriel's request, arranged her hair this morning as she had worn it years ago on Norcombe Hill, she seemed in his eyes remarkably like the girl of that fascinating dream, which, considering that she was now only three or four-and-twenty, was perhaps not very wonderful. In the church were Tall, Liddy, and the parson, and in a remarkably short space of time the deed was done.

The two sat down very quietly to tea in Bathsheba's parlour in the evening of the same day, for it had been arranged that Farmer Oak should go there to live, since he had as yet neither money, house, nor furniture worthy of the name, though he was on a sure way towards them, whilst Bathsheba was, comparatively, in a plethora of all three.

Just as Bathsheba was pouring out a cup of tea, their ears were greeted by the firing of a cannon, followed by what seemed like a tremendous blowing of trumpets, in the front of the house.

'There !' said Oak, laughing, 'I knew those fellows were up to something, by the look of their faces.'

Oak took up the light and went into the porch, followed by Bathsheba with a shawl over her head. The rays fell upon a group of male figures gathered upon the gravel in front, who, when they saw the newly-married couple in the porch, set up a loud 'Hurrah!' and at the same moment bang again went the cannon in the background, followed by a hideous clang of music from a drum, tambourine, clarionet, serpent, hautboy, tenor-viol, and double-bass—the only remaining relics of the true and original Weatherbury band—venerable worm-eaten instruments, which had celebrated in their own persons the victories of Marlborough, under the fingers of the forefathers of those who played them now. The performers came forward, and marched up to the front.

'Those bright boys, Mark Clark and Jan, are at the bottom of all this,' said Oak. 'Come in, souls, and have something to eat and drink wi' me and my wife.'

'Not to-night,' said Mr. Clark, with evident self-denial. 'Thank ye all the same; but we'll call at a more seemly time. However, we couldn't think of letting the day pass without a note of admiration of some sort. If ye could send a drop of som'at down to Warren's, why so it is. Here's long life and happiness to neighbour Oak and his comely bride!'

'Thank ye; thank ye all,' said Gabriel. 'A bit and a drop shall be sent to Warren's for ye at once. I had a thought that we might very likely get a salute of some sort from our old friends, and I was saying so to my wife but now.'

'Faith,' said Coggan, in a critical tone, turning to his companions, 'the man hev learnt to say "my wife" in a wonderful naterel way, considering how very youthful he is in wedlock as yet—hey, neighbours all?'

'I never heerd a skilful old married feller of twenty years' standing pipe "my wife" in a more used note than 'a did,' said Jacob Smallbury. 'It might have been a little more true to nater if't had been spoke a little chillier, but that wasn't to be expected just now.'

'That improvement will come wi' time,' said Jan, twirling his eye.

Then Oak laughed, and Bathsheba smiled (for she never laughed readily now), and their friends turned to go.

'Yes; I suppose that's the size o't,' said Joseph Poorgrass with a cheerful sigh as they moved away; 'and I wish him joy o' her; though I were once or twice upon saying to-day with holy Hosea, in my scripture ma .ner, which is my second nature, "Ephraim is joined to idols: let him alone." But since 'tis as 'tis, why, it might have been worse, and I feel my thanks accordingly.'

THE END

THE MAYOR OF CASTERBRIDGE

PREFACE

READERS of the following story who have not yet arrived at middle age are asked to bear in mind that, in the days recalled by the tale, the home Corn Trade, on which so much of the action turns, had an importance that can hardly be realized by those accustomed to the sixpenny loaf of the present date, and to the present indifference of the public to harvest weather.

The incidents narrated arise mainly out of three events, which chanced to range themselves in the order and at or about the intervals of time here given, in the real history of the town called Casterbridge and the neighbouring country. They were the sale of a wife by her husband, the uncertain harvests which immediately preceded the repeal of the Corn Laws, and the visit of a Royal personage to the aforesaid part of England.

The present edition of the volume contains nearly a chapter which has never yet appeared in any English copy, though it was printed in the serial issue of the tale, and in the American edition. The restoration was made at the instance of some good judges across the Atlantic, who strongly represented that the home edition suffered from the omission. Some shorter passages and names, omitted or altered for reasons which no longer exist, in the original printing of both English and American editions, have also been replaced or inserted for the first time.

The story is more particularly a study of one man's deeds and character than, perhaps, any other of those included in my little Exhibition of Wessex life. Objections have been raised to the Scotch language of Mr. Farfrae, the second character ; and one of his fellow-countrymen went so far as to declare that men beyond the Tweed did not and never could say "warrld," "cannet," "advairrtisment," and so on. As this gentleman's pronunciation in correcting me seemed to my Southron ear an exact repetition of what my spelling implied, I was not struck with the truth of his remark, and somehow we did not get any forwarder in the matter. It must be remembered that the Scotchman of the tale is represented not as he would appear to other Scotchmen, but as he would appear to people of outer regions. Moreover, no attempt is made herein to repro- duce his entire pronunciation phonetically, any more than that of the Wessex speakers. I should add, however, that this new edition of the book has had the accidental advantage of a critical overlooking by a professor of the tongue in question—one of undoubted authority :—in fact he is a gentleman who adopted it for urgent personal reasons in the first year of his existence.

Furthermore, a charming non-Scottish lady, of strict veracity and admitted penetration, the wife of a well-known Caledonian, came to the writer shortly after the story was

PREFACE

first published, and inquired if Farfrae were not drawn from her husband, for he seemed to her to be the living portrait of that (doubtless) happy man. It happened that I had never thought of her husband in constructing Farfrae. I trust therefore that Farfrae may be allowed to pass, if not as a Scotchman to Scotchmen, as a Scotchman to Southerners.

T. H.

February 1895.

I

ONE evening of late summer, before the present century had reached its thirtieth year, a young man and woman, the latter carrying a child, were approaching the large village of Weydon-Priors, in Upper Wessex, on foot. They were plainly but not ill clad, though the thick hoar of dust which had accumulated on their shoes and garments from an obviously long journey lent a disadvantageous shabbiness to their appearance just now.

The man was of fine figure, swarthy, and stern in aspect; and he showed in profile a facial angle so slightly inclined as to be almost perpendicular. He wore a short jacket of brown corduroy, newer than the remainder of his suit, which was a fustian waistcoat with white horn buttons, breeches of the same, tanned leggings, and a straw hat overlaid with black glazed canvas. At his back he carried by a looped strap a rush basket, from which protruded at one end the crutch of a hay-knife, a wimble for hay-bonds being also visible in the aperture. His measured, springless walk was the walk of the skilled countryman as distinct from the desultory shamble of the general labourer; while in the turn and plant of each foot there was, further, a dogged and cynical indifference, personal to himself, showing its presence even in the regularly inter-

I

changing fustian folds, now in the left leg, now in the right, as he paced along.

What was really peculiar, however, in this couple's progress, and would have attracted the attention of any casual observer otherwise disposed to overlook them, was the perfect silence they preserved. They walked side by side in such a way as to suggest afar off the low, easy, confidential chat of people full of reciprocity; but on closer view it could be discerned that the man was reading, or pretending to read, a ballad sheet which he kept before his eyes with some difficulty by the hand that was passed through the basket strap. Whether this apparent cause were the real cause, or whether it were an assumed one to escape an intercourse that would have been irksome to him, nobody but himself could have said precisely; but his taciturnity was unbroken, and the woman enjoyed no society whatever from his presence. Virtually she walked the highway alone, save for the child she bore. Sometimes the man's bent elbow almost touched her shoulder, for she kept as close to his side as was possible without actual contact; but she seemed to have no idea of taking his arm, nor he of offering it; and far from exhibiting surprise at his ignoring silence, she appeared to receive it as a natural thing. If any word at all were uttered by the little group, it was an occasional whisper of the woman to the child—a tiny girl in short clothes and blue boots of knitted yarn—and the murmured babble of the child in reply.

The chief—almost the only—attraction of the young woman's face was its mobility. When she looked down sideways to the girl she became pretty, and even handsome, particularly that in the action her features caught slantwise the rays of the strongly coloured sun, which made transparencies of her eyelids and nostrils, and set fire on her lips. When she plodded on in the shade of the hedge, silently thinking, she had the hard, halfapathetic expression of one who deems anything possible at the hands of Time and Chance, except, perhaps, fair play. The first phase was the work of Nature, the second probably of civilization.

That the man and woman were husband and wife, and the parents of the girl in arms, there could be little doubt. No other than such relationship would have accounted for the atmosphere of stale familiarity which the trio carried along with them like a nimbus as they moved down the road.

The wife mostly kept her eyes fixed ahead, though with little interest—the scene for that matter being one that might have been matched at almost any spot in any county in England at this time of the year; a road neither straight nor crooked, neither level nor hilly, bordered by hedges, trees, and other vegetation, which had entered the blackened-green stage of colour that the doomed leaves pass through on their way to dingy, and yellow, and red. The grassy margin of the bank, and the nearest hedgerow boughs, were powdered by the dust that had been stirred over them by hasty vehicles, the same dust as it lay on the road deadening their footfalls like a carpet; and this, with the aforesaid total absence of conversation, allowed every extraneous sound to be heard.

For a long time there was none, beyond the voice of a weak bird singing a trite old evening song that might doubtless have been heard on the hill at the same hour, and with the self-same trills, quavers, and breves, at any sunset of that season for centuries untold. But as they approached the village sundry distant shouts and rattles reached their ears from some elevated spot in that direction, as yet screened from view by foliage. When the outlying houses of Weydon-Priors could just be descried, the family group was met by a turnip-hoer with his hoe on his shoulder, and his dinner-bag suspended from it. The reader promptly glanced up.

3

'Any trade doing here?' he asked phlegmatically, designating the village in his van by a wave of the broadsheet. And thinking the labourer did not understand him, he added, 'Anything in the hay-trussing line?'

The turnip-hoer had already begun shaking his head. 'Why, save the man, what wisdom's in him that 'a should come to Weydon for a job of that sort this time o' year?'

'Then is there any house to let—a little small new cottage just a builded, or such like?' asked the other.

The pessimist still maintained a negative. 'Pulling down is more the nater of Weydon. There were five houses cleared away last year, and three this; and the volk nowhere to go—no, not so much as a thatched hurdle; that's the way o' Weydon-Priors.'

The hay-trusser, which he obviously was, nodded with some superciliousness. Looking towards the village, he continued, 'There is something going on here, however, is there not?'

'Ay. 'Tis Fair Day. Though what you hear now is little more than the clatter and scurry of getting away the money o' children and fools, for the real business is done earlier than this. I've been working within sound o't all day, but I didn't go up—not I. 'Twas no business of mine.'

The trusser and his family proceeded on their way, and soon entered the Fair-field, which showed standing-places and pens where many hundreds of horses and sheep had been exhibited and sold in the forenoon, but were now in great part taken away. At present, as their informant had observed, but little real business remained on hand, the chief being the sale by auction of a few inferior animals, that could not otherwise be disposed of, and had been absolutely refused by the better class of traders, who came and went early. Yet the crowd was denser now than during the morning

4

hours, the frivolous contingent of visitors, including journeymen out for a holiday, a stray soldier or two home on furlough, village shopkeepers, and the like, having latterly flocked in; persons whose activities found a congenial field among the peep-shows, toy-stands, waxworks, inspired monsters, disinterested medical men who travelled for the public good, thimble-riggers, nick-nack vendors, and readers of Fate.

Neither of our pedestrians had much heart for these things, and they looked around for a refreshment tent among the many which dotted the down. Two, which stood nearest to them in the ochreous haze of expiring sunlight, seemed almost equally inviting. One was formed of new, milk-hued canvas, and bore red flags on its summit; it announced 'Good Home-brewed Beer, Ale, and Cyder.' The other was less new; a little iron stove-pipe came out of it at the back, and in front appeared the placard, 'Good Furmity Sold Hear.' The man mentally weighed the two inscriptions, and inclined to the former tent.

'No—no—the other one,' said the woman. 'I always like furmity; and so does Elizabeth-Jane; and so will you. It is nourishing after a long hard day.'

'I've never tasted it,' said the man. However, he gave way to her representations, and they entered the furmity booth forthwith.

A rather numerous company appeared within, seated at the long narrow tables that ran down the tent on each side. At the upper end stood a stove, containing a charcoal fire, over which hung a large three-legged crock, sufficiently polished round the rim to show that it was made of bell-metal. A haggish creature of about fifty presided, in a white apron, which, as it threw an air of respectability over her as far as it extended, was made so wide as to reach nearly round her waist. She slowly stirred the contents of the pot. The dull scrape of her large spoon was audible throughout the tent as

5

she thus kept from burning the mixture of corn in the grain, milk, raisins, currants, and what not, that composed the antiquated slop in which she dealt. Vessels holding the separate ingredients stood on a white-clothed table of boards and trestles close by.

The young man and woman ordered a basin each of the mixture, steaming hot, and sat down to consume it at leisure. This was very well so far, for furmity, as the woman had said, was nourishing, and as proper a food as could be obtained within the four seas; though, to those not accustomed to it, the grains of wheat, swollen as large as lemon-pips, which floated on its surface, might have a deterrent effect at first.

But there was more in that tent than met the cursory glance; and the man, with the instinct of a perverse character, scented it quickly. After a mincing attack on his bowl, he watched the hag's proceedings from the corner of his eye, and saw the game she played. He winked to her, and passed up his basin in reply to her nod; when she took a bottle from under the table, slily measured out a quantity of its contents, and tipped the same into the man's furmity. The liquor poured in was rum. The man as slily sent back money in payment.

He found the concoction, thus strongly laced, much more to his satisfaction than it had been in its natural state. His wife had observed the proceeding with much uneasiness; but he persuaded her to have hers laced also, and she agreed to a milder allowance after some misgiving.

The man finished his basin, and called for another, the rum being signalled for in yet stronger proportion. The effect of it was soon apparent in his manner, and his wife but too sadly perceived that in strenuously steering off the rocks of the licensed liquor-tent she had only got into maelstrom depths here amongst the smugglers.

The child began to prattle impatiently, and the wife more than once said to her husband, 'Michael, how about our lodging? You know we may have trouble in getting it if we don't go soon.'

But he turned a deaf ear to those bird-like chirpings. He talked loud to the company. The child's black eyes, after slow, round, ruminating gazes at the candles when they were lighted, fell together; then they opened, then shut again, and she slept.

At the end of the first basin the man had risen to serenity; at the second he was jovial; at the third, argumentative; at the fourth, the qualities signified by the shape of his face, the occasional clench of his mouth, and the fiery spark of his dark eye, began to tell in his conduct; he was overbearing—even brilliantly quarrelsome.

The conversation took a high turn, as it often does on such occasions. The ruin of good men by bad wives, and, more particularly, the frustration of many a promising youth's high aims and hopes, and the extinction of his energies, by an early imprudent marriage, was the theme.

'I did for myself that way thoroughly,' said the trusser, with a contemplative bitterness that was well-nigh resentful. 'I married at eighteen, like the fool that I was; and this is the consequence o't.' He pointed at himself and family with a wave of the hand intended to bring out the penuriousness of the exhibition.

The young woman his wife, who seemed accustomed to such remarks, acted as if she did not hear them, and continued her intermittent private words on tender trifles to the sleeping and waking child, who was just big enough to be placed for a moment on the bench beside her when she wished to ease her arms. The man continued—

'I haven't more than fifteen shillings in the world,

and yet I am a good experienced hand in my line. I'd challenge England to beat me in the fodder business; and if I were a free man again, I'd be worth a thousand pound before I'd done o't. But a fellow never knows these little things till all chance of acting upon 'em is past.'

The auctioneer selling the old horses in the field outside could be heard saying, 'Now this is the last lot—now who'll take the last lot for a song? Shall I say forty shillings? 'Tis a very promising brood-mare, a trifle over five years old, and nothing the matter with the hoss at all, except that she's a little holler in the back and had her left eye knocked out by the kick of another, her own sister, coming along the road.'

'For my part I don't see why men who have got wives, and don't want 'em, shouldn't get rid of 'em as these gipsy fellows do their old horses,' said the man in the tent. 'Why shouldn't they put 'em up and sell 'em by auction to men who are in want of such articles? Hey? Why, begad, I'd sell mine this minute if anybody would buy her!'

'There's them that would do that,' some of the guests replied, looking at the woman, who was by no means ill-favoured.

'True,' said a smoking gentleman, whose coat had the fine polish about the collar, elbows, seams, and shoulder-blades that long-continued friction with grimy surfaces will produce, and which is usually more desired on furniture than on clothes. From his appearance he had possibly been in former time groom or coachman to some neighbouring county family. 'I've had my breedings in as good circles, I may say, as any man,' he added, 'and I know true cultivation, or nobody do; and I can declare she's got it—in the bone, mind ye, I say—as much as any female in the fair—though it may want a little bringing out.' Then, crossing his legs, he resumed his pipe with a nicely-adjusted gaze at a point in the air.

The fuddled young husband stared for a few seconds at this unexpected praise of his wife, half in doubt of the wisdom of his own attitude towards the possessor of such qualities. But he speedily lapsed into his former conviction, and said harshly—

'Well, then, now is your chance; I am open to an offer for this gem o' creation.'

She turned to her husband and murmured, 'Michael, you have talked this nonsense in public places before. A joke is a joke, but you may make it once too often, mind!'

'I know I've said it before; I meant it. All I want is a buyer.'

At the moment a swallow, one among the last of the season, which had by chance found its way through an opening into the upper part of the tent, flew to and fro in quick curves above their heads, causing all eyes to follow it absently. In watching the bird till it made its escape the assembled company neglected to respond to the workman's offer, and the subject dropped.

But a quarter of an hour later the man, who had gone on lacing his furmity more and more heavily, though he was either so strong-minded or such an intrepid toper that he still appeared fairly sober, recurred to the old strain, as in a musical fantasy the instrument fetches up the original theme. 'Here—I am waiting to know about this offer of mine. The woman is no good to me. Who'll have her?'

The company had by this time decidedly degenerated, and the renewed inquiry was received with a laugh of appreciation. The woman whispered; she was imploring and anxious: 'Come, come, it is getting dark, and this nonsense won't do. If you don't come along, I shall go without you. Come!'

She waited and waited; yet he did not move. In ten minutes the man broke in upon the desultory conversation of the furmity drinkers with, 'I asked this

question, and nobody answered to 't. Will any Jack
Rag or Tom Straw among ye buy my goods ? '

The woman's manner changed, and her face assumed
the grim shape and colour of which mention has been
made.

'Mike, Mike,' said she; 'this is getting serious.
Oh !—too serious ! '

'Will anybody buy her ? ' said the man.

'I wish somebody would,' said she firmly. 'Her
present owner is not at all to her liking ! '

'Nor you to mine,' said he. 'So we are agreed
about that. Gentlemen, you hear ? It's an agreement
to part. She shall take the girl if she wants to, and
go her ways. I'll take my tools, and go my ways.
'Tis simple as Scripture history. Now then, stand up,
Susan, and show yourself.'

'Don't, my chiel,' whispered a buxom staylace
dealer in voluminous petticoats, who sat near the
woman ; 'yer good man don't know what he's saying.'

The woman, however, did stand up. 'Now, who's
auctioneer ? ' cried the hay-trusser.

'I be,' promptly answered a short man, with a
nose resembling a copper knob, a damp voice, and eyes
like button-holes. 'Who'll make an offer for this lady ? '

The woman looked on the ground, as if she maintained her position by a supreme effort of will.

'Five shillings,' said some one, at which there was
a laugh.

'No insults,' said the husband. 'Who'll say a
guinea ? '

Nobody answered ; and the female dealer in stay-
laces interposed.

'Behave yerself moral, good man, for Heaven's
love ! Ah, what a cruelty is the poor soul married
to ! Bed and board is dear at some figures, 'pon my
'vation 'tis ! '

'Set it higher, auctioneer,' said the trusser.

'Two guineas!' said the auctioneer; and no one replied.

'If they don't take her for that, in ten seconds they'll have to give more,' said the husband. 'Very well. Now, auctioneer, add another.'

'Three guineas—going for three guineas!' said the rheumy man.

'No bid?' said the husband. 'Good Lord, why she's cost me fifty times the money, if a penny. Go on.'

'Four guineas!' cried the auctioneer.

'I'll tell ye what—I won't sell her for less than five,' said the husband, bringing down his fist so that the basins danced. 'I'll sell her for five guineas to any man that will pay me the money, and treat her well; and he shall have her for ever, and never hear aught o' me. But she shan't go for less. Now then—five guineas—and she's yours. Susan, you agree?'

She bowed her head with absolute indifference.

'Five guineas,' said the auctioneer, 'or she'll be withdrawn. Do anybody give it? The last time. Yes or no?'

'Yes,' said a loud voice from the doorway.

All eyes were turned. Standing in the triangular opening which formed the door of the tent was a sailor, who, unobserved by the rest, had arrived there within the last two or three minutes. A dead silence followed his affirmation.

'You say you do?' asked the husband, staring at him.

'I say so,' replied the sailor.

'Saying is one thing, and paying is another. Where's the money?'

The sailor hesitated a moment, looked anew at the woman, came in, unfolded five crisp pieces of paper, and threw them down upon the table-cloth. They were Bank-of-England notes for five pounds. Upon the face of this he chinked down the shillings severally—one, two, three, four, five.

The sight of real money in full amount, in answer to a challenge for the same till then deemed slightly hypothetical, had a great effect upon the spectators. Their eyes became riveted upon the faces of the chief actors, and then upon the notes as they lay, weighted by the shillings, on the table.

Up to this moment it could not positively have been asserted that the man, in spite of his tantalizing declaration, was really in earnest. The spectators had indeed taken the proceedings throughout as a piece of mirthful irony carried to extremes; and had assumed that, being out of work, he was, as a consequence, out of temper with the world, and society, and his nearest kin. But with the demand and response of real cash the jovial frivolity of the scene departed. A lurid colour seemed to fill the tent, and change the aspect of all therein. The mirth-wrinkles left the listeners' faces, and they waited with parting lips.

'Now,' said the woman, breaking the silence, so that her low dry voice sounded quite loud, 'before you go further, Michael, listen to me. If you touch that money, I and this girl go with the man. Mind, it is a joke no longer.'

'A joke? Of course it is not a joke!' shouted her husband, his resentment rising at her suggestion. 'I take the money: the sailor takes you. That's plain enough. It has been done elsewhere—and why not here?'

''Tis quite on the understanding that the young woman is willing,' said the sailor blandly. 'I wouldn't hurt her feelings for the world.'

'Faith, nor I,' said her husband. 'But she is willing, provided she can have the child. She said so only the other day when I talked o't!'

'That you swear?' said the sailor to her.

'I do,' said she, after glancing at her husband's face and seeing no repentance there.

'Very well, she shall have the child, and the bargain's complete,' said the trusser. He took the sailor's notes and deliberately folded them, and put them with the shillings in a high remote pocket, with an air of finality.

The sailor looked at the woman and smiled. 'Come along!' he said kindly. 'The little one too—the more the merrier!' She paused for an instant, with a close glance at him. Then dropping her eyes again, and saying nothing, she took up the child and followed him as he made towards the door. On reaching it, she turned, and pulling off her wedding-ring, flung it across the booth in the hay-trusser's face.

'Mike,' she said, 'I've lived with thee a couple of years, and had nothing but temper! Now I'm no more to 'ee; I'll try my luck elsewhere. 'Twill be better for me and the child, both. So good-bye!'

Seizing the sailor's arm with her right hand, and mounting the little girl on her left, she went out of the tent sobbing bitterly.

A stolid look of concern filled the husband's face, as if, after all, he had not quite anticipated this ending; and some of the guests laughed.

'Is she gone?' he said.

'Faith, ay; she gone clane enough,' said some rustics near the door.

He rose and walked to the entrance with the careful tread of one conscious of his alcoholic load. Some others followed, and they stood looking into the twilight. The difference between the peacefulness of inferior nature and the wilful hostilities of mankind was very apparent at this place. In contrast with the harshness of the act just ended within the tent was the sight of several horses crossing their necks and rubbing each other lovingly as they waited in patience to be harnessed for the homeward journey. Outside the fair, in the valleys and woods, all was quiet. The sun had recently set, and the west heaven was hung with rosy cloud, which seemed permanent, yet slowly changed. To watch it was like looking at some grand feat of stagery from a darkened auditorium. In presence of this scene, after the other, there was a natural instinct to abjure man as the blot on an otherwise kindly universe; till it was remembered that all terrestrial conditions were intermittent, and that mankind might some night be innocently sleeping when these quiet objects were raging loud.

'Where do the sailor live?' asked a spectator, when they had vainly gazed around.

'God knows that,' replied the man who had seen high life. 'He's without doubt a stranger here.'

'He came in about five minutes ago,' said the furmity woman, joining the rest with her hands on her hips. 'And then 'a stepped back, and then 'a looked in again. I'm not a penny the better for him.'

'Serves the husband well be-right,' said the stay-lace vendor. 'A comely respectable body like her—what can a man want more? I glory in the woman's sperrit. I'd ha' done it myself—od send if I wouldn't, if a husband had behaved so to me! I'd go, and 'a might call, and call, till his keacorn was raw; but I'd never come back — no, not till the great trumpet, would I!'

'Well, the woman will be better off,' said another of a more deliberative turn. 'For seafaring naters be very good shelter for shorn lambs, and the man do seem to have plenty of money, which is what she's not been used to lately, by all showings.'

'Mark me—I'll not go after her!' said the trusser, returning doggedly to his seat. 'Let her go! If she's up to such vagaries she must suffer for 'em. She'd no business to take the maid—'tis my maid;

14

and if it were the doing again she shouldn't have her !'

Perhaps from some little sense of having countenanced an indefensible proceeding, perhaps because it was late, the customers thinned away from the tent shortly after this episode. The man stretched his elbows forward on the table, leant his face upon his arms, and soon began to snore. The furmity seller decided to close for the night, and after seeing the rum-bottles, milk, corn, raisins, &c., that remained on hand, loaded into the cart, came to where the man reclined. She shook him, but could not wake him. As the tent was not to be struck that night, the fair continuing for two or three days, she decided to let the sleeper, who was obviously no tramp, stay where he was, and his basket with him. Extinguishing the last candle, and lowering the flap of the tent, she left it, and drove away.

II

THE morning sun was streaming through the crevices of the canvas when the man awoke. A warm glow pervaded the whole atmosphere of the marquee, and a single big blue fly buzzed musically round and round it. Besides the buzz of the fly there was not a sound. He looked about—at the benches—at the table supported by trestles—at his basket of tools—at the stove where the furmity had been boiled—at the empty basins—at some shed grains of wheat—at the corks which dotted the grassy floor. Among the odds and ends he discerned a little shining object, and picked it up. It was his wife's ring.

A confused picture of the events of the previous evening seemed to come back to him, and he thrust his hand into his breast-pocket. A rustling revealed the sailor's bank-notes thrust carelessly in.

This second verification of his dim memories was enough; he knew now they were not dreams. He remained seated, looking on the ground for some time. 'I must get out of this as soon as I can,' he said deliberately at last, with the air of one who could not catch his thoughts without pronouncing them. 'She's gone—to be sure she is—gone with that sailor who bought her, and little Elizabeth-Jane. We walked here, and I had the furmity, and rum in it—and sold her.

Yes, that's what's happened, and here am I. Now, what am I to do—am I sober enough to walk, I wonder?' He stood up, found that he was in fairly good condition for progress, unencumbered. Next he shouldered his tool basket, and found he could carry it. Then lifting the tent door he emerged into the open air.

Here the man looked around with gloomy curiosity. The freshness of the September morning inspired and braced him as he stood. He and his family had been weary when they arrived the night before, and they had observed but little of the place; so that he now beheld it as a new thing. It exhibited itself as the top of an open down, bounded on one extreme by a plantation, and approached by a winding road. At the bottom stood the village which lent its name to the upland, and the annual fair that was held thereon. The spot stretched downward into valleys, and onward to other uplands, dotted with barrows, and trenched with the remains of prehistoric forts. The whole scene lay under the rays of a newly risen sun, which had not as yet dried a single blade of the heavily dewed grass, whereon the shadows of the yellow and red vans were projected far away, those thrown by the felloe of each wheel being elongated in shape to the orbit of a comet. All the gipsies and showmen who had remained on the ground lay snug within their carts and tents, or wrapped in horse-cloths under them, and were silent and still as death, with the exception of an occasional snore that revealed their presence. But the Seven Sleepers had a dog; and dogs of the mysterious breeds that vagrants own, that are as much like cats as dogs, and as much like foxes as cats, also lay about here. A little one started up under one of the carts, barked as a matter of principle, and quickly lay down again. He was the only positive spectator of the hay-trusser's exit from the Weydon Fair-field.

This seemed to accord with his desire. He went on in silent thought, unheeding the yellowhammers which flitted about the hedges with straws in their bills, the crowns of the mushrooms, and the tinkling of local sheep-bells, whose wearers had had the good fortune not to be included in the fair. When he reached a lane, a good mile from the scene of the previous evening, the man pitched his basket, and leant upon a gate. A difficult problem or two occupied his mind.

'Did I tell my name to anybody last night, or didn't I tell my name?' he said to himself; and at last concluded that he did not. His general demeanour was enough to show how he was surprised and nettled that his wife had taken him so literally—as much could be seen in his face, and in the way he nibbled a straw which he pulled from the hedge. He knew that she must have been somewhat excited to do this; moreover, she must have believed that there was some sort of binding force in the transaction. On this latter point he felt almost certain, knowing her freedom from levity of character, and the extreme simplicity of her intellect. There may, too, have been enough recklessness and resentment beneath her ordinary placidity to make her stifle any momentary doubts. On a previous occasion when he had declared, during a fuddle, that he would dispose of her as he had done, she had replied that she would not hear him say that many times more before it happened, in the resigned tones of a fatalist. . . . 'Yet she knows I am not in my senses when I do that?' he exclaimed. 'Well, I must walk about till I find her. . . . Seize her, why didn't she know better than bring me into this disgrace!' he roared out. 'She wasn't queer if I was. 'Tis like Susan to show such idiotic simplicity. Meek—that meekness has done me more harm than the bitterest temper!'

When he was calmer, he turned to his original conviction that he must somehow find her and his little Elizabeth-Jane, and put up with the shame as best he could. It was of his own making, and he ought to bear it. But first he resolved to register an oath, a greater oath than he had ever sworn before: and to do it properly he required a fit place and imagery; for there was something fetichistic in this man's beliefs.

He shouldered his basket and moved on, casting his eyes inquisitively round upon the landscape as he walked, and at the distance of three or four miles perceived the roofs of a village and the tower of a church. He instantly made towards the latter object. The village was quite still, it being that motionless hour of rustic daily life which fills the interval between the departure of the field-labourers to their work, and the rising of their wives and daughters to prepare the breakfast for their return. Hence he reached the church without observation, and the door being only latched, he entered. The hay-trusser deposited his basket by the font, went up the nave till he reached the altar-rails, and opening the gate, entered the sacrarium, where he seemed to feel a sense of the strangeness for a moment; then he knelt upon the foot-pace. Dropping his head upon the clamped book which lay on the Communion-table, he said aloud—

'I, Michael Henchard, on this morning of the sixteenth of September, do take an oath here in this solemn place that I will avoid all strong liquors for the space of twenty years to come, being a year for every year that I have lived. And this I swear upon the book before me; and may I be strook dumb, blind, and helpless, if I break this my oath!'

When he had said it and kissed the big book, the hay-trusser arose, and seemed relieved at having made a start in a new direction. While standing in the porch a moment, he saw a thick jet of wood smoke suddenly start up from the red chimney of a cottage

near, and knew that the occupant had just lit her fire
He went round to the door, and the housewife agreed
to prepare him some breakfast for a trifling payment,
which was done. Then he started on the search for
his wife and child.

The perplexing nature of the undertaking became
apparent soon enough. Though he examined and
inquired, and walked hither and thither day after day,
no such characters as those he described had anywhere been seen since the evening of the fair. To add
to the difficulty, he could gain no sound of the sailor's
name. As money was short with him, he decided,
after some hesitation, to spend the sailor's money in
the prosecution of this search; but it was equally in
vain. The truth was, that a certain shyness of revealing his conduct prevented Michael Henchard from
following up the investigation with the loud hue-and-
cry such a pursuit demanded to render it effectual;
and it was probably for this reason that he obtained
no clue, though everything was done by him that did
not involve an explanation of the circumstances under
which he had lost her.

Weeks counted up to months, and still he searched
on, maintaining himself by small jobs of work in the
intervals. By this time he had arrived at a seaport,
and there he derived intelligence that persons answering
somewhat to his description had emigrated a little time
before. Then he said he would search no longer, and
that he would go and settle in the district which he had
had for some time in his mind. Next day he started,
journeying south-westward, and did not pause, except
for nights' lodgings, till he reached the town of Casterbridge, in a far distant part of Wessex.

III

THE highroad into the village of Weydon-Priors was again carpeted with dust. The trees had put on as of yore their aspect of dingy green, and where the Henchard family of three had once walked along, two persons not unconnected with that family walked now.

The scene in its broad aspect had so much of its previous character, even to the voices and rattle from the neighbouring village down, that it might for that matter have been the afternoon following the previously recorded episode. Change was only to be observed in details; but here it was obvious that a long procession of years had passed by. One of the two who walked the road was she who had figured as the young wife of Henchard on the previous occasion; now her face had lost much of its rotundity; her skin had undergone a textural change; and though her hair had not lost colour, it was considerably thinner than heretofore. She was dressed in the mourning clothes of a widow. Her companion, also in black, appeared as a well-formed young woman of eighteen, completely possessed of that ephemeral precious essence youth, which is itself beauty, irrespective of complexion or contour.

A glance was sufficient to inform the eye that this was Susan Henchard's grown-up daughter. While life's middle summer had set its hardening mark on the mother's face, her former spring-like specialities were transferred so dexterously by Time to the second figure, her child, that the absence of certain facts within her mother's knowledge from the girl's mind would have seemed for the moment, to one reflecting on those facts, to be a curious imperfection in Nature's powers of continuity.

They walked with joined hands, and it could be perceived that this was the act of simple affection. The daughter carried in her outer hand a withy basket of old-fashioned make; the mother a blue bundle, which contrasted oddly with her black stuff gown.

Reaching the outskirts of the village, they pursued the same track as formerly, and ascended to the fair. Here, too, it was evident that the years had told. Certain mechanical improvements might have been noticed in the roundabouts and highfliers, machines for testing rustic strength and weight, and in the erections devoted to shooting for nuts. But the real business of the fair had considerably dwindled. The new periodical great markets of neighbouring towns were beginning to interfere seriously with the trade carried on here for centuries. The pens for sheep, the tie-ropes for horses, were about half as long as they had been. The stalls of tailors, hosiers, coopers, linen-drapers, and other such trades had almost disappeared, and the vehicles were far less numerous. The mother and daughter threaded the crowd for some little distance, and then stood still.

'Why did we hinder our time by coming in here? I thought you wished to get onward?' said the maiden.

'Yes, my dear Elizabeth-Jane,' explained the other. 'But I had a fancy for looking up here.'

'Why?'

'It was here I first met with Newson—on such a day as this.'

'First met with father here? Yes, you have told me so before. And now he's drowned and gone from

22

us!' As she spoke the girl drew a card from her
pocket and looked at it with a sigh. It was edged with
black, and inscribed within a design resembling a mural
tablet were the words, 'In affectionate memory of
Richard Newson, mariner, who was unfortunately lost
at sea, in the month of November 184—, aged forty-
one years.'

'And it was here,' continued her mother, with more
hesitation, 'that I last saw the relation we are going to
look for—Mr. Michael Henchard.'

'What is his exact kin to us, mother? I have never
clearly had it told me.'

'He is, or was—for he may be dead—a connection
by marriage,' said her mother deliberately.

'That's exactly what you have said a score of times
before!' replied the young woman, looking about her
inattentively. 'He's not a near relation, I suppose?'

'Not by any means.'

'He was a hay-trusser, wasn't he, when you last
heard of him?'

'He was.'

'I suppose he never knew me?' the girl innocently
continued.

Mrs. Henchard paused for a moment, and answered
uneasily, 'Of course not, Elizabeth-Jane. But come
this way.' She moved on to another part of the field.

'It is not much use inquiring here for anybody, I
should think,' the daughter observed, as she gazed round
about. 'People at fairs change like the leaves of trees;
and I daresay you are the only one here to-day who was
here all those years ago.'

'I am not so sure of that,' said Mrs. Newson, as
she now called herself, keenly eyeing something under
a green bank a little way off. 'See there.'

The daughter looked in the direction signified. The
object pointed out was a tripod of sticks stuck into the
earth, from which hung a three-legged crock, kept hot

by a smouldering wood fire beneath. Over the pot stooped an old woman, haggard, wrinkled, and almost in rags. She stirred the contents of the pot with a large spoon, and occasionally croaked in a broken voice, 'Good furmity sold here!'

It was indeed the former mistress of the furmity tent—once thriving, cleanly, white-aproned, and chinking with money—now tentless, dirty, owning no tables or benches, and having scarce any customers except two small whitey-brown boys, who came up and asked for 'A ha'p'orth, please—good measure,' which she served in a couple of chipped yellow basins of commonest clay.

'She was here at that time,' resumed Mrs. Newson, making a step as if to draw nearer.

'Don't speak to her—it isn't respectable!' urged the other.

'I will just say a word—you, Elizabeth-Jane, can stay here.'

The girl was not loth, and turned to some stalls of coloured prints while her mother went forward. The old woman begged for the latter's custom as soon as she saw her, and responded to Mrs. Henchard-Newson's request for a pennyworth with more alacrity than she had shown in selling sixpennyworths in her younger days. When the *soi-disant* widow had taken the basin of thin poor slop that stood for the rich concoction of the former time, the hag opened a little basket behind the fire, and looking up slily, whispered, 'Just a thought o' rum in it?—smuggled, you know—say two penn'orth—'twill make it slip down like cordial!'

Her customer smiled bitterly at this survival of the old trick, and shook her head with a meaning the old woman was far from translating. She pretended to eat a little of the furmity with the leaden spoon offered, and as she did so, said blandly to the hag, 'You've seen better days?'

'Ah, ma'am—well ye may say it!' responded the old woman, opening the sluices of her heart forthwith. 'I've stood in this fair-ground, maid, wife, and widow, these nine-and-thirty year, and in that time have known what it was to do business with the richest stomachs in the land! Ma'am, you'd hardly believe that I was once the owner of a great pavilion-tent that was the attraction of the fair. Nobody could come, nobody could go, without having a dish of Mrs. Goodenough's furmity. I knew the clergy's taste, the dandy gent's taste; I knew the town's taste, the country's taste. I even knowed the taste of the coarse shameless females. But seize my life—the world's no memory; straightforward dealings don't bring profit—'tis the sly and the underhand that get on in these times!'

Mrs. Newson glanced round—her daughter was still bending over the distant stalls. 'Can you call to mind,' she said cautiously to the old woman, 'the sale of a wife by her husband in your tent eighteen years ago to-day?'

The hag reflected, and half shook her head. 'If it had been a big thing I should have minded it in a moment,' she said. 'I can mind every serious fight o' married parties, every murder, every manslaughter, even every pocket-picking—leastwise large ones—that 't has been my lot to witness. But a selling? Was it done quiet-like?'

'Well, yes. I think so.'

The furmity woman half shook her head again. 'And yet,' she said, 'I do. At any rate, I can mind a man doing something o' the sort—a man in a cord jacket, with a basket of tools; but, Lord bless ye, we don't gi'e it head-room, we don't, such as that. The only reason why I can mind the man is that he came back here to the next year's fair, and told me quite private-like that if a woman ever asked for him I was to say he had gone to—where?—Casterbridge—yes—

to Casterbridge, said he. But, Lord's my life, I shouldn't ha' thought of it again!'

Mrs. Newson would have rewarded the old woman as far as her small means afforded, had she not discreetly borne in mind that it was by that unscrupulous person's liquor her husband had been degraded. She briefly thanked her informant, and rejoined Elizabeth, who greeted her with, 'Mother, do let's go on—it was hardly respectable for you to buy refreshments there. I see none but the lowest do.'

'I have learned what I wanted, however,' said her mother quietly. 'The last time our relative visited this fair he said he was living at Casterbridge. It is a long, long way from here, and it was many years ago that he said it; but there I think we'll go.'

With this they descended out of the fair, and went onward to the village, where they obtained a night's lodging.

IV

HENCHARD'S wife acted for the best, but she had involved herself in difficulties. A hundred times she had been upon the point of telling her daughter, Elizabeth-Jane, the true story of her life, the tragical crisis of which had been the transaction at Weydon Fair, when she was not much older than the girl now beside her. But she had refrained. An innocent maiden had thus grown up in the belief that the relations between the genial sailor and her mother were the ordinary ones that they had always appeared to be. The risk of endangering a child's strong affection by disturbing ideas which had grown with her growth was to Mrs. Henchard too fearful a thing to contemplate. It had seemed, indeed, folly to think of making Elizabeth-Jane wise.

But Susan Henchard's fear of losing her dearly loved daughter's heart by a revelation had little to do with any sense of wrong-doing on her own part. Her simplicity—the original ground of Henchard's contempt for her—had allowed her to live on in the conviction that Newson had acquired a morally real and justifiable right to her by his purchase—though the exact bearings and legal limits of that right were vague. It may seem strange to sophisticated minds that a sane young matron could believe in the seriousness of such a transfer; and were there not numerous other instances of the same belief the thing might scarcely be credited. But she was by no means the first or last peasant woman who had religiously adhered to her purchaser, as too many rural records show.

The history of Susan Henchard's adventures in the interim can be told in two or three sentences. Absolutely helpless, she had been taken off to Canada, where they had lived several years without any great worldly success, though she worked as hard as any woman could to keep their cottage cheerful and well-provided. When Elizabeth-Jane was about twelve years old the three returned to England, and settled at Falmouth, where Newson made a living for a few years as boatman and general handy shoreman.

He then engaged in the Newfoundland trade, and it was during this period that Susan had an awakening. A friend to whom she confided her history ridiculed her grave acceptance of her position; and all was over with her peace of mind. When Newson came home at the end of one winter he saw that the delusion he had so carefully sustained had vanished for ever.

There was then a time of sadness, in which she told him her doubts if she could live with him longer. Newson left home again on the Newfoundland trade when the season came round. The news of his loss at sea a little later on solved a problem which had become torture to her meek conscience. She saw him no more.

Of Henchard they heard nothing. To the liege subjects of Labour, the England of those days was a continent, and a mile a geographical degree.

Elizabeth-Jane developed early into womanliness. One day, a month or so after receiving intelligence of Newson's death off the Bank of Newfoundland, when the girl was about eighteen, she was sitting on a willow chair in the cottage they still occupied, working twine nets for the fishermen. Her mother was in a back corner of the same room, engaged in the same labour; and dropping the heavy wood needle she was filling, she surveyed her daughter thoughtfully. The sun shone in at the door upon the young woman's head and hair, which was worn loose, so that the rays streamed into its depths as into a hazel copse. Her face, though somewhat wan and incomplete, possessed the raw materials of beauty in a promising degree. There was an under-handsomeness in it, struggling to reveal itself through the provisional curves of immaturity, and the casual disfigurements that resulted from the straitened circumstances of their lives. She was handsome in the bone, hardly as yet handsome in the flesh. She possibly might never be fully handsome, unless the carking accidents of her daily existence could be evaded before the mobile parts of her countenance had settled to their final mould.

The sight of the girl made her mother sad—not vaguely, but by logical inference. They both were still in that strait-waistcoat of poverty from which she had tried so many times to be delivered for the girl's sake. The woman had long perceived how zealously and constantly the young mind of her companion was struggling for enlargement; and yet now, in her eighteenth year, it still remained but little unfolded. The desire—sober and repressed—of Elizabeth-Jane's heart was indeed to see, to hear, and to understand. How could she become a woman of wider knowledge, higher repute—'better,' as she termed it—this was her constant inquiry of her mother. She sought further into things than other girls in her position ever did, and her mother groaned as she felt she could not aid in the search.

The sailor was now lost to them; and Susan's staunch, religious adherence to him as her husband in principle, till her views had been disturbed by enlightenment, was demanded no more. She asked herself whether the present moment, now that she was a free woman again, were not as opportune a one as she would find in a world where everything had been so inopportune, for making a desperate effort to advance Elizabeth. To pocket her pride and search for the first husband seemed, wisely or not, the best initiatory step. He had possibly drunk himself into his tomb. But he might, on the other hand, have had too much sense to do so; for in her time with him he had been given to bouts only, and was not a habitual drunkard.

At any rate, the propriety of returning to him, if he lived, was unquestionable. The awkwardness of searching for him lay in enlightening Elizabeth, a proceeding which her mother could not endure to contemplate. She finally resolved to undertake the search without confiding to the girl her former relations with Henchard, leaving it to him if they found him to take what steps he might choose to that end. This will account for their conversation at tne fair, and the half-informed state in which Elizabeth was led onward.

In this attitude they proceeded on their journey, trusting solely to the dim light afforded of Henchard's whereabouts by the furmity woman. The strictest economy was indispensable. Sometimes they might have been seen on foot, sometimes on farmers' waggons, sometimes in carriers' vans; and thus they drew near to Casterbridge. Elizabeth-Jane discovered to her alarm that her mother's health was not what it once had been, and there was ever and anon in her talk that renunciatory tone which showed that, but for the girl, she would not be very sorry to quit a life she was growing thoroughly weary of.

It was on a Friday evening, near the middle of September, and just before dusk, that they reached the summit of a hill within a mile of the place they sought. There were high-banked hedges to the coach-road here, and they mounted upon the green turf within, and sat down. The spot commanded a full view of the town and its environs.

'What an old-fashioned place it seems to be!' said Elizabeth-Jane, while her silent mother mused on other things than topography. 'It is huddled all together; and it is shut in by a square wall of trees, like a plot of garden ground by a box-edging.'

Its squareness was, indeed, the characteristic which most struck the eye in this antiquated borough, the borough of Casterbridge—at that time, recent as it was, untouched by the faintest sprinkle of modernism. It was compact as a box of dominoes. It had no suburbs—in the ordinary sense. Country and town met at a mathematical line.

To birds of the more soaring kind Casterbridge must have appeared on this fine evening as a mosaic-work of subdued reds, browns, greys, and crystals, held together by a rectangular frame of deep green. To the level eye of humanity it stood as an indistinct mass behind a dense stockade of limes and chestnuts, set in the midst of miles of rotund down and concave field. The mass became gradually dissected by the vision into towers, gables, chimneys, and casements, the highest glazings shining bleared and bloodshot with the coppery fire they caught from the belt of sunlit cloud in the west.

From the centre of each side of this tree-bound square ran avenues east, west, and south into the wide expanse of corn-land and combe to the distance of a mile or so. It was by one of these avenues that the pedestrians were about to enter. Before they had risen to proceed, two men passed outside the hedge, engaged in argumentative conversation.

'Why, surely,' said Elizabeth, as they receded, 'those men mentioned the name of Henchard in their talk—the name of our relative?'

'I thought so too,' said Mrs. Newson.

' That seems a hint to us that he is still here.'

' Yes.'

' Shall I run after them, and ask them about him '——

' No, no, no! Not for the world just yet. He may be in the workhouse, or in the stocks, for all we know.'

' Dear me—why should you think that, mother ? '

' 'Twas just something to say—that's all! But we must make private inquiries.'

Having sufficiently rested, they proceeded on their way at evenfall. The dense trees of the avenue rendered the road dark as a tunnel, though the open land on each side was still under a faint daylight; in other words, they passed down a midnight between two gloamings. The features of the town had a keen interest for Elizabeth's mother, now that the human side came to the fore. As soon as they had wandered about they could see that the stockade of gnarled trees which framed in Casterbridge was itself an avenue, standing on a low green bank or escarpment, with a ditch yet visible without. Within the avenue and bank was a wall more or less discontinuous, and within the wall were packed the abodes of the burghers.

Though the two women did not know it, these external features were but the ancient defences of the town, planted as a promenade.

The lamplights now glimmered through the engirdling trees, conveying a sense of great snugness and comfort inside, and rendering at the same time the unlighted country without strangely solitary and vacant in aspect, considering its nearness to life. The difference between burgh and champaign was increased, too, by sounds which now reached them above others—the notes of a brass band. The travellers returned into the High Street, where there were timber houses with overhanging stories, whose small-paned lattices were screened by dimity curtains on a drawing-string, and under whose barge-boards old cobwebs waved in the breeze. There were houses of brick-nogging, which derived their chief support from those adjoining. There were slate roofs patched with tiles, and tile roofs patched with slate, with occasionally a roof of thatch.

The agricultural and pastoral character of the people upon whom the town depended for its existence was shown by the class of objects displayed in the shop windows. Scythes, reap-hooks, sheep-shears, bill-hooks, spades, mattocks, and hoes at the ironmonger's; bee-hives, butter-firkins, churns, milking stools and pails, hay-rakes, field-flagons, and seed-lips at the cooper's; cart-ropes and plough-harness at the saddler's; carts, wheel-barrows, and mill-gear at the wheelwright's and machinist's; horse-embrocations at the chemist's; at the glover's and leather-cutter's, hedging-gloves, thatcher's knee-caps, ploughman's leggings, villager's pattens and clogs.

They came to a grizzled church, whose massive square tower rose unbroken into the darkening sky, the lower parts being illuminated by the nearest lamps sufficiently to show how completely the mortar from the joints of the stonework had been nibbled out by time and weather, which had planted in the crevices thus made little tufts of stone-crop and grass almost as far up as the very battlements. From this tower the clock struck eight, and thereupon a bell began to toll with a peremptory clang. The curfew was still rung in Casterbridge, and it was utilized by the inhabitants as a signal for shutting their shops. No sooner did the deep notes of the bell throb between the house-fronts than a clatter of shutters arose through the whole length of the High Street. In a few minutes business at Casterbridge was ended for the day.

Other clocks struck eight from time to time—one

gloomily from the gaol, another from the gable of an almshouse, with a preparative creak of machinery, more audible than the note of the bell; a row of tall, varnished case-clocks from the interior of a clock-maker's shop joined in one after another just as the shutters were enclosing them, like a row of actors delivering their final speeches before the fall of the curtain; then chimes were heard stammering out the Sicilian Mariners' Hymn; so that chronologists of the advanced school were appreciably on their way to the next hour before the whole business of the old one was satisfactorily wound up.

In an open space before the church walked a woman with her gown-sleeves rolled up so high that the edge of her under-linen was visible, and her skirt tucked up through her pocket hole. She carried a loaf under her arm from which she was pulling pieces of bread, and handing them to some other women who walked with her; which pieces they nibbled critically. The sight reminded Mrs. Henchard-Newson and her daughter that they had an appetite; and they inquired of the woman for the nearest baker's.

'Ye may as well look for manna-food as good bread in Casterbridge just now,' she said, after directing them. 'They can blare their trumpets and thump their drums, and have their roaring dinners'—waving her hand towards a point further along the street, where the brass band could be seen standing in front of an illuminated building—'but we must needs be put-to for want of a wholesome crust. There's less good bread than good beer in Casterbridge now.'

'And less good beer than swipes,' said a man with his hands in his pockets.

'How does it happen there's no good bread?' asked Mrs. Henchard.

'Oh, 'tis the corn-factor—he's the man that our millers and bakers all deal wi', and he has sold 'em growed wheat, which they didn't know was growed, so they say, till the dough ran all over the ovens like quicksilver; so that the loaves be as flat as toads, and like suet pudden inside. I've been a wife, and I've been a mother, and I never see such unprincipled bread in Casterbridge as this before.—But you must be a real stranger here not to know what's made all the poor volks plim like blowed blathers this week?'

'I am,' said Elizabeth's mother shyly.

Not wishing to be observed further till she knew more of her future in this place, she withdrew with her daughter from the speaker's side. Getting a couple of biscuits at the shop indicated as a temporary substitute for a meal, they next bent their steps instinctively to where the music was playing.

V

A FEW score yards brought them to the spot where the town band was now shaking the window-panes with the strains of 'The Roast Beef of Old England.'

The building before whose doors they had pitched their music-stands was the chief hotel in Casterbridge —namely, the King's Arms. A spacious bow-window projected into the street over the main portico, and from the open sashes came the babble of voices, the jingle of glasses, and the drawing of corks. The blinds, moreover, being left unclosed, the whole interior of this room could be surveyed from the top of some steps opposite, for which reason a knot of idlers had gathered there.

'We might, perhaps, after all, make a few inquiries about—our relation, Mr. Henchard,' whispered Mrs. Newson, who, since her entry into Casterbridge, had seemed strangely weak and agitated. 'And this, I think, would be a good place for trying it—just to ask, you know, how he stands in the town—if he is here, as I think he must be. You, Elizabeth-Jane, had better be the one to do it. I'm too worn out to do anything—pull down your fall first.'

She sat down upon the lowest step, and Elizabeth-Jane obeyed her directions and stood among the idlers.

'What's going on to-night?' asked the girl, after

singling out an old man, and standing by him long enough to acquire a neighbourly right of converse.

'Well, ye must be a stranger sure,' said the old man, without taking his eyes from the window. 'Why, 'tis a great public dinner of the gentle-people and such like leading volk—wi' the Mayor in the chair. As we plainer fellows baint invited, they leave the winder-shutters open that we may get jist a sense o't out here. If you mount the steps you can see 'em. That's Mr. Henchard, the Mayor, at the end of the table, a facing ye; and that's the Council men right and left. . . . Ah, lots of them when they begun life were no more than I be now!'

'Henchard!' said Elizabeth-Jane, surprised, but by no means suspecting the whole force of the revelation. She ascended to the top of the door-steps.

Her mother, though her head was bowed, had already caught from the inn-window tones that strangely riveted her attention, before the old man's words, 'Mr. Henchard, the Mayor,' reached her ears. She arose, and stepped up to her daughter's side as soon as she could do so without showing exceptional eagerness.

The interior of the hotel dining-room was spread out before her, with its tables, and glass, and plate, and inmates. Facing the window, in the chair of dignity, sat a man about forty years of age; of heavy frame, large features, and commanding voice; his general build being rather coarse than compact. He had a rich complexion, which verged on swarthiness, a flashing black eye, and dark, bushy brows and hair. When he indulged in an occasional loud laugh at some remark among the guests, his large mouth parted so far back as to show to the rays of the chandelier a full score or more of the two-and-thirty sound white teeth that he obviously still could boast of.

That laugh was not encouraging to strangers; and hence it may have been well that it was rarely heard.

Many theories might have been built upon it. It fell in well with conjectures of a temperament which would have no pity for weakness, but would be ready to yield ungrudging admiration to greatness and strength. Its producer's personal goodness, if he had any, would be of a very fitful cast—an occasional almost oppressive generosity rather than a mild and constant kindness.

Susan Henchard's husband—in law, at least—sat before them, matured in shape, stiffened in line, exaggerated in traits; disciplined, thought-marked—in a word, older. Elizabeth, encumbered with no recollections as her mother was, regarded him with nothing more than the keen curiosity and interest which the discovery of such unexpected social standing in the long-sought relative naturally begot. He was dressed in an old-fashioned evening suit, an expanse of frilled shirt showing on his broad breast; jewelled studs, and a heavy gold chain. Three glasses stood at his right hand; but, to his wife's surprise, the two for wine were empty, while the third, a tumbler, was half full of water.

When last she had seen him he was sitting in a corduroy jacket, fustian waistcoat and breeches, and tanned leather leggings, with a basin of hot furmity before him. Time, the magician, had wrought much here. Watching him, and thus thinking of past days, she became so moved that she shrank back against the jamb of the deep doorway to which the steps gave access, the shadow from it conveniently hiding her features. She forgot her daughter, till a touch from Elizabeth-Jane aroused her. 'Have you seen him, mother?' whispered the girl.

'Yes, yes,' answered her companion hastily. 'I have seen him, and it is enough for me! Now I only want to go—pass away—die.'

'Why—oh what?' She drew closer, and whispered in her mother's ear, 'Does he seem to you not likely to befriend us? I thought he looked a generous man.

What a gentleman he is, isn't he? and how his diamond studs shine! How strange that you should have said he might be in the stocks, or in the workhouse, or dead! Did ever anything go more by contraries! Why do you feel so afraid of him? I am not at all; I'll call upon him—he can but say he don't own such remote kin.'

'I don't know at all—I can't tell what to set about. I feel so down.'

'Don't be that, mother, now we have got here and all! Rest there where you be a little while—I will look on and find out more about him.'

'I don't think I can ever meet Mr. Henchard. He is not how I thought he would be—he overpowers me! I don't wish to see him any more.'

'But wait a little time and consider.'

Elizabeth-Jane had never been so much interested in anything in her life as in their present position, partly from the natural elation she felt at discovering herself akin to a coach; and she gazed again at the scene. The younger guests were talking and eating with animation; their elders were searching for tit-bits, and sniffing and grunting over their plates like sows nuzzling for acorns. Three drinks seemed to be sacred to the company—port, sherry, and rum; outside which old-established trinity few or no palates ranged.

A row of ancient rummers with ground figures on their sides, and each primed with a spoon, was now placed down the table, and these were promptly filled with grog at such high temperatures as to raise serious considerations for the articles exposed to its vapours. But Elizabeth-Jane noticed that, though this filling went on with great promptness up and down the table, nobody filled the Mayor's glass, who still drank large quantities of water from the tumbler behind the clump of crystal vessels intended for wine and spirits.

'They don't fill Mr. Henchard's wine-glasses,' she ventured to say to her elbow acquaintance, the old man.

'Oh no; don't ye know him to be the celebrated abstaining worthy of that name? He scorns all tempting liquors; never touches nothing. Oh yes, he've strong qualities that way. I have heard tell that he sware a gospel oath in by-gone times, and has bode by it ever since. So they don't press him, knowing it would be unbecoming in the face of that; for yer gospel oath is a serious thing.'

Another elderly man, hearing this discourse, now joined in by inquiring, 'How much longer have he got to suffer from it, Solomon Longways?'

'Another two year, they say. I don't know the why and the wherefore of his fixing such a time, for 'a never has told anybody. But 'tis exactly two calendar years longer, they say. A powerful mind to hold out so long!'

'True. . . . But there's great strength in hope. Knowing that in four-and-twenty months' time ye'll be out of your bondage, and able to make up for all you've suffered, by partaking without stint—why, it keeps a man up, no doubt.'

'No doubt, Christopher Coney, no doubt. And 'a must need such reflections—a lonely widow man,' said Longways.

'When did he lose his wife?' asked Elizabeth.

'I never knowed her. 'Twas afore he came to Casterbridge,' Solomon Longways replied, with terminative emphasis, as if the fact of his ignorance of Mrs. Henchard were sufficient to deprive her history of all interest. 'But I know that 'a's a banded tee-totaller, and that if any of his men be ever so little overtook by a drop, he's down upon 'em as stern as the Lord upon the jovial Jews.'

'Has he many men, then?' said Elizabeth-Jane.

'Many! Why, my good maid, he's the powerfullest member of the Town Council, and quite a principal man in the country round besides. Never a big dealing in wheat, barley, oats, hay, roots, and such-like but Henchard's got a hand in it. Ay, and he'll go into other things too; and that's where he makes his mistake. He worked his way up from nothing when 'a came here; and now he's a pillar of the town. Not but what he's been shaken a little to-year about this bad corn he has supplied in his contracts. I've seen the sun rise over Durnover Moor these nine-and-sixty year, and though Mr. Henchard has never cussed me unfairly ever since I've worked for'n, seeing I be but a little small man, I must say that I have never before tasted such rough bread as has been made from Henchard's wheat lately. 'Tis that growed out that ye could a'most call it malt, and there's a list at bottom o' the loaf as thick as the sole of one's shoe.'

The band now struck up another melody, and by the time it was ended the dinner was over, and speeches began to be made. The evening being calm, and the windows still open, these orations could be distinctly heard. Henchard's voice arose above the rest; he was telling a story of his hay-dealing experiences, in which he had outwitted a sharper who had been bent upon outwitting him.

'Ha-ha-ha!' responded his audience at the upshot of the story; and hilarity was general till a new voice arose with, 'This is all very well; but how about the bad bread?'

It came from the lower end of the table, where there sat a group of minor tradesmen who, although part of the company, appeared to be a little below the social level of the others; and who seemed to nourish a certain independence of opinion, and carry on discussions not quite in harmony with those at the head; just as the west end of a church is sometimes persistently found to sing out of time and tune with the leading spirits in the chancel.

This interruption about the bad bread afforded infinite satisfaction to the loungers outside, several of whom were in the mood which finds its pleasure in others' discomfiture; and hence they echoed pretty freely, 'Hey! How about the bad bread, Mr. Mayor?' Moreover, feeling none of the restraints of those who shared the feast, they could afford to add, 'You rather ought to tell the story o' that, sir!'

The interruption was sufficient to compel the Mayor to notice it.

'Well, I admit that the wheat turned out badly,' he said. 'But I was taken in in buying it as much as the bakers who bought it o' me.'

'And the poor folk who had to eat it whether or no,' said the inharmonious man outside the window.

Henchard's face darkened. There was temper under the thin bland surface—the temper which, artificially intensified, had banished a wife nearly a score of years before.

'You must make allowances for the accidents of a large business,' he said. 'You must bear in mind that the weather just at the harvest of that corn was worse than we have known it for years. However, I have mended my arrangements on account o't. Since I have found my business too large to be well looked after by myself alone, I have advertised for a thorough good man as manager of the corn department. When I've got him you will find these mistakes will no longer occur—matters will be better looked into.'

'But what are you going to do to repay us for the past?' inquired the man who had before spoken, and who seemed to be a baker or miller. 'Will you re-place the grown flour we've still got by sound grain?'

Henchard's face had become still more stern at these interruptions, and he drank from his tumbler of water

as if to calm himself or gain time. Instead of vouch-
safing a direct reply, he stiffly observed—

'If anybody will tell me how to turn grown wheat
into wholesome wheat, I'll take it back with pleasure.
But it can't be done.'

Henchard was not to be drawn again. Having said
this, he sat down.

VI

NOW the group outside the window had within the last few minutes been reinforced by new arrivals, some of them respectable shopkeepers and their assistants, who had come out for a whiff of air after putting up the shutters for the night; some of them of a lower class. Distinct from either there appeared a stranger —a young man of remarkably pleasant aspect—who carried in his hand a carpet-bag of the smart floral pattern prevalent in such articles at that time.

He was fair and ruddy, bright-eyed, and slight in build. He might possibly have passed by without stopping at all, or at most for half a minute to glance in at the scene, had not his advent coincided with the discussion on corn and bread; in which event this history had never been enacted. But the subject seemed to arrest him, and he whispered some inquiries of the other bystanders, and remained listening.

When he heard Henchard's closing words, 'It can't be done,' he smiled impulsively, drew out his pocket-book, and wrote down a few words by the aid of the light in the window. He tore out the leaf, folded and directed it, and seemed about to throw it in through the open sash upon the dining-table; but, on second thoughts, edged himself through the loiterers, till he reached the door of the hotel, where one of the waiters

who had been serving inside was now idly leaning
against the door-post.

'Give this to the Mayor at once,' he said, handing
in his hasty note.

Elizabeth-Jane had seen his movements and heard
the words, which attracted her both by their subject
and by their accent—a strange one for those parts. It
was quaint and northerly.

The waiter took the note, while the young stranger
continued—

'And can ye tell me of a respectable hotel that's
a little more moderate than this?'

The waiter glanced indifferently up and down the
street.

'They say the Three Mariners, just below here, is
a very good place,' he languidly answered; 'but I have
never stayed there myself.'

The Scotchman, as he seemed to be, thanked him,
and strolled on in the direction of the Three Mariners
aforesaid, apparently more concerned about the question of an inn than about the fate of his note, now that
the momentary impulse of writing it was over. While
he was disappearing slowly down the street the waiter
left the door, and Elizabeth-Jane saw with some interest
the note brought into the dining-room and handed to
the Mayor.

Henchard looked at it carelessly, unfolded it with
one hand, and glanced it through. Thereupon it was
curious to note an unexpected effect. The nettled,
clouded aspect which had held possession of his face
since the subject of his corn-dealings had been broached,
changed itself into one of arrested attention. He read
the note slowly, and fell into thought, not moody, but
fitfully intense, as that of a man who has been captured
by an idea.

By this time toasts and speeches had given place to
songs, the wheat subject being quite forgotten. Men

were putting their heads together in twos and threes, telling good stories, with pantomimic laughter which reached convulsive grimace. Some were beginning to look as if they did not know how they had come there, what they had come for, or how they were going to get home again; and provisionally sat on with a dazed smile. Square-built men showed a tendency to become hunchbacks; men with a dignified presence lost it in a curious obliquity of figure, in which their features grew disarranged and one-sided; whilst the heads of a few who had dined with extreme thoroughness were somehow sinking into their shoulders, the corners of their mouth and eyes being bent upwards by the subsidence. Only Henchard did not conform to these flexuous changes; he remained stately and vertical, silently thinking.

The clock struck nine. Elizabeth-Jane turned to her companion. 'The evening is drawing on, mother,' she said. 'What do you propose to do?'

She was surprised to find how irresolute her mother had become. 'We must get a place to lie down in,' she murmured. 'I have seen—Mr. Henchard; and that's all I wanted to do.'

'That's enough for to-night, at any rate,' Elizabeth-Jane replied soothingly. 'We can think to-morrow what is best to do about him. The question now is— is it not?—how shall we find a lodging?'

As her mother did not reply, Elizabeth-Jane's mind reverted to the words of the waiter, that the Three Mariners was an inn of moderate charges. A recommendation good for one person was probably good for another. 'Let's go where the young man has gone to,' she said. 'He is respectable. What do you say?'

Her mother assented, and down the street they went.

In the meantime the Mayor's thoughtfulness, engendered by the note as stated, continued to hold him in abstraction; till, whispering to his neighbour to take his place, he found opportunity to leave the chair. This was just after the departure of his wife and Elizabeth.

Outside the door of the assembly-room he saw the waiter, and beckoning to him, asked who brought the note which had been handed in a quarter of an hour before.

'A young man, sir—a sort of traveller. He was a Scotchman seemingly.'

'Did he say how he had got it?'

'He wrote it himself, sir, as he stood outside the window.'

'Oh—wrote it himself. . . . Is the young man in the hotel?'

'No, sir. He went to the Three Mariners, I believe.'

The Mayor walked up and down the vestibule of the hotel with his hands under his coat tails, as if he were merely seeking a cooler atmosphere than that of the room he had quitted. But there could be no doubt that he was in reality still possessed to the full by the new idea, whatever that might be. At length he went back to the door of the dining-room, paused, and found that the songs, toasts, and conversation were proceeding quite satisfactorily without his presence. The Corporation, private residents, and major and minor tradesmen had, in fact, gone in for comforting beverages to such an extent, that they had quite forgotten, not only the Mayor, but all those vast political, religious, and social differences which they felt necessary to maintain in the daytime, and which separated them like iron grills. Seeing this, the Mayor took his hat, and when the waiter had helped him on with a thin holland overcoat, went out and stood under the portico.

Very few persons were now in the street; and his eyes, by a sort of attraction, turned and dwelt upon a spot about a hundred yards further down. It was the

house to which the writer of the note had gone—the
Three Mariners—whose two prominent gables, bow-
window, and passage-light could be seen from where
he stood.   Having kept his eyes on it for a while, he
strolled in that direction.

This ancient house of accommodation for man and
beast, now, unfortunately, pulled down, was built of
mellow sandstone, with mullioned windows of the same
material, markedly out of perpendicular from the settlement of foundations.   The bay window projecting into
the street, whose interior was so popular among the
frequenters of the inn, was closed with shutters, in each
of which appeared a heart-shaped aperture, somewhat
more attenuated in the right and left ventricles than is
seen in Nature.   Inside these illuminated holes, at a
distance of about three inches, were ranged at this hour,
as every passer knew, the ruddy polls of Billy Wills the
glazier, Smart the shoemaker, Buzzford the general
dealer, and others of a secondary set of worthies, of
a grade somewhat below that of the diners at the
King's Arms, each with his yard of clay.

A four-centred Tudor arch was over the entrance,
and over the arch the signboard, now visible in the
rays of an opposite lamp.   Hereon the Mariners, who
had been represented by the artist as persons of two
dimensions only—in other words, flat as a shadow—
were standing in a row in paralyzed attitudes.   Being
on the sunny side of the street, the three comrades
had suffered largely from warping, splitting, fading, and
shrinkage, so that they were but a half-invisible film
upon the reality of the grain, and knots, and nails,
which composed the signboard.   As a matter of fact,
this state of things was not so much owing to Stannidge
the landlord's neglect, as from the lack of a painter
in Casterbridge who would undertake to reproduce the
features of men so traditional.

A long, narrow, dimly-lit passage gave access to the

inn, within which passage the horses going to their stalls at the back, and the coming and departing human guests, rubbed shoulders indiscriminately, the latter running no slight risk of having their toes trodden upón by the animals. The good stabling and the good ale of the Mariners, though somewhat difficult to reach on account of there being but this narrow way to both, were nevertheless perseveringly sought out by the sagacious old heads who knew what was what in Casterbridge.

Henchard stood without the inn for a few instants; then lowering the dignity of his presence as much as possible by buttoning the brown-holland coat over his shirt-front, and in other ways toning himself down to his ordinary everyday appearance, he entered the inn door.

VII

ELIZABETH-JANE and her mother had arrived some twenty minutes earlier. Outside the house they had stood and considered whether even this homely place, though recommended as moderate, might not be too serious in its prices for their light pockets. Finally, however, they had found courage to enter, and duly met Stannidge, the landlord ; a silent man, who drew and carried frothing measures to this room and to that, shoulder to shoulder with his waiting-maids—a stately slowness, however, entering into his ministrations by contrast with theirs, as became one whose service was somewhat optional. It would have been altogether optional but for the orders of the landlady, a person who sat in the bar, corporeally motionless, but with a flitting eye and quick ear, with which she observed and heard through the open door and hatchway the pressing needs of customers whom her husband overlooked though close at hand. Elizabeth and her mother were passively accepted as sojourners, and shown to a small bedroom under one of the gables, where they sat down.

The principle of the inn seemed to be to compensate for the antique awkwardness, crookedness, and obscurity of the passages, floors, and windows, by quantities of clean linen spread about everywhere, and this had a dazzling effect upon the travellers.

' 'Tis too good for us—we can't meet it ! ' said the elder woman, looking round the apartment with misgiving as soon as they were left alone.

' I fear it is, too,' said Elizabeth. ' But we must be respectable.'

' We must pay our way even before we must be respectable,' replied her mother. ' Mr. Henchard is too high for us to make ourselves known to him, I much fear ; so we've only our own pockets to depend on.'

' I know what I'll do,' said Elizabeth-Jane, after an interval of waiting, during which their needs seemed quite forgotten under the press of business below. And leaving the room, she descended the stairs and penetrated to the bar.

If there was one good thing more than another which characterized this single-hearted girl, it was a willingness to sacrifice her personal comfort and dignity to the common weal.

' As you seem busy here to-night, and mother's not well off, might I take out part of our accommodation by helping ? ' she asked of the landlady.

The latter, who remained as fixed in the arm-chair as if she had been melted into it when in a liquid state, and could not now be unstuck, looked the girl up and down inquiringly, with her hands on the chair-arms. Such arrangements as the one Elizabeth proposed were not uncommon in country villages ; but, though Casterbridge was old-fashioned, the custom was well-nigh obsolete here. The mistress of the house, however, was an easy woman to strangers, and she made no objection. Thereupon Elizabeth, being instructed by nods and motions from the taciturn landlord as to where she could find the different things, trotted up and down stairs with materials for her own and her parent's meal.

While she was doing this, the wood partition in the centre of the house thrilled to its centre with the tugging of a bell-pull upstairs. A bell below tinkled a note that was feebler in sound than the twanging of wires and cranks that had produced it.

' 'Tis the Scotch gentleman,' said the landlady omnisciently; and turning her eyes to Elizabeth, ' Now then, can you go and see if his supper is on the tray? If it is, you can take it up to him. The front room over this.'

Elizabeth-Jane, though hungry, willingly postponed serving herself awhile, and applied to the cook in the kitchen, whence she brought forth the tray of supper viands, and proceeded with it upstairs to the apartment indicated. The accommodation of the Three Mariners was far from spacious, despite the fair area of ground it covered. The room demanded by intrusive beams and rafters, partitions, passages, staircases, disused ovens, settles, and four-posters, left comparatively small quarters for human beings. Moreover, this being at a time before home-brewing was abandoned by the smaller victuallers, and a house in which the twelve-bushel strength was still religiously adhered to by the landlord in his ale, the quality of the liquor was the chief attraction of the premises, so that everything had to make way for utensils and operations in connection therewith. Thus Elizabeth found that the Scotchman was located in a room quite close to the small one that had been allotted to herself and her mother.

When she entered, nobody was present but the young man himself—the same whom she had seen lingering without the windows of the King's Arms Hotel. He was now idly reading a copy of the local paper, and was hardly conscious of her entry, so that she looked at him quite coolly, and saw how his forehead shone where the light caught it, and how nicely his hair was cut, and the sort of velvet-pile or down that was on the skin at the back of his neck, and how his cheek was so truly curved as to be part of a globe, and how clearly drawn were the lids and lashes which hid his bent eyes.

She set down the tray, spread his supper, and went away without a word. On her arrival below, the land-lady, who was as kind as she was fat and lazy, saw that Elizabeth-Jane was rather tired, though in her earnest-ness to be useful she was waiving her own needs altogether. Mrs. Stannidge thereupon said, with a considerate peremptoriness, that she and her mother had better take their own suppers if they meant to have any.

Elizabeth fetched their simple provisions, as she had fetched the Scotchman's, and went up to the little chamber where she had left her mother, noiselessly pushing open the door with the edge of the tray. To her surprise her mother, instead of being reclined on the bed where she had left her, was in an erect position, with lips parted. At Elizabeth's entry she lifted her finger.

The meaning of this was soon apparent. The room allotted to the two women had at one time served as a dressing-room to the Scotchman's chamber, as was evidenced by signs of a door of communication between them—now screwed up, and pasted over with the wall paper. But, as is frequently the case with hotels of far higher pretensions than the Three Mariners, every word spoken in either of these rooms was distinctly audible in the other. Such sounds came through now.

Thus silently conjured, Elizabeth deposited the tray, and her mother whispered as she drew near, ''Tis he.'

'Who?' said the girl.

'The Mayor.'

The tremors in Susan Henchard's tone might have led any person, but one so perfectly unsuspicious of the truth as the girl was, to surmise some closer

53

connection than the admitted simple kinship, as a means of accounting for them.

Two men were indeed talking in the adjoining chamber, the young Scotchman and Henchard, who, having entered the inn while Elizabeth-Jane was in the kitchen waiting for the supper, had been deferentially conducted upstairs by host Stannidge himself. The girl noiselessly laid out their little meal, and beckoned to her mother to join her, which Mrs. Henchard mechanically did, her attention being fixed on the conversation through the door.

'I merely strolled in on my way home to ask you a question about something that has excited my curiosity,' said the Mayor, with careless geniality. 'But I see you have not finished supper.'

'Ay, but I will be done in a little! Ye needn't go, sir. Take a seat. I've almost done, and it makes no difference at all.'

Henchard seemed to take the seat offered, and in a moment he resumed: 'Well, first I should ask, did you write this?' A rustling of paper followed.

'Yes, I did,' said the Scotchman.

'Then,' said Henchard, 'I am under the impression that we have met by accident while waiting for the morning to keep an appointment with each other? My name is Henchard; ha'n't you replied to an advertisement for a corn-factor's manager that I put into the paper—ha'n't you come here to see me about it?'

'No,' said the Scotchman, with some surprise.

'Surely you are the man,' went on Henchard insistingly, 'who arranged to come and see me? Joshua, Joshua, Jipp—Jopp—what was his name?'

'You're wrong!' said the young man 'My name is Donald Farfrae. It is true I am in the corren trade —but I have replied to no advairrtisment, and arranged to see no one. I am on my way to Bristol—from

54

there to the other side of the warrld, to try my fortune in the great wheat-growing districts of the West! I have some inventions useful to the trade, and there is no scope for developing them heere.'

'To America—well, well,' said Henchard, in a tone of disappointment, so strong as to make itself felt like a damp atmosphere. 'And yet I could have sworn you were the man!'

The Scotchman murmured another negative, and there was a silence, till Henchard resumed: 'Then I am truly and sincerely obliged to you for the few words you wrote on that paper.'

'It was nothing, sir.'

'Well, it has a great importance for me just now. This row about my grown wheat, which I declare to Heaven I didn't know to be bad till the people came complaining, has put me to my wits' end. I've some hundreds of quarters of it on hand; and if your renovating process will make it wholesome, why, you can see what a quag 'twould get me out of. I saw in a moment there might be truth in it. But I should like to have it proved; and of course you don't care to tell the steps of the process sufficiently for me to do that, without my paying ye well for't first.'

The young man reflected a moment or two. 'I don't know that I have any objection,' he said. 'I'm going to another country, and curing bad corn is not the line I'll take up there. Yes, I'll tell ye the whole of it—you'll make more out of it here than I will in a foreign country. Just look heere a minute, sir. I can show ye by a sample in my carpet-bag.'

The click of a lock followed, and there was a sifting and rustling; then a discussion about so many ounces to the bushel, and drying, and refrigerating, and so on.

'These few grains will be sufficient to show ye with,' came in the young fellow's voice; and after a pause, during which some operation seemed to be intently watched by them both, he exclaimed, ' There, now, do you taste that.'

' It's complete !—quite restored, or—well—nearly.'

' Quite enough restored to make good seconds out of it,' said the Scotchman. ' To fetch it back entirely is impossible ; Nature won't stand so much as that, but heere you go a great way towards it. Well, sir, that's the process ; I don't value it, for it can be but of little use in .countries where the weather is more settled than in ours ; and I'll be only too glad if it's of service to you.'

' But hearken to me,' pleaded Henchard. ' My business, you know, is in corn and in hay ; but I was brought up as a hay-trusser simply, and hay is what I understand best, though I now do more in corn than in the other. If you'll accept the place, you shall manage the corn branch entirely, and receive a commission in addition to salary.'

' You're liberal—very liberal ; but no, no—I cannet ! ' the young man still replied, with some distress in his accents.

' So be it ! ' said Henchard conclusively. ' Now— to change the subject—one good turn deserves.another ; don't stay to finish that miserable supper. Come to my house ; I can find something better for ye than cold ham and ale.'

Donald Farfrae was grateful—said he feared he must decline—that he wished to leave early next day.

' Very well,' said Henchard quickly, ' please yourself. But I tell you, young man, if this holds good for the bulk, as it has done for the sample, you have saved my credit, stranger though you be. What shall I pay you for this knowledge ? '

' Nothing at all, nothing at all. It may not prove necessary to ye to use it often, and I don't value it at all. I thought I might just as well let ye know, as you were in a difficulty, and they wer harrd upon ye.'

Henchard paused. 'I shan't soon forget this,' he said. 'And from a stranger! . . . I couldn't believe you were not the man I had engaged! Says I to 'myself " He knows who I am, and recommends himself by this stroke." And yet it turns out, after all, that you are not the man who answered my advertisement, but a stranger!'

'Ay, ay; that's so,' said the young man.

Henchard again suspended his words, and then his voice came thoughtfully: 'Your forehead, Farfrae, is something like my poor brother's—now dead and gone; and the nose, too, isn't unlike his. You must be, what —five foot nine, I reckon? I am six foot one and a half out of my shoes. But what of that? In my business, 'tis true that strength and bustle build up a firm. But judgment and knowledge are what keep it established. Unluckily, I am bad at science, Farfrae; bad at figures —a rule o' thumb sort of man. You are just the reverse—I can see that. I have been looking for such as you these two year, and yet you are not for me. Well, before I go, let me ask this: Though you are not the young man I thought you were, what's the difference? Can't ye stay just the same? Have you really made up your mind about this American notion? I won't mince matters. I feel you would be invaluable to me—that needn't be said—and if you will bide and be my manager, I will make it worth your while.'

' My plans are fixed,' said the young man, in negative tones. 'I have formed a scheme, and so we need na say any more about it. But will you not drink with me, sir? I find this Casterbridge ale warreming to the stomach.'

'No, no; I fain would, but I can't,' said Henchard gravely, the scraping of his chair informing the listeners that he was rising to leave. 'When I was a young man I went in for that sort of thing too strong—far too strong—and was well-nigh ruined by it! I did a deed on account of it which I shall be ashamed of to my dying day. It made such an impression on me that I swore, there and then, that·I'd drink nothing stronger than tea for as many years as I was old that day. I have kept my oath; and though, Farfrae, I am sometimes that dry in the dog days that I could drink a quarter-barrel to the pitching, I think o' my oath, and touch no strong drink at all.'

'I'll no' press ye, sir—I'll no' press ye. I respect your vow.'

'Well, I shall get a manager somewhere, no doubt,' said Henchard, with strong feeling in his tones. 'But it will be long before I see one that would suit me so well!'

The young man appeared much moved by Henchard's warm convictions of his value. He was silent till they reached the door. 'I wish I could stay—sincerely I would like to,' he replied. 'But no—it cannet be! it cannet! I want to see the warrld.'

VIII

THUS they parted; and Elizabeth-Jane and her mother remained each in her thoughts over their meal, the mother's face being strangely bright since Henchard's avowal of shame for a past action. The quivering of the partition to its core presently denoted that Donald Farfrae had again rung his bell, no doubt to have his supper removed; for humming a tune, and walking up and down, he seemed to be attracted by the lively bursts of conversation and melody from the general company below. He sauntered out upon the landing, and descended the staircase.

When Elizabeth-Jane had carried down his supper tray, and also that used by her mother and herself, she found the bustle of serving to be at its height below, as it always was at this hour. The young woman shrank from having anything to do with the ground-floor serving, and crept silently about observing the scene—so new to her, fresh from the seclusion of a seaside cottage. In the general sitting-room, which was large, she remarked the two or three dozen strong-backed chairs that stood round against the wall, each fitted with its genial occupant; the sanded floor; the black settle which, projecting endwise from the wall within the door, permitted Elizabeth to be a spectator of all that went on, without herself being particularly seen.

The young Scotchman had just joined the guests. These, in addition to the respectable master-tradesmen occupying the seats of privilege in the bow-window and its neighbourhood, included an inferior set at the un-lighted end, whose seats were mere benches against the wall, and who drank from cups instead of from glasses. Among the latter she noticed some of those personages who had stood outside the windows of the King's Arms.

Behind their backs was a small window, with a wheel ventilator in one of the panes, which would suddenly start off spinning with a jingling sound, as suddenly stop, and as suddenly start again.

While thus furtively making her survey, the opening words of a song greeted her ears from behind the settle, in a melody and accent of peculiar charm. There had been some singing before she came down; and now the Scotchman had made himself so soon at home that, at the request of some of the master-tradesmen, he, too, was favouring the room with a ditty.

Elizabeth-Jane was fond of music; she could not help pausing to listen; and the longer she listened the more she was enraptured. She had never heard any singing like this; and it was evident that the majority of the audience had not heard such frequently, for they were attentive to a much greater degree than usual. They neither whispered, nor drank, nor dipped their pipe-stems in their ale to moisten them, nor pushed the mug to their neighbours. The singer himself grew emotional, till she could imagine a tear in his eye as the words went on :—

' It's hame, and it's hame, hame fain would I be,
Oh hame, hame, hame to my ain countree !
There's an eye that ever weeps, and a fair face will be fain,
As I pass through Annan Water with my bonnie bands again ;
When the flower is in the bud, and the leaf upon the tree,
The lark shall sing me hame to my ain countree !'

There was a burst of applause, and a deep silence which was even more eloquent than the applause. It was of such a kind that the snapping of a pipe-stem too long for him by old Solomon Longways, who was one of those gathered at the shady end of the room, seemed a harsh and irreverent act. Then the ventilator in the window-pane spasmodically started off for a new spin, and the pathos of Donald's song was temporarily effaced.

''Twas not amiss — not at all amiss!' muttered Christopher Coney, who was also present. And removing his pipe a finger's breadth from his lips, he said aloud, 'Draw on with the next verse, young gentleman, please.'

'Yes. Let's have it again, stranger,' said the glazier, a stout, bucket-headed man, with a white apron rolled up round his waist. 'Folks don't lift up their hearts like that in this part of the world.' And turning aside, he said in undertones, 'Who is the young man?— Scotch, d'ye say?'

'Yes, straight from the mountains of Scotland, I believe,' replied Coney.

Young Farfrae repeated the last verse. It was plain that nothing so·pathetic had been heard at the Three Mariners for a considerable time. The difference of accent, the excitability of the singer, the intense local feeling, and the seriousness with which he worked himself up to a climax, surprised this set of worthies, who were only too prone to shut up their emotions with caustic words.

'Danged if our country down here is worth singing about like that!' continued the glazier, as the Scotchman again melodized with a dying fall, 'My ain countree!' 'When you take away from among us the fools and the rogues, and the lammigers, and the wanton hussies, and the slatterns, and such like, there's cust few left to ornament a song with in Casterbridge, or the country round.'

61

'True,' said Buzzford, the dealer, looking at the grain of the table. 'Casterbridge is a old, hoary place o' wickedness, by all account. 'Tis recorded in history that we rebelled against the King one or two hundred years ago, in the time of the Romans, and that lots of us was hanged on Gallows Hill, and quartered, and our different jints sent about the country like butcher's meat; and for my part I can well believe it.'

'What did ye come away from yer own country for, young maister, if ye be so wownded about it?' inquired Christopher Coney, from the background, with the tone of a man who preferred the original subject. 'Faith, it wasn't worth your while on our account, for, as Maister Billy Wills says, we be bruckle folk here—the best o' us hardly honest sometimes, what with hard winters, and so many mouths to fill, and God-a'mighty sending his little taties so terrible small to fill 'em with. We don't think about flowers and fair faces, not we—except in the shape o' cauliflowers and pigs' chaps.'

'But, no!' said Donald Farfrae, gazing round into their faces with earnest concern; 'the best of ye hardly honest—not that surely? None of ye has been stealing what didn't belong to him?'

'Lord! no, no!' said Solomon Longways, smiling grimly. 'That's only his random way o' speaking. 'A was always such a man of under-thoughts.' (And reprovingly towards Christopher): 'Don't ye be so over-familiar with a gentleman that ye know nothing of —and that's travelled a'most from the North Pole.'

Christopher Coney was silenced, and as he could get no public sympathy, he mumbled his feelings to himself: 'Be dazed, if I loved my country half as well as the young feller do, I'd live by claning my neighbour's pigsties afore I'd go away! For my part I've no more love for my country than I have for Botany Bay!'

'Come,' said Longways; 'let the young man draw onward with his ballet, or we shall be here all night.'

'That's all of it,' said the singer apologetically.

'Soul of my body, then we'll have another!' said the general dealer.

'Can you turn a strain to the ladies, sir?' inquired a fat woman with a figured purple apron, the waist-string of which was overhung so far by her sides as to be invisible.

'Let him breathe—let him breathe, Mother Cuxsom. He hain't got his second wind yet,' said the master glazier.

'Oh yes, but I have!' exclaimed the young man; and he at once rendered 'O Nannie' with faultless modulations, and another or two of the like sentiment, winding up at their earnest request with 'Auld Lang Syne.'

By this time he had completely taken possession of the hearts of the Three Mariners' inmates, including even old Coney. Notwithstanding an occasional odd gravity which awoke their sense of the ludicrous for the moment, they began to view him through a golden haze which the tone of his mind seemed to raise around him. Casterbridge had sentiment—Casterbridge had romance; but this stranger's sentiment was of differing quality. Or rather, perhaps, the difference was mainly superficial; he was to them like the poet of a new school who takes his contemporaries by storm; who is not really new, but is the first to articulate what all his listeners have felt, though but dumbly till then.

The silent landlord came and leant over the settle while the young man sang; and even Mrs. Stannidge managed to unstick herself from the framework of her chair in the bar, and get as far as the door-post, which movement she accomplished by rolling herself round, as a cask is trundled on the chine by a drayman without losing the perpendicular.

'And are you going to bide in Casterbridge, sir?' she asked.

'Ah—no!' said the Scotchman, with melancholy fatality in his voice, 'I'm only passing thirrough! I am on my way to Bristol, and on frae there to foreign parts.'

'We be truly sorry to hear it,' said Solomon Longways. 'We can ill afford to lose tuneful wynd-pipes like yours when they fall among us. And verily, to mak' acquaintance with a man a come from so far, from the land o' perpetual snow, as we may say, where wolves and wild boars and other dangerous animalcules be as common as blackbirds hereabout—why, 'tis a thing we can't do every day; and there's good sound information for bide-at-homes like we when such a man opens his mouth.'

'Nay, but ye mistake my country,' said the young man, looking round upon them with tragic fixity, till his eye lighted up and his cheek kindled with a sudden enthusiasm to right their errors. 'There are not perpetual snow and wolves at all in it!—except snow in winter, and—well—a little in summer just sometimes, and a "gaberlunzie" or two stalking about here and there, if ye may call them dangerous. Eh, but you should take a summer jarreny to Edinboro', and Arthur's Seat, and all round there, and then go on to the lochs, and all the Highland scenery—in May and June— and you would never say 'tis the land of wolves and perpetual snow!'

'Of course not—it stands to reason,' said Buzzford. ''Tis barren ignorance that leads to such words. He's a simple home-spun man, that never was fit for good company—think nothing of him, sir.'

'And do ye carry your flock bed, and your quilt, and your crock, and your bit of chiney? or do ye go in bare bones, as ⁑ may say?' inquired Christopher Coney.

'I've sent on my luggage—though it isn't much; for the voyage is long.' Donald's eyes dropped into a remote gaze as he added: 'But I said to myself, "Never a one of the prizes of life will I come by unless I undertake it!" and I decided to go.'

A general sense of regret, in which Elizabeth-Jane shared not least, made itself apparent in the company. As she looked at Farfrae from the back of the settle, she decided that his statements showed him to be no less thoughtful than his fascinating melodies revealed him to be cordial and impassioned. She admired the serious light in which he looked at serious things. He had seen no jest in ambiguities and roguery, as the Casterbridge toss-pots had done; and rightly not—there was none. She disliked those wretched humours of Christopher Coney and his tribe; and he did not appreciate them. He seemed to feel exactly as she felt about life and its surroundings—that they were a tragical, rather than a comical, thing; that though one could be gay on occasion, moments of gaiety were interludes, and no part of the actual drama. It was extraordinary how similar their views were.

Though it was still early, the young Scotchman expressed his wish to retire, whereupon the landlady whispered to Elizabeth to run upstairs and turn down his bed. She took a candlestick and proceeded on her mission, which was the act of a few moments only. When, candle in hand, she reached the top of the stairs on her way down again, Mr. Farfrae was at the foot coming up. She could not very well retreat; they met and passed in the turn of the staircase.

She must have appeared interesting in some way—notwithstanding her plain dress—or rather, possibly, in consequence of it, for she was a girl characterized by earnestness and soberness of mien, with which simple drapery accorded well. Her face flushed, too, at the slight awkwardness of the meeting, and she

passed him with her eyes bent on the candle-flame
that she carried just below her nose. Thus it happened
that when confronting her he smiled ; and then, with
the manner of a temporarily light-hearted man, who
has started himself on a flight of song whose momentum
he cannot readily check, he softly tuned an old ditty
that she seemed to suggest—

> ' As I came in by my bower door,
>   As day was waxin' wearie,
>   Oh wha came tripping down the stair
>   But bonnie Peg my dearie.'

Elizabeth-Jane, rather disconcerted, hastened on ; and
the Scotchman's voice died away, humming more of
the same within the closed door of his room.

Here the scene and sentiment ended for the present.
When, soon after, the girl rejoined her mother, the
latter was still in thought—on quite another matter
than a young man's song.

' We've made a mistake,' she whispered (that the
Scotchman might not overhear). ' On no account
ought ye to have helped serve here to-night. Not
because of ourselves, but for the sake of *him*. If he
should befriend us, and take us up, and then find out
what you did when staying here, 'twould grieve and
wound his natural pride as Mayor of the town.'

Elizabeth, who would perhaps have been more
alarmed at this than her mother had she known the
real relationship, was not much disturbed about it as
things stood. Her ' he ' was another man than her
poor mother's. ' For myself,' she said, ' I didn't at
all mind waiting a little upon him. He's so respectable, and educated—far above the rest of 'em in the inn.
They thought him very simple not to know their grim
broad way of talking about themselves here. But of
course he didn't know—he was too refined in his mind
to know such things ! ' Thus she earnestly pleaded.

Meanwhile, the 'he' of her mother was not so far away as even they thought. After leaving the Three Mariners he had sauntered up and down the empty High Street, passing and repassing the inn in his promenade. When the Scotchman sang, his voice had reached Henchard's ears through the heart-shaped holes in the window-shutters, and had led him to pause outside them a long while.

'To be sure, to be sure, how that fellow does draw me!' he had said to himself. 'I suppose 'tis because I'm so lonely. I'd have given him a third share in the business to have stayed!'

IX

WHEN Elizabeth-Jane opened the hinged casement next morning, the mellow air brought in the feel of imminent autumn almost as distinctly as if she had been in the remotest hamlet. Casterbridge was the complement of the rural life around; not its urban opposite. Bees and butterflies in the corn-fields at the top of the town, who desired to get to the meads at the bottom, took no circuitous course, but flew straight down High Street without any apparent consciousness that they were traversing strange latitudes. And in autumn airy spheres of thistledown floated into the same street, lodged upon the shop fronts, blew into drains; and innumerable tawny and yellow leaves skimmed along the pavement, and stole through people's doorways into their passages, with a hesitating scratch on the floor, like the skirts of timid visitors.

Hearing voices, one of which was close at hand, she withdrew her head, and glanced from behind the window-curtains. Mr. Henchard — now habited no longer as a great personage, but as a thriving man of business—was pausing on his way up the middle of the street, and the Scotchman was looking from the window adjoining her own. Henchard, it appeared, had gone a little way past the inn before he had noticed his acquaintance of the previous evening. He came back a few steps, Donald Farfrae opening the window further.

'And you are off soon, I suppose?' said Henchard upwards.

'Yes—almost this moment, sir,' said the other. 'Maybe I'll walk on till the coach makes up on me.'

'Which way?'

'The way ye are going.'

'Then shall we walk together to the top o' town?'

'If ye'll wait a minute,' said the Scotchman.

In a few minutes the latter emerged, bag in hand. Henchard looked at the bag as at an enemy. It showed there was no mistake about the young man's departure. 'Ah, my lad,' he said, 'you should have been a wise man, and have stayed with me.'

'Yes, yes—it might have been wiser,' said Donald, looking microscopically at the houses that were furthest off. 'It is only telling ye the truth when I say my plans are vague.'

They had by this time passed on from the precincts of the inn, and Elizabeth-Jane heard no more. She saw that they continued in conversation, Henchard turning to the other occasionally, and emphasizing some remark with a gesture. Thus they passed the King's Arms Hotel, the Market House, the churchyard wall, ascending to the upper end of the long street till they were small as two grains of corn; when they bent suddenly to the right into the Bristol Road, and were out of view.

'He was a good man—and he's gone,' she said to herself. 'I was nothing to him, and there was no reason why he should have wished me good-bye.'

The simple thought, with its latent sense of slight, had moulded itself out of the following little fact: when the Scotchman came out at the door he had by accident glanced up at her; and then he had looked away again without nodding, or smiling, or saying a word.

'You are still thinking, mother,' she said, when she turned inwards.

'Yes; I am thinking of Mr. Henchard's sudden liking for that young man. He was always so. Now, surely, if he takes so warmly to people who are not related to him at all, may he not take as warmly to his own kin?'

While they debated this question a procession of five large waggons went past, laden with hay up to the bedroom windows. They came in from the country, and the steaming horses had probably been travelling a great part of the night. To the shaft of each hung a little board, on which was painted in white letters, 'Henchard, corn-factor and hay-merchant.' The spectacle renewed his wife's conviction that, for her daughter's sake, she should strain a point to rejoin him.

The discussion was continued during breakfast, and the end of it was that Mrs. Henchard decided, for good or for ill, to send Elizabeth-Jane with a message to Henchard, to the effect that his relative Susan, a sailor's widow, was in the town; leaving it to him to say whether or not he would recognize her. What had brought her to this determination were chiefly two things. He had been described as a lonely widower; and he had expressed shame for a past transaction of his life. There was promise in both.

'If he says no,' she enjoined, as Elizabeth-Jane stood, bonnet on, ready to depart; 'if he thinks it does not become the good position he has reached to in the town, to own—to let us call on him as—his distant kinsfolk, say, "Then, sir, we would rather not intrude; we will leave Casterbridge as quietly as we have come, and go back to our own country." . . . I almost feel that I would rather he did say so, as I have not seen him for so many years, and we are so —little allied to him!'

'And if he say yes?' inquired the more sanguine one.

70

'In that case,' answered Mrs. Henchard cautiously, 'ask him to write me a note, saying when and how he will see us—or *me*.'

Elizabeth-Jane went a few steps towards the landing. 'And tell him,' continued her mother, 'that I fully know I have no claim upon him—that I am glad to find he is thriving; that I hope his life may be long and happy—there, go.' Thus with a half-hearted willingness, a smothered reluctance, did the poor forgiving woman start her unconscious daughter on this errand.

It was about ten o'clock, and market-day, when Elizabeth paced up the High Street, in no great hurry; for to herself her position was only that of a poor relation deputed to hunt up a rich one. The front doors of the private houses were mostly left open at this warm autumn time, no thought of umbrella stealers disturbing the minds of the placid burgesses. Hence, through the long, straight, entrance passages thus unclosed could be seen, as through tunnels, the mossy gardens at the back, glowing with nasturtiums, fuchsias, scarlet geraniums, 'bloody warriors,' snapdragons, and dahlias, this floral blaze being backed by crusted grey stone-work remaining from a yet remoter Casterbridge than the venerable one visible in the street. The old-fashioned fronts of these houses, which had older than old-fashioned backs, rose sheer from the pavement, into which the bow-windows protruded like bastions, necessitating a pleasing *chassez-déchassez* movement to the time-pressed pedestrian at every few yards. He was bound also to evolve other Terpsichorean figures in respect of door-steps, scrapers, cellar-hatches, church buttresses, and the overhanging angles of walls which, originally unobtrusive, had become bow-legged and knock-kneed.

In addition to these fixed obstacles which spoke so cheerfully of individual unrestraint as to boundaries, movables occupied the path and roadway to a perplexing extent. First the vans of the carriers in and out of Casterbridge, who hailed from Mellstock, Weatherbury, The Hintocks, Sherton-Abbas, Kingsbere, Overcombe, and many other towns and villages round. Their owners were numerous enough to be regarded as a tribe, and had almost distinctiveness enough to be regarded as a race. Their vans had just arrived, and were drawn up on each side of the street in close file, so as to form at places a wall between the pavement and the roadway. Moreover every shop pitched out half its contents upon trestles and boxes on the kerb, extending the display each week a little further and further into the roadway, despite the expostulations of the two feeble old constables, until there remained but a tortuous defile for carriages down the centre of the street, which afforded fine opportunities for skill with the reins. Over the pavement on the sunny side of the way hung shopblinds so constructed as to give the passenger's hat a smart buffet off his head, as from the unseen hands of Cranstoun's Goblin Page, celebrated in romantic lore.

Horses for sale were tied in rows, their forelegs on the pavement, their hind legs in the street, in which position they occasionally nipped little boys by the shoulder who were passing to school. And any inviting recess in front of a house that had been modestly kept back from the general line was utilized by pig-dealers as a pen for their stock.

The yeomen, farmers, dairymen, and townsfolk, who came to transact business in these ancient streets, spoke in other ways than by articulation. Not to hear the words of your interlocutor in metropolitan centres is to know nothing of his meaning. Here the face, the arms, the hat, the stick, the body throughout spoke equally with the tongue. To express satisfaction the Casterbridge market-man added to his utterance a broadening of the cheeks, a crevicing of the eyes, a throwing back of the shoulders, which was intelligible from the other end of the street. If he wondered, though all Henchard's carts and waggons were rattling past him, you knew it from perceiving the inside of his crimson mouth, and a target-like circling of his eyes. Deliberation caused sundry attacks on the moss of adjoining walls with the end of his stick, a change of his hat from the horizontal to the less so ; a sense of tediousness announced itself in a lowering of the person by spreading the knees to a lozenge-shaped aperture and contorting the arms. Chicanery, subterfuge, had hardly a place in the streets of this honest borough to all appearance ; and it was said that the lawyers in the Court House hard by occasionally threw in strong arguments for the other side out of pure generosity (though apparently by mischance) when advancing their own.

Thus Casterbridge was in most respects but the pole, focus, or nerve-knot of the surrounding country life; differing from the many manufacturing towns which are as foreign bodies set down, like boulders on a plain, in a green world with which they have nothing in common. Casterbridge lived by agriculture at one remove further from the fountain-head than the adjoining villages—no more. The townsfolk understood every fluctuation in the rustic's condition, for it affected their receipts as much as the labourer's ; they entered into the troubles and joys which moved the aristocratic families ten miles round—for the same reason. And even at the dinner-parties of the professional families the subjects of discussion were corn, cattle-disease, sowing and reaping, fencing and planting ; while politics were viewed by them less from their own standpoint of burgesses with rights and privileges than from the standpoint of their county neighbours.

All the venerable contrivances and confusions which

delighted the eye by their quaintness, and in a measure reasonableness, in this rare old market-town, were metropolitan novelties to the unpractised eyes of Elizabeth-Jane, fresh from netting fish-seines in a sea-side cottage. Very little inquiry was necessary to guide her footsteps. Henchard's house was one of the best, faced with dull red-and-grey old brick. The front door was open, and, as in other houses, she could see through the passage to the end of the garden—nearly a quarter of a mile off.

Mr. Henchard was not in the house, but in the store-yard. She was conducted into the mossy garden, and through a door in the wall, which was studded with rusty nails speaking of generations of fruit-trees that had been trained there. The door opened upon the yard, and here she was left to find him as she could. It was a place flanked by hay-barns, into which tons of fodder, all in trusses, were being packed from the waggons she had seen pass the inn that morning. On other sides of the yard were wooden granaries on stone staddles, to which access was given by Flemish ladders, and a store-house several floors high. Wherever the doors of these places were open, a closely packed throng of bursting wheat-sacks could be seen standing inside, with the air of awaiting a famine that would not come.

She wandered about this place, uncomfortably conscious of the impending interview, till she was quite weary of searching; she ventured to inquire of a boy in what quarter Mr. Henchard could be found. He directed her to an office which she had not seen before, and knocking at the door she was answered by a cry of 'Come in.'

Elizabeth turned the handle; and there stood before her, bending over some sample-bags on a table, not the corn-merchant, but the young Scotchman Mr. Farfrae—in the act of pouring some grains of wheat from one hand to the other. His hat hung on a peg behind him, and the roses of his carpet-bag glowed from the corner of the room.

Having toned her feelings and arranged words on her lips for Mr. Henchard, and for him alone, she was for the moment confounded.

'Yes, what is it?' said the Scotchman, like a man who permanently ruled there.

She said she wanted to see Mr. Henchard.

'Ah, yes; will you wait a minute? He's engaged just now,' said the young man, apparently not recognizing her as the girl at the inn. He handed her a chair, bade her sit down, and turned to his sample-bags again. While Elizabeth-Jane sits waiting in great amaze at the young man's presence we may briefly explain how he came there.

When the two new acquaintances had passed out of sight that morning towards the Bath and Bristol road they went on silently, except for a few commonplaces, till they had gone down an avenue on the town walls called the Chalk Walk, leading to an angle where the North and West escarpments met. From this high corner of the square earthworks a vast extent of country could be seen. A footpath ran steeply down the green slope, conducting from the shady promenade on the walls to a road at the bottom of the scarp. It was by this path the Scotchman had to descend.

'Well, here's success to ye,' said Henchard, holding out his right hand and leaning with his left upon the wicket which protected the descent. In the act there was the inelegance of one whose feelings are nipped and wishes defeated. 'I shall often think of this time, and of how you came at the very moment to throw a light upon my difficulty.'

Still holding the young man's hand he paused, and then added deliberately: 'Now I am not the man to let a cause be lost for want of a word. And before ye are gone for ever I'll speak. Once more, will ye stay?

There it is, flat and plain. You can see that it isn't all selfishness that makes me press 'ee; for my business is not quite so scientific as to require an intellect entirely out of the common. Others would do for the place without doubt. Some selfishness perhaps there is, but there is more; it isn't for me to repeat what. Come bide with me—and name your own terms. I'll agree to 'em willingly and 'ithout a word of gainsaying; for, hang it, Farfrae, I like thee well!'

The young man's hand remained steady in Henchard's for a moment or two. He looked over the fertile country that stretched beneath them, then backward along the shaded walk reaching to the top of the town. His face flushed.

'I never expected this—I did not!' he said. 'It's Providence! Should any one go against it? No; I'll not go to America, I'll stay and be your man!'

His hand, which had lain lifeless in Henchard's. returned the latter's grasp.

'Done,' said Henchard.

'Done,' said Donald Farfrae.

The face of Mr. Henchard beamed forth a satisfaction that was almost fierce in its strength. 'Now you are my friend!' he exclaimed. 'Come back to my house; let's clinch it at once by clear terms, so as to be comfortable in our minds.' Farfrae caught up his bag and retraced the North-West Avenue in Henchard's company as he had come. Henchard was all confidence now.

'I am the most distant fellow in the world when I don't care for a man,' he said. 'But when a man takes my fancy he takes it strong. Now I am sure you can eat another breakfast? You couldn't have eaten much so early, even if they had anything at that place to gi'e thee, which they hadn't; so come to my house and we will have a solid, staunch tuck-in, and settle terms in black-and-white if you like; though my word's my bond. I can always make a good meal ın the morning. I've got a splendid cold pigeon-pie going just now. You can have some home-brewed if you want to, you know.'

'It is too airly in the morning for that,' said Farfrae with a smile.

'Well, of course, I didn't know. I don't drink it because of my oath; but I am obliged to brew for my work-people.'

Thus talking they returned, and entered Henchard's premises by the back way or traffic entrance. Here the matter was settled over the breakfast, at which Henchard heaped the young Scotchman's plate to a prodigal fulness. He would not rest satisfied till Farfrae had written for his luggage from Bristol, and despatched the letter to the post-office. When it was done this man of strong impulses declared that his new friend should take up his abode in his house—at least till some suitable lodgings could be found.

He then took Farfrae round and showed him the place, and the stores of grain, and other stock; and finally entered the offices where the younger of them had already been discovered by Elizabeth.

X

WHILE she still sat under the Scotchman's eyes a man came up to the door, reaching it as Henchard opened the door of the inner office to admit Elizabeth. The new-comer stepped forward like the quicker cripple at Bethesda, and entered in her stead. She could hear his words to Henchard: 'Joshua Jopp, sir—by appointment—the new manager.'

'The new manager!—he's in his office,' said Henchard bluntly.

'In his office!' said the man, with a stultified air.

'I mentioned Thursday,' said Henchard; 'and as you did not keep your appointment, I have engaged another manager. At first I thought he must be you. Do you think I can wait when business is in question?'

'You said Thursday or Saturday, sir,' said the new-comer, pulling out a letter.

'Well, you are too late,' said the corn-factor. 'I can say no more.'

'You as good as engaged me,' murmured the man.

'Subject to an interview,' said Henchard. 'I am sorry for you—very sorry indeed. But it can't be helped.'

There was no more to be said, and the man came out, encountering Elizabeth-Jane in his passage. She could see that his mouth twitched with anger, and that bitter disappointment was written in his face everywhere.

Elizabeth-Jane now entered, and stood before the master of the premises. His dark pupils—which always seemed to have a red spark of light in them, though this could hardly be a physical fact—turned indifferently round under his dark brows until they rested on her figure. 'Now then, what is it, my young woman?' he said blandly.

'Can I speak to you—not on business, sir?' said she.

'Yes—I suppose.' He looked at her more thoughtfully.

'I am sent to tell you, sir,' she innocently went on, 'that a distant relative of yours by marriage, Susan Newson, a sailor's widow, is in the town; and to ask whether you would wish to see her.'

The rich *rouge-et-noir* of his countenance underwent a slight change. 'Oh—Susan is—still alive?' he asked with difficulty.

'Yes, sir.'

'Are you her daughter?'

'Yes, sir—her only daughter.'

'What — do you call yourself — your Christian name?'

'Elizabeth-Jane, sir.'

'Newson?'

'Elizabeth-Jane Newson.'

This at once suggested to Henchard that the transaction of his early married life at Weydon Fair was unrecorded in the family history. It was more than he could have expected. His wife had behaved kindly to him in return for his unkindness, and had never proclaimed her wrong to her child or to the world.

'I am—a good deal interested in your news,' he said. 'And as this is not a matter of business, but pleasure, suppose we go indoors.'

It was with a gentle delicacy of manner, surprising to Elizabeth, that he showed her out of the office, and through the outer room, where Donald Farfrae was overhauling bins and samples with the inquiring inspection of a beginner in charge. Henchard preceded her through the door in the wall to the suddenly changed scene of the garden and flowers, and onward into the house. The dining-room to which he introduced her still exhibited the remnants of the lavish breakfast laid for Farfrae. It was furnished to profusion with heavy mahogany furniture of the deepest red-Spanish hues. Pembroke tables, with leaves hanging so low that they well-nigh touched the floor, stood against the walls on legs and feet shaped like those of an elephant, and on one lay three huge folio volumes—a Family Bible, a 'Josephus,' and a 'Whole Duty of Man.' In the chimney corner was a fire-grate with a fluted semi-circular back, having urns and festoons cast in relief thereon; and the chairs were of the kind which, since that day, has cast lustre upon the names of Chippendale and Sheraton, though, in point of fact, their patterns may have been such as those illustrious carpenters never saw or heard of.

'Sit down—Elizabeth-Jane—sit down,' he said, with a shake in his voice as he uttered her name; and sitting down himself he allowed his hands to hang between his knees, while he looked upon the carpet. 'Your mother, then, is quite well?'

'She is rather worn out, sir, with travelling.'

'A sailor's widow—when did he die?'

'Father was lost last spring.'

Henchard winced at the word 'father,' thus applied. 'Do you and she come from abroad—America or Australia?' he asked.

'No. We have been in England some years. I was twelve when we came here from Canada.'

'Ah; exactly.' By such conversation he discovered

the circumstances which had enveloped his wife and her child in such total obscurity that he had long ago believed them to be in their graves. These things being clear, he returned to the present. 'And where is your mother staying?'

'At the Three Mariners.'

'And you are her daughter Elizabeth-Jane?' repeated Henchard. He arose, came close to her, and glanced in her face. 'I think,' he said, suddenly turning away with a wet eye, 'you shall take a note from me to your mother. I should like to see her. . . . She is not left very well off by her late husband?' His eye fell on Elizabeth's clothes, which, though a respectable suit of black, and her very best, were decidedly old-fashioned, even to Casterbridge eyes.

'Not very well,' she said, glad that he had divined this without her being obliged to express it.

He sat down at the table and wrote a few lines; next taking from his pocket-book a five-pound note, which he put in the envelope with the letter, adding to it, as by an after-thought, five shillings. Sealing the whole up carefully, he directed it to 'Mrs. Newson, Three Mariners Inn,' and handed the packet to Elizabeth.

'Deliver it to her personally, please,' said Henchard. 'Well, I am glad to see you here, Elizabeth-Jane—very glad. We must have a long talk together—but not just now.'

He took her hand at parting, and held it so warmly that she, who had known so little friendship, was much affected, and tears rose to her aerial-grey eyes. The instant that she was gone Henchard's state showed itself more distinctly; having shut the door, he sat in his dining-room stiffly erect, gazing at the opposite wall as if he read his history there.

'Begad!' he suddenly exclaimed, jumping up. 'I didn't think of that. Perhaps these are impostors— and Susan and the child dead after all!'

However, a something in Elizabeth-Jane soon assured him that, as regarded her, at least, there could be little doubt. And a few hours would settle the question of her mother's identity; for he had arranged in his note to see her that evening.

'It never rains but it pours!' said Henchard. His keenly excited interest in his new friend the Scotchman was now eclipsed by this event; and Donald Farfrae saw so little of him during the rest of the day that he wondered at the suddenness of his employer's moods.

In the meantime Elizabeth had reached the inn. Her mother, instead of taking the note with the curiosity of a poor woman expecting assistance, was much moved at sight of it. She did not read it at once, asking Elizabeth to describe her reception, and the very words Mr. Henchard used. Elizabeth's back was turned when her mother opened the letter. It ran thus :—

'Meet me at eight o'clock this evening, if you can, at the Ring on the Budmouth road. The place is easy to find. I can say no more now. The news upsets me almost. The girl seems to be in ignorance. Keep her so till I have seen you. M. H.'

He said nothing about the enclosure of five guineas. The amount was significant; it may tacitly have said to her that he bought her back again. She waited restlessly for the close of the day, telling Elizabeth-Jane that she was invited to see Mr. Henchard; that she would go alone. But she said nothing to show that the place of meeting was not at his house, nor did she hand the note to Elizabeth.

XI

THE Ring at Casterbridge was merely the local name of one of the finest Roman Amphitheatres, if not the very finest, remaining in Britain.

Casterbridge announced old Rome in every street, alley, and precinct. It looked Roman, bespoke the art of Rome, concealed dead men of Rome. It was impossible to dig more than a foot or two deep about the town fields and gardens without coming upon some tall soldier or other of the Empire, who had lain there in his silent unobtrusive rest for a space of fifteen hundred years. He was mostly found lying on his side, in an oval scoop in the chalk, like a chicken in its shell; his knees drawn up to his chest; sometimes with the remains of his spear against his arm; a fibula or brooch of bronze on his breast or forehead; an urn at his knees, a jar at his throat, a bottle at his mouth; and mystified conjecture pouring down upon him from the eyes of Casterbridge street boys and men, who had turned a moment to gaze at the familiar spectacle as they passed by.

Imaginative inhabitants, who would have felt an unpleasantness at the discovery of a comparatively modern skeleton in their gardens, were quite unmoved by these hoary shapes. They had lived so long ago, their time was so unlike the present, their hopes and motives were so widely removed from ours, that between them and the living there seemed to stretch a gulf too wide for even a spirit to pass.

The Amphitheatre was a huge circular enclosure, with a notch at opposite extremities of its diameter north and south. From its sloping internal form it might have been called the spittoon of the Jötuns. It was to Casterbridge what the ruined Coliseum is to modern Rome, and was nearly of the same magnitude. The dusk of evening was the proper hour at which a true impression of this suggestive place could be received. Standing in the middle of the arena at that time there by degrees became apparent its real vastness, which a cursory view from the summit at noon-day was apt to obscure. Melancholy, impressive, lonely, yet accessible from every part of the town, the historic circle was the frequent spot for appointments of a furtive kind. Intrigues were arranged there; tentative meetings were there experimented after divisions and feuds. But one kind of appointment—in itself the most common of any —seldom had place in the Amphitheatre: that of happy lovers.

Why, seeing that it was pre-eminently an airy, accessible, and sequestered spot for interviews, the cheerfullest form of those occurrences never took kindly to the soil of the ruin, would be a curious inquiry. Perhaps it was because its associations had about them something sinister. Its history proved that. Apart from the sanguinary nature of the games originally played therein, such incidents attached to its past as these: that for scores of years the town-gallows had stood at one corner; that in 1705 a woman who had murdered her husband was half-strangled and then burnt there in the presence of ten thousand spectators. Tradition reports that at a certain stage of the burning her heart burst and leapt out of her body, to the terror of them all, and that not one of those ten thousand people ever cared particularly for hot roast after that. In addition to these old tragedies, pugilistic encounters almost to the death had come off down to recent dates in that secluded arena, entirely invisible to the outside world, save by climbing to the top of the enclosure, which few townspeople in the daily round of their lives ever took the trouble to do. So that, though close to the turnpike-road, crimes might be perpetrated there unseen at mid-day.

Some boys had latterly tried to impart gaiety to the ruin by using the central arena as a cricket-ground. But the game usually languished, for the aforesaid reason— the dismal privacy which the earthen circle enforced, shutting out every appreciative passer's vision, every commendatory remark from outsiders—everything, except the sky; and to play at games in such circumstances was like acting to an empty house. Possibly, too, the boys were timid, for some old people said that at certain moments in the summer time, in broad daylight, persons sitting with a book, or dozing in the arena, had, on lifting their eyes, beheld the slopes lined with a gazing legion of Hadrian's soldiery as if watching the gladiatorial combat; and had heard the roar of their excited voices; that the scene would remain but a moment, like a lightning flash, and then disappear.

It was related that there still remained under the south entrance arched cells for the reception of the wild animals and athletes who took part in the games. The arena was still smooth and circular, as if used for its original purpose not so very long ago. The sloping pathways by which spectators had ascended to their seats were pathways yet. But the whole was grown over with grass, which now, at the end of summer, was bearded with withered bents that formed waves under the brush of the wind, returning to the attentive ear Æolian modulations, and detaining for moments the flying globes of thistledown.

Henchard had chosen this spot as being the safest

from observation which he could think of for meeting his long-lost wife, and at the same time as one easily to be found by a stranger after nightfall. As Mayor of the town, with a reputation to keep up, he could not invite her to come to his house till some definite course had been decided on.

Just before eight he approached the deserted earthwork, and entered by the south path which descended over the *débris* of the former dens. In a few moments he could discern a female figure creeping in by the great north gap, or public gateway. They met in the middle of the arena. Neither spoke just at first—there was no necessity for speech—and the poor woman leant against Henchard, who supported her in his arms.

'I don't drink,' he said in a low, halting, apologetic voice. 'You hear, Susan?—I don't drink now—I haven't since that night.' Those were his first words.

He felt her bow her head in acknowledgment that she understood. After a minute or two he again began:

'If I had known you were living, Susan! But there was every reason to suppose you and the child were dead and gone. I took every possible step to find you—travelled—advertised. My opinion at last was that you had started for some colony with that man, and had been drowned on your voyage out. Why did you keep silent like this?'

'O Michael! because of him—what other reason could there be? I thought I owed him faithfulness to the end of one of our lives—foolishly I believed there was something solemn and binding in the bargain; I thought that even in honour I dared not desert him when he had paid so much for me in good faith. I meet you now only as his widow—I consider myself that, and that I have no claim upon you. Had he not died, I should never have come—never! Of that you may be sure.'

86

'Tut-tut! How could you be so simple?'

'I don't know. Yet it would have been very wicked—if I had not thought like that!' said Susan, almost crying.

'Yes—yes—so it would. It is only that which makes me feel ye an innocent woman. But—to lead me into this!'

'What, Michael?' she asked, alarmed.

'Why, this difficulty about our living together again, and Elizabeth-Jane. She cannot be told all—she would so despise us both that—I could not bear it!'

'That was why she was brought up in ignorance of you. I could not bear it either.'

'Well—we must talk of a plan for keeping her in her present belief, and getting matters straight in spite of it. You have heard I am in a large way of business here—that I am Mayor of the town, and churchwarden, and I don't know what all?'

'Yes,' she murmured.

'These things, as well as the dread of the girl discovering our disgrace, makes it necessary to act with extreme caution. So that I don't see how you two can return openly to my house as the wife and daughter I once treated badly, and banished from me; and there's the rub o't.'

'We'll go away at once. I only came to see——'

'No, no, Susan; you are not to go—you mistake me!' he said, with kindly severity. 'I have thought of this plan: that you and Elizabeth take a cottage in the town as the widow Mrs. Newson and her daughter; that I meet you, court you, and marry you, Elizabeth-Jane coming to my house as my step-daughter. The thing is so natural and easy that it is half done in thinking o't. This would leave my shady, headstrong, disgraceful life as a young man absolutely unopened; the secret would be yours and mine only; and I should have the pleasure of seeing my own only child under my roof, as well as my wife.'

'I am quite in your hands, Michael,' she said meekly. 'I came here for the sake of Elizabeth; for myself, if you tell me to leave again to-morrow morning, and never come near you more, I am content to go.'

'Now, now; we don't want to hear that,' said Henchard gently. 'Of course you won't leave again. Think over the plan I have proposed for a few hours; and if you can't hit upon a better one we'll adopt it. I have to be away for a day or two on business, unfortunately; but during that time you can get lodgings — the only ones in the town fit for you are those over the china-shop in High Street—and you can also look for a cottage.'

'If the lodgings are in High Street they are dear, I suppose?'

'Never mind—you *must* start genteel if our plan is to be carried out. Look to me for money. Have you enough till I come back?'

'Quite,' said she.

'And are you comfortable at the inn?'

'O yes.'

'And the girl is quite safe from learning the shame of her case and ours?—that's what makes me most anxious of all.'

'You would be surprised to find how unlikely she is to dream of the truth. How could she ever suppose such a thing?'

'True!'

'I like the idea of repeating our marriage,' said Mrs. Henchard, after a pause. 'It seems the only right course, after all this. Now I think I must go back to Elizabeth-Jane, and tell her that our kinsman, Mr. Henchard, kindly wishes us to stay in the town.'

'Very well—arrange that yourself. I'll go some way with you.'

'No, no. Don't run any risk!' said his wife anxiously. 'I can find my way back—it is not late. Please let me go alone.'

'Right,' said Henchard. 'But just one word. Do you forgive me, Susan?'

She murmured something; but seemed to find it difficult to frame her answer.

'Never mind—all in good time,' said he. 'Judge me by my future works—good-bye!'

He retreated, and stood at the upper side of the Amphitheatre while his wife passed out through the lower way, and descended under the trees to the town. Then Henchard himself went homeward, going so fast, that by the time he reached his door he was almost upon the heels of the unconscious woman from whom he had just parted. He watched her up the street, and turned into his house.

XII

ON entering his own door, after watching his wife out of sight, the Mayor walked on through the tunnel-shaped passage into the garden, and thence by the back door towards the stores and granaries. A light shone from the office-window, and there being no blind to screen the interior, Henchard could see Donald Farfrae still seated where he had left him, initiating himself into the managerial work of the house by overhauling the books. Henchard entered, merely observing, 'Don't let me interrupt you, if ye will stay so late.'

He stood behind Farfrae's chair, watching his dexterity in clearing up the numerical fogs which had been allowed to grow so thick in Henchard's books as almost to baffle even the Scotchman's perspicacity. The corn-factor's mien was half admiring, and yet it was not without a dash of pity for the tastes of any one who could care to give his mind to such finnikin details. Henchard himself was mentally and physically unfit for grubbing subtleties from soiled paper; he had in a modern sense received the education of Achilles, and found penmanship a tantalizing art.

'You shall do no more to-night,' he said at length, spreading his great hand over the paper. 'There's time enough to-morrow. Come indoors with me and have some supper. Now you shall! I am determined on't.' He shut the account-books with friendly force.

Donald had wished to get to his lodgings; but he already saw that his friend and employer was a man who knew no moderation in his requests and impulses, and he yielded gracefully. He liked Henchard's warmth, even if it inconvenienced him; the great difference in their characters adding to the liking.

They locked up the office, and the young man followed his companion through the private little door which, admitting directly into Henchard's garden, permitted a passage from the utilitarian to the beautiful at one step. The garden was silent, dewy, and full of perfume. It extended a long way back from the house, first as lawn and flower-beds, then as fruit-garden, where the long-tied espaliers, as old as the old house itself, had grown so stout, and cramped, and gnarled that they had pulled their stakes out of the ground and stood distorted and writhing in vegetable agony, like leafy Laocoons. The flowers which smelt so sweetly were not discernible; and they passed through them into the house.

The hospitalities of the morning were repeated, and when they were over Henchard said, ' Pull your chair round to the fireplace, my dear fellow, and let's make a blaze—there's nothing I hate like a black grate, even in September.' He applied a light to the laid-in fuel, and a cheerful radiance spread around.

' It is odd,' said Henchard, ' that two men should meet as we have done on a purely business ground, and that at the end of the first day I should wish to speak to 'ee on a family matter. But, damn it all, I am a lonely man, Farfrae: I have nobody else to speak to; and why shouldn't I tell it to 'ee ? '

' I'll be glad to hear it, if I can be of any service,' said Donald, allowing his eyes to travel over the intricate wood-carvings of the chimney-piece, representing garlanded lyres, shields, and quivers, on either side of a draped ox-skull, and flanked by heads of Apollo and Diana in low relief.

'I've not been always what I am now,' continued Henchard, his firm deep voice being ever so little shaken. He was plainly under that strange influence which sometimes prompts men to confide to the new-found friend what they will not tell to the old. 'I began life as a working hay-trusser, and when I was eighteen I married on the strength o' my calling. Would you think me a married man?'

'I heard in the town that you were a widower.'

'Ah, yes—you would naturally have heard that. Well, I lost my wife eighteen years ago—by my own fault. . . . This is how it came about. One summer evening I was travelling for employment, and she was walking at my side, carrying the baby, our only child. We came to a booth in a country fair. I was a drinking man at that time.'

Henchard paused a moment, threw himself back so that his elbow rested on the table, his forehead being shaded by his hand, which, however, did not hide the marks of introspective inflexibility on his features as he narrated in fullest detail the incidents of the transaction with the sailor. The tinge of indifference which had at first been visible in the Scotchman now disappeared.

Henchard went on to describe his attempts to find his wife; the oath he swore; the solitary life he led during the years which followed. 'I have kept my oath for eighteen years,' he went on; 'I have risen to what you see me now.'

'Ay!'

'Well—no wife could I hear of in all that time; and being by nature something of a woman-hater, I have found it no hardship to keep at a distance from the sex. No wife could I hear of, I say, till this very day. And now—she has come back.'

'Come back, has she!'

'This morning—this very morning. And what's to be done?'

'Can ye no' take her and live with her, and make some amends?'

'That's what I've planned and proposed. But, Farfrae,' said Henchard gloomily, 'by doing right with Susan I wrong another innocent woman.'

'Ye don't say that?'

'In the nature of things, Farfrae, it is almost impossible that a man of my sort should have the good fortune to tide through twenty years o' life without making more blunders than one. It has been my custom for many years to run across to Jersey in the way of business, particularly in the potato and root season. I do a large trade wi' them in that line. Well, one autumn when stopping there I fell quite ill, and in my illness I sank into one of those gloomy fits I sometimes suffer from, on account o' the loneliness of my domestic life, when the world seems to have the blackness of hell, and, like Job, I could curse the day that gave me birth.'

'Ah, now, I never feel like it,' said Farfrae.

'Then pray to God that you never may, young man. While in this state I was taken pity on by a woman— a young lady I should call her, for she was of good family, well bred, and well educated—the daughter of some harum-scarum military officer who had got into difficulties, and had his pay sequestrated. He was dead now, and her mother too, and she was as lonely as I. This young creature was staying at the boarding-house where I happened to have my lodging; and when I was pulled down she took upon herself to nurse me. From that she got to have a foolish liking for me. Heaven knows why, for I wasn't worth it. But being together in the same house, and her feelings warm, we got naturally intimate. I won't go into particulars of what our relations were. It is enough to say that we honestly meant to marry. There arose a scandal, which did me no harm, but was of course ruin to her. Though, Farfrae, between you and me, as man and man, I solemnly declare that philandering with womankind has neither been my vice nor my virtue. She was terribly careless of appearances, and I was perhaps more, because o' my dreary state; and it was through this that the scandal arose. At last I was well, and came away. When I was gone she suffered much on my account, and didn't forget to tell me so in letters one after another; till, latterly, I felt I owed her something, and thought that, as I had not heard of Susan for so long, I would make this other one the only return I could make, and ask her if she would run the risk of Susan being alive (very slight as I believed) and marry me, such as I was. She jumped for joy, and we should no doubt soon have been married—but, behold, Susan appears!'

Donald showed his deep concern at a complication so far beyond the degree of his simple experiences.

'Now see what injury a man may cause around him! Even after that wrong-doing at the fair when I was young, if I had never been so selfish as to let this giddy girl devote herself to me over at Jersey, to the injury of her name, all might now be well. Yet, as it stands, I must bitterly disappoint one of these women; and it is the second. My first duty is to Susan—there's no doubt about that.'

'They are both in a very melancholy position, and that's true!' murmured Donald.

'They are! For myself I don't care—'twill all end one way. But these two.' Henchard paused in reverie. 'I feel I should like to treat the second, no less than the first, as kindly as a man can in such a case.'

'Ah, well, it cannet be helped!' said the other, with philosophic woefulness. 'You mun write to the young lady, and in your letter you must put it plain and honest that it turns out she cannet be your wife, the first having come back; that ye cannet see her more; and that— ye wish her weel.'

'That won't do. 'Od seize it, I must do a little more than that! I must—though she did always brag about her rich uncle or rich aunt, and her expectations from 'em—I must send a useful sum of money to her, I suppose—just as a little recompense, poor girl. . . . Now, will you help me in this, and draw up an explanation to her of all I've told ye, breaking it as gently as you can? I'm so bad at letters.'

'And I will.'

'Now, I haven't told you quite all yet. My wife Susan has my daughter with her—the baby that was in her arms at the fair; and this girl knows nothing of me beyond that I am some sort of relation by marriage. She has grown up in the belief that the sailor to whom I made over her mother, and who is now dead, was her father, and her mother's husband. What her mother has always felt, she and I together feel now—that we can't proclaim our disgrace to the girl by letting her know the truth. Now what would you do?—I want your advice.'

'I think I'd run the risk, and tell her the truth. She'll forgive ye both.'

'Never!' said Henchard. 'I am not going to let her know the truth. Her mother and I be going to marry again; and it will not only help us to keep our child's respect, but it will be more proper. Susan looks upon herself as the sailor's widow, and won't think o' living with me as formerly without another religious ceremony—and she's right.'

Farfrae thereupon said no more. The letter to the young Jersey woman was carefully framed by him, and the interview ended, Henchard saying, as the Scotchman left, 'I feel it a great relief, Farfrae, to tell some friend o' this! You see now that the Mayor of Casterbridge is not so thriving in his mind as it seems he might be from the state of his pocket.'

'I do. And I am sorry for ye!' said Farfrae.

When he was gone, Henchard copied the letter, and, enclosing a cheque, took it to the post-office, from which he walked back thoughtfully.

'Can it be that it will go off so easily!' he said. 'Poor thing—God knows! Now then, to make amends to Susan!'

XIII

THE cottage which Michael Henchard hired for his
wife Susan, under her name of Newson—in pursuance
of their plan—was in the upper or western part of
the town, near the wall, and the avenue which overshadowed it. The evening sun seemed to shine more
yellowly there than anywhere else this autumn—stretching its rays, as the hours grew later, under the lowest
sycamore boughs, and steeping the ground-floor of the
dwelling, with its green shutters, in a substratum of
radiance which the foliage screened from the upper
parts. Beneath these sycamores on the town walls
could be seen from the sitting-room the tumuli and
earth forts of the distant uplands; making it altogether
a pleasant spot, with the usual touch of melancholy
that a past-marked prospect lends.

As soon as the mother and daughter were comfortably installed, with a white-aproned servant and all
complete, Henchard paid them a visit, and remained to
tea. During the entertainment Elizabeth was carefully
hoodwinked by the very general tone of the conversation that prevailed—a proceeding which seemed to
afford some humour to Henchard, though his wife was
not particularly happy in it. The visit was repeated
again and again with business-like determination by
the Mayor, who seemed to have schooled himself into

a course of strict mechanical rightness towards this woman of prior claim, at any expense to the later one and to his own sentiments.

One afternoon the daughter was not indoors when Henchard came, and he said drily, 'This is a very good opportunity for me to ask you to name the happy day, Susan.'

The poor woman smiled faintly; she did not enjoy pleasantries on a situation into which she had entered solely for the sake of her girl's reputation. She liked them so little, indeed, that there was room for wonder why she had countenanced deception at all, and had not bravely let the girl know her history. But the flesh is weak; and the true explanation came in due course.

'O Michael!' she said, 'I am afraid all this is taking up your time and giving trouble—when I did not expect any such thing!' And she looked at him and at his dress as a man of affluence, and at the furniture he had provided for the room—ornate and lavish to her eyes.

'Not at all,' said Henchard, in rough benignity. 'This is only a cottage—it costs me next to nothing. And as to taking up my time'—here his red and black visage kindled with satisfaction—'I've a splendid fellow to superintend my business now—a man whose like I've never been able to lay hands on before. I shall soon be able to leave everything to him, and have more time to call my own than I've had for these last twenty years.'

Henchard's visits here grew so frequent and so regular that it soon became whispered, and then openly discussed, in Casterbridge, that the masterful, coercive Mayor of the town was captured and enervated by the genteel widow, Mrs. Newson. His well-known haughty indifference to the society of womankind, his silent avoidance of converse with the sex, contributed a piquancy to what would otherwise have been an unromantic matter enough. That such a poor fragile woman should be his choice was inexplicable, except on the ground that the engagement was a family affair in which sentimental passion had no place; for it was known that they were related in some way. Mrs. Henchard was so pale that the boys called her 'The Ghost.' Sometimes Henchard overheard this epithet when they passed together along the Walks—as the avenues on the walls were named—at which his face would darken with an expression of destructiveness towards the speakers ominous to see; but he said nothing.

He pressed on the preparations for his union, or rather reunion, with this pale creature in a dogged, unflinching spirit which did credit to his conscientiousness. Nobody would have conceived from his outward demeanour that there was no amatory fire or pulse of romance acting as stimulant to the bustle going on in his gaunt, great house; nothing but three large resolves —one, to make amends to his neglected Susan; another, to provide a comfortable home for Elizabeth-Jane under his paternal eye; and a third, to castigate himself with the thorns which these restitutory acts brought in their train; among them the lowering of his dignity in public opinion by marrying so comparatively humble a woman.

Susan Henchard entered a carriage for the first time in her life when she stepped into the plain brougham which drew up at the door on the wedding-day to take her and Elizabeth-Jane to church. It was a windless morning of warm November rain, which floated down like meal, and lay in a powdery form on the nap of hats and coats. Few people had gathered round the church door, though they were well packed within. The Scotchman, who assisted as groomsman, was of course the only one present, beyond the chief actors, who knew the true situation of the contracting parties He, however, was too inexperienced, too thoughtful, too judicial, too strongly conscious of the serious side of the business, to enter into the scene in its dramatic aspect. That required the special genius of Christopher Coney, Solomon Longways, Buzzford, and their fellows. But they knew nothing of the secret; though, as the time for coming out of church drew on, they gathered on the pavement adjoining, and expounded the subject according to their lights.

' 'Tis five-and-forty years since I had my settlement in this here town,' said Coney; ' but daze me if ever I see a man wait so long before to take so little! There's a chance even for thee after this, Nance Mockridge.' The remark was addressed to a woman who stood behind his shoulder—the same who had exhibited Henchard's bad bread in public when Elizabeth and her mother entered Casterbridge.

' Be cust if I'd marry any such as he, or thee either,' replied that lady. ' As for thee, Christopher, we know what ye be, and the less said the better. And as for he—well, there—(lowering her voice) 'tis said 'a was a poor parish 'prentice—I wouldn't say it for all the world —but 'a was a poor parish 'prentice, that began life wi' no more belonging to 'en than a carrion crow.'

' And now he's worth ever so much a minute,' murmured Longways. ' When a man is said to be worth so and so a minute, he's a man to be considered! '

Turning, he saw a circular disc reticulated with creases, and recognized the smiling countenance of the fat woman who had asked for another song at the Three Mariners. ' Well, Mother Cuxsom,' he said, ' how's this? Here's Mrs. Newson, a mere skellinton, has got another husband to keep her, while a woman of your tonnage have not.'

' I have not. Nor another to beat me. . . . Ah, yes, Cuxsom's gone, and so shall leather breeches ! '

'Yes; with the blessing of God leather breeches shall go.'

''Tisn't worth my old while to think of another husband,' continued Mrs. Cuxsom. 'And yet I'll lay my life I'm as respectable born as she.'

'True; your mother was a very good woman—I can mind her. She were rewarded by the Agricultural Society for having begot the greatest number of healthy children without parish assistance, and other virtuous marvels.'

''Twas that that kept us so low upon ground—that great family.'

'Ay. Where the pigs be many the wash runs thin.'

'And dostn't mind how mother would sing, Christopher?' continued Mrs. Cuxsom, kindling at the retrospection; 'and how we went with her to the party at Mellstock, do ye mind?—at old Dame Ledlow's, farmer Shinar's sister, do ye mind?—she we used to call Toad-skin, because her face were so yaller and freckled, do ye mind?'

'I do, hee-hee, I do!' said Christopher Coney.

'And well do I—for I was getting up husband-high at that time—one-half girl, and t'other half woman, as one may say. And canst mind'—she prodded Solomon's shoulder with her finger-tip, while her eyes twinkled between the crevices of their lids—'canst mind the sherry-wine, and the zilver-snuffers, and how Joan Dummett was took bad when we were coming home, and Jack Griggs was forced to carry her through the mud; and how 'a let her fall in Dairyman Sweet-apple's cow-barton, and we had to clane her gown wi' grass—never such a mess as 'a were in?'

'Ay—that I do—hee-hee, such doggery as there was in them ancient days, to be sure! Ah, the miles I used to walk then; and now I can hardly step over a furrow!'

Their reminiscences were cut short by the appearance

of the reunited pair—Henchard looking round upon the idlers with that ambiguous gaze of his, which at one moment seemed to mean satisfaction, and at another fiery disdain.

'Well—there's a difference between 'em, though he do call himself a teetotaller,' said Nance Mockridge. 'She'll wish her cake dough afore she's done of him. There's a bluebeardy look about 'en; and 'twill out in time.'

'Stuff—he's well enough! Some folk want their luck buttered. If I had a choice as wide as the ocean sea I wouldn't wish for a better man. A poor twanking woman like her—'tis a godsend for her, and hardly a pair of jumps or night-rail to her name.'

The plain little brougham drove off in the mist, and the idlers dispersed. 'Well, we hardly know how to look at things in these times!' said Solomon. 'There was a man dropped down dead yesterday, not so very many miles from here; and what wi' that, and this moist weather, 'tis scarce worth one's while to begin any work o' consequence to-day. I'm in such a low key with drinking nothing but small table ninepenny this last week or two that I shall call and warm up at the Mar'ners as I pass along.'

'I don't know but that I may as well go with 'ee, Solomon,' said Christopher; 'I'm as clammy as a cockle-snail.'

XIV

A MARTINMAS summer of Mrs. Henchard's life set in with her entry into her husband's large house and respectable social orbit; and it was as bright as such summers well can be. Lest she should pine for deeper affection than he could give, he made a point of showing some semblance of it in external action. Among other things he had the iron railings, that had smiled sadly in dull rust for the last eighty years, painted a bright green, and the heavy-barred, small-paned Georgian sash windows enlivened with three coats of white. He was as kind to her as a man, mayor, and churchwarden could possibly be. The house was large, the rooms lofty, and the landings wide; and the two unassuming women scarcely made a perceptible addition to its contents.

To Elizabeth-Jane the time was a most triumphant one. The freedom she experienced, the indulgence with which she was treated, went beyond her expectations. The reposeful, easy, affluent life to which her mother's marriage had introduced her was, in truth, the beginning of a great change in Elizabeth. She found she could have nice personal possessions and ornaments for the asking, and, as the mediæval saying puts it, 'Take, have, and keep, are pleasant words.' With peace of mind came development, and with development beauty. Knowledge—the result of great natural insight—she did not lack; learning, accomplishments—those, alas, she had not; but as the winter and spring passed by, her thin face and figure filled out in rounder and softer curves; the lines and contractions upon her young brow went away; the muddiness of skin which she had looked upon as her lot by nature departed with a change to abundance of good things, and a bloom came upon her cheek. Perhaps, too, her grey, thoughtful eyes revealed an arch gaiety sometimes; but this was infrequent; the sort of wisdom which looked from their pupils did not readily keep company with these lighter moods. Like all people who have known rough times, light-heartedness seemed to her too irrational and inconsequent to be indulged in except as a reckless dram now and then; for she had been too early habituated to anxious reasoning to drop the habit suddenly. She felt none of those ups and downs of spirit which beset so many people without cause; never—to paraphrase a recent poet—never a gloom in Elizabeth-Jane's soul but she well knew how it came there; and her present cheerfulness was fairly proportionate to her solid guarantees for the same.

It might have been supposed that, given a girl rapidly becoming good-looking, comfortably circumstanced, and for the first time in her life commanding ready money, she would go and make a fool of herself by dress. But no. The reasonableness of almost everything that Elizabeth did was nowhere more conspicuous than in this question of clothes. To keep in the rear of opportunity in matters of indulgence is as valuable a habit as to keep abreast of opportunity in matters of enterprise. This unsophisticated girl did it by an innate perceptiveness that was almost genius. Thus she refrained from bursting out like a water-flower that spring, and clothing herself in puffings and knick-knacks, as most of the Casterbridge girls would have done in her circumstances. Her triumph was tempered by circumspection; she had still that field-mouse fear of the coulter of destiny despite fair promise, which is common among the thoughtful who have suffered early from poverty and oppression.

'I won't be too gay on any account,' she would say to herself. 'It would be tempting Providence to hurl mother and me down, and afflict us again as He used to do.'

We now see her in a black silk bonnet, velvet mantle or silk spencer, dark dress, and carrying a sunshade. In this latter article she drew the line at fringe, and had it plain edged, with a little ivory ring for keeping it closed. It was odd about the necessity for that sunshade. She discovered that with the clarification of her complexion and the birth of pink cheeks her skin had grown more sensitive to the sun's rays. She protected those cheeks forthwith, deeming spotlessness part of womanliness.

Henchard had become very fond of her, and she went out with him more frequently than with her mother now. Her appearance one day was so attractive that he looked at her critically.

'I happened to have the ribbon by me, so I made it up,' she faltered, thinking him perhaps dissatisfied with some rather bright trimming she had donned for the first time.

'Ay—of course—to be sure,' he replied in his leonine way. 'Do as you like—or rather as your mother advises ye. 'Od send—I've nothing to say to't!'

Indoors she appeared with her hair divided by a parting that arched like a white rainbow from ear to ear. All in front of this line was covered with a thick encampment of curls; all behind was dressed smoothly, and drawn to a knob.

The three members of the family were sitting at breakfast one day, and Henchard was looking silently, as he often did, at this head of hair, which in colour was brown—rather light than dark. 'I thought Elizabeth-Jane's hair—didn't you tell me that Elizabeth-Jane's hair promised to be black when she was a baby?' he said to his wife.

She looked startled, jerked his foot warningly, and murmured, 'Did I?'

As soon as Elizabeth was gone to her own room Henchard resumed. 'Begad, I nearly forgot myself just now! What I meant was that the girl's hair certainly looked as if it would be darker, when she was a baby.'

'It did; but they alter so,' replied Susan.

'Their hair gets darker, I know—but I wasn't aware it lightened ever?'

'Oh yes.' And the same uneasy expression came out on her face, to which the future held the key. It passed as Henchard went on :

'Well, so much the better. Now, Susan, I want to have her called Miss Henchard—not Miss Newson. Lot's o' people do it already in carelessness—it is her legal name—so it may as well be made her usual name—I don't like t'other name at all for my own flesh and blood. I'll advertise it in the Casterbridge paper—that's the way they do it. She won't object.'

'No. Oh no. But——'

'Well, then, I shall do it,' said he, peremptorily. 'Surely, if she's willing, you must wish it as much as I?'

'Oh yes—if she agrees let us do it by all means,' she replied.

Then Mrs. Henchard acted somewhat inconsistently; it might have been called falsely, but that her manner was emotional and full of the earnestness of one who wishes to do right at great hazard. She went to Elizabeth-Jane, whom she found sewing in her own sitting-room upstairs, and told her what had been proposed about her surname. 'Can you agree—is it not a slight upon Newson—now he's dead and gone?'

Elizabeth reflected. 'I'll think of it, mother,' she answered.

When, later in the day, she saw Henchard, she adverted to the matter at once, in a way which showed that the line of feeling started by her mother had been persevered in. 'Do you wish this change so very much, sir?' she asked.

'Wish it? Why, my blessed fathers, what an ado you women make about a trifle! I proposed it—that's all. Now, 'Lizabeth-Jane, just please yourself. Curse me if I care what you do. Now, you understand, don't 'ee go agreeing to it to please me.'

Here the subject dropped, and nothing more was said, and nothing was done, and Elizabeth still passed as Miss Newson, and not by her legal name.

Meanwhile the great corn and hay traffic conducted by Henchard throve under the management of Donald Farfrae as it had never thriven before. It had formerly moved in jolts; now it went on oiled castors. The old crude *vivâ voce* system of Henchard, in which everything depended upon his memory, and bargains were made by the tongue alone, was swept away. Letters and ledgers took the place of 'I'll do't,' and 'you shall hae't;' and, as in all such cases of advance, the rugged picturesqueness of the old method disappeared with its inconveniences.

The position of Elizabeth-Jane's room—rather high in the house, so that it commanded a view of the hay-stores and granaries across the garden—afforded her opportunity for accurate observation of what went on there. She saw that Donald and Mr. Henchard were inseparables. When walking together Henchard would lay his arm familiarly on his manager's shoulder, as if

Farfrae were a younger brother, bearing so heavily that his slight figure bent under the weight. Occasionally she would hear a perfect cannonade of laughter from Henchard, arising from something Donald had said, the latter looking quite innocent and not laughing at all. In Henchard's somewhat lonely life he evidently found the young man as desirable for comradeship as he was useful for consultations. Donald's brightness of intellect maintained in the corn-factor the admiration it had won at the first hour of their meeting. The poor opinion, and but ill-concealed, that he entertained of the slim Farfrae's physical girth, strength, and dash, was more than counterbalanced by the immense respect he had for his brains.

Her quiet eye discerned that Henchard's tigerish affection for the younger man, his constant liking to have Farfrae near him, now and then resulted in a tendency to domineer, which, however, was checked in a moment when Donald exhibited marks of real offence. One day, looking down on their figures from on high, she heard the latter remark, as they stood in the doorway between garden and yard, that their habit of walking and driving about together rather neutralized Farfrae's value as a second pair of eyes, which should be used in places where the principal was not. 'Od damn it,' cried Henchard, 'what's all the world! I like a fellow to talk to. Now come along and hae some supper, and don't take too much thought about things, or ye'll drive me crazy.'

When she walked with her mother, on the other hand, she often beheld the Scotchman looking at them with a curious interest. The fact that he had met her at the Three Mariners was insufficient to account for it, since on the occasions on which she had entered his room he had never raised his eyes. Besides, it was at her mother more particularly than at herself that he looked, to Elizabeth-Jane's half-unconscious, simple-minded, perhaps pardonable, disappointment. Thus she could not account for this interest by her own attractiveness, and she decided that it might be apparent only—a way of turning his eyes that Mr. Farfrae had.

She did not divine the ample explanation of his manner, without personal vanity, that was afforded by the fact of Donald being the depositary of Henchard's confidence in respect of his past treatment of the pale, chastened mother who walked by her side. Her conjectures on that past never went further than faint ones based on things casually heard and seen—mere guesses that Henchard and her mother might have been lovers in their younger days, who had quarrelled and parted.

Casterbridge, as has been hinted, was a place deposited in the block upon a corn-field. There was no suburb in the modern sense, or transitional intermixture of town and down. It stood, with regard to the wide fertile land adjoining, clean-cut and distinct, like a chess-board on a green table-cloth. The farmer's boy could sit under his barley-mow and pitch a stone into the office-window of the town-clerk; reapers at work among the sheaves nodded to acquaintances standing on the pavement-corner; the red-robed judge, when he condemned a sheep-stealer, pronounced sentence to the tune of Baa, that floated in at the window from the remainder of the flock browsing hard by; and at executions the waiting crowd stood in a meadow immediately before the drop, out of which the cows had been temporarily driven to give the spectators room.

The corn grown on the upland side of the borough was garnered by farmers who lived in an eastern purlieu called Durnover. Here wheat-ricks overhung the old Roman street, and thrust their eaves against the church tower; green-thatched barns, with doorways as high as the gates of Solomon's temple, opened directly upon the main thoroughfare. Barns indeed were so numerous as to alternate with every half-dozen houses along the way. Here lived burgesses who daily walked the fallow; shepherds in an intra-mural squeeze. A street of farmers' homesteads—a street ruled by a mayor and corporation, yet echoing with the thump of the flail, the flutter of the winnowing-fan, and the purr of the milk into the pails—a street which had nothing urban in it whatever—this was the Durnover end of Casterbridge.

Henchard, as was natural, dealt largely with this nursery or bed of small farmers close at hand—and his waggons were often down that way. One day, when arrangements were in progress for getting home corn from one of the aforesaid farms, Elizabeth-Jane received a note by hand, asking her to oblige the writer by coming at once to a granary on Durnover Hill. As this was the granary whose contents Henchard was removing, she thought the request had something to do with his business, and proceeded thither as soon as she had put on her bonnet. The granary was just within the farm-yard, and stood on stone staddles, high enough for persons to walk under. The gates were open, but nobody was within. However, she entered and waited. Presently she saw a figure approaching the gate—that of Donald Farfrae. He looked up at the church clock, and came in. By some unaccountable shyness, some wish not to meet him there alone, she quickly ascended the step-ladder leading to the granary door, and entered it before he had seen her. Farfrae advanced, imagining himself in solitude; and a few drops of rain beginning to fall, he moved and stood under the shelter where she had just been standing. Here he leant against one of the staddles, and gave himself up to patience. He, too, was plainly expecting some one; could it be herself? if so, why? In a few minutes he looked at his watch, and then pulled out a note, a duplicate of the one she had herself received.

The situation began to be very awkward, and the longer she waited the more awkward it became. To emerge from a door just above his head and descend the ladder, and show she had been in hiding there, would look so very foolish, that she still waited on. A winnowing machine stood close beside her, and to relieve her suspense she gently moved the handle; whereupon a cloud of wheat husks flew out into her face, and covered her clothes and bonnet, and stuck into the fur of her victorine. He must have heard the slight movement, for he looked up, and then ascended the steps.

'Ah—it's Miss Newson,' he said as soon as he could see into the granary. 'I didn't know you were there. I have kept the appointment, and am at your service.'

'O Mr. Farfrae,' she faltered; 'so have I. But I didn't know it was you who wished to see me, otherwise I——'

'I wished to see you? Oh no—at least, that is, I am afraid there may be a mistake.'

'Didn't you ask me to come here? Didn't you write this?' Elizabeth held out her note.

'No. Indeed, at no hand would I have thought of it! And for you—didn't you ask me? This is not your writing?' And he held up his.

'By no means.'

'And is that really so! Then it's somebody wanting to see us both. Perhaps we would do well to wait a little longer.'

Acting on this consideration they lingered, Elizabeth-Jane's face being arranged to an expression of preternatural composure, and the young Scot, at every footstep in the street without, looking from under the granary to see if the passer were about to enter and declare himself their summoner. They watched individual drops of rain creeping down the thatch of the opposite rick—straw after straw—till they reached the bottom; but nobody came, and the granary roof began to drip.

'The person is not likely to be coming,' said Farfrae. 'It's a trick perhaps, and if so, it's a great pity to waste our time like this, and so much to be done.'

''Tis a great liberty,' said Elizabeth.

'It's true, Miss Newson. We'll hear news of this some day, depend on't, and who it was that did it. I wouldn't stand for it hindering myself; but you, Miss Newson '——

'I don't mind—much,' she replied.

'Neither do I.'

They lapsed again into silence. 'You are anxious to get back to Scotland, I suppose, Mr. Farfrae?' she inquired.

'Oh no, Miss Newson. Why would I be?'

'I only supposed you might be from the song you sang at the Three Mariners—about Scotland and home, I mean—which you seemed to feel so deep down in your heart; so that we all felt for you.'

'Ay—and I did sing there—I did —— But, Miss Newson '—and Donald's voice musically undulated between two semitones, as it always did when he became earnest—'it's well you feel a song, for a few minutes, and your eyes they get quite tearful; but you finish it, and for all you felt you don't mind it or think of it again for a long while. Oh no, I don't want to go back! Yet I'll sing the song to you wi' pleasure whenever you like. I could sing it now, and not mind at all!'

'Thank you, indeed. But I fear I must go—rain or no.'

'Ay! Then, Miss Newson, ye had better say nothing about this hoax, and take no heed of it. And if the person should say anything to you, be civil to him or her, as if you did not mind it—so you'll take the clever person's laugh away.' In speaking his eyes became fixed upon her dress, still sown with wheat husks. 'There's husks and dust on you. Perhaps you don't know it?' he said, in tones of extreme delicacy. 'And it's very bad to let rain come upon clothes when there's chaff on them. It washes in and spoils them. Let me help you—blowing is the best.'

As Elizabeth neither assented nor dissented, Donald Farfrae began blowing her back hair, and her side hair, and her neck, and the crown of her bonnet, and the fur of her victorine, Elizabeth saying, 'Oh, thank you,' at every puff. At last she was fairly clean, though Farfrae, having got over his first concern at the situation, seemed in no manner of hurry to be gone.

'Ah—now I'll go and get ye an umbrella,' he said.

She declined the offer, stepped out and was gone. Farfrae walked slowly after, looking thoughtfully at her diminishing figure, and whistling in undertones, 'As I came down through Cannobie.'

XV

AT first Miss Newson's budding beauty was not regarded with much interest by anybody in Casterbridge.
Donald Farfrae's gaze, it is true, was now attracted by
the Mayor's so-called step-daughter, but he was only
one. The truth is that she was but a poor illustrative
instance of the prophet Baruch's sly definition : 'The
virgin that loveth to go gay.'

When she walked abroad she seemed to be occupied
with an inner chamber of ideas, and to have slight need
for visible objects. She formed curious resolves on
checking gay fancies in the matter of clothes, because
it was inconsistent with her past life to blossom gaudily
the moment she had become possessed of money. But
nothing is more insidious than the evolution of wishes
from mere fancies, and of wants from mere wishes.
Henchard gave Elizabeth-Jane a box of delicately-tinted
gloves one spring day. She wanted to wear them to
show her appreciation of his kindness, but she had no
bonnet that would harmonize. As an artistic indulgence
she thought she would have such a bonnet. When she
had a bonnet that would go with the gloves she had
no dress that would go with the bonnet. It was now
absolutely necessary to finish ; she ordered the requisite article, and found that she had no sunshade to go
with the dress. In for a penny in for a pound ; she

bought the sunshade, and the whole structure was at last complete.

Everybody was attracted, and some said that her bygone simplicity was the art that conceals art, the 'delicate imposition' of Rochefoucauld; she had produced an effect, a contrast, and it had been done on purpose. As a matter of fact this was not true, but it had its result; for as soon as Casterbridge thought her artful it thought her worth notice. 'It is the first time in my life that I have been so much admired,' she said to herself; 'though perhaps it is by those whose admiration is not worth having.'

But Donald Farfrae admired her, too; and altogether the time was an exciting one; sex had never before asserted itself in her so strongly, for in former days she had perhaps been too impersonally human to be distinctively feminine. After an unprecedented success one day she came indoors, went upstairs, and leant upon her bed face downwards, quite forgetting the possible creasing and damage. 'Good Heaven,' she whispered, 'can it be? Here am I setting up as the town beauty!'

When she had thought it over, her usual fear of exaggerating appearances engendered a deep sadness. 'There is something wrong in all this,' she mused. 'If they only knew what an unfinished girl I am— that I can't talk Italian, or use globes, or show any of the accomplishments they learn at boarding-schools, how they would despise me! Better sell all this finery and buy myself grammar-books and dictionaries and a history of all the philosophies!'

She looked from the window, and saw Henchard and Farfrae in the hay-yard talking, with that impetuous cordiality on the Mayor's part, and genial modesty on the younger man's, that was now so generally observable in their intercourse. Friendship between man and man; what a rugged strength there was in it, as evinced by these two. And yet the seed that was to lift the foundation of this friendship was at that moment taking root in a chink of its structure.

It was about six o'clock; the men were dropping off homeward one by one. The last to leave was a round-shouldered, blinking young man of nineteen or twenty, whose mouth fell ajar on the slightest provocation, seemingly because there was no chin to support it. Henchard called aloud to him as he went out of the gate. 'Here—Abel Whittle!'

Whittle turned, and ran back a few steps. 'Yes, sir,' he said, in breathless deprecation, as if he knew what was coming next.

'Once more—be in time to-morrow morning. You see what's to be done, and you hear what I say, and you know I'm not going to be trifled with any longer.'

'Yes, sir.' Then Abel Whittle left, and Henchard and Farfrae; and Elizabeth saw no more of them.

Now there was good reason for this command on Henchard's part. Poor Abel, as he was called, had an inveterate habit of over-sleeping himself and coming late to his work. His anxious will was to be among the earliest; but if his comrades omitted to pull the string that he always tied round his great toe and left hanging out of the window for that purpose, his will was as wind. He did not arrive in time.

As he was often second hand at the hay-weighing, or at the crane which lifted the sacks, or was one of those who had to accompany the waggons into the country to fetch away stacks that had been purchased, this affliction of Abel's was productive of much inconvenience. For two mornings in the present week he had kept the others waiting nearly an hour; hence Henchard's threat. It now remained to be seen what would happen to-morrow.

Six o'clock struck, and there was no Whittle. At half-past six Henchard entered the yard; the waggon was horsed that Abel was to accompany; and the other man had been waiting twenty minutes. Then Henchard swore, and Whittle coming up breathless at that instant, the corn-factor turned on him, and declared with an oath that this was the last time; that if he were behind once more, by God, he would come and drag him out o' bed.

'There is sommit wrong in my make, your worshipful!' said Abel, 'especially in the inside, whereas my poor dumb brain gets as dead as a clot afore I've said my few scrags of prayers. Yes—it came on as a stripling, just afore I'd got man's wages, whereas I never enjoy my bed at all, for no sooner do I lie down than I be asleep, and afore I be awake I be up. I've fretted my gizzard green about it, maister, but what can I do? Now last night, afore I went to bed, I only had a scantling o' cheese and '——

'I don't want to hear it!' roared Henchard. 'Tomorrow the waggons must start at four, and if you're not here, stand clear. I'll mortify thy flesh for thee!'

'But let me clear up my points, your worshipful '——

Henchard turned away.

'He asked me and he questioned me, and then a' wouldn't hear my points!' said Abel, to the yard in general. 'Now, I shall twitch like a moment-hand all night to-night for fear o' him!'

The journey to be taken by the waggons next day was a long one, into Blackmoor Vale, and at four o'clock lanterns were moving about the yard. But Abel was missing. Before either of the other men could run to Abel's and warn him, Henchard appeared in the garden doorway. 'Where's Abel Whittle? Not come after all I've said? Now I'll carry out my word, by my blessed fathers—nothing else will do him any good! I'm going up that way.'

Henchard went off, entered Abel's house, a little cottage in Back Street, the door of which was never locked, because the inmates had nothing to lose.

Reaching Whittle's bedside, the corn-factor shouted a bass note so vigorously that Abel started up instantly, and beholding Henchard standing over him, was galvanized into spasmodic movements which had not much relation to getting on his clothes.

'Out of bed, sir, and off to the granary, or you leave my employ to-day! 'Tis to teach ye a lesson. March on; never mind your breeches!'

The unhappy Whittle threw on his sleeve waistcoat, and managed to get into his boots at the bottom of the stairs, while Henchard thrust his hat over his head. Whittle then trotted on down Back Street, Henchard walking sternly behind.

Just at this time Farfrae, who had been to Henchard's house to look for him, came out of the back gate, and saw something white fluttering in the morning gloom, which he soon perceived to be the part of Abel's shirt that showed below his waistcoat.

'For maircy's sake, what object's this?' said Farfrae, following Abel into the yard, Henchard being some way in the rear by this time.

'Ye see, Mr. Farfrae,' gibbered Abel with a resigned smile of terror, 'he said he'd mortify my flesh if so be I didn't get up sooner, and now he's a doing on't! Ye see it can't be helped, Mr. Farfrae; things do happen queer sometimes! Yes—I'll go to Blackmoor Vale half naked as I be, since he do command; but I shall kill myself afterwards; I can't outlive the disgrace; for the women-folk will be looking out of their winders at my mortification all the way along, and laughing me to scorn as a man 'ithout breeches! You know how I feel such things, Maister Farfrae, and how forlorn thoughts get hold upon me. Yes—I shall do myself harm—I feel it coming on!'

'Get back home, and slip on your breeches, and come to wark like a man! If ye go not, you'll ha'e your death standing there!'

'I'm afeard I mustn't! Mr. Henchard said'——

'I don't care what Mr. Henchard said, nor anybody else! 'Tis simple foolishness to do this. Go and dress yourself instantly, Whittle.'

'Hullo, hullo!' said Henchard, coming up behind. 'Who's sending him back?'

All the men looked towards Farfrae.

'I am,' said Donald. 'I say this joke has been carried far enough.'

'And I say it hasn't! Get up in the waggon, Whittle.'

'Not if I am manager,' said Farfrae. 'He either goes home, or I march out of this yard for good.'

Henchard looked at him with a face stern and red. But he paused for a moment, and their eyes met. Donald went up to him, for he saw in Henchard's look that he began to regret this.

'Come,' said Donald quietly, 'a man o' your position should ken better, sir! It is tyrannical and no worthy of you.'

''Tis not tyrannical!' murmured Henchard, like a sullen boy. 'It is to make him remember!' He presently added, in a tone of one bitterly hurt: 'Why did you speak to me before them like that, Farfrae? You might have stopped till we were alone. Ah—I know why! I've told ye the secret o' my life—fool that I was to do't—and you take advantage of me!'

'I had forgot it,' said Farfrae simply.

Henchard looked on the ground, said nothing more, and turned away. During the day Farfrae learnt from the men that Henchard had kept Abel's old mother in coals and snuff all the previous winter, which made him less antagonistic to the corn-factor. But Henchard continued moody and silent, and when one of the men inquired of him if some oats should be hoisted to an upper floor or not, he said shortly, 'Ask Mr. Farfrae. He's master here!'

Morally he was; there could be no doubt of it. Henchard, who had hitherto been the most admired man in his circle, was the most admired no longer. One day the daughters of a deceased farmer in Durnover wanted an opinion on the value of their haystack, and sent a messenger to ask Mr. Farfrae to oblige them with one. The messenger, who was a child, met in the yard not Farfrae, but Henchard.

'Very well,' he said. 'I'll come.'

'But please will Mr. Farfrae come?' said the child.

'I am going that way. . . . Why Mr. Farfrae?' said Henchard, with the fixed look of thought. 'Why do people always want Mr. Farfrae?'

'I suppose because they like him so—that's what they say.'

'Oh—I see—that's what they say—hey? They like him because he's cleverer than Mr. Henchard, and because he knows more; and, in short, Mr. Henchard can't hold a candle to him—hey?'

'Yes—that's just it, sir—some of it.'

'Oh, there's more? Of course there's more! What besides? Come, here's sixpence for a fairing.'

'"And he's better tempered, and Henchard's a fool to him," they say. And when some of the women were a walking home they said, "He's a diment— he's a chap o' wax—he's the best—he's the horse for my money," says they. And they said, "He's the most understanding man o' tnem two by long chalks. I wish he was the master instead of Henchard," they said.'

'They'll talk any nonsense,' Henchard replied with covered gloom. 'Well, you can go now. And *I* am coming to value the hay, d'ye hear?—I.' The boy departed, and Henchard murmured, 'Wish he were master here, do they?'

He went towards Durnover. On his way he overtook Farfrae. They walked on together, Henchard looking mostly on the ground.

'You're no yoursel' the day?' Donald inquired.

'Yes, I am very well,' said Henchard.

'But ye are a bit down—surely ye are down? Why, there's nothing to be angry about! 'Tis splendid stuff that we've got from Blackmoor Vale. By-the-by, the people in Durnover want their hay valued.'

'Yes. I am going there.'

'I'll go with ye.'

As Henchard did not reply, Donald practised a piece of music *sotto voce*, till, getting near the bereaved people's door, he stopped himself with—

'Ah, as their father is dead, I won't go on with such as that. How could I forget?'

'Do you care so very much about hurting folks' feelings?' observed Henchard with a half sneer. 'You do, I know—especially mine!'

'I am sorry if I have hurt yours, sir,' replied Donald, standing still, with a second expression of the same sentiment in the regretfulness of his face. 'Why should you say it—think it?'

The cloud lifted from Henchard's brow, and as Donald finished the corn-merchant turned to him, regarding his breast rather than his face.

'I have been hearing things that vexed me,' he said. ''Twas that made me short in my manner—made me overlook what you really are. Now, I don't want to go in here about this hay—Farfrae, you can do it better than I. They sent for ye, too. I have to attend a meeting of the Town Council at eleven, and 'tis drawing on for't.'

They parted thus in renewed friendship, Donald forbearing to ask Henchard for meanings that were not very plain to him. On Henchard's part there was now again repose; and yet, whenever he thought of Farfrae, it was with a dim dread; and he often regretted that he had told the young man his whole heart, and confided to him the secrets of his life.

XVI

ON this account Henchard's manner towards Farfrae insensibly became more reserved. He was courteous —too courteous—and Farfrae was quite surprised at the good breeding which now for the first time showed itself among the qualities of a man he had hitherto thought undisciplined, if warm and sincere. The cornfactor seldom or never again put his arm upon the young man's shoulder so as to nearly weigh him down with the pressure of mechanized friendship. He left off coming to Donald's lodgings and shouting into the passage, ' Hoy, Farfrae, boy, come and have some dinner with us! Don't sit here in solitary confinement! But in the daily routine of their business there was little change.

Thus their lives rolled on till a day of public rejoicing was suggested to the country at large in celebration of a national event that had recently taken place.

For some time Casterbridge, by nature slow, made no response. Then one day Donald Farfrae broached the subject to Henchard by asking if he would have any objection to lend some rick-cloths to himself and a few others, who contemplated getting up an entertainment of some sort on the day named, and required a shelter for the same, to which they might charge admission at the rate of so much a head.

'Have as many cloths as you like,' Henchard replied.

When his manager had gone about the business Henchard was fired with emulation. It certainly had been very remiss of him, as Mayor, he thought, to call no meeting ere this, to discuss what should be done on this holiday. But Farfrae had been so cursed quick in his movements as to give old-fashioned people in authority no chance of the initiative. However, it was not too late; and on second thoughts he determined to take upon his own shoulders the responsibility of organizing some amusements, if the other Councilmen would leave the matter in his hands. To this they quite readily agreed, the majority being fine old crusted characters who had a decided taste for living without worry.

So Henchard set about his preparations for a really brilliant thing—such as should be worthy of the venerable town. As for Farfrae's little affair, Henchard nearly forgot it; except once now and then when, on it coming into his mind, he said to himself, 'Charge admission at so much a head—just like a Scotchman!—who is going to pay anything a head?' The diversions which the Mayor intended to provide were to be entirely free.

He had grown so dependent upon Donald that he could scarcely resist calling him in to consult. But by sheer self-coercion he refrained. No, he thought, Farfrae would be suggesting such improvements in his damned luminous way, that in spite of himself he, Henchard, would sink to the position of second fiddle, and only scrape harmonies to his manager's talents.

Everybody applauded the Mayor's proposed entertainment, especially when it became known that he meant to pay for it all himself.

Close to the town was an elevated green spot surrounded by an ancient square earthwork—earthworks square, and not square, were as common as blackberries hereabout—a spot whereon the Casterbridge people usually held any kind of merry-making, meeting, or sheep-fair that required more space than the streets would afford. On one side it sloped to the river Froom, and from any point a view was obtained of the country round for many miles. This pleasant upland was to be the scene of Henchard's exploit.

He advertised about the town, in long posters of a pink colour, that games of all sorts would take place here; and set to work a little battalion of men under his own eye. They erected greasy-poles for climbing, with smoked hams and local cheeses at the top. They placed hurdles in rows for jumping over; across the river they laid a slippery pole, with a live pig of the neighbourhood tied at the other end, to become the property of the man who could walk over and get it. There were also provided wheelbarrows for racing, donkeys for the same, a stage for boxing, wrestling, and drawing blood generally; sacks for jumping in. Moreover, not forgetting his principles, Henchard provided a mammoth tea, of which everybody who lived in the borough was invited to partake without payment. The tables were laid parallel with the inner slope of the rampart, and awnings were stretched overhead.

Passing to and fro the Mayor beheld the unattractive exterior of Farfrae's erection in the West Walk, rick-cloths of different sizes and colours being hung up to the arching trees without any regard to appearance. He was easy in his mind now, for his own preparations far transcended these.

The morning came. The sky, which had been remarkably clear down to within a day or two, was overcast, and the weather threatening, the wind having an unmistakable hint of water in it. Henchard wished he had not been quite so sure about the continuance of a fair season. But it was too late to modify or postpone, and the proceedings went on. At twelve o'clock the rain began to fall, small and steady, commencing and increasing so insensibly that it was difficult to state exactly when dry weather ended or wet established itself. In an hour the slight moisture resolved itself into a monotonous smiting of earth by heaven, in torrents to which no end could be prognosticated.

A number of people had heroically gathered in the field, but by three o'clock Henchard discerned that his project was doomed to end in failure. The hams at the top of the poles dripped watered smoke in the form of a brown liquor, the pig shivered in the wind, the grain of the deal tables showed through the sticking table-cloths, for the awning allowed the rain to drift under at its will, and to enclose the sides at this hour seemed a useless undertaking. The landscape over the river disappeared; the wind played on the tent-cords in Æolian improvisations; and at length rose to such a pitch that the whole erection slanted to the ground, those who had taken shelter within it having to crawl out on their hands and knees.

But towards six the storm abated, and a drier breeze shook the moisture from the grass bents. It seemed possible to carry out the programme after all. The awning was set up again; the band was called out from its shelter, and ordered to begin, and where the tables had stood a place was cleared for dancing.

'But where are the folk?' said Henchard, after the lapse of half-an-hour, during which time only two men and a woman had stood up to dance. 'The shops are all shut. Why don't they come?'

'They are at Farfrae's affair in the West Walk,' answered a councilman who stood in the field with the Mayor.

'A few, I suppose. But where are the body o' 'em?'

'All out of doors are there.'

'Then the more fools they!'

Henchard walked away moodily. One or two young fellows gallantly came to climb the poles, to save the hams from being wasted; but as there were no spectators, and the whole scene presented the most melancholy appearance, Henchard gave orders that the proceedings were to be suspended, and the entertainment closed, the food to be distributed among the poor people of the town. In a short time nothing was left in the field but a few hurdles, the tents, and the poles.

Henchard returned to his house, had tea with his wife and daughter, and then walked out. It was now dusk. He soon saw that the tendency of all promenaders was towards a particular spot in the Walks, and eventually proceeded thither himself. The notes of a stringed band came from the enclosure that Farfrae had erected—the pavilion, as he called it—and when he reached it he perceived that a gigantic tent had been ingeniously constructed without poles or ropes. The densest point of the avenue of sycamores had been selected, where the boughs made a closely interlaced vault overhead; to these boughs the canvas had been hung, and a barrel roof was the result. The end towards the wind was enclosed, the other end was open. Henchard went round and saw the interior.

In form it was like the nave of a cathedral with one gable removed, but the scene within was anything but devotional. A reel or fling of some sort was in progress; and the usually sedate Farfrae was in the midst of the other dancers in the costume of a wild Highlander, flinging himself about and spinning to the tune. For a moment Henchard could not help laughing. Then he perceived the immense admiration for the Scotchman that revealed itself in the women's faces; and when this exhibition was over, and a new dance proposed, and Donald had disappeared for a time to return in his natural garments, he had an unlimited

choice of partners, every girl being in a coming-on disposition towards one who so thoroughly understood the
poetry of motion as he.

All the town crowded to the Walk, such a delightful
idea of a ball-room never having occurred to the inhabitants before. Among the rest of the onlookers were
Elizabeth and her mother—the former thoughtful yet
much interested, her eyes beaming with a longing lingering light, as if Nature had been advised by Correggio
in their creation. The dancing progressed with unabated
spirit, and Henchard walked and waited till his wife
should be disposed to go home. He did not care to
keep in the light, and when he went into the dark it was
worse, for there he heard remarks of a kind which were
becoming too frequent :

' Mr. Henchard's rejoicings couldn't say good morning to this,' said one. ' A man must be a headstrong
stunpoll to think folk would go up to that bleak place
to-day.'

The other answered that people said it was not only
in such things as those that the Mayor was wanting.
' Where would his business be if it were not for this
young fellow ? 'Twas verily Fortune sent him to Henchard. His accounts were like a bramblewood when
Mr. Farfrae came. He used to reckon his sacks by
chalk strokes all in a row like garden-palings, measure
his ricks by stretching with his arms, weigh his trusses
by a lift, judge his hay by a ' chaw,' and settle the price
with a curse. But now this accomplished young man
does it all by ciphering and mensuration. Then the
wheat—that sometimes used to taste so strongly of mice
when made into bread that people could fairly tell the
breed—Farfrae has a plan for purifying, so that nobody
would dream the smallest four-legged beast had walked
over it once. Oh yes, everybody is full of him, and the
care Mr. Henchard has to keep him, to be sure ! ' concluded this gentleman.

'But he won't do it for long, good-now,' said the other.

'No!' said Henchard to himself behind the tree. 'Or if he do, he'll be honeycombed clean out of all the character and standing that he's built up in these eighteen year!'

He went back to the dancing pavilion. Farfrae was footing a quaint little dance with Elizabeth-Jane—an old country thing, the only one she knew, and though he considerately toned down his movements to suit her demurer gait, the pattern of the shining little nails in the soles of his boots became familiar to the eyes of every bystander. The tune had enticed her into it; being a tune of a busy, vaulting, leaping sort—some low notes on the silver string of each fiddle, then a skipping on the small, like running up and down ladders— 'Miss M'Leod of Ayr' was its name, so Mr. Farfrae had said, and that it was very popular in his own country.

It was soon over, and the girl looked at Henchard for approval; but he did not give it. He seemed not to see her. 'Look here, Farfrae,' he said, like. one whose mind was elsewhere, 'I'll go to Port-Bredy Great Market to-morrow myself. You can stay and put things right in your clothes-box, and recover strength to your knees after your vagaries.' He planted on Donald an antagonistic glare that had begun as a smile.

Some other townsmen came up, and Donald drew aside. 'What's this, Henchard,' said Alderman Tubber, applying his thumb to the corn-factor like a cheese-taster. 'An opposition randy to yours, eh? Jack's as good as his master, eh? Cut ye out quite, hasn't he?'

'You see, Mr. Henchard,' said the lawyer, another good-natured friend, 'where you made the mistake was in going so far afield. You should have taken a leaf out of his book, and have had your sports in a sheltered place like this. But you didn't think of it, you see; and he did, and that's where he's beat you.'

'He'll be top-sawyer soon of you two, and carry all afore him,' added jocular Mr. Tubber.

'No,' said Henchard gloomily. 'He won't be that, because he's shortly going to leave me.' He looked towards Donald, who had again come near. 'Mr. Farfrae's time as my manager is drawing to a close—isn't it, Farfrae?'

The young man, who could now read the lines and folds of Henchard's strongly-traced face as if they were clear verbal inscriptions, quietly assented; and when people deplored the fact, and asked why it was, he simply replied that Mr. Henchard no longer required his help.

Henchard went home, apparently satisfied. But in the morning, when his jealous temper had passed away, his heart sank within him at what he had said and done. He was the more disturbed when he found that this time Farfrae was determined to take him at his word.

XVII

ELIZABETH-JANE had perceived from Henchard's manner that in assenting to dance she had made a mistake of some kind. In her simplicity she did not know what it was, till a hint from a nodding acquaintance enlightened her. As the Mayor's step-daughter, she learnt, she had not been quite in her place in treading a measure amid such a mixed throng as filled the dancing pavilion.

Thereupon her ears, cheeks, and chin glowed like live coals at the dawning of the idea that her tastes were not good enough for her position, and would bring her into disgrace.

This made her very miserable, and she looked about for her mother; but Mrs. Henchard, who had less idea of conventionality than Elizabeth herself, had gone away, leaving her daughter to return at her own pleasure. The latter moved on into the dark dense old avenues, or rather vaults of living woodwork, which ran along the town boundary, and stood reflecting.

A man followed in a few minutes, and her face being towards the shine from the tent, he recognized her. It was Farfrae—just come from the dialogue with Henchard which had signified his dismissal.

'And it's you, Miss Newson?—and I've been looking for ye everywhere!' he said, overcoming a sadness imparted by the estrangement with the corn-merchant. 'May I walk on with you as far as your street-corner?'

She thought there might be something wrong in this, but did not utter any objection. So together they went on, first down the West Walk, and then into the Bowling Walk, till Farfrae said, 'It's like that I'm going to leave you soon.'

She faltered 'Why?'

'Oh—as a mere matter of business—nothing more. But we'll not concern ourselves about it—it is for the best. I hoped to have another dance with you.'

She said she could not dance—in any proper way.

'Oh, but you do! It's the feeling for it rather than the learning of steps that makes pleasant dancers. . . . I fear I offended your father by getting up this! And now, perhaps, I'll have to go to another part o' the warrld altogether!'

This seemed such a melancholy prospect that Eliza-beth-Jane breathed a sigh—letting it off in fragments that he might not hear her. But darkness makes people truthful, and the Scotchman went on impulsively—perhaps he had heard her after all:

'I wish I was richer, Miss Newson; and your step-father had not been offended; I would ask you something in a short time—yes, I would ask you to-night. But that's not for me!'

What he would have asked her he did not say, and instead of encouraging him she remained incompetently silent. Thus afraid one of another, they continued their promenade along the walls till they got near the bottom of the Bowling Walk; twenty steps further and the trees would end, and the street-corner and lamps appear. In consciousness of this they stopped.

'I never found out who it was that sent us to Durn-over granary on a fool's errand that day,' said Donald, in his undulating tones. 'Did ye ever know yourself, Miss Newson?'

'Never,' said she.

'I wonder why they did it!'

'For fun, perhaps.'

'Perhaps it was not for fun. It might have been that they thought they would like us to stay waiting there, talking to one another? Ay, well! I hope you Casterbridge folk will no forget me if I go.'

'That I'm sure we won't!' she said earnestly. 'I —wish you wouldn't go at all.'

They had got into the lamplight. 'Now, I'll think over that,' said Donald Farfrae. 'And I'll not come up to your door; but part from you here; lest it make your father more angry still.'

They parted, Farfrae returning into the dark Bowling Walk, and Elizabeth-Jane going up the street. Without any consciousness of what she was doing she started running with all her might till she reached her father's door. 'Oh dear me—what am I at?' she thought, as she pulled up breathless.

Indoors she fell to conjecturing the meaning of Farfrae's enigmatic words about not daring to ask her what he fain would. Elizabeth, that silent observing woman, had long noted how. he was rising in favour among the townspeople; and knowing Henchard's nature now, she had feared that Farfrae's days as manager were numbered; so that the announcement gave her little surprise. Would Mr. Farfrae stay in Casterbridge despite his words and her father's dismissal? His occult breathings to her might be solvable by his course in that respect.

The next day was windy—so windy that walking in the garden she picked up a portion of the draft of a letter on business in Donald Farfrae's writing, which had flown over the wall from the office. The useless scrap she took indoors, and began to copy the caligraphy, which she much admired. The letter began 'Dear Sir,' and presently writing on a loose slip 'Eliza beth-Jane,' she laid the latter over 'Sir,' making the phrase 'Dear Elizabeth-Jane.' When she saw the effect a quick red ran up her face and warmed her through, though nobody was there to see what she had done. She quickly tore up the slip, and threw it away. After this she grew cool, and laughed at herself, walked about the room, and laughed again; not joyfully, but distressfully rather.

It was quickly known in Casterbridge that Farfrae and Henchard had decided to dispense with each other. Elizabeth-Jane's anxiety to know if Farfrae were going away from the town reached a pitch that disturbed her, for she could no longer conceal from herself the cause. At length the news reached her that he was not going to leave the place. A man following the same trade as Henchard, but on a very small scale, had sold his business to Farfrae, who was forthwith about to start as corn and hay-merchant on his own account.

Her heart fluttered when she heard of this step of Donald's, proving that he meant to remain; and yet, would a man who cared one little bit for her have endangered his suit by setting up a business in opposition to Mr. Henchard's? Surely not; and it must have been a passing impulse only which had led him to address her so softly.

To solve the problem whether her appearance on the evening of the dance were such as to inspire a fleeting love at first sight, she dressed herself up exactly as she had dressed then—the muslin, the spencer, the sandals, the parasol—and looked in the mirror. The picture glassed back was, in her opinion, precisely of such a kind as to inspire that fleeting regard, and no more—'just enough to make him silly, and not enough to keep him so,' she said luminously; and Elizabeth thought, in a much lower key, that by this time he had discovered how plain and homely was the informing spirit of that pretty outside.

Hence, when she felt her heart going out to him, she would say to herself with a mock pleasantry that carried an ache with it, ' No, no, Elizabeth-Jane—such dreams are not for you!' She tried to prevent herself from seeing him, and thinking of him; succeeding fairly well in the former attempt, in the latter not so completely.

Henchard, who had been hurt at finding that Farfrae did not mean to put up with his temper any longer, was incensed beyond measure when he learnt what the young man had done as an alternative. It was in the town-hall, after a council meeting, that he first became aware of Farfrae's *coup* for establishing himself independently in the town; and his voice might have been heard as far as the town-pump expressing his feelings to his fellow councilmen. Those tones showed that, though under a long reign of self-control he had become Mayor and churchwarden and what not, there was still the same unruly volcanic stuff beneath the rind of Michael Henchard as when he had sold his wife at Weydon Fair.

' Well, he's a friend of mine, and I'm a friend of his —or if we are not, what are we? 'Od send, if I've not been his friend, who has, I should like to know? Didn't he come here without a sound shoe to his voot? Didn't I keep him here—help him to a living? Didn't I help him to money, or whatever he wanted? I stuck out for no terms—I said " Name your own price." I'd have shared my last crust with that young fellow at one time, I liked him so well. And now he's defied me! But damn him, I'll have a tussle with him now—at fair buying and selling, mind—at fair buying and selling! And if I can't overbid such a stripling as he, then I'm not wo'th a varden! We'll show that we know our business as well as one here and there!'

His friends of the Corporation did not specially respond. Henchard was less popular now than he had

134

been when, nearly two years before, they had voted him to the chief magistracy on account of his amazing energy. While they had collectively profited by this quality of the corn-factor's, they had been made to wince individually on more than one occasion. So he went out of the hall and down the street alone.

Reaching home he seemed to recollect something with a sour satisfaction. He called Elizabeth-Jane. Seeing how he looked when she entered she appeared alarmed.

'Nothing to find fault with,' he said, observing her concern. 'Only I want to caution you, my dear. That man, Farfrae—it is about him. I've seen him talking to you two or three times—he danced with 'ee at the rejoicings, and came home with 'ee. Now, now, no blame to you. But just hearken: Have you made him any foolish promise? Gone the least bit beyond sniff and snaff at all?'

'No. I have promised him nothing.'

'Good. All's well that end's well. I particularly wish you not to see him again.'

'Very well, sir.'

'You promise?'

She hesitated for a moment, and then said—

'Yes, if you much wish it.'

'I do. He's an enemy to our house!'

When she had gone he sat down, and wrote in a heavy hand to Farfrae thus:—

'SIR,—I make request that henceforth you and my step-daughter be as strangers to each other. She on her part has promised to welcome no more addresses from you; and I trust, therefore, you will not attempt to force them upon her. M. HENCHARD.'

One would almost have supposed Henchard to have had policy to see that no better *modus vivendi* could be arrived at with Farfrae than by encouraging him to become his son-in-law. But such a scheme for buying over a rival had nothing to recommend it to the Mayor's headstrong faculties. With all domestic *finesse* of that kind he was hopelessly at variance. Loving a man or hating him, his diplomacy was as wrongheaded as a buffalo's; and his wife had not ventured to suggest the course which she, for many reasons, would have welcomed gladly.

Meanwhile, Donald Farfrae had opened the gates of commerce on his own account at a spot on Durnover Hill—as far as possible from Henchard's stores, and with every intention of keeping clear of his former friend and employer's customers. There was, it seemed to the younger man, room for both of them and to spare. The town was small, but the corn and hay-trade was proportionately large, and with his native sagacity he saw opportunity for a share of it.

So determined was he to do nothing which should seem like trade-antagonism to the Mayor that he refused his first customer—a large farmer of good repute—because Henchard and this man had dealt together within the preceding three months.

' He was once my friend,' said Farfrae, 'and it's not for me to take business from him. I am sorry to disappoint you, but I cannot hurt the trade of a man who's been so kind to me.'

In spite of this praiseworthy course the Scotchman's trade increased. Whether it were that his northern energy was an over-mastering force among the easy-going Wessex worthies, or whether it was sheer luck, the fact remained that whatever he touched he prospered in. Like Jacob in Padan-Aram, he would no sooner humbly limit himself to the ringstraked-and-spotted exceptions of trade, than the ringstraked-and-spotted would multiply and prevail.

But most probably luck had little to do with it.

Character is Fate, said Novalis, and Farfrae's character was just the reverse of Henchard's, who might not inaptly be described as Faust has been described—as a vehement gloomy being, who had quitted the ways of vulgar men, without light to guide him on a better way.

Farfrae duly received the request to discontinue attentions to Elizabeth-Jane. His acts of that kind had been so slight that the request was almost superfluous. Yet he had felt a considerable interest in her, and after some cogitation he decided that it would be as well to enact no Romeo part just then—for the young girl's sake no less than his own. Thus the incipient attachment was stifled down.

A time came when, avoid collision with his former friend as he might, Farfrae was compelled, in sheer self-defence, to close with Henchard in mortal commercial combat. He could no longer parry the fierce attacks of the latter by simple avoidance. As soon as their war of prices began everybody was interested, and some few guessed the end. It was, in some degree, Northern insight matched against Southron doggedness —the dirk against the cudgel—and Henchard's weapon was one which, if it did not deal ruin at the first or second stroke, left him afterwards well-nigh at his antagonist's mercy.

Almost every Saturday they encountered each other amid the crowd of farmers which thronged about the market-place in the weekly course of their business. Donald was always ready, and even anxious, to say a few friendly words; but the Mayor invariably gazed stormfully past him, like one who had endured and lost on his account, and could in no sense forgive the wrong; nor did Farfrae's snubbed manner of perplexity at all appease him. The large farmers, corn-merchants, millers, auctioneers, and others had each an official stall in the corn-market room, with their names painted thereon; and when to the familiar series of ' Henchard,'

'Everdene,' 'Shinar,' 'Darton,' and so on, was added one inscribed 'Farfrae,' in staring new letters, Henchard was stung into bitterness; like Bellerophon, he wandered away from the crowd, cankered in soul.

From that day Donald Farfrae's name was seldom mentioned in Henchard's house. If at breakfast or dinner Elizabeth-Jane's mother inadvertently alluded to her favourite's movements, the girl would implore her by a look to be silent; and her husband would say, 'What—are you, too, my enemy?'

XVIII

THERE came a shock which had been foreseen for some time by Elizabeth, as the box passenger foresees the approaching jerk from some channel across the highway.

Her mother was ill—too unwell to leave her room. Henchard, who treated her kindly, except in moments of irritation, sent at once for the richest, busiest doctor, whom he supposed to be the best. Bedtime came, and they burnt a light all night. In a day or two she rallied.

Elizabeth, who had been staying up, did not appear at breakfast on the second morning, and Henchard sat down alone. He was startled to see a letter for him from Jersey in a writing he knew too well, and had expected least to behold again. He took it up in his hands and looked at it as at a picture, a vision, a vista of past enactments; and then he read it as an unimportant finale to conjecture.

The writer said that she at length perceived how impossible it would be for any further communications to proceed between them now that his re-marriage had taken place. That such re-union had been the only straightforward course open to him she was bound to admit. 'On calm reflection, therefore,' she went on, 'I quite forgive you for landing me in such a dilemma, remem-

THE MAYOR OF CASTERBRIDGE

bering that you concealed nothing before our ill-advised acquaintance; and that you really did set before me in your grim way the fact of there being a certain risk in intimacy with you, slight as it seemed to be after eighteen years of silence on your wife's part. I thus look upon the whole as a misfortune of mine, and not a fault of yours.

'So that, Michael, I must ask you to overlook those letters with which I pestered you day after day in the heat of my feelings. They were written whilst I thought your conduct to me cruel; but now I know more particulars of the position you were in I see how inconsiderate my reproaches were.

'Now you will, I am sure, perceive that the one condition which will make any future happiness possible for me, is that the past connection between our lives be kept secret outside this isle. Speak of it I know you will not; and I can trust you not to write of it. One safeguard more remains to be mentioned — that no writings of mine, or trifling articles belonging to me, should be left in your possession through neglect or forgetfulness. To this end may I request you to return to me any such you may have, particularly the letters written in the first abandonment of feeling.

'For the handsome sum you forwarded to me as a plaster to the wound, I heartily thank you.

'I am now on my way to Bristol, to see my only relative. She is rich, and I hope will do something for me. I shall return through Casterbridge and Budmouth, where I shall take the packet-boat. Can you meet me with the letters and other trifles? I shall be in the coach which changes horses at the Antelope Hotel at half-past five Wednesday evening; I shall be wearing a Paisley shawl with a red centre, and thus may easily be found. I should prefer this plan of receiving them to having them sent. — I remain still, yours ever,

'LUCETTA.'

Henchard breathed heavily. 'Poor thing—better you had not known me! Upon my heart and soul, if ever I should be left in a position to carry out that marriage with thee, I *ought* to do it—I ought to do it, indeed!'

The contingency that he had in his mind was, of course, the death of Mrs. Henchard.

As requested, he sealed up Lucetta's letters, and put the parcel aside till the day she had appointed; this plan of returning them by hand being apparently a little *ruse* of the young lady for exchanging a word or two with him on past times. He would have preferred not to see her; but deeming that there could be no great harm in acquiescing thus far, he went at dusk and stood opposite the coach-office.

The evening was chilly, and the coach was late. Henchard crossed over to it while the horses were being changed; but there was no Lucetta inside or out. Concluding that something had happened to modify her arrangements he gave the matter up and went home, not without a sense of relief.

Meanwhile Mrs. Henchard was weakening visibly. She could not go out of doors any more. One day, after much thinking which seemed to distress her, she said she wanted to write something. A desk was put upon her bed with pen and paper, and at her request she was left alone. She remained writing for a short time, folded her paper carefully, called Elizabeth-Jane to bring a taper and wax, and then, still refusing assistance, sealed up the sheet, directed it, and locked it in her desk. She had directed it in these words:—

'*Mr. Michael Henchard. Not to be opened till Elizabeth-Jane's wedding-day.*'

The latter sat up with her mother to the utmost of her strength night after night. To learn to take the universe seriously there is no quicker way than to watch—to be a 'waker,' as the country-people call it. Between the hours at which the last toss-pot went by and the first sparrow shook himself, the silence in Casterbridge —barring the rare sound of the watchman—was broken in Elizabeth's ear only by the time-piece in the bedroom ticking frantically against the clock on the stairs; ticking harder and harder till it seemed to clang like a gong; and all this while the subtle-souled girl asking herself why she was born, why sitting in a room, and blinking at the candle; why things around her had taken the shape they wore in preference to every other possible shape. Why they stared at her so helplessly, as if waiting for the touch of some wand that should release them from terrestrial constraint; what that chaos called consciousness, which spun in her at this moment like a top, tended to, and began in. Her eyes fell together; she was awake, yet she was asleep.

A word from her mother roused her. Without preface, and as the continuation of a scene already progressing in her mind, Mrs. Henchard said: 'You remember the note sent to you and Mr. Farfrae—asking you to meet some one in Durnover Barton—and that you thought it was a trick to make fools of you?'

'Yes.'

'It was not to make fools of you—it was done to bring you together. 'Twas I did it.'

'Why?' said Elizabeth, with a start.

'I—wanted you to marry Mr. Farfrae.'

'O mother!' Elizabeth-Jane bent down her head so much that she looked quite into her own lap. But as her mother did not go on, she said, 'What reason?'

'Well, I had a reason. 'Twill out one day. I wish it could have been in my time! But there— nothing is as you wish it! Henchard hates him.'

'Perhaps they'll be friends again,' murmured the girl.

'I don't know—I don't know.' After this her

mother was silent, and dozed; and she spoke on the subject no more.

Some little time later on, Farfrae was passing Henchard's house on a Sunday morning, when he observed that the blinds were all down. He rang the bell so softly that it only sounded a single full note and a small one; and then he was informed that Mrs. Henchard was dead—just dead—that very hour.

At the town pump there were gathered when he passed a few old inhabitants, who came there for water whenever they had, as at present, spare time to fetch it, because it was purer from that original fount than from their own wells. Mrs. Cuxsom, who had been standing there for an indefinite time with her pitcher, was describing the incidents of Mrs. Henchard's death, as she had learnt them from the nurse.

'And she was as white as marble-stone,' said Mrs. Cuxsom. 'And likewise such a thoughtful woman, too—ah, poor soul—that a' minded every little thing that wanted tending. "Yes," says she, "when I'm gone, and my last breath's blowed, look in the top drawer o' the chest in the back room by the window, and you'll find all my coffin clothes; a piece of flannel —that's to put under me, and the little piece is to put under my head; and my new stockings for my feet—they are folded alongside, and all my other things. And there's four ounce pennies, the heaviest I could find, a tied up in bits of linen, for weights— two for my right eye and two for my left," she said. "And when you've used 'em, and my eyes don't open no more, bury the pennies, good souls, and don't ye go spending 'em, for I shouldn't like it. And open the windows as soon as I am carried out, and make it as cheerful as you can for Elizabeth-Jane." '

'Ah, poor heart!'

'Well, and Martha did it, and buried the ounce pennies in the garden. But if ye'll believe words, that man, Christopher Coney, went and dug 'em up, and spent 'em at the Three Mariners. "Faith," he said, "why should death rob life o' fourpence? Death's not of such good report that we should respect 'en to that extent," says he.'

' 'Twas a cannibal deed!' deprecated her listeners.

'Gad, then, I won't quite ha'e it,' said Solomon Longways. 'I say it to-day, and 'tis a Sunday morning, and I wouldn't speak wrongfully for a zilver zixpence at such a time. I don't see noo harm in it. To respect the dead is sound doxology; and I wouldn't sell skellintons—leastwise respectable skellintons—to be varnished for 'natomies, except I were out o' work. But money is scarce, and throats get dry. Why *should* death rob life o' fourpence? I say there was no treason in it.'

'Well, poor soul; she's helpless to hinder that or anything now,' answered Mother Cuxsom. 'And all her shining keys will be took from her, and her cupboards opened; and little things a' didn't wish seen, anybody will see; and her wishes and ways will all be as nothing!'

XIX

HENCHARD and Elizabeth sat conversing by the fire. It was three weeks after Mrs. Henchard's funeral; the candles were not lighted, and a restless, acrobatic flame, poised on a coal, called from the shady walls the smiles of all shapes that could respond—the old pier-glass, with gilt columns and huge entablature, the picture-frames, sundry knobs and handles, and the brass rosette at the bottom of each riband bell-pull on either side of the chimney-piece.

'Elizabeth, do you think much of old times?' said Henchard.

'Yes, sir; often,' said she.

'Who do you put in your pictures of 'em?'

'Mother and father—nobody else hardly.'

Henchard always looked like one bent on resisting pain when Elizabeth-Jane spoke of Richard Newson as 'father.' 'Ah! I am out of all that, am I not?' he said. . . . 'Was Newson a kind father?'

'Yes, sir; very.'

Henchard's face settled into an expression of stolid loneliness which gradually modulated into something softer. 'Suppose I had been your real father?' he said. 'Would you have cared for me as much as you cared for Richard Newson?'

'I can't think it,' she said quickly. 'I can think of no other as my father, except my father.'

Henchard's wife was dissevered from him by death; his friend and helper Farfrae by estrangement; Elizabeth-Jane by ignorance. It seemed to him that only óne of them could possibly be recalled, and that was the girl. His mind began vibrating between the wish to reveal himself to her, and the policy of leaving well alone, till he could no longer sit still. He walked up and down, and then he came and stood behind her chair, looking down upon the top of her head. He could no longer restrain his impulse. 'What did your mother tell you about me—my history?' he asked.

'That you were related by marriage.'

'She should have told more—before you knew me! Then my task would not have been such a hard one. .... Elizabeth, it is I who am your father, and not Richard Newson. Shame alone prevented your wretched parents from owning this to you while both of 'em were alive.'

The back of Elizabeth's head remained still, and her shoulders did not denote even the movements of breathing. Henchard went on: 'I'd rather have your scorn, your fear, anything than your ignorance; 'tis that I hate! Your mother and I were man and wife when we were young. What you saw was our second marriage. Your mother was too honest. We had thought each other dead—and—Newson became her husband.'

This was the nearest approach Henchard could make to the full truth. As far as he personally was concerned he would have screened nothing; but he showed a respect for the young girl's sex and years worthy of a better man.

When he had gone on to give details which a whole series of slight and unregarded incidents in her past life strangely corroborated; when, in short, she believed his story to be true, she became greatly agitated, and, turning round to the table, flung her face upon it weeping.

'Don't cry—don't cry!' said Henchard, with vehement pathos, 'I can't bear it, I won't bear it. I am your father; why should you cry? Am I so dreadful, so hateful to 'ee? Don't take against me, Elizabeth-Jane!' he cried, grasping her wet hand. 'Don't take against me—though I was a drinking man once, and used your mother roughly—I'll be kinder to you than *he* was! I'll do anything, if you will only look **upon** me as your father!'

She tried to stand up and confront him trustfully; but she could not; she was troubled at his presence, like the brethren at the avowal of Joseph.

'I don't want you to come to me all of a sudden,' said Henchard in jerks, and moving like a great tree in a wind. 'No, Elizabeth, I don't. I'll go away and not see you till to-morrow, or when you like; and then I'll show 'ee papers to prove my words. There, I am gone, and won't disturb you any more. . . . . 'Twas I that chose your name, my daughter; your mother wanted it Susan. There, don't forget 'twas I gave you your name!' He went out at the door and shut her softly in, and she heard him go away into the garden. But he had not done. Before she had moved, or in any way recovered from the effect of his disclosure, he reappeared.

'One word more, Elizabeth,' he said. 'You'll take my surname now—hey? Your mother was against it; but it will be much more pleasant to me. 'Tis legally yours, you know. But nobody need know that. You shall take it as if by choice. I'll talk to my lawyer— I don't know the law of it exactly; but will you do this—let me put a few lines into the newspaper that such is to be your name?'

'If it is my name I must have it, mustn't I?' she asked.

'Well, well; usage is everything in these matters.'

'I wonder why mother didn't wish it?'

'Oh, some whim of the poor soul's. Now get a bit of paper and draw up a paragraph as I shall tell you. But let's have a light.'

'I can see by the firelight,' she answered. 'Yes—I'd rather.'

'Very well.'

She got a piece of paper, and bending over the fender, wrote at his dictation words which he had evidently got by heart from some advertisement or other—words to the effect that she, the writer, hitherto known as Elizabeth-Jane Newson, was going to call herself Elizabeth-Jane Henchard forthwith. It was done, and fastened up, and directed to the office of the *Casterbridge Chronicle*.

'Now,' said Henchard, with the blaze of satisfaction that he always emitted when he had carried his point —though tenderness softened it this time—'I'll go upstairs and hunt for some documents that will prove it all to you. But I won't trouble you with them till to-morrow. Good night, my Elizabeth-Jane!'

He was gone before the bewildered girl could realize what it all meant, or adjust her filial sense to the new centre of gravity. She was thankful that he had left her to herself for the evening, and sat down over the fire. Here she remained in silence, and wept—not for her mother now, but for the genial sailor, Richard Newson, to whom she seemed doing a wrong.

Henchard, in the meantime, had gone upstairs. Papers of a domestic nature he kept in a drawer in his bedroom, and this he unlocked. Before turning them over he leant back and indulged in reposeful thought. Elizabeth was his at last, and she was a girl of such good sense and kind heart that she would be sure to like him. He was the kind of man to whom some human object for pouring out his heat upon— were it emotive or were it choleric—was almost a necessity. The craving of his heart for the re-establishment of this tenderest human tie had been great during his wife's lifetime, and now he had submitted to its mastery without reluctance and without fear. He bent over the drawer again, and proceeded in his search.

Among the other papers had been placed the contents of his wife's little desk, the keys of which had been handed to him at her request. Here was the letter addressed to him with the restriction, ' *Not to be opened till Elizabeth-Jane's wedding-day.*'

Mrs. Henchard, though more patient than her husband, had been no practical hand at anything. In sealing up the sheet, which was folded and tucked in without an envelope, in the old-fashioned way, she had overlaid the junction with a large mass of wax without the requisite under-touch of the same. The seal had cracked, and the letter was open. Henchard had no reason to suppose the restriction one of serious weight, and his feeling for his late wife had not been of the nature of deep respect. 'Some trifling fancy or other of poor Susan's, I suppose,' he said; and without curiosity he allowed his eyes to scan the letter :—

' MY DEAR MICHAEL,—For the good of all three of us, I have kept one thing a secret from you till now. I hope you will understand why; I think you will; though perhaps you may not forgive me. But, dear Michael, I have done it for the best. I shall be in my grave when you read this, and Elizabeth-Jane will have a home. Don't curse me, Mike—think of how I was situated. I can hardly write it, but here it is. Elizabeth-Jane is not your Elizabeth-Jane—the child who was in my arms when you sold me. No; she died three months after that, and this living one is my other husband's. I christened her by the same name we had given to the first, and she filled up the ache I felt at the other's loss. Michael, I am dying, and I might have held my tongue; but I could not. Tell

her husband of this or not, as you may judge; and
forgive, if you can, a woman you once deeply wronged,
as she forgives you.   SUSAN HENCHARD.'

Her husband regarded the paper as if it were a
window-pane through which he saw for miles. His
lip twitched, and he seemed to compress his frame, as
if to bear better. His usual habit was not to consider
whether destiny were hard upon him or not—the shape
of his ideas in cases of affliction being simply a moody
'I am to suffer, I perceive.' 'So much scourging as
this, then, is it for me?' But now through his
passionate head there stormed this thought—that the
blasting disclosure was what he had deserved.

His wife's extreme reluctance to have the girl's
name altered from Newson to Henchard was now
accounted for fully. It furnished another illustration
of that honesty in dishonesty which had characterized
her in other things.

He remained unnerved and purposeless for near a
couple of hours; till he suddenly said, 'Ah—I wonder
if it is true!'

He jumped up in an impulse, kicked off his slippers,
and went with a candle to the door of Elizabeth-Jane's
room, where he put his ear to the keyhole and listened.
She was breathing profoundly. Henchard softly turned
the handle, entered, and shading the light, approached
the bedside. Gradually bringing the light from behind
a screening curtain he held it in such a manner that
it fell slantwise on her face without shining on her eyes.
He steadfastly regarded her features.

They were fair: his were dark. But this was an
unimportant preliminary. In sleep there come to the
surface buried genealogical facts, ancestral curves, dead
men's traits, which the mobility of daytime animation
screens and overwhelms. In the present statuesque
repose of the young girl's countenance Richard Newson's

was unmistakably reflected. He could not endure the sight of her, and hastened away.

Misery taught him nothing more than defiant endurance of it. His wife was dead, and the first impulse for revenge died with the thought that she was beyond him. He looked out at the night as at a fiend. Henchard, like all his kind, was superstitious, and he could not help thinking that the concatenation of events this evening had produced was the scheme of some sinister intelligence bent on punishing him. Yet they had developed naturally. If he had not revealed his past history to Elizabeth he would not have searched the drawer for papers, and so on. The mockery was, that he should have no sooner taught a girl to claim the shelter of his paternity than he discovered her to have no kinship with him.

This ironical sequence of things angered him like an impish trick from a fellow-creature. Like Prester John's, his table had been spread, and infernal harpies had snatched up the food. He went out of the house, and moved sullenly onward down the pavement till he came to the bridge at the bottom of the High Street. Here he turned in upon a bypath on the river bank, skirting the north-eastern limits of the town.

These precincts embodied the mournful phases of Casterbridge life, as the south avenues embodied its cheerful moods. The whole way along here was sunless, even in summer time; in spring, white frosts lingered here when other places were steaming with warmth; while in winter it was the seed-field of all the aches, rheumatisms, and torturing cramps of the year. The Casterbridge doctors must have pined away for want of sufficient nourishment, but for the configuration of the landscape on the north-eastern side.

The river—slow, noiseless, and dark—the Schwarzwasser of Casterbridge—ran beneath a low cliff, the two together forming a defence which had rendered walls and artificial earthworks on this side unnecessary. Here were ruins of a Franciscan priory, and a mill attached to the same, the water of which roared down a back-hatch like the voice of desolation. Above the cliff, and behind the river, rose a pile of buildings, and in the front of the pile a square mass cut into the sky. It was like a pedestal lacking its statue. This missing feature, without which the design remained incomplete, was, in truth, the corpse of a man ; for the square mass formed the base of the gallows, the extensive buildings at the back being the county gaol. In the meadow where Henchard now walked the mob were wont to gather whenever an execution took place, and there to the tune of the roaring weir they stood and watched the spectacle.

The exaggeration which darkness imparted to the glooms of this region impressed Henchard more than he had expected. The lugubrious harmony of the spot with his domestic situation was too perfect for him, impatient of effects, scenes, and adumbrations. It reduced his heartburning to melancholy, and he exclaimed, 'Why the deuce did I come here!' He went on past the cottage in which the old local hangman had lived and died, in times before that calling was monopolized over all England by a single gentleman ; and climbed up by a steep back lane into the town.

For the sufferings of that night, engendered by his bitter disappointment, he might well have been pitied. He was like one who had half fainted, and could neither recover nor complete the swoon. In words he could blame his wife, but not in his heart ; and had he obeyed the wise directions outside her letter this pain would have been spared him for long—possibly for ever, Elizabeth-Jane seeming to show no ambition to quit her safe and secluded maiden courses for the speculative path of matrimony.

The morning came after this night of unrest, and

with it the necessity for a plan. He was far too self-willed to recede from a position, especially as it would involve humiliation. His daughter he had asserted her to be, and his daughter she should always think herself, no matter what hypocrisy it involved.

But he was ill-prepared for the first step in this new situation. The moment he came into the breakfast-room Elizabeth advanced with open confidence to him and took him by the arm.

'I have thought and thought all night of it,' she said frankly. 'And I see that everything must be as you say. And I am going to look upon you as the father that you are, and not to call you Mr. Henchard any more. It is so plain to me now. Indeed, father, it is. For, of course, you would not have done half the things you have done for me, and let me have my own way so entirely, and bought me presents, if I had only been your stepdaughter! He—Mr. Newson—whom my poor mother married by such a strange mistake' (Henchard was glad that he had disguised matters here), 'was very kind—oh, so kind!' (she spoke with tears in her eyes); 'but that is not the same thing as being one's real father after all. Now, father, breakfast is ready!' said she cheerfully.

Henchard bent and kissed her cheek. The moment and the act he had contemplated for weeks with a thrill of pleasure; yet it was no less than a miserable insipidity to him now that it had come. His reinstation of her mother had been chiefly for the girl's sake, and the fruition of the whole scheme was such dust and ashes as this.

XX

OF all the enigmas which ever confronted a girl there can have been seldom one like that which followed Henchard's announcement of himself to Elizabeth as her father. He had done it in an ardour and an agitation which had half carried the point of affection with her; yet, behold, from the next morning onwards his manner was constrained as she had never seen it before.

The coldness soon broke out into open chiding. One grievous failing of Elizabeth's was her occasional pretty and picturesque use of dialect words—those terrible marks of the beast to the truly genteel.

It was dinner-time—they never met except at meals—and she happened to say when he was rising from table, wishing to show him something, 'If you'll bide where you be a minute, father, I'll get it.'

'"Bide where you be,"' he echoed sharply. 'Good God, are you only fit to carry wash to a pig-trough, that ye use such words as those?'

She reddened with shame and sadness.

'I meant "Stay where you are," father,' she said, in a low, humble voice. 'I ought to have been more careful.'

He made no reply, and went out of the room.

The sharp reprimand was not lost upon her, and in time it came to pass that for 'fay' she said 'succeed; that she no longer spoke of 'dumbledores' but of

154

'humble bees;' no longer said of young men and women that they 'walked together,' but that they were 'engaged;' that she grew to talk of 'greggles' as 'wild hyacinths;' that when she had not slept she did not quaintly tell the servants next morning that she had been 'hag-rid,' but that she had 'suffered from indigestion.'

These improvements, however, are somewhat in advance of the story. Henchard, being uncultivated himself, was the bitterest critic the fair girl could possibly have had of her own lapses—really slight now, for she read omnivorously. A gratuitous ordeal was in store for her in the matter of her handwriting. She was passing the dining-room door one evening, and had occasion to go in for something. It was not till she had opened the door that she knew the Mayor was there in the company of a man with whom he transacted business.

'Here, Elizabeth-Jane,' he said, looking round at her, 'just write down what I tell you—a few words of an agreement for me and this gentleman to sign. I am a poor tool with a pen.'

'Be jowned, and so be I,' said the gentleman.

She brought forward blotting-book, paper, and ink, and sat down.

'Now then—"An agreement entered into this sixteenth day of October"—write that first.'

She started the pen in an elephantine march across the sheet. It was a splendid round, bold hand of her own conception, a style that would have stamped a woman as Minerva's own in more recent days. But other ideas reigned then : Henchard's creed was that proper young girls wrote ladies'-hand—nay, he believed that bristling characters were as innate and inseparable a part of refined womanhood as sex itself. Hence when, instead of scribbling, like the Princess Ida,—

> 'In such a hand as when a field of corn
> Bows all its ears before the roaring East,'

Elizabeth-Jane produced a line of chain-shot and sand-bags, he reddened in angry shame for her, and, peremptorily saying, ' Never mind—I'll finish it,' dismissed her there and then.

Her considerate disposition became a pitfall to her now. She was, it must be admitted, sometimes provokingly and unnecessarily willing to saddle herself with manual labours. She would go to the kitchen instead of ringing, ' Not to make Phœbe come up twice.' She went down on her knees, shovel in hand, when the cat overturned the coal-scuttle ; moreover, she would persistently thank the parlour - maid for everything, till one day, as soon as the girl was gone from the room, Henchard broke out with, ' Good God, why dostn't leave off thanking that girl as if she were a goddess-born ! Don't I pay her a dozen pound a year to do things for 'ee ? ' Elizabeth shrank so visibly at the exclamation that he became sorry a few minutes after, and said that he did not mean to be so rough.

These domestic exhibitions were the small protruding needle-rocks which suggested rather than revealed what was underneath. But his passion had less terror for her than his coldness. The increasing frequency of the latter mood told her the sad news that he disliked her with a growing dislike. The more interesting that her appearance and manners became under the softening influences which she could now command, and in her wisdom did command, the more she seemed to estrange him. Sometimes she caught him looking at her with a louring invidiousness that she could hardly bear. Not knowing his secret, it was a cruel mockery that she should for the first time excite his animosity when she had taken his surname.

But the most terrible ordeal was to come. Elizabeth had latterly been accustomed of an afternoon to present a cup of cider or ale and bread-and-cheese to Nance Mockridge, who worked in the yard, wimbling haybonds. Nance accepted this offering thankfully at first; afterwards as a matter of course. On a day when Henchard was on the premises he saw his step-daughter enter the hay-barn on this errand; and, as there was no clear spot on which to deposit the provisions, she at once set to work arranging two trusses of hay as a table, Mockridge meanwhile standing with her hands on her hips, easefully looking at the preparations on her behalf.

'Elizabeth, come here!' said Henchard; and she obeyed.

'Why do you lower yourself so confoundedly?' he said with suppressed passion. 'Haven't I told you o't fifty times? Hey? Making yourself a drudge for a common workwoman of such a character as hers! Why, ye'll disgrace me to the dust!'

Now these words were uttered loud enough to reach Nance inside the barn door, who fired up immediately at the slur upon her personal character. Coming to the door, she cried, regardless of consequences, 'Come to that, Mr. Michael Henchard, I can let 'ee know she've waited on worse!'

'Then she must have had more charity than sense,' said Henchard.

'Oh no, she hadn't. 'Twere not for charity but for hire; and at a public-house in this town!'

'It is not true!' cried Henchard indignantly.

'Just ask her,' said Nance, folding her naked arms in such a manner that she could comfortably scratch her elbows.

Henchard glanced at Elizabeth-Jane, whose complexion, now pink and white from confinement, lost nearly all of the former colour. 'What does this mean?' he said to her. 'Anything or nothing?'

'It is true,' said Elizabeth-Jane. 'But it was only——'

'Did you do it, or didn't you? Where was it?'

'At the Three Mariners; one evening for a little while, when we were staying there.'

Nance glanced triumphantly at Henchard, and sailed into the barn; for, assuming that she was to be discharged on the instant, she had resolved to make the most of her victory. Henchard, however, said nothing about discharging her. Unduly sensitive on such points by reason of his own past, he had the look of one completely ground down to the last indignity. Elizabeth followed him to the house like a culprit; but when she got inside she could not see him. Nor did she see him again that day.

Convinced of the scathing damage to his local repute and position that must have been caused by such a fact, though it had never before reached his own ears, Henchard showed a positive distaste for the presence of this girl not his own, whenever he encountered her. He mostly dined with the farmers at the market-room of one of the two chief hotels, leaving her in utter solitude. Could he have seen how she made use of those silent hours he might have found reason to reverse his judgment on her quality. She read and took notes incessantly, mastering facts with painful laboriousness, but never flinching from her self-imposed task. She began the study of Latin, incited by the Roman characteristics of the town she lived in. 'If I am not well-informed it shall be by no fault of my own,' she would say to herself through the tears that would occasionally glide down her peachy cheeks when she was fairly baffled by the portentous obscurity of many of these educational works.

Thus she lived on, a dumb, deep-feeling, great-eyed creature, construed by not a single contiguous being; quenching with patient fortitude her incipient interest in Farfrae, because it seemed to be one-sided, unmaidenly, and unwise. True, that for reasons best known to herself, she had, since Farfrae's dismissal, shifted her quarters from the back room affording a view of the yard (which she had occupied with such zest) to a front chamber overlooking the street; but as for the young man, whenever he passed the house he seldom or never turned his head.

Winter had almost come, and unsettled weather made her still more dependent upon indoor resources. But there were certain early winter days in Casterbridge—days of firmamental exhaustion which followed angry south-westerly tempests—when, if the sun shone, the air was like velvet. She seized on these days for her periodical visits to the spot where her mother lay buried—the still-used burial-ground of the old Roman-British city, whose curious feature was this, its continuity as a place of sepulture. Mrs. Henchard's dust mingled with the dust of women who lay ornamented with glass hair-pins and amber necklaces, and men who held in their mouths coins of Hadrian, Posthumus, and the Constantines.

Half-past ten in the morning was about her hour for seeking this spot—a time when the town avenues were deserted as the avenues of Karnac. Business had long since passed down them into its daily cells, and Leisure had not arrived there. So Elizabeth-Jane walked and read, or looked over the edge of the book to think, and thus reached the churchyard.

There, approaching her mother's grave, she saw a solitary dark figure in the middle of the gravel-walk. This figure, too, was reading; but not from a book: the words which engrossed it being the inscription on Mrs. Henchard's tombstone. The personage was in mourning like herself, was about her age and size, and might have been her wraith or double, but for the fact that it was a lady much more beautifully dressed than she. Indeed, comparatively indifferent as Elizabeth-Jane was to dress, unless for some temporary whim or purpose, her eyes were arrested by the artistic perfection of the lady's appearance. Her gait, too, had a flexuousness about it, which seemed to avoid angularity of movement less from choice than from predisposition. It was a revelation to Elizabeth that human beings could reach this stage of external development—she had never suspected it. She felt all the freshness and grace to be stolen from herself on the instant by the neighbourhood of such a stranger. And this was in face of the fact that Elizabeth could now have been writ handsome, while the young lady was simply pretty.

Had she been envious she might have hated the woman ; but she did not do that—she allowed herself the pleasure of feeling fascinated. She wondered where the lady had come from. The stumpy and practical walk of honest homeliness which mostly prevailed there, the two styles of dress thereabout, the simple and the mistaken, equally avouched that this figure was no Casterbridge woman's, even if a book in her hand resembling a guide-book had not also suggested it.

The stranger presently moved from the tombstone of Mrs. Henchard, and vanished behind the corner of the wall. Elizabeth went to the tomb herself; beside it were two footprints distinct in the soil, signifying that the lady had stood there a long time. She returned homeward, musing on what she had seen, as she might have mused on a rainbow or the Northern Lights, a rare butterfly or a cameo.

Interesting as things had been out of doors, at home it turned out to be one of her bad days. Henchard, whose two years' mayoralty was ending, had been made aware that he was not to be chosen to fill a vacancy in the list of aldermen ; and that Farfrae was likely to become one of the Council. This caused the unfortunate discovery that she had played the waiting-maid in the town of which he was Mayor to rankle in his mind yet more poisonously. He had learnt by personal inquiry at the time that it was to Donald Farfrae—that treacherous upstart — that she had thus humiliated herself. And though Mrs. Stannidge seemed to attach no great importance to the incident—the cheerful souls at the Three Mariners having exhausted its aspects long ago—such was Henchard's haughty spirit that the simple thrifty deed was regarded as little less than a social catastrophe by him.

Ever since the evening of his wife's arrival with her daughter there had been something in the air which had changed his luck. That dinner at the King's Arms with his friends had been Henchard's Austerlitz: he had had his successes since, but his course had not been upward. He was not to be numbered among the aldermen—that Peerage of burghers—as he had expected to be, and the consciousness of this soured him to-day.

'Well, where have you been?' he said to her, with off-hand laconism.

'I've been strolling in the Walks and churchyard, father, till I feel quite leery.' She clapped her hand to her mouth, but too late.

This was just enough to incense Henchard after the other crosses of the day. 'I *won't* have you talk like that!' he thundered. ' "Leery," indeed. One would think you worked upon a farm! One day I learn that you lend a hand in public-houses. Then I hear you talk like a clodhopper. I'm burned, if it goes on, this house can't hold us two.'

The only way of getting a single pleasant thought to go to sleep upon after this was by recalling the lady she had seen that day, and hoping she might see her again.

Meanwhile Henchard was sitting up, thinking over his jealous folly in forbidding Farfrae to pay his addresses to this girl who did not belong to him, when if he had allowed them to go on he might not have been encumbered with her. At last he said to himself with satisfaction as he jumped up and went to the writing-table : 'Ah! he'll think it means peace, and a marriage portion——not that I don't want my house to be troubled with her, and no portion at all!' He wrote as follows :——

'SIR,—On consideration, I don't wish to interfere with your courtship of Elizabeth-Jane, if you care for her. I therefore withdraw my objection ; excepting in this——that the business be not carried on in my house.——Yours,   M. HENCHARD.
'Mr. Farfrae.'

The morrow, being fairly fine, found Elizabeth-Jane again in the churchyard ; but while looking for the lady she was startled by the apparition of Farfrae, who passed outside the gate. He glanced up for a moment from a pocket-book in which he appeared to be making figures as he went ; whether or not he saw her he took no notice, and disappeared.

Unduly depressed by a sense of her own super-fluity, she thought he probably scorned her ; and quite broken in spirit, sat down on a bench. She fell into painful thought on her position, which ended with her saying quite loud, 'Oh, I wish I was dead with dear mother!'

Behind the bench was a little promenade under the wall where people sometimes walked instead of on the gravel. The bench seemed to be touched by something ; she looked round, and a face was bending over her, veiled, but still distinct, the face of the young woman she had seen yesterday.

Elizabeth-Jane looked confounded for a moment, knowing she had been overheard, though there was pleasure in her confusion. 'Yes, I heard you,' said the lady, in a vivacious voice, answering her look. 'What can have happened?'

'I don't—I can't tell you,' said Elizabeth, putting her hand to her face to hide a quick flush that had come.

There was no movement or word for a few seconds; then the girl felt that the young lady was sitting down beside her.

'I guess how it is with you,' said the latter. 'That was your mother.' She waved her hand towards the tombstone. Elizabeth looked up at her as if inquiring of herself whether there should be confidence. The lady's manner was so desirous, so anxious, that the girl decided there should be confidence. 'It was my mother,' she said, 'my only friend.'

'But your father, Mr. Henchard. He is living?'

'Yes, he is living,' said Elizabeth-Jane.

'Is he not kind to you?'

'I've no wish to complain of him.'

'There has been a disagreement?'

'A little.'

'Perhaps you were to blame,' suggested the stranger.

'I was—in many ways,' sighed the meek Elizabeth. 'I swept up the coals when the servant ought to have done it; and I said I was leery;—and he was angry with me.'

The lady seemed to warm towards her for that reply. 'Do you know the impression your words give me?' she said ingenuously. 'That he is a hot-tempered man—a little proud — perhaps ambitious; but not a bad man.' Her anxiety not to condemn Henchard, while siding with Elizabeth, was curious.

'Oh no; certainly not *bad*,' agreed the honest girl. 'And he has not even been unkind to me till lately—since mother died. But it has been very much to bear while it has lasted. All is owing to my defects, I daresay; and my defects are owing to my history.'

'What is your history?'

Elizabeth-Jane looked wistfully at her questioner. She

found that her questioner was looking at her; turned her eyes down; and then seemed compelled to look back again. 'My history is not gay or attractive,' she said: 'And yet I can tell it, if you really want to know.'

The lady assured her that she did want to know; whereupon Elizabeth-Jane told the tale of her life as she understood it, which was in general the true one, except that the sale at the fair had no part therein.

Contrary to the girl's expectation her new friend was not shocked. This cheered her; and it was not till she thought of returning to that home in which she had been treated so roughly of late that her spirits fell.

'I don't know how to return,' she murmured. 'I think of going away. But what can I do? Where can I go?'

'Perhaps it will be better soon,' said her friend gently. 'So I would not go far. Now what do you think of this: I shall soon want somebody to live in my house, partly as housekeeper, partly as companion; would you mind coming to me? But perhaps——'

'Oh yes,' cried Elizabeth, with tears in her eyes. 'I would, indeed—I would do anything to be independent; for then perhaps my father might get to love me. But, ah!'

'What?'

'I am no accomplished person. And a companion to *you* must be that.'

'Oh, not necessarily.'

'Not? But I can't help using rural words sometimes, when I don't mean to.'

'Never mind, I shall like to know them.'

'And—oh, I know I shan't do!'—she cried with a distressful laugh. 'I accidentally learned to write round hand instead of ladies'-hand. And, of course, you want some one who can write that?'

'Well, no.'

'What, not necessary to write ladies'-hand?' cried the joyous Elizabeth.

'Not at all.'

'But where do you live?'

'In Casterbridge, or rather I shall be living here after twelve o'clock to-day.'

Elizabeth, expressed her astonishment.

'I have been staying at Budmouth for a few days while my house was getting ready. The house I am going into is that one they call High Place Hall—the old stone one overlooking the Market. Two or three rooms are fit for occupation, though not all: I sleep there to-night for the first time. Now will you think over my proposal, and meet me here the first fine day next week, and say if you are still in the same mind?'

Elizabeth, her eyes shining at this prospect of a change from an unbearable position, joyfully assented; and the two parted at the gate of the churchyard.

XXI

As a maxim glibly repeated from childhood remains practically unmarked till some mature experience enforces it, so did this High Place Hall now for the first time really show itself to Elizabeth-Jane, though her ears had heard its name on a hundred occasions.

Her mind dwelt upon nothing else but the stranger, and the house, and her own chance of living there, all the rest of the day. In the afternoon she had occasion to pay a few bills in the town and do a little shopping, when she learnt that what was a new discovery to herself had become a common topic about the streets. High Place Hall was undergoing repair; a lady was coming there to live shortly; all the shop-people knew it, and had already discounted the chance of her being a customer.

Elizabeth-Jane could, however, add a capping touch to information so new to her in the bulk. The lady, she said, had arrived that day.

When the lamps were lighted, and it was yet not so dark as to render chimneys, attics, and roofs invisible, Elizabeth, almost with a lover's feeling, thought she would like to look at the outside of High Place Hall. She went up the street in that direction.

The Hall, with its grey *façade* and parapet, was the only residence of its sort so near the centre of the town. It had, in the first place, the characteristics of a country mansion—birds' nests in its chimneys, damp nooks where fungi grew, and irregularities of surface direct from Nature's trowel. At night the forms of passengers were patterned by the lamps in black shadows upon the pale walls.

This evening motes of straw lay around, and other signs of the premises having been in that lawless condition which accompanies the entry of a new tenant. The house was entirely of stone, and formed an example of dignity without great size. It was not altogether aristocratic, still less consequential, yet the old-fashioned stranger instinctively said, ' Blood built it, and Wealth enjoys it,' however vague his opinions of those accessories might be.

Yet as regards the enjoying it, the stranger would have been wrong, for until this very evening, when the new lady had arrived, the house had been empty for a year or two, while before that interval its occupancy had been irregular. The reason of its unpopularity was soon made manifest. Its rooms overlooked the market-place; and such a prospect from such a house was not considered desirable or seemly by its would-be occupiers.

Elizabeth's eyes sought the upper rooms, and saw lights there. The lady had obviously arrived. The impression that this woman of comparatively practised manner had made upon the studious girl's mind was so deep that she enjoyed standing under an opposite archway merely to think that the charming lady was inside the confronting walls, and to wonder what she was doing. Her admiration for the architecture of that front was entirely on account of the inmate it screened. Though for that matter the architecture deserved admiration, or at least study, on its own account. It was Palladian, and like most architecture erected since the Gothic age, was a compilation rather than a design. But its reasonableness made it impressive. It was not rich, but rich enough. A timely consciousness of the ultimate vanity of human architecture, no less than of other human things, had prevented artistic superfluity.

Men had till quite recently been going in and out with parcels and packing-cases, rendering the door and hall within like a public thoroughfare. Elizabeth trotted through the open door in the dusk, but becoming alarmed at her own temerity, she went quickly out again by another which stood open in the lofty wall of the back court. To her surprise she found herself in one of the little-used blind alleys of the town. Looking round at the door which had given her egress, by the light of the solitary lamp fixed in the alley, she saw that it was arched and old—older even than the house itself. The door was studded, and the keystone of the arch was a mask. Originally the mask had exhibited a comic leer, as could still be discerned; but generations of Casterbridge boys had thrown stones at the mask, aiming at its open mouth; and the blows thereof had chipped off the lips and jaws as if they had been eaten away by disease. The appearance was so ghastly by the weakly lamp glimmer that she could not bear to look at it—the first unpleasant feature of her visit.

The position of the queer old door and the odd presence of the leering mask suggested one thing above all others as appertaining to the mansion's past history —intrigue. By the alley it had been possible to come unseen from all sorts of quarters in the town—the old play-house, the old bull-stake, the old cock-pit, the pool wherein nameless infants had been used to disappear. High Place Hall could boast of its conveniences undoubtedly.

She turned to come away in the nearest direction homeward, which was up the alley, but hearing footsteps approaching in that quarter, and having no great wish to be found in such a place at such a time, she quickly retreated. There being no other way out, she stood behind a brick pier till the intruder should have gone his ways.

Had she watched she would have been surprised. She would have seen that the pedestrian on coming up made straight for the arched doorway : that as he paused with his hand upon the latch the lamplight fell upon the face of Henchard.

But Elizabeth-Jane clung so closely to her nook that she discerned nothing of this. Henchard passed in, as ignorant of her presence as she was ignorant of his identity, and disappeared in the darkness. Elizabeth came out a second time into the alley, and made the best of her way home.

Henchard's chiding, by begetting in her a nervous fear of doing anything definable as unlady-like, had operated thus curiously in keeping them unknown to each other at a critical moment. Much might have resulted from recognition—at the least a query on either side in one and the self-same form : What could he or she possibly be doing there?

Henchard, whatever his business at the lady's house, reached his own home only a few minutes later than Elizabeth-Jane. Her plan was to broach the question of leaving his roof this evening ; the events of the day had urged her to the course. But its execution depended upon his mood, and she anxiously awaited his manner towards her. She found that it had changed. He showed no further tendency to be angry ; he showed something worse. Absolute indifference had taken the place of irritability ; and his coldness was such that it encouraged her to departure, even more than hot temper could have done.

'Father, have you any objection to my going away?' she asked.

'Going away! No—none whatever. Where are you going?'

She thought it undesirable and unnecessary to say anything at present about her destination to one who took so little interest in her. He would know that soon enough. 'I have heard of an opportunity of getting more cultivated and finished, and being less idle,' she answered, with hesitation. 'A chance of a place in a household where I can have advantages of study, and seeing refined life.'

'Then make the best of it, in Heaven's name—if you can't get cultivated where you are.'

'You don't object?'

'Object—I? Ho—no! Not at all.' After a pause he said, 'But you won't have enough money for this lively scheme without help, you know? If you like I should be willing to make you an allowance, so that you be not bound to live upon the starvation wages refined folk are likely to pay 'ee.'

She thanked him for this offer.

'It had better be done properly,' he added after a pause. 'A small annuity is what I should like you to have—so as to be independent of me—and so that I may be independent of you. Would that please ye?'

'Certainly.'

'Then I'll see about it this very day.' He seemed relieved to get her off his hands by this arrangement, and as far as they were concerned the matter was settled. She now simply waited to see the lady again

The day and the hour came; but a drizzling rain fell. Elizabeth-Jane, having now changed her orbit from one of gay independence to laborious self-help, thought the weather good enough for such declined glory as hers, if her friend would only face it—a matter of doubt. She went to the boot-room where her pattens had hung ever since her apotheosis; took them down, had their mildewed leathers blacked, and put them on as she had done in old times. Thus mounted, and with cloak and umbrella, she went off to the place of appointment—intending, if the lady were not there, to call at the house.

One side of the churchyard—the side towards the weather—was sheltered by an ancient thatched mud wall whose eaves overhung as much as one or two feet. At the back of the wall was a corn-yard with its granary and barns—the place wherein she had met Farfrae many months earlier. Under the projection of the thatch she saw a figure. The young lady had come.

Her presence so exceptionally substantiated the girl's utmost hopes that she almost feared her good fortune. Fancies find room in the strongest minds. Here, in a churchyard old as civilization, in the worst of weathers, was a strange woman of curious fascinations never seen elsewhere: there might be some devilry about her presence. However, Elizabeth went on to the church tower, on whose summit the rope of a flag-staff rattled in the wind; and thus she came to the wall.

The lady had such a cheerful aspect in the drizzle that Elizabeth forgot her fancy. 'Well,' said the lady, a little of the whiteness of her teeth appearing with the word through the black fleece that protected her face, 'have you decided?'

'Yes, quite,' said the other eagerly.

'Your father is willing?'

'Yes.'

'Then come along.'

'When?'

'Now—as soon as you like. I had a good mind to send to you to come to my house, thinking you might not venture up here in the wind. But as I like getting out of doors, I thought I would come and see first.'

'It was my own thought.'

'That shows we shall agree. Then can you come to-day? My house is so hollow and dismal that I want some living thing there.'

' I think I might be able to,' said the girl, reflecting.

Voices were borne over to them at that instant on the wind and raindrops from the other side of the wall. There came such words as ' sacks,' ' quarters,' ' threshing,' ' tailing,' ' next Saturday's market,' each sentence being disorganized by the gusts like a face in a cracked mirror. Both the women listened.

' Who are those ? ' said the lady.

' One is my father. He rents that yard and barn.'

The lady seemed to forget the immediate business in listening to the technicalities of the corn trade. At last she said suddenly, ' Did you tell him where you were going to ? '

' No.'

' Oh—how was that ? '

' I thought it safer to get away first—as he is so uncertain in his temper.'

' Perhaps you are right. . . . Besides, I have never told you my name. It is Miss Templeman. . . . Are they gone—on the other side ? '

' No. They have only gone up into the granary.'

' Well, it is getting damp here. I shall expect you to-day—this evening, say, at six.'

' Which way shall I come, ma'am.'

' The front way—through the door. There is no other.'

Elizabeth-Jane had been thinking of the door in the alley.

' Perhaps, as you have not mentioned your destination, you may as well keep silent upon it till you are clear off. Who knows but that he may alter his mind ? '

Elizabeth-Jane shook her head. ' On consideration I don't fear it,' she said sadly. ' He has grown quite cold to me.'

' Very well. Six o'clock then.'

When they had emerged upon the open road and

parted, they found enough to do in holding their bowed umbrellas to the wind. Nevertheless the lady looked in at the corn-yard gates as she passed them, and paused on one foot for a moment. But nothing was visible there save the ricks, and the humpbacked barn, cushioned with moss, and the granary, rising against the church-tower behind, where the smacking of the rope against the flag-staff still went on.

Now Henchard had not the slightest suspicion that Elizabeth-Jane's movement was to be so prompt. Hence when, just before six, he reached home and saw a fly at the door from the King's Arms, and his step-daughter, with all her little bags and boxes, getting into it, he was taken by surprise.

'But you said I might go, father?' she explained through the carriage window.

'Said!—yes. But I thought you meant next month, or next year. 'Od, seize it—you take time by the forelock! This, then, is how you be going to treat me for all my trouble about ye?'

'O father! how can you speak like that? It is unjust of you!' she said with spirit.

'Well, well, have your own way,' he replied. He entered the house, and, seeing that all her things had not yet been.brought down, went up to her room to look on. He had never been there since she had occupied it. Evidences of her care, of her endeavours for improvement, were visible all around, in the form of books, sketches, maps, and little arrangements for tasteful effects. Henchard had known nothing of these efforts. He gazed at them, turned suddenly about, and came down to the door.

'Look here,' he said, in an altered voice—he never called her by name now—' don't 'ee go away from me. It may be I've spoke roughly to you—but I've been grieved beyond everything by you—there's something that caused it.'

'By me?' she said, with deep concern. 'What have I done?'

'I can't tell you now. But if you'll stop, and go on living as my daughter, I'll tell you all in time.'

But the proposal had come ten minutes too late. She was in the fly—was already, in imagination, at the house of the lady whose manner had such charms for her. 'Father,' she said, as considerately as she could, 'I think it best for us that I go on now. I need not stay long; I shall not be far away; and if you want me badly I can soon come back again.'

He nodded ever so slightly, as a receipt of her decision, and no more. 'You are not going far, you say. What will be your address, in case I wish to write to you? Or am I not to know?'

'Oh yes—certainly. It is only in the town—High Place Hall.'

'Where?' said Henchard, his face stilling.

She repeated the words. He neither moved nor spoke, and waving her hand to him in utmost friendliness, she signified to the flyman to drive up the street.

XXII

W E go back for a moment to the preceding night, to account for Henchard's attitude.

At the hour when Elizabeth-Jane was contemplating her stealthy reconnoitring excursion to the abode of the lady of her fancy, he had been not a little amazed at receiving a letter by hand in Lucetta's well-known characters. The self-repression, the resignation of her previous communication had vanished from her mood; she wrote with some of the natural lightness which had marked her in their early acquaintance.

'HIGH PLACE HALL.

'MY DEAR MR. HENCHARD,—Don't be surprised. It is for your good and mine, as I hope, that I have come to live at Casterbridge—for how long I cannot tell. That depends upon another; and he is a man, and a merchant, and a Mayor, and one who has the first right to my affections.

'Seriously, *mon ami*, I am not so light-hearted as I may seem to be from this. I have come here in consequence of hearing of the death of your wife—whom you used to think of as dead so many years before! Poor woman, she seems to have been a sufferer, though uncomplaining, and though weak in intellect not an imbecile. I am glad you acted fairly by her. As soon as I knew she was no more, it was brought home to me very forcibly by my conscience that I ought to endeavour to disperse the shade which my *étourderie* flung over my name, by asking you to carry out your promise to me. I hope you are of the same mind, and that you will take steps to this end. As, however, I did not know how you were situated, or what had happened since our separation, I decided to come and establish myself here before communicating with you.

'You probably feel as I do about this. I shall be able to see you in a day or two. Till then, farewell.— Yours,   LUCETTA.

'*P.S.*—I was unable to keep my appointment to meet you for a moment or two in passing through Caster-bridge the other day. My plans were altered by a family event, which it will surprise you to hear of.'

Henchard had already heard that High Place Hall was being prepared for a tenant. He said with a puzzled air to the first person he encountered, 'Who is coming to live at the Hall?'

'A lady of the name of Templeman, I believe, sir,' said his informant.

Henchard thought it over. 'Lucetta is related to her, I suppose,' he said to himself. 'Yes, I must put her in her proper position, undoubtedly.'

It was by no means with the oppression that would once have accompanied the thought that he regarded the moral necessity now; it was, indeed, with interest, if not warmth. His bitter disappointment at finding Eliza-beth-Jane to be none of his, and himself a childless man, had left an emotional void in Henchard that he uncon-sciously craved to fill. In this frame of mind, though without strong feeling, he had strolled up the blind alley and into High Place Hall by the postern at which Elizabeth had so nearly encountered him. He had gone on thence into the court, and inquired of a man whom he saw unpacking china from a crate, if Miss Le Sueur was living there. Miss Le Sueur had been the name under which he had known Lucetta—or 'Lucette,' as she had called herself at that time.

The man replied in the negative; that Miss Templeman only had come. Henchard went away, concluding that Lucetta had not as yet settled in.

He was in this interested stage of the inquiry when he witnessed Elizabeth-Jane's departure the next day. On hearing her announce the address, there suddenly took possession of him the strange thought that Lucetta and Miss Templeman were one and the same person, for he could recall that in her season of intimacy with him the name of the rich relative whom he had deemed somewhat a mythical personage had been given as Templeman. Though not a fortune-hunter, the possibility that Lucetta had been sublimed into a lady of means by some munificent testament on the part of this relative lent a charm to her image which it might not otherwise have acquired. He was getting on towards the dead level of middle age, when material things increasingly possess the mind.

But Henchard was not left long in suspense. Lucetta was rather addicted to scribbling, as had been shown by the torrent of letters after the *fiasco* in their marriage arrangements, and hardly had Elizabeth gone away when another note came to the Mayor's house from High Place Hall.

'I am in residence,' she said, 'and comfortable, though getting here has been a wearisome undertaking. You probably know what I am going to tell you, or do you not? My good Aunt Templeman, the banker's widow, whose very existence you used to doubt, much more her affluence, has lately died, and bequeathed some of her property to me. I will not enter into details except to say that I have taken her name—as a means of escape from mine, and its wrongs.

'I am now my own mistress, and have chosen to reside in Casterbridge—to be tenant of High Place Hall, that at least you may be put to no trouble if you wish to see me. My first intention was to keep you in ignorance of the changes in my life till you should meet me in the street; but I have thought better of this.

'You probably are aware of my arrangement with your daughter, and have doubtless laughed at the—what shall I call it?—practical joke (in all affection) of my getting her to live with me. But my first meeting with her was purely an accident. Do you see, Michael, partly why I have done it?—why, to give you an excuse for coming here as if to visit *her*, and thus to form my acquaintance naturally. She is a dear, good girl, and she thinks you have treated her with undue severity. You may have done so in your haste, but not deliberately, I am sure. As the result has been to bring her to me I am not disposed to upbraid you.—In haste, yours always, LUCETTA.'

The excitement which these announcements produced in Henchard's gloomy soul was to him most pleasurable. He sat over his dining-table long and dreamily, and by an almost mechanical transfer the sentiments which had run to waste since his estrangement from Elizabeth-Jane and Donald Farfrae gathered around Lucetta before they had grown dry. She was plainly in a very coming-on disposition for marriage. But what else could a poor woman be who had given her time and heart to him so thoughtlessly, at that former time, as to lose her credit by it? Probably conscience no less than affection had brought her here On the whole he did not blame her.

'The artful little woman!' he said, smiling (with reference to Lucetta's adroit and pleasant manœuvre with Elizabeth-Jane).

To feel that he would like to see Lucetta was with Henchard to start for her house. He put on his hat and went. It was between eight and nine o'clock when he reached her door. The answer brought him was that Miss Templeman was engaged for that evening; but that she would be happy to see him the next day.

'That's rather like giving herself airs!' he thought. 'And considering what we——' But after all, she plainly had not expected him, and he took the refusal quietly. Nevertheless he resolved not to go next day. 'These cursed women—there's not an inch of straight grain in 'em!' he said.

Let us follow the track of Mr. Henchard's thought as if it were a clue line, and view the interior of High Place Hall on this particular evening.

On Elizabeth-Jane's arrival she had been phlegmatically asked by an elderly woman to go upstairs and take off her things. She had replied with great earnestness that she would not think of giving that trouble, and on the instant divested herself of her bonnet and cloak in the passage. She was then conducted to the first door on the landing, and left to find her way further alone.

The room disclosed was prettily furnished as a boudoir or small drawing-room, and on a sofa with two cylindrical pillows reclined a dark-haired, large-eyed, pretty woman, of unmistakably French extraction on one side or the other. She was probably some years older than Elizabeth, and had a sparkling light in her eye. In front of the sofa was a small table, with a pack of cards scattered upon it faces upward.

The attitude had been so full of abandonment that she bounded up like a spring on hearing the door open.

Perceiving that it was Elizabeth she lapsed into ease, and came across to her with a reckless skip that innate grace only prevented from being boisterous.

'Why, you are late,' she said, taking hold of Elizabeth-Jane's hands.

'There were so many little things to put up.'

'And you seem dead-alive and tired. Let me try
to enliven you by some wonderful tricks I have learnt,
to kill time. Sit there and don't move.' She gathered
up the pack of cards, pulled the table in front of her,
and began to deal them rapidly, telling Elizabeth to
choose some.

'Well, have you chosen?' she asked, flinging down
the last card

'No,' stammered Elizabeth, arousing herself from
a reverie. 'I quite forgot, I was thinking of—you, and
me—and how strange it is that I am here.'

Miss Templeman looked at Elizabeth-Jane with interest, and laid down the cards. 'Ah! never mind,'
she said. 'I'll lie here while you sit by me; and we'll
talk.'

Elizabeth drew up silently to the head of the sofa,
but with obvious pleasure. It could be seen that in
years she was younger than her entertainer, while in
manner and general vision she seemed more of the
sage. Miss Templeman deposited herself on the sofa
in her former flexuous position, and throwing her arm
above her brow—somewhat in the pose of a well-
known conception of Titian's—talked up at Elizabeth-
Jane invertedly across her forehead and arm.

'I must tell you something,' she said. 'I wonder
if you have suspected it. I have only been mistress
of a large house and fortune a little while.'

'Oh! only a little while?' murmured Elizabeth-Jane,
her countenance slightly falling.

'As a girl I lived about in garrison towns and elsewhere with my father, till I was quite flighty and unsettled. He was an officer in the army. I should not
have mentioned this had I not thought it best you
should know the truth.'

'Yes, yes.' She looked thoughtfully round the
room—at the little square piano with brass inlayings,

at the window-curtains, at the lamp, at the fair and dark kings and queens on the card-table, and finally at the inverted face of Lucetta Templeman, whose large lustrous eyes had such an odd effect upside down.

Elizabeth's mind ran on acquirements to an almost morbid degree. 'You speak French and Italian fluently, no doubt,' she said. 'I have not been able to get beyond a wretched bit of Latin yet.'

'Well, for that matter, in my native isle speaking French does not go for much. It is rather the other way.'

'Where is your native isle?'

It was with rather more reluctance that Miss Templeman said, 'Jersey. There they speak French on one side of the street and English on the other, and a mixed tongue in the middle of the road. But it is a long time since I was there. Bath is where my people really belong to, though my ancestors in Jersey were as good as anybody in England. They were the Le Sueurs, an old family who have done great things in their time. I went back and lived there after my father's death. But I don't value such past matters, and am quite an English person in my feelings and tastes.'

Lucetta's tongue had for a moment outrun her discretion. She had arrived at Casterbridge as a Bath lady, and there were obvious reasons why Jersey should drop out of her life. But Elizabeth had tempted her to make free, and a deliberately formed resolve had been broken.

It could not, however, have been broken in safer company. Lucetta's words went no further, and after this day she was so much upon her guard that there appeared no chance of her identification with the young Jersey woman who had been Henchard's dear comrade at a critical time. Not the least amusing of her safeguards was her resolute avoidance of a French word, if one by accident came to her tongue more readily than its English equivalent. She shirked it with the suddenness of the weak Apostle at the accusation, 'Thy speech bewrayeth thee!'

Expectancy sat visibly upon Lucetta the next morning. She dressed herself for Mr. Henchard, and restlessly awaited his call before mid-day; as he did not come she waited on through the afternoon. But she did not tell Elizabeth that the person expected was the girl's stepfather.

They sat in adjoining windows of the same room in Lucetta's great stone mansion, netting, and looking out upon the market, which formed an animated scene. Elizabeth could see the crown of her stepfather's hat among the rest beneath, and was not aware that Lucetta watched the same object with yet intenser interest. He moved about amid the throng, at this point lively as an ant-hill; elsewhere more reposeful, and broken up by stalls of fruit and vegetables. The farmers as a rule preferred the open *carrefour* for their transactions, despite its inconvenient jostlings and the danger from crossing vehicles, to the gloomy sheltered market-room provided for them. Here they surged on this one day of the week, forming a little world of leggings, switches, and sample-bags; men of extensive stomachs, sloping like mountain sides; men whose heads in walking swayed as the trees in November gales; who in conversing varied their attitudes much, lowering themselves by spreading their knees, and thrusting their hands into the pockets of remote inner jackets. Their faces radiated tropical warmth; for though when at home their countenances varied with the seasons, their market-faces all the year round were glowing little fires.

All over-clothes here were worn as if they were an inconvenience, a hampering necessity. Some men were well-dressed; but the majority were careless in that respect, appearing in suits which were historical records of their wearer's deeds, sun-scorchings, and daily struggles for many years past. Yet many carried ruffled cheque-books in their pockets which regulated at the bank hard by a balance of never less than four figures. In fact, what these gibbous human shapes specially represented was ready money—money insistently ready —not ready next year like a nobleman's—often not merely ready at the bank like a professional man's, but ready in their large plump hands.

It happened that to-day there rose in the midst of them all two or three tall apple-trees standing as if they grew on the spot; till it was perceived that they were held by men from the cider-districts who came here to sell them, bringing the clay of their county on their boots. Elizabeth-Jane, who had often observed them, said, 'I wonder if the same trees come every week?'

'What trees?' said Lucetta, absorbed in watching for Henchard.

Elizabeth replied vaguely, for an incident checked her. Behind one of the trees stood Farfrae, briskly discussing a sample-bag with a farmer. Henchard had come up, accidentally encountering the young man, whose face seemed to inquire, 'Do we speak to each other?'

She saw her stepfather throw a shine into his eye, which answered 'No!' Elizabeth-Jane sighed.

'Are you particularly interested in anybody out there?' said Lucetta.

'Oh no,' said her companion, a quick red shooting over her face.

Luckily Farfrae's figure was immediately covered by the apple-tree.

Lucetta looked hard at her. 'Quite sure?' she said.

'Oh yes,' said Elizabeth-Jane.

Again Lucetta looked out. 'They are all farmers I suppose?' she said.

'No. There's Mr. Bulge—he's a wine merchant; there's Benjamin Brownlet — a horse dealer; and Kitson, the pig breeder; and Yopper, the auctioneer; besides maltsters, and millers—and so on.' Farfrae stood out quite distinctly now; but she did not mention him.

The Saturday afternoon slipped on thus desultorily. The market changed from the sample-showing hour to the idle hour before starting homewards, when tales were told. Henchard had not called on Lucetta, though he had stood so near. He must have been too busy, she thought. He would come on Sunday or Monday.

The days came, but not the visitor, though Lucetta repeated her dressing with scrupulous care. She was disheartened. It may at once be declared that Lucetta no longer bore towards Henchard all that warm allegiance which had characterized her in their first acquaintance ; the then unfortunate issue of things had chilled pure love considerably. But there remained a conscientious wish to bring about her union with him, now that there was nothing to hinder it—to right her position—which in itself was a happiness to sigh for. With strong social reasons on her side why their marriage should take place, there had ceased to be any worldly reason on his why it should be postponed, since she had succeeded to fortune.

Tuesday was the great Candlemas fair. At breakfast she said to Elizabeth-Jane quite coolly : ' I imagine your father may call to see you to-day. I suppose he stands close by in the market-place, with the rest of the corn-dealers ? '

She shook her head. ' He won't come.'

' Why ? '

' He has taken against me,' she said in a husky voice.

' You have quarrelled more deeply than I know of.'

Elizabeth, wishing to shield the man she believed
to be her father from any charge of unnatural dislike,
said 'Yes.'

'Then where you are is, of all places, the one he
will avoid?'

Elizabeth nodded sadly.

Lucetta looked blank, twitched up her lovely eyebrows and lip, and burst into hysterical sobs. Here
was a disaster—her ingenious scheme completely stultified!

'Oh, my dear Miss Templeman—what's the matter?'
cried her companion.

'I like your company much!' said Lucetta, as soon
as she could speak.

'Yes, yes—and so do I yours!' Elizabeth chimed
in soothingly.

'But—but——' She could not finish the sentence,
which was, naturally, that if Henchard had such a
rooted dislike for the girl as now seemed to be the
case, Elizabeth-Jane would have to be got rid of—a
disagreeable necessity.

A provisional resource suggested itself. 'Miss Henchard—will you go on an errand for me as soon
as breakfast is over?—Ah, that's very good of you.
Will you go and order——' Here she enumerated
several commissions at sundry shops, which would·
occupy Elizabeth's time for the next hour or two, at
least.

'And have you ever seen the Museum?'

Elizabeth-Jane had not.

'Then you should do so at once. You can finish
the morning by going there. It is an old house in a
back street—I forget where—but you'll find out—and
there are crowds of interesting things—skeletons, teeth,
old pots and pans, ancient boots and shoes, birds' eggs
—all charmingly instructive. You'll be sure to stay till
you get quite hungry.'

Elizabeth hastily put on her things and departed.
'I wonder why she wants to get rid of me to-day!' she
said sorrowfully, as she went. That her absence, rather
than her services or instruction, was in request, had
been readily apparent to Elizabeth-Jane, simple as she
seemed and difficult as it was to attribute a motive for
the desire.

She had not been gone ten minutes when one of
Lucetta's servants was sent to Henchard's with a note.
The contents were briefly :—

'DEAR MICHAEL,—You will be standing close to my
house to-day for two or three hours in the course of
your business, so do please call and see me. I am
sadly disappointed that you have not come before, for
can I help anxiety about my own equivocal relation to
you?—especially now my aunt's fortune has brought
me more prominently before society? Your daughter's
presence here may be the cause of your neglect; and
I have therefore sent her away for the morning. Say
you come on business—I shall be quite alone.
                                    'LUCETTA.'

When the messenger returned her mistress gave
directions that if a gentleman called he was to be
admitted at once, and sat down to await results.

Sentimentally she did not much care to see him—
his delays had wearied her; but it was necessary; and
with a sigh she arranged herself picturesquely in the
chair; first this way, then that; next so that the light
fell over her head. Next she flung herself on the couch
in the cyma-recta curve which so became her, and, with
her arm over her brow, looked towards the door. This,
she decided, was the best position after all; and thus
she remained till a man's step was heard on the stairs.
Whereupon Lucetta, forgetting her curve (for Nature
was too strong for Art as yet), jumped up, and ran and

hid herself behind one of the window-curtains in a freak of timidity. In spite of the waning of passion the situation was an agitating one—she had not seen Henchard since his (supposed) temporary parting from her in Jersey.

She could hear the servant showing the visitor into the room, shutting the door upon him, and leaving as if to go and look for her mistress. Lucetta flung back the curtain with a nervous greeting. The man before her was not Henchard.

XXIII

A CONJECTURE that her visitor might be some other person had, indeed, flashed through Lucetta's mind when she was on the point of bursting out; but it was just too late to recede.

He was years younger than the Mayor of Caster-bridge; fair, fresh, and slenderly handsome. He wore genteel cloth leggings with white buttons, polished boots with infinite lace holes, light cord breeches under a black velveteen coat and waistcoat; and he had a silver-topped switch in his hand. Lucetta blushed, and said with a curious mixture of pout and laugh on her face—'Oh, I've made a mistake!'

The visitor, on the contrary, did not laugh half a wrinkle.

'But I'm very sorry!' he said, in deprecating tones. 'I came and I inquired for Miss Henchard, and they showed me up heere, and in no case would I have caught ye so unmannerly if I had known!'

'I was the unmannerly one,' said she.

'But is it that I have come to the wrong house, madam?' said Mr. Farfrae, blinking a little in his bewilderment and nervously tapping his legging with his switch.

'Oh no, sir,—sit down. You must come and sit down now you are here,' replied Lucetta kindly, to relieve his embarrassment. 'Miss Henchard will be here directly.'

Now this was not strictly true; but that something about the young man—that hyperborean crispness, stringency, and charm, as of a well-braced musical instrument, which had awakened the interest of Henchard, and of Elizabeth-Jane, and of the Three Mariners' jovial crew, at sight, made his unexpected presence here attractive to Lucetta. He hesitated, looked at the chair, thought there was no danger in it (though there was), and sat down.

Farfrae's sudden entry was simply the result of Henchard's permission to him to see Elizabeth, if he were minded to woo her At first he had taken no notice of Henchard's brusque letter; but an exceptionally fortunate business transaction put him on good terms with everybody, and revealed to him that he could undeniably marry if he chose. Then who so pleasing, thrifty, and satisfactory in every way as Elizabeth-Jane? Apart from her personal recommendations, a reconciliation with his former friend Henchard would, in the natural course of things, flow from such a union. He therefore forgave the Mayor his curtness; and this morning on his way to the fair he had called at her house, where he learnt that she was staying at Miss Templeman's. A little stimulated at not finding her ready and waiting—so fanciful are men!—he hastened on to High Place Hall, to encounter no Elizabeth, but its mistress herself.

'The fair to-day seems a large one,' she said, when, by a natural deviation, their eyes sought the busy scene without. 'Your numerous fairs and markets keep me interested. How many things I think of while I watch from here!'

He seemed in doubt how to answer, and the babble without reached them as they sat—voices as of wavelets on a lopping sea, one ever and anon rising above the rest. 'Do you look out often?' he asked.

'Yes—very often.'

'Do you look for any one you know?'

Why should she have answered as she did?

'I look as at a picture merely. But,' she went on, turning pleasantly to him, 'I may do so now—I may look for you. You are always there, are you not? Ah —I don't mean it seriously! But it is amusing to look for somebody one knows in a crowd, even if one does not want him. It takes off the terrible oppressiveness of being surrounded by a throng, and having no point of junction with it through a single individual.'

'Ay! Maybe you'll be very lonely, ma'am?'

'Nobody knows how lonely.'

'But you are rich, they say?'

'If so, I don't know how to enjoy my riches. I came to Casterbridge thinking I should like to live here. But I wonder if I shall.'

'Where did ye come from, ma'am?'

'The neighbourhood of Bath.'

'And I from near Edinboro',' he murmured. 'It's better to stay at home, and that's true; but a man must live where his money is made. It is a great pity, but it's always so! Yet I've done very well this year. Oh yes,' he went on with ingenuous enthusiasm. 'You see that man with the drab kerseymere coat? I bought largely of him in the autumn when wheat was down, and then afterwards when it rose a little I sold off all I had! It brought only a small profit to me; while the farmers kept theirs, expecting higher figures—yes, though the rats were gnawing the ricks hollow. Just when I sold the markets went lower, and I bought up the corn of those who had been holding back at less price than my first purchases. And then,' cried Farfrae impetuously, his face alight, 'I sold it a few weeks after, when it happened to go up again! And so, by contenting

mysel' with small profits frequently repeated, I soon
made five hundred pounds—yes!'—(bringing down his
hand upon the table, and quite forgetting where he was)
—'while the others by keeping theirs in hand made
nothing at all!'

Lucetta regarded him with a critical interest. He
was quite a new type of person to her. At last his eye
fell upon the lady's and their glances met.

'Ay, now, I'm wearying you!' he exclaimed.

She said, 'No, indeed,' colouring a shade.

'What then?'

'Quite otherwise. You are most interesting.'

It was now Farfrae who showed the modest pink.

'I mean all you Scotchmen,' she added in hasty
correction. 'So free from Southern extremes. We
common people are all one way or the other—warm or
cold, passionate or frigid. You have both temperatures
going on in you at the same time.'

'But how do you mean that? Ye were best to
explain clearly, ma'am.'

'You are animated—then you are thinking of getting
on. You are sad the next moment—then you are
thinking of Scotland and friends.'

'Yes. I think of home sometimes!' he said simply.

'So do I—as far as I can. But it was an old
house where I· was born, and they pulled it down for
improvements, so I seem hardly to have any home to
think of now.'

Lucetta did not add, as she might have done, that
the house was in St. Helier, and not in Bath.

'But the mountains, and the mists and the rocks,
they are there! And don't they seem like home?'

She shook her head.

'They do to me—they do to me,' he murmured.
And his mind could be seen flying away northwards.
Whether its origin were national or personal, it was
quite true what Lucetta had said, that the curious

double strands in Farfrae's thread of life—the commercial and the romantic—were very distinct at times. Like the colours in a variegated cord those contrasts could be seen intertwisted, yet not mingling.

'You are wishing you were back again,' said she.

'Ah, no, ma'am,' said Farfrae, suddenly recalling himself.

The fair without the windows was now raging thick and loud. It was the chief hiring fair of the year, and differed quite from the market of a few days earlier. In substance it was a whitey-brown crowd flecked with white—this being the body of labourers waiting for places. The long bonnets of the women, like waggon-tilts, their cotton gowns and checked shawls, mixed with the carters' smockfrocks; for they, too, entered into the hiring. Among the rest, at the corner of the pavement, stood an old shepherd, who attracted the eyes of Lucetta and Farfrae by his stillness. He was evidently a chastened man. The battle of life had been a sharp one with him, for, to begin with, he was a man of small frame. He was now so bowed by hard work and years that, approaching from behind, a person could hardly see his head. He had planted the stem of his crook in the gutter, and was resting upon the bow, which was polished to silver brightness by the long friction of his hands. He had quite forgotten where he was, and what he had come for, his eyes being bent on the ground. A little way off negotiations were proceeding which had reference to him; but he did not hear them, and there seemed to be passing through his mind pleasant visions of the hiring successes of his prime, when his skill laid open to him any farm for the asking.

The negotiations were between a farmer from a distant county and the old man's son. In these there was a difficulty. The farmer would not take the crust without the crumb of the bargain, in other words, the old man without the younger; and the son had a sweetheart on his present farm, who stood by, waiting the issue with pale lips.

'I'm sorry to leave ye, Nelly,' said the young man with emotion. 'But, you see, I can't starve father, and he's out o' work at Lady-day. 'Tis only seventy mile.'

The girl's lips quivered. 'Seventy mile!' she murmured. 'Ah! 'tis enough! I shall never see 'ee again!' It was, indeed, a hopeless length of traction for Dan Cupid's magnet; for young men were young men at Casterbridge as elsewhere.

'Oh! no, no—I never shall,' she insisted, when he pressed her hand; and she turned her face to Lucetta's wall to hide her weeping. The farmer said he would give the young man half-an-hour for his answer, and went away, leaving the group sorrowing.

Lucetta's eyes, full of tears, met Farfrae's. His, too, to her surprise, were moist at the scene.

'It is very hard,' she said with strong feelings. 'Lovers ought not to be parted like that! Oh, if I had my wish, I'd let people live and love at their pleasure!'

'Maybe I can manage that they'll not be parted,' said Farfrae. 'I want a young carter; and perhaps I'll take the old man too—yes; he'll not be very expensive, and doubtless he will answer ma pairrpose somehow.'

'Oh, you are so good!' she cried, delighted. 'Go and tell them, and let me know if you have succeeded!'

Farfrae went out, and she saw him speak to the group. The eyes of all brightened; the bargain was soon struck. Farfrae returned to her immediately it was concluded.

'It is kind-hearted of you, indeed,' said Lucetta. 'For my part, I have resolved that all my servants shall have lovers if they want them! Do make the same resolve!'

Farfrae looked more serious, waving his head a half turn. 'I must be a little stricter than that,' he said.

'Why?'

'You are a—a thriving woman; and I am a struggling hay-and-corn merchant.'

'I am a very ambitious woman.'

'Ah, well, I cannet explain. I don't know how to talk to ladies, ambitious or no; and that's true,' said Donald with grave regret. 'I try to be civil to a' folk—no more!'

'I see you are as you say,' replied she, sensibly getting the upper hand in these exchanges of sentiment. Under this revelation of insight Farfrae again looked out of the window into the thick of the fair.

Two farmers met and shook hands, and being quite near the window their remarks could be heard as others' had been.

'Have you seen young Mr. Farfrae this morning?' asked one. 'He promised to meet me here at the stroke of twelve; but I've gone athwart and about the fair half-a-dozen times, and never a sign of him: though he's mostly a man to his word.'

'I quite forgot the engagement,' murmured Farfrae.

'Now you must go,' said she; 'must you not?'

'Yes,' he replied. But he still remained.

'You had better go,' she urged. 'You will lose a customer.'

'Now, Miss Templeman, you will make me angry,' exclaimed Farfrae.

'Then suppose you don't go; but stay a little longer?'

He looked anxiously at the farmer who was seeking him, and who just then ominously walked across to where Henchard was standing, and he looked into the room and at her. 'I like staying; but I fear I must go!' he said. 'Business ought not to be neglected, ought it?'

'Not for a single minute.'

'It's true. I'll come another time—if I may ma'am?'

'Certainly,' she said. 'What has happened to us to-day is very curious.'

'Something to think over when we are alone, it's like to be?'

'Oh, I don't know that. It is commonplace after all.'

'No, I'll not say that. Oh no!'

'Well, whatever it has been, it is now over; and the market calls you to be gone.'

'Yes, yes. Market—business! I wish there were no business in the warrld.'

Lucetta almost laughed — she would quite have laughed — but that there was a little emotion going in her at the time. 'How you change!' she said. 'You should not change like this.'

'I have never wished such things before,' said the Scotchman, with a simple, shamed, apologetic look for his weakness. 'It is only since coming here, and seeing you!'

'If that's the case, you had better not look at me any longer. Dear me, I feel I have quite demoralized you!'

'But look or look not, I will see you in my thoughts. Well, I'll go—thank you for the pleasure of this visit.'

'Thank you for staying.'

'Maybe I'll get into my market-mind when I've been out a few minutes,' he murmured. 'But I don't know —I don't know!'

As he went she said eagerly, 'You may hear them speak of me in Casterbridge as time goes on. If they tell you I'm a coquette, which some may, because of the incidents of my life, don't believe it, for I am not.'

'I swear I will not!' he said fervidly.

195

Thus the two. She had enkindled the young man's enthusiasm till he was quite brimming with sentiment; while he, from merely affording her a new form of idleness, had gone on to wake her serious solicitude. Why was this? They could not have told.

Lucetta as a young girl would hardly have looked at a tradesman. But her ups and downs, capped by her indiscretions with Henchard, had made her uncritical as to station. In her poverty she had met with repulse from the society to which she had belonged, and she had no great zest for renewing an attempt upon it now. Her heart longed for some ark into which it could fly and be at rest. Rough or smooth she did not care, so long as it was warm.

Farfrae was shown out, it having entirely escaped him that he had called to see Elizabeth. Lucetta at the window watched him threading the maze of farmers and farmers' men. She could see by his gait that he was conscious of her eyes, and her heart went out to him for his modesty—pleaded with her sense of his unfitness that he might be allowed to come again. He entered the market-house, and she could see him no more.

Three minutes later, when she had left the window, knocks, not of multitude but of strength, sounded through the house, and the waiting-maid tripped up.

'The Mayor,' she said.

Lucetta had reclined herself, and was looking dreamily through her fingers. She did not answer at once, and the maid repeated the information with the addition, 'And he's afraid he hasn't much time to spare, he says.'

'Oh! Then tell him that as I have a headache I won't detain him to-day.'

The message was taken down, and she heard the door close.

Lucetta had come to Casterbridge to quicken Henchard's feelings with regard to her. She had quickened them, and now she was indifferent to the achievement.

Her morning view of Elizabeth-Jane as a disturbing element changed, and she no longer felt strongly the necessity of getting rid of the girl for her stepfather's sake. When the young woman came in, sweetly unconscious of the turn in the tide, Lucetta went up to her, and said quite sincerely—

'I'm so glad you've come. You'll live with me a long time, won't you?'

Elizabeth as a watch-dog to keep her father off— what a new idea. Yet it was not unpleasing. Henchard had neglected her all these days, after compromising her indescribably in the past. The least he could have done when he found himself free, and herself affluent, would have been to respond heartily and promptly to her invitation.

Her emotions rose, fell, undulated, filled her with wild surmise at their suddenness; and so passed Lucetta's experiences of that day.

XXIV

POOR Elizabeth-Jane, little thinking what her malignant star had done to blast the budding attentions she had won from Donald Farfrae, was glad to hear Lucetta's words about remaining.

For in addition to Lucetta's house being a home, that raking view of the market-place which it afforded had as much attraction for her as for Lucetta. The *carrefour* was like the regulation Open Place in spectacular dramas, where the incidents that occur always happen to bear on the lives of the adjoining residents. Farmers, merchants, dairymen, quacks, hawkers, appeared there from week to week, and disappeared as the afternoon wasted away. It was the node of all orbits.

From Saturday to Saturday was as from day to day with the two young women now. In an emotional sense they did not live at all during the intervals. Wherever they might go wandering on other days, on market-day they were sure to- be at home. Both stole sly glances out of the window at Farfrae's shoulders and poll. His face they seldom saw, for, either through shyness, or not to disturb his mercantile mood, he avoided looking towards their quarters.

Thus things went on, till a certain market-morning brought a new sensation. Elizabeth and Lucetta were sitting at breakfast when a parcel containing two dresses arrived for the latter from London. She called Elizabeth from her breakfast, and entering her friend's bedroom Elizabeth saw the gowns spread out on the bed, one of a deep cherry colour, the other lighter—a glove lying at the end of each sleeve, a bonnet at the top of each neck, and parasols across the gloves, Lucetta standing beside the suggested human figure in an attitude of contemplation.

'I wouldn't think so hard about it,' said Elizabeth, marking the intensity with which Lucetta was alternating the question whether this or that would suit best.

'But settling upon new clothes is so trying,' said Lucetta. 'You are that person' (pointing to one of the arrangements), 'or you are *that* totally different person' (pointing to the other), 'for the whole of the coming spring: and one of the two, you don't know which, may turn out to be very objectionable.'

It was finally decided by Miss Templeman that she would be the cherry-coloured person at all hazards. The dress was pronounced to be a fit, and Lucetta walked with it into the front room, Elizabeth following her.

The morning was exceptionally bright for the time of year. The sun fell so flat on the houses and pavement opposite Lucetta's residence that they poured their brightness into her rooms. Suddenly, after a rumbling of wheels, there were added to this steady light a fantastic series of circling irradiations upon the ceiling, and the companions turned to the window. Immediately opposite a vehicle of strange description had come to a stand still, as if it had been placed there for exhibition.

It was the new-fashioned agricultural implement called a horse-drill, till then unknown, in its modern shape, in this part of the country, where the venerable seed-lip was still used for sowing as in the days of the Heptarchy. Its arrival created about as much sensation in the corn-market as a flying machine would create at Charing Cross. The farmers crowded round it, women drew near it, children crept under and into it. The machine was painted in bright hues of green, yellow, and red, and it resembled as a whole a compound of hornet, grasshopper, and shrimp, magnified enormously. Or it might have been likened to an upright musical instrument with the front gone. That was how it struck Lucetta. 'Why, it is a sort of agricultural piano,' she said.

'It has something to do with corn,' said Elizabeth.

'I wonder who thought of introducing it here?'

Donald Farfrae was in the minds of both as the innovator, for though not a farmer he was closely leagued with farming operations. And as if in response to their thought he came up at that moment, looked at the machine, walked round it, and handled it as if he knew something about its make. The two watchers had inwardly started at his coming, and Elizabeth left the window, went to the back of the room, and stood as if absorbed in the panelling of the wall. She hardly knew that she had done this till Lucetta, animated by the conjunction of her new attire with the sight of Farfrae, spoke out: 'Let us go and look at the instrument, whatever it is.'

Elizabeth-Jane's bonnet and shawl were pitchforked on in a moment, and they went out. Among all the agriculturists gathering round, the only appropriate possessor of the new machine seemed to be Lucetta, because she alone rivalled it in colour.

They examined it curiously; observing the rows of trumpet-shaped tubes one within the other, the little scoops, like revolving salt-spoons, which tossed the seed into the upper ends of the tubes that conducted it to the ground; till somebody said, 'Good morning, Elizabeth-Jane.' She looked up, and there was her stepfather.

His greeting had been somewhat dry and thunderous, and Elizabeth-Jane, embarrassed out of her equanimity,

stammered at random, 'This is the lady I live with,
father—Miss Templeman.'

Henchard put his hand to his hat, which he brought
down with a great wave till it met his body at the
knee. Miss Templeman bowed. 'I am happy to
become acquainted with you, Mr. Henchard,' she said.
'This is a curious machine.'

'Yes,' Henchard replied; and he proceeded to explain it, and still more forcibly to ridicule it.

'Who brought it here?' said Lucetta.

'Oh, don't ask me, ma'am!' said Henchard. 'The
thing—why 'tis impossible it should act. 'Twas brought
here by one of our machinists on the recommendation
of a jumped-up jackanapes of a fellow who thinks——'
His eye caught Elizabeth-Jane's imploring face, and he
stopped, probably thinking that the suit might be progressing.

He turned to go away. Then something seemed
to occur which his stepdaughter fancied must really be
a hallucination of hers. A murmur apparently came
from Henchard's lips in which she detected the words,
'You refused to see me!' reproachfully addressed to
Lucetta. She could not believe that they had been
uttered by her stepfather; unless, indeed, they might have
been spoken to one of the yellow-gaitered farmers near
them. Yet Lucetta seemed silent; and then all thought
of the incident was dissipated by the humming of a
song, which sounded as though from the interior of the
machine. Henchard had by this time vanished into the
market-house, and both the women glanced towards the
corn-drill. They could see behind it the bent back of a
man who was pushing his head into the internal works to
master their simple secrets. The hummed song went on—

> ' 'Tw—s on a s—m—r aftern—n,
> A wee be—re the s—n w—nt d—n,
> When Kitty wi' a braw n—w g—wn
> C—me ow're the h—lls to Gowrie.'

Elizabeth-Jane had apprehended the singer in a moment, and looked guilty of she did not know what. Lucetta next recognized him, and more mistress of herself said archly, ' The " Lass of Gowrie " from the inside of a seed-drill—what a phenomenon ! '

Satisfied at last with his investigation, the young man stood upright, and met their eyes across the summit.

' We are looking at the wonderful new drill,' Miss Templeman said. ' But practically it is a stupid thing —is it not ? ' she added, on the strength of Henchard's information.

' Stupid ? Oh no ! ' said Farfrae gravely. ' It will revolutionize sowing heerabout ! No more sowers flinging their seed about broadcast, so that some falls by the wayside and some among thorns, and all that. Each grain will go straight to its intended place, and nowhere else whatever ! '

' Then the romance of the sower is gone for good,' observed Elizabeth-Jane, who felt herself at one with Farfrae in Bible-reading at least. ' " He that observeth the wind shall not sow," so the Preacher said ; but his words will not be to the point any more. How things change ! '

' Ay ; ay. . . . It must be so ! ' Donald admitted, his gaze fixing itself on a blank point far away. ' But the machines are already very common in the East and North of England,' he added apologetically.

Lucetta seemed to be rather outside this train of sentiment, her acquaintance with the Scriptures being somewhat limited. ' Is the machine yours ? ' she asked of Farfrae.

' Oh no, madam,' said he, becoming embarrassed and deferential at the sound of her voice, though with Elizabeth-Jane he was quite at his ease. ' No, no—I merely recommended that it should be got.'

In the silence which followed Farfrae appeared only

conscious of her; to have passed from perception of Elizabeth into a brighter sphere of existence than she appertained to. Lucetta, discerning that he was much mixed that day, partly in his mercantile mood and partly in his romantic one, said gaily to him—

'Well, don't forsake the machine for us,' and went indoors with her companion.

The latter felt that she had been in the way, though why was unaccountable to her. Lucetta explained the matter somewhat by saying, when they were again in the sitting-room—

'I had occasion to speak to Mr. Farfrae the other day, and so I knew him this morning.'

Lucetta was very kind towards Elizabeth that day Together they saw the market thicken, and in course of time thin away with the slow decline of the sun towards the upper end of the town, its rays taking the street endways and enfilading the long thorough-fare from top to bottom. The gigs and vans disappeared one by one till there was not a vehicle in the street. The time of the riding world was over; the pedestrian world held sway. Field labourers and their wives and children trooped in from the villages for their weekly shopping, and instead of a rattle of wheels and a tramp of horses ruling the sound as earlier, there was nothing but the shuffle of many feet. All the implements were gone; all the farmers; all the moneyed class. The character of the town's trading had changed from bulk to multiplicity, and pence were handled now as pounds had been handled earlier in the day.

Lucetta and Elizabeth looked out upon this, for though it was night, and the street lamps were lighted, they had kept their shutters unclosed. In the faint blink of the fire they spoke more freely.

'Your father was distant with you,' said Lucetta.

'Yes.' And having forgotten the momentary

mystery of Henchard's seeming speech to Lucetta, she continued, ' It is because he does not think I am respectable. I have tried to be so more than you can imagine, but in vain! My mother's separation from my father was unfortunate for me. You don't know what it is to have shadows like that upon your life.'

Lucetta seemed to wince. ' I do not—of that kind precisely,' she said, ' but you may feel a—sense of disgrace—shame—in other ways.'

' Have you ever had any such feeling ? ' said the younger innocently.

' Oh no,' said Lucetta quickly. ' I was thinking of —what happens sometimes when women get themselves in strange positions in the eyes of the world from no fault of their own.'

' It must make them very unhappy afterwards.'

' It makes them anxious ; for might not other women despise them ? '

' Not altogether despise them. Yet not quite like or respect them.'

Lucetta winced again. Her past was by no means secure from investigation, even in Casterbridge. For one thing, Henchard had never returned to her the cloud of letters she had written and sent him in her first excitement. Possibly they were destroyed ; but she could have wished that they had never been written.

The rencounter with Farfrae and his bearing towards Lucetta had made the reflective Elizabeth more observant of her brilliant and amiable companion. A few days afterwards, when her eyes met Lucetta's as the latter was going out, she somehow knew that Miss Templeman was nourishing a hope of seeing the attractive Scotchman. The fact was printed large all over Lucetta's cheeks and eyes to any one who read her as Elizabeth-Jane was beginning to do. Lucetta passed on and closed the street door.

A seer's spirit took possession of Elizabeth, impelling

her to sit down by the fire, and divine events so surely from data already her own that they could be held as witnessed. She followed Lucetta thus mentally—saw her encounter Donald somewhere as if by chance—saw him wear his special look when meeting women, with an added intensity because this one was Lucetta. She depicted his impassioned manner; beheld the indecision of both between their lothness to separate and their desire not to be observed; depicted their shaking of hands; how they probably parted with frigidity in their general contour and movements, only in the smaller features showing the spark of passion, thus invisible to all but themselves. This discerning silent witch had not done thinking of these things when Lucetta came noiselessly behind her, and made her start.

It was all true as she had pictured—she could have sworn it. Lucetta had a heightened luminousness in her eye over and above the advanced colour of her cheeks.

'You've seen Mr. Farfrae,' said Elizabeth demurely.

'Yes,' said Lucetta. 'How did you know?'

She knelt down on the hearth and took her friend's hands excitedly in her own. But after all she did not say when or how she had seen him or what he had said.

That night she became restless; in the morning she was feverish; and at breakfast-time she told her companion that she had something on her mind—something which concerned a person in whom she was interested much. Elizabeth was earnest to listen and sympathize.

'This person—a lady—once admired a man much —very much,' she said tentatively.

'Ah,' said Elizabeth-Jane.

'They were intimate—rather. He did not think so deeply of her as she did of him. But in an impulsive moment, purely out of reparation, he proposed to make her his wife. She agreed. But there was an unexpected hitch in the proceedings; though she had been so far compromised with him that she felt she could never belong to another man, as a pure matter of conscience, even if she should wish to. After that they were much apart, heard nothing of each other for a long time, and she felt her life quite closed up for her.'

' Ah——poor girl!'

' She suffered much on account of him; though I should add that he could not altogether be blamed for what had happened. At last the obstacle which separated them was providentially removed; and he came to marry her.'

' How delightful!'

' But in the interval she——my poor friend——had seen a man she liked better than him. Now comes the point: Could she in honour dismiss the first?'

' A new man she liked better——that's bad!'

' Yes,' said Lucetta, looking pained at a boy who was swinging the town pump-handle. ' It is bad! Though you must remember that she was forced into an equivocal position with the first man by an accident——that he was not so well educated or refined as the second, and that she had discovered some qualities in the first that rendered him less desirable as a husband than she had at first thought him to be.'

' I cannot answer,' said Elizabeth-Jane thoughtfully. ' It is so difficult. It wants a Pope to settle that!'

' You prefer not to, perhaps?' Lucetta showed in her appealing tone how much she leant on Elizabeth's judgment.

' Yes, Miss Templeman,' admitted Elizabeth. ' I would rather not say.'

Nevertheless, Lucetta seemed relieved by the simple fact of having opened out the situation a little, and was slowly convalescent of her headache. ' Bring me a looking-glass. How do I appear to people?' she said languidly.

' Well——a little worn,' answered Elizabeth, eyeing her

206

as a critic eyes a doubtful painting; fetching the glass she enabled Lucetta to survey herself in it, which Lucetta anxiously did.

' I wonder if I wear well, as times go!' she observed after a while.

' Yes—fairly.

' Where am I worst?'

' Under your eyes—I notice a little brownness there.'

' Yes. That is my worst place, I know. How many years more do you think I shall last before I get hopelessly plain?'

There was something curious in the way in which Elizabeth, though the younger, had come to play the part of experienced sage in these discussions. ' It may be five years,' she said judicially. ' Or, with a quiet life, as many as ten. With no love you might calculate on ten.'

Lucetta seemed to reflect on this as on an unalterable, impartial verdict. She told Elizabeth-Jane no more of the past attachment she had roughly adumbrated as the experiences of a third person; and Elizabeth, who in spite of her philosophy was very tender-hearted, wept that night in bed at the thought that her pretty, rich Lucetta did not treat her to the full confidence of names and dates in her confessions. For by the ' she ' of Lucetta's story Elizabeth had not been beguiled.

XXV

THE next phase of the supersession of Henchard in Lucetta's heart was an experiment in calling on her performed by Farfrae with some apparent trepidation. Conventionally speaking, he conversed with both Miss Templeman and her companion; but in fact it was rather that Elizabeth sat invisible in the room. Donald appeared not to see her at all, and answered her wise little remarks with curtly indifferent monosyllables, his looks and faculties hanging on the woman who could boast of a more Protean variety in her phases, moods, opinions, and also principles, than could Elizabeth. Lucetta had persisted in dragging her into the circle; but she had remained like an awkward third point which that circle would not touch.

Susan Henchard's daughter bore up against the frosty ache of the treatment, as she had borne up under worse things, and contrived as soon as possible to get out of the inharmonious room without being missed. The Scotchman seemed hardly the same Farfrae who had danced with her, and walked with her, in a delicate poise between love and friendship— that period in the history of a love when alone it can be said to be unalloyed with pain.

She stoically looked from her bedroom window, and contemplated her fate as if it were written on the top of the church-tower hard by. 'Yes,' she said at last, bringing down her palm upon the sill with a pat: '*He* is the second man of that story she told me!'

All this time Henchard's smouldering sentiments towards Lucetta had been fanned into higher and higher inflammation by the circumstances of the case. He was discovering that the young woman, for whom he once felt a pitying warmth, which had been almost chilled out of him by reflection, was, when now qualified with a slight inaccessibility and a more matured beauty, the very being to make him satisfied with life. Day after day proved to him, by her silence, that it was no use to think of bringing her round by holding aloof; so he gave in, and called upon her again, Elizabeth-Jane being absent.

He crossed the room to her with a heavy tread of some awkwardness, his strong, warm gaze upon her— like the sun beside the moon in comparison with Farfrae's modest look—and with something of a hail-fellow bearing, as, indeed, was not unnatural. But she seemed so transubstantiated by her change of position, and held out her hand to him in such cool friendship, that he became deferential, and sat down with a perceptible loss of power. He understood but little of fashion in dress, yet enough to feel himself inadequate in appearance beside her whom he had hitherto been dreaming of as almost his property. She said something very polite about his being good enough to call. This caused him to recover balance. He looked her oddly in the face, losing his awe.

'Why, of course I have called, Lucetta,' he said. 'What does that nonsense mean? You know I couldn't have helped myself if I had wished—that is, if I had any kindness at all. I've called to say that I am ready, as soon as custom will permit, to give you my name, in return for your devotion, and what you lost by it, in thinking too little of yourself and too much of me; to say that you can fix the day or month, with my full consent, whenever in your opinion it would be seemly: you know more of these things than I.'

'It is full early yet,' she said evasively.

'Yes, yes; I suppose it is. But you know, Lucetta, I felt directly my poor ill-used Susan died, and when I could not bear the idea of marrying again, that after what had happened between us it was my duty not to let any unnecessary delay occur before putting things to rights. Still, I wouldn't call in a hurry, because—well, you can guess how this money you've come into made me feel.' His voice slowly fell; he was conscious that in this room his accents and manner wore a roughness not observable in the street. He looked about the room, at the novel hangings and ingenious furniture with which she had surrounded herself.

'Upon my life, I didn't know such furniture as this could be bought in Casterbridge,' he said.

'Nor can it be,' said she. 'Nor will it till fifty years more of civilization have passed over the town. It took a waggon and four horses to get it here.'

'H'm. The fact is, your setting up like this makes my bearing towards you rather awkward.'

'Why?'

An answer was not really needed, and he did not furnish one. 'Well,' he went on, 'there's nobody in the world I would have wished to see enter into this wealth before you, Lucetta, and nobody, I am sure, who will become it more.' He turned to her with congratulatory admiration so fervid that she shrank somewhat, notwithstanding that she knew him so well.

'I am greatly obliged to you for all that,' said she, rather with an air of speaking ritual. The stint of reciprocal feeling was perceived, and Henchard showed chagrin at once—nobody was more quick to show that than he.

'You may be obliged or not for't. Though the things I say may not have the polish of what you've lately learnt to expect for the first time in your life, they are real, my lady Lucetta.'

'That's rather a rude way of speaking to me,' pouted Lucetta, with stormy eyes.

'Not at all!' replied Henchard hotly. 'But there, there, I don't want to quarrel with 'ee. I come with an honest proposal for silencing your Jersey enemies, and you ought to be thankful.'

'How can you speak so!' she answered, firing quickly. 'Knowing that my only crime was the indulging in a foolish girl's passion for you with too little regard for correctness, and that I was what *I* call innocent all the time they called me guilty, you ought not to be so cutting! I suffered enough at that worrying time, when you wrote to tell me of your wife's return, and my consequent dismissal, and if I am a little independent now, surely the privilege is due to me!'

'Yes, it is,' he said. 'But it is not by what is, in this life, but by what appears, that you are judged; and I therefore think you ought to accept me—for your own good name's sake. What is known in your native Jersey may get known here.'

'How you keep on about Jersey! I am English!'

'Yes, yes. Well, what do you say to my proposal?'

For the first time in their acquaintance Lucetta had the move; and yet she was backward. 'For the present let things be,' she said with some embarrassment. 'Treat me as an acquaintance; and I'll treat you as one. Time will——' she stopped; and he said nothing to fill the gap for awhile, there being no pressure of half acquaintance to drive them into speech if they were not minded for it.

'That's the way the wind blows, is it?' he said at last grimly, nodding an affirmative to his own thoughts.

A yellow flood of reflected sunlight filled the room for a few instants. It was produced by the passing of a load of newly trussed hay from the country, in a waggon marked with Farfrae's name. Beside it rode Farfrae himself on horseback. Lucetta's face became —as a woman's face becomes when the man she loves rises upon her gaze like an apparition.

A turn of the eye by Henchard, a glance from the window, and the secret of her inaccessibility would have been revealed. But Henchard in estimating her tone was looking down so plumb-straight that he did not note the warm consciousness upon Lucetta's face.

'I shouldn't have thought it—I shouldn't have thought it of women!' he said emphatically by-and-by, rising and shaking himself into activity; while Lucetta was so anxious to divert him from any suspicion of the truth, that she asked him to be in no hurry. Bringing him some apples, she insisted upon paring one for him.

He would not take it. 'No, no; such is not for me,' he said drily, and moved to the door. At going out he turned his eye upon her.

'You came to live in Casterbridge entirely on my account,' he said. 'Yet now you are here you won't have anything to say to my offer!'

He had hardly gone down the staircase when she dropped upon the sofa, and jumped up again in a fit of desperation. 'I will love him!' she cried passionately; 'as for *him*—he's hot-tempered and stern, and it would be madness to bind myself to him knowing that. I won't be a slave to the past—I'll love where I choose!'

Yet having decided to break away from Henchard, one might have supposed her capable of aiming higher than Farfrae. But Lucetta reasoned nothing: she feared hard words from the people with whom she had been earlier associated; she had no relatives left; and with native lightness of heart took kindly to what fate offered.

Elizabeth-Jane, surveying the position of Lucetta between her two lovers from the crystalline sphere of a straightforward mind, did not fail to perceive that her father, as she called him, and Donald Farfrae became more desperately enamoured of her friend every day. On Farfrae's side it was the unforced passion of youth. On Henchard's the artificially stimulated coveting of maturer age.

The pain she experienced from the almost absolute obliviousness to her existence that was shown by the pair of them became at times half dissipated by her sense of its humorousness. When Lucetta had pricked her finger they were as deeply concerned as if she were dying; when she herself had been seriously sick or in danger they uttered a conventional word of sympathy at the news, and forgot all about it immediately. But, as regarded Henchard, this perception of hers also caused her some filial grief; she could not help asking what she had done to be neglected so, after the professions of solicitude he had made. As regarded Farfrae, she thought, after honest reflection, that it was quite natural. What was she beside Lucetta?—as one of the 'meaner beauties of the night,' when the moon had risen in the skies.

She had learnt the lesson of renunciation, and was as familiar with the wreck of each day's wishes as with the diurnal setting of the sun. If her earthly career had taught her few book philosophies it had at least well practised her in this. Yet her experience had consisted less in a series of pure disappointments than in a series of substitutions. Continually it had happened that what she had desired had not been granted her, and that what had been granted her she had not desired. So she viewed with an approach to equanimity the now cancelled days when Donald had been her undeclared lover, and wondered what unwished-for thing Heaven might send her in place of him.

XXVI

IT chanced that on a fine spring morning Henchard and Farfrae met in the chestnut-walk which ran along the south wall of the town. Each had just come out from his early breakfast, and there was not another soul near. Henchard was reading a letter from Lucetta, sent in answer to a note from him, in which she made some excuse for not immediately granting him a second interview that he had desired.

Donald had no wish to enter into conversation with his former friend on their present constrained terms; neither would he pass him in scowling silence. He nodded, and Henchard did the same. They had receded from each other several paces when a voice cried 'Farfrae!' It was Henchard's, who stood regarding him.

'Do you remember,' said Henchard, as if it were the presence of the thought and not of the man which made him speak, 'do you remember my story of that second woman—who suffered for her thoughtless intimacy with me?'

'I do,' said Farfrae.

'Do you remember my telling 'ee how it all began, and how it ended?'

'Yes.'

'Well, I have offered to marry her now that I can;

215

but she won't marry me. Now what would you think of her—I put it to you?'

'Well, ye owe her nothing more now,' said Farfrae heartily.

'It is true,' said Henchard, and went on.

That he had looked up from a letter to ask his questions completely shut out from Farfrae's mind all vision of Lucetta as the culprit. Indeed, her present position was so different from that of the young woman of Henchard's story as of itself to be sufficient to blind him absolutely to her identity. As for Henchard, he was reassured by Farfrae's words and manner against a suspicion which had crossed his mind. They were not those of a conscious rival.

Yet that there was rivalry by some one he was firmly persuaded. He could feel it in the air around Lucetta, see it in the turn of her pen. There was an antagonistic force in exercise, so that when he had tried to hang near her he seemed standing in a refluent current. That it was not innate caprice he was more and more certain. Her windows gleamed as if they did not want him; her curtains seemed to hang slily, as if they screened an ousting presence. To discover whose presence that was—whether really Farfrae's after all, or another's—he exerted himself to the utmost to see her again; and at length succeeded.

At the interview, when she offered him tea, he made it a point to launch a cautious inquiry if she knew Mr. Farfrae.

Oh yes, she knew him, she declared; she could not help knowing almost everybody in Casterbridge, living in such a gazebo over the centre and arena of the town.

'Pleasant young fellow,' said Henchard.

'Yes,' said Lucetta.

'We both know him,' said kind Elizabeth-Jane, to relieve her companion's divined embarrassment.

There was a knock at the door; literally, three full knocks and a little one at the end.

'That kind of knock means half-and-half—somebody between gentle and simple,' said the corn-merchant to himself. 'I shouldn't wonder therefore if it is he.' In a few seconds surely enough Donald walked in.

Lucetta was full of little fidgets and flutters, which increased Henchard's suspicions without affording any special proof of their correctness. He was well-nigh ferocious at the sense of the queer situation in which he stood towards this woman. One who had re-proached him for deserting her when calumniated, who had urged claims upon his consideration on that ac-count, who had lived waiting for him, who at the first decent moment had come to ask him to rectify, by making her his, the false position into which she had placed herself for his sake; such she had been. And now he sat at her tea-table eager to gain her atten-tion, and, in his amatory rage, feeling the other man present to be a villain, just as any young fool of a lover might feel.

They sat stiffly side by side at the darkening table, like some Tuscan painting of the two disciples supping at Emmaus. Lucetta, forming the third and chief figure, was opposite them; Elizabeth-Jane, being out of the game, and out of the group, could observe from afar all things: that there were long spaces of taci-turnity, when all exterior circumstance was subdued to the touch of spoons and china, the click of a heel on the pavement under the window, the passing of a wheelbarrow or cart, the whistling of the carter, the gush of water into householders' buckets at the town-pump opposite; the exchange of greetings among their neighbours, and the rattle of the yokes by which they carried off their evening supply.

'More bread-and-butter?' said Lucetta to Henchard

and Farfrae equally, holding out between them a plateful of long slices. Henchard took a slice by one end and Donald by the other; each feeling certain he was the man meant; neither let go, and the slice came in two.

'Oh—I am so sorry!' cried Lucetta, with a nervous titter. Farfrae tried to laugh; but he was too much in love to see the incident in any but a tragic light.

'How ridiculous of all three of them!' said Elizabeth to herself.

Henchard left the house with a ton of conjecture, though without a grain of proof, that the counter-attraction was Farfrae; and therefore he would not make up his mind. Yet to Elizabeth-Jane it was plain as the town-pump that Donald and Lucetta were incipient lovers. More than once, in spite of her care, Lucetta had been unable to restrain her glance from flitting across into Farfrae's eyes like a bird to its nest. But Henchard was constructed upon too large a scale to discern such minutiæ as these by an evening light, which to him were as the notes of an insect that lie above the compass of the human ear.

But he was disturbed. And the sense of occult rivalry in suitorship was so much superadded to the palpable rivalry of their business lives. To the coarse materiality of that rivalry it added an inflaming soul.

The thus vitalized antagonism took the form of action by Henchard sending for Jopp, the manager originally displaced by Farfrae's arrival. Henchard had frequently met this man about the streets, observed that his clothing spoke of neediness, heard that he lived in Mixen Lane—a back slum of the town, the *pis aller* of Casterbridge domiciliation—itself almost a proof that a man had reached a stage when he would not stick at trifles.

Jopp came after dark, by the gates of the store-yard, and felt his way through the hay and straw to the office where Henchard sat in solitude awaiting him.

' I am again out of a foreman,' said the corn-factor. 'Are you in a place?'

' Not so much as a beggar's, sir.'

' How much do you ask?'

Jopp named his price, which was very moderate.

' When can you come?'

' At this hour and moment, sir,' said Jopp, who, standing hands-pocketed at the street corner till the sun had faded the shoulders of his coat to scarecrow green, had regularly watched Henchard in the market-place, measured him, and learnt him, by virtue of the power which the still man has in his stillness of knowing the busy one better than he knows himself. Jopp, too, had had a convenient experience; he was the only one in Casterbridge besides Henchard and the close-lipped Elizabeth who knew that Lucetta came truly from Jersey, and but proximately from Bath. 'I know Jersey, too, sir,' he said. 'Was living there when you used to do business that way. Oh yes—have often seen ye there.'

' Indeed! Very good. Then the thing is settled. The testimonials you showed me when you first tried for't are sufficient.'

That characters deteriorate in time of need possibly did not occur to Henchard. Jopp said, 'Thank you,' and stood more firmly, in the consciousness that at last he officially belonged to that spot.

' Now,' said Henchard, digging his strong eyes into Jopp's face, ' one thing is necessary to me, as the biggest corn-and-hay-dealer in these parts. The Scotchman, who's taking the town trade so bold into his hands, must be cut out. D'ye hear? We two can't live side by side—that's clear and certain.'

' I've seen it all,' said Jopp.

' By fair competition I mean, of course,' Henchard continued. ' But as hard, keen, and unflinching as fair —rather more so. By such a desperate bid against him for the farmers' custom as will grind him into the ground—starve him out. I've capital, mind ye, and I can do it.'

' I'm all that way of thinking,' said the new foreman. Jopp's dislike of Farfrae as the man who had once usurped his place, while it made him a willing tool, made him, at the same time, commercially as unsafe a colleague as Henchard could have chosen.

' I sometimes think,' he added, ' that he must have some glass that he sees next year in. He has such a knack of making everything bring him fortune.'

' He's deep beyond all honest men's discerning ; but we must make him shallower. We'll under-sell him, and over-buy him, and so snuff him out.'

They then entered into specific details of the process by which this would be accomplished, and parted at a late hour.

Elizabeth-Jane heard by accident that Jopp had been engaged by her stepfather. She was so fully convinced that he was not the right man for the place that, at the risk of making Henchard angry, she expressed her apprehension to him when they met. But it was done to no purpose. Henchard shut up her argument with a sharp rebuff.

The season's weather seemed to favour their scheme. The time was in the years immediately before foreign competition had revolutionized the trade in grain, when still, as from the earliest ages, the wheat quotations from month to month depended entirely upon the home harvest. A bad harvest, or the prospect of one, would double the price of corn in a few weeks ; and the promise of a good yield would lower it as rapidly. Prices were like the roads of the period, steep in gradient, reflecting in their phases the local conditions, without engineering, levellings, or averages.

The farmer's income was ruled by the wheat-crop within his own horizon, and the wheat-crop by the weather. Thus, in person, he became a sort of flesh-barometer, with feelers always directed to the sky and wind around him. The local atmosphere was every-thing to him; the atmospheres of other countries a matter of indifference. The people, too, who were not farmers, the rural multitude, saw in the god of the weather a more important personage than they do now. Indeed, the feeling of the peasantry in this matter was so intense as to be almost unrealizable in these equable days. Their impulse was well-nigh to prostrate them-selves in lamentation before untimely rains and tempests, which came as the Alastor of those households whose crime it was to be poor.

After midsummer they watched the weather-cocks as men waiting in antechambers watch the lackey. Sun elated them; quiet rain sobered them; weeks of watery tempest stupefied them. That aspect of the sky which they now regard as disagreeable they then beheld as furious.

It was June, and the weather was very unfavourable. Casterbridge, being, as it were, the bell-board on which all the adjacent hamlets and villages sounded their notes, was decidedly dull. Instead of new articles in the shop-windows, those that had been rejected in the foregoing summer were brought out again; superseded reap-hooks, badly-shaped rakes, shop-worn leggings, and time-stiffened water-tights reappeared, furbished up as near to new as possible.

Henchard, backed by Jopp, read a disastrous gar-nering, and resolved to base his strategy against Farfrae upon that reading. But before acting he wished—what so many have wished—that he could know for cer-tain what was at present only strong probability. He was superstitious—as such headstrong natures often are—and he nourished in his mind an idea bearing on the matter; an idea he shrank from disclosing even to Jopp.

In a lonely hamlet a few miles from the town—so lonely, that what are called lonely villages were teeming by comparison—there lived a man of curious repute as a forecaster or weather-prophet. The way to his house was crooked and miry—even difficult in the present unpropitious season. One evening when it was raining so heavily that ivy and laurel resounded like distant musketry, and an out-door man could be excused for shrouding himself to his ears and eyes, such a shrouded figure on foot might have been perceived travelling in the direction of the hazel-copse which dripped over the prophet's cot. The turnpike-road became a lane, the lane a cart-track, the cart-track a bridle-path, the bridle-path a foot-way, the foot-way overgrown. The solitary walker slipped here and there, and stumbled over the natural springes formed by the brambles, till at length he reached the house, which, with its garden, was surrounded with a high, dense hedge. The cottage, comparatively a large one, had been built of mud by the occupier's own hands, and thatched also by himself. Here he had always lived, and here it was assumed he would die.

He existed on unseen supplies; for it was an anomalous thing that while there was hardly a soul in the neighbourhood but affected to laugh at this man's assertions, uttering the formula, 'There's nothing in 'em,' with full assurance on the surface of their faces, very few of them were unbelievers in their secret hearts. Whenever they consulted him they did it 'for a fancy.' When they paid him they said, ' Just a trifle for Christmas,' or 'Candlemas,' as the case might be.

He would have preferred more honesty in his clients, and less sham ridicule; but fundamental belief consoled him for superficial irony. As stated, he was enabled to live; people supported him with their backs turned. He was sometimes astonished that men could profess so little and believe so much at his house, when at church they professed so much and believed so little.

Behind his back he was called 'Wide-oh,' on account of his reputation; to his face 'Mr.' Fall.

The hedge of his garden formed an arch over the entrance, and a door was inserted as in a wall. Outside the door the tall traveller stopped, bandaged his face with a handkerchief as if he were suffering from tooth-ache, and went up the path. The window shutters were not closed, and he could see the prophet within, preparing his supper.

In answer to the knock Fall came to the door, candle in hand. The visitor stepped back a little from the light, and said, 'Can I speak to ye?' in significant tones. The other's invitation to come in was responded to by the country formula, 'This will do, thank ye,' after which the householder has no alternative but to come out. He placed the candle on the corner of the dresser, took his hat from a nail, and joined the stranger in the porch, shutting the door behind him.

'I've long heard that you can—do things of a sort?' began the other, repressing his individuality as much as he could.

'Maybe so, Mr. Henchard,' said the weather-caster.

'Ah—why do you call me that?' asked the visitor with a start.

'Because it's your name. Feeling you'd come, I've waited for ye; and thinking you might be leery from your walk, I laid two supper plates—look ye here.' He threw open the door and disclosed the supper-table, at which appeared a second chair, knife and fork, plate and mug, as he had declared.

Henchard felt like Saul at his reception by Samuel; he remained in silence for a few moments, then throw-ing off the disguise of frigidity which he had hitherto

preserved, he said, 'Then I have not come in vain.
. . . Now, for instance, can ye charm away warts?'

'Without trouble.'

'Cure the evil?'

'That I've done.—with consideration—if they will
wear the toad-bag by night as well as by day.'

'Forecast the weather?'

'With labour and time.'

'Then take this,' said Henchard. ''Tis a crown-
piece. Now, what is the harvest fortnight to be? When
can I know?'

'I've worked it out already, and you can know at
once.' (The fact was that five farmers had already been
there on the same errand from different parts of the
country.) 'By the sun, moon, and stars, by the clouds,
the winds, the trees, and grass, the candle-flame and
swallows, the smell of the herbs; likewise by the cats'
eyes, the ravens, the leeches, the spiders, and the dung-
mixen, the last fortnight in August will be—rain and
tempest.'

'You are not certain, of course?'

'As one can be in a world where all's unsure. 'Twill
be more like living in Revelations this autumn than in
England. Shall I sketch it out for ye in a scheme?'

'Oh no, no,' said Henchard. 'I don't altogether
believe in forecasts, come to second thoughts on such.
But I——'

'You don't—you don't—'tis quite understood,'
said Wide-oh, without a sound of scorn. 'You
have given me a crown because you've one too many.
But won't you join me at supper, now 'tis waiting
and all?'   .

Henchard would gladly have joined; for the savour
of the stew had floated from the cottage into the porch
with such appetizing distinctness, that the meat, the
onions, the pepper, and the herbs could be severally
recognized by his nose. But as sitting down to hob-

and-nob there would have seemed to mark him too implicitly as the weather-caster's apostle, he declined, and went his way.

The next Saturday Henchard bought grain to such an enormous extent that there was quite a talk about his purchases among his neighbours, the lawyer, the wine merchant, and the doctor; also on the next, and on all available days. When his granaries were full to choking, all the weathercocks of Casterbridge creaked and set their faces in another direction, as if tired of the south-west. The weather changed; the sunlight, which had been like tin for weeks, assumed the hues of topaz. The temperament of the welkin passed from the phlegmatic to the sanguine; an excellent harvest was almost a certainty; and as a consequence prices rushed down.

All these transformations, lovely to the outsider, to the wrong-headed corn-dealer were terrible. He was reminded of what he had well known before, that a man might gamble upon the square green areas of fields as readily as upon those of a card-room.

Henchard had backed bad weather, and apparently lost. He had mistaken the turn of the flood for the turn of the ebb. His dealings had been so extensive that settlement could not long be postponed, and to settle, he was obliged to sell off corn that he had bought only a few weeks before at figures higher by many shillings a quarter. Much of the corn he had never seen; it had not even been moved from the ricks in which it lay stacked miles away. Thus he lost heavily.

In the blaze of an early August day he met Farfrae in the market-place. Farfrae knew of his dealings (though he did not guess their intended bearing on himself) and commiserated him; for since their exchange of words in the South Walk they had been on stiffly speaking terms. Henchard for the moment, appeared to resent the sympathy; but he suddenly took a careless turn.

'Ho, no, no!—nothing serious, man!' he cried with fierce gaiety. 'These things always happen, don't they? I know it has been said that figures have touched me tight lately; but is that anything rare? The case is not so bad as folk make out perhaps. And dammy, a man must be a fool to mind the common hazards of trade!'

But he had to enter the Casterbridge Bank that day for reasons which had never before sent him there— and to sit a long time in the partners' room with a constrained bearing. It was rumoured soon after that much real property, as well as vast stores of produce, in the town and neighbourhood, which had stood in Henchard's name, was actually the property of his bankers.

Coming down the steps of the bank he encountered Jopp. The gloomy transactions just completed within had added fever to the original sting of Farfrae's sympathy that morning, which Henchard fancied might be satire disguised, so that Jopp met with anything but a bland reception. The latter was in the act of taking off his hat to wipe his forehead, and saying, 'A fine hot day,' to an acquaintance.

'You can wipe and wipe, and say, "A fine hot day," can ye!' cried Henchard in a savage undertone, imprisoning Jopp between himself and the bank wall. 'If it hadn't been for your blasted advice it might have been a fine day enough! Why did ye let me go on, hey?—when a word of doubt from you or anybody would have made me think twice! For you can never be sure of weather till 'tis past.'

'My advice, sir, was to do what you thought best.'

'A useful fellow! And the sooner you help somebody else in that way the better!' Henchard continued his address to Jopp in similar terms till it ended in Jopp's dismissal there and then, Henchard turning upon his heel and leaving him.

'You shall be sorry for this, sir; sorry as a man can be!' said Jopp, standing pale, and looking after the corn-merchant as he disappeared in the crowd of market-men hard by.

XXVII

IT was the eve of harvest. Prices being low Farfrae was buying. As was usual, after reckoning too surely on famine weather, the local farmers had flown to the other extreme, and (in Farfrae's opinion) were selling off too recklessly—calculating with just a trifle too much certainty upon an abundant yield. So he went on buying old corn at its comparatively ridiculous price : for the produce of the previous year, though not large, had been of excellent quality.

When Henchard had squared his affairs in a disastrous way, and got rid of his burdensome purchases at a monstrous loss, the harvest began. There were three days of excellent weather, and then—' What if that curst conjuror should be right after all ! ' said Henchard.

The fact was, that no sooner had the sickles begun to play than the atmosphere suddenly felt as if cress would grow in it without other nourishment. It rubbed people's cheeks like damp flannel when they walked abroad. There was a gusty, high, warm wind ; isolated raindrops starred the window-panes at remote distances : the sunlight would flap out like a quickly opened fan, throw the pattern of the window upon the floor of the room in a milky, colourless shine, and withdraw as suddenly as it had appeared.

From that day and hour it was clear that there

was not to be so successful an ingathering after all.
If Henchard had only waited long enough he might
at least have avoided loss, though he had not made a
profit. But the momentum of his character knew no
patience. At this turn of the scales he remained
silent. The movements of his mind seemed to tend to
the thought that some power was working against him.

'I wonder,' he asked himself with eerie misgiving;
'I wonder if it can be that somebody has been roasting
a waxen image of me, or stirring an unholy brew to
confound me! I don't believe in such power; and
yet—what if they should ha' been doing it!' Even
he could not admit that the perpetrator, if any, might
be Farfrae. These isolated hours of superstition came
to Henchard in time of moody depression, when all
his practical largeness of view had oozed out of him.

Meanwhile Donald Farfrae prospered. He had purchased in so depressed a market that the present
moderate stiffness of prices was sufficient to pile for
him a large heap of gold where a little one had been.

'Why, he'll soon be Mayor!' said Henchard. It
was indeed hard that the speaker should, of all others,
have to follow the triumphal chariot of this man to
the Capitol.

The rivalry of the masters was taken up by the men.

September night-shades had fallen upon Casterbridge; the clocks had struck half-past eight, and the
moon had risen. The streets of the town were
curiously silent for such a comparatively early hour.
A sound of jangling horse-bells and heavy wheels
passed up the street. These were followed by angry
voices outside Lucetta's house, which led her and
Elizabeth-Jane to run to the windows, and pull up
the blinds.

The opposite Market House and Town Hall abutted
against its next neighbour the Church except in the
lower storey, where an arched thoroughfare gave

admittance to a large square called Bull Stake. A stone post rose in the midst, to which the oxen had formerly been tied for baiting with dogs to make them tender before they were killed in the adjoining shambles. In a corner stood the stocks.

The thoroughfare leading to this spot was now blocked by two four-horse waggons and horses, one laden with hay-trusses, the leaders having already passed each other, and become entangled head to tail. The passage of the vehicles might have been practicable if empty; but built up with hay to the bedroom windows as one was, it was impossible.

'You must have done it a' purpose!' said Farfrae's waggoners. 'You can hear my horses' bells half-a-mile such a night as this!'

'If ye'd been minding your business instead of zwailing along in such a gawk-hammer way, you would have zeed me!' retorted the wroth representative of Henchard.

However, according to the strict rule of the road it appeared that Henchard's man was most in the wrong; he therefore attempted to back into the High Street. In doing this the near hind-wheel rose against the churchyard wall, and the whole mountainous load went over, two of the four wheels rising in the air, and the legs of the thill horse.

Instead of considering how to gather up the load, the two men closed in a fight with their fists. Before the first round was quite over Henchard came upon the spot, somebody having run for him.

Henchard sent the two men staggering in contrary directions by collaring one with each hand, turned to the horse that was down, and extricated him after some trouble. He then inquired into the circumstances; and seeing the state of his waggon and its load, began hotly rating Farfrae's man.

Lucetta and Elizabeth-Jane had by this time run

down to the door and opened it, whence they watched
the bright heap of new hay lying in the moon's rays,
and passed and re-passed by the forms of Henchard
and the waggoners. The women had witnessed what
nobody else had seen—the origin of the mishap; and
Lucetta spoke.

'I saw it all, Mr. Henchard,' she cried; 'and your
man was most in the wrong!'

Henchard paused in his harangue and turned. 'Oh,
I didn't notice you, Miss Templeman,' said he. 'My
man in the wrong? Ah, to be sure; to be sure! But
I beg your pardon notwithstanding. The other's is
the empty waggon, and he must have been most to
blame for coming on.'

'No; I saw it, too,' said Elizabeth-Jane. 'And I
can assure you he couldn't help it.'

'You can't trust *their* senses!' murmured Henchard's
man.

'Why not?' asked Henchard sharply.

'Why, you see, sir, all the women side with Farfrae
—being a damn young dand—of the sort that he is—
one that creeps into a maid's heart like the giddying
worm into a sheep's brain—making crooked seem
straight to their eyes!'

'But do you know what that lady is you talk about
in such a fashion? Do you know that I pay my
attentions to her, and have for some time? Just be
careful!'

'Not I. I know nothing, sir, outside eight shillings
a week.'

'And that Mr. Farfrae is well aware of that? He's
sharp in trade, but he wouldn't do anything so underhand as what you hint at.'

Whether because Lucetta heard this low dialogue,
or not, her white figure disappeared from her doorway
inward, and the door was shut before Henchard could
reach it to converse with her further. This disappointed

him, for he had been sufficiently disturbed by what the
man had said to wish to speak to her more closely.
While pausing the old constable came up.

'Just see that nobody drives against that hay and
waggon to-night, Stubberd,' said the corn-merchant. 'It
must bide till the morning, for all hands are in the
fields still. And if any coach or road-waggon wants to
come along, tell 'em they must go round by the back
street, and be hanged to 'em. . . . Any case to-morrow
up in Hall?'

'Yes, sir. One in number, sir.'

'Oh, what's that?'

'An old flagrant female, sir, swearing and committing
a nuisance in a horrible profane manner against the
church wall, sir, as if 'twere no more than a pot-house!
That's all, sir.'

'Oh. The Mayor's out o' town, isn't he?'

'He is, sir.'

'Very well, then I'll be there. · Don't forget to keep
an eye on that hay. Good night t'ye.'

During those moments Henchard had determined to
follow up Lucetta, notwithstanding her elusiveness, and
he knocked for admission.

The answer he received was an expression of Miss
Templeman's sorrow at being unable to see him again
that evening, because she had an engagement to go out.

Henchard walked away from the door to the opposite
side of the street, and stood by his hay in a lonely
reverie, the constable having strolled elsewhere, and the
horses being removed. Though the moon was not
bright as yet there were no lamps lighted, and he entered
the shadow of one of the projecting jambs which formed
the thoroughfare to Bull Stake; here he watched Lucetta's
door.

Candle-lights were flitting in and out of her bedroom,
and it was obvious that she was dressing for the appointment, whatever the nature of that might be at such

an hour. The lights disappeared, the clock struck nine, and almost at the moment Farfrae came round the opposite corner and knocked. That she had been waiting just inside for him was certain, for she instantly opened the door herself. They went together by the way of a back lane westward, avoiding the front street; guessing at last where they were going, he determined to follow.

The harvest had been so delayed by the capricious weather, that whenever a fine day occurred all sinews were strained to save what could be saved of the damaged crops. On account of the rapid shortening of the days the harvesters worked by moonlight. Hence to-night the wheat-fields abutting on the two sides of the square formed by Casterbridge town were animated by the gathering hands. Their shouts and laughter had reached Henchard at the Market House, while he stood there waiting, and he had little doubt from the turn which Farfrae and Lucetta had taken that they were bound for the spot.

Nearly the whole town had gone into the fields. The Casterbridge populace still retained the primitive habit of helping one another in time of need; and thus, though the corn belonged to the farming section of the little community—that inhabiting the Durnover quarter—the remainder was no less interested in the labour of getting it home.

Reaching the end of the lane Henchard crossed the shaded avenue on the walls, slid down the green rampart, and stood amongst the stubble. The 'stitches' or shocks rose like tents about the yellow expanse, those in the distance becoming lost in the moonlit hazes.

He had entered at a point removed from the scene of immediate operations; but two others had entered at that place, and he could see them winding among the shocks. They were paying no regard to the direction of their walk, whose vague serpentining soon began to bear down towards Henchard. A meeting promised to be awkward, and he therefore stepped into the hollow of the nearest shock, and sat down.

'You have my leave,' Lucetta was saying gaily. 'Speak what you like.'

'Well, then,' replied Farfrae, with the unmistakable inflection of the lover pure, which Henchard had never heard in full resonance on his lips before, 'you are sure to be much sought after for your position, wealth, talents, and beauty. But will ye resist the temptation to be one of those ladies with lots of admirers—ay—and be content to have only a homely one?'

'And he the speaker?' said she, laughing. 'Very well, sir, what next?'

'Ah! I'm afraid that what I feel will make me forget my manners!'

'Then I hope you'll never have any, if you lack them only for that cause.' After some broken words, which Henchard lost, she added, 'Are you sure you won't be jealous?'

Farfrae seemed to assure her that he would not, by taking her hand.

'You are convinced, Donald, that I love nobody else,' she presently said. 'But I should wish to have my own way in some things.'

'In everything! What special thing did you mean?'

'If I wished not to live always in Casterbridge, for instance; on finding that I should not be happy here?'

Henchard did not hear the reply; he might have done so and much more, but he did not care to play the eavesdropper. They went on towards the scene of activity, where the sheaves were being handed, a dozen a minute, upon the carts and waggons which carried them away.

Lucetta insisted on parting from Farfrae when they drew near the workpeople. He had some business with them, and, though he entreated her to wait a few minutes, she was inexorable, and tripped off homeward alone.

Henchard thereupon left the field, and followed her. His state of mind was such that on reaching Lucetta's door he did not knock, but opened it, and walked straight up to her sitting-room, expecting to find her there. But the room was empty, and he perceived that in his haste he had somehow passed her on the way hither. He had not to wait many minutes, however, for he soon heard her dress rustling in the hall, followed by a soft closing of the door. In a moment she appeared.

The light was so low that she did not notice Henchard at first. As soon as she saw him she uttered a little cry, almost of terror.

' How can you frighten me so ? ' she exclaimed, with a flushed face. ' It is past ten o'clock, and you have no right to surprise me here at such a time.'

' I don't know that I've not the right. At any rate, I have the excuse. Is it so necessary that I should stop to think of manners and customs ? '

' It is too late for propriety, and might injure me.'

' I called an hour ago, and you would not see me, and I thought you were in when I called now. It is you, Lucetta, who are doing wrong. It is not proper in 'ee to throw me over like this. I have a little matter to remind you of, which you seem to forget.'

She sank into a chair, and turned pale.

' I don't want to hear it—I don't want to hear it ! ' she said through her hands, as he, standing close to the edge of her gown, began to allude to the Jersey days.

' But you ought to hear it,' said he.

' It came to nothing ; and through you. Then why not leave me the freedom that I gained with such sorrow ! Had I found that you proposed to marry me for pure love I might have felt bound now. But I soon learnt that you had planned it out of mere charity—almost as an unpleasant duty—because I had nursed you, and compromised myself, and you thought you must repay me. After that I did not care for you so deeply as before.'

' Why did you come here to find me, then ? '

' I thought I ought to marry you for conscience' sake, since you were free, even though I—did not like you so well.'

' And why then don't you think so now ? '

She was silent. It was only too obvious that con science had ruled well enough till new love had intervened, and usurped that rule. In feeling this she herself forgot for the moment her partially justifying argument—that having discovered Henchard's infirmities of temper, she had some excuse for not risking her happiness in his hands after once escaping them. The only thing she could say was, ' I was a poor girl then ; and now my circumstances have altered, so I am hardly the same person.'

' That's true. And it makes the case awkward for me. But I don't want to touch your money. I am quite willing that every penny of your property shall remain to your personal use. Besides, that argument has nothing in it. The man you are thinking of is no better than I.'

' If you were as good as he you would leave me ! ' she cried passionately.

This unluckily aroused Henchard. ' You cannot in honour refuse me,' he said. ' And unless you give me your promise this very night to be my wife, before a witness, I'll reveal our intimacy—in common fairness to other men ! '

A look of resignation settled upon her. Henchard saw its bitterness ; and had Lucetta's heart been given to any other man in the world than Farfrae he would probably have had pity upon her at that moment. But the supplanter was the upstart (as Henchard called him) who had mounted into prominence upon his shoulders, and he could bring himself to show no mercy.

Without another word she rang the bell, and directed that Elizabeth-Jane should be fetched from her room. The latter appeared, surprised in the midst of her lucubrations. As soon as she saw Henchard she went across to him dutifully.

'Elizabeth-Jane,' he said, taking her hand, 'I want you to hear this.' And turning to Lucetta: 'Will you, or will you not, marry me?'

'If you—wish it, I must agree!'

'You say yes?'

'I do.'

No sooner had she given the promise than she fell back in a fainting state.

'What dreadful thing drives her to say this, father, when it is such a pain to her?' asked Elizabeth, kneeling down by Lucetta. 'Don't compel her to do anything against her will! I have lived with her, and know that she cannot bear much.'

'Don't be a no'thern simpleton!' said Henchard drily. 'This promise will leave him free for you, if you want him, won't it?'

At this Lucetta seemed to wake from her swoon with a start.

'Him? Who are you talking about?' she said wildly.

'Nobody, as far as I am concerned,' said Elizabeth firmly.

'Oh—well. Then it is my mistake,' said Henchard. 'But the business is between me and Miss Templeman. She agrees to be my wife.'

'But don't dwell on it just now,' entreated Elizabeth, holding Lucetta's hand.

'I don't wish to, if she promises,' said Henchard.

'I have, I have,' groaned Lucetta, her limbs hanging like flails, from very misery and faintness. 'Michael, please don't argue it any more!'

'I will not,' he said. And taking up his hat he went away.

Elizabeth-Jane continued to kneel by Lucetta. 'What is this?' she said. 'You called my father "Michael" as if you knew him well? And how is it he has got this power over you, that you promise to marry him against your will? Ah—you have many many secrets from me!'

'Perhaps you have some from me,' Lucetta murmured, with closed eyes, little thinking, however, so unsuspicious was she, that the secret of Elizabeth's heart concerned the young man who had caused this damage to her own.

'I would not—do anything against you at all!' stammered Elizabeth, keeping in all signs of emotion till she was ready to burst. 'I cannot understand how my father can command you so; I don't sympathize with him in it at all. I'll go to him and ask him to release you.'

'No, no,' said Lucetta. 'Let it all be.'

XXVIII

THE next morning Henchard went to the Town Hall opposite Lucetta's house, to attend Petty Sessions, being still a magistrate for the year by virtue of his late position as Mayor. In passing he looked up at her windows, but nothing of her was to be seen.

Henchard, as a Justice of the Peace, may at first seem to be an even greater incongruity than Shallow and Silence themselves. But his rough and ready perceptions, his sledge-hammer directness, had often served him better than nice legal knowledge in despatching such simple business as fell to his hands in this Court. To-day, Dr. Chalkfield, the Mayor for the year, being absent, the corn-merchant took the big chair, his eyes still abstractedly stretching out of the window to the ashlar front of High Place Hall.

There was one case only, and the offender stood before him. She was an old woman of mottled countenance, attired in a shawl of that nameless tertiary hue which comes, but cannot be made—a hue neither tawny, russet, hazel, nor ash ; a sticky black bonnet that seemed to have been worn in the country of the Psalmist where the clouds drop fatness ; and an apron that had been white in times so comparatively recent as still to contrast visibly with the rest of her clothes. The steeped aspect of the woman as a whole showed her to be no native of the country-side or even of a country-town.

She looked cursorily at Henchard and the second magistrate, and Henchard looked at her, with a momentary pause, as if she had reminded him indistinctly of somebody or something which passed from his mind as quickly as it had come. 'Well, and what has she been doing?' he said, looking down at the charge-sheet.

'She is charged, sir, with the offence of disorderly female and nuisance,' whispered Stubberd.

'Where did she do that?' said the other magistrate.

'By the church, sir, of all the horrible places in the world!—I caught her in the act, your worship.'

'Stand back then,' said Henchard, 'and let's hear what you've got to say.'

Stubberd was sworn, the magistrate's clerk dipped his pen, Henchard being no note-taker himself, and the constable began—

'Hearing a' illegal noise I went down the street at twenty-five minutes past eleven P.M. on the night of the fifth instinct, Hannah Dominy. When I had——'

'Don't go on so fast, Stubberd,' said the clerk.

The constable waited, with his eyes on the clerk's pen, till the latter stopped scratching, and said, 'yes.' Stubberd continued: 'When I had proceeded to the spot, I saw defendant at another spot, namely, the gutter.' He paused, watching the point of the clerk's pen again.

'Gutter, yes, Stubberd.'

'Spot measuring twelve feet nine inches or thereabouts, from where I——' Still careful not to outrun the clerk's penmanship, Stubberd pulled up again; for having got his evidence by heart, it was immaterial to him whereabouts he broke off.

'I object to that,' spoke up the old woman, '"spot

measuring twelve feet nine or thereabouts from where I," is not good evidence !'

The magistrates consulted, and the second one said that the bench was of opinion that twelve feet nine inches from a man on his oath was admissible evidence.

Stubberd, with a suppressed gaze of victorious rectitude at the old woman, continued : 'Was standing myself. She was wambling about quite dangerous to the thoroughfare, and when I approached to draw near, she insulted me.'

' "Insulted me." . . . Yes, what did she say ? '

' She said, " Put away that dee lantern," she says.'

' Yes.'

' Says she, " Dost hear, old turmit-head ? Put away that dee lantern. I have floored fellows a dee sight finer-looking than a dee fool like thee, you son of a bee, dee me if I haint," she says.'

' I object to that conversation !' interposed the old woman. 'I was not capable enough to hear what I said, and what is said out of my hearing is not evidence.'

There was another stoppage for consultation, a book was referred to, and finally Stubberd was allowed to go on again. The truth was that the old woman had appeared in court so many more times than the magistrates themselves, that they were obliged to keep a sharp look-out upon their procedure. However, when Stubberd had rambled on a little further, Henchard broke out impatiently, ' Come—we don't want to hear any more of them cust D's and B's ! Say the words out like a man, and don't be so modest, Stubberd; or else leave it alone !' Turning to the woman, ' Now then, have you any questions to ask him, or anything to say ? '

' Yes,' she replied with a twinkle in her eye; and the clerk dipped his pen.

' Twenty years ago I was a selling of furmity in a tent at Weydon Fair——'

' " Twenty years ago "—well, that's beginning at the beginning; suppose you go back to the Creation ! ' said the clerk, not without satire.

But Henchard stared, and quite forgot what was evidence and what was not.

' A man and a woman with a little child came into my tent,' the woman continued. ' They sat down and had a basin apiece. Ah, Lord's my life ! I was of a more respectable station in the world then than I am now, being a land smuggler in a large way of business ; and I used to season my furmity with rum for them who asked for't. I did it for the man ; and then he had more and more ; till at last he quarrelled with his wife, and offered to sell her to the highest bidder. A sailor came in and bid five guineas, and paid the money, and led her away. And the man who sold his wife in that fashion is the man sitting there in the great big chair.' The speaker concluded by nodding her head at Henchard, and folding her arms.

Everybody looked at Henchard. His face seemed strange, and in tint as if it had been powdered over with ashes. ' We don't want to hear your life and adventures,' said the second magistrate sharply, filling the pause which followed. ' You've been asked if you've anything to say bearing on the case.'

' That bears on the case. It proves that he's no better than I, and has no right to sit there in judgment upon me.'

' 'Tis a concocted story,' said the clerk. ' So hold your tongue ! '

' No—'tis true.' The words came from Henchard. ' 'Tis as true as the light,' he said slowly. ' And upon my soul, it does prove that I'm no better than she ! And to keep out of any temptation to treat her hard for her revenge, I'll leave her to you.'

The sensation in the court was indescribably great. Henchard left the chair, and came out, passing through a group of people on the steps and outside that was much larger than usual; for it seemed that the old furmity dealer had mysteriously hinted to the denizens of the lane in which she had been lodging since her arrival, that she knew a queer thing or two about their great local man Mr. Henchard, if she chose to tell it. This had brought them hither.

'Why are there so many idlers round the Town Hall to-day?' said Lucetta to her servant when the case was over. She had risen late, and had just looked out of the window.

'Oh, please, ma'am, 'tis this larry about Mr. Henchard. A woman has proved that before he became a gentleman he sold his wife for five guineas in a booth at a fair.'

In all the accounts which Henchard had given her of the separation from his wife Susan for so many years, of his belief in her death, and so on, he had never clearly explained the actual and immediate cause of that separation. The story she now heard for the first time.

A gradual misery overspread Lucetta's face as she dwelt upon the promise wrung from her the night before. At bottom, then, Henchard was this. How terrible a contingency for a woman who should commit herself to his care.

During the day she went out to the Ring, and to other places, not coming in till nearly dusk. As soon as she saw Elizabeth-Jane after her return indoors she told her that she had resolved to go away from home to the seaside for a few days—to Port-Bredy; Casterbridge was so gloomy.

Elizabeth, seeing that she looked wan and disturbed, encouraged her in the idea, thinking a change would afford her relief. She could not help suspecting that the gloom which seemed to have come over Casterbridge in Lucetta's eyes might be partially owing to the fact that Farfrae was away from home.

Elizabeth saw her friend depart for Port-Bredy, and took charge of High Place Hall till her return. After two or three days of solitude and incessant rain Henchard called at the house. He seemed disappointed to hear of Lucetta's absence, and though he nodded with outward indifference, he went away handling his beard with a nettled mien.

The next day he called again. ' Is she come now ? ' he asked.

' Yes. She returned this morning,' replied his stepdaughter. ' But she is not indoors. She has gone for a walk along the turnpike-road to Port-Bredy. She will be home by dusk.'

After a few words, which only served to reveal his restless impatience, he left the house again.

XXIX

AT this hour Lucetta was bounding along the road to Port-Bredy just as Elizabeth had announced. That she had chosen for her afternoon walk the road along which she had returned to Casterbridge three hours earlier in a carriage was curious—if anything should be called curious in concatenations of phenomena wherein each is known to have its accounting cause. It was the day of the chief market—Saturday—and Farfrae for once had been missed from his corn-stand in the dealers' room. Nevertheless, it was known that he would be home that night—'for Sunday,' as Casterbridge expressed it.

Lucetta, in continuing her walk, had at length reached the end of the ranked trees which bordered the highway in this and other directions out of the town. This end marked a mile; and here she stopped.

The spot was a vale between two gentle acclivities, and the road, still adhering to its Roman foundation, stretched onward straight as a surveyor's line till lost to sight on the most distant ridge. There was neither hedge nor tree in the prospect now, the road clinging to the stubbly expanse of corn-land like a stripe to an undulating garment. Near her was a barn—the single building of any kind within her horizon.

She strained her eyes up the lessening road, but

nothing appeared thereon—not so much as 'a speck. She sighed one word—' Donald ! ' and turned her face to the town for retreat.

Here the case was different. A single figure was approaching her—Elizabeth-Jane's.

Lucetta, in spite of her loneliness, seemed a little vexed. Elizabeth's face, as soon as she recognized her friend, shaped itself into affectionate lines while yet beyond speaking distance. ' I suddenly thought I would come and meet you,' she said, smiling.

Lucetta's reply was taken from her lips by an un-expected diversion. A by-road on her right hand descended from the fields into the highway at the point where she stood, and down the track a bull was rambling uncertainly towards her and Elizabeth, who, facing the other way, did not observe him.

In the latter quarter of each year cattle were at once the mainstay and the terror of families about Casterbridge and its neighbourhood, where breeding was carried on with Abrahamic success. The head of stock driven into and out of the town at this season to be sold by the local auctioneer was very large; and all these horned beasts, in travelling to and fro, sent women and children to shelter as nothing else could do. In the main the animals would have walked along quietly enough; but the Casterbridge tradition was that to drive stock it was indispensable that hideous cries, coupled with Yahoo antics and gestures, should be used, large sticks flourished, stray dogs called in, and in general everything done that was likely to infuriate the viciously disposed and terrify the mild. Nothing was commoner than for a householder, on going out of his parlour, to find his hall or passage full of little children, nursemaids, aged women, or a ladies' school, who apologized for their presence by saying, ' A bull passing down street from the sale.'

Lucetta and Elizabeth regarded the animal in doubt,

he meanwhile drawing vaguely towards them. It was a large specimen of the breed, in colour rich dun, though disfigured at present by splotches of mud about his seamy sides. His horns were thick and tipped with brass; his two nostrils like the Thames Tunnel as seen in the perspective toys of yore. Between them, through the gristle of his nose, was a stout copper ring, welded on, and irremovable as Gurth's collar of brass. To the ring was attached an ash staff about a yard long, which the bull with the motions of his head flung about like a flail.

It was not till they observed this dangling stick that the young women were really alarmed; for it revealed to them that the bull was an old one, too savage to be driven, which had in some way escaped, the staff being the means by which the drover controlled him and kept his horns at arms' length.

They looked round for some shelter or hiding-place, and thought of the barn hard by. As long as they had kept their eyes on the bull he had shown some deference in his manner of approach; but no sooner did they turn their backs to seek the barn than he tossed his head, and decided to thoroughly terrify them. This caused the two helpless girls to run wildly, whereupon the bull advanced in a deliberate charge.

The barn stood behind a green slimy pond, and it was closed save as to one of the usual pair of doors facing them, which had been propped open by a hurdle-stake, and for this opening they made. The interior had been cleared by a recent bout of threshing, except at one end, where there was a stack of dry clover. Elizabeth-Jane took in the situation. 'We must climb up there,' she said.

But before they had even approached it they heard the bull scampering through the pond without, and in a second he dashed into the barn, knocking down the hurdle-stake in passing; the heavy door slammed behind him; and all three were imprisoned in the barn together. The mistaken creature saw them, and stalked towards the end of the barn into which they had fled. The girls doubled so adroitly that their pursuer was against the wall when the fugitives were already half way to the other end. By the time that his length would allow him to turn and follow them thither they had crossed over; thus the pursuit went on, the hot air from his nostrils blowing over them like a sirocco, and not a moment being attainable by Elizabeth or Lucetta in which to open the door. What might have happened had their situation continued cannot be said; but in a a few moments a rattling of the door distracted their adversary's attention, and a man appeared. He ran forward towards the leading-staff, seized it, and wrenched the animal's head as if he would snap it off. The wrench was in reality so violent that the thick neck seemed to have lost its stiffness and to become half paralysed, whilst the nose dropped blood. The premeditated human contrivance of the nose-ring was too cunning for impulsive brute force, and the creature flinched.

The man was seen in the partial gloom to be large-framed and unhesitating. He led the bull to the door, and the light revealed Henchard. He made the bull fast without, and re-entered to the succour of Lucetta; for he had not perceived Elizabeth, who had climbed on to the clover-heap. Lucetta was hysterical, and Henchard took her in his arms and carried her to the door.

'You—have saved me!' she cried, as soon as she could speak.

'I have returned your kindness,' he responded tenderly. 'You once saved me.'

'How—comes it to be you—you?' she asked, not heeding his reply.

'I came out here to look for you. I have been wanting to tell you something these two or three days;

but you have been away, and I could not. Perhaps you cannot talk now?'

'Oh—no! Where is Elizabeth?'

'Here am I!' cried the missing one cheerfully; and without waiting for the ladder to be placed she slid down the face of the clover-stack to the floor.

Henchard supporting Lucetta on one side, and Elizabeth-Jane on the other, they went slowly along the rising road. They had reached the top and were descending again when Lucetta, now much recovered, recollected that she had dropped her muff in the barn.

'I'll run back,' said Elizabeth-Jane. 'I don't mind it at all, as I am not tired as you are.' She thereupon hastened down again to the barn, the others pursuing their way.

Elizabeth soon found the muff, such an article being by no means small at that time. Coming out she paused to look for a moment at the bull, now rather to be pitied with his bleeding nose, having perhaps rather intended a practical joke than a murder. Henchard had secured him by jamming the staff into the hinge of the barn-door, and wedging it there with a stake. At length she turned to hasten onward, after her contemplation, when she saw a green-and-black gig approaching from the contrary direction, the vehicle being driven by Farfrae.

His presence here seemed to explain Lucetta's walk that way. Donald saw her, drew up, and was hastily made acquainted with what had occurred. At Elizabeth-Jane mentioning how greatly Lucetta had been jeopardized, he exhibited an agitation different in kind no less than in intensity from any she had seen in him before. He became so absorbed in the circumstances that he scarcely had sufficient knowledge of what he was doing to think of helping her up beside him.

'She has gone on with Mr. Henchard, you say?' he inquired at last.

'Yes. He is taking her home. They are almost there by this time.'

'And you are sure she can get home?'

Elizabeth-Jane was quite sure.

'Your stepfather saved her?'

'Entirely.'

Farfrae checked his horse's pace; she guessed why. He was thinking that it would be best not to intrude on the other two just now. Henchard had saved Lucetta, and to provoke a possible exhibition of her deeper affection for himself was as ungenerous as it was unwise.

The immediate subject of their talk being exhausted, she felt more embarrassed at sitting thus beside her past lover; but soon the two figures of the others were visible at the entrance to the town. The face of the woman was frequently turned back, but Farfrae did not whip on the horse. When these reached the town walls Henchard and his companion had disappeared down the street; Farfrae set down Elizabeth-Jane, on her expressing a particular wish to alight there, and drove round to the stables at the back of his lodgings.

On this account he entered the house through his garden, and going up to his apartments found them in a particularly disturbed state, his boxes being hauled out upon the landing, and his bookcase standing in three pieces. These phenomena, however, seemed to cause him not the least surprise. 'When will everything be sent up?' he said to the mistress of the house, who was superintending.

'I am afraid not before eight, sir,' said she. 'You see we wasn't aware till this morning that you were going to move, or we could have been forwarder.'

'A—well, never mind, never mind!' said Farfrae cheerily. 'Eight o'clock will do well enough if it be not later. Now, don't ye be standing here talking, or it will be twelve, I doubt.' Thus speaking he went out by the front door and up the street.

During this interval Henchard and Lucetta had had experiences of a different kind. After Elizabeth's departure for the muff, the corn-merchant opened himself frankly, holding her hand within his arm, though she would fain have withdrawn it. 'Dear Lucetta, I have been very, very anxious to see you these two or three days,' he said; 'ever since I saw you last! I have thought over the way I got your promise that night. You said to me, 'If I were a man I should not insist.' That cut me deep. I felt that there was some truth in it. I don't want to make you wretched; and to marry me just now would do that as nothing else could—it is but too plain. Therefore I agree to an indefinite engagement—to put off all thought of marriage for a year or two.'

'But—but—can I do nothing of a different kind?' said Lucetta. 'I am full of gratitude to you—you have saved my life. And your care of me is like coals of fire on my head! I am a monied person now. Surely I can do something in return for your goodness—something practical?'

Henchard remained in thought. He had evidently not expected this. 'There is one thing you might do, Lucetta,' he said. 'But not exactly of that kind.'

'Then of what kind is it?' she asked with renewed misgiving.

'I must tell you a secret to ask it.—— You may have heard that I have been unlucky this year? I did what I have never done before—speculated rashly; and I lost. That's just put me in a strait.'

'And you would wish me to advance some money?'

'No, no!' said Henchard, almost in anger. 'I'm not the man to sponge on a woman, even though she may be so nearly my own as you. No, Lucetta; what you can do is this; and it would save me. My great creditor is Grower, and it is at his hands I shall suffer if at anybody's ; while a fortnight's forbearance on his part would be enough to allow me to pull through. This may be got out of him in one way—that you would let it be known to him that you are my intended —that we are to be quietly married in the next fort-night.—— Now stop, you haven't heard all! Let · him have this story, without, of course, any prejudice to the fact that the actual engagement between us is to be a long one. Nobody else need know : you could go with me to Mr. Grower and just let me speak to ye before him as if we were on such terms. We'll ask him to keep it secret. He will willingly wait then. At the fortnight's end I shall be able to face him ; and I can coolly tell him all is postponed between us for a year or two. Not a soul in the town need know how you've helped me. Since you wish to be of use, there's your way.'

It being now what the people called the ' pinking in ' of the day, that is, the quarter-hour just before dusk, he did not at first observe the result of his own words upon her.

' If it were anything else,' she began, and the dryness of her lips was represented in her voice.

' But it is such a little thing ! ' he said, with a deep reproach. ' Less than you have offered—just the beginning of what you have so lately promised ! I could have told him as much myself, but he would not have believed me.'

' It is not because I won't—it is because I absolutely can't,' she said, with rising distress.

' You are provoking ! ' he burst out. ' It is enough to make me force you to carry out at once what you have promised.'

' I cannot ! ' she insisted desperately.

'Why? When I have only within these few minutes released you from your promise to do the thing off-hand.'

' Because——he was a witness ! '

' Witness ?   Of what ? '

' If I must tell you——.   Don't, don't upbraid me ! '

' Well !   Let's hear what you mean ? '

' Witness of my marriage—Mr. Grower was ! '

' Marriage ? '

' Yes.   With Mr. Farfrae.   O Michael !   I am already his wife.   We were married this week at Port-Bredy. There were reasons against our doing it here.   Mr. Grower was a witness because he happened to be at Port-Bredy at the time.'

.Henchard stood as if idiotized.   She was so alarmed at his silence that she murmured something about lending him sufficient money to tide over the perilous fortnight.

' Married him ? ' said Henchard at length.   ' My good—what, married him whilst—bound to marry me ? '

' It was like this,' she explained, with tears in her eyes and quavers in her voice ;   ' don't—don't be cruel ! I loved him so much, and I thought you might tell him of the past—and that grieved me !   And then, when I had promised you, I learnt of the rumour that you had—sold your first wife at a fair, like a horse or cow !   How could I keep my promise after hearing that ?   I could not risk myself in your hands ;   it would have been letting myself down to take your name after such a scandal.   But I knew I should lose Donald if I did not secure him at once—for you would carry out your threat of telling him of our former acquaintance, as long as there was a chance of keeping me for yourself by doing so.   But you will not do so now, will you, Michael ;   for it is too late to separate us ? '

The notes of St. Peter's bells in full peal had been wafted to them while he spoke ;   and now the genial thumping of the town band, renowned for its unstinted use of the drum-stick, throbbed down the street.

'Then this racket they are making is on account of it, I suppose?' said he.

'Yes—I think he has told them, or else Mr. Grower has. . . . May I leave you now? My—he was detained at Port-Bredy to-day, and sent me on a few hours before him.'

'Then it is *his wife's* life I have saved this afternoon.'

'Yes—and he will be for ever grateful to you.'

'I am much obliged to him. . . . Oh, you false woman!' burst from Henchard. 'You promised me!'

'Yes, yes! But it was under compulsion, and I did not know all your past——'

'And now I've a mind to punish you as you deserve! One word to this bran-new husband of how you courted me, and your precious happiness is blown to atoms!'

'Michael—pity me, and be generous!'

'You don't deserve pity! You did; but you don't now.'

'I'll help you to pay off your debt.'

'A pensioner of Farfrae's wife—not I! Don't stay with me longer—I shall say something worse. Go home!'

She disappeared under the trees of the south walk as the band came round the corner, awaking the echoes of every stock and stone in celebration of her happiness. Lucetta took no heed, but ran up the back street and reached her own home unperceived.

XXX

FARFRAE'S words to his landlady had referred to the removal of his boxes and other effects from his late lodgings to Lucetta's house. The work was not heavy, but it had been much hindered on account of the frequent pauses necessitated by exclamations of surprise at the event, of which the good woman had been briefly informed by letter a few hours earlier.

At the last moment of leaving Port-Bredy, Farfrae, like John Gilpin, had been detained by important customers, whom, even in the exceptional circumstances, he was not the man to neglect. Moreover, there was a convenience in Lucetta arriving first at her house. Nobody there as yet knew what had happened; and she was best in a position to break the news to the inmates, and give directions for her husband's accommodation. He had, therefore, sent on his two-days' bride in a hired brougham, whilst he went across the country to a certain group of wheat and barley ricks a few miles off, telling her the hour at which he might be expected the same evening. This accounted for her trotting out to meet him after their separation of four hours.

By a strenuous effort, after leaving Henchard, she calmed herself in readiness to receive Donald at High Place Hall when he came on from his lodgings. One supreme fact empowered her to this, the sense that, come what would, she had secured him. Half-an-hour after her arrival he walked in, and she met him with a relieved gladness, which a month's perilous absence could not have intensified.

'There is one thing I have not done; and yet it is important,' she said earnestly, when she had finished talking about the adventure with the bull. 'That is, broken the news of our marriage to my dear Elizabeth-Jane.'

'Ah, and you have not?' he said thoughtfully. 'I gave her a lift from the barn homewards; but I did not tell her either; for I thought she might have heard of it in the town, and was keeping back her congratulations from shyness, and all that.'

'She can hardly have heard of it. But I'll find out; I'll go to her now. And, Donald, you don't mind her living on with me just the same as before? She is so quiet and unassuming.'

'Oh no, indeed I don't,' Farfrae answered with, perhaps, a faint awkwardness. 'But I wonder if she would care to?'

'Oh yes!' said Lucetta eagerly. 'I am sure she would like to. Besides, poor thing, she has no other home.'

Farfrae looked at her, and saw that she did not suspect the secret of her more reserved friend. He liked her all the better for the blindness. 'Arrange as you like with her, by all means,' he said. 'It is I who have come to your house, not you to mine.'

'I'll run and speak to her,' said Lucetta.

When she got upstairs to Elizabeth-Jane's room, the latter had taken off her out-door things, and was resting over a book. Lucetta found in a moment that she had not yet learnt the news.

'I did not come down to you, Miss Templeman,' she said simply. 'I was coming to ask if you had quite recovered from your fright, but I found you had a visitor. What are the bells ringing for, I wonder? And the band, too, is playing. Somebody must be married; or else they are practising for Christmas.'

Lucetta uttered a vague 'Yes,' and seating herself by the other young woman, looked musingly at her. 'What a lonely creature you are,' she presently said; 'never knowing what's going on, or what people are talking about everywhere with keen interest. You should get out, and gossip about as other women do, and then you wouldn't be obliged to ask me a question of that kind. Well, now, I have something to tell you.'

Elizabeth-Jane said she was so glad, and made herself receptive.

'I must go rather a long way back,' said Lucetta, the difficulty of explaining herself satisfactorily to the pondering one beside her growing more apparent at each syllable. 'You remember that trying case of conscience I told you of some time ago—about the first lover, and the second lover?' She let out in jerky phrases a leading word or two of the story she had told.

'Oh yes—I remember; the story of *your friend*,' said Elizabeth drily, regarding the irises of Lucetta's eyes as though to catch their exact shade. 'The two lovers—the old and the new: how she wanted to marry the second, but felt she ought to marry the first; so that the good she would have done she did not, and the evil that she would not, that she did—exactly like the Apostle Paul.'

'Oh no; she didn't do evil exactly!' said Lucetta hastily.

'But you said that she—or as I may say *you*'— answered Elizabeth, dropping the mask, 'were in honour and conscience bound to marry the first?'

Lucetta's blush at being seen through came and went again before she replied anxiously, ' You will never breathe this, will you, Elizabeth-Jane ? '

' Certainly not, if you say not.'

' Then I will tell you that the case is more complicated—worse, in fact—than it seemed in my story. I and the first man were thrown together in a strange way, and felt that we ought to be united, as the world had talked of us. He was a widower, as he supposed. He had not heard of his first wife for many years. But the wife returned, and we parted. She is now dead ; and the husband comes paying me addresses again, saying, " Now we'll complete our purpose." But, Elizabeth-Jane, all this amounts to a new courtship of me by him ; I was absolved from all vows by the return of the other woman.'

' Have you not lately renewed your promise ? ' said the younger with quiet surmise. She had divined Man Number One.

' That was wrung from me by a threat.'

' Yes, it was. But I think when any one gets coupled up with a man in the past so unfortunately as you have done, she ought to become his wife, if she can, even if she were not the sinning party.'

Lucetta's countenance lost its sparkle. ' He turned out to be a man I should be afraid to marry,' she pleaded. ' Really afraid ! And it was not till after my renewed promise that I knew it.'

' Then there is only one course left to honesty. You must remain a single woman.'

' But think again ! Do consider——'

' I am certain,' interrupted her companion hardily. ' I have guessed very well who the man is. My father ; and I say it is him or nobody for you.'

Any suspicion of impropriety was to Elizabeth-Jane like a red rag to a bull. Her craving for correctness of procedure was, indeed, almost vicious. Owing to her early troubles with regard to her mother, a semblance of irregularity had terrors for her which those whose names are safeguarded from suspicion know nothing of. 'You ought to marry Mr. Henchard or nobody—certainly not another man!' she went on with a quivering lip, in whose movement two passions shared.

'I don't admit that!' said Lucetta passionately.

'Admit it or not, it is true!'

Lucetta covered her eyes with her right hand, as if she could plead no more, holding out her left to Elizabeth-Jane.

'Why, you *have* married him!' cried the latter, jumping up with pleasure after a glance at Lucetta's fingers. 'When did you do it? Why did you not tell me, instead of teasing me like this? How very honourable of you! He did treat my mother badly once, it seems, in a moment of intoxication. And it is true that he is stern sometimes. But you will rule him entirely, I am sure, with your beauty and wealth and accomplishments. You are the woman he will adore, and we shall all three be happy together now!'

'Oh, my Elizabeth-Jane!' cried Lucetta distressfully. ''Tis somebody else that I have married! I was so desperate—so afraid of being forced to anything else—so afraid of revelations that would quench his love for me, that I resolved to do it off-hand, come what might, and purchase a week of happiness at any cost!'

'You—have—married Mr. Farfrae!' cried Elizabeth-Jane, in Nathan tones.

Lucetta bowed. She had recovered herself.

'The bells are ringing on that account,' she said. 'My husband is downstairs. He will live here till a more suitable house is ready for us; and I have told him that I want you to stay with me just as before.'

'Let me think of it alone,' the girl quickly replied, corking up the turmoil of her feeling with grand control.

'You shall. I am sure we shall be happy together.'

Lucetta departed to join Donald below, a vague uneasiness floating over her joy at seeing him quite at home there. Not on account of her friend Elizabeth did she feel it: for of the bearings of Elizabeth-Jane's emotions she had not the least suspicion; but on Henchard's alone.

Now the instant decision of Susan Henchard's daughter was to dwell in that house no more. Apart from her estimate of the propriety of Lucetta's conduct, Farfrae had been so nearly her avowed lover that she felt she could not abide there.

It was still early in the evening when she hastily put on her things and went out. In a few minutes, knowing the ground, she had found a suitable lodging, and arranged to enter it that night. Returning and entering noiselessly she took off her pretty dress and arrayed herself in a plain one, packing up the other to keep as her best; for she would have to be very economical now. She wrote a note to leave for Lucetta, who was closely shut up in the drawing-room with Farfrae; and then Elizabeth-Jane called a man with a wheelbarrow; and seeing her boxes put into it she trotted off down the street to her rooms. They were in the street in which Henchard lived, and almost opposite his door.

Here she sat down and considered the means of subsistence. The little annual sum settled on her by her stepfather would keep body and soul together. A wonderful skill in netting of all sorts—acquired in childhood by making seines in Newson's home—might serve her in good stead; and her studies, which were pursued unremittingly, might serve her in still better.

By this time the marriage that had taken place was known throughout Casterbridge; had been discussed noisily on kerbstones, confidentially behind counters, and jovially at the Three Mariners. Whether Farfrae would sell his business and set up for a gentleman on his wife's money, or whether he would show independence enough to stick to his trade in spite of his brilliant alliance, was a great point of interest.

XXXI

THE retort of the furmity-woman before the magistrates had spread; and in four-and-twenty hours there was not a person in Casterbridge who remained unacquainted with the story of Henchard's mad freak at Weydon Priors Fair, long years before. The amends he had made in after life were lost sight of in the dramatic glare of the original act. Had the incident been well-known of old and always, it might by this time have grown to be lightly regarded as the rather tall wild oat, but well-nigh the single one, of a young man with whom the steady and mature (if somewhat headstrong) burgher of to-day had scarcely a point in common. But the act having lain as dead and buried ever since, the interspace of years was unperceived; and the black spot of his youth wore the aspect of a recent crime.

Small as the court incident had been in itself, it formed the edge or turn in the incline of Henchard's fortunes. On that day—almost at that minute—he passed the ridge of prosperity and honour, and began to descend rapidly on the other side. It was strange how soon he sank in esteem. Socially he had received a startling fillip downwards; and, having already lost commercial buoyancy from rash transactions, the velocity of his descent in both aspects became accelerated every hour.

He now gazed more at the pavements, and less at the house-fronts, when he walked about; more at the feet and leggings of men, and less into the pupils of their eyes with the blazing regard which formerly had made them blink.

New events combined to undo him. It had been a bad year for others besides himself, and the heavy failure of a debtor whom he had trusted generously completed the overthrow of his tottering credit. And now, in his desperation, he failed to preserve that strict correspondence between bulk and sample, which is the soul of commerce in grain. For this, one of his men was mainly to blame; that worthy, in his great un-wisdom, having picked over the sample of an enormous quantity of second-rate corn which Henchard had in hand, and removed the pinched, blasted, and smutted grains in great numbers. The produce, if honestly offered, would have created no scandal; but the blun-der of misrepresentation, coming at such a moment, dragged Henchard's name into the ditch.

The details of his failure were of the ordinary kind. One day Elizabeth-Jane was passing the King's Arms, when she saw people bustling in and out more than usual when there was no market. A bystander in-formed her, with some surprise at her ignorance, that it was a meeting of the Commissioners under Mr. Henchard's bankruptcy. She felt quite tearful, and when she heard that he was present in the hotel she wished to go in and see him, but was advised not to intrude that day.

The room in which debtor and creditors had as-sembled was a front one, and Henchard, looking out of the window, had caught sight of Elizabeth-Jane through the wire blind. His examination had closed, and the creditors were leaving. The appearance of Elizabeth threw him into a reverie; till, turning his face from the window, and towering above all the rest, he called their attention for a moment more. His countenance had somewhat changed from its flush of prosperity; the black hair and whiskers were the same as ever, but a film of ash was over the rest.

'Gentlemen,' he said, 'over and above the assets that we've been talking about, and that appear on the balance-sheet, there be these. It all belongs to ye, as much as everything else I've got, and I don't wish to keep it from you, not I.' Saying this, he took his gold watch from his pocket, and laid it on the table; then his purse—the yellow canvas money-bag, such as was carried by all farmers and dealers—untying it, and shaking the money out upon the table beside the watch. The latter he drew back quickly for an instant, to remove the hair-guard made and given him by Lucetta. 'There, now you have all I've got in the world,' he said. 'And I wish for your sakes 'twas more.'

The creditors, farmers almost to a man, looked at the watch, and at the money, and into the street; when Farmer James Everdene spoke.

'No, no, Henchard,' he said warmly. 'We don't want that. 'Tis honourable in ye; but keep it. What do you say, neighbours—do ye agree?'

'Ay, sure: we don't wish it at all,' said Grower, another creditor.

'Let him keep it, of course,' murmured another in the background—a silent, reserved young man, named Boldwood; and the rest responded unanimously.

'Well,' said the senior Commissioner, addressing Henchard, 'though the case is a desperate one, I am bound to admit that I have never met a debtor who behaved more fairly. I've proved the balance-sheet to be as honestly made out as it could possibly be; we have had no trouble; there have been no evasions and no concealments. The rashness of dealing which led to this unhappy situation is obvious enough; but as far as I can see every attempt has been made to avoid wronging anybody.'

Henchard was more affected by this than he cared to let them perceive, and he turned aside to the window again. A general murmur of agreement followed the Commissioner's words; and the meeting dispersed. When they were gone Henchard regarded the watch they had returned to him. ' 'Tisn't mine by rights,' he said to himself. ' Why the devil didn't they take it?—I don't want what don't belong to me!' Moved by a recollection he took the watch to the maker's just opposite, sold it there and then for what the trades-man offered, and went with the proceeds to one among the smaller of his creditors, a cottager of Durnover, in straitened circumstances, to whom he handed the money.

When everything was ticketed that Henchard had owned, and the auctions were in progress, there was quite a sympathetic reaction in the town, which till then for some time past had done nothing but con-demn him. Now that Henchard's whole career was pictured distinctly to his neighbours, and they could see how admirably he had used his one talent of energy to create a position of affluence out of absolutely nothing—which was really all he could show when he came to the town as a journeyman hay-trusser, with his wimble and knife in his basket—they wondered and regretted his fall.

Try as she might, Elizabeth could never meet with him. She believed in him still, though nobody else did; and she wanted to be allowed to forgive him for his roughness to her, and to help him in his trouble.

She wrote to him; he did not reply. She then went to his house—the great house she had lived in so happily for a time—with its front of dun brick, vitrified here and there, and its heavy sash-bars—but Henchard was to be found there no more. The ex-Mayor had left the home of his prosperity, and gone into Jopp's cottage by the Priory Mill—the sad purlieu to which he had wandered on the night of his discovery that she was not his daughter. Thither she went.

Elizabeth thought it odd that he had fixed on this spot to retire to, but assumed that necessity had no choice. Trees which seemed old enough to have been planted by the friars still stood around, and the back hatch of the original mill yet formed a cascade which had raised its terrific roar for centuries. The cottage itself was built of old stones from the long dismantled Priory, scraps of tracery, moulded window-jambs, and arch-labels, being mixed in with the rubble of the walls.

In this cottage he occupied a couple of rooms, Jopp, whom Henchard had employed, abused, cajoled, and dismissed by turns, being the householder. But even here her stepfather could not be seen.

'Not by his daughter?' pleaded Elizabeth.

'By nobody—at present: that's his order,' she was informed.

Afterwards she was passing by the corn-stores and hay-barns which had been the headquarters of his business. She knew that he ruled there no longer; but it was with amazement that she regarded the familiar gateway. A smear of decisive lead-coloured paint had been laid on to obliterate Henchard's name, though its letters dimly loomed through like ships in a fog. Over these, in fresh white, spread the name of Farfrae.

Abel Whittle was edging his skeleton in at the wicket, and she said, 'Mr. Farfrae is master here?'

'Yaas, Miss Henchet,' he said, 'Mr. Farfrae have bought the concern and all of we work-folk with it; and 'tis better for us than 'twas—though I shouldn't say that to you as a daughter-law. We work harder, but we bain't made afeard now. It was fear made my few poor hairs so thin! No busting out, no slamming of doors, no meddling with yer eternal soul and all

that; and though 'tis a shilling a week less I'm the
richer man; for what's all the world if yer mind is
always in a larry, Miss Henchet?'

The intelligence was in a general sense true; and
Henchard's stores, which had remained in a paralyzed
condition during the settlement of his bankruptcy, were
stirred into activity again when the new tenant had possession.   Thenceforward the full sacks, looped with the
shining chain, went scurrying up and down under the
cat-head, hairy arms were thrust out from the different
door-ways, and the grain was hauled in; trusses of
hay were tossed anew in and out of the barns, and
the wimbles creaked; while the scales and steelyards
began to be busy where guess-work had formerly been
the rule.

XXXII

TWO bridges stood near the lower part of Caster-bridge town. The first, of weather-stained brick, was immediately at the end of High Street, where a diverging branch from that thoroughfare ran round to the low-lying Durnover lanes ; so that the precincts of the bridge formed the merging point of respectability and indigence. The second bridge, of stone, was further out on the highway—in fact, fairly in the meadows, though still within the town boundary.

These bridges had speaking countenances. Every projection in each was worn down to obtuseness, partly by weather, more by friction from generations of loungers, whose toes and heels had from year to year made restless movements against these parapets, as they had stood there meditating on the aspect of affairs. In the case of the more friable bricks and stones even the flat faces were worn into hollows by the same mixed mechanism. The masonry of the top was clamped with iron at each joint; since it had been no uncommon thing for desperate men to wrench the coping off and throw it down the river, in reckless defiance of the magistrates.

For to this pair of bridges gravitated all the failures of the town; those who had failed in business, in love, in sobriety, in crime. Why the unhappy hereabout usually chose the bridges for their meditations in preference to a railing, a gate, or a stile, was not so clear.

There was a marked difference of quality between the personages who haunted the near bridge of brick, and the personages who haunted the far one of stone. Those of lowest character preferred the former, adjoining the town; they did not mind the glare of the public eye. They had been of comparatively no account during their successes; and, though they might feel dispirited, they had no particular sense of shame in their ruin. Their hands were mostly kept in their pockets; they wore a leather strap round their waists, and boots that required a great deal of lacing, but seemed never to get any. Instead of sighing at their adversities they spat, and instead of saying the iron had entered into their souls, they said they were down on their luck. Jopp in his times of distress had often stood here; so had Mother Cuxsom, Christopher Coney, and poor Abel Whittle.

The *misérables* who would pause on the remoter bridge were of a politer stamp. They included bankrupts, hypochondriacs, persons who were what is called 'out of a situation' from fault or lucklessness, the inefficient of the professional class—shabby-genteel men, who did not know how to get rid of the weary time between breakfast and dinner, and the yet more weary time between dinner and dark. The eyes of this species were mostly directed over the parapet upon the running water below. A man seen there looking thus fixedly into the river was pretty sure to be one whom the world did not treat kindly for some reason or other. While one in straits on the townward bridge did not mind who saw him so, and kept his back to the parapet to survey the passers-by, one in straits on this never faced the road, never turned his head at coming footsteps, but, sensitive to his own condition, watched the current whenever a stranger approached,

as if some strange fish interested him, though every
finned thing had been poached out of the river years
before.

There and thus they would muse; if their grief were
the grief of oppression they would wish themselves
kings; if their grief were poverty, wish themselves
millionaires; if sin, they would wish they were saints or
angels; if despised love, that they were some much-
courted Adonis of county fame. Some had been
known to stand and think so long with this fixed gaze
downward, that eventually they had allowed their poor
carcases to follow that gaze; and they were discovered
the next morning in the pool beneath out of reach of
their troubles.

To this bridge came Henchard, as other unfor-
tunates had come before him, his way thither being
by the riverside path on the chilly edge of the town.
Here he was standing one windy afternoon when
Durnover church clock struck five. While the gusts
were bringing the notes to his ears across the damp
intervening flat a man passed behind him, and greeted
Henchard by name. Henchard turned slightly, and
saw that the comer was Jopp, his old foreman, now
employed elsewhere, to whom, though he hated him, he
had gone for lodgings because Jopp was the one man
in Casterbridge whose observation and opinion the fallen
corn-merchant despised to the point of indifference.

Henchard returned him a scarcely perceptible nod,
and Jopp stopped.

'He and she are gone into their new house to-day,'
said Jopp.

'Oh,' said Henchard absently. 'Which house is
that?'

'Your old one.'

'Gone into my house?' And, starting up, Henchard
added, '*My* house of all others in the town!'

'Well, as somebody was sure to live there, and

you couldn't, it can do ye no harm that he's the man.'

It was quite true : he felt that it was doing him no harm. Farfrae, who had already taken the yards and stores, had acquired possession of the house for the obvious convenience of its contiguity. And yet this act of his taking up residence within those roomy chambers while he, their former tenant, lived in a cottage, galled Henchard indescribably.

Jopp continued : 'And you heard of that fellow who bought all the best furniture at your sale? He was bidding for no other than Farfrae all the while! It has never been moved out of the house, as he'd already got the lease.'

' My furniture too! Surely he'll buy my body and soul likewise ! '

' There's no saying he won't, if you be willing to sell.' And having planted these wounds in the heart of his once imperious master, Jopp went on his way; while Henchard stared and stared into the racing river till the bridge seemed moving backward with him.

The low land grew blacker, and the sky a deeper grey. When the landscape looked like a picture blotted in with ink, another traveller approached the great stone bridge.' He was driving a gig, his direction being also townwards. On the round of the middle of the arch the gig stopped. ' Mr. Henchard?' came from it in the voice of Farfrae. Henchard turned his face.

Finding that he had guessed rightly, Farfrae told the man who accompanied him to drive home; while he alighted, and went up to his former friend.

' I have heard that you think of emigrating, Mr. Henchard,' he said. ' Is it true? I have a real reason for asking.'

Henchard withheld his answer for several instants, and then said, ' Yes; it is true. I am going where you were going to a few years ago, when I prevented you and got you to bide here. 'Tis turn and turn about, isn't it! Do ye mind how we stood like this in the Chalk Walk when I persuaded ye to stay? You then stood without a chattel to your name, and I was the master of the house in Corn Street. But now I stand without a stick or a rág, and the master of that house is you.'

'Yes, yes; that's so! It's the way o' the warrld,' said Farfrae.

'Ha, ha, true!' cried Henchard, throwing himself into a mood of jocularity. 'Up and down! I'm used to it. What's the odds after all!'

'Now listen to me, if it's no taking up your time,' said Farfrae, 'just as I listened to you. Don't go. Stay at home.'

'But I can do nothing else, man!' said Henchard scornfully. 'The little money I have will just keep body and soul together for a few weeks, and no more. I have not felt inclined to go back to journey-work yet; but I can't stay doing nothing, and my best chance is elsewhere.'

'No; but what I propose is this—if ye will listen. Come and live in your old house. We can spare some rooms very well—I am sure my wife would not mind it at all—until there's an opening for ye.'

Henchard started. Probably the picture drawn by the unsuspecting Donald of himself under the same roof with Lucetta was too striking to be received with equanimity. 'No, no,' he said gruffly; 'we should quarrel.'

'You should hae a part to yourself,' said Farfrae; 'and nobody to interfere wi' you. It will be a deal healthier than down there by the river where you live now.'

Still Henchard refused. 'You don't know what you ask,' he said. 'However, I can do no less than thank 'ee.'

They walked into the town together side by side, as they had done when Henchard persuaded the young Scotchman to remain. 'Will you come in and have some supper?' said Farfrae, when they reached the middle of the town, where their paths diverged right and left.

'No, no.'

'By-the-bye, I had nearly forgot. I bought a good deal of your furniture.'

'So I have heard.'

'Well, it was no that I wanted it so very much for myself; but I wish ye to pick out all that you care to have—such things as may be endeared to ye by associations, or particularly suited to your use. And take them to your own house—it will not be depriving me; we can do with less very well, and I will have plenty of opportunities of getting more.'

'What—give it to me for nothing?' said Henchard. 'But you paid the creditors for it!'

'Ah, yes; but maybe it's worth more to you than it is to me.'

Henchard was a little moved. 'I—sometimes think I've wronged ye!' he said, in tones which showed the disquietude that the night shades hid in his face. He shook Farfrae abruptly by the hand, and hastened away as if unwilling to betray himself further. Farfrae saw him turn through the thoroughfare into Bull Stake and vanish down towards the Priory Mill.

Meanwhile Elizabeth-Jane, in an upper room no larger than the Prophet's chamber, and with the silk attire of her palmy days packed away in a box, was netting with great industry between the hours which she devoted to studying such books as she could get hold of.

Her lodgings being nearly opposite her stepfather's former residence, now Farfrae's, she could see Donald and Lucetta speeding in and out of their door with all the bounding enthusiasm of their situation. She avoided looking that way as much as possible, but it was hardly in human nature to keep the eyes averted when the door slammed.

While living on thus quietly she heard the news that Henchard had caught cold and was confined to his room—possibly a result of standing about the meads in damp weather. She went off to his house at once. This time she was determined not to be denied admittance, and made her way upstairs. He was sitting up in the bed with a greatcoat round him, and at first resented her intrusion. 'Go away—go away,' he said. 'I don't like to see ye!'

'But, father——'

'I don't like to see ye,' he repeated.

However, the ice was broken, and she remained. She made the room more comfortable, gave directions to the people below, and by the time she went away had reconciled her stepfather to her visiting him.

The effect, either of her ministrations or of her mere presence, was a rapid recovery. He soon was well enough to go out; and now things seemed to wear a new colour in his eyes. He no longer thought of emigration, and thought more of Elizabeth. The having nothing to do made him more dreary than any other circumstance; and one day, with better views of Farfrae than he had held for some time, and a sense that honest work was not a thing to be ashamed of, he stoically went down to Farfrae's yard and asked to be taken on as a journeyman hay-trusser. He was engaged at once. This hiring of Henchard was done through a foreman, Farfrae feeling that it was undesirable to come personally in contact with the ex-cornfactor more than was absolutely necessary. While anxious to help him he was well aware by this time of his uncertain temper, and thought reserved relations best. For the same reason his orders to Henchard to proceed to this and that country farm trussing in the usual way were always given through a third person.

For a time these arrangements worked well, it being the custom to truss in the respective stack-yards, before bringing it away, the hay bought at the different farms about the neighbourhood; so that Henchard was often absent at such places the whole week long. When this was all done, and Henchard had become in a measure broken in, he came to work daily on the home premises like the rest. And thus the once flourishing merchant and Mayor and what not stood as a day-labourer in the barns and granaries he formerly had owned.

'I have worked as a journeyman before now, ha'n't I?' he would say in his defiant way; 'and why shouldn't I do it again?' But he looked a far different journeyman from the one he had been in his earlier days. Then he had worn clean, suitable clothes, light and cheerful in hue; leggings yellow as marigolds, corduroys immaculate as new flax, and a neckerchief like a flower-garden. Now he wore the remains of an old blue cloth suit of his gentlemanly times, a rusty silk hat, and a once black satin stock, soiled and shabby. Clad thus, he went to and fro, still comparatively an active man—for he was not much over forty—and saw with the other men in the yard Donald Farfrae going in and out the green door that led to the garden, and the big house, and Lucetta.

At the beginning of the winter it was rumoured about Casterbridge that Mr. Farfrae, already in the Town Council, was to be proposed for Mayor in a year or two.

'Yes; she was wise, she was wise in her generation!' said Henchard to himself when he heard of this one day on his way to Farfrae's hay-barn. He thought it over as he wimbled his bonds, and the piece of news acted as a reviviscent breath to that old view of his—of Donald Farfrae as his triumphant rival who rode rough-shod over him.

'A fellow of his age going to be Mayor, indeed!' he murmured with a corner-drawn smile on his mouth. 'But 'tis her money that floats en upward. Ha-ha—how cust odd it is! Here be I, his former master, working for him as man, and he the man standing as master, with my house and my furniture and my what-you-may-call wife all his own.'

He repeated these things a hundred times a day. During the whole period of his acquaintance with Lucetta he had never wished to claim her as his own so desperately as he now regretted her loss. It was no mercenary hankering after her fortune that moved him; though that fortune had been the means of making her so much the more desired by giving her the air of independence and sauciness which attracts men of his composition. It had given her servants, house, and fine clothing—a setting that invested Lucetta with a startling novelty in the eyes of him who had known her in her narrow days.

He accordingly lapsed into moodiness, and at every allusion to the possibility of Farfrae's near election to the municipal chair his former hatred of the Scotchman returned. Concurrently with this he underwent a moral change. It resulted in his significantly saying every now and then, in tones of recklessness, 'Only a fortnight more!'—'Only a dozen days!' and so forth, lessening his figures day by day.

'Why d'ye say only a dozen days?' asked Solomon Longways as he worked beside Henchard in the granary weighing oats.

'Because in twelve days I shall be released from my oath.'

'What oath?'

'The oath to drink no spirituous liquid. In twelve

days it will be twenty years since I swore it, and then I mean to enjoy myself, please God!'

Elizabeth-Jane sat at her window one Sunday, and while there she heard in the street below a conversation which introduced Henchard's name. She was wondering what was the matter, when a third person who was passing by asked the question in her mind.

'Michael Henchard have busted out drinking after taking nothing for twenty years!'

Elizabeth-Jane jumped up, put on her things, and went out.

XXXIII

AT this date there prevailed in Casterbridge a convivial custom—scarcely recognized as such, yet none the less established. On the afternoon of every Sunday a large contingent of the Casterbridge journeymen—steady church-goers and sedate characters—having attended service; filed from the church doors across the way to the Three Mariners Inn. The rear was usually brought up by the choir, with their bass-viols, fiddles, and flutes under their arms.

The great point, the point of honour, on these sacred occasions was for each man to strictly limit himself to half-a-pint of liquor. This scrupulosity was so well understood by the landlord, that the whole company was served in cups of that measure. They were all exactly alike—straight-sided, with leafless lime-trees done in eel-brown on the sides—one towards the drinker's lips, the other confronting his comrade. To wonder how many of these cups the landlord possessed altogether was a favourite exercise of children in the marvellous. Forty at least might have been seen at these times in the large room, forming a ring round the margin of the great sixteen-legged oak table, like the monolithic circle at Stonehenge in its pristine days. Outside and above the forty cups came a circle of forty smoke-jets from forty clay pipes; outside the pipes the countenances of the forty church-goers, supported at the back by a circle of forty chairs.

The conversation was not the conversation of week-days, but a thing altogether finer in point and higher in tone. They invariably discussed the sermon, dissecting it; weighing it, as above or below the average —the general tendency being to regard it as a scientific feat or performance which had no relation to their own lives, except as between critics and the thing criticized. The bass-viol player and the clerk usually spoke with more authority than the rest on account of their official connection with the preacher.

Now the Three Mariners was the inn chosen by Henchard as the place for closing his long term of dramless years. He had so timed his entry as to be well established in the large room by the time the forty church-goers entered to their customary cups. The flush upon his face proclaimed at once that the vow of twenty years had lapsed, and the era of recklessness begun anew. He was seated on a small table, drawn up to the side of the massive oak board reserved for the churchmen, a few of whom nodded to him as they took their places, and said, ' How be ye, Mr. Henchard ? Quite a stranger here.'

Henchard did not take the trouble to reply for a few moments, and his eyes rested on his stretched-out legs and boots. ' Yes,' he said at length ; ' that's true. I've been down in spirit for weeks ; some of ye know the cause. I am better now ; but not quite serene. I want you fellows of the choir to strike up a tune ; and what with that and this brew of Stannidge's, I am in hopes of getting altogether out of my minor key.'

' With all my heart,' said the first fiddle. ' We've let back our strings, that's true ; but we can soon pull 'em up again. Sound A, neighbours, and give the man a stave.'

' I don't care a curse what the words be,' said

Henchard. 'Hymns, ballets, or rantipole rubbish; the Rogue's March or the cherubim's warble—'tis all the same to me if 'tis good harmony, and well put out.'

'Well—heh, heh—it may be we can do that, and not a man among us that have sat in the gallery less than twenty year,' said the leader of the band. 'As 'tis Sunday, neighbours, suppose we raise the Fourth Psa'am, to Samuel Wakely's tune, as improved by me?'

'Hang Samuel Wakely's tune, as improved by thee!' said Henchard. 'Chuck across one of your psalters—old Wiltshire is the only tune worth singing —the psalm-tune that would make my blood ebb and flow like the sea when I was a steady chap. I'll find some words to fit en.' He took one of the psalters, and began turning over the leaves.

Chancing to look out of the window at that moment he saw a flock of people passing by, and perceived them to be the congregation of the upper church, now just dismissed, their sermon having been a longer one than that the lower parish was favoured with. Among the rest of the leading inhabitants walked Mr. Councillor Farfrae, with Lucetta upon his arm, the observed and imitated of all the smaller tradesmen's womankind. Henchard's mouth changed a little, and he continued to turn over the leaves.

'Now then,' he said, 'Psalm the Hundred-and-Ninth, to the tune of Wiltshire: verses ten to fifteen. I gi'e ye the words:

> " His seed shall orphans be, his wife
> A widow plunged in grief;
> His vagrant children beg their bread
> Where none can give relief.

> ' His ill-got riches shall be made
> To usurers a prey;
> The fruit of all his toil shall be
> By strangers borne away.

" None shall be found that to his wants
    Their mercy will extend,
Or to his helpless orphan seed
    The least assistance lend.

" A swift destruction soon shall seize
    On his unhappy race;
And the next age his hated name
    Shall utterly deface." '

'I know the Psa'am—I know the Psa'am!' said the leader hastily; 'but I would as lief not sing it. 'Twasn't made for singing. We chose it once when the gipsy stole the pa'son's mare, thinking to please him, but he were quite upset. Whatever Servant David were thinking about when he made a Psalm that nobody can sing without disgracing himself, I can't fathom! Now then, the Fourth Psalm, to Samuel Wakely's tune, as improved by me.'

''Od seize your sauce—I tell ye to sing the Hundred-and-Ninth, to Wiltshire, and sing it you shall!' roared Henchard. 'Not a single one of all the droning crew of ye goes out of this room till that Psalm is sung!' He slipped off the table, seized the poker, and going to the door placed his back against it. 'Now then, go ahead, if you don't wish to have your cust pates broke!'

'Don't 'ee, don't 'ee take on so!—As 'tis the Sabbath-day, and 'tis Servant David's words and not ours, perhaps we don't mind for once, hey?' said one of the terrified choir, looking round upon the rest. So the instruments were tuned and the comminatory verses sung.

'Thank ye, thank ye,' said Henchard in a softened voice, his eyes growing downcast, and his manner that of a man much moved by the strains. 'Don't you blame David,' he went on in low tones, shaking his head without raising his eyes. 'He knew what he was about when he wrote that! . . . If I could afford it, be hanged if I wouldn't keep a church choir at my own expense to play and sing to me at these low, dark times of my life. But the bitter thing is, that when I was rich I didn't need what I could have, and now I be poor I can't have what I need!'

While they paused, Lucetta and Farfrae passed again, this time homeward, it being their custom to take, like others, a short walk out on the highway and back, between church and tea-time. 'There's the man we've been singing about,' said Henchard.

The players and singers turned their heads, and saw his meaning. 'Heaven forbid!' said the bass-player.

''Tis the man,' repeated Henchard doggedly.

'Then if I'd known,' said the performer on the clarionet solemnly, 'that 'twas meant for a living man, nothing should have drawn out of my wynd-pipe the breath for that Psalm, so help me!'

'Nor from mine,' said the first singer. 'But, thought I, as it was made so long ago, and so far away, perhaps there isn't much in it, so I'll oblige a neighbour; for there's nothing to be said against the tune.'

'Ah, my boys, you've sung it,' cried Henchard triumphantly. 'As for him, it was partly by his songs that he got over me, and heaved me out. . . . I could double him up like that—and yet I don't.' He laid the poker across his knee, bent it as if it were a twig, flung it down, and came away from the door.

It was at this time that Elizabeth-Jane, having heard where her stepfather was, entered the room with a pale and agonized countenance. The choir and the rest of the company moved off, in accordance with their half-pint regulation. Elizabeth-Jane went up to Henchard, and entreated him to accompany her home.

By this hour the volcanic fires of his nature had burnt down, and having drunk no great quantity as yet, he was inclined to acquiesce. She took his arm, and together they went on. Henchard walked blankly, like a blind man, repeating to himself the last words of the singers—

> ' And the next age his hated name
> Shall utterly deface ! '

At length he said to her, ' I am a man to my word. I have kept my oath for twenty years ; and now I can drink with a good conscience. . . . . If I don't do for him—well, I am a fearful practical joker when I choose ! He has taken away everything from me, and by heavens, if I meet him I won't answer for my deeds ! '

These half-uttered words alarmed Elizabeth—all the more by reason of the still determination of Henchard's mien.

' What will you do ? ' she asked cautiously, while trembling with disquietude, and guessing Henchard's allusion only too well.

Henchard did not answer, and they went on till they had reached his cottage. ' May I come in ? ' she said.

' No, no ; not to-day,' said Henchard ; and she went away ; feeling that to caution Farfrae was almost her duty, as it was certainly her strong desire.

As on the Sunday, so on the week-days, Farfrae and Lucetta might have been seen flitting about the town like two butterflies—or rather like a bee and a butterfly in league for life. She seemed to take no pleasure in going anywhere except in her husband's company ; and hence when business would not permit him to waste an afternoon she remained indoors, waiting for the time to pass till his return, her face being visible to Elizabeth-Jane from her window aloft. The latter, however, did not say to herself that Farfrae should be thankful for such devotion, but, full of her reading, she cited Rosalind's exclamation: 'Mistress, know yourself; down on your knees and thank Heaven fasting for a good man's love.'

She kept her eye upon Henchard also. One day he answered her inquiry for his health by saying that he could not endure Abel Whittle's pitying eyes upon him while they worked together in the yard. 'He is such a fool,' said Henchard, 'that he can never get out of his mind the time when I was master there.'

'I'll come and wimble for you instead of him, if you will allow me,' said she. Her motive on going to the yard was to get an opportunity of observing the general position of affairs on Farfrae's premises now that her stepfather was a workman there. Henchard's threats had alarmed her so much, that she wished to see his behaviour when the two were face to face.

For two or three days after her arrival Donald did not make any appearance. Then one afternoon the green door opened, and through came, first Farfrae, and at his heels Lucetta. Donald brought his wife forward without hesitation, it being obvious that he had no suspicion whatever of any antecedents in common between her and the now journeyman hay-trusser.

Henchard did not turn his eyes toward either of the pair, keeping them fixed on the bond he twisted, as if that alone absorbed him. A feeling of delicacy, which ever prompted Farfrae to avoid anything that might seem like triumphing over a fallen rival, led him to keep away from the hay-barn where Henchard and his daughter were working, and to go on to the corn department. Meanwhile Lucetta, never having been informed that Henchard had entered her husband's service, rambled straight on to the barn, where she came suddenly upon Henchard, and gave vent to a little 'Oh!' which the happy and busy Donald was too far off to hear. Henchard, with withering humility of demeanour, touched the brim of his hat to her as

Whittle and the rest had done, to which she breathed
a dead-alive ' Good afternoon.'

' I beg your pardon, ma'am ? ' said Henchard, as if
he had not heard.

' I said good afternoon,' she faltered.

' Oh yes, good afternoon, ma'am,' he replied, touching his hat again. ' I am glad to see you, ma'am.'
Lucetta looked embarrassed, and Henchard continued :
' For we humble workmen here feel it a great honour
that a lady should look in and take an interest in us.'

She glanced at him entreatingly; the sarcasm was
too bitter, too unendurable.

' Can you tell me the time, ma'am ? ' he asked.

' Yes,' she said hastily ; ' half-past four.'

' Thank ye. An hour and a half longer before we
are released from work. Ah, ma'am, we of the lower
classes know nothing of the gay leisure that such as
you enjoy ! '

As soon as she could do so Lucetta left him, nodded
and smiled to Elizabeth-Jane, and joined her husband
at the other end of the enclosure, where she could be
seen leading him away by the outer gates, so as to
avoid passing Henchard again. That she had been
taken by surprise was obvious. The result of this
casual rencounter was that the next morning a note
was put into Henchard's hand by the postman.

' Will you,' said Lucetta, with as much bitterness
as she could put into a small communication, ' will
you kindly undertake not to speak to me in the biting
undertones you used to-day, if I walk through the
yard at any time? I bear you no ill-will, and I am
only too glad that you should have employment of my
dear husband; but in common fairness treat me as
his wife, and do not try to make me wretched by
covert sneers. I have committed no crime, and done
you no injury.'

' Poor fool ! ' said Henchard with fond savagery,

285

holding out the note. ' To know no better than commit herself in writing like this! Why, if I were to show that to her dear husband—pooh! ' He threw the letter into the fire.

Lucetta took care not to come again among the hay and corn. She would rather have died than run the risk of encountering Henchard at such close quarters a second time. The gulf between them was growing wider every day. Farfrae was always considerate to his fallen acquaintance; but it was impossible that he should not, by degrees, cease to regard the ex-corn-merchant as more than one of his other workmen. Henchard saw this, and concealed his feelings under a cover of stolidity, fortifying his heart by drinking more freely at the Three Mariners every evening.

Often did Elizabeth-Jane, in her endeavours to prevent his taking other liquor, carry tea to him in a little basket at five o'clock. Arriving one day on this errand, she found her stepfather was measuring up clover-seed and rape-seed in the corn-stores on the top floor, and she ascended to him. Each floor had a door opening into the air under a cat-head, from which a chain dangled for hoisting the sacks.

When Elizabeth's head rose through the trap she perceived that the upper door was open, and that her stepfather and Farfrae stood just within it in conversation, Farfrae being nearest the dizzy edge, and Henchard a little way behind. Not to interrupt them she remained on the steps without raising her head any higher. While waiting thus she saw—or fancied she saw, for she had a terror of feeling certain—her stepfather slowly raise his hand to a level behind Farfrae's shoulders, a curious expression taking possession of his face. The young man was quite unconscious of the action, which was so indirect that, if Farfrae had observed it, he might almost have regarded it as an idle outstretching of the arm. But it would have been possible, by a comparatively light touch, to push Farfrae off his balance, and send him head over heels into the air.

Elizabeth felt quite sick at heart on thinking of what this *might* have meant. As soon as they turned she mechanically took the tea to Henchard, left it, and went away. Reflecting, she endeavoured to assure herself that the movement was an idle eccentricity, and no more. Yet, on the other hand, his subordinate position in an establishment where he once had been master might be acting on him like an irritant poison; and she finally resolved to caution Donald.

XXXIV

NEXT morning, accordingly, she rose at five o'clock, and went into the street. It was not yet light; a dense fog prevailed, and the town was as silent as it was dark, except that from the rectangular avenues which framed in the borough there came a chorus of tiny rappings, caused by the fall of water drops condensed on the boughs; now it was wafted from the West Walk, now from the South Walk; and then from both quarters simultaneously. She moved on to the bottom of Corn Street, and, knowing his time well, waited only a few minutes before she heard the familiar bang of his door, and then his quick walk towards her. She met him at the point where the last tree of the engirding avenue flanked the last house in the street.

He could hardly discern her till, glancing inquiringly, he said, 'What—Miss Henchard—and are ye up so early?'

She asked him to pardon her for waylaying him at such an unseemly time. 'But I am anxious to mention something,' she said. 'And I wished not to alarm Mrs. Farfrae by calling.'

'Yes?' said he, with the cheeriness of a superior. 'And what may it be? It's very kind of ye, I'm sure.'

She now felt the difficulty of conveying to his mind the exact aspect of possibilities in her own. But she somehow began, and introduced Henchard's name. 'I sometimes fear,' she said with an effort, 'that he may be betrayed into some attempt to—insult you, sir.'

'But we are the best of friends?'

'Or to play some practical joke upon you, sir. Remember that he has been hardly used.'

'But we are quite friendly?'

'Or to do something—that would injure you— hurt you—wound you.' Every word cost her twice its length of pain. And she could see that Farfrae was still incredulous. Henchard, a poor man in his employ, was not, to Farfrae's view, the Henchard who had ruled him. Yet he was not only the same man, but that man, with his sinister qualities, formerly latent, quickened into life by his buffetings.

Farfrae, happy, and thinking no evil, persisted in making light of her fears. Thus they parted, and she went homeward, journeymen now being in the street, waggoners going to the harness-makers for articles left to be repaired, farm-horses going to the shoeing-smiths, and the sons of labour being generally on the move. Elizabeth entered her lodging unhappily, thinking she had done no good, and only made herself appear foolish by her weak note of warning.

But Donald Farfrae was one of those men upon whom an incident is never absolutely lost. He revised impressions from a subsequent point of view, and the impulsive judgment of the moment was not always his permanent one. The vision of Elizabeth's earnest face in the rimy dawn came back to him several times during the day. Knowing the solidity of her character, he did not treat her hints altogether as idle sounds.

But he did not desist from a kindly scheme on Henchard's account that engaged him just then; and when he met Lawyer Joyce, the town-clerk, later in the day, he spoke of it as if nothing had occurred to damp it.

'About that little seedsman's shop,' he said; 'the shop overlooking the churchyard, which is to let. It is not for myself I want it, but for our unlucky fellow-townsman, Henchard. It would be a new beginning for him, if a small one; and I have told the Council that I would head a private subscription among them to set him up in it—that I would be fifty pounds, if they would make up the other fifty among them.'

'Yes, yes; so I've heard; and there's nothing to say against it for that matter,' the town-clerk replied, in his plain, frank way. 'But, Farfrae, others see what you don't. Henchard hates ye—ay, hates ye; and 'tis right that you should know it. To my knowledge he was at the Three Mariners last night, saying in public that about you which a man ought not to say about another.'

'Is that so—and is that so?' said Farfrae, looking down. 'Why should he do it?' added the young man bitterly; 'what harm have I done him that he should try to wrong me?'

'God only knows,' said Joyce, lifting his eyebrows. 'It shows much long-suffering in you to put up with him, and keep him in your employ.'

'But I cannet discharge a man who was once a good friend to me? How can I forget that when I came here 'twas he enabled me to make a footing for mysel'? No, no. As long as I've a day's wark to offer he shall do it if he chooses. 'Tis not I who will deny him such a little as that. But I'll drop the idea of establishing him in a shop till I can think more about it.'

It grieved Farfrae much to give up this scheme. But a damp having been thrown over it by these and other voices in the air, he went and countermanded his orders. The then occupier of the shop was in it when Farfrae spoke to him, and feeling it necessary to give some explanation of his withdrawal from the negotiation, Donald mentioned Henchard's name, and stated that the intentions of the Council had been changed.

The occupier was much disappointed, and straight-way informed Henchard, as soon as he saw him, that a scheme of the Council for setting him up in a shop had been knocked on the head by Farfrae. And thus out of error enmity grew.

When Farfrae got indoors that evening the tea-kettle was singing on the high hob of the semi-egg-shaped grate. Lucetta, light as a sylph, ran forward and seized his hands, whereupon Farfrae duly kissed her.

'Oh!' she cried playfully, turning to the window. 'See—the blinds are not drawn down, and the people can look in—what a scandal!'

When the candles were lighted, the curtains drawn, and the twain sat at tea, she noticed that he looked serious. Without directly inquiring why, she let her eyes linger solicitously on his face.

'Who has called?' he absently asked. 'Any folk for me?'

'No,' said Lucetta. 'What's the matter, Donald?'

'Well—nothing worth talking of,' he responded sadly.

'Then, never mind it. You will get through it. Scotchmen are always lucky.'

'No—not always!' he said, shaking his head gloomily as he contemplated a crumb on the table. 'I know many who have not been so! There was Sandy Mac-farlane, who started to America to try his fortune, and he was drowned; and Archibald Leith, he was murdered! And poor Willie Dunbleeze and Maitland Macfreeze—they fell into bad courses, and went the way of all such!'

'Why—you old goosey—I was only speaking in a general sense, of course! You are always so literal

Now when we have finished tea, sing me that funny song about high-heeled shoon and siller tags, and the one-and-forty wooers.'

'No, no. I couldna sing to-night! It's Henchard —he hates me; so that I may not be his friend if I would. I would understand why there should be a wee bit envy; but I cannet see a reason for the whole intensity of what he feels. Now, can you, Lucetta? It is more like old-fashioned rivalry in love than just a bit of rivalry in trade.'

Lucetta had grown somewhat wan. 'No,' she replied.

'I give him employment—I cannet refuse it. But neither can I blind myself to the fact that with a man of passions such as his, there is no safeguard for conduct!'

'What have you heard—O Donald, dearest?' said Lucetta in alarm. The words on her lips were 'anything about me?'—but she did not utter them. She could not, however, suppress her agitation, and her eyes filled with tears.

'No, no—it is not so serious as ye fancy,' declared Farfrae soothingly; though he did not know its seriousness so well as she.

'I wish you would do what we have talked of,' mournfully remarked Lucetta. 'Give up business, and go away from here. We have plenty of money, and why should we stay?'

Farfrae seemed seriously disposed to discuss this move, and they talked thereon till a visitor was announced. Their neighbour Alderman Vatt came in.

'You've heard, I suppose, of poor Doctor Chalkfield's death? Yes—died this afternoon at five,' said Mr. Vatt. Chalkfield was the Councilman who had succeeded to the Mayoralty in the preceding November.

Farfrae was sorry at the intelligence, and Mr. Vatt continued: 'Well, we know he's been going some days, and as his family is well provided for we must take it all as it is. Now I have called to ask ye this—quite privately. If I should nominate 'ee to succeed him, and there should be no particular opposition, will 'ee accept the chair?'

'But there are folk whose turn is before mine; and I'm over young, and maybe thought pushing!' said Farfrae after a pause.

'Not at all. I don't speak for myself only, several have named it. You won't refuse?'

'We thought of going away,' interposed Lucetta, looking at Farfrae anxiously.

'It was only a fancy,' Farfrae murmured. 'I wouldna refuse if it is the wish of a respectable majority in the Council.'

'Very well, then, look upon yourself as elected. We have had older men long enough.'

When he was gone Farfrae said musingly, 'See now how it's ourselves that are ruled by the powers above us! We plan this, but we do that. If they want to make me Mayor I will stay, and Henchard must rave as he will.'

From this evening onward Lucetta was very uneasy. If she had not been imprudence incarnate, she would not have acted as she did when she met Henchard by accident a day or two later. It was in the bustle of the market, when no one could readily notice their discourse.

'Michael,' said she, 'I must again ask you what I asked you months ago—to return me any letters or papers of mine that you may have—unless you have destroyed them! You must see how desirable it is that the time at Jersey should be blotted out, for the good of all parties.'

'Why, bless the woman!—I packed up every scrap of your handwriting to give you in the coach—but you never appeared.'

She explained how the death of her aunt had prevented her taking the journey on that day. ' And what
became of the parcel then? ' she asked.

He could not say—he would consider. When she
was gone he recollected that he had left a heap of useless papers in his former dining-room safe—built up in
the wall of his old house—now occupied by Farfrae.
The letters might have been amongst them.

A grotesque grin shaped itself on Henchard's face.
Had that safe been opened?

On the very evening which followed this there was
a great ringing of bells in Casterbridge, and the combined brass, wood, catgut, and leather bands played
round the town with more prodigality of percussion-
notes than ever. Farfrae was Mayor—the two-hun-
dredth odd of a series forming an elective dynasty
dating back to the days of Charles I.—and the fair
Lucetta was the courted of the town. . . . But, ah!
that worm i' the bud—Henchard; what he could tell!

He, in the meantime, festering with indignation at
some erroneous intelligence of Farfrae's opposition to
the scheme for installing him in the little seed-shop,
was greeted with the news of the municipal election
(which, by reason of Farfrae's comparative youth and
his Scottish nativity—a thing unprecedented in the
case—had an interest far beyond the ordinary). The
bell-ringing and the band-playing, loud as Tamer-
lane's trumpet, goaded the downfallen Henchard indescribably · the ousting now seemed to him to be
complete.

The next morning he went to the corn-yard as
usual, and about eleven o'clock Donald entered through
the green door, with no trace of the worshipful about
him. The yet more emphatic change of places between
him and Henchard which this election had established
renewed a slight embarrassment in the manner of the
modest younger man; but Henchard showed the front

of one who had overlooked all this; and Farfrae met his amenities half-way at once.

'I was going to ask you,' said Henchard, 'about a packet that I may possibly have left in my old safe in the dining-room.' He added particulars.

'If so, it is there now,' said Farfrae. 'I have never opened the safe at all as yet; for I keep ma papers at the bank, to sleep easy o' nights.'

'It was not of much consequence—to me,' said Henchard. 'But I'll call for it this evening, if you don't mind?'

It was quite late when he fulfilled his promise. He had primed himself with grog, as he did very frequently now, and a curl of sardonic humour hung on his lip as he approached the house, as though he were contemplating some terrible form of amusement. Whatever it was, the incident of his entry did not diminish its force, this being his first visit to the house since he had lived there as owner. The ring of the bell spoke to him like the voice of a familiar drudge who had been bribed to forsake him; the movements of the doors were revivals of dead days.

Farfrae invited him into the dining-room, where he at once unlocked the iron safe built into the wall, *his*, Henchard's safe, made by an ingenious locksmith under his direction. Farfrae drew thence the parcel, and other papers, with apologies for not having returned them.

'Never mind,' said Henchard drily. 'The fact is they are letters mostly. . . . Yes,' he went on, sitting down and unfolding Lucetta's passionate bundle, 'here they be. That ever I should see 'em again! I hope Mrs. Farfrae is well after her exertions of yesterday?'

'She has felt a bit weary; and has gone to bed early on that account.'

Henchard returned to the letters, sorting them over with interest, Farfrae being seated at the other end of the dining-table. 'You don't forget, of course,' he resumed, 'that curious chapter in the history of my past, which I told you of, and that you gave me some assistance in? These letters are, in fact, related to that unhappy business. Though, thank God, it is all over. now.'

'What became of the poor woman?' asked Farfrae.

'Luckily she married, and married well,' said Henchard. 'So that these reproaches she poured out on me do not now cause me any twinges, as they might otherwise have done. . . . Just listen to what an angry woman will say!'

Farfrae, willing to humour Henchard, though quite uninterested, and bursting with yawns, gave well-mannered attention.

'"For me,"' Henchard read, '"there is practically no future. A creature too unconventionally devoted to you—who feels it impossible that she can be wife of any other man; and who is yet no more to you than the first woman you meet in the street—such am I. I quite acquit you of any intention to wrong me, yet you are the door through which wrong has come to me. That in the event of your present wife's death you will place me in her position is a consolation so far as it goes—but how far does it go? Thus I sit here, forsaken by my few acquaintance, and forsaken by you!"'

'That's how she went on to me,' said Henchard, 'acres of words like that, when what had happened was what I could not cure.'

'Yes,' said Farfrae absently, 'it is the way wi' women.' But the fact was that he knew very little of the sex; yet detecting a sort of resemblance in style between the effusions of the woman he worshipped and those of the supposed stranger, he concluded that Aphrodite ever spoke thus, whosesoever the personality she assumed.

Henchard unfolded another letter, and read it through

likewise, stopping at the subscription as before. 'Her name I don't give,' he said blandly. 'As I didn't marry her, and another man did, I can scarcely do that in fairness to her."

'Tr-rue, tr-rue,' said Farfrae. 'But why didn't you marry her when your wife Susan died?' Farfrae asked this, and the other questions, in the comfortably indifferent tone of one whom the matter very remotely concerned.

'Ah—well you may ask that!' said Henchard, the new-moon-shaped grin adumbrating itself again upon his mouth. 'In spite of all her protestations, when I came forward to do so, as in generosity bound, she was not the woman for me.'

'She had already married another—maybe?'

Henchard seemed to think it would be sailing too near the wind to descend further into particulars, and he answered 'Yes.'

'The young lady must have had a heart that bore transplanting very readily!'

'She had, she had,' said Henchard emphatically.

He opened a third and fourth letter, and read. This time he approached the conclusion as if the signature were indeed coming with the rest. But again he stopped short. The truth was that, as may be divined, he had quite intended to effect a grand catastrophe at the end of this drama by reading out the name; he had come to the house with no other thought. But sitting here in cold blood he could not do it. Such a wrecking of hearts appalled even him. His quality was such that he could have annihilated them both in the heat of action; but to accomplish the deed by oral poison was beyond the nerve of his enmity.

XXXV

As Donald stated, Lucetta had retired early to her room because of fatigue. She had, however, not gone to rest, but sat in the bedside chair reading, and thinking over the events of the day. At the ringing of the door-bell by Henchard she wondered who it should be that would call at that comparatively late hour. The dining-room was almost under her bedroom; she could hear that somebody was admitted there, and presently the indistinct murmur of a person reading became audible.

The usual time for Donald's arrival upstairs came and passed, yet still the reading and conversation went on. This was very singular. She could think of nothing but that some extraordinary crime had been committed, and that the visitor, whoever he might be, was reading an account of it from a special edition of the *Casterbridge Chronicle*. At last she left the room, and descended the stairs. The dining-room door was ajar, and in the silence of the resting household the voice and the words were recognizable before she reached the lower flight. She stood transfixed. Her own words greeted her, in Henchard's voice, like spirits from the grave.

Lucetta leant upon the banister with her cheek against the smooth hand-rail, as if she would make a friend of it in her misery. Rigid in this position, more and more words fell successively upon her ear. But what amazed her most was the tone of her husband. He spoke merely in the accents of a man who made a present of his time.

'One word,' he was saying, as the crackling of paper denoted that Henchard was unfolding yet another sheet. 'Is it quite fair to this young woman's memory to read at such length to a stranger what was intended for your eye alone?'

'Well, yes,' said Henchard. 'By not giving her name I make it an example of all womankind, and not a scandal to one.'

'If I were you I would destroy them,' said Farfrae, giving more thought to the letters than he had hitherto done. 'As another man's wife it would injure the woman if it were known.'

'No, I shall not destroy them,' murmured Henchard, putting the letters away. Then he arose, and Lucetta heard no more.

She went back to her bedroom in a semi-paralyzed state. For very fear she could not undress, but sat on the edge of the bed, waiting. Would Henchard let out the secret in his parting words? Her suspense was terrible. Had she confessed all to Donald in their early acquaintance he might possibly have got over it, and married her just the same—unlikely as it had once seemed; but, for her or any one else to tell him now would be fatal.

The door slammed; she could hear her husband bolting it. After looking round in his customary way he came leisurely up the stairs. The spark in her eyes well-nigh went out when he appeared round the bedroom door. Her gaze hung doubtful for a moment, then to her joyous amazement she saw that he looked at her with the rallying smile of one who had just been relieved of a scene that was irksome. She could hold out no longer, and sobbed hysterically.

When he had restored her Farfrae naturally enough spoke of Henchard. 'Of all men he was the least desirable as a visitor,' he said; 'but it is my belief that he's just a bit crazed. He has been reading to me a long lot of letters relating to his past life; and I could do no less than indulge him by listening.'

This was sufficient. Henchard, then, had not told. Henchard's last words to Farfrae, in short, as he stood on the door-step, had been these: 'Well—I'm much obliged to 'ee for listening. I may tell more about her some day.'

Finding this, she was much perplexed as to Henchard's motives in opening the matter at all; for in such cases we attribute to an enemy a power of consistent action which we never find in ourselves or in our friends; and forget that abortive efforts from want of heart are as possible to revenge as to generosity.

Next morning Lucetta remained in bed, meditating how to parry this incipient attack. The bold stroke of telling Donald the truth, dimly conceived, was yet too bold; for she dreaded lest, in doing so, he, like the rest of the world, should believe that the episode was rather her fault than her misfortune. She decided to employ persuasion—not with Donald, but with the enemy himself. It seemed the only practicable weapon left her as a woman. Having laid her plan she rose, and wrote to him who kept her on these tenterhooks :—

'I overheard your interview with my husband last night, and saw the drift of your revenge. The very thought of it crushes me! Have pity on a distressed woman! If you could see me you would relent. You do not know how anxiety has told upon me lately. I will be at the Ring at the time you leave work—just before the sun goes down. Please come that way. I cannot rest till I have seen you face to face, and heard from your mouth that you will carry this horse-play no further.'

To herself she said, on closing up this appeal : ' If ever tears and pleadings have served the weak to fight the strong, let them do so now ! '

With this view she made a toilette which differed from all she had ever attempted before. To heighten her natural attractions had hitherto been the unvarying endeavour of her adult life, and one in which she was no novice. But now she neglected this, and even proceeded to impair the natural presentation. She had not slept all the previous night, and this had produced upon her naturally pretty though slightly worn features the aspect of a countenance ageing prematurely from extreme sorrow. She selected—as much from want of spirit as design—her poorest, plainest, and longest discarded attire.

To avoid the contingency of being recognized she veiled herself, and slipped out of the house quickly. The sun was resting on the hill like a drop of blood on an eyelid by the time she had got up the road opposite the amphitheatre, which she speedily entered. The interior was shadowy, and emphatic of the absence of every living thing.

She was not disappointed in the fearful hope with which she awaited him. Henchard came over the top, descended, and Lucetta waited breathlessly. But having reached the arena she saw a change in his bearing : he stood still, at a little distance from her ; she could not think why.

Nor could any one else have known. The truth was that in appointing this spot, and this hour, for the rendezvous, Lucetta had unwittingly backed up her entreaty by the strongest argument she could have used outside words, with this man of moods, glooms, and superstitions. Her figure in the midst of the huge enclosure, the unusual plainness of her dress, her attitude of hope and appeal, so strongly revived in his soul the memory of another ill-used woman who had stood

there and thus in bygone days, and had now passed
away into her rest, that he was unmanned, and his
heart smote him for having attempted reprisals on
one of a sex so weak. When he approached her,
and before she had spoken a word, her point was half
gained.

His manner as he had come down had been one
of cynical carelessness; but he now put away his
grim half-smile, and said, in a kindly subdued tone,
'Good-night t'ye. Of course I'm glad to come if you
want me.'

'Oh, thank you,' she said apprehensively.

'I am sorry to see 'ee looking so ill,' he stammered,
with unconcealed compunction.

She shook her head. 'How can you be sorry,' she
asked, 'when you deliberately cause it?'

'What!' said Henchard uneasily. 'Is it anything
I have done that has pulled you down like that?'

'It is all your doing,' said she. 'I have no other
grief. My happiness would be secure enough but for
your threats. O Michael! don't wreck me like this!
You might think that you have done enough! When
I came here I was a young woman; now I am rapidly
becoming an old one. Neither my husband nor any
other man will regard me with interest long.'

Henchard was disarmed. His old feeling of super-
cilious pity for womankind in general was intensified
by this suppliant appearing here as the double of the
first. Moreover, that thoughtless want of foresight
which had led to all her trouble remained with poor
Lucetta still; she had come to meet him here in this
compromising way without perceiving the risk. Such
a woman was very small deer to hunt; he felt ashamed,
lost all zest and desire to humiliate Lucetta there and
then, and no longer envied Farfrae his bargain. He
had married money, but nothing more. Henchard was
anxious to wash his hands of the game.

'Well, what do you want me to do?' he said gently. 'I am sure I shall be very willing. My reading of those letters was only a sort of practical joke, and I revealed nothing.'

'To give me back the letters and any papers you may have that breathe of matrimony or worse.'

'So be it. Every scrap shall be yours. . . . But, between you and me, Lucetta, he is sure to find out something of the matter, sooner or later.'

'Ah!' she said with eager tremulousness; 'but not till I have proved myself a faithful and deserving wife to him, and then he may forgive me everything!'

Henchard silently looked at her: he almost envied Farfrae such love as that, even now. 'H'm—I hope so,' he said. 'But you shall have the letters without fail. And your secret shall be kept. I swear it.'

'How good you are!—how shall I get them?'

He reflected, and said he would send them the next morning. 'Now don't doubt me,' he added. 'I can keep my word.'

XXXVI

RETURNING from her appointment Lucetta saw a man waiting by the lamp nearest to her own door. When she stopped to go in he came and spoke to her. It was Jopp.

He begged her pardon for addressing her. But he had heard that Mr. Farfrae had been applied to by a neighbouring corn-merchant to recommend a working partner; if so, he wished to offer himself. He could give good security, and had stated as much to Mr. Farfrae in a letter; but he would feel much obliged if Lucetta would say a word in his favour to her husband.

'It is a thing I know nothing about,' said Lucetta coldly.

'But you can testify to my trustworthiness better than anybody, ma'am,' said Jopp. 'I was in Jersey several years, and knew you there by sight.'

'Indeed,' she replied. 'But I knew nothing of you.'

'I think, ma'am, that a word 'or two from you would secure for me what I covet very much,' he persisted.

She steadily refused to have anything to do with the affair, and, cutting him short, because of her anxiety to get indoors before her husband should miss her, left him on the pavement.

He watched her till she had vanished, and then went home. When he got there he sat down in the fireless chimney corner looking at the iron dogs, and the wood laid across them for heating the morning kettle. A movement upstairs disturbed him, and Henchard came down from his bed-room, where he seemed to have been rummaging boxes.

'I wish,' said Henchard, 'you would do me a service, Jopp, now—to-night, I mean, if you can. Leave this at Mrs. Farfrae's for her. I should take it myself, of course, but I don't wish to be seen there.'

He handed a package in brown paper, sealed. Henchard had been as good as his word. Immediately on coming indoors he had searched over his few belongings; and every scrap of Lucetta's writing that he possessed was here. Jopp indifferently expressed his willingness.

'Well, how have ye got on to-day?' his lodger asked. 'Any prospect of an opening?'

'I am afraid not,' said Jopp, who had not told the other of his application to Farfrae.

'There never will be in Casterbridge,' declared Henchard decisively. 'You must roam further afield.' He said good-night to Jopp, and returned to his own part of the house.

Jopp sat on till his eyes were attracted by the shadow of the candle-snuff on the wall, and looking at the original he found that it had formed itself into a head like a red-hot cauliflower. Henchard's packet next met his gaze. He knew there had been something of the nature of wooing between Henchard and the now Mrs. Farfrae; and his vague ideas on the subject narrowed themselves down to these: Henchard had a parcel belonging to Mrs. Farfrae, and he had reasons for not returning that parcel to her in person. What could be inside it? So he went on and on till, animated by resentment at Lucetta's haughtiness, as he thought it, and curiosity to learn if there were any weak sides to this transaction with Henchard, he examined the package. The pen and all its relations being awkward tools in Henchard's hands, he had affixed the seals without an impression, it never occurring to him that the efficacy of such a fastening depended on this. Jopp was far less of a tyro; he lifted one of the seals with his penknife, peeped in at the end thus opened, saw that the bundle consisted of letters; and, having satisfied himself thus far, sealed up the end again by simply softening the wax with the candle, and went off with the parcel as requested.

His path was by the river-side at the foot of the town. Coming into the light at the bridge which stood at the end of High Street, he beheld lounging thereon Mother Cuxsom and Nance Mockridge.

'We be just going down Mixen Lane way, to look into Peter's Finger afore creeping to bed,' said Mrs. Cuxsom. 'There's a fiddle and tambourine going on there. Lord, what's all the world—do ye come along too, Jopp—'twon't hinder ye five minutes.'

Jopp had mostly kept himself out of this company, but present circumstances made him somewhat more reckless than usual, and without many words he decided to go to his destination that way.

Though the upper part of Durnover was mainly composed of a curious congeries of barns and farm-steads, there was a less picturesque side to the parish. This was Mixen Lane, now in great part pulled down.

Mixen Lane was the Adullam of all the surrounding villages. It was the hiding-place of those who were in distress, and in debt, and trouble of every kind. Farm-labourers and other peasants, who combined a little poaching with their farming, and a little brawling and bibbing with their poaching, found themselves sooner or later in Mixen Lane. Rural mechanics too idle to mechanize, rural servants too rebellious to serve, drifted or were forced into Mixen Lane.

The lane and its surrounding thicket of thatched cottages stretched out like a spit into the moist and misty lowland. Much that was sad, much that was low, some things that were baneful, could be seen in Mixen Lane. Vice ran freely in and out certain of the doors of the neighbourhood; recklessness dwelt under the roof with the crooked chimney; shame in some bow-windows; theft (in times of privation) in the thatched and mud-walled houses by the sallows. Even slaughter had not been altogether unknown here. In a block of cottages up an alley there might have been erected an altar to disease in years gone by. Such was Mixen Lane in the times when Henchard and Farfrae were Mayors.

Yet this mildewed leaf in the sturdy and flourishing Casterbridge plant lay close to the open country; not a hundred yards from a row of noble elms, and commanding a view across the moor of airy uplands and corn-fields, and mansions of the great. A brook divided the moor from the tenements, and to outward view there was no way across it—no way to the houses but round about by the road. But under every householder's stairs there was kept a mysterious plank nine inches wide; which plank was a secret bridge.

If you, as one of those refugee householders, came in from business after dark—and this was the business time here—you stealthily crossed the moor, approached the border of the aforesaid brook, and whistled opposite the house to which you belonged. A shape thereupon made its appearance on the other side bearing the bridge on end against the sky; it was lowered; you crossed, and a hand helped you to land yourself, together with the pheasants and hares gathered from neighbouring manors. You sold them slily the next morning, and the day after you stood before the magistrates, with the eyes of all your sympathizing neighbours concentrated on your back. You disappeared for a time; then you were again found quietly living in Mixen Lane.

Walking along the 'lane at dusk the stranger was struck by two or three peculiar features therein. One was an intermittent rumbling from the back premises of the inn half-way up; this meant a skittle alley. Another was the extensive prevalence of whistling in the various domiciles—a piped note of some kind coming from nearly every open door. Another was the frequency of white aprons over dingy gowns among the women around the doorways. A white apron is a suspicious vesture in situations where spotlessness is difficult; moreover, the industry and cleanliness which the white apron expressed were belied by the postures and gaits of the women who wore it—their knuckles being mostly on their hips (an attitude which lent them the aspect of two-handled mugs), and their shoulders against doorposts; while there was a curious alacrity in the turn of each honest woman's head upon her neck, and in the twirl of her honest eyes, at any noise resembling a masculine footfall along the lane.

Yet amid so much that was bad needy respectability also found a home. Under some of the roofs abode pure and virtuous souls whose presence there was due to the iron hand of necessity, and to that alone. Families from decayed villages—families of that once bulky, but now nearly extinct, section of village society called 'liviers,' or lifeholders—copy-holders and others, whose roof-trees had fallen for some reason or other, compelling them to quit the rural spot that had been their home for generations—came here, unless they chose to lie under a hedge by the wayside.

The inn called Peter's Finger was the church of Mixen Lane.

It was centrally situate, as such places should be,

and bore about the same social relation to the Three
Mariners as the latter bore to the King's Arms. At
first sight the inn was so respectable as to be puzzling.
The front door was kept shut, and the step was so clean
that evidently but few persons entered over its sanded
surface. But at the corner of the public-house was an
alley, a mere slit, dividing it from the next building.
Half-way up the alley was a narrow door, shiny and
paintless from the rub of infinite hands and shoulders.
This was the actual entrance to the inn.

A pedestrian would be seen abstractedly passing
along Mixen Lane; and then, in a moment, he would
vanish, causing the gazer to blink like Ashton at the
disappearance of Ravenswood. That abstracted pedestrian had edged into the slit by the adroit fillip of his
person sideways; from the slit he edged into the tavern
by a similar exercise of skill.

The company at the Three Mariners were persons
of quality in comparison with the company which
gathered here; though it must be admitted that the
lowest fringe of the Mariner's party touched the crest
of Peter's at points. Waifs and strays of all sorts
loitered about here. The landlady was a virtuous
woman, who had been unjustly sent to gaol as an
accessory to something or other after the fact. She
underwent her year, and had worn a martyr's countenance ever since, except at times of meeting the
constable who apprehended her, when she winked her
eye.

To this house Jopp and his acquaintances had
arrived. The settles on which they sat down were
thin and tall, their tops being guyed by pieces of twine
to hooks in the ceiling; for when the guests grew
boisterous the settles would rock and overturn without some such security. The thunder of bowls echoed
from the backyard; swingels hung behind the blower
of the chimney; and ex-poachers and ex-gamekeepers,

whom squires had persecuted without a cause, sat elbowing each other—men who in past times had met in fights under the moon, till lapse of sentences on the one part, and loss of favour and expulsion from service on the other, brought them here together to a common level, where they sat calmly discussing old times.

'Dos't mind how you could jerk a trout ashore with a bramble, and not ruffle the stream, Charl?' a deposed keeper was saying. ''Twas at that I caught 'ee once, if you can mind?'

'That can I. But the worst larry for me was that pheasant business at Yalbury Wood. Your wife swore false that time, Joe—oh, by Gad, she did—there's no denying it.'

'How was that?' asked Jopp.

'Why—Joe closed wi' me, and we rolled down to-gether, close to his garden hedge. Hearing the noise, out ran his wife with the oven pyle, and it being dark under the trees she couldn't see which was uppermost. "Where beest thee, Joe, under or top?" she screeched. "Oh—under, by Gad!" says he. She then began to rap down upon my skull, back, and ribs, with the pyle till we'd roll over again. "Where beest now, dear Joe, under or top?" she'd scream again. By George, 'twas through her I was took! And then when we got up in hall she sware that the cock pheasant was one of her rearing, when 'twas not your bird at all, Joe; 'twas Squire Brown's bird—that's whose 'twas—one that we'd picked off as we passed his wood, an hour afore. It did hurt my feelings to be so wronged! . . . . Ah well—'tis over now.'

'I might have had ye days afore that,' said the keeper. 'I was within a few yards of ye dozens of times, with a sight more of birds than that poor one.'

'Yes—'tis not our greatest doings that the world gets wind of,' said the furmity-woman, who, lately settled in this purlieu, sat among the rest. Having

travelled a great deal in her time, she spoke with cos
mopolitan largeness of idea. It was she who presently
asked Jopp what was the parcel he kept so snugly
under his arm.

'Ah, therein lies a grand secret,' said Jopp. 'It is
the passion of love. To think that a woman should
love one man so well, and hate another so unmerci-
fully.'

'Who's the object of your meditation, sir?'

'One that stands high in this town. I'd like to
shame her! Upon my life, 'twould be as good as a
play to read her love-letters, the proud piece of silk
and wax-work! For 'tis her love-letters that I've got
here.'

'Love-letters? then let's hear 'em, good soul,' said
Mother Cuxsom. 'Lord, do ye mind, Richard, what
fools we used to be when we were younger? Getting
a schoolboy to write ours for us; and giving him a
penny, do ye mind, not to tell other folks what he'd
put inside, do ye mind?'

By this time Jopp had pushed his finger under the
seals, and unfastened the letters, tumbling them over
and picking up one here and there at random, which
he read aloud. These passages soon began to uncover
the secret which Lucetta had so earnestly hoped to
keep buried, though the epistles, being allusive only,
did not make it altogether plain.

'Mrs. Farfrae wrote that!' said Nance Mockridge.
''Tis a humbling thing for us, as respectable women,
that one of the same sex could do it. And now she's
vowed herself to another man!'·

'So much the better for her,' said the aged furmity-
woman. 'Ah, I saved her from a real bad marriage,
and she's never been the one to thank me.'

'I say, what a good foundation for a skimmity-ride,'
said Nance.

'True,' said Mrs. Cuxsom, reflecting. ''Tis as good

311

a ground for a skimmity-ride as ever I knowed; and it ought not to be wasted. The last one seen in Casterbridge must have been ten years ago, if a day.'

At this moment there was a shrill whistle, and the landlady said to the man who had been called Charl, ' 'Tis Jim coming in. Would ye go and let down the bridge for me?'

Without replying Charl and his comrade Joe rose, and receiving a lantern from her went out at the back door and down the garden-path, which ended abruptly at the edge of the stream already mentioned. Beyond the stream was the open moor, from which a clammy breeze smote upon their faces as they advanced. Taking up the board that had lain in readiness, one of them lowered it across the water, and the instant its further end touched the ground footsteps entered upon it, and there appeared from the shade a stalwart man with straps round his knees, a double-barrelled gun under his arm and some birds slung up behind him. They asked him if he had had much luck.

'Not much,' he said indifferently. 'All safe inside?'

Receiving a reply in the affirmative he went on inwards, the others withdrawing the bridge and beginning to retreat in his rear. Before, however, they had entered the house a cry of 'Ahoy' from the moor led them to pause.

The cry was repeated. They pushed the lantern into an out-house, and went back to the brink of the stream.

'Ahoy—is this the way to Casterbridge?' said some one from the other side.

'Not in particular,' said Charl. 'There's a river afore ye.'

'I don't care—here's for through it!' said the man in the moor. 'I've had travelling enough for to-day.'

'Stop a minute, then,' said Charl, finding that the man was no enemy. 'Joe, bring the plank and lantern; here's somebody that's lost his way. You should have kept along the turnpike road, friend, and not have strook across here.'

'I should—as I see now. But I saw a light here, and says I to myself, that's a short cut, depend on't.'

The plank was now lowered; and the stranger's form shaped itself from the darkness. He was a middle-aged man, with hair and whiskers prematurely grey, and a broad and genial face. He had crossed on the plank without hesitation, and seemed to see nothing odd in the transit. He thanked them, and walked between them up the garden. 'What place is this?' he asked, when they reached the door.

'A public-house.'

'Ah. Perhaps it will suit me to put up at. Now then, come in and wet your whistle at my expense for the lift over you have given me.'

They followed him into the inn, where the increased light exhibited him as one who would stand higher in an estimate by the eye than in one by the ear. He was dressed with a certain clumsy richness—his coat being furred, and his head covered by a cap of seal-skin, which, though the nights were chilly, must have been warm for the day time, spring being somewhat advanced. In his hand he carried a small mahogany case, strapped, and clamped with brass.

Apparently surprised at the kind of company which confronted him through the kitchen door, he at once abandoned his idea of putting up at the house; but taking the situation lightly, he called for glasses of the best, paid for them as he stood in the passage, and turned to proceed on his way by the front door. This was barred, and while the landlady was unfastening it the conversation about the skimmington was continued in the sitting-room, and reached his ears.

'What do they mean by a "skimmity-ride"?' he asked.

'Oh, sir!' said the landlady, swinging her long ear-rings with deprecating modesty; ''tis a' old foolish thing they do in these parts when a man's wife is—well, not too particularly his own. But as a respectable householder I don't encourage it.'

'Still, are they going to do it shortly? It is a good sight to see, I suppose?'

'Well, sir!' she simpered. And then, bursting into naturalness, and glancing from the corner of her eye, ''Tis the funniest thing under the sun! And it costs money.'

'Ah! I remember hearing of some such thing. Now I shall be in Casterbridge for two or three weeks to come, and should not mind seeing the performance. Wait a moment.' He turned back, entered the sitting-room, and said, 'Here, good folks; I should like to see the old custom you are talking of, and I don't mind being something towards it—take that.' He threw a sovereign on the table and returned to the landlady at the door, of whom, having inquired the way into the town, he took his leave.

'There were more where that one came from,' said Charl, when the sovereign had been taken up and handed to the landlady for safe keeping. 'By George! we ought to have got a few more while we had him here.'

'No, no,' answered the landlady. 'This is a re-spectable house, thank God! And I'll have nothing done but what's honourable.'

'Well,' said Jopp; 'now we'll consider the business begun, and will soon get it in train.'

'We will!' said Nance. 'A good laugh warms my heart more than a cordial, and that's the truth on't.'

Jopp gathered up the letters, and it being now somewhat late, he did not attempt to call at Farfrae's with them that night. He reached home, sealed them up as before, and delivered the parcel at its address next morning. Within an hour its contents were reduced to ashes by Lucetta, who, poor soul! was inclined to fall down on her knees in thankfulness that at last no evidence remained of the unlucky episode with Henchard in her past. For though hers had been rather the laxity of inadvertence than of intention, that episode, if known, was not the less likely to operate fatally between herself and her husband.

XXXVII

SUCH was the state of things when the current affairs of Casterbridge were interrupted by an event of such magnitude that its influence reached to the lowest social stratum there, stirring the depths of its society simultaneously with the preparations for the skimmington. It was one of those excitements which, when they move a country town, leave a permanent mark upon its chronicles, as a warm summer permanently marks the ring in the tree-trunk corresponding to its date.

A Royal Personage was about to pass through the borough, on his course further west, to inaugurate an immense engineering work out that way. He had consented to halt half-an-hour or so in the town, and to receive an address from the corporation of Casterbridge, which, as a representative centre of husbandry, wished thus to express its sense of the great services he had rendered to agricultural science and economics, by his zealous promotion of designs for placing the art of farming on a more scientific footing.

Royalty had not been seen in Casterbridge since the days of the third King George, and then only by candlelight for a few minutes, when that monarch, on a night-journey, had stopped to change horses at the King's Arms. The inhabitants therefore decided to make a thorough *fête carillonnée* of the unwonted

316

occasion. Half-an-hour's pause was not long, it is true; but much might be done in it by a judicious grouping of incidents, above all, if the weather were fine.

The address was prepared on parchment, by an artist who was handy at ornamental lettering, and was laid on with the best gold-leaf and colours that the sign-painter had in his shop. The Council met on the Tuesday before the appointed day, to arrange the details of procedure. While they were sitting, the door of the Council Chamber standing open, they heard a heavy footstep coming up the stairs. It advanced along the passage, and Henchard entered the room, in clothes of frayed and threadbare shabbiness, the very clothes which he had used to wear in the primal days when he had sat among them.

'I have a feeling,' he said, advancing to the table and laying his hand upon the green cloth, 'that I should like to join ye in this reception of our illustrious visitor. I suppose I could walk with the rest?'

Embarrassed glances were exchanged by the Council, and Grower nearly ate the end of his quill-pen, so gnawed he it during the silence. Farfrae, the young Mayor, who by virtue of his office sat in the large chair, intuitively caught the sense of the meeting, and as spokesman was obliged to utter it, glad as he would have been that the duty should have fallen to another tongue.

'I hardly see that it would be proper, Mr. Henchard,' said he. 'The Council are the Council, and as ye are no longer one of the body, there would be an irregularity in the proceeding. If ye were included, why not others?'

'I have a particular reason for wishing to assist at the ceremony.'

Farfrae looked round. 'I think I have expressed the feeling of the Council,' he said.

'Yes, yes,' from Dr. Bath, Lawyer Long, Alderman Tubber, and several more.

'Then I am not to be allowed to have anything to do with it officially?'

'I am afraid so; it is out of the question, indeed. But of course you can see the doings full well, such as they are to be, like the rest of the spectators.'

Henchard did not reply to that very obvious suggestion, and, turning on his heel, went away.

It had been only a passing fancy of his, but opposition crystallized it into a determination. 'I'll welcome his Royal Highness, or nobody shall!' he went about saying. 'I am not going to be sat upon by Farfrae, or any of the rest of the paltry crew! You shall see.'

The eventful morning was bright, a full-faced sun confronting early window-gazers eastward, and all perceived (for they were practised in weather-lore) that there was permanence in the glow. Visitors soon began to flock in from county houses, villages, remote copses, and lonely uplands, the latter in oiled boots and tilt bonnets, to see the reception, or if not to see it, at any rate to be near it. There was hardly a workman in the town who did not put a clean shirt on. Solomon Longways, Christopher Coney, Buzzford, and the rest of that fraternity, showed their sense of the occasion by advancing their customary eleven o'clock pint to half-past ten; from which they found a difficulty in getting back to the proper hour for several days.

Henchard had determined to do no work that day. He primed himself in the morning with a glass of rum, and walking down the street met Elizabeth-Jane, whom he had not seen for a week. 'It was lucky,' he said to her, 'my twenty years had expired before this came on, or I should never have had the nerve to carry it out.'

'Carry out what?' said she, alarmed.

'This welcome I am going to give our Royal visitor.'

She was perplexed. 'Shall we go and see it together?' she said.

'See it! I have other fish to fry. You see it. It will be worth seeing!'

She could do nothing to elucidate this, and decked herself out with a heavy heart. As the appointed time drew near she got sight again of her stepfather. She thought he was going to the Three Mariners; but no, he elbowed his way through the gay throng to the shop of Woolfrey, the draper. She waited in the crowd without.

In a few minutes he emerged, wearing, to her surprise, a brilliant rosette, while more surprising still, in his hand he carried a flag, of somewhat homely construction, formed by tacking one of the small Union Jacks, which abounded in the town to-day, to the end of a deal wand—probably the roller from a piece of calico. Henchard rolled up his flag on the doorstep, put it under his arm, and went down the street.

Suddenly the taller members of the crowd turned their heads, and the shorter stood on tiptoe. It was said that the Royal *cortège* approached. The railway had stretched out an arm towards Casterbridge at this time, but had not reached it by several miles as yet; so that the intervening distance, as well as the remainder of the journey, was to be traversed by road, in the old fashion. People thus waited—the county families in their carriages, the masses on foot—and watched the far-stretching London highway to the ringing of bells and chatter of tongues.

From the background Elizabeth-Jane watched the scene. Some seats had been arranged from which ladies could witness the spectacle, and the front seat was occupied by Lucetta, the Mayor's wife, just at present. In the road under her eyes stood Henchard. She appeared so bright and pretty that, as it seemed, he was experiencing the momentary weakness of wishing for her notice. But he was far from attractive to a woman's eye, ruled as that is so largely by the super- ficies of things. He was not only a journeyman, unable to appear as he formerly had appeared, but he disdained to appear as well as he might. Everybody else, from the Mayor to the washerwoman, shone in new ves- ture according to means; but Henchard had doggedly retained the fretted and weather-beaten garments of bygone years.

Hence, alas, this occurred : Lucetta's eyes slid over him to this side and to that without anchoring on a feature—as gaily dressed women's eyes will too often do on such occasions. Her manner signified quite plainly that she meant to know him in public no more.

But she was never tired of watching Donald, as he stood in animated converse with his friends a few yards off, wearing round his young neck the official gold chain with great square links, like that round the Royal unicorn. Every trifling emotion that her husband showed as he talked had its reflex on her face and lips, which moved in little duplicates to his. She was living his part rather than her own, and cared for no one's situation but Farfrae's that day.

At length a man stationed at the furthest turn of the high road, namely, on the second bridge of which mention has been made, gave a signal; and the Cor- poration in their robes proceeded from the front of the Town Hall to the archway erected at the entrance to the town. The carriages containing the Royal visitor and his suite arrived at the spot in a cloud of dust, a procession was formed, and the whole came on to the Town Hall at a walking pace.

This spot was the centre of interest. There were a few clear yards in front of the Royal carriage; and into this space a man stepped before any one could prevent him. It was Henchard. He had unrolled his private flag, and removing his hat he advanced to the side of the slowing vehicle, waving the Union Jack to and fro with his left hand, while he blandly held out his right to the illustrious Personage.

All the ladies said with bated breath, ' Oh, look there!' and Lucetta was ready to faint. Elizabeth-Jane peeped through the shoulders of those in front, saw what it was, and was terrified; and then her interest in the spectacle as a strange phenomenon got the better of her fear.

Farfrae, with Mayoral authority, immediately rose to the occasion. He seized Henchard by the shoulder, dragged him back, and told him roughly to be off. Henchard's eyes met his, and Farfrae observed the fierce light in them, despite his excitement and irritation. For a moment Henchard stood his ground rigidly; then by an unaccountable impulse gave way and retired. Farfrae glanced to the ladies' gallery, and saw that his Calphurnia's cheek was pale.

' Why—it is your husband's old patron!' said Mrs. Blowbody, a lady of the neighbourhood who sat beside Lucetta.

' Patron!' said Donald's wife with quick indignation.

' Do you say the man is an acquaintance of Mr. Farfrae's?' observed Mrs. Bath, the physician's wife, a new-comer to the town, through her recent marriage with the doctor.

' He works for my husband,' said Lucetta.

' Oh—is that all? They have been saying to me that it was through him your husband first got · a footing in Casterbridge. What stories people will tell!'

' They will indeed. It was not so at all. Donald's genius would have enabled him to get a footing anywhere, without anybody's help! He would have been just the same if there had been no Henchard in the world.'

It was partly Lucetta's ignorance of the circumstances of Donald's arrival which led her to speak thus; partly the sensation that everybody seemed bent on snubbing her at this triumphant time. The incident had occupied but a few moments, but it was necessarily witnessed by the Royal personage, who, however, with practised tact, affected not to have noticed anything unusual. He alighted, the Mayor advanced, the address was read; the visitor replied, then said a few words to Farfrae, and shook hands with Lucetta as the Mayor's wife. The ceremony occupied but a few minutes, and the carriages rattled heavily as Pharaoh's chariots down Corn Street and out upon the Budmouth Road, in continuation of the journey coastward.

In the crowd stood Coney, Buzzford, and Longways. 'Some difference between him now and when he zung at the Dree Mariners,' said the first. ''Tis wonderful how he could get a lady of her quality to go snacks wi' en in such quick time.'

'True. Yet how folk do worship fine clothes! Now there's a better-looking woman than she that nobody notices at all, because she's akin to that hontish fellow Henchard.'

. 'I could worship ye, Buzz, for saying that,' remarked Nance Mockridge. 'I do like to see the trimming pulled off such Christmas candles. I am quite unequal to the part of villain myself, or I'd gi'e all my small silver to see that lady toppered. . . . And perhaps I shall soon,' she added significantly.

'That's not a noble passiont for a 'oman to keep up,' said Longways.

Nance did not reply, but every one knew what she meant. The ideas diffused by the reading of Lucetta's letters at Peter's Finger had condensed into a scandal, which was spreading like a miasmatic fog through

Mixen Lane, and thence up the back streets of Casterbridge.

This mixed assemblage of idlers known to each other presently fell apart into two bands, by a process of natural selection, the frequenters of Peter's Finger going off Mixen Lane-wards, where most of them lived, while Coney, Buzzford, Longways, and that connection remained in the street.

'You know what's brewing down there, I suppose?' said Buzzford mysteriously to the others.

Coney looked at him. 'Not the skimmity-ride?'

Buzzford nodded.

'I have my doubts if it will be carried out,' said Longways. 'If they are getting it up they are keeping it mighty close.'

'I heard they were thinking of it a fortnight ago, at all events.'

'If I were sure o't I'd lay information,' said Longways emphatically. ''Tis too rough a joke, and apt to wake riots in towns. We know that the Scotchman is a right enough man, and that his lady has been a right enough 'oman since she came here, and if there was anything wrong about her afore, that's their business, not ours.'

Coney reflected. Farfrae was still liked in the community; but it must be owned that, as the Mayor and man of money, engrossed with affairs and ambitions, he had lost in the eyes of the poorer inhabitants something of that wondrous charm which he had had for them as a light-hearted, penniless young man, who sang ditties as readily as the birds in the trees. Hence the anxiety to keep him from annoyance showed not quite the ardour that would have animated it in former days.

'Suppose we make inquiration into it, Christopher,' continued Longways; 'and if we find there's really anything in it, drop a letter to them most concerned, and advise 'em to keep out of the way?'

This course was decided on, and the group separated, Buzzford saying to Coney, 'Come, my ancient friend; let's move on. There's nothing more to see here."

These well-intentioned ones would have been surprised had they known how ripe the great jocular plot really was. 'Yes, to-night,' Jopp had said to the Peter's party at the corner of Mixen Lane. 'As a wind-up to the Royal visit the hit will be all the more pat by reason of their great elevation to-day.'

To him, at least, it was not a joke, but a retaliation.

XXXVIII

THE proceedings had been brief — too brief — to Lucetta, whom an intoxicating *Weltlust* had fairly mastered; but they had brought her a great triumph nevertheless. The shake of the Royal hand still lingered in her fingers; and the chit-chat she had overheard, that her husband might possibly receive the honour of knighthood, though idle to a. degree, seemed not the wildest vision; stranger things had occurred to men so good and captivating as her Scotchman was.

After the collision with the Mayor, Henchard had withdrawn behind the ladies' stand; and there he stood, regarding with a stare of abstraction the spot on the lappel of his coat where Farfrae's hand had seized it. He put his own hand there, as if he could hardly realize such an outrage from one whom it had once been his wont to treat with ardent generosity. While pausing in this half-stupefied state the conversation of Lucetta with the other ladies reached his ears; and he distinctly heard her deny him—deny that he had assisted Donald, that he was anything more than a common journeyman.

He moved on homeward, and met Jopp in the archway to the Bull Stake. 'So you've had a snub,' said Jopp.

' And what if I have ? ' answered Henchard sternly.

' Why, I've had one too, so we are both under the same cold shade.' He briefly related his attempt to win Lucetta's intercession.

Henchard merely heard his story, without taking it deeply in. His own relation to Farfrae and Lucetta overshadowed all kindred ones. He went on saying brokenly to himself, ' She has supplicated to me in her time; and now her tongue won't own me nor her eyes see me ! . . . And he—how angry he looked. He drove me back as if I were a bull breaking fence. . . . I took it like a lamb, for I saw it could not be settled there. He can rub brine on a green wound ! . . . But he shall pay for it, and she shall be sorry. It must come to a tussle—face to face; and then we'll see how a coxcomb can front a man ! '

Without further reflection the fallen merchant, bent on some wild purpose, ate a hasty dinner, and went forth to find Farfrae. After being injured by him as a rival, and snubbed by him as a journeyman, the crowning degradation had been reserved for this day —that he should be shaken at the collar by him as a vagabond in the face of the whole town.

The crowds had dispersed. But for the green arches which still stood as they were erected Casterbridge life had resumed its ordinary shape. Henchard went down Corn Street till he came to Farfrae's house, where he knocked, and left a message that he would be glad to see his employer at the granaries as soon as he conveniently could come there. Having done this he proceeded round to the back and entered the yard.

Nobody was present, for, as he had been aware, the labourers and carters were enjoying a half-holiday on account of the events of the morning—though the carters would have to return for a short time later on, to feed and litter down the horses. He had reached the

granary steps and was about to ascend, when he said
to himself aloud, ' I'm stronger than he.'

Henchard returned to a shed, where he selected a
short piece of rope from several pieces that were lying
about; hitching one end of this to a nail, he took the
other in his right hand and turned himself bodily
round, while keeping his arm against his side; by this
contrivance he pinioned the latter effectively. He now
went up the ladders to the top floor of the corn-
stores.

It was empty, except of a few sacks, and at the
further end was the door often mentioned, opening
under the cathead and chain that hoisted the sacks.
He fixed the door open, and looked over the sill.
There was a depth of thirty or forty feet to the ground;
here was the spot on which he had been standing with
Farfrae when Elizabeth-Jane had seen him lift his arm,
with many misgivings as to what the movement por-
tended.

He retired a few steps into the loft and waited.
From this elevated perch his eye could sweep the roofs
round about, the upper parts of the luxurious chestnut
trees, now delicate in leaves of a week's age, and the
drooping boughs of the limes; Farfrae's garden and
the green door leading therefrom. In course of time
—he could not say how long—that green door opened
and Farfrae came through. He was dressed as if for
a journey. The low light of the nearing evening caught
his head and face when he emerged from the shadow
of the wall, warming them to a complexion of flame-
colour. Henchard watched him with his mouth firmly
set, the squareness of his jaw and the verticality of
his profile being unduly marked.

Farfrae came on with one hand in his pocket, and
humming a tune in a way which told that the words
were most in his mind. They were those of the song
he had sung when he arrived years before at the Three

Mariners, a poor young man, adventuring for life and fortune, and scarcely knowing whitherward :—

> ' " And here's a hand, my trusty fiere,
>   And gie's a hand o' thine." '

Nothing moved Henchard like an old melody. He sank back. ' No; I can't do it!' he gasped. ' Why does the infernal fool begin that now!'

At length Farfrae was silent, and Henchard looked out of the loft door. ' Will ye come up here?' he said.

' Ay, man,' said Farfrae. ' I couldn't see ye. What's wrang?'

A minute later Henchard heard his feet on the lowest ladder. He heard him land on the first floor, ascend and land on the second, begin the ascent to the third. And then his head rose through the trap behind.

' What are you doing up here at this time?' he asked, coming forward. ' Why didn't ye take your holiday like the rest of the men?' He spoke in a tone which had just severity enough in it to show that he remembered the untoward event of the forenoon.

Henchard said nothing; but, going back, he closed the stair hatchway, and stamped upon it so that it went tight into its frame; he next turned to the wondering young man, who by this time observed that one of Henchard's arms was bound to his side.

' Now,' said Henchard quietly, ' we stand face to face—man and man. Your money and your fine wife no longer lift 'ee above me as they did but now, and my poverty does not press me down.'

' What does it all mean?' asked Farfrae simply

' Wait a bit, my lad. You should ha' thought twice before you affronted to extremes a man who had nothing to lose. I've stood your rivalry, which ruined me, and your snubbing, which humbled me; but your hustling, that disgraced me, I won't stand!'

Farfrae warmed a little at this. 'Ye'd no business there,' he said.

'As much as any one among ye! What, you forward stripling, tell a man of my age he'd no business there!' The anger-vein swelled in his forehead as he spoke.

'You insulted Royalty, Henchard; and 'twas my duty, as the chief magistrate, to stop you.'

'Royalty be damned,' said Henchard. 'I am as loyal as you, come to that!'

'I am not here to argue. Wait till you cool doon, wait till you cool; and you will see things the same way as I do.'

'You may be the one to cool first,' said Henchard grimly. 'Now this is the case. Here be we, in this four-square loft, to finish out that little wrestle you began this morning. There's the door, forty foot above ground. One of us two puts the other out by that door—the master stays inside. If he likes he may go down afterwards and give the alarm that the other has fallen out by accident—or he may tell the truth—that's his business. As the strongest man I've tied one arm to take no advantage of 'ee. D'ye understand? Then here's at 'ee!'

There was no time for Farfrae to do aught but one thing, to close with Henchard, for the latter had come on at once. It was a wrestling match, the object of each being to give his antagonist a back fall; and on Henchard's part, unquestionably, that it should be through the door.

At the outset Henchard's hold by his only hand, the right, was on the left side of Farfrae's collar, which he firmly grappled, the latter holding Henchard by his collar with the contrary hand. With his right he endeavoured to get hold of his antagonist's left arm, which, however, he could not do, so adroitly did Henchard keep it in the rear as he gazed upon the lowered eyes of his fair and slim antagonist.

Henchard planted the first toe forward, Farfrae crossing him with his; and thus far the struggle had very much the appearance of the ordinary wrestling of those parts. Several minutes were passed by them in this attitude, the pair rocking and writhing like trees in a gale, both preserving an absolute silence. By this time their breathing could be heard. Then Farfrae tried to get hold of the other side of Henchard's collar, which was resisted by the larger man exerting all his force in a wrenching movement, and this part of the struggle ended by his forcing Farfrae down on his knees by sheer pressure of one of his muscular arms. Hampered as he was, however, he could not keep him there, and Farfrae finding his feet again the struggle proceeded as before.

By a whirl Henchard brought Donald dangerously near the precipice; seeing his position the Scotchman for the first time locked himself to his adversary, and all the efforts of that infuriated Prince of Darkness— as he might have been called from his appearance just now—were inadequate to lift or loosen Farfrae for a time. By an extraordinary effort he succeeded at last, though not until they had got far back again from the fatal door. In doing so Henchard contrived to turn Farfrae a complete somersault. Had Henchard's other arm been free it would have been all over with Farfrae then. But again he regained his feet, wrenching Henchard's arm considerably, and causing him sharp pain, as could be seen from the twitching of his face. He instantly delivered the younger man an annihilating turn by the left fore-hip, as it used to be expressed, and following up his advantage thrust him towards the door, never loosening his hold till Farfrae's fair head was hanging over the window-sill, and his arm dangling down outside the wall.

'Now,' said Henchard between his gasps, 'this is the end of what you began this morning. Your life is in my hands.'

'Then take it, take it!' said Farfrae. 'Ye've wished to long enough!'

Henchard looked down upon him in silence, and their eyes met. 'O Farfrae!—that's not true!' he said bitterly. 'God is my witness that no man ever loved another as I did thee at one time. . . . And now—though I came here to kill 'ee, I cannot hurt thee! Go and give me in charge—do what you will —I care nothing for what comes of me!'

He withdrew to the back part of the loft, and flung himself into a corner upon some sacks, in the abandonment of remorse. Farfrae regarded him in silence; then went to the hatch, and descended through it. Henchard would fain have recalled him; but his tongue failed in its task, and the young man's steps died on his ear.

Henchard took his full measure of shame and self-reproach. The scenes of his first acquaintance with Farfrae rushed back upon him—that time when the curious mixture of romance and thrift in the young man's composition so commanded his heart that Farfrae could play upon him as on an instrument. So thoroughly subdued was he that he remained on the sacks in a crouching attitude, unusual for a man, and for such a man. Its womanliness sat tragically on the figure of so stern a piece of virility. He heard a conversation below, the opening of the coach-house door, and the putting in of a horse, but took no notice.

Here he stayed till the thin shades thickened to opaque obscurity, and the loft-door became an oblong of gray light—the only visible shape around. At length he arose, shook the dust from his clothes wearily, felt his way to the hatch, and gropingly descended the steps till he stood in the yard.

'He thought highly of me once,' he murmured. 'Now he'll hate me and despise me for ever!'

He became possessed by an overpowering wish to see Farfrae again that night, and by some desperate pleading to attempt the well-nigh impossible task of winning pardon for his late mad attack. But as he walked towards Farfrae's door, he recalled the un-heeded doings in the yard while he had lain above in a sort of stupor. Farfrae he remembered had gone to the stable and put the horse into the gig; while doing so, Whittle had brought him a letter; Farfrae had then said that he would not go towards Budmouth as he had intended—that he was unexpectedly summoned to Weatherbury, and meant to call at Mellstock on his way thither, that place lying but one or two miles out of his course.

He must have come prepared for a journey when he first arrived in the yard, unsuspecting enmity; and he must have driven off (though in a changed direction) without saying a word to any one on what had occurred between themselves.

It would therefore be useless to call at Farfrae's house till very late.

There was no help for it but to wait till his return, though waiting was almost torture to his restless and self-accusing soul. He walked about the streets and outskirts of the town, lingering here and there till he reached the stone bridge of which mention has been made, an accustomed halting-place with him now. Here he spent a long time, the purl of waters through the weirs meeting his ear, and the Casterbridge lights glimmering at no great distance off.

While leaning thus upon the parapet, his listless attention was awakened by sounds of an unaccustomed kind from the town quarter. They were a confusion of rhythmical noises, to which the streets added yet more confusion by encumbering them with echoes. His first incurious thought that the clangour arose from the town band, engaged in an attempt to round off a memorable day by a burst of evening harmony, was contradicted by certain peculiarities of reverberation. But inexplicability did not rouse him to more than a cursory heed ; his sense of degradation was too strong for the admission of foreign ideas ; and he leant against the parapet as before.

XXXIX

WHEN Farfrae descended out of the loft breathless from his encounter with Henchard, he paused at the bottom to recover himself. He arrived at the yard with the intention of putting the horse into the gig himself (all the men having a holiday), and driving to a village on the Budmouth Road. Despite the fearful struggle he decided still to persevere in his journey, so as to recover himself before going indoors and meeting the eyes of Lucetta. He wished to consider his course in a case so serious.

When he was just on the point of driving off, Whittle arrived with a note badly addressed, and bearing the word 'immediate' upon the outside. On opening it he was surprised to see that it was unsigned. It contained a brief request that he would go to Weather-bury that evening about some business which he was conducting there. Farfrae knew nothing that could make it pressing; but as he was bent upon going out he yielded to the anonymous request, particularly as he had a call to make at Mellstock which could be included in the same tour. Thereupon he told Whittle of his change of direction, in words which Henchard had overheard; and set out on his way. Farfrae had not directed his man to take the message indoors, and Whittle had not been supposed to do so on his own responsibility.

Now the anonymous letter was the well-intentioned but clumsy contrivance of Longways and other of Farfrae's men, to get him out of the way for the evening, in order that the satirical mummery should fall flat, if it were attempted. By giving open information they would have brought down upon their heads the vengeance of those among their comrades who enjoyed these boisterous old games; and therefore the plan of sending a letter recommended itself by its indirectness.

For poor Lucetta they took no protective measure, believing with the majority there was some truth in the scandal, which she would have to bear as she best might.

It was about eight o'clock, and Lucetta was sitting in the drawing-room alone. Night had set in for more than half-an-hour, but she had not had the candles lighted, for when Farfrae was away she preferred waiting for him by the firelight, and, if it were not too cold, keeping one of the window-sashes a little way open that the sound of his wheels might reach her ears early. She was leaning back in her chair, in a more hopeful mood than she had enjoyed since her marriage. The day had been such a success; and the temporary uneasiness which Henchard's show of effrontery had wrought in her disappeared with the quiet disappearance of Henchard himself under her husband's reproof. The floating evidences of her absurd passion for him, and its consequences, had been destroyed, and she really seemed to have no cause for fear.

The reverie in which these and other subjects mingled was disturbed by a hubbub in the distance, that increased moment by moment. It did not greatly surprise her, the afternoon having been given up to recreation by a majority of the populace since the passage of the Royal equipages. But her attention was at once riveted to the matter by the voice of a maid-servant next door, who spoke from an upper

335

window across the street to some other maid even more elevated than she.

'Which way be they going now?' inquired the first with interest.

'I can't be sure for a moment,' said the second, 'because of the malter's chimbley. Oh yes—I can see 'em. Well, I declare, I declare!'

'What, what?' from the first, more enthusiastically.

'They are coming up Corn Street after all! They sit back to back!'

'What—two of 'em—are there two figures?'

'Yes. Two images on a donkey, back to back, their elbows tied to one another's! She's facing the head, and he's facing the tail.'

'Is it meant for anybody particular?'

'Well—it mid be. The man has got on a blue coat and kerseymere leggings; he has black whiskers, and a reddish face. 'Tis a stuffed figure, with a mask.'

The din was increasing now—then it lessened a little.

'There—I shan't see, after all!' cried the disappointed first maid.

'They have gone into a back street—that's all,' said the one who occupied the enviable position in the attic. 'There—now I have got 'em all endways nicely!'

'What's the woman like? Just say, and I can tell in a moment if 'tis meant for one I've in mind.'

'My—why—'tis dressed just as *she* was dressed when she sat in the front seat at the time the play-actors came to the Town Hall!'

Lucetta started to her feet; and almost at the instant the door of the room was quickly and softly opened. Elizabeth-Jane advanced into the firelight.

'I have come to see you,' she said breathlessly. 'I did not stop to knock—forgive me! I see you have not shut your shutters, and the window is open.'

Without waiting for Lucetta's reply she crossed quickly to the window, and pulled out one of the shutters. Lucetta glided to her side. 'Let it be— hush!' she said peremptorily, in a dry voice, while she seized Elizabeth-Jane by the hand, and held up her finger. Their intercourse had been so low and hurried that not a word had been lost of the conversation without; which had thus proceeded :—

'Her neck is uncovered, and her hair in bands, and her back-comb in place; she's got on a puce silk, and white stockings, and coloured shoes.'

Again Elizabeth-Jane attempted to close the window, but Lucetta held her by main force.

'Tis me!' she said, with a face pale as death. 'A procession—a scandal—an effigy of me, and him!'

The look of Elizabeth betrayed that the latter knew it already.

'Let us shut it out,' coaxed Elizabeth-Jane, noting that the rigid wildness of Lucetta's features were growing yet more rigid and wild with the nearing of the noise and laughter. 'Let us shut it out!'

'It is of no use!' she shrieked out. 'He will see it, won't he? Donald will see it! He is just coming home—and it will break his heart—he will never love me any more—and oh, it will kill me— kill me!'

Elizabeth-Jane was frantic now. 'Oh, can't something be done to stop it?' she cried. 'Is there nobody to do it—not one?'

She relinquished Lucetta's hands, and ran to the door. Lucetta herself, saying recklessly, 'I will see it!' turned to the window, threw up the sash, and went out upon the balcony. Elizabeth immediately followed her, and put her arm round her to pull her in. Lucetta's eyes were straight upon the spectacle of the uncanny revel, now advancing rapidly. The numerous lights around the two effigies threw them up into lurid distinctness; it was impossible to mistake the pair for other than the intended victims.

'Come in, come in,' implored Elizabeth; 'and let me shut the window!'

'She's me—she's me—even to the parasol—my green parasol!' cried Lucetta, with a wild laugh as she stepped in. She stood motionless for one second— then fell heavily to the floor.

Almost at the instant of her fall the rude music of the skimmington ceased. The roars of sarcastic laughter went off in ripples, and the trampling died out like the rustle of a spent wind. Elizabeth was only indirectly conscious of this; she had rung the bell, and was bending over Lucetta, who remained convulsed on the carpet in the paroxysms of an epileptic seizure. She rang again and again, in vain; the probability being that the servants had all run out of the house to see more of the Demoniac Sabbath than they could see within.

At last Farfrae's man, who had been agape on the door-step, came up; then the cook. The shutters, hastily pushed to by Elizabeth, were quite closed, a light was obtained, Lucetta carried to her room, and the man sent off for a doctor. While Elizabeth was undressing her she recovered consciousness; but as soon as she remembered what had passed the fit returned.

The doctor arrived with unhoped-for promptitude; he had been standing at his door, like others, wondering what the uproar meant. As soon as he saw the unhappy sufferer he said, in answer to Elizabeth's mute appeal, 'This is serious.'

'It is a fit,' Elizabeth said.

'Yes. But a fit in the present state of her health means mischief. You must send at once for Mr. Farfrae. Where is he?'

'He has driven into the country, sir,' said the

parlour-maid; 'to some place on the Budmouth Road. He's likely to be back soon.'

'Never mind; he must be sent for, in case he should not hurry.' The doctor returned to the bed-side again. The man was despatched, and they soon heard him clattering out of the yard at the back.

Meanwhile Mr. Benjamin Grower, that prominent burgess of whom mention has been already made, hearing the din of cleavers, tongs, tambourines, kits, crouds, humstrums, serpents, rams'-horns, and other historical kinds of music as he sat indoors in the High Street, had put on his hat and gone out to learn the cause. He came to the corner above Farfrae's, and soon guessed the nature of the proceedings; for being a native of the town he had witnessed such rough jests before. His first move was to search hither and thither for the constables; there were two in the town, shrivelled men whom he ultimately found in hiding up an alley, yet more shrivelled than usual, having some not ungrounded fears that they might be roughly handled if seen.

'What can we two poor lammigers do against such a multitude!' expostulated Stubberd, in answer to Mr. Grower's chiding. ''Tis tempting 'em to commit *felo de se* upon us, and that would be the death of the per-petrator; and we wouldn't be the cause of a fellow-creature's death on no account, not we!'

'Get some help, then! Here, I'll come with you. We'll see what a few words of authority can do. Quick now; have you got your staves?'

'We didn't want the folk to notice us as law officers, being so short-handed, sir; so we pushed our Gover'-ment staves up this water-pipe.'

'Out with 'em, and come along, for Heaven's sake! Ah, here's Mr. Blowbody; that's lucky.' (Blowbody was the third of the three borough magistrates.)

'Well, what's the row?' said Blowbody. 'Got their names—hey?'

'No. Now,' said Grower to one of the constables, 'you go with Mr. Blowbody round by the Old Walk and come up the street; and I'll go with Stubberd straight forward. By this plan we shall have 'em between us. Get their names only: no attack or interruption.'

Thus they started. But as Stubberd with Mr. Grower advanced into Corn Street, whence the sounds had proceeded, they were surprised that no procession could be seen. They passed Farfrae's, and looked to the end of the street. The lamp flames waved, the Walk trees soughed, a few loungers stood about with their hands in their pockets. Everything was as usual.

'Have you seen a motley crowd, making a disturbance?' Grower said magisterially to one of these in a fustian jacket, who smoked a short pipe and wore straps round his knees.

'Beg yer pardon, sir?' blandly said the person addressed, who was no other than Charl, of Peter's Finger. Mr. Grower repeated the words.

Charl shook his head to the zero of childlike ignorance. 'No; we haven't seen anything; have we, Joe? And you was here afore I.'

Joseph was quite as blank as the other in his reply.

'H'm—that's odd,' said Mr. Grower. 'Ah—here's a respectable man coming that I know by sight. Have you,' he inquired, addressing the nearing shape of Jopp, 'have you seen any gang of fellows making a devil of a noise—skimmington riding, or something of the sort?'

'Oh no—nothing, sir,' Jopp replied, as if receiving the most singular news. 'But I've not been far to-night, so perhaps——'

'Oh, 'twas here—just here,' said the magistrate.

'Now I've noticed, come to think o't, that the wind in the Walk trees makes a peculiar poetical-like murmur to-night, sir; more than common; so perhaps 'twas that?' Jopp suggested, as he rearranged his hand in his greatcoat pocket (where it ingeniously supported a pair of kitchen tongs and a cow's horn, thrust up under his waistcoat).

'No, no, no,—d'ye think I'm a fool? Constable, come this way. They must have gone into the back street.'

Neither in back street nor in front street, however, could the disturbers be perceived; and,Blowbody and the second constable, who came up at this time, brought similar intelligence. Effigies, donkey, lanterns, band, all had disappeared like the crew of *Comus*.

'Now,' said Mr. Grower, 'there's only one thing more we can do. Get ye half-a-dozen helpers, and go in a body to Mixen Lane, and into Peter's Finger. I'm much mistaken if you don't find a clue to the perpetrators there.'

The rusty jointed executors of the law mustered assistance as soon as they could, and the whole party marched off to the lane of notoriety. It was no rapid matter to get there at night, not a lamp or glimmer of any sort offering itself to light the way, except an occasional pale radiance through some window-curtain, or through the chink of some door which could not be closed because of the smoky chimney within. At last they entered the inn boldly, by the till then bolted front-door, after a prolonged knocking, of loudness commensurate with the importance of their standing.

In the settles of the large room, guyed to the ceiling by cords as usual for stability, an ordinary group sat drinking and smoking with statuesque quiet of demeanour. The landlady looked mildly at the invaders, saying in honest accents, 'Good evening, gentlemen; there's plenty of room. I hope there's nothing amiss?'

They looked round the room. 'Surely,' said Stubberd to one of the men, 'I saw you by now in Corn Street—Mr. Grower spoke to 'ee?'

The man, who was Charl, shook his head absently. 'I've been here this last hour, hain't I, Nance?' he said to the woman who meditatively sipped her ale near him.

'Faith, that you have. I came in for my quiet supper-time half-pint, and you was here then, as was all the rest.'

The other constable was facing the clock-case, where he saw reflected in the glass a quick motion by the landlady. Turning sharply, he caught her closing the oven-door.

'Something curious about that oven, ma'am!' he observed advancing, opening it, and drawing out a tambourine.

'Oh,' she said, apologetically, 'that's what we keep here to use when there's a little quiet dancing. You see damp weather spoils it, so I put it there to keep it dry.'

The constable nodded knowingly; but what he knew was nothing. Nohow could anything be elicited from this mute and inoffensive assembly. In a few minutes the investigators went out, and joining those of their auxiliaries who had been left at the door, they pursued their way elsewhither.

XL

LONG before this time Henchard, weary of his ruminations on the bridge, had repaired towards the town. When he stood at the bottom of the street a procession burst upon his view, in the act of turning out of an alley just above him. The lanterns, horns, and multitude startled him; he saw the mounted images, and knew what it all meant.

They crossed the way, entered another street, and disappeared. He turned back a few steps and was lost in grave reflection, finally wending his way homeward by the obscure river-side path. Unable to rest there, he went to his stepdaughter's lodging, and was told that Elizabeth-Jane had gone to Mrs. Farfrae's. Like one acting in obedience to a charm, and with a nameless apprehension, he followed in the same direction, in the hope of meeting her, the roysterers having vanished. Disappointed in this, he gave the gentlest of pulls to the door-bell, and then learnt particulars of what had occurred, together with the doctor's imperative orders that Farfrae should be brought home, and how they had set out to meet him on the Budmouth Road.

'But he has gone to Mellstock and Weatherbury!' exclaimed Henchard, now unspeakably grieved. 'Not Budmouth way at all.'

343

But, alas! for Henchard; he had lost his good name. They would not believe him, taking his words but as the frothy utterances of recklessness. Though Lucetta's life seemed at that moment to depend upon her husband's return (she being in great mental agony lest he should never know the unexaggerated truth of her past relations with Henchard), no messenger was despatched towards Weatherbury. Henchard, in a state of bitter anxiety and contrition, determined to seek Farfrae himself.

To this end he hastened down the town, ran along the eastern road over Durnover moor, up the hill beyond, and thus onward in the moderate darkness of this spring night till he had reached a second and almost a third hill about three miles distant. In Yalbury Bottom, the plain at the foot of the hill, he listened. At first nothing, beyond his own heart-throbs, was to be heard but the slow wind making its moan among the masses of spruce and larch of Yalbury Wood which clothed the heights on either hand; but presently there came the sound of light wheels whetting their felloes against the newly stoned patches of road, accompanied by the distant glimmer of lights.

He knew it was Farfrae's gig descending the hill from an indescribable personality in its noise, the vehicle having been his own till bought by the Scotchman at the sale of his effects. Henchard thereupon retraced his steps, the gig coming up with him as its driver slackened speed at the foot of the decline.

It was a point in the highway near which the road to Mellstock branched off from the homeward direction. By diverging to that village, as he had intended to do, Farfrae might probably delay his return by a couple of hours. It soon appeared that his intention was to do so still, the light swerving towards Cuckoo Lane, the by-road aforesaid. Farfrae's off gig-lamp flashed in

Henchard's face. At the same time, Farfrae discerned his late antagonist.

'Farfrae—Mr. Farfrae!' cried the breathless Henchard, holding up his hand.

Farfrae allowed the horse to turn several steps into the branch lane before he pulled up. He then drew rein, and said 'Yes?' over his shoulder, as one would towards a pronounced enemy.

'Come back to Casterbridge at once!' Henchard said. 'There's something wrong at your house—requiring your return. I've run all the way here on purpose to tell ye.'

Farfrae was silent, and at his silence Henchard's soul sank within him. Why had he not, before this, thought of what was only too obvious? He who, four hours earlier, had enticed Farfrae into a deadly wrestle, stood now in the darkness of late night-time on a lonely road, inviting him to come a particular way, where he might have confederates, instead of his purposed way, where there might be a better opportunity of guarding himself from attack. Henchard could almost feel this view of things in course of passage through Farfrae's mind.

'I have to go to Mellstock,' said Farfrae coldly, as he loosened his rein to move on.

'But,' implored Henchard, 'the matter is more serious than your business at Mellstock. It is—your wife! She is ill. I can tell you particulars as we go along.'

The very agitation and abruptness of Henchard increased Farfrae's suspicion that this was a *ruse* to decoy him on to the next wood, where might be effectually compassed what, from policy or want of nerve, Henchard had failed to do earlier in the day. He started the horse.

'I know what you think,' deprecated Henchard, running after, almost bowed down with despair as he perceived the image of unscrupulous villainy that he assumed in his former friend's eyes. 'But I am not what you think!' he cried hoarsely. 'Believe me, Farfrae; I have come entirely on your own and your wife's account. She is in danger. I know no more; and they want you to come. Your man has gone the other way in a mistake. O Farfrae! don't mistrust me—I am a wretched man; but my heart is true to you still!'

Farfrae, however, did distrust him utterly. He knew his wife was with child, but he had left her not long ago in perfect health; and Henchard's treachery was more credible than his story. He had in his time heard bitter ironies from Henchard's lips, and there might be ironies now. He quickened the horse's pace, and had soon risen into the high country lying between there and Mellstock, Henchard's spasmodic run after him lending yet more substance to his thought of evil purposes.

The gig and its driver lessened against the sky in Henchard's eyes; his exertions for Farfrae's good had been in vain. Over this repentant sinner, at least, there was to be no joy in heaven. He cursed himself like a less scrupulous Job, as a vehement man will do when he loses self-respect, the last mental prop under poverty. To this he had come after a time of emotional darkness of which the adjoining woodland shade afforded inadequate illustration. Presently he began to walk back again along the way by which he had arrived. Farfrae should at all events have no reason for delay upon the road by seeing him there when he took his journey homeward later on.

Arriving at Casterbridge, Henchard went again to Farfrae's house to make inquiries. As soon as the door opened anxious faces confronted his from the staircase, hall, and landing; and they all said in grievous disappointment, 'Oh—it is not he!' The man, finding his mistake, had long since returned, and all hopes had been centred upon Henchard.

'But haven't you found him?' said the doctor.

'Yes. . . . I cannot tell ye!' Henchard replied as he sank down on a chair within the entrance. 'He can't be home for two hours.'

'H'm,' said the physician, returning upstairs.

'How is she?' asked Henchard of Elizabeth, who formed one of the group.

'In great danger, father. Her anxiety to see her husband makes her fearfully restless. Poor woman— I fear they have killed her!'

Henchard regarded the sympathetic speaker for a few instants as if she struck him in a new light; then, without further remark, went out of the door and onward to his lonely cottage. So much for man's rivalry, he thought. Death was to have the oyster, and Farfrae and himself the shells. But about Elizabeth-Jane; in the midst of his gloom she seemed to him as a pin-point of light. He had liked the look of her face as she answered him from the stairs. There had been affection in it, and above all things what he desired now was affection from anything that was good and pure. She was not his own; yet, for the first time, he had a faint dream that he might get to like her as his own, —if she would only continue to love him.

Jopp was just going to bed when Henchard got home. As the latter entered the door Jopp said, 'This is rather bad about Mrs. Farfrae's illness.'

'Yes,' said Henchard shortly, though little dreaming of Jopp's complicity in the night's harlequinade, and raising his eyes just sufficiently to observe that Jopp's face was lined with anxiety.

'Somebody has called for you,' continued Jopp, when Henchard was shutting himself into his own apartment. 'A kind of traveller, or sea-captain of some sort.'

' Oh !—who could he be ? '

' He seemed a well-be-doing man—had grey hair and a broadish face; but he gave no name, and no message.'

' Nor do I gi'e him any attention.' And, saying this, Henchard closed his door.

The divergence to Mellstock delayed Farfrae's return very nearly the two hours of Henchard's estimate. Among the other urgent reasons for his presence had been the need of his authority to send to Budmouth for a second physician; and when at length Farfrae did come back he was in a state bordering on distraction at his misconception of Henchard's motives.

A messenger was despatched to Budmouth, late as it had grown; the night wore on, and the other doctor came in the small hours. Lucetta had been much soothed by Donald's arrival; he seldom or never left her side; and when, immediately after his entry, she had tried to lisp out to him the secret which so oppressed her, he checked her feeble words, lest talking should be dangerous, assuring her there was plenty of time to tell him everything.

Up to this time he knew nothing of the skimming-ton-ride. The dangerous illness and miscarriage of Mrs. Farfrae was soon rumoured through the town, and an apprehensive guess having been given as to its cause by the leaders in the exploit, compunction and fear threw a dead silence over all particulars of their orgie; while those immediately around Lucetta would not venture to add to her husband's distress by alluding to the subject.

What, and how much, Farfrae's wife ultimately explained to him of her past entanglement with Henchard, when they were alone in the solitude of that sad night, cannot be told. That she informed him of the bare facts of her peculiar intimacy with the corn-merchant became plain from Farfrae's own statements. But in respect of her subsequent conduct—her motive in coming to Casterbridge to unite herself with Henchard —her assumed justification in abandoning him when she discovered reasons for fearing him (though in truth her inconsequent passion for another man at first sight had most to do with that abandonment)—her method of reconciling to her conscience a marriage with the second when she was in a measure committed to the first: to what extent she spoke of these things remained Farfrae's secret alone.

Besides the watchman who called the hours and weather in Casterbridge that night there walked a figure up and down Corn Street hardly less frequently. It was Henchard's, whose retiring to rest had proved itself a futility as soon as attempted; and he gave it up to go hither and thither, and make inquiries about the patient every now and then. He called as much on Farfrae's account as on Lucetta's, and on Elizabeth-Jane's even more than on either's. Shorn one by one of all other interests, his life seemed centering on the personality of the stepdaughter whose presence but recently he could not endure. To see her on each occasion of his inquiry at Lucetta's was a comfort to him.

The last of his calls was made about four o'clock in the morning, in the steely light of dawn. Lucifer was fading into day across Durnover Moor, the sparrows were just alighting into the street, and the hens had begun to cackle from the outhouses. When within a few yards of Farfrae's he saw the door gently opened, and a servant raise her hand to the knocker, to untie the piece of cloth which had muffled it. He went across, the sparrows in his way scarcely flying up from the road-litter, so little did they believe in human aggression at so early a time.

'Why do you take off that?' said Henchard.

She turned in some surprise at his presence, and did not answer for an instant or two.   Recognizing him, she said, 'Because they may knock as loud as they will; she will never hear it any more.'

XLI

HENCHARD went home. The morning having now fully broke he lit his fire, and sat abstractedly beside it. He had not sat there long when a gentle footstep approached the house and entered the passage, a finger tapping lightly at the door. Henchard's face brightened, for he knew the motions to be Elizabeth's. She came into his room, looking wan and sad.

' Have you heard?' she asked. ' Mrs. Farfrae! She is—dead! Yes, indeed—about an hour ago!'

'I know it,' said Henchard. ' I have but lately come in from there. It is so very good of 'ee, Elizabeth, to come and tell me. You must be so tired out, too, with sitting up. Now do you bide here with me this morning. You can go and rest in the other room; and I will call 'ee when breakfast is ready.'

To please him, and herself—for his recent kindliness was winning a surprised gratitude from the lonely girl —she did as he bade her, and lay down on a sort of couch which Henchard had rigged up out of a settle in the adjoining room. She could hear him moving about in his preparations; but her mind ran most strongly on Lucetta, whose death, in such fulness of life, and amid such cheerful hopes of maternity, was appallingly unexpected. Presently she fell asleep.

Meanwhile her stepfather in the outer room had set

the breakfast in readiness; but finding that she dozed he would not call her; he waited on, looking into the fire and keeping the kettle boiling with housewifely care, as if it were an honour to have her in his house. In truth, a great change had come over him with regard to her, and he was developing the dream of a future lit by her filial presence, as though that way alone could happiness lie.

He was disturbed by another knock at the door, and rose to open it, rather deprecating a call from anybody just then. A stoutly built man stood on the doorstep, with an alien, unfamiliar air about his figure and bearing—an air which might have been called colonial by people of cosmopolitan experience. It was the man who had asked the way at Peter's Finger. Henchard nodded, and looked inquiry.

'Good morning, good morning,' said the stranger with profuse heartiness. 'Is it Mr. Henchard I am talking to?'

'My name is Henchard.'

'Then I caught 'ee at home—that's right. Morning's the time for business, says I. Can I have a few words with you?'

'By all means,' Henchard answered, showing the way in.

'You may remember me?' said his visitor, seating himself.

Henchard observed him indifferently, and shook his head.

'Well—perhaps you may not. My name is Newson.'

Henchard's face and eyes seemed to die. The other did not notice it. 'I know the name well,' Henchard said at last, looking on the floor.

'I make no doubt of that. Well, the fact is, I've been looking for 'ee this fortnight past. I landed at Havenpool and went through Casterbridge on my way to Falmouth, and when I got there, they told me you

had some years before been living at Casterbridge.
Back came I again, and by long and by late I got here
by coach, ten minutes ago. " He lives down by the
mill," says they. So here I am. Now—that transaction between us some twenty years agone—'tis that
I've called about. 'Twas a curious business. I was
younger then than I am now, and perhaps the less said
about it, in one sense, the better.'

' Curious business! 'Twas worse than curious.
I cannot even allow that I'm the man you met then.
I was not in my senses, and a man's senses are him-
self.'

' We were young and thoughtless,' said Newson.
' However, I've come to mend matters rather than
open arguments. Poor Susan—her's was a strange
experience.'

' It was.'

' She was a warm-hearted, home-spun woman. She
was not what they call shrewd or sharp at all—better
she had been.'

' She was not.'

' As you in all likelihood know, she was simple-
minded enough to think that the sale was in a way
binding. She was as guiltless o' wrong-doing in that
particular as a saint in the clouds.'

' I know it, I know it. I found it out directly,'
said Henchard, still with averted eyes. ' There lay
the sting o't to me. If she had seen it as what it
was, she would never have left me. Never! But how
should she be expected to know? What advantages
had she? None. She could write her own name,
and no more.'

' Well, it was not in my heart to undeceive her
when the deed was done,' said the sailor of former
days. ' I thought, and there was not much vanity in
thinking it, that she would be happier with me. She
was fairly happy, and I never would have undeceived

353

her till the day of her death. Your child died; she had another, and all went well. But a time came— mind me, a time always does come. A time came —it was some while after she and I and the child returned from America—when somebody she had confided her history to, told her my claim to her was a mockery, and made a jest of her belief in my right. After that she was never happy with me. She pined and pined, and socked and sighed. She said she must leave me, and then came the question of our child. Then a man advised me how to act, and I did it, for I thought it was best. I left her at Falmouth, and went off to sea. When I got to the other side of the Atlantic there was a storm, and it was supposed that a lot of us, including myself, had been washed overboard. I got ashore at Newfoundland, and then I asked myself what I should do. ' Since I'm here, here I'll bide,' I thought to myself; ' 'twill be most kindness to her, now she's taken against me, to let her believe me lost; for,' I thought, ' while she supposes us both alive she'll be miserable; but if she thinks me dead she'll go back to him, and the child will have a home.' I've never returned to this country till a month ago, and I found that, as I had supposed, she went to you, and my daughter with her. They told me in Falmouth that Susan was, dead. But my Elizabeth-Jane—where is she?'

' Dead likewise,' said Henchard doggedly. ' Surely you learnt that too?'

The sailor started up, and took an enervated pace or two down the room. ' Dead!' he said, in a low voice. ' Then what's the use of my money to me?'

Henchard, without answering, shook his head, as if that were rather a question for Newson himself than for him.

' Where is she buried?' the traveller inquired.

' Beside her mother,' said Henchard, in the same stolid tones.

354

'When did she die?'

'A year ago and more,' replied the other without hesitation.

The sailor continued standing. Henchard never looked up from the floor. At last Newson said : ' My journey hither has been for nothing! I may as well go as I came! It has served me right. I'll trouble you no longer.'

Henchard heard the retreating footsteps of Newson upon the sanded floor, the mechanical lifting of the latch, the slow opening and closing of the door that was natural to a baulked or dejected man ; but he did not turn his head. Newson's shadow passed the window. He was gone.

Then Henchard, scarcely believing the evidence of his senses, rose from his seat, amazed at what he had done. It had been the impulse of a moment. The regard he had lately acquired for Elizabeth, the new-sprung hope of his loneliness that she would be to him a daughter of whom he could feel as proud as of the actual daughter she still believed herself to be, had been stimulated by the unexpected coming of Newson to a greedy exclusiveness in relation to her ; so that the sudden prospect of her loss had caused him to speak mad lies like a child, in pure mockery of consequences. He had expected questions to close in round him, and unmask his fabrication in five minutes ; yet such questioning had not come. But surely they would come ; Newson's departure could be but momentary ; he would learn all by inquiries in the town ; and return to curse him, and carry his last treasure away !

He hastily put on his hat, and went out in the direction that Newson had taken. Newson's back was soon visible up the road. Henchard followed ; and saw his visitor stop at the King's Arms, where the morning coach which had brought him waited half-an-hour for another coach which crossed there. The coach

Newson had come by was now about to move again. Newson mounted; his luggage was put in, and in a few minutes the vehicle disappeared with him.

He had not so much as turned his head. It was an act of simple faith in Henchard's words—faith so simple as to be almost sublime. The young sailor who had taken Susan Henchard on the spur of the moment, and on the faith of a glance at her face, more than twenty years before, was still living and acting under the form of the grizzled traveller who had taken Henchard's words on trust so absolute as to shame him as he stood.

Was Elizabeth-Jane to remain his by virtue of this hardy invention of a moment? 'Perhaps not for long,' said he. Newson might converse with his fellow-travellers, some of whom might be Casterbridge people; and the trick would be discovered.

This probability threw Henchard into a defensive attitude, and instead of considering how best to right the wrong, and acquaint Elizabeth's father with the truth at once, he bethought himself of ways to keep the position he had accidentally won. Towards the young woman herself his affection grew more jealously strong with each new hazard to which his claim to her was exposed.

He watched the distant highway, expecting to see Newson return on foot, enlightened and indignant, to claim his child. But no figure appeared. Possibly he had spoken to nobody on the coach, but buried his grief in his own heart.

His grief!—what was it, after all, to that which he, Henchard, would feel at the loss of her? Newson's affection, cooled by years, could not equal his who had been constantly in her presence. And thus his jealous soul speciously argued to excuse the separation of father and child.

He returned to the house half expecting that she would have vanished. No; there she was—just coming out from the inner room, the marks of sleep upon her eyelids, and exhibiting a generally refreshed air.

'O father!' she said, smiling. 'I had no sooner lain down than I napped, though I did not mean to? I wonder I did not dream about poor Mrs. Farfrae, after thinking of her so; but I did not. How strange it is that we do not often dream of latest events, absorbing as they may be.'

'I am glad you have been able to sleep,' he said, taking her hand with anxious proprietorship—an act which gave her a pleasant surprise.

They sat down to breakfast, and Elizabeth-Jane's thoughts reverted to Lucetta. Their sadness added charm to a countenance whose beauty had ever lain in its meditative soberness.

'Father,' she said, as soon as she recalled herself to the outspread meal, 'it is so kind of you to get this nice breakfast with your own hands, and I idly asleep the while.'

'I do it every day,' he replied. 'You have left me; everybody has left me; how should I live but by my own hands.'

'You are very lonely, are you not?'

'Ay, child—to a degree that you know nothing of! It is my own fault. You are the only one who has been near me for weeks. And you will come no more.'

'Why do you say that? Indeed I will, if you would like to see me.'

Henchard signified dubiousness. Though he had so lately hoped that Elizabeth-Jane might again live in his house as daughter, he would not ask her to do so now. Newson might return at any moment, and what Elizabeth would think of him for his deception it were best to bear apart from her.

When they had breakfasted his stepdaughter still lingered, till the moment arrived at which Henchard was accustomed to go to his daily work. Then she arose, and with assurances of coming again, soon went up the hill in the morning sunlight.

'At this moment her heart is as warm towards me as mine is towards her; she would live with me here in this humble cottage for the asking! Yet before the evening probably he will have come; and then she will scorn me!'

This reflection, constantly repeated by Henchard to himself, accompanied him everywhere through the day. His mood was no longer that of the rebellious, ironical, reckless misadventurer; but the leaden gloom of one who has lost all that can make life interesting, or even tolerable. There would remain nobody for him to be proud of, nobody to fortify him; for Elizabeth-Jane would soon be but as a stranger, and worse. Susan, Farfrae, Lucetta, Elizabeth—all had gone from him, one after one, either by his fault or by his misfortune.

In place of them he had no interest, hobby, or desire. If he could have summoned music to his aid, his existence might even now have been borne; for with Henchard music was of regal power. The merest trumpet or organ tone was enough to move him, and high harmonies transubstantiated him. But fate had ordained that he should be unable to call up this Divine spirit in his need.

The whole land ahead of him was as darkness itself; there was nothing to come, nothing to wait for. Yet in the natural course of life he might possibly have to linger on earth another thirty or forty years—scoffed at; at best pitied.

The thought of it was unendurable.

To the east of Casterbridge lay moors and meadows, through which much water flowed. The wanderer in this direction, who should stand still for a few moments on a quiet night, might hear singular symphonies from these waters, as from a lampless orchestra, all playing in their sundry tones, from near and far parts of the moor. At a hole in a rotten weir they executed a recitative; where a tributary brook fell over a stone breastwork they trilled cheerily; under an arch they performed a metallic cymballing; and at Durnover Hole they hissed. The spot at which their instrumentation rose loudest was a place called Ten Hatches, whence during high springs there proceeded a very fugue of sounds.

The river here was deep and strong at all times, and the hatches on this account were raised and lowered by cogs and a winch. A path led from the second bridge over the highway (so often mentioned) to these Hatches, crossing the stream at their head by a narrow plank-bridge. But after night-fall human beings were seldom found going that way, the path leading to no place in particular, and the passage being dangerous.

Henchard, however, leaving the town by the east road, proceeded to the second, or stone bridge, and thence struck into this path of solitude, following its course beside the stream till the dark shapes of the Ten Hatches cut the sheen thrown upon the river by the weak lustre that still lingered in the west. In a second or two he stood beside the weir-hole where the water was at its deepest. He looked backwards and forwards, and no creature appeared in view. He then took off his coat and hat, and stood on the brink of the stream with his hands clasped in front of him.

While his eyes were bent on the water beneath, there slowly became visible a something floating in the circular pool formed by the wash of centuries; the pool he was intending to make his death-bed. At first it was indistinct, by reason of the shadow from the bank; but it emerged thence, and took shape, which was that of a human body, lying stiff and stark upon the surface of the stream.

In the circular current imparted by the central flow the form was brought forward, till it passed under his

359

eyes; and then he perceived with a sense of horror that it was *himself.* Not a man somewhat resembling him, but one in all respects his counterpart, his actual double, was floating as if dead in Ten Hatches Hole.

The sense of the supernatural was strong in this unhappy man, and he turned away as one might have done in the actual presence of an appalling miracle. He covered his eyes and bowed his head. Without looking again into the stream he took his coat and hat, and went slowly away.

Presently he found himself by the door of his own dwelling. To his surprise Elizabeth-Jane was standing there. She came forward, spoke, called him ' father ' just as before. Newson, then, had not even yet returned.

' I thought you seemed very sad this morning,' she said, ' so I have come again to see you. Not that I am anything but sad myself. But everybody and everything seem against you so; and I know you must be suffering.'

How this woman divined things! Yet she had not divined their whole extremity.

He said to her, ' Are miracles still worked, do ye think, Elizabeth? I am not a read man. I don't know so much as I could wish. I have tried to peruse and learn all my life; but the more I try to know the more ignorant I seem.'

' I don't quite think there are any miracles now-a-days,' she said.

' No interference in the case of desperate intentions, for instance? Well, perhaps not, in a direct way. Perhaps not. But will you come and walk with me, and I will show 'ee what I mean.'

She agreed willingly, and he took her over the highway, and by the lonely path to Ten Hatches. He walked restlessly, as if some haunting shade, unseen of her, hovered round him and troubled his glance. She would gladly have talked of Lucetta, but feared to disturb him. When they got near the weir he stood still, and asked her to go forward and look into the pool, and tell him what she saw.

She went, and soon returned to him. 'Nothing,' she said.

'Go again,' said Henchard, 'and look narrowly.'

She proceeded to the river brink a second time. On her return, after some delay, she told him that she saw something floating there; but what it was she could not discern. It seemed to be a bundle of old clothes.

'Are they like mine?' asked Henchard.

'Well — they are. Dear me — I wonder if —— Father, let us go away!'

'Go and look once more; and then we will get home.'

She went back, and he could see her stoop till her head was close to the margin of the pool. She started up, and hastened back to his side.

'Well,' said Henchard; 'what do you say now?'

'Let us go home.'

'But tell me — do — what is it floating there?'

'The effigy,' she answered hastily. 'They must have thrown it into the river, higher up amongst the willows, to get rid of it in their alarm at discovery; and it must have floated down here.'

'Ah — to be sure — the image o' me! But where is the other? Why that one only? . . . That performance of theirs killed her, but kept me alive!'

Elizabeth-Jane thought and thought of these words 'kept me alive,' as they slowly retraced their way to the town, and at length guessed their meaning. 'Father! — I will not leave you alone like this!' she cried. 'May I live with you, and tend upon you, as I used to do? I do not mind your being poor. I would have agreed to come this morning, but you did not ask me.'

'May you come to me?' he cried bitterly. 'Elizabeth, don't mock me! If you only would come!'

'I will,' said she.

'How will you forgive all my roughness in former days? You cannot!'

'I have forgotten it. Talk of that no more.'

Thus she assured him, and arranged their plans for reunion; and at length each went home. Then Henchard shaved for the first time during many days, and put on clean linen, and combed his hair: and was as a man resuscitated thenceforward.

The next morning the fact turned out to be as Elizabeth-Jane had stated; the effigy was discovered by a cowherd, and that of Lucetta a little higher up in the same stream. But as little as possible was said of the matter, and the figures were privately destroyed.

Despite this natural solution of the mystery, Henchard no less regarded it as an intervention that the figure should have been floating there. Elizabeth-Jane heard him say, 'Who is such a reprobate as I! And yet it seems that even I be in Somebody's hand!'

XLII

BUT the emotional conviction that he was in Somebody's hand began to die out of Henchard's breast as time slowly removed into distance the event which had given that feeling birth. The apparition of Newson haunted him. He would surely return.

Yet Newson did not arrive. Lucetta had been borne along the churchyard path; Casterbridge had for the last time turned its regard upon her, before proceeding to its work as if she had never lived. But Elizabeth remained undisturbed in the belief of her relationship to Henchard, and now shared his home. Perhaps, after all, Newson was gone for ever.

In due time the bereaved Farfrae had learnt the, at least, proximate cause of Lucetta's illness and death; and his first impulse was naturally enough to wreak vengeance in the name of the law upon the perpetrators of the mischief. He resolved to wait till the funeral was over ere he moved in the matter. The time having come he reflected. Disastrous as the result had been, it was obviously in no way foreseen or intended by the thoughtless crew who arranged the motley procession. The tempting prospect of putting to the blush people who stand at the head of affairs

THE MAYOR OF CASTERBRIDGE

—that supreme and piquant enjoyment of those who writhe under the heel of the same—had alone animated them, so far as he could see; for he knew nothing of Jopp's incitements. Other considerations were also involved. Lucetta had confessed everything to him before her death, and it was not altogether desirable to make much ado about her history, alike for her sake, for Henchard's, and for his own. To regard the event as an untoward accident seemed, to Farfrae, truest consideration for the dead one's memory, as well as best philosophy.

Henchard and himself mutually forbore to meet. For Elizabeth's sake the former had fettered his pride sufficiently to accept the small seed business which some of the Town Council, headed by Farfrae, had purchased, to afford him a new opening. Had he been only personally concerned, Henchard, without doubt, would have declined assistance even remotely brought about by the man whom he had so fiercely assailed. But the sympathy of the girl seemed necessary to his very existence; and on her account pride itself wore the garments of humility.

Here they settled themselves; and on each day of their lives Henchard anticipated her every wish with a watchfulness in which paternal regard was heightened by a burning jealous dread of rivalry. Yet that Newson would ever now return to Casterbridge to claim her as a daughter there was little reason to suppose. He was a wanderer and a stranger, almost an alien; he had not seen his daughter for several years; his affection for her could not in the nature of things be keen; other interests would probably soon obscure his recollections of her, and prevent any such renewal of inquiry into the past as would lead to a discovery that she was still a creature of the present. To satisfy his conscience somewhat, Henchard repeated to himself that the lie which had retained for him the coveted treasure had not been deliberately told to that end, but had come from him as the last defiant word of an irony which took no thought of consequences. Furthermore he pleaded within himself that no Newson could love her as he loved her, or would tend her to his life's extremity as he was prepared to do cheerfully.

Thus they lived on in the shop overlooking the churchyard, and nothing occurred to mark their days during the remainder of the year. Going out but seldom, and never on a market-day, they saw Donald Farfrae only at rarest intervals, and then mostly as a transitory object in the distance of the street. Yet he was pursuing his ordinary avocations, smiling mechanically to fellow - tradesmen, and arguing with bargainers — as bereaved men do after a while.

Time, in his own grey style,' taught Farfrae how to estimate his experience of Lucetta—all that it was, and all that it was not. There are men whose hearts insist upon a dogged fidelity to some image or cause, thrown by chance into their keeping, long after their judgment has pronounced it no rarity—even the reverse, indeed ; and without them the band of the worthy is incomplete. But Farfrae was not of those. It was inevitable that the insight, briskness, and rapidity of his nature' should take him out of the dead blank which his loss threw about him. He could not but perceive that by the death of Lucetta he had exchanged a looming misery for a simple sorrow. After that revelation of her history, which must have come sooner or later in any circumstances, it was hard to believe that life with her would have been productive of further happiness.

But as a memory, notwithstanding such conditions, Lucetta's image still lived on with him, her weaknesses provoking only the gentlest criticism, and her sufferings attenuating wrath at her concealments to a momentary spark now and then.

By the end of a year Henchard's little retail seed and grain shop, not much larger than a cupboard, had developed its trade considerably, and the stepfather and daughter enjoyed much serenity in the pleasant, sunny corner in which it stood. The quiet bearing of one who brimmed with an inner activity characterized Elizabeth-Jane at this period. She took long walks into the country two or three times a week, mostly in the direction of Budmouth. Sometimes it occurred to him that when she sat with him in the evening after these invigorating walks she was civil rather than affectionate; and he was troubled; one more bitter regret being added to those he had already experienced at having, by his severe censorship, frozen up her precious affection when originally offered.

She had her own way in everything now. In going and coming, in buying and selling, her word was law.

'You have got a new muff, Elizabeth,' he said to her one day quite humbly.

'Yes; I bought it,' she said.

He looked at it again as it lay on an adjoining table. The fur was of a glossy brown, and, though he was no judge of such articles, he thought it seemed an unusually good one for her to possess.

'Rather costly, I suppose, my dear, was it not?' he hazarded.

'It was rather above my figure,' she said quietly. 'But it is not showy.'

'Oh no,' said the netted lion, anxious not to pique her in the least.

Some little time after, when the year had advanced into another spring, he paused opposite her empty bedroom in passing it. He thought of the time when she had cleared out of his then large and handsome house in Corn Street, in consequence of his dislike and harshness, and he had looked into her chamber in just the same way. The present room was much humbler, but what struck him about it was the abundance of books lying everywhere. Their number and quality made the meagre furniture that supported them seem absurdly disproportionate. Some, indeed many, must have been recently purchased ; and though he encouraged her to buy in reason, he had no notion that she indulged her innate passion so extensively in proportion to the narrowness of their income. For the first time he felt a little hurt by what he thought her extravagance, and resolved to say a word to her about it. But, before he had found the courage to speak, an event happened which set his thoughts flying in quite another direction.

The busy time of the seed trade was over ; and the quiet weeks that preceded the hay-season had come —setting their special stamp upon Casterbridge by thronging the market with wood rakes, new waggons in yellow, green, and. red, formidable scythes, and pitchforks of prong sufficient to skewer up a small family. Henchard, contrary to his wont, went out one Saturday afternoon towards the market-place, from a curious feeling that he would like to pass a few minutes on the spot of his former triumphs. Farfrae, to whom he was still a comparative stranger, stood a few steps below the Corn Exchange door—a usual position with him at this hour—and he appeared lost in thought about something he was looking at a little way off.

Henchard's eyes followed Farfrae's, and he saw that the object of his gaze was no sample-showing farmer, but his own stepdaughter, who had just come out of a shop over the way. She, on her part, was quite unconscious of his attention, and in this was less fortunate than those young women whose very plumes, like those of Juno's bird, are set with Argus eyes whenever possible admirers are within ken.

Henchard went away, thinking that perhaps there was nothing significant after all in Farfrae's look at Elizabeth-Jane at that juncture. Yet he could not forget that the Scotchman had once shown a tender interest in her, of a fleeting kind. Thereupon promptly came to the surface that idiosyncrasy of Henchard's which had ruled his courses from the beginning, and had mainly made him what he was. Instead of thinking that a union between his cherished stepdaughter and the energetic thriving Donald was a thing to be desired for her good and his own, he hated the very possibility.

Time had been when such instinctive opposition would have taken shape in action. But he was not now the Henchard of former days. He schooled himself to accept her will, in this as in other matters, as absolute and unquestionable. He dreaded lest an antagonistic word should lose for him such regard as he had regained from her by his devotion, feeling that to retain this under separation was better than to incur her dislike by keeping her near.

But the mere thought of such separation fevered his spirit much, and in the evening he said, with the stillness of suspense: 'Have you seen Mr. Farfrae to-day, Elizabeth?'

Elizabeth-Jane started at the question; and it was with some confusion that she replied 'No.'

'Oh—that's right—that's right. . . . It was only that I saw him in the street when we both were there.' He was wondering if her embarrassment justified him in a new suspicion—that the long walks which she had latterly been taking, that the new books which had so surprised him, had anything to do with the young man. She did not enlighten him, and lest silence should allow her to shape thoughts unfavourable to their present friendly relations, he diverted the discourse into another channel.

Henchard was, by original make, the last man to act stealthily, for good or for evil. But the *solicitus timor* of his love—the dependence upon Elizabeth's regard into which he had declined (or, in another sense, to which he had advanced)—denaturalized him. He would often weigh and consider for hours together the meaning of such and such a deed or phrase of hers, when a blunt settling question would formerly have been his first instinct. And now, uneasy at the thought of a passion for Farfrae which should entirely displace her mild filial sympathy with himself, he observed her going and coming more narrowly.

There was nothing secret in Elizabeth-Jane's movements beyond what habitual reserve induced; and it may at once be owned on her account that she was guilty of occasional conversations with Donald when they chanced to meet. Whatever the origin of her walks on the Budmouth Road, her return from those walks was often coincident with Farfrae's emergence from Corn Street for a twenty minutes' blow on that rather windy highway—just to winnow the seeds and chaff out of him before sitting down to tea, as he said. Henchard became aware of this by going to the Ring, and, screened by its enclosure, keeping his eye upon the road till he saw them meet. His face assumed an expression of extreme anguish.

'Of her, too, he means to rob me!' he whispered. 'But he has the right. I do not wish to interfere.'

The meeting, in truth, was of a very innocent kind, and matters were by no means so far advanced between the young people as Henchard's jealous grief inferred. Could he have heard such conversation as passed he would have been enlightened thus much :—

He.—'You like walking this way, Miss Henchard —and is it not so?' (uttered in his undulatory accents, and with an appraising, pondering gaze at her).

369

She.—'Oh yes. I have chosen this road latterly. I have no great reason for it.'

He.—'But that may make a reason for others.'

She (reddening).—'I don't know that. My reason, however, such as it is, is that I wish to get a glimpse of the sea every day.'

He.—'Is it a secret why?'

She (reluctantly).—'Yes.'

He (with the pathos of one of his native ballads).— 'Ah, I doubt there will be any good in secrets! A secret cast a deep shadow over my life. And well you know what it was.'

Elizabeth admitted that she did, but she refrained from confessing why the sea attracted her. She could not herself account for it fully, not knowing the secret possibly to be that, in addition to early marine associations, her blood was a sailor's.

'Thank you for those new books, Mr. Farfrae,' she added shyly. 'I wonder if I ought to accept so many!'

'Ay! why not? It gives me more pleasure to get them for you, than you to have them!'

'It cannot!'

They proceeded along the road together till they reached the town, and their paths diverged.

Henchard vowed that he would leave them to their own devices, put nothing in the way of their courses, whatever they might mean. If he were doomed to be bereft of her, so it must be. In the situation which their marriage would create he could see no *locus standi* for himself at all. Farfrae would never recognize him more than superciliously; his poverty ensured that, no less than his past conduct. And so Elizabeth would grow to be a stranger to him, and the end of his life would be friendless solitude.

With such a possibility impending he could not help watchfulness. Indeed, within certain lines, he had the

right to keep an eye upon her as his charge. The meetings seemed to become matters of course with them on
special days of the week.

At last full proof was given him. He was standing
behind a wall close to the place at which Farfrae encountered her. He heard the young man address her
as ' Dearest Elizabeth-Jane,' and then kiss her, the girl
looking quickly round to assure herself that nobody
was near.

When they were gone their way Henchard came
out from the wall, and mournfully followed them to
Casterbridge. The chief looming trouble in this
engagement had not decreased. Both Farfrae and
Elizabeth-Jane, unlike the rest of the people, must
suppose Elizabeth to be his actual daughter, from
his own assertion while he himself had the same belief; and though Farfrae must have so far forgiven
him as to have no objection to own him as a father-
in-law, intimate they could never be. Thus would
the girl, who was his only friend, be withdrawn from
him by degrees through her husband's influence, and
learn to despise him.

Had she lost her heart to any other man in the
world than the one he had rivalled, cursed, wrestled
with for life in days before his spirit was broken,
Henchard would have said, ' I am content.' But
content with the prospect as now depicted was hard
to acquire.

There is an outer chamber of the brain in which
thoughts unowned, unsolicited, and of noxious kind,
are sometimes allowed to wander for a moment prior
to being sent off whence they came. One of these
thoughts sailed into Henchard's ken now.

Suppose he were to communicate to Farfrae the
fact that his betrothed was not the child of Michael
Henchard at all—legally, nobody's child; how would
that correct and leading townsman receive the informa-

tion? He might possibly forsake Elizabeth-Jane, and then she would be her stepsire's own again.

Henchard shuddered, and exclaimed, 'God forbid such a thing! Why should I still be subject to these visitations of the devil, when I try so hard to keep him away?'

XLIII

WHAT Henchard saw thus early was, naturally enough, seen at a little later date by other people. That Mr. Farfrae 'walked with that bankrupt Henchard's stepdaughter, of all women,' became a common topic in the town, the simple perambulating term being used hereabout to signify a wooing; and the nineteen superior young ladies of Casterbridge, who had each looked upon herself as the only woman capable of making the merchant Councilman happy, indignantly left off going to the church Farfrae attended, left off conscious mannerisms, left off putting him in their prayers at night amongst their blood relations; in short, reverted to their natural courses.

Perhaps the only inhabitants of the town to whom this looming choice of the Scotchman's gave unmixed satisfaction were the members of the philosophic party, which included Longways, Christopher Coney, Billy Wills, Mr. Buzzford, and the like. The Three Mariners having been, years before, the house in which they had witnessed the young man and woman's first and humble appearance on the Casterbridge stage, they took a kindly interest in their career, not unconnected, perhaps, with visions of festive treatment at their hands hereafter. Mrs. Stannidge, having rolled into the large parlour one evening, and said that it was a wonder such a man

373

as Mr. Farfrae, 'a pillow of the town,' who might have chosen one of the daughters of the professional men, or private residents, should stoop so low, Coney ventured to disagree with her.

'No, ma'am, no wonder at all. 'Tis she that's a stooping to he—that's my opinion. A widow man— whose first wife was no credit to him—what is it for a young perusing woman, that's her own mistress and well-liked? But as a neat patching up of things I see much good in it. When a man have put up a tomb of best marble-stone to the other one, as he've done, and weeped his fill, and thought it all over, and said to himself, "T'other took me in; I knowed this one first; she's a sensible piece for a partner, and there's no faithful woman in high life now;"—well, he may do worse than not to take her, if she's tender-inclined.'

Thus they talked at the Mariners. But we must guard against a too liberal use of the conventional declaration that a great sensation was caused by the prospective event, that all the gossips' tongues were set wagging thereby, and so on, even though such a declaration might lend some eclat to the career of our poor only heroine. When all has been said about busy rumourers, a superficial and temporary thing is the interest of anybody in affairs which do not directly touch them. It would be a truer representation to say that Casterbridge (ever excepting the nineteen young ladies) looked up for a moment at the news, and withdrawing its attention, went on labouring and victualling, bringing up its children, and burying its dead, without caring a tittle for Farfrae's domestic plans.

Not a hint of the matter was thrown out to her stepfather by Elizabeth herself or by Farfrae either. Reasoning on the cause of their reticence he concluded that, estimating him by his past, the throbbing pair were afraid to broach the subject, and looked upon him as an irksome obstacle whom they would be heartily glad to get out of the way. Embittered as he was against society, this moody view of himself took deeper and deeper hold of Henchard, till the daily necessity of facing mankind, and of them particularly Elizabeth-Jane, became well-nigh more than he could endure. His health declined; he became morbidly sensitive. He wished he could escape those who did not want him, and hide his head for ever.

But what if he were mistaken in his views, and there were no necessity that his own absolute separation from her should be involved in the incident of her marriage?

He proceeded to draw a picture of the alternative— himself living like a fangless lion about the back rooms. of a house in which his stepdaughter was mistress; an inoffensive old man, tenderly smiled on by Elizabeth, and good-naturedly tolerated by her husband. It was terrible to his pride to think of descending so low; and yet, for the girl's sake he might put up with anything; even from Farfrae; even snubbings and masterful tongue scourgings. The privilege of being in the house she occupied would almost outweigh the personal humiliation.

Whether this were a dim possibility or the reverse, the courtship — which it evidently now was — had an absorbing interest for him.

Elizabeth, as has been said, often took her walks on the Budmouth Road, and Farfrae as often made it convenient to create an accidental meeting with her there. A quarter of a mile from the highway was the pre-historic fort called Mai Dun, of huge dimensions and many ramparts, within or upon whose enclosures a human being, as seen from the road, was but an insignificant speck. Hither Henchard often resorted, glass in hand, and scanned the hedgeless *Via*—for it was the original track laid out by the legions of the Empire—to a distance of two or three miles, his object being to read the progress of affairs between Farfrae and his charmer.

One day Henchard was at this spot when a masculine figure came along the road from Budmouth, and lingered. Applying his telescope to his eye Henchard expected that Farfrae's features would be disclosed as usual. But the lenses revealed that to-day the man was not Elizabeth-Jane's lover.

It was one clothed as a merchant captain; and as he turned in his scrutiny of the road he revealed his face. Henchard lived a lifetime the moment he saw it. The face was Newson's.

Henchard dropped the glass, and for some seconds made no other movement. Newson waited, and Henchard waited—if that could be called a waiting which was a transfixture. But Elizabeth-Jane did not come. Something or other had caused her to neglect her customary walk that day. Perhaps Farfrae and she had chosen another road for variety's sake. But what did that amount to? She might be here to-morrow, and in any case Newson, if bent on a private meeting and a revelation of the truth to her, would soon make his opportunity.

Then he would tell her not only of his paternity, but of the ruse by which he had been once sent away. Elizabeth's strict nature would cause her for the first time to despise her stepfather, would root out his image as that of an arch-deceiver, and Newson would reign in her heart in his stead.

But Newson did not see anything of her that morning. Having stood still awhile he at last retraced his steps, and Henchard felt like a condemned man who has a few hours' respite. When he reached his own house he found her there.

' O father ! ' she said innocently, ' I have had a letter —a strange one—not signed. Somebody has asked me to meet him, either on the Budmouth Road at noon to-day, or in the evening at Mr. Farfrae's. He says he came to see me some time ago, but a trick was played him, so that he did not. I don't understand it; but between you and me I think Donald is at the bottom of the mystery, and that it is a relation of his who wants to pass an opinion on his choice. But I did not like to go till I had seen you. Shall I go?'

Henchard replied heavily, 'Yes; go.'

The question of his remaining in Casterbridge was for ever disposed of by this closing in of Newson on the scene. Henchard was not the man to stand the certainty of condemnation on a matter so near his heart. And being an old hand at bearing anguish in silence, and haughty withal, he resolved to make as light as he could of his intention, while immediately taking his measures.

He surprised the young woman, whom he had looked upon as his all in this world, by saying to her, as if he did not care about her more: 'I am going to leave Casterbridge, Elizabeth-Jane.'

'Leave Casterbridge!' she cried, 'and leave—me?'

'Yes, this little shop can be managed by you alone as well as by us both; I don't care about shops and streets and folk—I would rather get into the country by myself, out of sight, and follow my own ways, and leave you to yours.'

She looked down, and her tears fell silently. It naturally seemed to her that this resolve of his had come on account of her attachment, and its probable result. She showed her devotion to Farfrae, however, by mastering her emotion and speaking out.

'I am sorry you have decided on this,' she said with difficult firmness. 'For I thought it probable—possible—that I might marry Mr. Farfrae some little time hence, and I did not know that you disapproved of the step!'

377

'I approve of anything you desire to do, Izzy,' said Henchard huskily. 'If I did not approve, it would be no matter! I wish to go away. My presence might make things awkward in the future; and, in short, it is best that I go.'

Nothing that her affection could urge would induce him to reconsider his determination; for she could not urge what she did not know—that when she should learn he was not related to her other than as a step-parent she would refrain from despising him, and that when she knew what he had done to keep her in ignorance she would refrain from hating him. It was his conviction that she would not so refrain; and there existed as yet neither word nor event which could argue it away.

'Then,' she said at last, 'you will not be able to come to my wedding; and that is not as it ought to be.'

'I don't want to see it—I don't want to see it!' he exclaimed; adding more softly, 'but think of me sometimes in your future life—you'll do that, Izzy?— think of me when you are living as the wife of the richest, the foremost man in the town, and don't let my sins, *when you know them all*, cause 'ee to quite forget that though I loved 'ee late I loved 'ee well.'

'It is because of Donald!' she sobbed.

'I don't forbid you to marry him,' said Henchard. Promise not to quite forget me when——' He meant when Newson should come.

She promised mechanically, in her agitation; and the same evening at dusk Henchard left the town, to whose development he had been one of the chief stimulants for many years. During the day he had bought a new tool-basket, cleaned up his old hay-knife and wimble, set himself up in fresh leggings, knee-naps and corduroys, and in other ways gone back to the working clothes of his young manhood, discarding for ever the shabby-genteel suit of cloth and rusty silk hat that since his decline had characterized him in the Casterbridge street as a man who had seen better days.

He went secretly and alone, not a soul of the many who had known him being aware of his departure. Elizabeth-Jane accompanied him as far as the second bridge on the highway—for the hour of her appointment with the unguessed visitor at Farfrae's had not yet arrived—and parted from him with unfeigned wonder and sorrow—keeping him back a minute or two before finally letting him go. She watched his form diminish across the moor, the yellow straw basket at his back moving up and down with each tread, and the creases behind his knees coming and going alternately till she could no longer see them. Though she did not know it, Henchard formed at this moment much the same picture as he had presented when entering Casterbridge for the first time nearly a quarter of a century before ; except, to be sure, that the serious addition to his years had considerably lessened the spring of his stride, that his state of hopelessness had weakened him, and imparted to his shoulders, as weighted by the basket, a perceptible bend.

He went on till he came to the first milestone, which stood in the bank, half way up a steep hill. He rested his basket on the top of the stone, placed his elbows on it, and gave way to a convulsive ; twitch, which was worse than a sob, because it was so hard and so dry.

'If I had only got her with me—if I only had ! ' he said. ' Hard work would be nothing to me then ! But that was not to be. I—Cain—go alone as I deserve—an outcast and a vagabond. But my punishment is *not* greater than I can bear ! '

He sternly subdued his anguish, shouldered his basket, and went on.

Elizabeth, in the meantime, had breathed him a sigh,

recovered her equanimity, and turned her face to Casterbridge. Before she had reached the first house she was
met in her walk by Donald Farfrae. This was evidently not their first meeting that day; they joined
hands without ceremony, and Farfrae anxiously asked,
' And is he gone—and did you tell him?—I mean of
the other matter—not of ours.'

' He is gone; and I told him all I knew of your
friend. Donald, who is he?'

' Well, well, dearie; you will know soon about
that. And Mr. Henchard will hear of it if he does not
go far.'

' He will go far—he's bent upon getting out of sight
and sound!'

She walked beside her lover, and when they reached
the Town Pump turned with him into Corn Street,
instead of going straight on to her own door. At
Farfrae's house they stopped and went in.

Farfrae flung open the door of the ground-floor
sitting-room, saying, ' There he is waiting for you,' and
Elizabeth entered. In the arm-chair sat the broad-faced
genial man who had called on Henchard on a memorable morning between one and two years before this
time, and whom the latter had seen mount the coach
and depart within half-an-hour of his arrival. It was
Richard Newson. The meeting with the light-hearted
father from whom she had been separated half-a-dozen
years, as if by death, need hardly be detailed. It was
an affecting one, apart from the question of paternity.
Henchard's departure was in a moment explained.
When the true facts came to be handled, the difficulty
of restoring her to her old belief in Newson was not
so great as might have seemed likely, for Henchard's
conduct itself was a proof that those facts were true.
Moreover, she had grown up under Newson's paternal
care; and even had Henchard been her father in
nature, this father in early domiciliation might

almost have carried the point against him, when the incidents of her parting with Henchard had a little worn off.

Newson's pride in what she had grown up to be was more than he could express. He kissed her again and again.

' I've saved you the trouble to come and meet me— ha-ha!' said Newson. 'The fact is that Mr. Farfrae here, he said, "Come up and stop with me for a day or two, Captain Newson, and I'll bring her round." "Faith," says I, " so I will ; " and here I am.'

'Well, Henchard is gone,' said Farfrae, shutting the door. 'He has done it all voluntarily, and, as I gather from Elizabeth, he has been very nice with her. I was got rather uneasy; but all is as it should be, and we will have no more difficulties at all.'

' Now, that's very much as I thought,' said Newson, looking into the face of each by turns. 'I said to myself, ay, a hundred times, when I tried to get a peep at her unknown to herself—" Depend upon it, 'tis best that I should live on quiet for a few days like this till something turns up for the better." I now know you are all right, and what can I wish for more ? '

' Well, Captain Newson, I will be glad to see ye here every day now, since it can do no harm,' said Farfrae. 'And what I've been thinking is, that the wedding may as well be kept under my own roof, the house being large, and you being in lodgings by yourself—so that a great deal of trouble and expense would be saved ye ?—and 'tis a convenience when a couple's married not to hae far to go to get home ! '

' With all my heart,' said Captain Newson ; ' since, as ye say, it can do no harm, now poor Henchard's gone ; though I wouldn't have done it otherwise, or put myself in his way at all; for I've already in my lifetime been an intruder into his family quite as far as politeness can be expected to put up with. But what do the young woman say herself about it? Elizabeth, my child, come and hearken to what we be talking about, and not bide staring out o' the window as if ye didn't hear.'

' Donald and you must settle it,' murmured Elizabeth, still keeping up a scrutinizing gaze at some small object in the street.

' Well, then,' continued Newson, turning anew to Farfrae with a face expressing thorough entry into the subject, ' that's how we'll have it. And, Mr. Farfrae, as you provide so much, and houseroom, and all that, I'll do my part in the drinkables, and see to the rum and schiedam—maybe a dozen jars will be sufficient, as many of the folk will be ladies, and perhaps they won't drink hard enough to make a high average in the reckoning? But you know best. I've provided for men and shipmates times enough, but I'm as ignorant as a child how many glasses of grog a woman, that's not a drinking woman, is expected to consume at these ceremonies?'

' Oh, none—we'll no want much of that—oh no!' said Farfrae, shaking his head with appalled gravity. ' Do you leave all to me.'

When they had gone a little further in these particulars Newson, leaning back in his chair and smiling reflectively at the ceiling, said, ' I've never told ye, or have I, Mr. Farfrae, how Henchard put me off the scent that time?'

He expressed ignorance of what the Captain alluded to.

' Ah, I thought I hadn't. I resolved that I would not, I remember, not to hurt the man's name. But now he's gone I can tell ye. Why, I came to Casterbridge nine or ten months before that day last week that I found ye out. I had been here twice before then. The first time I passed through the town on my way westward, not knowing Elizabeth lived here. Then hearing at some place—I forget where—that a man of the name of Henchard had been mayor here, I came back, and called at his house one morning. The joker!—he said Elizabeth-Jane had died years ago.'

Elizabeth now gave earnest heed to his story.

'Now, it never crossed my mind that the man was selling me a packet,' continued Newson. 'And, if you'll believe me, I was that upset, that I went back to the coach that had brought me, and took passage onward without lying in the town half-an-hour. Ha-ha!—'twas a good joke, and well carried out, and I give the man credit for't!'

Elizabeth-Jane was amazed at the intelligence. 'A joke?—oh no!' she cried. 'Then he kept you from me, father, all those months, when you might have been here?'

The father admitted that such was the case.

'He ought not to have done it!' said Farfrae.

Elizabeth sighed. 'I said I would never forget him. But oh! I think I ought to forget him now!'

Newson, like a good many rovers and sojourners among strange men and strange moralities, failed to perceive the enormity of Henchard's crime, notwithstanding that he himself had been the chief sufferer therefrom. Indeed, the attack upon the absent culprit waxing serious, he began to take Henchard's part.

'Well, 'twas not ten words that he said, after all,' Newson pleaded. 'And how could he know that I should be such a simpleton as to believe him? 'Twas as much my fault as his, poor fellow!'

'No,' said Elizabeth-Jane firmly, in her revulsion of feeling. 'He knew your disposition—you always were so trusting, father; I've heard my mother say so hundreds of times—and he did it to wrong you. After weaning me from you these five years by saying he was my father, he should not have done this.'

Thus they conversed; and there was nobody to set before Elizabeth any extenuation of the absent one's deceit. Even had he been present Henchard might scarce have pleaded it, so little did he value himself or his good name.

'Well, well—never mind—it is all over and past,' said Newson good-naturedly. 'Now, about this wedding again.'

XLIV

MEANWHILE, the man of their talk had pursued his solitary way eastward till weariness overtook him, and he looked about for a place of rest. His heart was so exacerbated at parting from the girl that he could not face an inn, or even a household of the most humble kind; and entering a field he lay down under a wheatrick, feeling no want of food. The very heaviness of his soul caused him to sleep profoundly.

The bright autumn sun shining into his eyes across the stubble awoke him the next morning early. He opened his basket, and ate for his breakfast what he had packed for his supper; and in doing so overhauled the remainder of his kit. Although everything he brought necessitated carriage at his own back, he had secreted among his tools a few of Elizabeth-Jane's cast-off belongings, in the shape of gloves, shoes, a scrap of her handwriting, and the like; and in his pocket he carried a curl of her hair. Having looked at these things he closed them up again, and went onward.

During five consecutive days Henchard's rush basket rode along upon his shoulder between the highway hedges, the new yellow of the rushes catching the eye of an occasional field-labourer as he glanced over the quickset, together with the wayfarer's hat and head,

385

and down-turned face, over which the twig shadows moved in endless procession. It now became apparent that the direction of his journey was Weydon Priors, which he reached on the afternoon of the sixth day.

The renowned hill, whereon the annual fair had been held for so many generations, was now bare of human beings, and almost of aught besides. A few sheep grazed thereabout, but these ran off when Henchard halted upon the summit. He deposited his basket upon the turf, and looked about with sad curiosity; till he discovered the road by which his wife and himself had entered, on the upland so memorable to both, two or three-and-twenty years before.

'Yes, we came up that way,' he said, after ascertaining his bearings. 'She was carrying the baby, and I was reading a ballet-sheet. Then we crossed about here—she so sad and weary, and I speaking to her hardly at all, because of my cursed pride and mortification at being poor. Then we saw the tent—that must have stood more this way.' He walked to another spot; it was not really where the tent had stood, but it seemed so to him. 'Here we went in, and here we sat down. I faced this way. Then I drank, and committed my crime. It must have been just on that very pixy-ring that she was standing when she said her last words to me before going off with him; I can hear their sound now, and the sound of her sobs: "O Mike! I've lived with thee all this while, and had nothing but temper. Now I'm no more to 'ee—I'll try my luck elsewhere."'

He experienced not only the bitterness of a man who finds, in looking back upon an ambitious course, that what he has sacrificed in sentiment was worth as much as what he has gained in substance; but the superadded bitterness of seeing his very recantation nullified. He had been sorry for all this long ago;

but his attempts to replace ambition by love had been as fully foiled as his ambition itself. His wronged wife had foiled them by a fraud so grandly simple as to be almost a virtue. It was an odd sequence that out of all this wronging of social law came that flower of Nature, Elizabeth. Part of his wish to wash his hands of life arose from his perceptions of its contrarious inconsistencies—of Nature's jaunty readiness to support unorthodox social principles.

He intended to go on from this place—visited as an act of penance—into another part of the country altogether. But he could not help thinking of Elizabeth, and the quarter of the horizon in which she lived. Out of this it happened that the centrifugal tendency imparted by weariness of the world was counteracted by the centripetal influence of his love for his stepdaughter. As a consequence, instead of following a straight course yet further away from Casterbridge, Henchard gradually, almost unconsciously, deflected from that right line of his first intention; till, by degrees, his path, like that of the Canadian woodsman, became part of a circle, of which Casterbridge formed the centre. In ascending any particular hill, he ascertained the bearings as nearly as he could by means of the sun, moon, or stars, and settled in his mind the exact direction in which Casterbridge and Elizabeth-Jane lay. Sneering at himself for his weakness, he yet every hour—nay, every few minutes—conjectured her actions for the time being— her sitting down and rising up, her goings and comings, till thought of Newson's and Farfrae's counter-influence would pass like a cold blast over a pool, and efface her image. And then he would say of himself, ' O you fool! All this about a daughter who is no daughter of thine ! '

At length he obtained employment at his own occupation of hay-trusser, work of that sort being in demand at this autumn time. The scene of his hiring was a pastoral farm near the old western highway, whose course was the channel of all such communications as passed between the busy centres of novelty and the remote Wessex boroughs. He had chosen the neighbourhood of this artery from a sense that, situated here, though at a distance of fifty miles, he was virtually nearer to her whose welfare was so dear than he would be at a road-less spot only half as remote.

And thus Henchard found himself again on the pre-cise standing which he had occupied five-and-twenty years before. Externally there was nothing to hinder his making another start on the upward slope, and by his new lights achieving higher things than his soul in its half-formed state had been able to accomplish. But the ingenious machinery contrived by the Gods for re-ducing human possibilities of amelioration to a minimum —which arranges that wisdom to do shall come *pari passu* with the departure of zest for doing—stood in the way of all that. He had no wish to make an arena a second time of a world that had become a mere painted scene to him.

Very often, as his hay-knife crunched down among the sweet-smelling grassy stems, he would survey man-kind and say to himself: ' Here and everywhere be folk dying before their time like frosted leaves, though wanted by their families, the country, and the world; while I, an outcast, an encumberer of the ground, wanted by nobody, and despised by all, live on against my will ! '

He often kept an eager ear upon the conversation of those who passed along the road—not from a general curiosity by any means—but in the hope that among these travellers to and from Casterbridge some would, sooner or later, speak of that place. The distance, however, was too great to lend much probability to his desire; and the highest result of his attention to way-side words was that he did indeed hear the name

'Casterbridge' uttered one day by the driver of a road-waggon. Henchard ran to the gate of the field he worked in, and hailed the speaker, who was a stranger.

'Yes—I've come from there, maister,' he said, in answer to Henchard's inquiry. 'I trade up and down, ye know; though, what with this travelling without horses that's getting so common, my work will soon be done.'

'Anything moving in the old place, mid I ask?'

'All the same as usual.'

'I've heard that Mr. Farfrae, the late mayor, is thinking of getting married. Now is that true or not?'

'I couldn't say for the life o' me. Oh no, I should think not.'

'But yes, John—you forget,' said a woman inside the waggon-tilt. 'What were them packages we carr'd there at the beginning o' the week? Surely they said a wedding was coming off soon—on Martin's Day?'

The man declared he remembered nothing about it; and the waggon went on jangling over the hill.

Henchard was convinced that the woman's memory served her well. The date was an extremely probable one, there being no reason for delay on either side. He might, for that matter, write and inquire of Elizabeth; but his instinct for sequestration had made the course difficult. Yet before he left her, she had said that for him to be absent from her wedding was not as she wished it to be.

The remembrance would continually revive in him now that it was not Elizabeth and Farfrae who had driven him away from them, but his own haughty sense that his presence was no longer desired. He had assumed the return of Newson, without absolute proof that the Captain meant to return; still less that Elizabeth-Jane would welcome him; and with no proof whatever that if he did return he would stay. What if he had been mistaken in his views; if there had been no necessity that his own absolute separation from her he loved should be involved in these untoward incidents? To make one more attempt to be near her : to go back · to see her, to plead his cause before her, to ask forgiveness for his fraud, to endeavour strenuously to hold his own in her love; it was worth the risk of repulse, ay, of life itself.

But how to initiate this reversal of all his former resolves, without causing husband and wife to despise him for his inconsistency, was a question which made him tremble and brood.

He cut and cut his trusses two days more, and then he concluded his hesitancies by a sudden reckless determination to go to the wedding festivity. Neither writing nor message would be expected of him. She had regretted his decision to be absent—his unanticipated presence would fill the little unsatisfied corner that would probably have place in her just heart without him.

To intrude as little of his personality as possible upon a gay event with which that personality could show nothing in keeping, he decided not to make his appearance till evening—when stiffness would have worn off, and a gentle wish to let bygones be bygones would exercise its sway in all hearts.

He started on foot, two mornings before St. Martin's-tide, allowing himself about sixteen miles to perform for each of the three days' journey, reckoning the wedding-day as one. There was only one town, Shottsford, of any importance along his course, and here he stopped on the second night, not only to rest, but to prepare himself for the next evening.

Possessing no clothes but the working suit he stood in—now stained and distorted by their two months of hard usage, he entered a shop to make some purchases which should put him, externally at any rate, a little in harmony with the prevailing tone of the morrow. A rough yet respectable coat and hat, a new shirt and neck-cloth, were the chief of these; and having satisfied himself that in appearance at least he would not now offend her, he proceeded to the more interesting particular of buying her some present.

What should that present be? He walked up and down the street, regarding dubiously the display in the shop windows, from a gloomy sense that what he might most like to give her would be beyond his miserable pocket. At length a caged goldfinch met his eye. The cage was a plain and small one, the shop humble, and on inquiry he concluded he could afford the modest sum asked. A sheet of newspaper was tied round the little creature's wire prison, and with the wrapped up cage in his hand Henchard sought a lodging for the night.

Next day he set out upon the last stage, and was soon within the district which had been his trading-ground in bygone years. Part of the distance he travelled by carrier, seating himself in the darkest corner at the back of that trader's van; and as the other passengers, mainly women going short journeys, mounted and alighted in front of Henchard, they talked over much local news, not the least portion of this being the wedding then in course of celebration at the town they were nearing. It appeared from their accounts that the town band had been hired for the evening party, and, lest the convivial instincts of that body should get the better of their skill, the further step had been taken of engaging the string band from Budmouth, so that there would be a reserve of harmony to fall back upon in case of need.

He heard, however, but few particulars beyond those known to him already, the incident of the deepest interest on the journey being the soft pealing of the Casterbridge bells, which reached the travellers' ears while the van paused on the top of Yalbury Hill to have the drag lowered. The time was just after twelve o'clock.

Those notes were a signal that all had gone well; that there had been no slip 'twixt cup and lip in this case; that Elizabeth-Jane and Donald Farfrae were man and wife.

Henchard did not care to ride any further with his chattering companions after hearing this sound. Indeed, it quite unmanned him; and in pursuance of his plan of not showing himself in Casterbridge street till evening, lest he should mortify Farfrae and his bride, he alighted here, with his bundle and bird-cage, and was soon left as a lonely figure on the broad white highway.

It was the hill near which he had waited to meet Farfrae, almost two years earlier, to tell him of the serious illness of his wife Lucetta. The place was unchanged; the same larches sighed the same notes; but Farfrae had another wife—and, as Henchard knew, a better one. He only hoped that Elizabeth-Jane had obtained a better home than had been hers at the former time.

He passed the remainder of the afternoon in a curious high-strung condition, unable to do much but think of the approaching meeting with her, and sadly satirize himself for his emotions thereon, as a Samson shorn. Such an innovation on Casterbridge customs as a flitting of bridegroom and bride from the town immediately after the ceremony, was not likely, but if it should have taken place he would wait till their return. To assure himself on this point he asked a market-man when near the borough if the newly-married couple had gone away, and was promptly informed that they had not; they were at that hour, according to all accounts, entertaining a houseful of guests at their home in Corn Street.

Henchard dusted his boots, washed his hands at the river-side, and proceeded up the town under the feeble lamps. He need have made no inquiries beforehand, for on drawing near Farfrae's residence it was plain to the least observant that festivity prevailed within, and that Donald himself shared it, his voice being distinctly audible in the street, giving strong expression to a song of his dear native country, that he loved so well as never to have revisited it. Idlers were standing on the pavement in front; and wishing to escape the notice of these Henchard passed quickly on to the door.

It was wide open; the hall was lighted extravagantly, and people were going up and down the stairs. His courage failed him; to enter footsore, laden, and poorly dressed into the midst of such resplendency, was to bring needless humiliation upon her he loved, if not to court repulse from her husband. Accordingly he went round into the street at the back that he knew so well, entered the garden, and came quietly into the house through the kitchen, temporarily depositing the bird and cage under a bush outside, to lessen the awkwardness of his arrival.

Solitude and sadness had so emolliated Henchard that he now feared circumstances he would formerly have scorned, and he began to wish that he had not taken upon himself to arrive at such a juncture. However, his progress was made unexpectedly easy by his discovering alone in the kitchen an elderly woman who seemed to be acting as provisional housekeeper during the convulsions from which Farfrae's establishment was just then suffering. She was one of those people whom nothing surprises, and though to her, a total stranger, his request must have seemed odd, she willingly volunteered to go up and inform the master and mistress of the house that 'a humble old friend' had come.

On second thoughts she said that he had better not wait in the kitchen, but come up into the little back-parlour, which was empty. He thereupon followed her thither, and she left him. Just as she had got across the landing to the door of the best parlour a dance was struck up, and she returned to say that she would wait till that was over before announcing him—Mr. and Mrs. Farfrae having both joined in the figure.

The door of the front room had been taken off its hinges to give more space, and that of the room Henchard sat in being ajar, he could see fractional parts of the dancers whenever their gyrations brought them near the doorway, chiefly in the shape of the skirts of dresses and streaming curls of hair; together with about three-fifths of the band, in profile, including the restless shadow of a fiddler's elbow, and the tip of the bass-viol bow.

The gaiety jarred upon Henchard's spirits; and he could not quite understand why Farfrae, a much-sobered man, and a widower, who had had his trials, should have cared for it all, notwithstanding the fact that he was quite a young man still, and quickly kindled to enthusiasm by dance and song. That the quiet Elizabeth, who had long ago appraised life at a moderate value, and who knew, in spite of her maidenhood, that marriage was as a rule no dancing matter, should have had zest for this revelry surprised him still more. However, young people could not be quite old people, he concluded, and custom was omnipotent.

With the progress of the dance the performers spread out somewhat, and then for the first time he caught a glimpse of the once despised daughter who had mastered him, and made his heart ache. She was in a dress of white silk or satin, he was not near enough to say which—snowy white, without a tinge of milk or cream; and the expression of her face was one of nervous pleasure rather than of gaiety. Presently Farfrae came round, his exuberant Scotch movement making him conspicuous in a moment. The pair were not dancing together, but Henchard could discern that whenever the changes of the figure made them the partners of a moment, their emotions breathed a much subtler essence than at other times.

By degrees Henchard became aware that the measure was trod by some one who out-Farfraed Farfrae in saltatory intenseness. This was strange, and it was stranger to find that the eclipsing personage was Elizabeth-Jane's partner. The first time that Henchard saw him he was sweeping grandly round, his head quivering and low down, his legs in the form of an X and his back towards the door. The next time he came round in the other direction, his white waistcoat preceding his face, and his toes preceding his white waistcoat. That happy face—Henchard's complete discomfiture lay in it. It was Newson's, who had indeed come and supplanted him.

Henchard pushed to the door, and for some seconds made no other movement. He rose to his feet, and stood like a dark ruin, obscured by ' the shade from his own soul upthrown.'

But he was no longer the man to stand these reverses unmoved. His agitation was great, and he would fain have been gone, but before he could leave the dance had ended, the housekeeper had informed Elizabeth-Jane of the stranger who awaited her, and she entered the room immediately.

' Oh—it is—Mr. Henchard ! ' she said, starting back.

' What ; Elizabeth ? ' he cried, as he seized her hand.

'What do you say?—*Mr.* Henchard? Don't, don't scourge me like that! Call me worthless old Henchard —anything—but don't 'ee be so cold as this! Oh, my maid—I see you have another—a real father in my place. Then you know all; but don't give all your thought to him! Do ye save a little room for me!'

She flushed up, and gently drew her hand away. ' I could have loved you always—I would have, gladly,' said she. ' But how can I when I know you have deceived me so—so bitterly deceived me! You persuaded me that my father was not my father—allowed me to live on in ignorance of the truth for years; and then when he, my warm-hearted real father, came to find me, cruelly sent him away with a wicked invention of my death, which nearly broke his heart. Oh how can I love, or do anything more for, a man who has served us like this!'

Henchard's lips half parted to begin an explanation. But he shut them up like a vice, and uttered not a sound. How should he, there and then, set before her with any effect the palliatives of his great faults—that he had himself been deceived in her identity at first, till informed by her mother's letter that his own child had died; that, in the second accusation, his lie had been the last desperate throw of a gamester who loved her affection better than his own honour? Among the many hindrances to such a pleading, not the least was this, that he did not sufficiently value himself to lessen his sufferings by strenuous appeal or elaborate argument.

Waiving, therefore, his privilege of self-defence, he regarded only her discomposure. ' Don't ye distress yourself on my account,' he said, with proud superiority. ' I would not wish it—at such a time, too, as this. I have done wrong in coming to 'ee—I see my error. But it is only for once, so forgive it. I'll never trouble 'ee again, Elizabeth-Jane—no, not to my dying day! Good-night. Good-bye!'

Then, before she could collect her thoughts, Henchard went out from her rooms, and departed from the house by the back way as he had come; and she saw him no more.

XLV

IT was about a month after the day which closed as in the last chapter. Elizabeth-Jane had grown accustomed to the novelty of her situation, and the only difference between Donald's movements now and formerly was, that he hastened indoors rather more quickly after business hours than he had been in the habit of doing for some time.

Newson had stayed in Casterbridge three days after the wedding party (whose gaiety, as might have been surmised, was of his making rather than of the married couple's), and was stared at and honoured as became the returned Crusoe of the hour. But whether or not because Casterbridge was difficult to excite by dramatic returns and disappearances, through having been for centuries an assize town, in which sensational exits from the world, antipodean absences, and such like, were half-yearly occurrences, the inhabitants did not altogether lose their equanimity on his account. On the fourth morning he was discovered disconsolately climbing a hill, in his craving to get a glimpse of the sea from somewhere or other. The contiguity of salt water proved to be such a necessity of his existence that he preferred Budmouth as a place of residence, notwithstanding the society of his daughter in the other town. Thither he went, and settled in lodgings in a green-shuttered cottage which had a bow-window, jutting out sufficiently to afford glimpses of a vertical strip of blue sea to any one opening the sash, and leaning forward far enough to look through a narrow lane of tall intervening houses.

Elizabeth-Jane was standing in the middle of her upstairs parlour, critically surveying some re-arrangement of articles, with her head to one side, when the housemaid came in with the announcement, 'Oh, please ma'am, we know now how that bird-cage came there.'

In exploring her new domain during the first week of residence, gazing with critical satisfaction on this cheerful room and that, penetrating cautiously into dark cellars, sallying forth with gingerly tread to the garden, now leaf-strewn with autumn winds, and thus, like a wise field-marshal, estimating the capabilities of the site whereon she was about to open her house-keeping campaign—Mrs. Donald Farfrae had discovered in a screened corner a new bird-cage, shrouded in newspaper, and at the bottom of the cage a little ball of feathers—the dead body of a goldfinch. Nobody could tell her how the bird and cage had come there; though that the poor little songster had been starved to death was evident. The sadness of the incident had made an impression on her. She had not been able to forget it for days, despite Farfrae's tender banter; and now when the matter had been nearly forgotten it was again revived.

'Oh, please ma'am, we know how that bird-cage came there. That farmer's man who called on the evening of the wedding—he was seen wi' it in his hand as he came up the street; and 'tis thoughted that he put it down while he came in with his message, and then went away forgetting where he had left it.'

This was enough to set Elizabeth thinking, and in thinking she seized hold of the idea, at one feminine bound, that the caged bird had been brought by Hen-

chard for her, as a wedding gift and token of repentance. He had not expressed to her any regrets or
excuses for what he had done in the past; but it was
a part of his nature to extenuate nothing, and live on
as one of his own worst accusers. She went out,
looked at the cage, buried the starved little singer, and
from that hour her heart softened towards the self-
alienated man.

When her husband came in she told him her solution of the bird-cage mystery; and begged Donald to
help her in finding out, as soon as possible, whither
Henchard had banished himself, that she might make
her peace with him; try to do something to render his
life less that of an outcast, and more tolerable to him.
Although Farfrae had never so passionately liked Henchard as Henchard had liked him, he had, on the other
hand, never so passionately hated in the same direction
as his former friend had done; and he was therefore
not the least indisposed to assist Elizabeth-Jane in her
laudable plan.

But it was by no means easy to set about discovering Henchard. He had apparently sunk into the earth
on leaving Mr. and Mrs. Farfrae's door. Elizabeth-
Jane remembered what he had once attempted; and
trembled.

But though she did not know it, Henchard had
become a changed man since then—as far, that is, as
change of emotional basis can justify such a radical
phrase; and she needed not to fear. In a few days
Farfrae's inquiries elicited that Henchard had been
seen, by one who knew him, walking steadily along the
Melchester highway eastward, at twelve o'clock at night
—in other words, retracing his steps on the road by
which he had come.

This was enough; and the next morning Farfrae
might have been discovered driving his gig out of
Casterbridge in that direction, Elizabeth-Jane sitting

beside him, wrapped in a thick flat fur—the victorine of the period—her complexion somewhat richer than formerly, and an incipient matronly dignity, which the serene Minerva-eyes of one 'whose gestures beamed with mind' made becoming, settling on her face. Having herself arrived at a promising haven from at least the grosser troubles of her life, her object was to place Henchard in some similar quietude before he should sink into that lower stage of existence which was only too possible to him now.

After driving along the highway for a few miles they made further inquiries, and learnt of a road-mender, who had been working thereabouts for weeks, that he had observed such a man at the time mentioned; he had left the Melchester coach-road at Weatherbury by a forking highway which skirted the north of Egdon Heath. Into this road they directed the horse's head, and soon were bowling across that ancient country whose surface never had been stirred to a finger's depth, save by the scratchings of rabbits, since brushed by the feet of the earliest tribes. The tumuli these had left behind, dun and shagged with heather, jutted roundly into the sky from the uplands, as though they were the full breasts of Diana Multimammia supinely extended there.

They searched Egdon, but found no Henchard. Farfrae drove onward, and by the afternoon reached the neighbourhood of some extension of the heath to the north of Anglebury, a prominent feature of which, in the form of a blasted clump of firs on the summit of a hill, they soon passed under. That the road they were following had, up to this point, been Henchard's track on foot they were pretty certain; but the ramifications which now began to reveal themselves in the route made further progress in the right direction a matter of pure guess-work, and Donald strongly advised his wife to give up the search in person, and trust to other means for obtaining news of her stepfather. They were now a score of miles at least from home, but, by resting the horse for a couple of hours at a village they had just traversed, it would be possible to get back to Caster-bridge that same day; while to go much further afield would reduce them to the necessity of camping out for the night; 'and that will make a hole in a sovereign,' said Farfrae. She pondered the position, and agreed with him.

He accordingly drew rein, but before reversing their direction paused a moment, and looked vaguely round upon the wide country which the elevated position dis-closed. While they looked, a solitary human form came from under the clump of trees, and crossed ahead of them. The person was some labourer; his gait was shambling, his regard fixed in front of him as absolutely as if he wore blinkers; and in his hand he carried a few sticks. Having crossed the road he descended into a ravine, where a cottage revealed itself, which he entered.

'If it were not so far away from Casterbridge I should say that must be poor Whittle. 'Tis just like him,' observed Elizabeth-Jane.

'And it may be Whittle, for he's never been to the yard these three weeks, going away without saying any word at all; and I owing him for two days' work, with-out knowing who to pay it to.'

The possibility led them to alight, and at least make an inquiry at the cottage. Farfrae hitched the reins to the gate-post, and they approached what was of humble dwellings surely the humblest. The walls, built of kneaded clay originally faced with a trowel, had been worn by years of rain-washings to a lumpy crumbling surface, channelled and sunken from its plane, its gray rents held together here and there by a leafy strap of ivy which could scarcely find substance enough for the purpose. Leaves from the fence had been blown into the corners of the doorway, and lay there undisturbed.

The door was ajar; Farfrae knocked; and he who stood before them was Whittle, as they had conjectured.

His face showed marks of deep sadness, his eyes lighting on them with an unfocused gaze; and he still held in his hand the few sticks he had been out to gather. As soon as he recognized them he started.

'What, Abel Whittle; is it that ye are here?' said Farfrae.

'Ay, yes, sir! You see he was kind-like to mother when she wer here below, though 'a was rough to me.'

'Who are you talking of?'

'Oh, sir—Mr. Henchet! Didn't ye know it? He's just gone—about half-an-hour ago, by the sun; for I've got no watch to my name.'

'Not—dead?' faltered Elizabeth-Jane.

'Yes, ma'am, he's gone! He was kind-like to mother when she wer here below, sending her the best ship-coal, and hardly any ashes from it at all; and taties, and such-like that were very needful to her. I seed en go down street on the night of your worship-ful's wedding to the lady at yer side, and I thought he looked low and faltering. And I followed en over the road, and he turned and zeed me, and said "You go back!" But I followed, and he turned again, and said, "Do you hear, sir? Go back!" But I zeed that he was low, and I followed on still. Then 'a said, "Whittle, what do ye follow me for when I've told ye to go back all these times?" And I said, "Because, sir, I see things be bad with 'ee, and ye wer kind-like to mother if ye were rough to me, and I would fain be kind-like to you." Then he walked on, and I followed; and he never complained at me no more. We walked on like that all night; and in the blue o' the morning, when 'twas hardly day, I looked ahead o' me, and I zeed that he wambled, and could hardly drag along. By that time we had got past here, but I had seen that this house was empty as I went by, and I got him to come back; and I took down the boards from the windows, and helped him inside. "What, Whittle," he said, "and can ye really be such a poor fond fool as to care for such a wretch as I!" Then I went on further, and some neighbourly woodmen lent me a bed, and a chair, and a few other traps, and we brought 'em here, and made him as comfortable as we could. But he didn't gain strength, for you see, ma'am, he couldn't eat—no, no appetite at all—and he got weaker; and to-day he died. One of the neighbours have gone to get a man to measure him.'

'Dear me—is that so!' said Farfrae.

As for Elizabeth, she said nothing.

'Upon the head of his bed he pinned a piece of paper, with some writing upon it,' continued Abel Whittle. 'But not being a man o' letters, I can't read writing; so I don't know what it is. I can get it and show ye.'

They stood in silence while he ran into the cottage; returning in a moment with a crumpled scrap of paper. On it there was pencilled as follows :—

'MICHAEL HENCHARD'S WILL.

'That Elizabeth-Jane Farfrae be not told of my death, or made to grieve on account of me.

'& that I be not bury'd in consecrated ground.

'& that no sexton be asked to toll the bell.

'& that nobody is wished to see my dead body.

'& that no murners walk behind me at my funeral.

'& that no flours be planted on my grave.

'& that no man remember me.

'To this I put my name.

'MICHAEL HENCHARD.'

'What are we to do?' said Donald, when he had handed the paper to her.

She could not answer distinctly. 'O Donald!' she said at last through her tears, 'what bitterness lies there!

Oh I would not have minded so much if it had not been for that last parting ! . . . But there's no altering —so it must be.'

What Henchard had written in the anguish of his dying was respected as far as practicable by Elizabeth-Jane, though less from a sense of the sacredness of last words, as such, than from her independent knowledge that the man who wrote them meant what he said. She knew the directions to be a piece of the same stuff that his whole life was made of, and hence were not to be tampered with to give herself a mournful pleasure, or her husband credit for large-heartedness.

All was over at last, even her regrets for having misunderstood him on his last visit, for not having searched him out sooner, though these were deep and sharp for a good while. From this time forward Elizabeth-Jane found herself in a latitude of calm weather, kindly and grateful in itself, and doubly so after the Capharnaum in which some of her preceding years had been spent. As the lively and sparkling emotions of her early married life cohered into an equable serenity, the finer movements of her nature found scope in discovering to the narrow-lived ones around her the secret (as she had once learnt it) of making limited opportunities endurable; which she deemed to consist in the cunning enlargement, by a species of microscopic treatment, of those minute forms of satisfaction that offer themselves to everybody not in positive pain; which, thus handled, have much of the same inspiriting effect upon life as wider interests cursorily embraced.

Her teaching had a reflex action upon herself, insomuch that she thought she could perceive no great personal difference between being respected in the nether parts of Casterbridge, and glorified at the uppermost end of the social world. Her position was, indeed, to a marked degree one that, in the common phrase, afforded much to be thankful for. That she was not demonstratively thankful was no fault of hers. Her experience had been of a kind to teach her, rightly or wrongly, that the doubtful honour of a brief transit through a sorry world hardly called for effusiveness, even when the path was suddenly irradiated at some half-way point by daybeams rich as hers. But her strong sense that neither she nor any human being deserved less than was given, did not blind her to the fact that there were others receiving less who had deserved much more. And in being forced to class herself among the fortunate she did not cease to wonder at the persistence of the unforeseen, when the one to whom such unbroken tranquillity had been accorded in the adult stage was she whose youth had seemed to teach that happiness was but the occasional episode in a general drama of pain.

THE END